THE JAKE FONKO SERIES: BOOKS 4, 5, & 6

Fonko in the Sun, Fonko Bolo, & The Mother of All Fonkos

B. HESSE PFLINGGER

Copyright © 2014 - 2015 G. Ray Funkhouser. All rights reserved.

This book is a work of fiction. Similarities to actual events, places, persons or other entities is coincidental.

The Jake Fonko Series: Books 4, 5 & 6/B. Hesse Pflingger. – 1st ed.

CONTENTS

The Jake Fonko Series	v
Fonko in the Sun	1
Fonko Bolo	189
The Mother of All Fonkos	415
Fonko Go Home (Book 7)	625

THE JAKE FONKO SERIES

Jake Fonko M.I.A.
Fonko on the Carpet
Fonko's Errand Go Boom
Fonko in the Sun
Fonko Bolo
The Mother of All Fonkos
Fonko Go Home
To Russia With Fonko
The Fonko Connection
The Jake Fonko Series: 1, 2 & 3 Box Set
The Jake Fonko Series: 4, 5 & 6 Box Set

All Jake Fonko titles are now available on Amazon at **bit.ly/jakefonko**.

GRAND CAYMAN - GRENADA 1983

FONKO IN THE SUN

A JAKE FONKO ADVENTURE
B. HESSE PFLINGGER

PREFACE
Editor's Note

I am pleased to call the reader's attention to an innovative feature we introduce in *Fonko in the Sun*—background music. To the best of my knowledge, no serious scholarly text has previously attempted this.

There is an interesting story behind our innovation. One day I looked up from my notes for my lecture course, Trends 101, to find that without exception, every student in the room was not looking at me, but rather at some handheld gadget. I assumed they must be taking notes on recording devices and continued on with the day's lesson, but afterward, I asked my research assistant, Dr. Bertha Sikorski, about it. She explained that it happens in all the lecture courses these days—the students were sending messages to friends via "texting" or "tweeting," or were watching pornography or "YouTube." Pornography I understood, but texting, tweeting and YouTube were new concepts to me.

Dr. Sikorski explained them, and I was particularly taken with YouTube. Astounding! Anybody and everybody posting videos, movies, music, just about everything one can imagine! I spent the afternoon exploring YouTube on my desktop computer, amazed at the wealth of materials available. I even found original David Frost and William F. Buckley Jr. TV interviews. It was clear to me that YouTube could become as valuable a source of insight into contemporary history as Wikipedia is proving to be.

This occurred while my publisher was preparing *Fonko in the Sun* for publication. Dr. Sikorski had recently seen a film by a Mr. James Cliff, *The Harder They Come*, and she was taken by the music of Jamaica (where that film is set). She thought it would be "cool" to assemble a "playlist" to complement the text of our book, and she prevailed on our colleagues to "give it a shot." The two of us spent many enjoyable evenings combing through the reggae and calypso songs that so enliven those exotic islands, and the result is a series of chapter headings reflecting song titles that one can easily access on YouTube.

My hope is that this feature will enhance your appreciation of Jake Fonko's remarkable adventures in the Caribbean Islands by providing a flavor of the environs and people he encountered.

B. Hesse Pflingger, PhD
Professor of Contemporary History
California State University, Cucamonga

JOHNNY TOO BAD

They handed me the suitcase, and then the three guys started for the door, and I watched them go. They were good looking young fellows, wore good clothes, and they looked like they had plenty of money. As they turned out the door to the right, a closed car came down the street toward them. The first thing a pane of glass went, and the bullet smashed into a row of bottles on the showcase wall to the right. I heard the gun going and, bop, bop, bop; there were bottles smashing all along the wall.

I jumped behind the bar and peered through the bartender's cut-out passageway. The car was stopped, and there were two men crouched down by it. One had an Uzi and the other had a sawed-off automatic shotgun. The one with the Uzi was an African-American. The other was swarthy and wore cutoffs and a loose, untucked cotton shirt with an Island design.

One of the boys was facedown in a growing seep of blood. Another was behind a parked beer delivery van. He'd pulled out a Glock and taken a wild shot around the back of the van. The African-American with the Uzi got his face almost to the street and gave the back of the van a burst from underneath, and sure enough, one came down. He flopped there, putting his hands over his head, and the guy in cutoffs shot at him with the shotgun while the African-American put in a fresh clip.

The third fellow pulled the one who was hit back by the legs to behind the van, and I saw the African-American getting his face down on the paving to give them another burst. Then I saw a man in uniform step clear of the van and get the guy in cutoffs with the S&W revolver he had. He shot twice over the African-American's head, and once low. At ten feet, the African-American shot him in the belly with the Uzi, with what must have been the last shot in it because I saw him throw it down, and the cop sat down hard and went over forwards. He was trying to get another shot off with his revolver when the African-American took the shotgun that was lying beside his buddy and blew the side of his head off. Some African-American.

Okay, I've got to say something here. Professor Pflingger insisted that I refer to the guy with the Uzi as an "African-American," but the fact is, we were in neither Africa nor America. This happened in George Town, on Grand Cayman Island, in the Caribbean Sea south of Cuba. I'd have used some other descriptor, but Professor Pflingger would accept no substitutes for the current, politically-correct term. He's one of those university types that call a shovel "a manually-operated dirt-moving device," rather than speak plain English.

Professor Pflingger insisted on "shovel" too. He even had problems with "manually."

* * *

No matter how cynical you become, it's never enough to keep up. Lily Tomlin never spoke truer words than that. You might think an ex-surf rat who'd been around the barn a few times would be mentally hardened enough to brush off just about anything by age 35, but even after my go-rounds with the Khmer Rouge, the Shah's family and John DeLorean, I still cannot get my mind around some of the stuff that went down in those sun-drenched tropical islands in 1983. Corruption? Terrorism? Brutality? Payoffs? Double-dealing? Treason? Death squads? Black helicopters? Fraud and grand theft on a global scale? You ain't seen nothin' yet.

I'd gone down to the Caribbean on a gig arranged through a guy that knew a guy that knew a guy. Probably I should blame it all on a spate of cockiness that had nudged me into the danger zone. I'd gotten away with a satchel of Irish rebel gun-running money, you see. I'd saved Maggie Thatcher's life. And the rumor was circulating that I'd been covertly running a mole in the KGB, who'd tipped me off about Russia's invasion of Afghanistan. Of course, that was just Emil Grotesqcu, but fat chance of explaining *that* to anybody. Even if I wanted to I couldn't, being legally enjoined from discussing anything about my erstwhile CIA career, mercifully now eight years in the past. In the shadow world of covert ops nobody knows what's *really* going on—even the guys involved—making me in some influential circles an international man of mystery. Truth be told, I was just a freelance gun for hire, sort of, but the more I denied being a deep-cover covert op, the more people believed the rumors that I was a CIA super-agent must be true. Those ill-founded beliefs helped me hustle business, but they carried some serious downsides too. As will soon become clear.

So an increasing volume of shady proposals was coming my way, enough of them that I could pick and choose. Naturally, I chose the ones that offered the best pay for the least danger, steering clear of problems prospective clients brought to my Malibu door that entailed violent solutions. Damn right. Violence hurts, in case you've never been involved in any. Who needs that? And then there was the money angle, I might as well admit it. My 1975 Corvette called for a long-overdue upgrade. Maggie Thatcher's "thank-you" DeLorean DMC-12 hadn't been a worthy replacement, so I gave it to Steve Spielberg for *Back to the Future*. Not that I had to have the biggest, newest, fastest, flashiest ride on the block, but repairs and upkeep had outstripped my Vette's usefulness. So lately I'd been looking longingly at new model Vettes, Porches, Alfa Romeos, Audis... any of which would bite big into my ready cash.

Plus I had a little too much time on my hands. Dana Wehrli had met her destiny and gotten The Call. Three months previously, she'd hied off to Cheyenne, Wyoming, for a weather babe gig on the ABC affiliate there, with intimations of bigger and better career steps if that went well. From what I'd heard about Wyoming weather, she'd have plenty to report on, but her departure left me bereft. Southern California abounds in blonde beach bunnies, sure, but none that matched up to Dana.

Thus, for one reason and another, I wound up in George Town, on Grand Cayman Island. I knew the man who alerted me to the job well enough to trust his assurances. He said he knew the guy who'd contacted him well enough to vouch for him. So I assumed that the client who'd put out the feeler must be reasonably up-and-up too. It was a delivery job, ferrying some undefined valuable item from George Town to a private party, specifics to be revealed (where have I heard *that* before?). Having once been an unknowing mule to Grand Cayman for Charlie Goldenman's casino skim, I insisted on guarantees that the job didn't involve black money. No, I was told, definitely not black money. Illegal merchandise? No, no, a thousand times no! So I signed on: Fly down to the Caymans, make a one-day delivery, fly back and earn a five-figure paycheck, plus expenses. They'd fronted half the fee. It was cool. Just like money from home.

What they say about "ASSUME"—it makes an ASS of U and ME.

The first-class flight from LAX (connecting through MIA) set me down at the George Town airport the day before I was to collect the parcel. I figured that was all the time I needed as the job wasn't taxing enough to bother with a three-hour jetlag-adjust. All my essentials fit in a small duffel bag, which had to go through luggage check owing to the silenced SIG Sauer I packed along (licensed to carry). It was mid-October, the muggy summer tropical steam bath giving way to the balmy breezes that draw the tourists. The Caymans aren't much as West Indies islands go, small, low and scrubby, with mangrove forests along some of the coast and fairly nice beaches elsewhere. Rain avoids those islands; water's a problem. They are noteworthy for two things: superb scuba diving on some of the best coral reefs in the world and offshore banking. The Caymans don't qualify as a five-star tourist destination, but doubtful money flocks there from every dark corner of the world. Not that large banks impose over the streets and boulevards, no. Typically, a Cayman Island bank amounts to a brass plaque on a building facade, a mail drop, some filing cabinets and phones and computers through which various currencies in large denominations are received, logged in and hidden away. George Town boasts modern buildings, but they're low-rise: no one would mistake the place for the looming canyons of Wall Street, especially considering the Caribbean squalor a few blocks away.

The phone by the bed woke me up a little after 0800 (0500. PST). A harried voice told me to be in the hotel bar downstairs in twenty minutes, where I'd get the parcel and instructions. That gave me time to clean up and dress, though no margin for breakfast. I figured I could see to that after I received the goods. The bar, with a big window overlooking the street, was open but not yet serving. A black porter in a more or less uniform sat idly against the far wall, apparently not yet on duty. Or maybe he was. Those islands have never been a refuge for workaholics.

"It's a puzzlement, mon," he remarked in the Islands sing-song.

"What's a puzzlement?" I asked.

"They robbed de bank last night. Mon, that bank don't got no money in the vaults. My friend Johnson one time go there to change some dollars; they tell him they don't do that. So what they rob?"

"Which bank they hit?"

"That BCCI. Bank of Credit and someting or other. Down the road. Late last night. They say watchman was shot, maybe killed. Everybody talking, nobody knowing."

Three swarthy young men bustled through the front door of the hotel, right on time. One of them carried a Haliburton aluminum two-suiter. The other two stationed themselves by the window, keeping a wary eye on their back-trail. "Jake Fonko?" the guy with the suitcase asked me. He had a Latino accent.

"I'm Fonko," I replied. "You're the man who called me?"

"Yes sir. This is the item you are to deliver." He handed me the case. It was heavier than I'd expected, real heavy. Heavier than lots of money, even. "You take it out to the airport right away. Get a taxi. A helicopter is waiting for you. It's the only one. You can't miss it."

"Shit!" one of his pals at the window exclaimed. "Here they come. Let's vamoose!" They drew pistols, dashed out the door and took off down the street. Then all hell broke loose.

* * *

AFTER THE FIRING STOPPED, AND THE STREET QUIETED DOWN, the African-American looked around, sizing up the situation. Four bodies sprawled here and there, littering the street and sidewalk with gore and blood puddles. He checked the shotgun for load, paused to consider his next move. Then he looked up and noticed me, standing in the bar behind the shattered window. He took a couple steps, bent down and retrieved his Uzi. Tucking the shotgun under his elbow, he calmly swapped Uzi clips and started toward the hotel door. No one seemed inclined to interfere.

This "African American" business is getting tiresome. Enough PC crap. He was a black man, okay? A very dark shade of Negro. Large. With dreadlocks. Homicidal. And most importantly, intent on taking that suitcase away from me.

The porter was cowering on his chair against the wall. Me, I didn't need a written invitation. I grabbed the case and clutched it to my belly with both arms, like a fullback hitting the line against a goal-line stand. I dashed into the lobby, pivoted and plunged down a corridor toward the back of the building. My mind was running at warp speed. Extra clothes. Field gear. Passport. Return ticket. Travelers cheques. SIG and silencer. Everything essential but my wallet was back in my room, with no chance of getting to it. A few hundred bucks and some credit cards, all I had on me. The rest of my kit I'd have to come back for later. Much later. Right this minute, it was run-for-my-life. I reached the end of the corridor and glanced back to see the gunman just starting after me. I had a good head start on him and a good chance that I could outrun him, even schlepping that suitcase. The back door of the hotel put me in an alleyway. One end of the alley opened to a main street, the best bet to find a taxi, so I loped down there. Down the block, a beat-up Chevy cab sat at a corner taxi stand, good enough for me. I started for it just as the gunman emerged from the hotel and spotted me.

The driver was leaning languidly against the side of his car. "Twenty bucks American if you can get me to the airport twice as fast as usual," I declared.

"Yes sah!" he replied, straightening up and springing to action. We piled into the cab, and he started the engine. As the car lurched away from the curb, the gunman came around the end of the alley. We were out of his range before he could react.

The airport wasn't far, lying alongside the sparkling blue sea less than a mile away from the town center. The cabbie got me there with a ride that a NASCAR driver wouldn't dare try on the track, scattering dust, roadside trash, pedestrians and cyclists, and cowing all other drivers into making way. Across the runway sat a weathered Huey chopper, rotor idling. I had the driver shoot me directly to the passenger side, bounced out and slapped a twenty into his palm. As he gushed his gratitude, I saw the gunmen's car arrive at the airport entrance. I cut his effusions off with a hearty wave and clambered into the chopper.

"Howdy, Fonko, long time no see," said the pilot

DRAGONFLY! Sitting there big as life, togged out in camo cargo pants, a well-used safari shirt and a flight helmet.

No time for niceties. "The guy in that approaching car means to shoot me full of holes," I said. "We ready to roll?"

"Up, up and away," he remarked, and he hit the throttle. The rotor gained speed, raising us from the tarmac and accelerating us into the clear blue sky. By the time the car reached the helipad, trying to bring us down with an Uzi would have been a futile gesture, and the gunman was pro enough to realize it.

DRAGONFLY, you may remember from my first memoir, was the CIA code name for Clyde Driffter, the renegade CIA ex-agent I'd been dispatched to Phnom Penh by the Agency to find in the closing days of the Viet Nam war. He'd reluctantly ferried me and Soh Soon back to civilization from his stronghold in the Cambodian hills, after which I'd hoped never again to lay eyes on him. He'd been a crack chopper jockey for Air America, a key player in the Laotian War-That-Wasn't before a B-52 bombing raid in Cambodia sent him over the edge. After that... well, aside from being an international gunrunner, a drug smuggler and a psychopathic killer he wasn't a bad sort, I suppose. He still looked the aw-shucks Nebraska farm boy, though the ensuing years of outdoor work had weathered his face and left a generous crinkle of wrinkles around his perpetually combat-alert eyes.

"I don't get it," I said as we vaulted aloft. "What the hell kind of job is this?"

"I'm not sure, myself," he said, "but it sounded like easy money, and I'm in no position to be choosy. "

"Okay, but what about *me*? How did I get involved?"

"I asked for you. They told me I should get a good man to ride shotgun. The amount they're paying, I figured they wanted the best, and you're the best."

"What? After that Cambodia mess?"

"No hard feelings about Cambodia, Fonko. It was a dirty situation, but you played fair. We both come out clean. I've been keeping tabs on you since then, been hearin' things. Cambodia was no fluke. The goddamn KGB has an operation keepin' tabs on you. Those sonsabitches don't fuck around."

If you only knew, I thought. "Don't put too much stock in things you hear," I said. "What's this job, then?"

"That suitcase you brought on board. We're taking it to Cuba."

"*Cuba?* Jesus Christ, you gotta be kidding! Nobody told me about Cuba. What are we delivering?"

"I don't know. Like I said, I'm in no position to be choosy."

We'd reached cruising altitude, whapping north over the shimmering sea. "You have anything to eat on board? I had to butt out in a hurry, skipped breakfast."

"The guy on your tail didn't give you a time out for a coffee break? There's some chow in the locker behind us. Help yourself."

I squeezed between the forward seats and found a cooler in the cargo bay. It held sandwiches, chocolate bars, apples, bananas, a jug of iced tea, some bottles of water. Beside it sat a small arsenal of assault rifles, sidearms and rocket launchers. I grabbed some grub and returned to my seat. "Expecting trouble?" I asked between bites.

"They told me to come prepared, just in case. Always a good idea to pack along some rations. As well as some Heckler & Koch G3s and Redeyes." We flew along in silence while I finished eating. Then Driffter said, "Okay, let's take a look."

"Look at what?"

"What we're carrying. Damned if I'm going to deliver something sight unseen. Must be valuable, what they're paying us to carry it 200 miles and smuggle it into Cuba. Come on, open the case. Let's see what it is."

I was curious too. The latches were locked. Driffter reached into a pocket on his leg and came up with a switchblade knife. I popped the locks with it and raised the lid, and... what the hell? "It's books. And some file folders. And these boxes..." I tugged one open. "... computer floppy disks."

"Any identification on any of it?" Driffter asked.

I flipped through a file folder. Then I picked out one of the books and rifled through a few pages. "Some of it's in English, but some's in a foreign language I don't recognize," I said. "Columns of figures, big numbers. It seems to have to do with The Bank of Credit and Commerce International. Wait a second. I bet that's the bank that was robbed last night."

"Bank robbery last night? Where?"

"George Town, down the street from my hotel. The hotel porter was talking about it. Said he couldn't figure out what they'd steal. There was no money at the bank."

"Maybe that's the stuff they stole. Lemme see one of those books." I handed it to him, and he leafed through the pages. "BCCI," he muttered, "The Bank of Crooks and Criminals... This is a ledger book. What about the others?"

I did a quick shuffle through. "They're all like that one. What's the deal with the foreign writing?"

"Urdu," Driffter said. "That's a Pakistani bank; that's their language. International operation, huge scale. One of the biggest banks in the world, branches everywhere. Big Middle Eastern Arab oil money behind it. I've done some business with them. A lot of guys in my line of work use BCCI..." He looked more closely at the ledger columns and nodded his head.

"Can you make anything out of it?" I asked.

"Enough," he said. "I picked up a little Urdu along the way. These are handwritten bank ledgers, seems like we have the last couple years' books here. Put this back and hand me one of those file folders."

The files looked all about the same to me, so I stowed the ledger and grabbed one at random and gave it to him. He laid it open on his lap, started turning through the sheets. He'd pick one up and hold it where he could read it, scan it and then put it back. Sometimes he'd nod his head. Most of the pages were written in, apparently, Urdu. The ones I saw in English were business correspondence. I couldn't make out anything important in them, but Driffter was becoming increasingly animated. He finished the one file, asked for another and scanned some of the papers.

"Interesting..." he muttered. "...what the hell's International Credit and Investment Company?" There were a dozen more files, but after he finished the second one he passed it back and didn't ask for any others. There was no point checking out the several boxes of computer floppies. "So, somebody stole these out of

BCCI on Grand Cayman Island," he said. "It's bank records and business agreements, and now we're carting them to Cuba. For who?"

"Don't ask me, I just got here myself," I said. "Does your chopper have the range for this trip? Cuba's more than 200 miles from the Caymans. Hueys are good for what, about 250 max?"

"We'll make it there with gas to spare. It's got extra fuel tanks, and they were full when we took off."

"That's over 400 miles round trip. What about getting back?"

"It's an old trick; I fell for it the first time they pulled it. At the delivery point, they think they've got us over a barrel because we'll have to refuel. They figure to hold us up for the return fuel, maybe stiff us on what we're owed. Leverage on us, threaten to leave us high and dry in Cuba. Don't sweat it, it's covered. We're gonna set down and refuel before we deliver."

"You've got connections in Cuba?"

"Connections all over the place, Fonko. Thanks to some unfortunate circumstances my retirement plans turned to shit, and I've been workin' hard ever since. There's a landing spot manned by some soldiers with government gas to sell. Even with my expenses, I'll come ahead on the half they down-paid, and I mean to head back home with the other half in my pocket. Hold on…" He peered into the rearview mirror, then craned around and looked aft, "…we may have some company…" I turned in my seat. A little plane, far to the rear, was gaining on us. "It must have come out of Grand Cayman. Cessna 210, if I'm not mistaken. About 60 knots faster than us. Overtake us in five minutes. Go back there and grab one of them H&Ks. They're military models. Use full-auto. Open a port on both sides. You ever do air-to-air combat?"

"I stood in as door gunner in Nam a few times, but it was mostly M-60 suppression fire at ground targets. Can't say that I ever hit much of anything."

"Air-to-air geometry is tricky. They're moving, and we're moving, and there's a hundred fifty knots of wind resistance. Those clips have no tracers, so you can't track your rounds. That

Cessna ain't a combat plane. They'll have to pass alongside and shoot from the windows, same as us. If it comes to shooting, lead 'em a little more than if we were stationary. Your fire will be movin' forward, because we're movin' forward, but wind resistance will retard it. Not likely you'll hit 'em, the idea is to keep 'em at a distance. Put on a helmet and get yourself braced. I may have to bounce us around some." He turned the radio up, bringing hisses and crackles. We got a hail from the plane as it closed on us. Driffter ignored it.

I went back to the cargo bay, donned a helmet and hoisted one of the guns, clicked in a clip, chambered a round. Twenty rounds to a clip. Short bursts only. We waited.

"They're comin' in on the starboard side," Driffter said. "Don't shoot on the first pass. Let's see what they do. No way they're gonna hit us, shootin' out a window." With a 60 knot differential they buzzed by as fast as a car would go by if you were standing beside a freeway. It was a spiffy civilian single-engine plane, high-winged, the tropical sun sparkling off its bright-white surfaces. Was it the guy with the Uzi? Didn't get a good look. "Nothin' happenin'." Driffter said. After a minute he added, "They're loopin' back around. Looks like they'll pass to port this time. If they get within fifty yards give 'em a burst, otherwise leave 'em be."

The Cessna approached at one hundred yards away, then weaved in closer. I saw flashes at the window behind the pilot, but we took no hits. Following Driffter's instructions, I tried to lead them a little more than normal, aiming slightly high, and tapped the trigger as they zipped past. It startled me. Aerial combat commenced and was gone in seconds. Nothing in my jungle warfare experience compared. It would take a lot of training, not to mention superfast reflexes, to be any good at it. They veered away, and again we waited.

"Here they come," Driffter announced. "Looks like they're approachin' high, going to pass to port again, descending as they pull abreast. Lead 'em forward and low, don't wait for them to fire first this time." This time, I was better prepared. The Cessna came in as expected, a gun barrel out a window. They were going to brush closer in this time, and I let go three short bursts, starting as soon as they cleared our rotor above and behind us, leading them all the way through the pass. The last burst emptied the clip. I quick-swapped it for a full one, but by that time they were gone. Instead of returning for another try the pilot peeled away and headed back where they came from. "You might have hit something, but leastways you discouraged 'em. We're more than halfway there now, comin' up on Cuban airspace. I think that's the last visitors we're gonna see for the time being."

"Cuban interceptors?"

"Naw, that's covered. We're expected."

I put the rifle back in the stack and took the co-pilot seat. "Fill me in, Clyde. What's been happening? You said something about unfortunate circumstances."

"It's the way of the world," he sighed. "You win some, you lose some. I'm a trader—find the markets where the money is, line up suppliers, buy low, sell high, deliver the goods. So I was doin' right well in the Golden Triangle with arms, drugs, gold, gemstones, what have you. Made a pretty good pile, stashed it in a Swiss bank. Never had no experience in managing finances, but I figured my money was in good hands. If your Swiss banker jumps out a window, follow him and you'll make money, you ever hear that one? So I left it to them to invest it. They put it into an investment plan called IOS—International Offshore something, or maybe Investors Offshore, I don't know, didn't give a shit. It was Swiss bankers, after all. Wasn't paying much attention, busy as I was with my trading operations. Well, some skunk named Vesco took control of the fund and stripped its assets, ran off with $200,000,000 including my stake, and I lost every last dime. So I kept on pluggin', and by the time you paid your visit in Cambodia, I'd accumulated a good inventory of high-end weapons, drugs, gold and rubies. Had it all in the chopper when we hauled ass out of Cambodia. It was enough to tide me over, get me launched into business somewhere else.

"I thought I'd got away with it, but then your Chinese girlfriend had her daddy locate me, and she guided a CIA raiding party that took it all while I was away. Wasn't much I could do, not so much because of the CIA, but her daddy is Old Man Poon of Hong Kong, a customer I wouldn't want to tangle with. Well, there I was, dead broke and stranded. Had to take what work I could get, mostly runnin' guns for Africans dead set on slaughterin' each other. Spent a number years workin' south of the Sahara, sellin' guns to anybody with something to trade. Zimbabwe. Liberia. Uganda. Angola. Congo. Mozambique. Zaire. Nigeria. The things I saw, fit to gag a battlefield buzzard. Goddamn, what a filthy place, a fuckin' pesthole. And don't get me started on the UN so-called Peacekeepers. Pedophiles sans Frontiers," he snorted, "with rules of engagement to avoid engaging with anybody. Give me Southeast Asia any day of the week. At least folks there keep themselves clean and serve decent food.

"Then I heard things was percolatin' around the Caribbean. Drug traffic shifted from the Golden Triangle to Colombia and Mexico. Independence movements in the islands, takeovers and revolts in Salvador, Ecuador, Nicaragua, just about everywhere. So I bailed out of Africa, happiest day of my life, couldn't clear out fast enough. Came away with a stake to set up shop here, found it more to my likin'. Shit, blue-haired old ladies come down here for vacations; the place is a damned paradise. So I've been movin' drugs and money around, runnin' arms for the revolutionaries, as well as for the governments they're revoltin' against. Small scale stuff, a lot of competition, get too big, and the Big Boys come after you... just makin' myself useful, you might say. I take what work I can get. This job we're on looked like easy money, one day's work plus prep time and expenses. After that go-round with the Cessna, I'm not sure that it's gonna be so easy, though…"

An interesting tale Drifter told. At least now I had an idea how Soh Soon paid for her Jaguar. It was a two-hour flight from Grand Cayman. Drifter and I passed the time swapping war stories, and as you can imagine from what I've said about him, he had some amazing stories to tell. Umm... try "horrifying"? Our chat didn't set my mind at ease, far from it. With every mile we covered, I regretted more and more having taken on this job. And as I was to discover, the shootout in George Town and our duel with the Cessna only marked the beginning of my adventure.

Land soon loomed in the distance. Cuba's the biggest island in the region, 750 miles east to west, with as much area as the state of Pennsylvania. From where we approached it stretched from horizon to horizon, might as well be a mainland. I scanned one of Driffter's maps to get a fix on location. We were coming in a little west of center, near a coastal city, Trinidad. Driffter got on the radio and made a couple calls. He then checked his bearings and altered course a little east. We flew in low over the coast, passing across some islands, a few inviting beaches, and a lot of swamp. We presently set down at a little airfield inserted among crop fields. Didn't see much activity as we landed. A squad of Cuban soldiers hustled over with a battered, grease-stained tank truck and set about refueling the Huey, wasting no time. The job done, Driffter passed a handful of hundreds to their leader, and the troops drove away happy. Communism hadn't entirely killed the capitalist spirit, it seemed.

"Delivery's scheduled in an hour at a landing strip about twenty-five miles further inland," Driffter said. "Take it easy, Jake. Have some lunch. Stretch your legs. And make sure those weapons are loaded."

Driffter claimed some shade under the chopper, cat-napping on a blanket he'd spread out. I killed the time with a reconnoiter around the airstrip. Having never been to Cuba, I wanted to see what I could, even in that short a time. The land along the southern coast of Cuba was mostly flat, agricultural. Palm trees. Some scrub. Rural poor and shabby. Down the road a piece a little settlement, not big enough to qualify as a village, just a clutch of squalid shacks. Other than the squad that refueled us, nothing seemed to be moving very quickly. No Benjamins circulating, I suppose. The few people I encountered eyed me with suspicion. I was surprised at the vintage American cars —1950s Fords, Chevys, Buicks, Pontiacs—still running and looking well-cared for. I covered a couple miles and returned to the airstrip, and presently Driffter announced it was time to leave. He slipped back to the cargo bay and strapped on a holster. He'd be packing a .44 magnum Desert Eagle with a brushed chrome finish—a hand-cannon that, just pointed at you, carried almost enough impact to knock you to the ground. "Get yourself a G3," he told me.

"Expecting trouble?"

"Don't know what to expect, so best arrive prepared," he said. He started the engine, warmed it up, and we lifted off. A few minutes later we came upon another small airstrip, just a dirt runway and a couple rundown sheds, apparently deserted except for a Mercedes sedan. Driffter landed the chopper out of pistol range and throttled the rotors down to a slow idle. And then we sat there.

Two Latino men climbed out of the Merc and strolled over, walking a professionally-trained distance apart. They wore tropical weight suits, with bright floral ties, and neat panama hats. Their pointed-toe shoes gleamed in the midday sun. One of them asked up to Driffter, "Do you bring a package for us?" He had a Spanish accent.

"Depends on who you are," Driffter drawled.

"We're the ones collecting the delivery," said the other man, "the package."

"Sorry, I don't work with delivery boys," Driffter replied.

"The boss sent us. He said you are to give us the package."

"Do you have the money?" Driffter asked.

"No. The boss has the money. You give us the package. We take it to the boss. If he's satisfied, we'll bring the money back."

I looked around the strip. I could see no means of refueling. "We need gasolina for the ride back to George Town," I said. "Where's the gasolina?"

"The boss has the gasolina," was the reply. I looked at Driffter, and he gave me a sly smile and a wink. "Cover them," he muttered to me. I shifted my G3 into a ready grip.

Driffter took off his flight helmet, set it aside and swung his legs around from in front of the seat. Keeping a close eye on the two men, he dropped down to the ground and drew his pistol in one motion. "You," he said to one of the men, "what's your name?"

"Enrique."

"Enrique, you step over here, take your time." Enrique walked slowly to Driffter. Driffter patted him down, extracting an automatic pistol, which he tossed back toward the chopper. "You," he said to the other, "what's your name?"

"Jorge."

"Okay, Jorge. You see my co-pilot there in the cockpit has an assault rifle. His gun is aimed at your belly. He is a very accurate shot. Now, I want to see the boss. Himself. Right here. Where is he?"

"Oh, a long way away," said Jorge. "That's why he sent us to receive the package. Because he is a long way away."

"That's okay. We'll wait here as long as it takes. You want to take the car and go fetch him? Can you call him on a phone?"

"I have a phone," Jorge admitted.

"That's good. Okay. So would you please call the boss and tell him we want to deliver his package to him. And tell him to bring the money and the gasolina. But before you do that, I want you to take your pistola out and toss it to me. Remember, my co-pilot in the helicopter has his rifle aimed at your belly. Okay?"

Jorge hesitated. He was flustered. He was embarrassed. He resented the hell out of this. But finally he pulled an automatic out of a shoulder holster, looked at it in fond farewell, and reluctantly tossed it at Driffter's feet. "Good," Clyde said. "Now call the boss and ask him to join us here. So we can deliver his package to him."

"I haven't seen no package yet," Jorge protested. "How do I know if you got the package? I can't tell the boss if I don't know you got the package."

"Jake," Driffter said, "get the package and hold it out where they can see it." I went back to the cargo bay, hefted the aluminum suitcase, brought it to the chopper door and held it out. "See," said Driffter, "there's the package. It's all right, everything's there. We'll deliver it to the boss, and collect our money and gasolina and be on our way, and everything will be all right." Jorge looked at me with the suitcase and then at Driffter with the big pistola. He went back to the car, came up with a cell phone, and made the call.

The boss couldn't have been too far away because in less than ten minutes another Mercedes, with a driver and a passenger, came down the dirt track, pulled onto the airstrip and stopped a few yards away. The passenger door swung open, and a man eased out and stood up straight. He was in expensive tropical clothes, tall and a little beefy, with a beard similar to Fidel Castro's. Designer sunglasses notwithstanding, the greying hair, weathered face and jittery way he handled his cigarette contradicted the in-control image he tried hard to project. This was one troubled man.

Driffter holstered his pistol and gestured to me to keep everything covered. He stepped up to the man. "We've brought a package across from Grand Cayman Island. Who do I have the pleasure of addressin'?" he asked.

"I'm Robert Vesco," the boss replied. "I'm the guy who hired you. You're wasting my time. I'd appreciate it if you and your pal would hand over my package."

BABALU

"You're THE Robert Vesco?" Driffter gasped. "The one who ran off with $200 million from that IOS fund?"

"Half right. I'm that Vesco, and I ran IOS for a while, but Bernie Cornfeld had that company screwed, blued and tattooed before I ever got there. I was trying to save it, couldn't bring it off, and then the SEC fucked me over, and I had to find some place with no extradition treaty to stay for a while until things cool off."

"Goddammit, I lost every cent I had in IOS," Driffter said, growing more heated. "Seems to me if you got away with that much you could come up with my stake."

"Well, I didn't get away with that much," Vesco said coolly. "And I sure can't come up with your so-called stake. I'm up against it myself. That's why you brought that package. Bastards ripped me off, and I'm trying to locate my money. Say, how about if you don't wave that gun around? Making me nervous."

"That so? Maybe I'll do more than just wave it. We've brought your package. You owe us the rest of the fee. And you also owe me $230,000."

Vesco looked at Driffter, shook his head and chuckled. "I don't fucking believe this," he said. "I'm trying to retrieve $70,000,000, and you come whining to me about $230,000? That's rich, you penny-ante redneck. Who the hell do you think you are, anyway?"

Some things you don't say to some people, and Vesco just then nailed it. Driffter's eyes flashed, and he drilled them into Vesco's like he was doing a root canal. "I'm Clyde P. Driffter, formerly with Air America and the Central Intelligence Agency, and now representing the United States of Go Fuck Yourself, you slick-assed crook."

Vesco was one of those operators who could turn on a dime and radiate charm when he needed to, and he knew he needed to. "Calm down, Mr. Driffter," he said, suddenly soothingly. "Look, there was never any $200 million. That was a figure the SEC—Sees Everything Crooked—made up for the sake of publicity. They had it in for IOS, and they had it in for me. Now, the IOS was just a Ponzi scheme. Bernie Cornfeld ran a bunch of offshore mutual funds, had a big sales force conning U.S. servicemen in Germany into investing with him. Superior returns. No taxes. Sure. That was the story. In reality, he lived large off the incoming money, ran a lifestyle Hugh Hefner would envy, took it right out of the funds. It appeared that IOS funds were coining money only because the incoming was greater than what he spent on mansions, girls and parties, and he cooked the books to show portfolio gains. When I took control, IOS was a sinking ship, leaking money in every direction. The SEC tried every way they could think of to indict Cornfeld and close down IOS. Now me, they were after me because I'd come too far too fast—a poor boy from Detroit who became one of the richest men in the U.S. in just a few years. I must be doing something illegal, right? Wrong. I was just smarter than their clerks. Of course I used shell companies, options, warrants, forward contracts, hedges, big leverage. It's high finance, not a lemonade stand. You leverage, then you re-leverage. You shift into tax shelters and tax havens, reissue stock, swap companies around, use every edge and every dodge you can find. It's the only way to stay ahead of the big corporations. They don't play patty-cake.

Okay, maybe I sailed a little close to the wind here and there. You can't keep track; they change the laws every day. I had a team of the best lawyers in the business, but the upshot is that the SEC had to have something to show for all the resources they'd devoted to shutting me down, and they finally got something to indict me on. I had to clear out with what I could. Self-preservation, that's all.

"Look, here's the situation. The people who ripped me off, I know the money disappeared into the Bank of Credit and Commerce International. So I hired some people to, er, requisition their records over on Grand Cayman. That's what you carried over here. With those records, I think I can ferret out my money. And if I do, I'd certainly be happy to make good on your stake. And that's doing more than I'm required to do by law. The SEC ruled the IOS in violation of every law on the books. So as an American overseas, using undeclared funds and paying no taxes, technically your BCCI deposits were illegal, with no recourse."

"I wouldn't know anything about all that. I had the money in a Swiss bank account, and my manager invested it in IOS."

"Oh, well, then it's all right, isn't it? A Swiss bank account? So the IRS wouldn't find out about it? And I suppose you made your money perfectly legally running a dry cleaning shop or a McDonald's franchise?"

Driffter guffawed. "Vesco, I haven't done anything legal since the age of 15. Legality is neither here nor there. The issue is, you screwed me out of $230,000. What I'm thinking is, if you can't come across with it right here and now, I'll bet what's in that suitcase is worth a hell of a lot more than a quarter million to somebody else. And I bet I can find a cash buyer."

Vesco took a half step closer to Driffter, locking eyes with him. "You know why I paid you so much to ferry that stuff over here? Because it's records of the financial transactions of every crook, scumbag and dictator in the Caribbean. Not to mention the Western Hemisphere. Not to mention the whole fucking world. I heard from my contact in George Town that you've already been shot at, and that's just a taste. Here in Cuba I'm safe, Castro's protecting me, but if you take those documents out of here, it's open season. Give me the stuff. I've got your money here in my car, and there's a tank truck five minutes away. Gas you up and you can go home. Deal done, okay?"

"You've told me nothing so far that I haven't dealt with worse, before," said Driffter.

"You think? Pal, you have no idea, no fucking idea, not the first fucking inkling of the first fucking hint, what you're getting yourself into. BCCI is a Third World bank, the biggest bank in the world that isn't controlled by white people. It's Muslims. From Pakistan. You want to mess with Muslims? The guys that rack up virgins in Paradise for killing infidels? They'd like their records back because their operations are very dark, very secret. But that's just the beginning. Let me give you a rundown of their clientele, the folks who do those very dark, very secret deals, who don't want records of their very dark, very secret deals falling into the wrong hands. Just off the top of my head—every oil sheik in the Middle East; Saddam Hussein; Manuel Noriega; Iranian ayatollahs; the Colombian Medellin drug cartel, Pablo Escobar's boys; the CIA and the KGB finance their covert ops through BCCI; mafia families send their money there; Armand Hammer does illegal deals with the Russians for Occidental Petroleum; hmm, there's the Palestine Liberation Organization, also the Mossad; the Sandinistas, the Contras, and tin-pot dictators here, there and everywhere. And let me tell you another—Jimmy Carter, Bert Lance, Andrew Young, Clark Clifford—Democrat honchos up to their ears in BCCI-related illegal banking in the U.S. You think Democrats are just a bunch of touchy-feely tree-huggers? Boy, you do not know Democrats. And ponder this: that's just a list of the ones I've heard of. The BCCI clientele you *don't* know about, they're the ones you have to worry about.

"Now, you leave this island with the contents of that suitcase, and you are going to soon meet a number of people you most assuredly do not want to know. But don't worry, you won't know them for long, just as long as it takes them to get that suitcase away from you, however they have to do it. I'm safe with it here in Cuba. Castro is interested in it too, so nobody is going to come here after it, his secret police will see to that. But with the contents of that valise, off this island, you'll be ducks in a shooting gallery."

It was clear enough to me. Give him the goods, collect our paychecks and blow this joint. But Driffter's eyes had grown brighter and brighter as Vesco's tale unfolded. "Jake," he said, "I think we can do better than the deal he's offering. What I've seen in that valise, I know people who'd pay a lot more for it than he will."

"I don't see where I'd fit into a scheme like that. I vote we deliver the goods, get paid and go home."

"Oh, I'd give you a fair split for ridin' shotgun—60 - 40 after my expenses. We're talkin' six figures for your share, easy."

Vesco was listening in disbelief. "Are you guys crazy? Nobody's going to pay you for that stuff. They'll just kill you and take it away."

Driffter ignored him. "We've got plenty of fuel to get us to safety. He's just bluffin'. Dammit, he stole my stake, and he owes me big. This'll settle the score. Look, Fonko, I'm leaving with that valise. Stay here if you want." He left the issue hanging while I looked from him to Vesco, to the shiny suitcase, to the shabby airstrip, to the hostile hills in the western distance...

"Well, you with me, Fonko?" he demanded, "Or do you want to stay here and spend the next ten years in a Cuban jail?"

What's that old Jack Benny joke? *Your money or your life! Don't rush me, I'm thinking!* I wish I'd had a little time to think about it.

"Let's go," I said.

"Okay," he said. "Now, first we got to take care of a few things. Stow the case and bring your G3 down here." I did as told. "Keep 'em covered. Now, gentlemen," he said, turning to the three men with their hands up, "hand over your phones. One at a time, and do it slow." In turn, Driffter received a phone from each, tossed it on the ground and stomped it with his heel. He then walked to the parked cars. He threw open the door of the first Mercedes, rummaged around and came out with another phone, also an Uzi. He stomped the phone, then raised his .44 Magnum Desert Eagle and deliberately fired a shot through the hood.

"Hey, wait a minute," yelled Vesco. "You can't do that. It isn't my car. It's a government car."

"Calm down," Driffter said. "Cubans are good at fixin' cars, have it back on the road in no time. What's a couple of Mercs to a guy with $200 million, anyway?"

"I'm telling you; I don't *have* $200 million!"

Driffter strolled over to the other Mercedes and repeated the routine—no Uzi this time. Both cars disabled, he came back to the chopper, pausing to pick up the discarded pistols and remove their clips, which he slipped into one of the pockets of his cargo pants. He tossed the pistols back on the dirt runway. "Mount up, and we're gone," he told me. We climbed up into the cockpit, me still holding the G3 on Vesco and his partners. Driffter added the Uzi to his arsenal in the cargo bay. I stowed the suitcase.

"You'll regret this," Vesco yelled as Driffter throttled the rotor up from idle. "You cannot even imagine how much you'll regret this!"

"Always a pleasure doin' business with you," Driffter replied with a big smile and a hearty wave. I doubt Vesco could hear him as we lifted off the strip and surged away from the airstrip, but the gesture clearly further pissed him off.

"What's with the cars?" I asked.

"Just a normal precaution, a delaying tactic. I didn't want them getting help too soon. As for the cars, if I make what I expect to on this deal, I'll buy Fidel a couple new Mercs. I do a little business in Cuba, surely don't want to queer it. That was to give a little head start, get us into the mountains before they scramble a plane after us. I figure we've got an hour, be halfway to Jamaica by then."

"Jamaica?"

"Can't very well go back to Grand Cayman. Jamaica's the only friendly land in range. That's all right. I sometimes work out of Jamaica, have friends there. We'll just go east to the Sierra Maestra, slip through the valleys and line up with Jamaica, then pop across the Strait and set down in the mountains. I figure we've got maybe an hour before Vesco and his boys can get some opposition organized. Put on a helmet, strap yourself in and keep a sharp eye on the horizon."

And so we flew down the coast of Cuba, skimming over rolling hills and green farm fields, streams and rivers flowing south, woods here and there, bypassing towns and villages. Driffter kept us low, under radar detection and close enough to the ground to make Cuba's rural squalor—shabby shacks, ragtag peasants, bare-assed infants, malnourished livestock, hand labor tending vast fields of sugar cane—apparent as we streamed above it. This would have been a comedy of errors, were anything funny about it. I sign on for a simple delivery job, and the next thing I know I'm a paperless fugitive fleeing the Cuban military, the sidekick of an international desperado. But there I was, and now that I'd gotten into partnership with Driffter, I needed more information. "Clyde," I said, "what's the big deal about BCCI? That was quite a client list Vesco rattled off. Why is that rogue's gallery doing business with a Pakistani bank significant?"

"Well, there's lots of things going on," he replied. "I've done a little business with BCCI myself. Let's take a simple example that I'm familiar with, gun-running. You're moving goods and large amounts of money between dodgy countries with different currencies. Say I sell a load of rifles to rebels in Nigeria and get paid in Nigerian nairas. BCCI comes in handy because they have operations just about everywhere, especially where Western banks aren't doing business. Nairas are no good outside Nigeria, so I deposit my nairas at BCCI in Lagos, and then I can draw it out somewhere else in U.S. dollars, BCCI making the conversion. They'll take a big bite, but it's worth it because it's easy and risk-free.

"Then there's money laundering. A lot of dirty money finds its way to BCCI. Governments can't necessarily monitor the deposits going in, but when, say, a mafia family or a front for a drug syndicate comes up with a sudden big boodle, warning flags go up in Customs, the IRS, the Fed, lots of places. Tax issues? Origin of the money? What they can do is deposit the money at one of BCCI's subsidiaries, then take out a loan for the same amount less fees at another subsidiary. Loan's never paid back; BCCI keeps the deposit, and nobody taxes money you borrow. Doesn't show up on the watch lists. So casino skim, drug money, what have you will find its way there. Especially international dirty money—Colombian, Mexican drug cartels. Less evidence for their governments to compile.

"It helps money disappear, too. Say some old African Strong Man wheedles a few million in humanitarian aid from Uncle Sugar. The only human he's gonna aid is himself. A lot of aid money goes unaccounted for. It used to wind up in numbered Swiss accounts, but nowadays it's finding its way to BCCI. Convenient, untraceable, and more their own kind of people, you might say. No way Uncle Sugar's ever gonna follow that money into BCCI.

"Vesco mentioned covert ops. Covert ops means paying for weapons, supplies, transportation, troops, also bribes and contributions to the right parties. Some of it's illegal, some of it you don't want anybody to be able to follow the money trail. In the case of the CIA, the Reagan people especially don't want to give the Democrats any ammunition. You want to keep it all dark, and that's where BCCI comes in. Your money's accessible wherever you might need it, and no traceable records because being an offshore bank they aren't subject to any government's regulations, except maybe Pakistan's, and all the Muslims care about is you don't charge interest. CIA uses BCCI, so does the KGB, no doubt the Mossad, the PLO, and God only knows who else out there.

"I don't know anything about the Carter crowd he mentioned. Maybe BCCI wants to set up an operation in the U.S.? It'd be an endless source of deposits, and once a bank gets the deposits, it can create money against it at ten to one, or even higher. That's the ticket—banks mint their own money by making loans."

"Okay, I get the idea," I said. "Vesco said something about shell companies. I suppose BCCI would be useful there, too. And for any other financial scams somebody wants to keep out of sight. Bribery? That's another possibility. A U.S. defense contractor wants to sell some planes to a third world government, where every palm needs a little grease. So the company deposits a million in an account at BCCI, and the Slobovian major domo draws that same million out of his local branch. Now you see it, now you don't."

"No end to the angles Vesco might play," Driffter reflected. "So he wanted those records to track down the money, he says was stolen from him, and he also could use them to blackmail the thieves into returning it. Or any other thieves, and the woods are full of them. That bribery angle, for example. The defense company CEO faces prosecution for bribery; the Slobovian government faces embarrassment, maybe the U.S. government honcho that okayed the deal is lookin' at an investigation. I see his point about being safe in Cuba. Hell, Castro must be one of BCCI's best clients. But now that we have those records, some rough customers will be taking an interest in us. The sooner I can peddle it off, the better. There's no cash in that suitcase, but it's chock full of money to be made. I've got an idea where I can turn a good dollar on it, but it's gonna take some delicate dealing. I'm thinkin' it through as we go."

On we flew, eating up distance not nearly fast enough for me. I wanted Cuba in the rearview mirror; I wanted to be in friendly territory, out of this deal and shut of Driffter. He knew his stuff, though, sorry to say: dead on his estimate, about an hour after we left Vesco, he remarked, "Company incoming. Best you get back into the cabin, grab a G3, get yourself secure and get ready for combat."

"Combat? What do you see?"

"A fighter-jet, coming high out of the northwest, probably based in Havana. He's runnin' a search pattern. He'll spot us in a few minutes, no place for us to hide over open country. Don't worry about the first pass. He'll just buzz us, takin' stock of the situation. I don't think you'll have much chance to get a shot at him, but be ready just in case." In a short while a fighter jet whooshed by several hundred feet above us, a helluva lot faster than the Cessna, then began a long, high loop back around. Driffter abandoned his steady course toward the mountains and took to weaving to and fro and bobbing up and down in unpredictable patterns. The jet buzzed by us again, closer this time, there and gone in a flash. Down close like that, big as all outdoors and scary as hell.

"I'm supposed to take him on with an assault rifle? Fat chance."

"We'll have to do our best with what we have. He'll try to force us down, pay it no mind. I've played this game before. He'll try it a time or two more, and if we don't respond then he'll open up. It's a MIG-21. Good plane at altitude, gave our flyboys a go in Nam. But useless down on the deck. They're supersonic. Performance goes all to hell when they have to slow down for this kind of combat. Anyhow, Cuban pilots aren't worth shit. No shootin'-war experience, only school training, and not much of that."

The green-blue peaks of the Sierra Maestra had appeared ahead to the east and drew steadily closer. The MIG buzzed us from the rear once more, then circled and came in from the front, the closing speeds far faster than from the rear. He dipped toward us head on, then veered back up and screamed above our rotor with an ear-busting roar, "He may try some gunfire on the next run," Driffter remarked, "no chance of hitting us from abeam. Closing speeds coming in from the front are 'way too short. He'll have to come in from behind, but even so he's got just split seconds to line us up for a shot. They should have sent out something suitable for ground support," he tsked. Sure enough, after a few minutes a swarm of tracer whipped above us, the jet following in a split second.

"I used to dodge these guys in Nam, nothin' to it," Driffter remarked. "The pilots are trained for air to air combat against similar craft, rockets from a half mile away at 800 knots or more.

Two tactics. Either come from high above, take your shot and dive away below. Or come up from below, shoot and loop around for another pass. Can't do either with us this low to the ground. So he's gotta line up for a shot coming on a flat trajectory from dead behind us, and he can't aim the plane too low, or he'll hit the ground before he can pull out. So he can't help but shoot high. I'll juke and jive a little just to make sure. Here he comes." Drifter suddenly threw the chopper to the right and dropped it down to within a few yards of the ground. Tracer passed high left, a football field off target, as the jet roared by.

Drifter veered the chopper over toward some low foothills and took advantage of what cover he could find in terrain features. "He's got time for maybe one more pass, and then we'll be in that valley up ahead. Once we're in there, there's nothing he can do, and I don't think they'll have time to scramble any aircraft more suitable." Drifter headed directly for a dark cleavage separating two looming mountains, steep and greenly wooded. "Here he comes, oh shit!" He hit the throttle hard and threw the chopper up and to the left. A rocket zipped by where we'd just been and flew on to explode in a field ahead of us. As we passed over the settling dust, Drifter said, "Bastard damn near got lucky. That's his last shot at us for a while, anyhow. No way he's gonna draw a bead on us in the valleys."

This was getting hairy. Before the MIG could get around for another pass Drifter steered us into a welcoming cleft, its twists and turns drawing us deeply between forested ridges of the fabled Sierra Maestra. I resumed the co-pilot seat, strapped myself in tight and found myself wrenching through a wild ride to put Mr. Toad to shame. Might have been kind of fun if a MIG hadn't had killing us in mind. Drifter's CIA code name was DRAGONFLY, and he'd been a Laotian legend. I got it. Damn, the sonofabitch could fly a chopper. He slipped through the depths of valleys hugging the mountain slopes that afforded the best protection until the last possible moment, unerringly found a pass to the south, bobbed up, through and over, then flowed down the next declivity into another valley without giving the circling MIG a chance at a shot. The Sierra Maestra was mostly too wild for much sign of humanity, occasional shacks and settlements down on the floors, but in one of the valleys an odd construction caught my eye. "What the hell's that?" I asked.

"Where?"

"Off to the right, in that little notch between the slopes. Looks like a giant vacuum cleaner."

"Oh yeah, I see it. Don't know. Could be some kind of air defense installation the Russkies put there. Could be a charcoal plant. Maybe a sawmill? Probably not a sugar refinery, they'd have it closer to the plantations. Cubans don't build things according to the same specs we use. Could be anything."

It faded away behind us as we mounted the slope and slipped over yet another ridge. "In a few minutes, we're going to clear the mountains and hit the coast, and the MIG's going to make another pass at us. He don't want to return to base empty-handed. I don't like those rockets. I think we'd best return fire."

"What's the point? There's no way in hell I'll ever wing him with an assault rifle. He won't even notice."

"Ever use a Redeye?"

"Never had any use for them on LRRP patrols, no."

"It's sort of like a bazooka, shoulder-launched, heat-seeking. It's designed for surface-to-air against slower-movin' craft, but it's the best firepower we got. Go back and get one, I'll show you what to do." I unstrapped myself and groped my way to the cargo bay, bracing myself on any surface reachable against the buck-and-weaving of the chopper. Driffter pointed out the safety/actuator, led me through the get-ready, showed me the trigger. "He'll fire another rocket at us and pass us by, above our rotor," he said. "I'm gonna bank over as he goes by to give you a clear field of fire. The second he comes abreast put your sight on his tailpipe. A MIG could outrun it at top speed, but he's slowed way down here. You'll get one shot, so make it count."

So then it was a matter of waiting as we sped through the

valley, vaulted the final mountain ridge and slid toward the coast margin. The MIG couldn't follow us down the slope. He circled around, high above, as we cleared the shoreline and started across the open sea. I rehearsed firing the Redeye. Seemed simple enough—aim, shoot and high tech does the rest. "He's got enough space behind us for him to make a run at us. Ready on the right side. Here he comes." Taking aim and making my shot at the moment of opportunity amidst Driffter's bouncing the chopper around was the challenge. I braced myself as best I could at the open port on the right. "Here comes the rocket!" Driffter shouted. It hissed below us. "Up and at 'em!" He banked the Huey hard over to the left, exposing my port to the passing jet. It was all I could do to keep from being tossed across the cargo bay and out the other port, but I got the shot off.

The MIG started its climb. "Guess I missed him," I said.

"Give it a sec. It's chasing his tailpipe, and it can turn inside the arc he's taking." Presently an explosion flashed orange at the tail of the MIG. "God damn; you got him!" Driffter exclaimed. Sure enough. The plane faltered in its climb and went into a crazy spin. A dark object popped out of it, and then a chute opened, the pilot ejecting.

"We're home free?" I asked hopefully.

"Don't we wish. I've had enough of this trip, want to get it behind us. That's probably the last we'll see of Cubans, but there's still another hundred miles over open sea, and I'm afraid the word has gotten out by now. They know about the robbery at BCCI. They know we took off with the suitcase from Grand Cayman. They'll be checkin' your hotel, find your stuff. They can ID my chopper. I wouldn't be surprised if Vesco put out an APB on us, so they'll know we left Cuba, and Jamaica is the only possible destination. We just shot down a Cuban jet, and they'll hear all about that plenty pronto."

"They? What 'they'?"

"Why, every damn body with an interest in the contents of that suitcase, a mighty big legion of 'theys'."

"How are we doing for fuel?"

"Evading the MIG used up more than I like, but we'll probably make it, just barely."

With that disquieting thought in mind, I settled into my seat as we whapwhapwhapped our way across the empty sea, staying low. The deep blue surface showed a little swell, no chop to speak of. We buzzed fishing boats here and there, passed over a big Bertram motor cruiser and a couple of big sailing yachts scudding along outside Cuban waters, a lovely day for a leisurely helicopter jaunt about the exotic blue Caribbean. If only. As the day leaned toward sunset Jamaica's grey mountain peaks peeked over the horizon, then grew in the distance—forty miles away, fifteen or twenty minutes maybe?

What a twenty minutes it was soon to be! "Shit, now we're in for it," spat Drifter. "Incomin' chopper on the east horizon."

I peered to the east, couldn't make out anything. Drifter had pilot's eyes, he surely did. Presently I espied a little black dot. It was like the scene in *Lawrence of Arabia* at the waterhole, where a distant blur materializes into a murderous brigand on camelback. Except this was no raghead with a muzzleloader, it was a combat aircraft. Drifter suddenly put the Huey into a stomach-dropping climb. "What is it?" I asked.

"A Cobra," he said. "We need altitude. That MIG was no problem, but this will be."

"We called Cobras 'flying tanks'," I said. "Attack helicopters, great for air strikes."

"Good for a lot of things, and it's got us outgunned and outclassed. They're hopped-up Hueys, a little faster, a lot of firepower. If I was them, I'd try to get above us—they could fire down, we couldn't fire up through the rotor."

As it closed on us, I made out that it was black, no markings. "Who is it?"

"From their bearing, they must of come from Gitmo. Meaning American. Shit, it's always something! Little problem here, Fonko. I've never done chopper to chopper combat. None of America's enemies had combat choppers, except the Russkies, and we never went head to head with them. Never encountered any in Africa, either. We're wingin' it here; no pun intended—makin' it up as we go along. One thing for sure, we can't let them get above us. If they get directly over us, they can ride us to the deck. They'll stay there, keep us from rising and take away our lift with their downdraft. I'm trying for maneuvering room. Only a couple things in our favor. The Huey's a little nimbler with a higher rate of climb and a higher operating ceiling. They have to line up nose-on to shoot at us whereas we don't. And we've got a better pilot... I hope."

Driffter turned up the radio as we continued to climb. As we reached 5000 feet, sure enough a hail squawked out. "Huey, Huey, come in."

"Might's well see what they have to say." He picked up the mike. "This is the Huey. Identify yourselves, you in the Cobra."

"Negative on that. Big mean bastards is all you need to know. We're going to escort you to the nearest landing point. Reduce your altitude, follow a course on 218 degrees heading."

"They mean to take us down on the Jamaican coast," Driffter breathed. "Fuck that. Get back in the cargo bay. Ready a Redeye and grab a G3." Into the mike he said, "Identify yourselves. I don't take orders from strangers."

"You're kidding! Come off it, the jig's up, Driffter. We're your worst nightmares. Take a 218 heading and come quietly, or we'll blow your sorry ass out of the sky."

"Shit, they know me. Get ready for the ride of your life, Fonko." He leveled out and goosed the chopper toward the looming hills, the coast now maybe fifteen miles distant. The Cobra closed in fast and climbed above us. They had maybe 10 knots speed advantage, not huge but helpful. Driffter peeled away. As the Cobra came around to face us, he turned and went into another climb, getting above the Cobra. It became a cat-and-mouse dance, Driffter snatching distance toward the island every chance he got. This couldn't be good for fuel economy. The Cobra looped away, then came in at us. A cascade of sparks in the nose sent a raft of tracer fifty yards ahead of us, the obligatory shot across the bow. Jesus—an M197 Gatling gun, 1500 rounds per minute! And me with a 20-round clip in a G3.

"Driffter, quit fucking around and take your chopper in," the radio squawked. "We aren't going to waste any more time here."

"Shouldn't we just give it up? " I asked. "They could blow us away any time they want. It's Americans. We can work it out?"

"Maybe *you* can, Fonko, but there's some matters outstanding between me and the CIA. My Cambodia operation. That Sea Sprite I hijacked. Those CIA guys I shanghaied. Not to mention some other activities I've been involved in since then. There's no such thing as statute of limitations with the CIA. They get their hands on me, I'm as good as strung up."

"Hey, what about *me*?"

"Fonko, you're okay, wish I could do better for you, but in the present circumstances..." He banked the Huey, quickly scooted down under them, then climbed behind them while they rotated around to meet us. "They can only shoot at us lined up nose-on. I don't mean to sit still long enough for that to happen." As the Cobra oriented toward us, we banked and peeled away, another spritz of tracer missing us aft. By not much. I smelled urine in the cockpit.

"Okay, I think we better return fire. No way you can bring it down with a G3, no use tryin'. I'll try to set you up to go after the pilot."

"I'm supposed to shoot at Americans?"

"I know you didn't sign up for this. Neither did I. But at this moment, it's them or us, and the odds are in their favor. Get ready with a G3 and have an extra clip at hand. The relative speeds here are different from with MIGs and Cessnas, we'll practically be stationary in effect. I'll try to give you a clear shot. It'll be close to point blank range, don't worry about elevation. I don't know about windage, so empty your clip sweeping from about ten yards out one side, across the windshield to ten yards off the other. If there's time, give 'em another clip."

"But…" I couldn't get more than that out. As the Cobra maneuvered into position, Driffter suddenly turned broadside to it. "Now!" he shouted. What else could I do? The black chopper faced us from about fifty yards away. The gunfight at the OK Corral, a mile in the sky. I swept my sights across their windshield, my finger on the trigger. I popped the clip, jammed in another and raised the gun again, and their nose spouted sparks. I heard some loud thunks, our plexiglass windows filled with big spiderwebs, and Driffter let out a huff. We hadn't changed position, so I fired off the second clip, same as the first but crossing from the other side. "Get us the hell out of here!" I screamed. The whole exchange had lasted less than ten seconds. Driffter may have taken one, but it didn't slow him down. He put us into a winding dive, flinging us closer in toward land. I could now see shoreline clearly.

"I think you drew blood," Driffter gasped, pain warping his voice. "They aren't reacting, should be on our tail. I'm going to haul ass for yonder hills. You get that other Redeye and stand by. If they come after us, it's our only hope. But maybe they won't. They're stretching their combat radius."

The Cobra, or at least its crew, must have been ailing. It did not follow us in hot pursuit. Just as well, as shooting down an American chopper, even if unidentified and on the attack, I didn't want on my resume. They somehow knew Driffter manned our controls, but with luck, not of my complicity, so if we landed safely out of sight in the mountains, maybe I had a chance of getting out of this with skin and freedom intact.

If we landed safely. Driffter's breath rasped with effort. The fuel gauge indicated fumes. A fiery half-disk bade farewell over the horizon. We passed over Montego Bay, having provided four-star entertainment for thrill-hungry vacationers at the resorts. "You know what we saw down in Jamaica, Melissa? They had an honest-to-God dogfight between helicopters! With rockets and stuff!"

"Oh yeah? I bet some resort staged it? Like those pirate ships in Key West?"

We kept our altitude around 2000 feet across the coastal flats and into the mountains. I looked aft, no sign of the Cobra. Driffter steered us deep into a valley as the motor sputtered. The chopper slowed and angled down. Driffter backed off of the rotor as best he could to ease our descent, and the shadowed hillside forest swooped up toward our shredded windshields in welcome.

JAMAICA FAREWELL

Driffter's Huey piled into a hillside at thirty miles per hour, fortunately hitting soft ground among undergrowth and saplings, and came to rest propped out at an angle on its nose. The gear in the cargo bay lay in a heap behind the bulkhead. Nothing hard and heavy had flown forward and brained us. So far, so good. We weren't hung up in high branches. We hadn't wrapped our nose around a solid tree trunk. My safety belt held, and my helmet kept the bump my head took against the roof from amounting to injury. Drifter slumped over toward the controls, held in place by his seatbelt, laboring through each breath. His chest oozed blood into his shirt front. His left pant leg was torn and bloody around the calf. His crotch and below were soaked. No dishonor there. "Only my laundryman knew how scared I was," the chopper pilots used to say.

"Fonko," he gasped. "I think I messed up some internals when we come in."

"Let's get you out of here onto solid ground and see what gives," I said.

"Don't trouble yourself," he rasped. "You're in travelin' condition? Good. Nothin' you can do for me. Save yourself. Get to a road and send the medics up for me. Maybe I'll make it, maybe I won't. "

"Come on, Clyde. I'll get you out of this. We brought guys in worse shape than you out of the jungle in 1970."

"Don't kid yourself, Fonko. We ain't a squad of Marines. You don't have MedEvac back up. A damn fool's errand to try to hump me out of the mountains. You'd never make it, only kill us both in the attempt. Look, get down to a road. Send people up after me..." He coughed, labored to catch his breath. "The party's over for me." The next breath came harder for him. He looked sideways at me. "A man..." he gasped. He looked at me plaintively with his country-boy eyes.

"Which man?" I asked him.

"A man," he said again very flatly, very slowly, talking with a dry mouth. "Now the way things are, the way they go no matter what no." He looked very, very tired. "Like trying to pass cars on the top of hills. On that road in Cuba. On any road. Anywhere. Just like that. I mean how things are. The way that they been going. For a while yes sure all right. Maybe with luck. A man." Obviously in great pain. Dread entering eyes that had 'til then shown no fear. "A man," he continued, looking at me. "One man ain't got. No man alone now." He stopped. "No matter how a man alone ain't got no bloody fucking chance."

He shut his eyes. It had taken him a long time to get it out, and it had taken all of his life to learn it.

His dying words? He wasn't dead yet, still had a pulse. But he was right, I couldn't carry him down the mountain, and military honor didn't apply here. Truth be told, he was, to put it charitably, an international outlaw. More bluntly, one of the world's worst people. Wouldn't be missed or mourned, except by other thugs and crooks, and by them only as a matter of business never to be done and IOUs never to be covered. There's only so much a man can do. Getting myself out of there would be trouble enough. Driffter had taken his shot, had taken many shots in his cowboy life, and there he was.

So now what? I took stock of the situation. I'm on a hillside deep in a Jamaican jungle with a soon-to-be-dead body, and a suitcase full of stuff people wouldn't stop at killing me for. And I better do something fast, as the curious will soon gather, and I sure don't want to have to explain all this to any authorities. I'm in street clothes suitable for doing business in a tropical town, not for traversing jungle. At least I was wearing my desert boots—better than deck shoes or penny loafers. I'd no idea of the Jamaican terrain except that it had mountains down the middle and the capital, Kingston, lay on the southern coast. According to Harry Belafonte, the nights are gay, and the sun shines daily on the mountain top. A lot of help, that.

Speaking of nights, darkness was falling fast. The mountains were inhabited, I noticed shacks and little settlements in pockets and clearings as we came in. A crashing chopper surely doesn't happen every day. People will come, and who knows who? I pushed debris out of the way and crawled into the cargo bay to see what I could salvage. Not much useful. I pulled some blankets out of the tangle, uncovering the food locker. I wrestled that loose and opened it. A few sandwiches remained, as well as some bottles of water. Not much tea in the jug, and certainly no longer iced. I took two bottles of water for myself and took the third back into the cockpit to see if Driffter needed something to drink. Still out, couldn't rouse a response. I figured to leave some water and some food for him should he come out of his funk, and take the rest. What else? The Uzi we'd taken off Vesco's thug was awkward for a man on foot in the jungle, but I rummaged around and located a Glock automatic with a full clip, which wouldn't over-burden me. What about the aluminum suitcase? Should I be sensible, leave it there and be rid of its curse? On the other hand, it must be worth a lot to somebody. Might give me some compensation from my inconvenience, maybe some bargaining leverage, which I might well need in getting out of this jam. I decided I'd tote it along for a while and see what developed.

Plus it was a handy carrying case for the trek out of the woods.

I opened it to stow the food and the Glock, and what the...? The ledger books and the disks were still there, but the file folders had gone missing. How could that have happened? But what difference did it make? I couldn't make any sense of them anyhow. What the hell, it lightened the load and left room for the goods I'd be carrying. I repacked it, made a blanket roll, gathered my gear and set out down the slope. The trees were mostly evergreens, not hardwoods like Indochina's jungles. The undergrowth was not thick or densely entangled, easy enough to bushwhack until I came across a trail of sorts leading down toward the canyon floor. In the dark, I groped my way into a little clearing a ways off the trail and set up camp for the night. I won't say I felt at home in that jungle, because who feels at home in jungles, besides people born and raised in them? They're hot, steamy, sticky, itchy and creepy. They harbor diseases and little critters that want to feast on your fluids. But I'd spent a year patrolling the jungles in Nam, knew my way around them. Jamaica was far from the worst I'd spent a night in. There weren't even any predators or poisonous snakes, as far as I knew. It had been a fraught day. I'd survived six flight hours in a chopper piloted by a madman. I'd bucked a shootout, three aerial dogfights and a helicopter crash. I needed shuteye. I laid a blanket over a level patch, crushed the vegetation beneath it to some semblance of comfort, rigged the other blanket overhead for a canopy, folded some of the ground cloth over the suitcase for a pillow of sorts and hit the rack, letting chirpy, squawky, hooty night noises lull me to sleep.

* * *

I SLEPT FITFULLY. AT ONE POINT I THOUGHT I HEARD VOICES passing along the trail I'd used, but I didn't rouse myself to investigate. They weren't bothering me, and the last thing I wanted was company. I awakened for good before dawn, checked myself over for wear and tear and decided I'd survived the night. My overhead blanket had absorbed the light sprinkle of rain misting down. The air was moist but warm. I ate half the food I had, drank a little water. I'd save the rest for the heat of the day when hiking downslope sweated me thirsty. From what I'd observed as we flew in, we weren't too far into the mountains, the coast lying no more than ten miles down the stream in the canyon.

In the light of day I inventoried my kit. A pistol with nine rounds. Enough food and water to get me through the day. In my wallet $248 American, plus AmEx and MasterCard plastic. My only ID was my California driver's license, no passport. A pocket comb. A ballpoint pen. Not your basic survival assembly, but I was on a densely populated, fertile, friendly island, not a trackless wilderness—situation not desperate. I hadn't gone far from the chopper, so I assembled my gear, laid it out of sight in the clearing and climbed the slope back to the chopper to see if anything else useful might be there. I left the trail and crept through the underbrush as quietly as I could to where I could observe it, then waited. Nothing. Nobody. I approached it and found the cockpit and the cargo bay doors open. Driffter was gone! Who? How? What? Screw it. Nobody was in sight. The gear in the cargo bay had been thoroughly tossed. The rifles and Uzi had been taken, among other things. I sorted through what remained, found nothing useful. The food I'd left behind was gone. No problem. No time to linger. I returned to my clearing, packed up my gear to make it as portable as I could. Left the blankets in a heap on the ground and set out.

The trail got easier the further I descended. As days in the jungle go, this one went pretty well, with flowering plants all over the place, the trees and bushes full of birds. Lower down in areas cleared of trees I passed some huts, apparently not in use now. Creeks fed the stream, which became a small river tumbling down over rocks and ridges. When lost always follow water downstream, is the rule of thumb, and age-old wisdom again did the trick. Downhill quick-marching is hell on the knees, but you go fast. By early afternoon I reached a little settlement, a cluster of shacks mostly, where a paved country road crossed a bridge over the river.

The people out and about, black every one, watched me warily from their distance. A white man coming down out of the mountains where a helicopter had disappeared had to be an object of curiosity.

A cement block building crudely painted in bright, raw colors and designs, topped by a rusted corrugated roof, stood at the roadside and seemed to be a general store. I went in and asked the man tending the counter if he spoke English. He did, in the local patois, sing-songy with a rippling rhythm, punctuated with "mon." I won't try to transcribe it here. Listen to some reggae music if you want to hear a sample. Even with my limited foreign language skills I could follow it, no worse than American ghetto slang. I asked how to get to Kingston. He told me a bus stopped there, the ride to Kingston more than 200 km, take "mos de day, de nex one come soon." He didn't ask any questions, though I'm sure there were answers he'd have loved to hear. He changed some American dollars into Jamaican ones. I bought a bus ticket, a coke, some rolls and jerky to eat just then, and cookies and bananas for a snack on the way. I sat on a bench in the shade to eat lunch while I waited. A young man in a white T-shirt and faded jeans went into the store. I sensed a hushed discussion inside, then the young man rushed out. Presently I saw him burst from behind a shack on a bicycle, a scrawny dog yapping up a ruckus as it chased him down the road.

A banged-up old bus, covered with exotic graffiti from stem to stern, lurched to a stop across from the store. A few people got off, and I followed the several who climbed on. I threaded my way through luggage, parcels and protruding limbs to a seat in the rear and settled in next to a dignified, grey-haired man. I positioned my aluminum case behind my legs, leaving little forward clearance for my knees, and surveyed my fellow passengers. They comprised a motley collection of types and burdens. Fat, brightly-swathed mamas with squirmy children. School-agers toting books. Young men bent on missions unknown. Judging from the array on the roof-rack, some had wares to market, others had packed well-used trunks and bags for extended stays. At least I wasn't sharing my seat with a cage full of roosters.

As the driver finished his break and took his seat a large, well-polished white BMW rushed to a stop by the roadside shop. Two sharply dressed black men with dark glasses got out and strode in through the door. As we pulled away, they rushed outside looking up and down the road. Uh oh. I bent over and stayed down until we were well underway on the road. Then I took another look at my fellow riders. I was the only white person on the bus, or anywhere in sight. Another uh oh. With my straight dark hair, my olive complexion, my changeling face and my slightly less than average height I've always been able to blend into any crowd outside of sub-Saharan Africa. Those talents got me a job as a Hollywood extra when I was in high school, and they've gotten me through tight spots in my later adventures. I hadn't thought of the Caribbean, which I have since learned was exploiting black African plantation slave labor centuries before it caught on in the U.S. of A, and whose present demographics reflect that history. My immediate goal was to evade capture by ill-meaning parties unknown. My immediate difficulty was, I was in a population where I stood out like Mama Cass in a bathing beauty lineup.

"Are you a tourist, sir?" my seatmate asked. In contrast to the storekeeper, he was well spoken.

"Mmmm, in a way," I said. "Taking in the sights. Going off the beaten track, seeing how the people live."

"Poorly, but happily," he replied. "Where are you staying?"

"Nowhere in particular. I'm in transit right now." Tourists! A crowd I could blend into while I got my bearings. The bus lumbered along at a good clip, traffic being light out in the country at that hour. I couldn't spot the BMW. If the storekeeper told them I'd bought a ticket to Kingston, they might figure to hang back and intercept the bus there. "The fact is, I haven't yet decided on my next destination. Perhaps you could recommend a good place for a tourist?"

"Ochos Rios is very popular with the American tourists," he

said. "A good selection of hotels, many shops, world-renowned beaches. Tourist cruise ships stop there regularly. But you'll learn little about how, as you put it, the people in Jamaica live. Too pricey for Jamaicans, but I gather that Americans find it a bargain."

"A day or two at the beach would be refreshing. Where is Ochos Rios?"

"We'll be arriving there in about an hour."

And so, after a ride of fits, starts, lurches and high-speed chicken around mountain curves, we did. "Kingston ticket no good no more for you stopping here, mon," the bus driver informed me. "Muss buy nudder one." I assured him it was no problem and alit. I scanned the parking area, spotted no white BMWs. The beach resorts and hotels lay a moderate walk away, but that shiny aluminum case in my hand was a beacon to all evildoers. I needed to minimize my visibility. I had a taxi drive me to a shop that sold luggage and travel gear where I bought a comfortable, nondescript backpack, a canvas book bag for the ledgers and a little case for the computer discs. Much less awkward to tote, and feather-light compared to the packs I used to hump in the LRRPs. In the cab, I transferred my gear from the two-suiter. When he dropped me off in front of an econo-class hotel a ways back from the beach, I paid him off and was going to leave the aluminum suitcase in the back seat until it occurred to me that anyone curious could quickly find out where the man who left it had been last seen. Better to leave it behind in the hotel.

The hotel clerk had a room for the night and accepted my AmEx card, though he wouldn't give me a cash advance on it. I had enough money for the time being, and I'd be in Kingston tomorrow. I'd have been disappointed with my bare-bones room if I'd squandered all my savings on a two-week vacation there, but it suited the situation. I shoved the aluminum case under the bed, shrugged the backpack onto my shoulders and went out on another errand—camo gear. I broke a U.S. $50 into Jamaican at a money changer, then strolled along the main shopping street until

I came to a vendor hawking tourist plumage. Shorts were out of the question for what I had to do, but I bought a loose cotton T-shirt, lemon yellow, lime green sporting a picture of Bob Marley. Also, a crushable Panama hat with a bright red band. Voila! All I needed was a zoom-lens Canon to hang around my neck and a sunburned wife nagging at me. I stuffed the shirt I'd been wearing into the pack and strolled out to blend in with my fellow vacationers. I spotted a pharmacy nearby, picked up basic toiletries. Next stop was a beachfront tiki bar, for a Heineken and a bite to eat. Ochos Rios was a gorgeous spot, all right, that sweeping arc of white sand. A placid bay, ideal for parasailing and windsurfing and general blissing out, but no surf to speak of. Can't have everything. The bar sat toward the east end of the bay, affording a glimpse of the sunset, always a treat in the tropics. Shore boats were shuttling day-trippers back to a big cruise ship anchored out in the harbor.

So now what? I couldn't get back in the states without a passport, nor did I dare return to Grand Cayman to retrieve mine. There must be a U.S. Consulate in Kingston that does that sort of thing, so I'd pursue that tomorrow. Maybe the clerk at the hotel desk could advise me. And then lay low until a flight out? How long would that take to arrange? Topping up my cash would be helpful. As best I could tell from the tourist guides I picked up in the hotel lobby, Kingston was about 70 miles over the mountains, several hours by bus. Were I not an international party of interest, the operation would go like Caribbean clockwork. As it was, I had to keep to the shadows and walk with measured step. I nursed a couple after-dinner beers and listened to a steel band until mid-evening. My eyelids went drooping. Time for a much-needed sleep. I hoisted my pack and headed back to the hotel.

As the clerk handed me my room key, he said, "Mr. Fonko, some men came asking after you earlier."

"Could you describe them?"

"Rough hombres. Latino. Three of them. I, of course, told them nothing, but they were insistent, said they knew you were here. They said they would be back."

Not the bunch in the BMW. Then who? How did they know to look for me here? "Had you by any chance entered my credit card charge in your system before they showed up?"

"The bookkeeper did before he quit work at 5 p.m."

They can trace me through credit card transactions? Whoever they are? Because of banking connections with BCCI? Shit. "I'll bet you twenty dollars American you can't put me in another room, far away from my present one."

"Mr. Fonko, I'm sorry to say you lose that bet. I happen to have an available room at the other end of the top floor."

"I never win anything," I said, fishing a twenty out of my wallet. "This transfer won't be recorded in your books, will it?"

"How can it? It never happened. Sleep well."

My first day in Jamaica and already two packs of punks dogged my trail. Sleep well? Right. "Say, by the way, I need to replace a lost passport. American. Where would I do that?"

"It happens from time to time. The American Consulate in Kingston can help you with that, I think."

* * *

NEXT MORNING, I STEPPED OUT OF THE ELEVATOR TO A HUBBUB in the hotel lobby. The night clerk had been murdered. A room had been broken into. The one I'd moved out of. Which meant they'd found the empty suitcase. Which meant they knew I still had the stuff, but not the suitcase. I hurried back to my room, assembled my kit, checked out and exited via the back door. I didn't spot any tails as I hurried to the beachfront. Probably, they didn't know what I looked like. I found a crowded restaurant to grab breakfast and do some thinking. I couldn't linger in Ochos Rios, clearly. Getting back to the States was my only hope, but for that I'd need a passport, so my next move must be to hit the American Consulate. I walked to a row of resort hotels along the beach to see about a ride to Kingston. A sleek tourist bus stood at the curb at the entrance to one, boarding sun-broiled vacationers, and I counted too few to fill it. I sidled up to the driver, asked some questions. It was a package tour, heading to the Kingston airport for a flight back to Chicago. He was amenable to a little bribe and welcomed me aboard.

The bus followed the coast, passed resorts along the shoreline and veered inland through forests and plantations, as pretty a roadside as I'd ever seen. The driver pointed out Ian Fleming's cliffside house, to the delight of the James Bond fans (*Octopussy* was a big film hit that year). Jamaican countryside driving was a stop-and-start blood sport. When the traffic moved, it defied death. Beat-up cars passed on blind curves, darting back in between trucks and school buses the last split second before a head-on collision with a taxicab. Dreadlocked men on Japanese motorbikes whipped around the bus, banking and weaving through shoulder-width spaces between lines of speeding traffic in opposing lanes. Then the whole mess came to a halt as opposing drivers faced off over the right of way on a narrow bridge. During one delay, I went up the aisle and asked the bus driver about the American Consulate. He told me we'd pass close by, and he agreed to drop me off on a nearby cross street. At Port Maria, we swung inland and commenced a headlong ride over the Blue Mountains that had the terrified Midwesterners all but praying for deliverance. After the driver rampaged us through a stretch of twists and curves that would baffle a pretzel maker, the road leveled off, calmed down and straightened out. The driver brought the bus to a stop and motioned me forward. "Just a little ways down Oxford Road here," he said, pointing. "You can't miss it." I thanked him and debarked.

On the flat in a nice area of town, Oxford Road comprised a commercial district of hotels, restaurants, office buildings, diplomatic outposts and the New Kingston Shopping Mall, interspersed with palms, lawns and hedges. Having the address of the Consulate would have made it easier not to miss. A single story stand-alone office building with a discreet nameplate, it took me a while to locate. Not many people walked the street in the midday sun, no crowd to blend into, so I sort of stood out. I wasn't garbed for a diplomatic reception, but I was an American in need of a temporary passport. Thanks to my night in the hotel, I was at least cleaned up and presentable, and they probably had to deal with bewildered tourists in Bob Marley T-shirts three times every day. I walked through the entrance into the lobby. The clerk on duty greeted me and asked how he could help me.

"I need a temporary passport, or possibly a replacement."

"You already have an American passport?"

"Yes, but not with me."

"You have a passport, but not with you? Why do you need a new passport? How did you get into Jamaica with no passport?"

Oops. "Oh, I had it when I left the States, but I lost it."

"Where did you lose it? Was it stolen?"

"No, I lost it on the cruise ship. Had a few drinks, got a little frisky on the afterdeck and it blew overboard."

"I see. What cruise ship is that?"

"The one at Ochos Rios. It's anchored in the harbor. I came into town about the passport. Have to have a replacement, or at least temporary documents, before the ship leaves tomorrow morning."

"And what cruise line would that be?" He was taking notes. This was not going where I wanted it to.

"Carnival. Carnival Cruises." I'd seen their ads somewhere—Fun Ship Cruises. Did they do them in the Caribbean? I had a feeling I'd soon find out.

"Have you any American identification?"

"I have a California driver's license in my wallet, if that will help."

"It would. Could I take a look?" I took it out of my wallet and passed it to him. He examined it, took some more notes and handed it back.

"Okay. American tourists lose passports all the time. I'll take your information to our passport desk; we'll fix you up with something and get you back to your cruise ship, don't worry. Can you come back here a little later in the day, say around 3 p.m.?"

"Sure. I'll be here." I went back outside wondering if I'd screwed myself with my phony yarn. But the truth—that I'd crash landed in a chopper flying out of Cuba with the proceeds of a bloody bank robbery on Grand Cayman—would that have been better? Everything depended on how diligently they checked out the tale I told. I had a few hours to kill—what to do but wait and see and hope for the best?

It was past noon, so I picked out a restaurant up the road and sat down to an American lunch. Out the window I noticed three shabby men, seemed to be blind, tapping slowly along the sidewalk with white sticks. They appeared mixed-race, bulky, bowed over as they shuffled along. The first one wore blue glasses and held a tin cup against the crook of his white stick. The others' eyes were squinted shut. The right hand of the second man was on the first man's shoulder and the right hand of the third man on the second's. A dingy black motor hearse with black plumes on the corners of the roof came slowly up the street and stopped beside them, the driver conferring with the man in the lead. Then a strange thing, the three blind men looked up at the restaurant as though they could see it. The hearse pulled back into traffic, and the three men went tap-tap-tapping away along the walkway. They were looking for me? How would they know? Somebody questioned the bus driver, maybe?

I still had some time before 3 p.m. A low profile being advisable, I found an out of the way spot in an alleyway behind the Pegasus Hotel where I could sit in the shade and plot some strategy. If the passport desk put any effort into verifying my story I wouldn't be getting a new one any time soon. Worse than that, what would they do after I'd showed up after spinning a fancy yarn? How much of the true story was circulating? How much of it would reach the Consulate? Obviously, some people already knew more than was healthy for me.

Should I get stuck here, my cash wouldn't last much longer. I wondered if a local bank would let me tap my AmEx card, or maybe an American bank would be a better bet? I verged on getting up and searching for a bank when I heard tap-tap-tapping drawing nearer around the building's corner. I rose to my feet with my backpack in my hand, edged closer to the corner and waited in the shadow. The three blind men I'd seen on the street suddenly surged around the corner, looking for me and reaching inside their coats. They spotted me and drew silenced pistols. Unfortunately for them, they'd stayed bunched together, and I stood closer than they'd anticipated. Street-fight rule of thumb: run from a knife but charge a gun. Figuring them as sneaks, not warriors, I took a big lunge forward and with a swift, two-hand basketball pass thrust my heavy backpack in the face of the man in the middle, sending him staggering backwards and flat on his ass. I distracted the one on the left with a sharp jab to the solar plexus, leaving him gasping. The one on my right couldn't line up a shot into the swirling action. I swiveled, grabbed his gun arm with both hands, twisted it up behind his back until his shoulder dislocated, then pitched him to the ground. I turned and fell on the one struggling under the backpack. I wrenched his pistol out of his grasp and turned it on him, shot him in the temple. His suppressor was a good one, emitting a modest "thwip"— wouldn't draw a crowd. I put the other two out of their misery with it as well.

Ranger training in jungle warfare comes in handy from time to time.

They'd staged their assault when nobody was close by, but somebody would surely soon happen along. In my current circumstances, a silenced pistol would be more useful than the one I'd taken out of the chopper. I wasn't familiar with the guns my assailants carried, but they'd do. I slipped the one in my hand into my backpack and added the clips from the other two, wiped fingerprints off the guns. I straightened my shirt, dusted off my pants, slid my arms through the pack straps, put my hat back on and strolled out to Oxford Road. The black hearse sat parked a few yards down the street, motor running in readiness to scoot up the alley for a pickup—my corpse. When the driver saw me emerge he put it in gear and sped away.

Now what? Would the hearse come charging back with reinforcements? Would the police nab me on suspicion when they showed up? Hang around until 3 o'clock to find out whether my yarn fooled the passport desk? No way. Time to haul ass. I looked up and down the road, located a taxi sitting by a Texaco gas station down the street and headed for it. The driver was in the shade of his vehicle, sipping a Coke. "Is there an American bank in town?" I asked him.

"Yes sah, de Citibank," he said.

"Take me there," I said.

"Yas sah." We headed down toward the center of town. He took me through a district where the streets jammed up with honking cars and shouting drivers. People—preponderantly black and poor-looking— thronged the sidewalks. The scene rang with reggae, throbbed lively, sultry, colorful. Presently the cabbie swung into a more well-appointed business district, contained and quieter. We passed down an avenue lined by office buildings and came to a stop. "Here de Citibank," he announced.

I scoped out the street. People here dressed for business. My Marley Tee wouldn't play well. "Take me where they sell clothes," I said.

"Yas sah." He drove to another street where vendors of clothing, hats, doo-dads, knick-knacks, most everything else, hawked their goods. Climbing out, I gave him enough U.S. dollars to put a smile on his lips. I found a stand with dress-style shirts, picked out a conservative design in my size. I bought a subdued baseball cap and stowed the panama. I donned the dress shirt on over my Tee and tucked both in, ready for business. Too warm for the day, but presentable. And different enough from whatever description of me might have spread. That done, I walked the few blocks back to Citibank.

The teller said she was not able to advance cash against my MasterCard on the strength of my California driver's license. She thought the American Express office would be a better bet. I followed her directions and arrived there a half hour before closing time. The clerk ran my card, read the screen and told me there was a problem with my account. She'd have to see if it covered overseas cash advances. She told me to take a seat in the lobby while she checked it out, then disappeared through a door. What gives with this?

Rather than establish myself as a sitting duck, I hoisted my backpack, ducked outside, crossed the street and took a table by the window inside a little café down the way from the AmEx office. I ordered a cup of coffee and watched the AmEx entrance. It wasn't long before a pair of sharply dressed, swarthy men showed up, scanned the street and went in. They came out quickly, looked both ways and separated hurriedly to cover both directions. The hell? Just from running my card?

This was getting disturbing. People saw me tear out of Grand Cayman with Driffter. I'm still checked in at the hotel, and they have my stuff. Vesco sounded the alarm, no telling how widely. A ton of people saw me with the aluminum suitcase, all the way to Ochos Rios. They're tracking me through my credit cards. The Feds had me in their sights. I felt like a stalked teenager in *Friday the 13th Part XVI*. Jason's after me! How do I get away? Where can I turn? I could surrender the BCCI stuff to the U.S. Embassy here, but then I'd have to explain how I came by it and how I got it here. And it wouldn't surprise me if I'd broken a few laws in the process—transporting stolen goods, shooting down a Cuban fighter jet, spraying a U.S. chopper with gunfire, entering Jamaica illegally, greasing three assassins—just for starters. I could just ditch it somewhere, but people would still be coming after me to locate it, and I had no doubt they'd work me over rather than settling for "I dunno" as my answer. Plus the BCCI swag could give me bargaining power, which I might sorely need. I was stuck with it for the time being.

Time for an identity switch. The AmEx clerk had seen me in a dress shirt, so I peeled it off and stuffed it in the pack. Switch hats. Back to Joe Tourist in a Marley Tee, just arrived in Kingston town.

Then I noticed the headline on the *Daily Gleaner* at the corner news stand:

Murder at Ochos Rios Hotel: Missing American Suspect at Large

Shit.

Forget passports and pocket money. Now my priority was to get the hell out of Jamaica. Too many people were onto me. The airport was no-go: they'd have that staked out for sure, and anyhow I couldn't exit without a passport. Only one other option for leaving an island—by boat. Of course, they'd be looking for me there too, so booking any ordinary boat ride was risky. Then, what other kind of boat? Kingston had a big, busy harbor. Cruise ships, tankers, freighters, what else?

Better take a look. I went out on the street, flagged a taxi, aimed him at the harbor. I told him to drive along the shoreline slowly. The modern, industrialized part of the harbor offered no help. Tankers and ore freighters had destinations far removed from my desires. We rolled by an older, shabbier section of the harbor that seemed more promising, with several boats that looked like local haulers. We passed a small, beat-up old freight boat, the *John B,* tied wharfside where trucks full of green bananas were congregating. A half mile down the way we came to a café shack, and I had the driver let me off there. After he'd driven out of sight, I shrugged into my pack and walked back to the banana boat. A man who seemed to be the captain was directing banana trucks as they gathered on the dock.

I lowered my pack to the ground and stood by, watching the activity for a few minutes. "Where are you taking the bananas?" I asked him.

"To Haiti, mon," he replied. "Sailin' me bananas to Haiti."

I watched the drivers maneuver their trucks. "I could use a ride to Haiti," I said. "You have space for a passenger?"

"Got an extra bunk in the foc'sle. When you plannin' on goin' Haiti?"

"As soon as possible. When you putting to sea?"

"Break of day tomorrow."

"The men load the bananas during the night?"

"Yes, mon. They labors be easier after the sun go down, it not bein' so hot, you know. The ladin' crew show up here a little later, have a drink of rum. Then they work all night, stack bananas 'til the morning come. When daylight come I tally their banana, 'cause they wanna go home. Soon's that done, we cast off for Haiti. Get to Port au Prince the next mornin'. That suit you?"

"Yes it does. My name's Jake Fonko." I put out my hand.

"I'm Captain Quarrel," he said, giving my hand a hearty shake. "Will be a pleasure havin' you aboard."

"Why do you take Jamaica bananas to Haiti? Doesn't Haiti have their own bananas?"

"Jamaica grow plenty of bananas, Haiti folk have plenty of nothin'. De American Uncle Sugar govment send 'em Haitians hoomanitarian aid. Which Baby Doc put in his own pocket, him bein' hoomanitarian as de nex' bloke. What hoomanitarian aid he overlook, he leave for de people, small change enough to pay for Jamaica bananas, ha ha."

"Would it be all right if I sleep on board tonight?"

"No problem, Mr. Fonko. I have a boy show you down to the foc'sle. You take care down there, might be deadly black tarantula, ha ha."

I stowed my gear under an empty bunk and went back topside. With both my Jamaica disguises blown, I put on the shirt I'd worn when I left Grand Cayman. I lurked out of sight until night had fallen good and dark, then furtively made my way down to the café. Brightly lit and busy, it filled with boisterous workingman's chatter, day crews going off work, night crews coming on. The day's chalkboard scrawl featured goat stew and rice, fine by me. I gobbled it and returned to the *John B* as quickly as I could. I'd have loved to hang out in that lively café a little longer, but staying out of sight was imperative. Back on board I watched the banana loaders from inside the cabin. Five huge, sweaty, muscle-rippling black men toted stalks of bananas into the hold like they were delivering sacks of Kitty Litter. These guys were wasting their time in Kingston: they should have been the offensive line for some NFL team.

I turned in early and passed a restful night down in the foc'sle, tarantulas notwithstanding. I awoke before daybreak and was emerging to run down and grab breakfast at the café when Mr. Quarrel stopped me at the top of the companionway.

"Mr. Fonko, just one moment. I hear some bad fellows come to de harbor last night, be askin' around about an American with a suitcase. I know nothin' about any of dat, but you better be keepin' an eye out. Dem bad fellows, dey tell me, plenty bad men."

"You don't think it's safe to run down to the café for a minute?"

"My advice is not do dat. Better if you eat with me in de cabin. Plenty good food." He ushered me in. A weathered table was neatly set. A pile of fresh fruit, a platter of sweet pastry, strong Blue Mountain coffee, and the cook was turning out scrambled eggs. Plenty good food indeed.

As we ate I remarked, "I thought bananas were yellow, but last night I saw them load red ones, purple ones, green ones."

"Dem yellow ones, dey United Fruit Company banana, for the Yankee market. For the islands market they come all colors, all shapes, all sizes. Yellow, red, purple ones. Big ones, little ones. Six foot, seven foot, eight foot bunch. Pick 'em green so dey travel nice, ripen after dey get to market."

"Mr. Quarrel, have you always been in this business, trading Jamaica bananas to Haiti?"

"Only last few years. One time I had a guano business—bird shit, you know. Hauled it out of Crab Key off de coast. Sold it to Americans, dey want put on their strawberries. Why dey do dat? I put sugar on mine, taste mo' bettah. But den dey blow up Crab Key, blow it clean away. No more guano business. Strange

Chinaman own dat island, he a very bad man, don't miss workin' for him. Banana business better, more steadier."

Quarrel looked me up and down. "You know, Mr. Fonko, I think maybe you a bit of bad man yourself. But dere only one of you, and many of dem other bad men maybe lookin' for you? Go back down de foc'sle for a time. After we clear past the harbor mouth, den it safe for you up here."

ZOMBIE JAMBOREE

THE BOAT RIDE TO HAITI WENT WITHOUT INCIDENT. The weather was benign, the waters calm, Captain Quarrel a skillful seaman and good company. Apparently, I had not been observed departing on the *John B*; at least, we'd not been pursued or harassed. The route from Kingston to Port au Prince included only a short stretch over open water between the islands. During the night, we'd entered the long bay leading to Port au Prince. Haiti—the entire island it shares with the Dominican Republic, Hispaniola, actually—was mountainous, reaching nearly 9000 feet. Quarrel and I, over strong morning coffee, watched the sun rise over the approaching peaks. "We be there in a couple hours, Mr. Fonko," he said. "What business you have in Haiti anyhow?"

"As you know, bad men are after me on Jamaica. Haiti's the nearest place I could get away from them safely."

"They not after you on Haiti as well?"

"They may well be, but I think my odds are better someplace other than Jamaica."

"I'm hopin' you right, but nobody's odds is better on Haiti. Haiti one bad place, mon. The people are poor. The government is evil. Baby Doc, he follow in Papa Doc's footsteps, evil man. You step out of line in Haiti, him Tonton Macoutes step on you, maybe turn you into a zombie."

"What are the Tonton Macoutes?"

"They like a police force, but not police because no law for Tonton Macoutes. Judge, jury and executioner right on de spot. Oh, maybe not like dat for a white man, but bad enough, put you in jail, beat you up a bit, just not so bad as for black man. Even worse for black woman. De police, dey just want a little pourboire, grease de palm, you know, give 'em a few gourdes and dey go away happy. Tonton Macoutes, dey take de bribe, den do you anyhow."

"Do they wear uniforms? How do I recognize them?"

"Some wear uniforms, some dress sharp, all of dem wear big dark glasses, all of dem look well fed. Dey everywhere, watchin' watchin' watchin'. So a man mus be careful his step everywhere."

The sun had ascended high enough to unleash shades of blue out to sea, but in the long bay leading to Port au Prince the water nearer shore had a sludgy brown caste. Quarrel explained that the Haitian mountains had long been cleared of trees and other vegetation for firewood and charcoal manufacture, leaving the bare topsoil to wash into the sea with the rain runoff. He gave me a look through his binoculars. Yes, the hills surrounding the city were bare indeed, some scrub and brown weeds but not much else. No surprise that grazing goats had the anorexic bodies of high fashion models.

From the water the city didn't look so bad, seemed to have a few parks and trees here and there, some broad avenues, some dignified buildings. It appeared low, flat, the highest buildings just a few stories tall and bright white in the oppressive sun glare. Domes here and there, a few spires. Not much very modern-looking—no glass-façade high rises. Nestled between hills on both arms surrounding the bay and backed up by mountains, the city sat in a heat-trapping basin, its morning air already as stifling and foul as Bangkok at its worst. Just standing on deck in the morning breeze, sweat plastered my Bob Marley T-shirt to my torso.

We landed mid-morning, tying up along the banana dock, a

rickety wharf. Loaders loitered around awaiting work to commence when the trucks arrived. I put on my baseball hat, shouldered my backpack and put a foot on the gangway to shore. "You take care now," advised Quarrel. "My advice to you, go to the main road, have a taxi get you to a hotel straightaway, do not linger on the streets here. You should know, Haiti was French colony in de old days, not English like Jamaica. French de official language here. However, mos de Haiti people speak Creole. You find English speakin' mon straightaway, that be best for you."

I thanked him for his advice, as well as for a most pleasant boat ride, and mounted the plank to the wharf. It fronted an older section of the waterfront whose pilings, deck, warehouses and office shacks confessed timeless years of weather, abuse and vandalism. Wood was splintered and splayed; corrugated iron walls and roofs patched, dented and rust-rotted. The waiting loaders sat, squatted and leaned against anything upright in what shade they could find, eying me from under droopy lids as I started toward the streets.

An emaciated, raggedy man emerged from an alley to intercept me, his hand out for a handout. Avoiding eye contact, I walked beyond him. He fell in behind, chanting "dollah, dollah, dollah..." Another shambling scarecrow joined our little parade, close on my heels. And another and another. By the time I'd walked the two blocks to a busy waterfront road, I'd collected a regiment comprising every disease, defect, disability, dilapidation, degeneracy and deformity known to modern medicine and ancient legend. Noisy, insistent, wild-eyed, filthy and foul-smelling, they beseeched me from every side, tugging at my clothing, pack and bare arms. Was I in danger? I began to think that I might be. I threw elbows around, causing the ones nearest me to back off in bewilderment. One of them shouted "Blan!" then rattled off a speech in a language I'd never heard before. The crowd broke into loud laughter and started chanting "Blan, blan, blan." Another one made a speech, evoking more riotous laughter. Then, pressed by their comrades behind them, they oozed back toward me. I no longer wondered if I might be in danger. Yep, no doubt about it. Starving, desperate, and they 'way outnumbered me.

I saw no clear path to the street through the reeking mob, decided to make one of my own and plowed into what seemed the weakest part of their defensive line. As I reached the curbside of Boulevard Harry Truman, a black Mercedes screeched to a halt, the four men inside sizing up my roiling entourage from behind black sunglasses. Two police cars pulled up behind it. I spotted a taxi at the curb about fifty yards down the street and made a break for it. The crowd of beggars surged after me, whereupon a squad of police piled out of their cars and waded into the swarm, whaling on everybody within reach with long batons. Thumps and thwacks punctuated shouts and yowls of pain. Instantly, my beseechers morphed from threatening to pitiable, but I didn't linger to empathize with their plight—let 'em feel their own pain. I hustled into the taxi and said just about all the French I knew, "Hotel. Anglais." I looked back at the seething mob. Two men had emerged from the Mercedes and were pointing their arms at the crowd. I heard pistols pop. The cab driver peeled away not a moment too soon. I kept lookout abaft. The Merc didn't follow us.

The scene that greets the visitor as he approaches from the sea, I soon discovered, was just a wee bit deceptive. The shining white buildings were Haitian government buildings, for example, the Palais National and a museum. There were a couple semi-lux hotels on Boulevard Jean-Jacques Dessalines. My driver pulled up to one and stopped. No, too easy for anyone to find me there, if they'd even take me with no passport. "Speak English?" I tentatively asked the driver.

"Little," he replied.

"Too expensive for this hotel. Money too much. Take me to English hotel, cheap cheap." He nodded and re-entered the crawling stream of traffic. Presently we departed the high rent district of gleaming government buildings and confronted actual Port au Prince. The streets narrowed and jammed up, teeming with battered cars and trucks, riders laboring along under their loads on rusted bicycles, and pedestrians and overloaded porters needy of a lifetime of square meals. What seemed to be a middle class district by Haitian standards would qualify as an American big city slum, except that the Haitian version looked less prosperous. Shabby, low buildings with corrugated steel roofs, their facades painted in screaming raw colors—scarlet, yellow, electric blues, acid greens—offered a variety of products and services. What they might be I can't say, as even the signs still legible were in French. Street vendors spilled out over the curbs into the dusty, crumbling road. The street crowds predominately came in darker shades of African black, no white people in sight and not even many mulattos. The male uniform was threadbare white T-shirts and faded blue jeans. The women, many of them balancing burdens atop their heads, sported long, brightly colored cotton dresses and bandanas. Off the business avenues, I caught glimpses down what passed for residential streets, shanties desperate despite the bright paint covering their rust and rot, piled on top of equally desperate shanties. And all of it grinding slowly along in a murky basin of fetid tropical steam heat. The only comparably poor housing I'd ever seen was peasant villages during my tours in Nam and Cambodia, but those at least were functioning communities in the rice paddies, not the sorry despair of Haitian slums. On the other hand, Haiti was more colorful.

Our route left the slums and entered a district of once elegant mansions embellished with towers and gables, weathered gingerbread wood carvings and rusting ironwork filigree and lacework, interspersed with neglected houses of more modern design. They sat on overgrown but undernourished plots strewn with non-biodegradable trash. The driver rolled down an eroded gravel driveway flanked by wind-shattered banana palms to, according to its weather-ravaged sign, "Hotel Trianon." It occupied a decent sized plot of ground whose gardens had been well-landscaped in some distant past. It was a good-sized building. A verandah overhung with a roof missing half its shingles spanned the front. Towers, balconies and wood fretwork decorations, all of which cried out for rehab and three coats of fresh paint, gave the impression of something out of an old Charles Addams *New Yorker* cartoon. I half expected to find Angelica Huston as "Morticia" greeting me from behind the reception counter.

Instead, I was met by a weedy, greying Britisher. "My name is Brown," he said, advancing toward me. "Welcome to Hotel Trianon."

"Pleased to meet you, Mr. Brown," I said. "I'm Jake Fonko. I told the cab driver to take me to an English hotel, and we ended up here. You're the manager?"

"No, the owner. You're lucky. He could have done worse by you. How much did you pay him, if I may ask?"

"I didn't have any local currency, so I gave him an American five dollar bill. He seemed happy enough with it." "As well he should. That's a week's wages here. But not enough to cause trouble, I think. Some Americans have over-tipped to the extent that we were beset with hordes come to offer their services."

"I need a room for a while. Anything available?"

"Oh yes," said Mr. Brown. "That's never a problem at Hotel Trianon. Perhaps up on the third floor? You can have the Barrymore Room. John Barrymore once stayed in it. We even have his bar bills, in case you want verification."

"If it was good enough for The Great Profile, it's good enough for me. When did that happen?"

"About 50 years ago, I think. I don't remember rightly. I was just a little nipper then. Let's sign you in. Could I see your passport, please?"

"I'm having difficulties about that right now," I said. "I lost it on Grand Cayman. I hitched a ride to here on a banana boat from Kingston. Is it a problem?"

"Not to Hotel Trianon, but you'd better have a good story for the authorities. I suggest you get yourself in a proper frame of mind for the inevitable official visit, concoct a good story. Newly arriving white men are always persons of interest. Why would a white person in his right mind sneak in here? They'd like to know."

"I kept an eye out. There were police around when I caught the cab, but they didn't follow me. They were too busy beating up the crowd of beggars I'd attracted."

"No need for the police to waste their time tagging after you—they know the cab, they'll question the driver. Was there by chance in the vicinity a Mercedes with men in sky blue uniforms wearing sunglasses?"

"Sunglasses, yes. I didn't notice their clothing. Were those Tonton Macoutes? My boat captain warned me about them. What are they, secret police?"

"Tontons Macoute," he corrected me. "Nothing secret about them. They're everywhere, some in uniform, some in plain clothes, all of them government thugs. 'Uncle Gunnysack,' the Haitian bogeyman. It's an old Creole myth. Tonton Macoute comes around and puts bad children in his gunnysack. Most people they come around to see would gladly trade being put in a gunnysack for the treatment they get. They'll be showing up to talk to you, count on that. You see, whites of any shade are privileged in Haiti, not only pure Caucasians, but also mulattos and the Syrian shopkeepers. Non-blacks are only 5% of the population, but they own the place. Baby Doc's of a slightly lighter hue, possibly quadroon. It's the reverse of where we come from. In the U.S. and U.K., any black and you're a black. Here, any white and you're a white, privileged. But not immune." I told him about the crowd of beggars taunting me. "That's what they do when a white intrudes on a black situation and gives offense. 'Blan' is from the French word for 'white'—'blanc.' They compete with derisive stories and rhymes about 'blans,' the winner the one who draws the biggest laugh from the crowd. Harmless fun for them. Unsettling for a foreigner fresh off the boat. Speaking of which, you came from Kingston on a banana boat, with no passport or papers? You don't happen to have a gun in your pack, do you? If so, let's get it hidden. That would bring trouble you don't want. I'll settle you in your room; then we'll see where things stand."

He led me up the stairs. The John Barrymore room was

spacious and comfortable, if shopworn. The windows looked down on the entrance and driveway. I dropped my pack on the dresser. He assured me my room would be searched, so we found a secure hidey-hole for my two pistols. And then located a different one to stash my pack. I surely didn't want the Tontons getting into that. He led me back downstairs to the lobby. "Through that portal is the bar and the restaurant," he explained. "The swimming pool's out the rear entrance. Right now we're refilling it, but you should be able to use it tomorrow morning."

"Refilling it?"

"We had to drain it. The Secretary of Social Welfare committed suicide in it last night, slashed his wrists and his throat. The other guests wouldn't swim in the water after that, so we thought it best to drain it. It's an American young couple. They like to swim naked in the pool at night. It isn't lit. Hate to bother you, but I need to ask. How do you intend to handle the bill? Hotel Trianon isn't expensive, but we do like to be paid for our hospitality."

"Would an American Express card do?"

"Regrettably, no. We aren't set up for American credit cards yet."

Money was an encroaching problem. I thought about it. "Could I make a telephone call to the U.S. from here?"

"In theory, yes. The telephone service is spotty, so it may take some time."

"Let's give it a try." I wrote down the office and home numbers of Evanston, my lawyer, ex-spook stepfather. It would be mid-afternoon in Pacific Palisades. No telling where he'd be at this hour. Overseas calls had to be placed through a central exchange. Mr. Brown dialed it and placed both calls. "They'll let us know when they connect."

"Is your phone secure?" I asked.

"Of course not. The government eavesdrops here."

"Then maybe I'd better tell you a little more about my situation." He took me into the bar, sat us down under a ceiling fan and stood for a round. For which at that moment I was deeply grateful. I related an edited version of the past couple days' adventures.

"Sticky wicket," he said. "No passport, no money and pursued by assassins. We have an American Consulate here. How about giving them a try?"

"I could, but it's possible the U.S. government is after me too. The list of BCCI clientele is pretty cosmopolitan and could include our own Central Intelligence Agency. I couldn't wait around in Kingston to see what the Consulate had in mind, but if they checked my case with any care, they'd have had questions whose answers would raise more questions. With the Consulate here, my odds are even worse. At least in Jamaica, I had a cruise ship for an alibi."

We sipped our drinks. We mulled over possible resolutions. He brought another round to the table. The telephone rang. He went to the desk and answered it. "It's a Mr. Wheeler. Your call?" he told me.

I went over and put the phone to my ear. "This is Jake. Hello?"

"Evanston here. What's up? You're calling from Haiti?"

"Yes. I have to be brief and cryptic. Number one, could you get a thousand dollars into the hands of Mr. Brown at the Hotel Trianon here? I'm good for it. I'll put him on the line for the details. Number two. Can you think of a way for me to get back into the U.S. without a passport?"

"It's tricky getting money into Haiti, but I can do that. You can enter the U.S. from Puerto Rico without a passport. Can you get to Puerto Rico from there?"

I turned to Mr. Brown. "Can I get to Puerto Rico from here?"

"From here it would be difficult. From Santo Domingo over the mountains, they have boat service."

Back to Evanston. "Can do. Do you know anyone in Santo Domingo I could contact?"

"Probably. I'll come up with something and get it to you. Anything else?"

"That's it for now. Here's Mr. Brown." I handed the phone

over, leaving it to them to square away routing and account numbers.

They settled things up, and Mr. Brown ushered me out to a table on the verandah with a third round of drinks. "Might as well relax and take in the tropical ambiance while we wait for the Tontons Macoute to show up," he said. He told me something of the Haitian people. Poor. Desperate. Terrified. Superstitious. Warm-hearted. Suspicious to the point of paranoia. Unreliable. Undisciplined. Some good individuals, but collectively a miserable lot. A white Mercedes sedan turned into the driveway and crunched to a stop at the stoop. "You wait here," Brown said, and he rose and went down the step to meet them. Two large, sun-glassed black men in well-tailored, well-pressed tropical weight civilian clothes got out to confer with him. They chatted amicably, then mounted the worn wood steps together, Brown in the lead by a pace.

"These gentlemen would like to have a word with you," Brown said. "Just a formality. They like to greet all our American guests. Gentlemen, this is Mr. Jake Fonko."

The larger of the two, apparently in command, stepped forward. "Pleased to meet you, Mr. Fonko. How are you finding our humble island?" He didn't offer a hand to shake.

"Mmmm, colorful. Lively. A place in which a native son can take pride."

"Quite so. So you arrived this morning on a banana boat, I understand? And where did your trip originate?"

"Jamaica."

"Yes, Jamaica sends us many fine bananas. So it slipped your mind to register your entry with the immigration department in the Customs Building?"

"I intended to, but I was assailed by a mob of beggars, and getting free of them distracted me from doing that. I plan to take care of it once I get settled here."

"Yes, that would be wise. Could I see your passport, please?"

"I don't have it with me."

"Of course. Why would you have it with you? It is in your luggage? I will wait for you while you get it." For a guy who with impunity could have me beaten to a pulp and tossed in solitary, he was exceedingly polite.

"What I meant to say is, I do not have my passport here in Haiti."

"Oh, I misunderstood. How did you arrive in these islands with no passport?"

"I had it when I arrived, but then I lost it on Jamaica, maybe stolen. So I had to come here with no passport. I was going to the American Consulate tomorrow to have it replaced."

"I see. Yes, that is the correct path to follow. But, tell me, why did you not take up your case with the Consulate in Kingston?"

I've never walked into a quicksand bog, but it must feel something like this. "The passport desk was closed when I went in. I had to leave the island before they opened the next day. Excuse me, is this an official inquiry?"

"Oh, no, no. Just an informal ushering you in, you know. Perhaps you could come into our office tomorrow, and we will see to the formalities. Mr. Brown can provide you with a driver who knows the way. After you visit your American Consulate, of course. With new passport in hand, I am sure there will be no difficulties. Pleased to have met you, Mr. Fonko." With that and no further words, the two men went back to their car, got in and eased around the parking area and back out to the street.

"Well, he seemed like a nice enough guy," I remarked as they drove away.

"He'd slit your throat for nothing because it's his job," Brown replied. "Not to mention his pleasure. I'll have Joseph run you down to the American Consulate first thing in the morning. If they can come up with paperwork, that may get you by. Or maybe you could take refuge in the Embassy. Otherwise, you've got a rough day ahead of you. If a local had that conversation with that man, he'd be defecating in his drawers right now."

I found something to read until the dinner hour, ate in the

hotel restaurant with the other guests and some walk-ins (the place may have been rundown, but the chef was first rate), and after that hung around Hotel Trianon for the rest of the evening. What else? Go out on the town looking for excitement? I took the opportunity to wash my underpants and two of my three shirts, hoping I'd have a chance to do a little shopping tomorrow after I finished business.

The tropic sun rose next morning, casting palm shadows over the filled swimming pool. It had enough length for brisk laps, which, wearing Jockey shorts, I found refreshing and relaxing. After toweling down, I checked my washing. Shirts still a little damp, but dry enough to wear. I hung my underpants in the bright morning sun and went without for the time being. Mr. Brown joined me for breakfast. "Your Mr. Wheeler said he'd transmit the money to the American Express office, in the form of travelers cheques. The banks here are loath to hand out hard currency, but you'd need a bushel basket to carry a thousand U.S. dollars' worth of gourdes."

"What's?"

"Gourdes—that is, gourds—loom large here. They yield a staple food, and then the natives use the shells for drinking vessels, so they named the currency after them too. The office opens at ten. I'll see to our business there while Joseph swings you by the American Consulate."

"Could you change some Jamaican dollars to gourdes? A little pocket money just in case..."

"Certainly." He went behind the reception desk and unlocked the cash drawer.

I showed him the remainder of my Jamaican money. "Would this get me through the day?"

"The day? More like a week." He counted out an array of Haitian bills and lay them on the counter. "Here's an assortment of ones, twos, fives and tens and a bunch twenty-fives. Fifty gourdes is a large amount, to the natives."

The shirt I'd worn when this fiasco began in the George Town hotel barroom was lightweight, with long sleeves. Thinking it suitable for official business with the passport people, I put it on that morning, and a good thing I did. Joseph, Mr. Brown's driver/porter/handyman, drove me through town and parked in front of the American Consulate. He turned off the motor, opened the car's windows wide and sat back to wait in the car while I went in. I introduced myself to the clerk as needing help concerning a passport. "Certainly, Mr. Fonko. I'll get someone from the passport desk for you. Right this way." He led me to a small conference room, seated me at a table and offered me coffee. Sure, why not? After what seemed a long gap he returned with a cup of coffee on a saucer, set it before me and said, "It'll be just a few minutes." He then went out, shutting the door behind him. And locked it.

Shit! The word must be out. Oh, I'd get refuge in the Embassy, right. And maybe a free ride back to the States. In shackles. They'd even provide an armed guard at no extra charge. I made a quick survey of the room. The walls were cement or cinderblock, under plaster—nothing serious was made of wood in this climate. The room's single window had been designed to resist a rampaging mob. From the outside. How about the inside? I considered trying to throw a chair through it until it dawned on me that it opened out from the inside. All standing between me and freedom was a bug screen. I swung the windows wide, punched the screen loose from its frame, ripped the hole wider and climbed through. It let out on a garden of sorts, from the first floor level. I dropped into a flower bed and made a bent-over dash through trees, palms and bushes to a fence at the rear of the grounds. I vaulted that sucker in a flash, landing in an alleyway. I had a rough idea where we were in town, one of the better districts, too far from Hotel Trianon to get there on foot. I needed cover. I needed mobility. No way could I get back to the car and Joseph without being spotted, and security would have been alerted by now.

I trotted to the end of the alleyway and looked up and down the street. It was wide and open, busy with traffic, no pedestrian crowd to melt into. Some sort of wildly-decorated vehicle pulled up to a clutch of people standing at the curb. It may once have been a truck or van but now resembled a jitney-bus that had survived an explosion in a Day-Glo paint factory. Any old port. I joined the passenger queue. As each climbed aboard he gave the driver money. I offered him five gourdes, which he accepted with a smile. Every seat was taken, so I grabbed a handhold. No one seemed much interested in my presence. The bus wound through the city discharging and taking on riders. Finally it pulled up in a parking lot next to a huge, busy market. Here was the crowd I needed, except everyone in sight was black. How to blend in? I sure didn't want another mob chanting "blan blan" at me.

I found the answer at my feet, literally. A shoeshine man had set up shop by the bus stop. I squatted down and examined his array of polish—brown, cordovan, black, tan, neutral. The dark brown looked about right. I held out ten gourdes and pointed to it. He looked at the bill, and then the dark brown shoe polish, then at my khaki suede desert boots, and then he looked at me quizzically. He shrugged and motioned me to put a foot on his shoeshine stand. I shook my head "no," pointed again at the brown polish, and motioned him to give it to me. He took my money, handed me the polish and watched me with interest. I picked up his brown polish rag, dabbed some polish on it and started applying it to my face. With that, he broke into a big smile. When I thought I'd finished, he took the rag and touched up a few spots I'd missed. I tipped him another tenner, stood up, put my baseball cap on backwards, shoved my still-Caucasian hands in my pockets and wandered in among the market throng.

My disguise wouldn't pass close examination, but all I needed was enough camo as I hunted up a taxi that no one would remember seeing a white man that morning. The bus had brought me to Marche de Fer, the Iron Market, the main one in town. Like every other third-world native market, it was cramped and aromatic, but this one was impoverished compared to others I'd seen around the world. It resounded with the haggling of women in bright cotton dresses. Everything a Haitian family might need or want, from fresh vegetables and live chickens to hardware and voodoo accessories, was for sale. Stacks of canned goods—some rusting, some with peeling labels, some unlabeled entirely—covered tables, cupboards, shelves and plots of baked earth. Sagging baskets of corn, millet, rice, and spices spilled out onto the ground. Food stalls didn't draw me in. The most popular dish, as well as the most appetizing fare on offer, was some sort of corn porridge mixed with milk and sugar, cooked in a big tin can over a wood fire, served in a tin cup, eaten with a spoon.

Glad I'd had a hearty breakfast at the hotel before I'd left with Joseph, I squirmed and slithered through the stalls and pandemonium, giving any Tontons I spotted a wide berth until I located a cab. By the time the driver deposited me at Hotel Trianon my expedition had used up the morning. The driver laughed when my white-man hand passed him a generous helping of gourdes. I hurried up the stoop and into the lobby. Mr. Brown sat behind the reception counter, bent over some business. He at first didn't recognize me. When he did, he chortled, "Well, Mr. Fonko, might there be an interesting story behind this?"

Joseph hadn't yet returned. I recounted my adventure at the American Consulate, giving Brown a chuckle. "My cover's blown here," I said. "I'd better head for Santo Domingo without delay. How did it go at the American Express office?"

"The clerk at American Express told me the Los Angeles office hadn't opened for business yet, but that the transfer of funds should go through soon. Your Mr. Wheeler a little while ago telexed a name and contact information in Santo Domingo. Can you wait another hour or two for the money?"

"The Americans aren't going to come after me here—they don't even know where I am—but the Tontons might. Let me run up to my room and take this shoe polish off. Do you have any cold cream or skin lotion? While I'm taking care of that, think about the best way for me to get to Santo Domingo."

Removing the shoe polish required a lot of lotion and the sacrifice of one of the hotel's bath towels. Midway through the task, I noticed a Mercedes pull up in the driveway three floors below, two sun-glassed heavies piling out and disappearing under the verandah roof. I scooped up lotion and towel and quietly went out into the hallway, trying doors for a place to hole up. A maid's closet left just enough room for me to squeeze in. As I pulled the door closed, footsteps clambered up the stairs.

They took their time tossing my room. No big deal. I'd spent longer periods in worse closets facing worse dangers (see Book One). They found nothing incriminating, of course: Brown had stashed my gear well. After the sounds of the Tontons faded down the stairwell, I gave them ten more minutes, then cracked the door open. Saw and heard nothing amiss. Crept back to my room. Peeped out the window through the sheer curtain. The Mercedes had left. I finished scouring my face of shoe polish, shuffled my clothes into presentability and went down to talk to Brown.

"I told them you'd gone to the American Embassy, hadn't returned yet," he said. "Fortunately, Joseph isn't on hand to give my tale the lie. You're not on the Tonton Macoute Ten Most-Wanted list yet, but they did say you have some items with you that would be of interest to the Haitian government. Definitely, you ought to clear out of here without further delay."

"Any good ideas about doing that?"

"Your best bet is to go over the mountains. There are two main border crossings, one north and one south. I'd advise Jimani, the southern crossing, the most-direct route to Santo Domingo. There's a bus, but they'll be watching those, and your blackface get-up won't fool anybody who's looking for you. A contractor I know in town has a project ongoing in a village, La Source, and he is always trucking building materials up there. If he could smuggle you to La Source, a missionary friend of mine could guide you across the border."

Joseph showed up with the car, and Brown dispatched him to the contractor. His place of business was a distance away, but sounding him out by phone would alert the Tontons. Then Brown called American Express. The money had been wired, so Brown called a taxi and left to take care of that, leaving a black assistant in charge of the desk. I holed up in my room, keeping a watch on the driveway. It wasn't long before a grey, late model Honda pulled up at the entrance and a thuggish man got out. Inquiries at the desk rapidly escalated to loud threats and then slaps and cries, then a thud and silence. Heavy footsteps clumped up to the second floor, and then the third. I hadn't time to get my pistol, so I grabbed a heavy glass ashtray, stepped behind the locked door and waited. A knock. Another. Some hard bangs. And then a kick blasted the door open, and a man charged into the room, revolver at the ready. I stepped up from behind and clouted him on the temple with the ashtray, and he went down. First things first, I pulled the cord from the bed lamp and hog-tied him. I stuffed a hand towel in his mouth and secured it by wrapping a pillow case tightly around his head. Put his gun in a dresser door. And then I searched him—a page from the hotel register book in his hand, but no ID. No car keys. Also, no sunglasses. At least he wasn't a Tonton.

I went downstairs, looked for Brown's assistant. He lay unconscious behind the desk, knocked out. The register book had been flung to the ground. The car keys were in the ignition. It was a rental. I drove his car down the road and around the corner, wiped the door handle, keys and steering wheel with my hankie, and left it there for somebody to steal.

Brown returned from the AmEx office, travelers cheques in hand. I told him about my little to-do. "No idea who?"

"No ID. Nothing in the car. I left him tied up and gagged in my room. Any point in questioning him?"

"Only if it makes a difference to you. A rented car means he's not Haiti government, meaning he's no concern of theirs. We'll have to get him out of here, but let's see what Joseph comes back with before we decide what to do."

Joseph returned with good news. For a modest consideration, the contractor would take me up with materials he was delivering to La Source that evening, night deliveries occasioning less traffic and fewer roadblock shakedowns. Hotel Trianon was on his way. He'd stop by after dusk. Brown came back with cheques in $50s. He said $100 would take care of everything; I insisted on $150. He signed the others over to me. One problem solved. For the time being. We took a table in the bar for a late afternoon happy hour, me prepared to scurry up the stairs at first sign of intruders. The cook fixed me an early dinner. The contractor's truck pulled in as I finished it. He, Brown and I went up to my room.

My visitor had come to. Squatting behind him (no sense enabling him to ID me), I unwrapped his head. He was not a happy camper. We tried, in every language we could muster, to find out whom he represented. He just glared at us. After he had spat at Brown, I stuffed the towel back in his mouth and re-wrapped him. "We can dump him someplace," the contractor suggested. Excellent idea. We lugged him downstairs, stuffed him in the back of the truck with the cinder blocks and sacks of cement and covered him with a tarp.

"What about a little disguise?" Brown suggested. He went into a room off the lobby and came back with glasses, a fake mustache, a safari-type shirt and a topee pith helmet. "Things people have left behind. It may help in the dark," he said. What the heck? I put them on. "Oh, and pack that thug's revolver along. You'll find out why in La Source."

It was about 40 miles up Route Nationale 40, one of the longest 40 miles I'd ever traveled. The road was narrow and potholed, traffic was slow, and once we cleared the city, the grades into the mountains were steep. The two roadblocks we ran into just shook us down for a few gourdes and didn't slow us up much. I couldn't make out much of the countryside in the dark. Flimsy huts along the verge, skinny people trudging along ("Zombies," the contractor said, then laughed), trash of all kinds everywhere. If ever a place could have benefited from "Adopt-a-Highway"... At a wide spot on the shoulder in a little valley where the contractor could see the road for a distance in both directions, he pulled to a stop and waited until the coast was clear. Then we jumped out, pulled the tarp off our thug, dragged him out of the truck and laid him beside the road.

"Somebody will find him and turn him loose," the contractor assured me. "The Tontons dump people out here all the time. Usually not this much alive, though."

We reached La Scale around 10 p.m.—three hours to cover 40 miles. The contractor brought the truck up to a small white church. "Mr. Brown contacted the priest (NOTE: no names, don't want trouble finding my friends). He'll put you up for the night and get you across the border in the morning." I asked him if U.S. $50 was enough for the ride. More than enough, he said, but it was the smallest I had. I signed a cheque back to Brown, explaining that Brown could cash it and pay him, leaving no paper linking him with me.

The priest was still up and expecting me. He welcomed me into his residence, a modest and, considering the context, well-kept bungalow. It was a Catholic mission, but the church itself was like none I'd ever seen. The Christ and the saints were all black, amid exotic, electric-hued pictures, relics and symbols, more African than Western. "Most Haitians consider themselves Catholic," he explained. "But also, most Haitians believe in voodoo. So over the years we've created a fusion, keeping the essence and the rites of Catholicism but yielding to local customs. I think we do the people some good. I hope so," he concluded. He showed me to an alcove with a narrow, simple bed in it. "Sleep well. We'll get you across the border in the morning."

I was up early, as was the priest. He took me into his bare-bones kitchen cum dining room, sat me on a pine bench at a small wood table and gave me a cup of hair-raising strength coffee. "You'll have to excuse our cuisine this morning," he said. "We share the diet of the people." He cooked his own food in battered pots on a wood stove. He dished up plates of rice and beans, added chunks of bread, and sat down with me. I've never balked at modest peasant food, but the bread qualified as barely edible. In response to my ill-concealed revulsion he said, "There's no wheat flour outside of Port au Prince and little enough there. We use manioc for flour. It's terrible, but it's what we have. Agriculture in Haiti is the poorest of the poor. Topsoil has eroded away, so even though every inch of arable land is cultivated, and the farmers work very hard, crops are sparse. In a few hours, things will be better for you. Alas, they will never be better for the Haitians."

We'd finished eating and were having a second cup of coffee when we heard a car drive up, and then a rap on the door. The priest said something, and a young black woman in a bright, full cotton dress came in. "She'll take you to the border crossing. She does speak a little English." I assembled my gear and came out, sans mustache and glasses, ready to go.

"Can I pay you something for your trouble?" I asked the priest. "A donation for the poor or whatever?"

"Not money, no. But Mr. Brown said you had some guns with you. Perhaps you could share with us? There are rebels here in the mountains, well-meaning men, good men. I don't know that they have much chance of overthrowing Mr. Duvalier and his Tontons, but what can one do? Certainly guns would aid their cause."

I dug into my backpack. There was the Glock I salvaged out of the chopper. There was the revolver I took from the hood yesterday. And the automatic I collected in Jamaica. "I only need one," I said. "Here's two for your boys." I kept the automatic with its silencer and the extra clips.

"I will pass them along, with much gratitude. Are you ready to leave?" he asked the girl. She motioned me to come.

She drove us in a faded VW Bug, battered but running decently. "The border is just a few miles," she said, "but you need papers to get across, which I understand you do not have. The Dominican Republic is not welcoming of Haitians, nor of undocumented foreigners. So I will take you most of the way, and then you must go across country to Jimani, avoiding border control. Feel like a little hike this fine morning?"

Up in the mountains it wasn't as hot as in town, at least. "Sure, let's do it."

The village comprised whitewashed mud houses, with straw or rusted sheet iron roofs, interspersed with banana palms, stunted trees, dusty shrubs and trash. On the way out, I noticed a large group of raucous boys, each with a big plastic tub. They were standing in a line of sorts, rough housing and cavorting as boys do the world over. But nobody bothered the boys walking away with their plastic tubs on their heads. "What's happening there?" I asked.

"They gather at the standpipe each morning. It's the town's only decent source of water. So they fill their tubs and take them back home balanced on their heads. They're little boys in line, but grown-ups after they fill their tubs."

La Source sat near a huge lake. It reminded me of Mono Lake in the California Sierras—a big body of blue water surrounded by desolate hills and mountains. Except that Mono Lake wasn't surrounded by trash and garbage and a multitude of destitute black people. We drove beside the lake for a couple of miles. As we approached a roadside shack with clearly painted, official-looking signs in French and English, a soldier stepped out and waved us to a halt. Uh oh. I unzipped my pack and was reaching for my pistol. She cautioned me off. The soldier came to her window. She rolled it down, and he said something. She answered. Then she opened the door. "Don't worry," she whispered to me. "This won't take a minute." The soldier escorted her into the shack. I scrunched down in my seat, pulled my topee hat down over my face and did my best to avoid curious eyes.

She returned to the car and resumed the driver's seat. "It's a little game we play," she explained. "He tells me I've got contraband hidden in my petticoats. I tell him that if he does a personal inspection he will find that isn't true. So we take a little time together in his guard shack. I think he wants to marry me. We'll see."

The road continued along the lake, then took a swing southerly. She ran the car down a dirt track to the right for a half mile. "The border is another half mile ahead. You will want to go off the trail and walk south through the brush down this valley, maybe a mile just to be sure. Then turn directly east and walk maybe five miles until you come to a river. You may find trails. It's a popular route. Follow the river, and it will take you directly into Jimani."

I thanked her for the ride, gave her the rest of my gourdes and set off across the bleak landscape. In twenty minutes, I turned toward where the sun had risen and left Haiti behind me, hopefully forever. Gun-running? Ha! Clyde Driffter had nothing on me.

007 SHANTY TOWN

The early morning hour, the high mountain elevation and October weather made the dusty hike not only endurable but after pressure-cooker Port au Prince, positively exhilarating. I strode along in good spirits, my pack light on my back, reveling in the cool, dry air. Judging from the trash and litter along the way, it obviously was a popular route for Haitians without papers, or whose business in the Dominican Republic wouldn't pass muster with the guards manning the gate. Crossing that border compared to the point in *The Wizard of Oz* at which Dorothy wakes up after the cyclone—from black-and-white Kansas farmland to Technicolor Oz. It didn't happen that abruptly, but I soon found the forested, green, well-tended land I entered quite an improvement over Haiti's dusty, grimy, squalid landscape.

Beyond that border, lighter skinned folks became more abundant, Latinos rather than Blacks or Mulattos. I discarded my topee pith helmet, the fake mustache and the glasses that Mr. Brown gave me. No need for a phony disguise, this crowd I could blend into. I followed the river road into Jimani, a border town of a few thousand. Its population looked better fed and cared for than the village I'd just left. Not that Jimani folks enjoyed country club lifestyles, but at least naked kids with starvation-bulged bellies weren't trailing along behind me with tiny hands out and desperate eyes. Jimani didn't compare with Tijuana for border town action, primarily because the other side of the border wasn't bursting with Gringo money to spend on trinkets, booze, drugs and whores. Rather, an outpost far from population centers, it served as a barrier forestalling a Haitian influx from pressing further into the Dominican Republic.

I bought some chow from a food vendor in the town marketplace, a plate of spicy pork, rice and black beans, with a couple corn tortillas, and washed it down with a warm beer. A welcome upgrade over Haiti street food. My Southern California Spanish sufficed to get directions from the vendor to the town bus stop. The ticket clerk sold me a seat on one leaving for Santo Domingo within the hour.

The crow route from Jimani to Santo Domingo covers about 150 miles, but on the ground my trip stretched a lot further. The route followed a network of well-paved rural highways, numbers 46, 44 and 2, mostly through forested hills and farmland. Route 46 skirted along the edge of Sierra Baoruco National Park, as inviting a garden spot of tropical paradise as I'd seen. The island, Hispaniola, lies about 20 degrees north latitude, giving the lush mountains and valleys a balmy climate, not the steam bath of equatorial jungle. The plantations and small-hold farms on the coastal flats didn't rise above third-world, of course, but by that standard seemed prosperous. The roads weren't trash-littered, and the people I saw from the bus wore non-patched, non-tattered clothing. Yes, I could appreciate why they'd strive to keep Haitian hordes from spilling over the border.

The bus made stops to let off and take on passengers, including restroom breaks and an afternoon half hour for eats and a leg-stretch in the town of Bani. We rolled into Santo Domingo central bus terminal around dinnertime. I got an assortment of empanadas at a nearby food stall—chicken, shrimp, pork, smothered in spicy sauces—and a cold beer to wash them down with.

Outside the tourist orbit, Spanish was the lingua franca, which I knew enough of at least to get around. I pulled out the name and address Evanston had telexed to Hotel Trianon, and showed it to a cab driver. He studied it, then motioned me in. I had no idea of the Santo Domingo city layout, but the route we followed put me on guard. The guy supposedly was one of Evanston's many overseas contacts, and Evanston had a lot of money. Assuming that his cronies must be in the same lines of business, I'd envisaged a palm-shaded bungalow by the sea. Instead, the driver took us through the modern city center, past some well-preserved and maintained traditional districts, and into a hillside slum. I don't mean to imply it was in the same league as the plywood/tarpaper/rusty-roofed horrors of Port au Prince, but it didn't seem the kind of place anybody affluent would live voluntarily. The neighborhood comprised housing blocks of cement and plastered cinderblocks, some painted, some their natural grey, cascading down low hills and spilling out on the flat below. They weren't decrepit and falling-down, but definitely a little more decor, or at least a fresh coat of whitewash would brighten the place. The cab wound up through twisted, narrow streets and stopped in front of a larger place, the one highest up on the hillside. A rusted American sedan sat parked in a little bay let into the road. A chubby cat disappeared under it as I got out. I checked the address I'd been given. Yep, unless we were in the wrong neighborhood entirely, this was the place.

I climbed a steep stairway to a bare cement porch jutting from an unadorned concrete façade. Lights showed through barred front windows. The dark hardwood front door had native designs carved into it. I tapped the knocker—it made a heavier sound than I'd expected. I heard voices inside, then determined footsteps. A concealed sliding panel opened, and hostile eyes peered out. "What do you want?"

"I'm looking for Bond at this address." (I'm codenaming Evanston's contact "Bond;" he deserves his anonymity.)

"Who are you?"

"Jake Fonko. I got your name from Evanston Wheeler. He said I should contact you here."

"Ev Wheeler? Well, shit goddamn. Just a minute." He snapped the peephole shut. Some locks clicked, and the door swung open. "Come on in, what'd you say your name was?"

The cabbie had been waiting below to make sure we'd got the right place. I'd paid him, and now I waved him away. "Jake Fonko," I replied. I stepped past him into the foyer. The door made a deep thud when he closed it, the locks loud clinks. The carved hardwood, it turned out, fronted heavy metal. The place was larger than it looked from outside, and if not luxurious, it was definitely comfortable. The front windows commanded a sweeping view of Santo Domingo.

"Jake Fonko… seems to me I've heard of you… you did some things with the CIA, is that it?" Bond deviated from the Sean Connery movie character in every way possible. About Evanston's age—60ish—he wore a loose fitting flowered tropical-weight cotton shirt that draped over a beer-gut. His droopy shorts hung below his knees, leaving hairy legs descending through puffy ankles to scuffed deck shoes. His face was more florid than tanned, punctuated by a pencil-mustache. A cross-pate sweep of slicked down grey hair made a vain attempt to camouflage a receded hairline.

"Nothing that I can talk about," I said.

"CIA guys do a lot of things like that. So, what does old Ev have to say?"

"Not much. I needed a friendly in Santo Domingo on short notice, and he came up with your name. Where do you know him from?"

"The OSS. We both worked there in World War Two. I was in field ops, and Ev was one of my liaisons. Wild times. You needed a friendly? What's up? Hey, let's go in the living room, get comfortable. Can I get you anything?"

"Right now, could you point me to a bathroom? I've suddenly developed an overwhelming urge to take a dump."

He ushered me to a powder room in the hallway, and I just made it to the crapper. Shit! Literally.

"Happens to everybody down here, especially from street food," Bond reassured me when I rejoined him. "I'll get you some cement pills. Plug you right up. Unless it's something serious you picked up in Haiti, you'll be good as new in the morning." He pointed to a leather easy chair. "Have a seat." He disappeared into the hallway. I saw in the kitchen a young Latina woman, humming to herself as she busied herself with something. Bond returned shortly with a small bottle in his hand and passed it to me. "Lupe," he shouted out to the kitchen, "could you bring our guest a glass with some ice in it? And some more ice for me?" Back to me, he said, "How about a little rum to wash those pills down with?"

Why not? Lupe brought the glasses and ice, along with cut limes and a cold bottle of Coca-Cola, and Bond introduced us. She was in her twenties, I'd guess. Butterscotch skin, long, straight brown hair, face shaped around Indian features. Bond thanked her in Spanish. She smiled warmly at both of us and left, and Bond filled our glasses from the half-emptied liter bottle on the table. A brand of rum I'd never seen before, local I assumed. They make a lot of it down there. I splashed in some Coke and squeezed lime juice into the mix.

"So, what's the deal?" he asked. I gave him an edited version of the last several days, skipping over a lot of detail and stressing that I'd left George Town without my passport and was now carrying items that parties unknown were willing to kill me for. "So, what do you want?" he asked. "You looking for a buyer? You want protection? What?"

"Right now, just dispose of this stuff and get back to the States safely," I said.

"Let's have a look at what you got," he said.

I hesitated. I didn't know this guy from a fire hydrant. On first impression, he wasn't somebody I'd naturally pick for a friend, much less as point man on patrol. I scoped out his place. We sat on leather chairs in a spacious room, tidy and tastefully decorated.

"Nice place you have," I remarked. "Not what you'd expect, just looking at it from outside."

"It suits me," he said. "The location's affordable and convenient, and it's easy to keep a low profile here. I don't live down to the appearance of the neighborhood, by any means. You'd be surprised at what's inside some of the houses here. Not everybody in a slum is poor."

"You're working here in Santo Domingo? What're you doing these days?"

"Mmmm, a little of this, a little of that. Targets of opportunity, you might say."

"You'd been in field ops for the OSS, you said? I was a Ranger, myself. Did a year's tour with the LRRPs in Nam, late 60s."

"Good outfit, tough service. I didn't do a lot of combat. They had me working as a go-between with the Partisans in Yugoslavia, arranging things, monitoring arms drops. Talk about tough, man, them Serbs, you won't find anybody tougher. So, what's Ev up to these days? We haven't really kept much in touch. Somebody in the Network must have put him onto me. Not many of our kind of guys here to choose from, I guess."

"He's an international lawyer. He does all right, gets around. Has a lot of contacts in surprising places."

"Ev was okay. Yeah, he was a lawyer back then, fresh out of Harvard Law. Did his work mostly in the office, a desk job, though not paper-pushing. I'm not surprised he stayed with lawyering. He was good."

"How about you? After the war, what?"

"Followed my nose. I was good at field ops, got along with indigs. Liked the adrenalin rush. Worked for the government for a few years, then went freelance in the earliest days of Nam, when we moved in after France hung it up. No place for me in that, leave it to the young fellows, I thought. Saw opportunities here in the Caribbean, been here ever since. So, tell me more about this stuff you're carrying."

I'd have to eventually. I gave him more details about the BCCI robbery, Driffter, Jamaica, Haiti. "You were flying with Clyde Driffter?" he asked, surprised. "Jesus."

"What about Driffter?"

"He's well known in certain circles. You say he was hit in the dogfight, injured in the crash, dying? And when you went back he was gone?" He guffawed. "That bastard has more lives than a cat. I think he's pulled that possum act before. Let's take a look at your parcels."

I sat my pack on the coffee table before us and pulled out the ledgers. Bond riffled through one. "Bank records," he muttered. "Looks like deposits, transfers, withdrawals, chronologically. English and Urdu. And people are chasing you for this? What kind of people?"

"So far I haven't been able to ID anybody. Maybe even the U.S. government." I told him about being locked up in the Haiti Consulate. "Maybe this is a clue, this gun I took off the gang of blind men in Kingston. I've never seen one of these before."

I fished the automatic out of the pack. He looked it over. "It's a CZ 75," he said, hefting it. "Czech. Good weapon. It's Iron Curtain gear. Those guys all had these? They use any language you could recognize?" He turned it over, this way and that, sighted down the barrel.

"Never uttered a peep. No ID on them. I kept the gun, figured it might come in handy."

"Well, they could be from a Red terrorist outfit. Or somebody's secret police. Maybe the KGB? Or they could be from some outfit Moscow supports—Shining Path in Peru? Sandinistas in Nicaragua? Castro? The PLO? Doesn't narrow it down much. And you and Driffter were taking this to... who?"

"Robert Vesco, in Cuba."

Bond guffawed again. "Clyde Driffter meets Robert Vesco! That's a horror movie title for you! Jake, you do keep some A-list company. Why did Vesco want this stuff?"

"He claimed $70,000,000 of his money disappeared, and he

believed he could trace it into BCCI with these records. What's the deal with Vesco?"

"Deal is the right word. The guy is deals personified. Came out of Detroit, scuffled and scrambled his way up. Through mergers, and leverage, and smoke and mirrors he assembled what on the surface was a major conglomerate—International Controls, ICC. Made the *Forbes* list of 'Richest Americans,' got his picture on the cover of *Fortune*, while still in his 30s—'The Bootstrap Kid,' somebody called him. Smart, hardworking, a quick mind for figures and an instinct for weakness. But also manipulative, evasive, aggressive, abrasive. Nobody you wanted to have working against you. As Bernie Cornfeld found out.

"Cornfeld put together Investors Overseas Services in the 50s. The idea was to sell mutual funds to GIs in Europe in small increments. 'I'll make you a millionaire' and 'Do you sincerely want to be rich?' were his catchphrases. His idea took off; he put a huge, aggressive sales force to work, and pretty soon he was raking in dough with both hands. And spending it just as fast, the original jet-setter. I mean, the guy was brilliant, but a flake. Lived large, hung around with Hugh Hefner, always had half-naked, gorgeous broads draped over him. Where was he getting his spending cash? Good question. Some was borrowed money, some came off the top of the funds, some came out of the stockholders' pockets. Other People's Money. good old OPM.

"In the 60s IOS started coming apart. The SEC got on his case, looking into fraudulent claims and schemes. The IRS took an interest in overseas Americans using IOS to evade taxes. IOS started hemorrhaging money, investors redeeming their funds and heading for the hills. In the early 70s Vesco saw all those millions of dollars just sitting there, saw that IOS was going under, so he elbowed his way into control through his company, ICC, claiming he could rescue it.

"Now, by that time, Vesco had moved his headquarters to Nassau, in the Bahamas, offshore operations being, let's say, more 'flexible' than under U.S. jurisdiction. Plus he liked to gamble on

Paradise Island. The SEC came after him. When he decamped to Norman Cay, the FBI suspected drug dealing, that being a narcotics center. Everybody was trying to extradite him. Money was flying around all over the place. It'd take an army of investigators, attorneys and accountants to have any hope of making sense of it at this point. Vesco himself had a legion of lawyers and spies, even mounted a machine gun on his yacht to fend off the Coast Guard if it tried to board. He found refuge in Costa Rica for a few years, was a pal of their president, played the public benefactor, had armed bodyguards. Lived the life there, but last year he had a falling out, or maybe ran out of ready cash, and moved on to Cuba. The intriguing question is, why did he want the BCCI stuff?"

"Wanted to track down some missing money, is what he said."

"Maybe. Maybe he had something else in mind. You said there were some disks. Could I take a look? I've got a little computer in my office."

What the hell? I was curious too. I pulled the case of disks out of my pack, and we went to a back room. He turned on his computer and let it warm up, then slipped a floppy into the slot.

The system refused to read it. Tried another one. Same result.

"I don't think they're blank. Could be locked. Could be in some strange code. God only knows what Pakistanis would use."

I put the disks back in the pack, and we returned to the living room for rum and war stories. Lupe sat quietly and politely, didn't have much to say. Finally, I'd had it. Between the day's travel and my case of the squirts, I was bushed. Bond showed me to a guest room. I stowed the pack under the bed and didn't last a minute after I hit the sheets.

* * *

BOND'S CEMENT PILLS HELD FIRM, LEAVING ME IN DECENT FETTLE when I woke up, even had an appetite. Lupe put out a breakfast of eggs and fried local salami with sweet rolls, and I had a feeling everything would stay in where it belonged. Just a quick case of overnight trots, not something more permanent like amoebic dysentery.

Bond and I chased breakfast with mugs of hot, spiced coffee, and he told me a little more about his situation. "I segued into the CIA after the OSS disbanded, but never really felt at home there, Yalies took the place over, and I was just a fullback from Ohio. At war's end that pipsqueak Tito shut us out of Yugoslavia, so no place for me there. Did one thing and another for The Company. The last straw was Guatemala, where the CIA helped throw out Arbenz in '54. Supposed to be preventing a communist takeover, but it seemed like we were really protecting United Fruit's banana plantations from land reform. I didn't like pushing peasants around for government salary. Nam was the last straw. Word reached me that Trujillo paid good money for foreign advisors, so I came over here, been here ever since. Trujillo was a bastard, no doubt about it, but he was *our* bastard, as they say, a staunch anti-communist. He was dictatorial and brutal, but under him this was one of the best-run islands in the Caribbean. Put in infrastructure, built up the economy, established law and order. Corrupt as hell, of course —it's the game they all play in these parts. Worth mega-millions by the time I arrived.

"The opposition took him out in 1961, shot him up in his Chevy Bel Air. Rumor had it that the CIA was behind the plotters. Don't know about that, but it was bad news for me, had to scramble for a few years. Things picked up when Balanguer won the election in '66; I'd known him through Trujillo. That put me back in business, lasted until '78. Since then, I've had to scratch up work elsewhere. Nobody wanted any part of Trujillo's people anymore. Can't complain, it was gravy while it lasted.

"I did learn one thing, though. Job security. You can have a good run freelancing for a while. But watch out. When that well ran dry, I found myself out of the loop, a has-been, watching the new fellows step in and take over. It's like people I know who dreamed of being writers, or artists, or dancers, or actors, or rock stars. A miniscule few make it big in those fields. Most get nowhere, quickly realize they've no future in it and take up something else. The unlucky ones have just enough talent to rise a few rungs up the ladder, make a living, nurture their dreams until they're too old to get into some other line of work. Oh, most are capable people, so they don't wind up living on dog food, but they find the last half of their lives a struggle against diminishing returns, spending their nights wondering where they took the wrong turn. That's where I'm at right now. A few irons in the fire, but I'm having to stretch harder to find income."

"Times get tough, but something always turns up," I remarked, for the sake of saying something, though I hadn't a clue what I was talking about. That angle hadn't occurred to me before. Was I hearing an ominous warning about me and my career as a freelance whatever-it-is-that-I-do? So far, so good, up to then. Was I one of the lucky ones? Or one of those others? I'd think about it tomorrow. Right now I have more immediate problems to solve. "I need to take care of a few errands. How's the city center here? Good banks, stores, etc.?"

"It's about the best spot in the Caribbean, prosperous, safe and orderly, has a solid middle class. Coming from Port au Prince, you'll think you died and went to heaven. Walk down to the busy avenue at the bottom of the hill—get a cab into town, about a half hour ride."

I washed up, got my gear in order and told Bond I'd be back in the afternoon. "You can leave your pack here if you like. It'll be safe," he suggested.

"I'd just as soon keep it with me," I said. "Do you know of a good bank in town?" He gave me a couple names, and I set out down the hill. He was right: compared to Port au Prince, Santo Domingo was paradise on earth. Downtown was spacious, clean and modern. Whatever he'd done wrong, Trujillo had done a lot right. My first errand was changing my travelers cheques into currency. No problem. The official currency was pesos, but U.S. dollars were popular. I signed the cheques and emerged with about $800 in my pocket, plus a fistful of pesos. Next on the to-do list:

clothing. I'd been living in the same pants and underwear too many days. In addition to cheap street wear, I picked up a black, long-sleeved pullover and black trousers. I blended in well, strolling among the Santo Domingo crowd, but the way things had been going, I thought it prudent to have some night-stalking duds on hand, just in case. Then I dropped in at a clean-looking café for lunch.

There, I pondered the question: now what? In the last couple days, I'd been on an island where they spoke English, one where they spoke Spanish, another with sort of English, another with sort of French, and now another one where they spoke Spanish. All sovereign nations, presumably they required passports, but I'd gotten by without one. I didn't think I'd left a trail anyone could follow, but the depth of surveillance so far unsettled me, unseen eyes and ears everywhere. No point hitting the U.S. Consulate for a passport. So my only option was Puerto Rico, from where I could return to the U.S. without one. But the people tracking me could figure that out too, and by now they'd know I'd left Haiti—to where else but here? Flying out, or taking a regular ferry, I'd have to show ID. Which meant I'd need a privately operated boat. I had a taxi take me to the waterfront. It seemed mostly commercial, not much charter activity. I got out and strolled around, asking people about fishing. The consensus recommended Bayahibe on the eastern end of the island.

I got back to Bond's by late afternoon. I briefed him on the situation. "Well, I can get you to Bayahibe, all right. Plenty of charter possibilities there. Plus, maybe less visibility. People looking for you would have the Puerto Rico angle covered, but if we snuck you out of Bayahibe you might get a little jump on them. Leaving here before daybreak in the morning, it's about two hours drive."

One point of affinity between Bond and the CIA crowd I'd met was, he did enjoy his booze. I don't believe a liter bottle would last him two days. After dinner we sat and drank, though I didn't try to keep up with him. Couldn't have. He said he'd get me up early for our drive, and we hit the sack. In the middle of the night I sensed somebody in my room and snapped to full wakefulness. The intruder was down on the floor, groping under the bed. I quietly pulled my cover aside, then rolled out on top of him. I bounced off, wrenched him over on his back and lay on top of his arm, my fist at his windpipe.

"Uncle," he gasped. "I give. White flag. You win." It was Bond.

"What's the deal?" I asked.

"Oh, nothing much. I just wanted to see those ledger books in your pack."

"Why didn't you ask?"

"Would have given the game away. You might have said no."

I got off him and let him sit up. "What's in the ledgers?"

"I did some business through BCCI that I'd rather didn't come to light, and who knows where those books are going to end up. I was thinking that if I just took a page out of July 1981, and another one out of October 1980, no harm done, and I'd feel a lot safer."

"Well hell, why not?" I said. "Can we take care of it in the morning?"

Then he shushed me. I could hear a quiet, coded ticking coming from his bedroom. "Intruder at the rear of the house," he whispered. "Get your gun, keep low, meet me in the kitchen." He disappeared out the door. As I tied my shoes, Lupe in her nightgown passed by, slinking toward the front door pistol in hand. I crouched into the kitchen. Bond was waiting. "In the overhead cupboard, next to the back door, you'll find a sliding panel. It's a gun port, looks through a trellis on the outside. Cover me through that. I'll go out and see to this."

He opened a door I thought was a broom closet and disappeared through it. I couldn't see much outside through the port, no moon, no city lights, but there seemed to be somebody moving around. Then I heard a brief but violent scuffle. "Jake?" Bond asked through the gun port, "Everything's okay. You can open the door. Come on out."

A disguised door on the building ell stood open. A black-dressed body was sprawled in front of the window he'd been trying to jimmy. Bond went back inside, returned with a flashlight. "Jake, go back to the end of the opposite ell and stay in the shadows. Keep that gun ready," Bond whispered. I took my position, and he shone the light on the body. It was a Latino man. Bond switched the flashlight off and motioned me over. "No ID, but from the tattoos I'd say he's from one of the Colombian drug cartels. Not an assassin, just a sneak thief. Doesn't amount to a threat. Let's get back inside."

He called to Lupe. She closed the front port, came into the kitchen and exchanged a few words with Bond. "Nothing out front, she said. Usually they work in pairs, so there may be another one lurking out there."

"Does this happen often?" I asked him. "You seem to have it down to a science."

"Not often," Bond said, "but the kind of work I'm in, you take precautions. You might have noticed; this house is designed to be defended—blank front wall, back patio enclosed by opposite ells. Only one approach—from the hill behind—and I've got sensors all over out there. Well, Jake, my boy, I fear your cover's blown."

"How?"

"Probably when you signed over your travelers cheques. A bank clerk bribed to look out for your name would pass it along when he saw it. If you'd let your pack out of your sight, it'd have disappeared before you turned back around, but nobody was going to mug you for it downtown in broad daylight. Maybe word got out that a Gringo went around the harbor asking about chartering a boat to San Juan. Obviously you were tracked back to here."

"So now what?"

"First, I call a pal at the morgue. They'll dispose of the guy. Then how about we grab a bite and head for Bayahibe? Umm, any chance of a look at those ledgers?"

I told him to help himself. He sat down at the table with the two books in question, flipped to the months of interest, and ran down the columns of entries with his finger. He carefully cut out a page from each book. "Okay, that's it. I'd love to spend a few days with that material, but we've gotta get you out of here. Then they'll be out of *my* hair, at least." I got my kit together, and we went to the front door. He handed me a pork-pie hat. "Put this on. Just a sec," he said, picking up a device from a side table. He poked a button. I heard the car below on the street start. "Another precaution," he remarked as he replaced the device. "If they're going to bomb my car, at least I won't be in it. They mean us no harm, they just want the stuff in your pack, though they'd kill you to get it. But you never know; some of those guys are dumb enough to blow us up with the stuff. The guy out back, he's a grunt, expendable. His partner's out there somewhere, but I don't think he'll risk a shootout. Okay, guns at the ready, just in case. Move out."

We clambered down the stairs and piled into the car. The engine sounded better than the exterior looked. "What, a stealth car?" I asked.

"It's camo'ed-up a little, yeah. Top shape, working wise. Here we go." We wound through the narrow roads. As we pulled away from the slum onto a main avenue, I noticed a car falling in behind us. It must have followed along out of the slum, lights off. Bond noticed it too. "No need to worry about that for now. When we get out of town on the highway, we'll deal with him. Relax."

Bond drove straightforwardly through the city to the coastal highway, Number 3. It was good road, and traffic was light. "I could outrun him any time I want, but he'd eventually catch up. We need to put him out of action before I drop you off." We sped on for nearly an hour. A few miles beyond a small town, La Romana, Bond slowed to the point where the following driver could track his taillights, then continued around a wide sweep in the road to the north. In about a mile he turned into a side road, then sped up until we rounded a blind turn. He stopped the car, doused the lights, reached across me and opened the glove compartment. He pulled out an S&W .44 magnum revolver and climbed out of the car. Our shadow came around the corner. Bond took a two-hand stance and fired two shots at the hood, stopping the car abruptly. He fired another shot through the passenger side of the windshield, then jumped back in and hit the gas. "Blew out his engine. That'll keep him there for a while," he said, handing me the gun. "This piece would stop a Tiger Tank. Put it back in the glove compartment."

"I saw a sign to Bayahibe back there."

"You did, but I took the road to Bahia de Yuma." Bond drove a fast 20 miles, winding through low hills. The way the car took the curves, he must know a good custom shop—Detroit suspensions don't handle like that. We stopped. "Now get in the back and lay down out of sight. You asked around in Santo Domingo about Bayahibe, so they're expecting you'll go there. It'll look like I dropped you down at Bahia de Yuma. It might, in fact, have been a better choice, but I have a compadre in Bayahibe." We drove back and hurtled past where the disabled car sat. "Stay down for a while," Bond said. After a time, he stopped again. "Bayahibe's about five miles down this road. I don't want anyone to see this car there. You'll reach it at daybreak. Go to the charter marina and find Santiago. Ask him how the fishing is." I climbed out and shouldered my pack. "Just a sec, give me that hat." I passed it to him. "Hand me the attaché case on the floor back there." I did. He sat it on the passenger seat, opened it and pushed a button. A man's torso inflated from it and popped up beside him. He put the pork-pie hat on its head. "They're going to see me heading back toward Santo Domingo with you. Halfway back, I'll pull over in a town with major crossroads, deflate this thing and drive back home alone. Should confuse 'em long enough for you to get away, and with you gone they won't bother me anymore. Good luck, Jake. Take care."

"Thanks for the lessons in tradecraft, Bond. Anything I can do for you, repay the hospitality?"

"Those ledger pages cover it. Hey, it was fun, added some excitement to some dull days. Give my greetings to Ev the next time you see him. Tell him that if he ever needs anything done down here, I'm his man. Good hunting." I wished him likewise. He turned the car around and drove off.

The sun painted high wispy clouds in the eastern sky with pastel oranges and pinks but had not yet topped the horizon. A balmy breeze and the pungent smell of chaparral made for a pleasant early morning hike. I fast-marched maybe four miles before I met a man coming toward me on the road. I asked him where I'd find the fishing boats, and he gave me directions. Another mile and I reached Bayahibe, a resort and fishing village fronting on a bay with a stretch of fine sandy beach. A fleet of outrigger-equipped boats sat placidly in their slips in the pre-dawn gloom at a small marina, crews fussing them into readiness for the day's charters. Fishermen, Americans mostly, were starting to trail over from the hotels, eager for a go at the deep's denizens. I asked a deckhand for Santiago, and he pointed out a big Hatteras cruiser in a slip on the other side.

A paunchy, middle-aged local man lay stretched out on a cushioned bench along the cockpit, on the other side of the fighting chair, his weathered captain's cap tilted over his eyes. "Senor Santiago?" I asked.

He rolled over and looked at me. "Do you know somebody?"

What kind of question was this? Know who, from where? Take a best guess. "Bond. In Santo Domingo I know Bond," I said.

The man levered himself upright. "I like people that know people," he said wryly. "You know Bond, you say. So therefore...?"

I looked the boat over. "Bond said to ask you, how's the fishing?" I said.

"You a fisherman?"

"I've done some fishing."

"Then you know the answer to that question."

"It was great yesterday. Tomorrow will be even better. But today, not so good."

He straightened his cap on his head. "So you want to go fishing today?"

"Maybe. Is your boat available for a day's charter?"

"Si. But this is not my boat. My boat's over there." He pointed down the dock. "What kind of fishing you want? Inshore? Offshore? Blue water? Billfish? Santiago does it all. The wahoo are biting, they say. Ever hook a wahoo? They give you a good fight."

"Show me your boat."

He eased himself up off the cushion, came across the cockpit, lithely mounted the gunwale and dropped down on the pier beside me, rocking the boat against its lines. He motioned me to follow him. His boat, a 36-foot Sea Ray cruiser, had seen better days, needed a good scrub and some varnish on the brightwork. I leaned down to see the waterline. The hull was clean enough, anyhow.

I looked around, ensured that no one was within earshot. "I need a boat ride to San Juan."

"I know a boat you could get on."

"How soon could we leave? I'm in a hurry to get out of here."

"It's gassed up. I just need to run over to the store and provision us, take a few minutes. Three hundred U.S. for the trip?"

"How long does it take?"

"Have you there tomorrow morning. Mayaguez is closer. Two hundred to Magayuez, then you take the bus to San Juan. Cheaper. Maybe quicker."

People would be expecting me to show up in San Juan. On the other hand, the ferryboats ran to Mayaguez. They'd be watching there too. Be safer on the boat than traveling overland. "All the way to San Juan."

"Hokay," he said. "Be back in a minute. You want to come along?"

"Better if I stay down below out of sight. Get what you want. I'll eat anything. I could use a little breakfast right now."

"Sure thing. Can I give my cousins a free ride?"

I looked the boat up and down. It seemed close quarters. "How you going to get them all inside?"

"It's just two guys. It's good weather. They'll sleep in the cockpit. Good deckhands, handy in the event of trouble. They got girlfriends in San Juan, no work for them here today."

I went below. The saloon, larger than it looked from the dock, was shipshape. I hung out in the forepeak, well out of sight. He and his cousins showed up twenty minutes later. They stowed the stuff, did a little prepping and cast off. We rumbled out of the marina just after daybreak, convoyed with two spiffy fly-bridge cruisers full of fishermen eager to drink beer, drown bait and burn themselves lobster red. We cleared the harbor and Santiago, set course toward the rising sun.

THE HARDER THEY COME

THE BOAT RIDE TO SAN JUAN, PUERTO RICO, STARTED OFF WELL. Santiago said it was about 200 miles, so we'd be arriving in pre-dawn darkness, which suited me just fine. His cousins, able crewmen when called upon, mostly kept to themselves. Santiago claimed to make his living as a charter boat operator, taking wealthy Gringos out on billfish quests. Marlin and sailfish abounded in those waters, and he'd do runs out to the Gulf Stream if a client were willing to pay for it. However, he claimed, he'd had a run of bad luck, 84 days without a client catching anything worthwhile. Once, he told me, a client caught the biggest marlin anyone had ever seen, only to have the sharks eat it before they could get it back to port, nothing but the head left. Another piece of bad luck he lamented was the Gringo, who'd lost Santiago's best rod and reel through carelessness, and then stiffed him for three weeks of charter fees. He'd had to supplement his income by hiring himself out to Bond and others for occasional "projects," as he called them.

Well, I don't know. Fishermen are known for being great story-tellers. At any rate, the weather was calm; Santiago skippered the boat skillfully, and he'd provisioned the trip well. I sat in the fighting chair sipping my way through Heinekens from the cooler, gazing aft and letting tension evaporate under the clear blue tropical sky as we burbled along at fifteen knots. Until we passed below Isla de Mona, a barren little mound in the middle of otherwise empty blue water. Deserted except for a lighthouse, it lay about 50 miles off Puerto Rico's eastern edge. A speck crept up over the horizon off our port side, coming from the direction of Puerto Rico. Its heading seemed on a vector to cut us off.

"I don't like the look of this," Santiago remarked from behind his binoculars.

"What's the problem?"

"It's a Bertram cruiser, not a kind of boat to be out here at this hour. If it was going around PR, no need for it to be this far out, it'd stay inshore. The good fishing is in the other direction from where it's coming. There's no destinations to the south of us, so on that heading there's no place it could be going, except to meet us."

"Are we in danger?"

"I don't know. Maybe you could tell me? I didn't ask your business, maybe I should know? Some men came around to the docks two days ago, asked everybody to tell them if they saw a Gringo named Jake, said they'd pay good moneys. You know about this Jake? Are any bodies after you?"

"Not me personally, but some rough customers would like to get their hands on what's in my pack."

Santiago pushed the throttles ahead, and his boat picked up speed with a jolt. "Bond is my friend, and Bond's friends are my friends. We should change our plans a little, I think. Maybe you'd like to go to Ponce or Salinas instead of San Juan? On the south side of the island. To get to San Juan, we have to get past that guy. We go to the south side; he won't catch us."

"Any old port," I said. Santiago altered course to ESE. He shouted something to his cousins that aroused them from their below-deck reverie.

"Their boat, they think they have the speed to catch us, but they don't," Santiago said. "When I took up doing projects for people, they had my boat fixed up for me a little. Bigger engines. Some adjustments to the planing hull. But let's see what that other boat does. No need to give away the game. Maybe they're just wealthy Gringos taking their whores out for a boat ride on a sunny day."

The other boat altered course to intercept. Santiago upped the throttles a little more. We ran along for a couple more hours, the other boat settling in on our wake, gaining a little but never getting nearer than a mile or so. Puerto Rico peeped over the northeastern horizon and grew steadily larger and darker. To the west of us, the light began shifting orange as the sun dropped toward the horizon. Then the boat behind began visibly gaining on us.

"Sonofabitch means to catch us just off the island, right around sundown. But he won't." Santiago let the other boat draw nearer, maybe a quarter mile off, still gaining, then matched his speed to theirs. I heard a gunshot in the distance. His cousins came up on deck with rifles and took seats in the cockpit.

We came abreast of the tip of Puerto Rico, and Santiago took us in toward shore. "Tricky waters around here," he remarked. "Many reefs. Great diving. Good inshore fishing. Sometimes I'll take dive trips over here when the fish aren't biting." He slowed the boat a knot or two, allowing the boat behind to close a little, and headed toward an island reaching out from shore. "Over here, especially good reefs," he said, slowing the boat again as we drew toward the island. "But you gotta know the waters."

Our pursuers drew a little closer. Another gunshot. "They can't hit a moving target from a moving platform at this range," Santiago observed. The cousins took fighting positions in the stern, nevertheless. Seemed like billfish chartering might not be their only day job. Daylight was beginning to fade away as we veered over toward the mainland. A gap between it and the island opened up, and Santiago goosed the throttles up a little. The boat behind increased speed and again closed on us. Santiago said something to the cousins, and they let go a fusillade in its direction. It returned desultory fire. Santiago seemed unconcerned. He sped up a little more and so did the following boat, now only a couple hundred yards behind. "Should of got 'em on the last reef," he remarked. "They've done some things to that boat too." We came into a passage bookended by house-sized boulders at 20 knots and suddenly he hit the throttles hard. The boat did a nautical version of a wheelie, accelerating and rising up on its tail. We scooted through the passage and a quarter mile beyond at 35 knots. The boat behind stopped abruptly.

"It's a little shallower through there," Santiago said as he eased off on the throttle and altered course away from shore. "That was our last chance. The tide was just right. If that didn't work, we'd have to run for it and hope to lose them in the dark. And if they had radar on board, we couldn't. We're in the clear now. I'm heading out where I don't have to worry about depth. We don't have no worries about them no more," he said, motioning back with his head. "They ripped out their hull."

* * *

Darkness fell. We continued on for a couple hours, running at 15 knots without lights. "This worries me," I told Santiago. "People are expecting me to come to Puerto Rico because it's the only place from where I can go to the U.S. with no passport. But somebody told somebody something, so somebody knew I was arriving today. That boat has a radio, so they'll have reported this. It's only a matter of time before others come looking. You mentioned Ponce and Salinas on the southern shore. Maybe there'll be people looking for me there too, now that we've headed for the south side. Any way you can land me without detection?"

"There's a little town between Ponce and Salinas, Potata Pastillo. I can slip in there with no lights, drop you off and then continue on to Salinas. You get a taxi to Mercedita Airport by the highway; that's about five miles, you still maybe got time to catch a late bus to San Juan. Anybody in Salinas asks me, I put you ashore at Ponce, no idea where you went after that."

"Your cousins won't get to see their girlfriends in San Juan."

"No problem. They got girlfriends in Salinas. "

Presently, Santiago steered us quietly toward the town dock at Potata Pastillo. I went below and put on my black outfit—no point standing out. He brought his boat up alongside and slowed it to a crawl. He wished me luck; I hopped down off the gunwale with my pack, and he turned his boat immediately back out toward open water. Within a few seconds, they'd got beyond the reach of the waterfront lights and disappeared into the night. I scampered away from the waterfront nightlights and took refuge in the shadows to get my bearings. Even as sought-after as I seemed to be, I figured there couldn't be lookouts posted everywhere. The various outfits that wanted the BCCI records couldn't possibly be working in concert, so each would have limited manpower, only enough to deploy in the most likely spots.

The town center wasn't far from the docks. A few bars and cantinas did lively business, but most shops had shuttered up. I found a cab waiting at a taxi stand, the driver catnapping. He spoke good English and the U.S. dollar was the official PR currency —no complications there. He was game for a ride to the bus stop by the airport. I asked him about catching a flight from there to the U.S., but he advised me it was small, local flights only. Most planes to America went out of Luis Munoz Marin airport in San Juan. He estimated a good chance that a publico bus might come by and pick me up. They ran on the highway from Ponce to San Juan, but scheduling depended on the drivers. Sometimes they waited until the bus filled with riders, but also sometimes the driver at the end of the day found himself on the far side of the island and was in a hurry to get back home. I decided to take my chances, figuring that if worse came to worst I could sleep rough and catch one in the morning. Luck favored me. Within a half hour, a bus lumbered up. I donned a tourist shirt over my black top, stepped out of the shadows and flagged it down, clambered aboard and took a seat. Unlike the buses in Jamaica and Haiti, it wasn't teeming with rural life, rather rode half-empty. Neither was it in a breakneck hurry. The driver stopped at villages and crossroads to pick up or discharge passengers. Nobody seemed inclined to interfere with me.

The ride covered about 60 miles over the central mountains. I gather Puerto Rico is lushly scenic, but I didn't see enough in the dark to appreciate it. We arrived in San Juan's central district somewhat before 10 p.m. I took a chance that surveillance teams had chucked it in for the night and asked a well-dressed passerby where I could find a nearby businessman's hotel. He mentioned several and recommended one where, he claimed, salesmen from around the region stayed when they came to town. That suited me —my cash was running low, and salesmen typically traveled on the cheap so they could pocket their per diems.

I spent some time that night and the next morning strategizing my egress. This could be my make-it-or-break-it, so I wanted it to come off. If they had my passport, they also might have my picture, a passport photo anyhow. Sketchy resemblance, but why take a chance? After breakfast, I found a barber and had my hair restyled. I bought an eyebrow pencil at a pharmacia and used it to thicken my eyebrows and dab on a sleazy mustache, aids to blending into the local flow. Then I undertook to recon the strength and disposition of the opposing force. Dressing in a shirt I'd bought in Santo Domingo that no one had seen me wearing, I rode a cab to the airport. A scan of the departures board showed a number of flights to various cities in the U.S., by a variety of carriers. In normal times, I'd simply pick out a flight, go to the ticket counter with my AmEx card, pop over to Miami, and that would be that, no problemo. Too bad times weren't normal. I strolled around the departure lounges, no clues there. People awaited their boarding calls, sat in anticipation of arriving loved ones, or were reading or having a bite to eat. No telling who, if anyone, was staked out for me. The time to find out was now, rather than when I showed up with boarding pass in eager hand.

I'd have to flush 'em out. An information brochure provided airport phone numbers. I located a bank of phones with a white courtesy phone nearby and called the airport information number. "I need to reach a passenger with an urgent message. He is there in the airport waiting to board his flight. Could you please page Mr. Jake Fonko for me?"

They could. The page went out. After a credible interval, I picked up the courtesy phone. "This is Jake Fonko. You paged me?"

"Yes, you have a phone call," said the operator. "I'll connect you." I heard a click, then "Go ahead."

"Jake Fonko here," I said into the courtesy phone.

Dropping my voice an octave, I replied into the pay phone, "Mr. Fonko, I am the contact you were told to meet. The password is 'Day O'. It is urgent that I meet with you without delay." "That's the password, all right. Okay. Where do you want to meet?"

"By the Hertz rental car desk. In five minutes. And bring your package with you."

"Could you make it ten minutes? I can be there in ten."

"Okay, ten minutes, by the Hertz desk. Do not fail." I hung up the pay phone, and then the courtesy phone.

I noticed men stirring at departure gates and in bars and eateries and duty free shops around the building. Several got up from lounges and casually strolled in the direction of the rental car desks. I estimated it would take about three minutes to reach the rental cars, so I took the long way around and joined a clutch of arriving passengers. I sauntered past Avis, Budget, Hertz and National and out the door to the sidewalk, scoping the situation with peripheral vision. Holy shit! The collection of hoods and thugs milling around, affecting bored disinterest while looking sideways at each other, was a tableau worthy of Hitchcock. At least two mafiosi viewed one another with wary suspicion from opposite sides of the room. Slick Latinos loitered languidly. Pasty-faced Iron Curtain Europeans shifted their gaze behind sunglasses. Mustached Arabs and furtive Pakistanis lurked here and there. Military types in mufti glanced around alertly. Bureaucrats—government? corporate?—kept a nervous eye on the others. No East Asians that I noticed—they must have their own crooked banks. Several in the crowd seemed familiar, may have caught a glimpse of them on previous islands. A number of them consulted a sheet of paper as they scanned passersby. INTERPOL could have scooped up the lot for their haul of the century. Too bad they're never around when you need them.

I emerged onto the sidewalk, kept right on sauntering to the taxi queue and took the first one available back to my hotel.

I later heard about the melee in the San Juan airport, touched off by hotheads from two rival South American political movements. The newspapers never reported it. Must have been unsettling for the tourists seeking vacation wheels.

This required further analysis and planning.

* * *

THE PROBLEM OF RETURNING TO THE STATES LOOMED LARGEST, but also my cash was drained. I'd been on the run now for a week, and even traveling on the cheap, it's not cheap. Puerto Rico being practically part of America, my credit cards and California ID would work here—nobody would insist on a passport. Of course, the minute I used either, my name went public, blowing my cover for any minion who'd been hit up for information about "Jake the Gringo." My recon tactic served its purpose, but it also alerted the hostiles that I was on site. I'd registered as Zak Fahnke, an alias I'd used comfortably since my Iranian gig, so my hotel room was secure enough for a while but I'd be wise to do a Speedy Gonzales out of Puerto Rico. I couldn't catch a flight back to the U.S. out of the international airport, nor could I do much else about alternate transport home with the legions looking to intercept me. At this point, I couldn't even ditch the BCCI loot and just head home without it. Pursuers would waylay me and beat the crap out of me to find out where it was. The only thing for it was to keep moving and work out an escape plan.

So... where next, and how do I get there? This being a businessman's hotel, the desk clerk would know about connections to other islands. He had an up-to-date airline directory as well as a list of other airfields on the island. There were a couple dozen, some servicing local short-hop airlines, others private aircraft at resort sites, and some handling both types. The nearest field of any consequence was on the east coast at Fajardo. My bankroll would cover cab fare out there and back, but not much else. For lack of any better ideas, I cleaned off my fake mustache, returned my eyebrows to normal, and set out after an early lunch.

The commercial terminal at Fajardo hosted several small Caribbean airlines providing puddle-jump flights to islands down the Antilles chain. That made sense to me: I couldn't retrace my previous route, so I might as well head further out and see if I could make something turn up. However, a discreet inspection of the departure area revealed a few lurking thugs like the ones I'd flushed out at the main airport. Somebody or other seemed to be on hand to thwart me at every turn. I eased out of the main terminal and inconspicuously found my way to the hangars for private aircraft. A man in an office there explained to me about chartering a plane. Pretty expensive, and you couldn't just walk in and take off. "What about people with private planes?" I asked him. "Where do they hang out?"

"They don't really hang out. They fly in here, go about their business, fly back out. Usually they land close to where they stay. A number of them own places down here. Some come to resorts. The Cessna over there, it belongs to a guy who likes to fly around the islands." He pointed to a spiffy high-wing plane, smaller than the one that attacked us off Grand Cayman.

"He planning any flights out soon?"

"You'd have to ask him. I thought I saw him over by that hangar."

I thanked him and ambled over where he pointed. It was shady inside the hangar but not much cooler, had that greasy rubbery musty smell of mechanical equipment. It housed a few small planes and various kinds of plane-tending gear. A short, pudgy middle-aged man sat at a desk filling out papers. "Excuse me, sir," I asked him. "Is that your Cessna out there?"

"What about it?"

"Fred in the charter office told me you fly around the islands a lot. I wonder if you might be planning a flight any time soon?"

"What about it?"

"I need a ride to another island. If you have room for a passenger, I'll spring for your gas."

"What island did you have in mind?"

"I'm flexible, just doing the grand tour. Where you headed?"

"Sint Maarten. Ever hear of it?"

"To be honest, no. I'm new in these parts. What's the story on Sint Maarten?"

"Half French, half Dutch. Quiet place, so-so beaches. Has casinos. The food's good on the French side."

"It very far away?"

"Hour and a half."

"Sounds like a place worth visiting. I'm Jake. If you've got an extra seat in your plane, I'd sure appreciate a ride over. "

He looked me up and down. "I'm flying alone. I wouldn't mind a little company if you're traveling light. Not much room for luggage. I'm Homer." He extended his hand, and we shook. "I was fixing to leave this afternoon. That suit you?"

"Couldn't be better. I'll have to go back to San Juan and get my gear. Be back in maybe an hour?"

"That'll work. We can take off as soon as you get back."

I'd have to work quickly. I had a taxi take me to the American Express office in town, told him to wait outside with the motor running. I got two thousand in t-cheques on the strength of my card, hopped back in the cab and directed him to my hotel. Told him to wait with the motor running. Threw my stuff in my pack, settled my bill, cashed some t-cheques for mad money and scrambled back into the cab. Had him hightail it back to Fajardo. I'd used my name twice, and there was a chance somebody'd noticed the cab, but I gambled that I had enough of a jump to avoid a high-speed chase with guns blazing.

We made it back to Fajardo within the hour I'd stipulated, encountering no trouble en route. Homer stood in the shade outside the hanger, catching a little breeze, sipping a styrofoam cup of coffee. When he saw me approaching, he tossed the dregs out and dropped the cup in a trashcan. "That was quicker'n I'd expected. Most folks don't estimate their time that well. You want to take a piss before we take off? No restroom aboard. In the hangar there, past the office door." A thoughtful suggestion.

When I came out he was waiting by the plane. He'd opened the passenger door for me. "Toss your pack behind the seat and climb on in," he said. I did so, he took the pilot's seat, and he turned the engine over. After a little warm-up, we rolled out onto the runway. A couple cars arrived in a hurry at the door of the little airport terminal, their riders hopping out and bustling in, but of course cars are always arriving at airports and they could just be travelers running late. My cab had already picked up a fare and headed back to San Juan. No one was going to question the driver right away. I'd stayed inconspicuous, and with luck nobody noticed me departing. Homer taxied out to the end of the runway, lined his craft up, hit the throttle and had us airborne in a jiffy. To my great relief, I'd gotten away from Puerto Rico free and clear. Except that I'd overlooked that Homer had filed a flight plan.

* * *

"So after I restructured the company and got my people in place," Homer was telling me, "it turned out they didn't need me on hand much at all. So I decided it was high time I enjoyed life a little. Took some flyin' lessons, something I'd always wanted to do. Liked it so much I bought this plane, started flyin' it around to see what the U.S. looked like. Oh, I'd traveled around before, but for business. Land in some city, take a cab to a hotel downtown, take another cab to some factory in the industrial boondocks, spend the day cooped up indoors, fly back to home. Never took time to see the sights, enjoy anything. Always had some other urgent business to attend to."

"You spend much time down here in the islands?" I asked.

"Just gettin' started on that. First I wanted to see America. Great place. Every state's a little different from the others, always something interesting."

"You don't bring your family along?"

"No family to speak of. Divorced. Wife said I paid too much attention to business, not enough to her. She was right. Kids are grown up, livin' their own lives, not close, I was always away on business. Can't complain. Doin' what I want to do now, floating along on dividend checks, consulting fees, investments, what have you—the money rolls in. Reapin' the rewards of my youthful energies, you might say."

"So what kind of company did you put together?"

"Manufacturing. Plastic and rubber items. Small things. Household items."

"Any products I might have heard of?"

"Sure. Urinal screens. Ever look down while you're pissin' and see a Barnard Co. urinal screen? Those little rubber mats with holes in it that stop the butts from cloggin' the drain?"

"Now that you mention it, I've noticed them here and there... Ummm, not that's any of my business, but I don't think I'd put my name in a situation like that."

"Neither would I," Homer chuckled. "My name's Buckle, not Barnard."

"So Barnard was one of those companies you bought?"

"No, that's my own company. I named that particular product myself, in honor of Jon Barnard. Jon, you see, was high school class president and football star, rich man's son, arrogant asshole. I was the class nebbish, grew up poor, studyin' hard, workin' after-school jobs, determined to get ahead in life. Jon was into fun and good times, treated me like shit, made me the butt of his jokes. I had a girlfriend for a while, not homecoming queen but good enough for me. Jon took it on himself to romance her, just to show me up, took her away from me, and I never got her back. Anyhow, when I developed that product line I thought back on Jon Barnard. It's my little joke. Fact is, I've always had the last laugh on him, doin' work I liked and now enjoyin' my money while he never left our hometown, still slavin' away in an auto parts store, stuck with a fat wife and paying alimony to his former high school sweetheart, the homecoming queen. Turned out ugly as sin and twice as mean."

Thus we passed the time. Homer flew as low as regulations allowed, following the scenery rather than a strict flight path, taking in the sights like a kid on a carnival midway. We skimmed by St. Thomas and St. John in the American Virgins, then reached the British Virgins. "Great little bar down there," Homer said, pointing to an island north of St. John. "Foxy's. On Jost van Dyke Island. New Year's Eve you can walk across the anchorage from one deck to the next. Provided you're sober enough to walk."

We were aloft above a string of emerald gems in a deep azure setting—Tortolla, Virgin Gorda, Anegada—with a parallel string across the channel and a sprinkling of neat little cays scattered around them. A goddam paradise on earth lay before my eyes. And I'd been impressed with the California seacoast? You could fit the whole thing from Malibu to Huntington Beach around one of these beauties. Catalina Island? I thought about other islands off California, and it dawned on me that Catalina is the only inhabited island on America's entire west coast, from the Mexican border to the mouth of Puget Sound, and it amounted to peanuts compared to any one of these. A scrub-covered patch of hills 25 miles off Long Beach represented the best we had? I hadn't been overwhelmed by Paradise Island in the Bahamas, where the Shah holed up, but the Antilles reached a higher dimension. Too bad an allstar team of the world's hoods dogged my trail. I could really stop and enjoy this place.

"Up yonder is Sint Maarten." Homer pointed to another island in the sun, emerging over the horizon. "We'll touch down there in a jiffy. Jake, from what you've said and not said, I get the impression you're on the run."

"Some people are after what's in my backpack. It's nothing personal."

"Running contraband? Illegal substances? If I'm in danger of being busted for drugs, tell me before we land, and I can deal with it."

"There's nothing illegal about the stuff; it's some business records, that's all. Transporting stolen goods is the worst they could accuse you of, and you know nothing about that because I didn't tell you."

"Business records? What business? Some kind of offshore shenanigans?"

"It has to do with BCCI. I guess you could say it's some kind of offshore shenanigan."

"You picked a winner—BCCI, the crookedest bank in the world. I've never done business with BCCI, always kept my affairs on the up-and-up and the straight and narrow. So, what are you planning to do on Sint Maarten?"

"No plans. I'm just trying to get away from the guys who are after me and find my way back to the U.S. Every shady outfit in the world wants those BCCI records, and they're just a few steps behind me. My passport got left in my hotel room on Grand Cayman, so they know my name and probably have my picture. It seems people are tracking any banking I do, and spies ask about me everywhere. I hoped to get back home from Puerto Rico, but they had the airport staked out. If I can find a bolt hole for a spell, I'll maybe be able to work out a way home."

"Why don't you just go to the U.S. counsel here and get your passport straightened out?"

"Because apparently the U.S. government is one of the parties that's after what I'm carrying. They tried to lock me up in Haiti."

"Sorry, I can't help you," he said. "I'm not heading home anytime soon, and anyhow people-smuggling's not my racket. I'd have to clear customs, so if there's an APB on you, they'd nab you there. We've, uh, got one problem right here and now. I filed a flight plan that included a passenger list, and I made up a last name for you—a technicality that nobody would much attend to. But I did put your first name as 'Jake', nationality American, so that's there for anybody looking for an American named 'Jake'. Didn't realize you had no passport. That's a more serious technicality, but there're ways. I'll get you into Sint Maarten, and after that, my advice is, try your luck on the French islands—St. Barts, Guadeloupe, Martinique. They're relatively civilized and orderly. You don't need a passport traveling from one to the next. The official language is French, but where white people gather they'll understand English. And greasing a palm or two will go a long way. You might even score a false passport if you can make your way to Martinique. Things are available there."

The plane descended toward another beach-bordered, lush green island. "Thanks for the info and advice, Homer," I said. "How much do I owe you for the gas? A couple hundred cover it?"

"You owe me nothing," he said. "I was headed here anyhow. Appreciated your company, Jake. Let's get on the ground, and I'll show you how to get around customs on Sint Maarten."

I SHOT THE SHERIFF

"We're goin' in on the French side of the island," Homer explained. "The French airport, Esperance, is geared to private craft, smaller prop jobs, local commuter flights. The international airport's on the Dutch side. Clearin' customs here is more or less a formality, but they do expect it. What I'll do is take the plane to the parkin' area, down the runway from the terminal. There's some cover adjacent to it. You slip out of the plane and duck into the bushes. From there you can make it to the road. I'll tell the customs agent that you're straightening out something in the plane, be along in a minute. Then I'll be on my way. You'll be on your own, of course."

"Where should I go once I find the road?"

"Depends on what you want to do. You want to go to Martinique, you'd best take a cab to the Dutch side, catch a plane, but I think you might need a passport for that. For St. Barts, you could catch a ferry down at the Dutch marina. Don't know about passports there, never used the ferry. Maybe your best bet's to go into Philipsburg and get the lay of the land. Find a place to stay there, get a good night's sleep and think out your plans. It's a small island. Folks take American money."

As we neared the Island I could see that it lacked Puerto Rico's lushness. The center was scrub-covered hills, the shore areas built up and tourist-oriented. Homer brought the plane down and taxied over to where a clutch of small planes like his sat. "Follow the road east, you'll reach the coast, it's a mile or two. From there, you can get a cab to Philipsburg. Good luck." I climbed down to the tarmac and shouldered my pack. "Hold on there, Jake," Homer said. "Seems to be a welcomin' committee comin' our way."

I squatted down and peered around the landing gear from beneath the plane. Three uniformed men had come out of the terminal buildings and walked briskly in our direction, focused on our plane. I kept low, using the plane as cover, and duck-walked down the side of the runway a few yards, then angled across the grassy verge toward the bushes. Then I noticed a pair of men get out of a car beside the road across the runway, scramble over the fence and take up tracking me from the other side. I straightened up and increased my speed. Both groups kept pace, gaining a little on me. They'd pulled within hailing distance, and I was considering making a run for it, when I heard a shot—pop—and one of the guys in uniform went down. Ranger training kicking in, I hit the deck too. It was like popcorn in a microwave oven. Pop—another shot as the uniforms dropped to crouches and one of them fired a shot across the runway, hitting nothing. The other guys took an answering shot—pop. A few more shots, from both sides—pop pop pop. And then a bunch erupted poppity-pop, both groups retreating in a hurry, firing wildly as they ran. Meantime, I slithered over the grass toward the scrub that lined the runway. I reached it, clambered over a low fence and dove in. Concealed, I parted some palm fronds to see what was going on. The guys with the car took off in it. The guys in the uniforms bustled into their building, propping up their buddy between them on their shoulders. Odd. I don't think either group fired that first shot. Then where did it come from? From some other thugs on my trail? Where were they? Why provoke a gunfight?

So there I was, hunkered down in bushes, undergrowth, cacti

and low trees. I fished out from my pack a shirt with earth colors, changed it with what I was wearing and crouch-walked through the scrub to a road. Following Homer's advice, I quick-marched toward the east. This island was built up, out here with shabby shacks and businesses with hand-lettered signs lining the road. I thought the guys in the car might show up, so I kept to cover as best I could, but nobody bothered me.

After a few twists, turns and false starts the streets took me through a better district of nice villas and bungalows, and I soon found myself on a long beach of white sand and gentle surf. Several smaller islands dotted the deep blue ocean beyond the mouth of the bay. The stretch above the beach was thick with villas, beach houses, mid-range hotels and palm-festooned resorts. White slatted lounge chairs, brightly colored umbrellas and sunbathing tourists filled the strand. Kids scampered around, but few people played in the water. Several yachts with sails furled bobbed at anchor in the bay. Wind-surfers skimmed hither and thither. A couple of speedboats towed parasails high above—must be quite a view from up there. Locals, mostly colored men, hawked the usual beach paraphernalia and doo-dads, their patter alternating between French and English. I bought a straw beach hat from one, a little camo to suit the scene.

Not being in beach duds, I stuck close to the buildings that bordered the strand and walked along until a tiki-bar next to the sand caught my attention. It was getting toward late afternoon; the place was not crowded. I was ready for some refreshment and a bite to eat, so I took a table next to the beach, ordered a beer and a shrimp basket and scoped out the situation. As I weighed the alternatives Homer proposed, a dinghy from one of the anchored yachts came in through the surf. Its three passengers—two men and a woman—hopped out, pulled it up far enough that it wouldn't drift away and trudged up the sandy slope into the bar. They took a table not far from mine and ordered Pina Colladas. I gathered from their conversation that they were Americans and that their next destination was St. Barts.

I shifted around in my seat. "Excuse me," I said. "I couldn't help but overhear. You're heading for St. Barts? What, in one of those sailboats?"

"That's right. You're an American?" the woman in the group answered. She was a pert little brunette wearing a bikini under a loose, unbuttoned cotton top.

"From California. Malibu. You're Americans too?"

"From Philadelphia."

"And you're cruising around these islands in a yacht? How do you do that? Do you own it?"

"We're in a ski club," one of the men, suntanned and husky, put in. The other man, though balding, looked a little younger, closer to my age. "In the off-season we have a sailing program, several weekend trips on Chesapeake Bay and one big trip. This is our big trip—two weeks around these islands. Last year we did two weeks around Greece."

"What, you hire a boat and skipper and so forth?"

"Oh, no. We bareboat charter. We have four boats on this trip, six to a boat. We have our own skippers, and everybody else is the crew, and we do our own cooking. Everybody pitches in. It's like camping out in an aqueous format. Are you into sailing?"

"More of a surfer, actually," I said. "I've been out on other people's boats, but I don't know much about it."

"It's a great sport," said the woman. "The amazing thing, it's so cheap when you do it this way. A resort here would cost you a fortune. What are you doing down here?" she asked, noting my pack. "Backpacking around the islands or something?"

"That's about it," I replied. "Drifting hither and yon as the breezes blow me. The reason my ears perked up is that I heard you mention St. Barts. That's close by here? I could use a lift over there if you've got room and it's on your way."

"We're having a last drink on Orient Bay here, then sailing over to St. Barts. It's about 15 miles, but we're going to sail around a little and then overnight at Ile Fourche, about halfway there. The bunks on the boat are all full, but if you don't mind sleeping in the cockpit, sure, we'll give you a ride over."

"Oh wow!" the woman exclaimed. "Will you look at that!" She indicated a big, blubbery naked man sloshing along in the shallows. "It's a nude beach, but there oughta be some kinds of restrictions. That's gross."

I hadn't noticed the bare-ass aspect. I scanned the shore, and sure enough, lots of folks sported full body tans, most of them middle-aged couples, pot-bellied men or plain-faced, pudgy women and all of them Europeans. "It's like what we used to say about Stanford when I went to UCLA," I remarked. "Nine out of ten California girls are pretty, and the tenth one goes to Stanford. Seems to apply to nude beaches as well." The woman laughed harder than the two men.

They finished their drinks. "Time to shove off," said the older man. "You want to come along, let's go." I settled my check, took off my desert boots and socks, tied the laces and draped them around my neck, rolled up my khakis and followed them down to their skiff. I helped them launch it, pushed it out free of the bottom and hopped aboard. The younger man yanked the outboard motor to life and scooted us out to one of the anchored boats.

The older of the men was John, the woman was Sally, his wife. John skippered this boat and organized the trip. The younger man was George, Sally's brother. On board were Bobbie, his wife, and Ray and Judy. Thinking it best to keep Jake Fonko low-profiled, I introduced myself as Jack Philco, my CIA cover name for my misadventures in Saigon and Cambodia. We climbed up a chrome-plated ladder onto a 40-foot sloop, as big a sailboat as I'd ever ridden on, though smaller than some where I'd enjoyed dockside parties. John got on the radio and checked with the other three boats in the group—all signaled readiness. I helped Ray haul up the anchor while John started the engine. We cleared the bay, George raised the mainsail, Sally and Judy unfurled the roller-jib, and the balmy breeze wafted us off toward St. Barts.

I'd puttered around with little sailboats—Sunfish and the like—and wasn't bad at windsurfing, but this was a new deal for me. John, it turned out, worked for a utility company and was ex-Coast Guard. His wife sold real estate. George and Bobbie worked in a factory in North Carolina. Ray taught college, and Judy worked as a research scientist. I'd always assumed you had to be a millionaire to go yachting in the Caribbean, and here a bunch of ordinary Americans my age were having a whale of a time and saving money at it. Out at sea, sailing a yacht seemed pretty basic, though more complicated than running a Sunfish. Let the sails out wide when the wind's behind you, crank them in closer amidships when you head closer to the direction of the wind. Steer the bow through the wind and shift the sails to the other side when you want to go the other way. It had an entirely different feel from powerboats, smooth and quiet. John explained that the tricky part with sailboats was handling them under power in close quarters.

The flotilla took its time getting to Ile Fourche, but nobody was in a hurry. Once out in the channel, the breeze picked up. Ray turned the boat upwind, heeling it over sharply, and we screamed forward through the wind, sea foam burbling past the leeward rail and us bracing ourselves up on our seats to windward. Cheap thrills at six miles per hour. It was fun. "You use a motor boat to get from one place to another," John observed. "But in a sailboat, you're where you want to be." As we sailed along, they told me more about their cruising vacations. Boats could be chartered all over the world; companies brokered them for individual owners. With a 40 foot sloop, you had your sleeping accommodations and transportation right there under your feet. Beyond the price of the charter, you paid for food, booze and incidental expenses. Cooking on board was cheap, and you couldn't beat a sailboat cockpit for atmospheric drinking and dining. You could drop anchor anywhere conditions permitted, for example near snorkeling reefs and off island towns and beaches. Plus, Ray pointed out, being on a sailboat gave you plenty of interesting things to do between meals. The catch was, you had to know how to sail, but there were classes you could take.

It brought to my mind Marina del Rey, that vast yacht basin near LAX that serves Los Angeles. I'd been down there for boat parties, to hit nautical-themed bars or to rendezvous with dates. All those big, gleaming yachts and cruisers sat lined up in their slips, so few of them venturing out to sea. Now I understood. Where would they go? Catalina offers the only offshore destination, and it boasts cold water, a small pebble beach and limited activity ashore. It was a long, hard sail for not much to do once you got there. Cruising up and down the coast took you into open sea, often in very fierce channel winds. To arrive where? This boat made about 5 or 6 knots, meaning 60 miles in a full day of sailing if all went well. So from Marina del Rey you could reach Newport Beach? Or Ventura? In ideal conditions. And then? So, California's nouveau rich reached the pinnacle, realized their dream of owning a sailboat, bought a yachting cap, took their prize out a few times, discovered that it was a lot of work and travail, and after the first season used it mostly as an offsite rec room. But down here you had this chain of gorgeous islands offering warm, clear water. Coral reefs. Coconut palms. Sheltered anchorages. Palm-shaded beaches with soft sand. Steady, gentle breezes year 'round (umm... hurricanes excepted). Exotic little ports. Further north lay Florida and the Bahamas. Sally said their ski club did weekenders on Chesapeake Bay. Lots of places to go there too. As glorious as it was, California didn't have everything, I was forced to admit.

We reached Ile Fourche, essentially a crescent of scrubby hills surrounding a quiet little bay, at cocktail time. While Judy and Bobbie prepped dinner, George set up the barbecue on the stern railing, and John brought out ice, big cans of tropical fruit juice, and bottles of rum. We ate sitting around the cockpit. Food always tastes better by a campfire out in the wild, and the same held true watching the sun set from a yacht at anchor. I volunteered to wash the dishes, a task everyone was happy to give to me.

Two of the other boats had rafted together, and after dinner we all piled into the dinghy and rowed over. The others in the group were much the same as on our boat—a nurse, a teacher, a paving contractor, a farmer and his family, a couple engineers, secretaries and so forth—practical people. What they had in common was a love of sailing and an aura of competence. They represented what the Malibu/Hollywood crowd back home called "real people"—the butts on the seats, the eyeballs on the screen that the entertainment and advertising industries craved and courted. And how did the "real people" party? Rum punch based on whatever fruit juice was at hand. Cold beer from the can. Jokes. Sailing stories. The day's adventures (Sally, given to dramatics, got a lot of mileage out of the 400 pound naked man). Reggae music, show tunes and sea shanties on the tape deck. Polite gossip and chit chat about families and friends. No big brandy sifters featuring a rainbow helping of pills. No coke lines. No haze of cannabis smoke. No perverts parading their depravities. No Egomobiles clogging up the street and the driveway. No battles of the bucks. No couples disappearing to back bedrooms in various combinations. No histrionics. No shrieking, phony laughter. No nervous deal seeking. No ambitious starlet wannabes requisitioned for purposes of jollying up stag men and wayward husbands.

It was sort of refreshing. Me being a guest, an outsider and someone who sought a low profile, I perched out of the way atop the cabin and quietly appreciated a relaxing evening.

The party ended at around ten, and everyone returned to their boats. I set up on the cockpit's starboard cushion and put on an extra shirt against night chill. A tropical shower passed over in the wee hours, but compared to some nights I'd spent on patrol in Nam, this was the Ritz. John woke up the boat by playing a "reveille" tape, then switched to local radio weather reports interspersed with reggae music. Sally came up the companionway in a bikini and demonstrated the principles of the "Joy bath." No, not a tropical group-grope. Joy dish detergent sudses up in salt water, so boat hygiene consisted of diving overboard, climbing back onto the stern diving platform, lathering yourself up from a squeeze bottle of Joy, then diving back in to rinse it off. The final step was a quick rinse with the boat's fresh water from the stern hose. George was about my size and lent me his extra bathing suit. In no time at all I was ready to face the day.

For breakfast, the cooking chores passed to John and George, I again washing up after we polished off eggs and sausage. We spotted some sea turtles in the bay. I had on George's trunks, still damp, so I borrowed a mask and flippers and went over the side. The bay held no reefs to speak of, but there were tropical fish aplenty in the shallows, and I chased the turtles for a while. This was a routine I could get into.

We weighed anchor a little after nine. St. Bart's wasn't far, and we joined the traffic into Gustavia harbor, the four boats anchoring well before noon. I wanted to be on my way, so I offered to spring for lunch for shipmates as a parting gesture. Needless to say, no one said no. We dinghied in, tied up at the town dock and trooped up the hill to a restaurant with a view of the harbor. Gustavia, the main town on St. Barts, sat back in a spacious bay. Similarly to Port au Prince, the surrounding hills turned it into a heat-collector, sauna-muggy even by late morning. Unsimilarly to Port au Prince, it was well-kept and expensive-looking. The shops along the streets as likely sold designer goods as tourist trinkets. I noticed at a newsstand/bookstore the local newspaper headlining a story about a Marxist coup on Grenada, wherever that was. According to Clyde Driffter, rebellions and revolts regularly erupted around the Caribbean basin, so I passed it off as no big deal. I'd get current on the news when I found the time to sit still and catch my breath.

We ate out on the shaded patio, enjoying the cooler sea breezes that reached over the hills to the restaurant. I spotted our boat down below and was surprised to realize that, at 40 foot length, the largest sailboat I'd ever gone out on, our group had the smallest yachts at anchor. St. Barts, I learned, was one of the pricier islands in the chain, populated with villas owned by wealthy

Europeans—particularly the French—and a favorite vacation destination of the jet set.

When we finished lunch, I didn't want to tarry, so I thanked my shipmates for a lovely time and told them I was going to scout out a place to stay a few days on St. Barts. Their plan was to sail the boats around the island to a hospitable bay on the other side. I bade them a fond farewell, sincerely meant, however on behalf of Jack Philco, no forwarding address. Then I shouldered my pack and strode down the hill to the shopping district. I'd worn desert boots continuously for over a week, and not only were they showing wear and tear, but they weren't suitable for the kind of traveling I'd been doing. I bought some good running shoes from a boutique, styled in black in case I needed them for night work. At a men's store, I got a swimsuit and a pair of casual trousers—my khakis were getting reeky from constant wear. I figured that the people pursuing my BCCI stuff had bribed bank personnel throughout the island chain to keep an eye out for "Jake Fonko," and possibly they could monitor some credit card transactions, though not always instantaneously. But no way could every shop clerk in the Caribbean be on Red Alert. I paid for everything on St. Barts with my MasterCard to conserve my cash. That left some traces behind, but I'd be off the island before the transactions reached the banks, where they might be monitored.

My last purchase was a black canvas duffle bag with a shoulder strap, as by now people would be looking for somebody with a backpack. I stuffed said backpack and my new duds into it, put on my Panama hat, and hiked to the St. Barts airport in my new shoes. It wasn't far—around the harbor and up over a hill to one of the funkier airstrips I'd seen since the makeshift ones in the Nam boondocks. As I made my way toward the terminal building, a two-engine, high wing Air Antilles commuter plane swooped down low over the brow of the hill, brushed close above cars on the road, and landed on a short, down-sloping runway that ended at a little bay on the other side of the island from Gustavia. According to shop clerks I'd obliquely queried, several local companies ran puddle-jump service around the islands, and I figured to catch one to Martinique.

I was dismayed, therefore, to see a couple of thuggish men loitering in the waiting area, checking out incoming customers. From my sojourn in Iran, I'd bet they hailed from that part of the world. Staying as far away from them as I could, I checked the departures board. It listed no flights to Martinique, but several went to Guadeloupe, one leaving shortly, probably the plane I'd seen just land. Guadeloupe, a French island just north of Martinique, lay in the right direction, and I was in no position to be choosy.

One of the men held a sheet of paper in his hand, and as I studied the departure schedule, he and his pal looked back and forth between the paper and me, showing increasing interest in me. Couldn't very well knock them out of my way or gun them down, so I tried a different tack. My changeling face got me a part-time job as a movie extra when I was a high school kid. Maybe it still worked. I walked directly up to them, and they back-stepped a pace. "You are looking at me, my friends? Is there some way I can help you?" I asked. They looked at each other shiftily. "What do you have there?" I said, reaching for the piece of paper. The fellow drew back further, but I persisted. "You are looking for somebody? Maybe the person on this paper? Let me see it. Perhaps I can help you."

He passed me the paper, a blow-up of my passport photo. Must have been the same sheet the troops in the Puerto Rico airport were consulting. I studied it carefully. "Hey, this man looks something like me," I remarked. "How about that! He's younger, I think (about eight years younger, as I'd gotten the passport in 1975 when I returned from Cambodia)... hmmm, he styles his hair differently. I think he must be a large man, maybe about six feet and one inch, judging from the way he's built (I'm 5' 10", but muscular)... and, look here, he has a scar on his face." The latter was a little stray line across a cheek, courtesy of the Xerox machine. They were examining the photo more closely, taking doubtful glances at me.

"You know what, I think I saw this man over in Gustavia town this very morning."

That got their attention. "You seen this guy? Where you see him?"

"Now where was it, let me think... it was at a restaurant! The one up on the hillside above the harbor, I didn't notice the name of it. He was sitting on the balcony with some people. It struck me then, how he looks like me. He had a backpack, I remember. Why do you seek him?"

"Just talk to him, that's all. How long ago you see him?"

"I came from there only a few minutes ago. You go over to that restaurant, show them your picture, they may recognize this man." I didn't doubt they would. I'd left a big tip. The guys looked at one another, each hoping the other would decide the next move. I handed the paper back to the one nearest the door and helped them along by gently guiding him in that direction. "If you hurry, you may find him still there," I urged. "They were lingering over coffees."

That got them moving. They scurried out to the taxi stand. I went to the ticket desk whose flight to Guadeloupe was preparing for departure. They had a seat available, and they booked Jack Philco through to Martinique with a twenty minute layover. I boarded the plane, and soon we rolled down the runway and vaulted into the blue sky over the sailboats at anchor and sunbathers laid out on the bright white arc of beach. By now, my shipmates would be back aboard, en route to the exquisite little bay I just left.

SWEET AND DANDY

Puddle-jump flights fascinate me. You sit in a small cabin open to the cockpit, so you watch over the pilot's shoulder where the plane is going, and you visualize yourself taking over the controls and bringing it in when he and the co-pilot collapse. Thank God that opportunity never arises, of course—I can do without white-knucklers. Both legs of my flight to Martinique went without incident. Good weather held—piles of distant cumulus clouds framed blue skies, and bright sunlight drew maximum color from the green islands and indigo sea we flowed over. I'd disclosed my name when I signed travelers cheques for my air ticket, but the first hop was short, too little time for Evil to marshal its Forces, and with luck, perhaps no one would notice right away that I'd be ricocheting off to Martinique. My plane change encountered no resistance, and the connecting flight took off on schedule, bringing me to Martinique by mid afternoon. It was a large island. Our flight path took us over a volcano in the ruggedly mountainous north, then down to a sea level airport toward the southern end.

It had a good-sized terminal, servicing international jet traffic. Commuter flights operated out of one end of it. Five other travelers arrived with me. I hung back after the others had deplaned, sitting in a crouch so as not to be visible from the ground, waiting for the flight crew to wind up their duties. It didn't take them long, and I left the plane with them. The ground crew had dropped my duffle on the tarmac by the cargo hatch. No one had rushed out to snatch it—my pursuers sought a man with a backpack. I hoisted the strap over my shoulder and ambled along with the pilots, quizzing them about Martinique, their work, their travels, anything to keep them engaged until we were inside the terminal building. They stopped at their airline office to log in. The commuter terminal was clear. I thanked them for a good flight and veered off to the main concourse. I gave it a quick survey, turned up nothing threatening. I came to a waiting area with a crowd, stopped there and took a seat amidst the throng.

And there I sat thinking. Because I'd arrived with no battle plan. What the hell was I doing here? I'd had to butt out of Puerto Rico. Homer suggested the French islands, said they were hospitable, told me I might find my way to a forged passport on Martinique. But details cried out for attention, like, now that I'm here, where do I go, where do I stay, how do I get there? What do I do next? And how much time do I have? As I sorted through my options a big jet rolled up to a gate on the other side of the concourse. It had American markings. Curious, I went to the arrivals board to see where it originated. I found no listed entry for that time slot, nor at any time near it. An animated horde of passengers streamed out—mostly men and women in their 20s and 30s, some older couples and a few odd strays. They were Americans, all right, numbering about a hundred, noisy and self-absorbed. This was a crowd I could blend into, so I gathered up my duffle bag, put on my baseball cap and joined the parade. Pasty-faced and bewildered, they were soaking up the exotic atmosphere, as exotic as any modern air terminal is likely to be, at any rate. Several women in charge herded them to baggage claim. I fell in by an unattached, pretty-ish 20-something woman. "Where are you all coming from?" I asked her.

"New York City," she said. She was rubber-necking several directions at once, taking it all in while keeping an eye out for her bag. "Wow, isn't this something!" she gushed.

"I didn't see any flights from New York on the arrivals schedule."

"Well, I don't know how they do those schedules. It's a charter flight. Maybe that's why it isn't listed."

"I think you nailed it," I said. A charter from New York. If anyone hoped to spot me arriving in Martinique, they'd have a hard time, for I'd fallen into perfect cover. It was as if somebody had taken a giant shop-vac, siphoned up several Manhattan singles bars and shaken out the bag into the Martinique Airport arrivals concourse. The crowd congregated around baggage claim as it delivered a mélange of suitcases and carry-ons. They collected their goods, and the guides steered them out to several shiny new buses. What the hell, why not? Wherever they were being taken, it got me out of the air terminal and beyond watchful eyes. I could always get a taxi to somewhere else once we arrived at our destination. I followed the crowd, boarded a bus and took a window seat. A stoked young yuppie took the seat beside me, and his raring-to-go buddies filled seats ahead, behind and across the aisle. They ignored me totally while we waited, while we rode and when we arrived, which was fine by me.

I'd thought maybe we were headed to Fort-de-France, the capital city, or possibly a resort hotel, but the ride took us quite a distance through hills, past local settlements (mostly black, but not as run down as some I'd seen), along tree-shaded and scrub-bordered rural lanes, down the middle of a plantation of some sort (coconut palms?), finally stopping on a parking lot fronting a walkway through a portal set off by palm trees. Inside the portal, a lively gauntlet of saronged and swim-suited, joyful young white people sporting various degrees of sunburn swayed and gyrated. As we trooped in they chorused a silly song and did a kind of cheerleader routine with their hands in time to their song. No, it wasn't an outpost of some weird religious sect. "Welcome to Club Med!" they enthused as we filed by. "Party time!"

* * *

WE NEWCOMERS TROOPED INTO A COMPOUND OF LOW-LYING, whitewashed buildings, and our greeters lost interest and dispersed to other fun. We were directed to queue up for check-in and room assignments. Not belonging here in the first place, I saw no point to joining that. Instead, I toted my duffle over to a tropic-themed, open-air bar with ceiling fans and laid it down below my stool. A tanned, cute, fit-looking barmaid in short-shorts and a sleeveless top came over. "How does a man get a drink around here?" I asked her.

"He orders one from me. What can I get for you?" She had a European accent.

"What does a Heineken go for?"

"One bead," she said.

"I just arrived. Beads?"

"Bar beads. You buy them at registration. Wine is free with meals, and the cocktail parties are complimentary, but for other drinks you use bar beads. It saves a lot of trouble, not having to deal with money. Like the doors on the rooms. No keys. Can you imagine what a confusion to issue keys in a beach resort like this? Drunks losing them all over the place?"

"No door locks? Theft isn't a problem?"

"Everybody deposits their valuables in the company safe room when they check in."

"I haven't yet checked in, thought a little thirst-relief would improve my day before I got down to business, so I'm short of beads at the moment," I said. "You look like a sporting woman. I'll bet you twenty American dollars you can't find me a cold Heineken's."

"A high roll, my friend," she said. She went to the taps, expertly drew a big plastic cup of foamy goodness and brought it to me. "You lose," she declared with a twinkle.

"I never have any luck," I sighed, slipping a folded bill into her palm. "Thank you." My first swallow hit the spot after a long, busy, hot journey. As did all the subsequent swallows. As I verged on finishing the brew, the barmaid came by my spot again.

"Here's a bauble for you to wear," she said, handing me a little bracelet of brown plastic pop-out beads. "It's safe to take them in the ocean, they float," she added.

"Merci," I said. "That's correct, isn't it? Martinique's a French island?"

"Oui," she said. "And Club Med's a French company. Almost all the G O's are French."

"G O's?"

"*Gentile Organizers*. The guests are G M's—*Gentile Members*. Technically, they're members of the Club. They'll explain that at orientation. Over there in the theater," she said, indicating the direction with a toss of her head. My crop of G M's, having taken possession of their rooms, now gathered and took seats.

"Are these beads good for meals too?" I asked.

"Meals, entertainment and activities are included in the price as clearly stated in your agreement."

"Oh yes, I forgot," I said. "I'm a slow learner." Well, that was good news. All I needed now was a place to sleep. I took my duffle over and seated myself beneath a ceiling fan at the rear of a covered amphitheater, an open-air construction with tiered seats and tables overlooking a stage. Some G O's, all personable, tanned and photogenic, laid out the program: Activities. Loads of activities. Facilities. Comprehensive facilities. Meals. Lavish buffet meals. Policies. Minimal policies. Anything goes, the sky's the limit. Once you got in, nobody watched too closely.

I returned to the bar and sidled up to the bartender. "I wonder if I could leave my bag out of sight behind the bar for a little while?" I asked, showing a folded ten dollar bill in my palm. "And perhaps you could keep an eye on it?"

"My pleasure, Monsieur," he said, accepting my bill with one hand and my duffle with the other. Both promptly vanished from view. "You will reclaim it before we close the bar? I cannot guarantee it after hours." I assured him I'd be back after dinner and ordered another beer. A good thing the barmaid laid those beads on me—I'd neared the end of my U.S. bills, and attempting to cash a t-cheque here would court complications.

Dinner hour arrived and the G M's came trooping in. They divided roughly into three groups. Sunburnt singles who'd been here a while arrived in boisterous cliques and headed straight for the buffet lines. Pasty-faced, overwhelmed singles who'd come this afternoon joined a food line where hostesses, er, G O's, shunted them to tables. And a bunch of older people, mostly couples, gathered at a section of tables they'd staked out. I joined the third group, more my age and demeanor. They welcomed me and made place. Meals were served a la buffet: the selection was wide, the cuisine quality superb, the table wine unlimited. Yay for the French! Tables of younger G M's got raucous—youth on the make far from home. The people I joined had a different slant on Club Med. They were veteran G M's, and they came because Club Meds were, like bareboat sailboat charters, a roaring bargain as resorts went. Good food, good settings, good service, good vibes. They filled me in on the routine, and they didn't ask questions. Most G M's came for one or two weeks, arriving on charter flights from specific, central locations,. So the crowd varied from one week to another, for example sometimes singles out of the New York metro, other times midwestern schoolteachers assembled at Chicago's O'Hare. Martinique had a reputation as one of the wilder Club Meds, but they told me it was pretty tame. No drugs. No orgies. A nude beach and some hanky panky was as depraved as it got. Family-friendly Club Meds offered organized children's activities. The G O's were an impressive bunch, they said, talented athletes and performers, and unexcelled at showing a wide variety of G M's a good time.

I'd landed in another segment of "real people," distinct from my erstwhile sailing buddies. Club Med was summer camp for adults, more an East Coast kind of thing. Out in Malibu we'd heard of it, but no one I knew had ever been to one. We lived in our own resort, after all, and should we be struck by a yen to Get Away From It All, we had our favored holiday destinations—Maui, Cabo, Aspen, Tahoe, Taos. The sailing group was active and earnest. Club Med G M's tended to be passive and hedonistic, into pointless fun and simple games. I knew their tribe well: their Southern California cousins kept the LA singles bar scene going.

Following dinner, I took in some of the floorshow in the amphitheater. Tonight featured amateur night for G M talent, and a Jewish guy from New York did some passable schtick about the new Tehran Club Med. "The hostages are the G M's and the terrorists are the G O's" drew a hearty laugh, including from me. The other would-be lounge acts didn't amount to much. I left and cruised the bar until I found a clutch of obviously two-week people whooping it up with booze-fueled banter, catchphrases and bad jokes. At a lull, I leaned in and said, "Excuse me guys, but maybe you can help. My roommate is entertaining a lady tonight, so I need a place to crash. Anybody know of a spare bed to be had?"

That set them abuzz with a fresh round of banter, catchphrases and bad jokes. When they'd exhausted the possibilities, a sandy-looking blonde said, "You should go talk to Denise. Her roommate's been shacked up with a copywriter the last couple of nights." Touching off a new round of etc. etc. etc. "That's Denise, second table over, with the carrot top," she added when the babble died down.

I made sure I had the right table and the correct carrot top in my sights, thanked them and sauntered over. Denise sat chatting with a small group of bored-looking lounge lizards. "Excuse me, Denise?" I said. She looked up and gave me her attention. "My name is Jack. Your friends over there (I pointed at the group) said you might be able to help a gent in distress." I explained my plight, embellishing it a bit.

"Not exactly friends," she sniffed. "I haven't even seen my so-called roommate for the past two days," she said. "I wouldn't be surprised if they'd ran off together by now. Is this a permanent arrangement you're looking for, Jack?"

"No, just for tonight. I'd be surprised if their romance lasts even that long."

"Have a seat and let's get acquainted," she said, turning away from the group toward a nearby, empty table. "I could use another Mai Tai," she added. She led me over, and the rest didn't seem sorry to see her leave.

I flagged a barmaid, er, G O, and ordered drinks. "So where are you from?" Denise asked. Her face had a vaguely rodent-like quality, and her curly, strawberry hair had been absorbing salt, sand and tropical sun for a couple days, during which she hadn't washed it. Slender verging on skinny, with cracks in the skin of her bare heels, she looked a little worse for wear. Early-thirties, I estimated, though she looked older. Her long fingernails, polished to carmine perfection, suggested she didn't live by strenuous physical labor (administrative assistant at a head-hunting firm, I later learned).

"Los Angeles," I said.

"I went there once, to Hollywood," she said. "Took the Universal Studio tour. Did Disneyland. Wasn't impressed." She fished a pack of Benson and Hedges cigarettes from a side pocket in the floppy seersucker tunic she wore over a two-piece swimsuit, offered me one (declined it), put one in her mouth and handed me her lighter. "I didn't know any charter flights from LA to here had come in," she said as I lighted her up.

"I flew down from St. Barts."

"Really? You came in by yourself? They only run charter flights from cities, I thought. St. Barts is one of these islands down here?" She expelled a smoke plume roofward.

"It's a few islands north. I negotiated a special arrangement. I was yachting in those waters, so flying down from there was more convenient. Cost a little more, but worth it."

"You get around," she said. "Yachting. Wow. You own a yacht down here in the islands?"

"Friends of mine."

"Good friends to have."

"Some of my friends have yachts, some don't. It takes all kinds. So, do you come to Club Med often?" I asked to change the subject.

"This is my first time. My first time to a tropical island, actually. My divorce just became final so I thought I should celebrate, you know? Some celebration. It's not as wild as everybody said, and I'm not much of a beach person anyway. Yachts might be better, except I get seasick. So tell me about yourself. What's your sign?"

That tired old pick-up line. I gave her a sign that worked in LA: "Slippery when wet."

She chortled, then guffawed, then laughed out loud. "Tell me more," she said, moving closer and resting a manicured hand on my thigh. Two rounds of Mai Tais and beers later I got my duffle bag from the bartender, and Denise led me to her room. It was small and basic, the Club Med concept dictating that you should participate in Paradise, not hole up in a hotel room. I'd barely set my gear down when she started massaging my neck. "Muscular," she murmured. "Mmmm... I like that." Obviously she expected me to respond, so I turned to her and instantly got a bear hug and a mouthful of cigarette-smoked tongue. Ah well...

Club Med beds weren't designed with wide-ranging romping in mind, but that didn't impede Denise. A very insistent woman, and I'll bet she back-seat drives, too. The old fraternity saying is, "The worst piece of ass I ever had was fantastic," but that's just youthful inexperience braying. Afterwards, she took over the bathroom and returned all ready for bed, having greased, slaked, and slathered her face and the rest of her body with a variety of potions, lotions and ointments. I hugged her dearly, told her she was a woman like none I'd ever met and retreated to the empty bed, hoping she wouldn't awaken in the wee hours with ideas.

Somewhere on Manhattan Island, a happy ex-husband was turning in for the night.

We went another round in the morning, causing me to cross gigolo off my list of possible fallback careers. I took the opportunity to shave and otherwise catch up on a couple days of grooming. I noticed my hair had grown enough longer than my passport photo to aid deception. When I came out of the bathroom, she said, "You've got a backpack in here? Why do you need both?"

Nosy bitch was snooping in my duffle bag. "You never know what to expect," I said. "Be prepared, that's my motto." I guided her hand out of it and resolutely zipped it shut. She hadn't gotten all the way into the backpack, or she'd have a lot more questions than that.

"Just getting to know you, hon," she said, not sheepishly enough.

"Let's go hit the breakfast line," I suggested. She clasped my hand and pulled me along.

You can't beat French pastries for breakfast, and there was plenty more besides. I especially appreciated the spread of fresh tropical fruit. Afterwards, I excused myself on grounds of wanting to look into some things, promising to meet her for lunch. An escape route was what I needed to look into. I put on a resort-y outfit, got into my running shoes and donned my backpack. Better not to leave it in an unlocked room with a snoop. I explored the compound boundary to boundary amidst a bustle of activity. Players sweated through morning volleyball. A group formed up for the morning snorkeling excursion. Down on the sand, a lithe G O led calisthenics. A speedboat gave a queue of eager beginners turns on water skis from off the pier. Joggers at the shoreline splashed their earnest ways along. Ping-pongers traded slams. Tennis players volleyed across their courts. Swimmers pounded out laps in the quiet water of the cove. A notice board announced football and field hockey tournaments slated for the afternoon. Concrete canyon critters couldn't ask for a better place to unleash pent-up urban energies.

The Club occupied a tree-sheltered salient with a sandy shoreline on a peninsula at the southern end of Martinique—a fine location for a resort, but awkward for getting to somewhere else. A barbed wire-topped chain link fence defined its perimeter. Good for keeping the indigs at bay, but getting over it would be awkward. I could skirt it at the waterline, but hiking out along the beach I'd be too exposed. The front portal offered the only viable exit. Out along the road I could find some cover, but I'd have to locate a ride. No way I could hoof it to Fort-de-France. I figured one more night here at Club Med to settle my nerves—though I'd spend it anywhere, even on the beach, even in the scrub, rather than with Denise—then I'd go see what shakes in the big city.

My plan changed abruptly when Denise intercepted me en route to the dining hall. "Did you see those guys?" she asked. "These two guys were going around asking everybody if they'd seen an American named Jake. They showed me a picture. He looks something like you."

Shit. "I've been getting that a lot down here," I said. "Some guys on St. Barts showed me that picture, too. Uncanny, how people can look alike. Describe the guys you saw?"

"You know, average Americans, about your age. Clean cut. Office-type clothes. Looked kind of tough."

Not the pair from St. Barts. "Denise, I just remembered something I have to do. Go on ahead, take a table in a conspicuous spot, and I'll join you in a few minutes. After lunch we'll hit the nude beach together." She greeted that with a smile, and I hurried back to the room for my kit. The first thing I did was pull my pistol out of the backpack and swap in a full clip. I returned it, silencer still attached, to the backpack, changed to traveling clothes and transferred everything else from the duffle to the backpack—a tight squeeze, had to leave a few things behind. I folded the duffle bag and secured it in the shoulder straps.

I strode through the grounds to the portal, where a pair of burly G O's in jock-strap swim trunks stepped out of a palm-fronded shack, blocking my way. "Excuse me, M'seur. How can we help you?" one asked. The notion of somebody escaping apparently contradicted the Club Med concept.

"No problem, I'm just going out here for a few minutes," I said.

"For G M's that is not permitted," said the other. "For safety reasons, you understand."

"Of course, of course," I said. "I appreciate your concern, but it is all right. It is for my training program. I must three times every day run two miles with my pack on. My sponsors insist on it."

"Training program? What are you training for?"

"The Ecuador to Brazil Endurance Marathon," I said, letting my imagination run wild. "It is an international event intended to call attention to the cause of saving the Amazon rainforest. I am sponsored by a major American petroleum company, Exxon Corporation, you of course have heard of it. They wish to portray themselves as allies of the environment, so they are sponsoring four entrants."

"I have heard of Exxon Corporation, but I have never heard of this race."

"That's because this is the first time for it. It will be announced later in the year with great fanfare. Contestants in teams of four will race through the jungle with packs in a relay, each leg 100 miles, over several days. Every country will have a team, some countries more than one. This week I am training for the sprint trials. So I will run as fast as I can through the trees along the road, one mile out and one mile back. You can help me, if you would be so kind."

By now they were intrigued. "Help you? How?"

"I have been training very hard, and this morning I'm hoping to achieve my personal best time. My sponsors insist on verification by witnesses. So we'll say that the portal is the start and finish line, and, I notice you have a wristwatch, if you would time me I would be very thankful. I think it will take about eight minutes."

"Running two four-minute miles through trees with a pack? Impossible!" one of them exclaimed.

"No one can do that!" the other man chimed in.

"As I said, it would be my personal best time. I haven't done it yet. But how can a man attain excellence if he does not set a high aspiration? Wish me luck, gentlemen. I have been steadily improving. Today may be the day! Ready, set, go!" I took off down the driveway to the road at a brisk trot, leaving them glued to the wristwatch. I rounded a bend out of their sight and stopped to catch my breath. Then I walked fast to the palm tree plantation along the road. Planted in rows, it offered less cover than I'd have liked, but it was better than nothing. I got beyond the palms, went by some buildings, then spotted a denser stand of trees and scrub further along. I plunged in. It meant slower going, but it was dense concealment. I figured to put more distance between me and Club Med, then emerge and see about a taxi. I hadn't gone far when I heard a car pull up along the road abreast of my woods, and then two car doors shut. I couldn't see them, and they couldn't see me, but I soon sensed people clumsily following my trail. The gatekeepers must have ratted me out to the two Americans. I sped up, ranging further away from the roadside, then doubled back and slipped into ambush position, pistol at the ready.

Presently two men answering Denise's description came struggling along in my tracks. I let them get ahead, waiting to see if they were on point. No, no one followed, it was just them. I crept out and stalked them quietly until they reached a little clearing.

"Gentlemen," I announced, "please put your hands up and turn around." They did. I gestured with my pistol for them to stand further apart. They complied promptly. Pistols with silencers are more intimidating than pistols without. "Now, take off your clothes," I ordered.

"Aw, come on," one protested.

"It's a warm day," I said. "You'll get them back. Hey, isn't that better than if I shoot you in the balls?" I lowered my pistol to that sight line on one of them. Against the possibility that I wasn't just joshing, they dutifully stripped. Beefy men—the two of them could probably take me in a fair fight. "The shoes, too... now, back away." They did so, wincing at each step. I quickly frisked through their two piles, locating two automatic pistols. I threw the clips into the bushes in one direction, and the guns in another. One of them had a phone. I tossed that in the bushes too.

"Who do you work for?" I asked.

"Wouldn't you like to know," one answered. I fired a shot between his ankles. "Clark Clifford," he replied quickly.

"Isn't he some political honcho?" I asked. "Some big Democrat?"

"As honcho as they come," said the other.

"What does he want with me?" I asked.

"Not you personally. You've got some stuff he wants. He sent us after it. Look, he'll pay you for it."

"How much?"

"He didn't tell us. We're supposed to get it that's all."

"How about you give me a contact number, and I'll get back to him."

"No can do. Look, we're just hired hands, work for an agency. Come with us, and we'll see what he'll cough up, but no way are we to give you ID or any connecting information."

"That so?" I reached down and fished out one of their wallets. It contained several business cards, and I pocketed them all. An address book turned up, and I slipped that in a pocket too. Then I thought of something. "You've got a lot of cash there. I'm running short. How about if I sign you a Traveler's Cheque for a hundred and take some of your bills?"

"Help yourself," he said. He gave me his name. I signed over a cheque and substituted it for a fifty, three tens and a twenty. "A pleasure to do business with you, gentlemen," I said. "Tell Mr. Clifford, I may be contacting him in the near future." I tossed their shoes into the brush in different directions, noting the dismay on their faces. I told them to step into the trees away from our path and lie down, and when they had done so, I broke for the road. I took a chance, going out in plain sight along the road, but they seemed to be working alone. I marched along with my thumb out. I reached a little market crossroads before anybody stopped to pick me up, and there I found a cab willing to carry me to Fort-de-France.

If those two bumblers could find me, I had no security on Martinique, and false passport or not I had to get away. I couldn't fly out on an international flight with no passport, and backtracking on a commuter to one of the other French islands was foreclosed. Moving further along to another island by boat was the only possibility, but the ride I'd cadged with the sailing club was a windfall. I'd need a boat for hire. I had the cabbie drop me off by a Fort-de-France waterfront saloon where he said the local skippers hung out. I might be able to find a ride with a boat skipper to some other island without being spotted. I couldn't think of any other place to turn.

Working men filled several tables in the dim, sour room. I got a beer and a sandwich and opened my ears. Most of the palaver was in French. One table sounded American. A man in a uniform stood beside it, addressing a one-armed man seated there behind a down-to-dregs schooner of beer.

"Where were you last night?" the uniform said.

"Here and at home."

"How late were you here?"

"Until the place closed."

"Anybody see you here?"

"What's the matter? You think I'd steal my own boat? What would I do with it?"

"I just asked you where you were. Don't get plugged."

"I'm not plugged. I was plugged when you Custom guys seized my boat without any proof there was anything on it."

They carried on for a while, getting nowhere until the Customs officer finally threw in the towel and stalked out. I gave the table time to settle down, then went over. "You're an American?" I asked.

"Sure," he said. He was wide-shouldered and tall. His blond hair was further sunburned nearly to white. He had broad mongol cheekbones, narrow eyes and a nose broken at the bridge. His shirtsleeve was pinned up to his shoulder "Harry Morgan, formerly of Key West, Florida." He looked like the real deal.

"I'm Jake Fonko, California. I need a boat ride. How well do you know these islands?"

"Pretty well. Where do you want to go?"

"That's just it. I could use some advice. People are after me (he looked squintily at me)... no, not the law. I haven't broken any laws. People want something I've got. It's not contraband, either. Everything's legal. What I need is a bolt-hole, a civilized place that's inaccessible. I need a little breathing room so I can contact people and work something out. I guess that's a pretty tall order?"

"Say, I know just the kind of place. Mustique Island, south of there. It's a private island. Wealthy Brits own it, the Queen and the Princesses and all them Earls and Dukes and Lords. Has a little town on it. The most secure airport in the Caribbean. Only one entry port for boats, and only yachts at that. Of course, if you want secrecy, you'd have to find a way around all that."

"How about wading in? How are the beaches?"

"Yeah, a lot of good beaches. I could get you in that way, sure. The problem is, Customs impounded my boat."

"Why'd they do that?"

"See, they suspected I was smuggling. But they didn't find any evidence. Seized the boat anyhow. It's my living. How am I supposed to make a living?"

"What would you charge to run somebody down to Mustique? If you had your boat, I mean?"

"Figure a hundred miles, more or less. Have to come back. Four hundred dollars, say. If I had my boat. I don't want to fool with this, but what choice do I got?"

"Is there a way to get your boat out of Customs? Pay a fine or something?"

"No, that won't do it. These Frenchies want me off the water. They haven't set a fine yet, they haven't even heard my case. They'll keep my boat as long as they can. Here's an idea. Supposing you was to force me to take my boat off the Customs dock, at gunpoint, say? Sure, that'll work. Then they couldn't blame me, see? On account of you forced me to do it."

"I hold a gun on you, and you get your boat, and you take me down to Mustique? You really think we could get away with it?"

"My boat's tied up at the Customs dock. We go over there, and when the guard goes to the other end of his round, that'll give us enough time. You want to do this tonight? It'll get dark soon, then we'll go over there."

"I didn't ask for any of this, and if you've got to do it, you've got to do it," I said.

* * *

THE CUSTOMS BUILDING AND ITS DOCK FILLED A STRETCH ALONG the harbor. Harry Morgan led me to a slip where the Customs boats—patrol craft and runabouts—were tied up. His boat, an old cruiser, was off by its lonesome. It had been through the mill. The paint was scratched, faded and mismatched. Rust trailed off metalwork. Bullet holes scarred the cabin and the cockpit. We lurked behind a shed while the guard passed by the boat and continued away, his shadow jumping and shifting from dock light to dock light as he ambled along below them in the sultry night air.

"Here's how it'll go," Harry whispered. "I'll come out on the dock in plain view with my hands up, see, and you'll be right behind me with the gun in my back. And you better have the safety on. You'll tell me to get in and start the boat, and then you'll cast off the lines. Once we get clear, I'll douse the lights and we'll run in the dark. We'll be at Mustique before daybreak, sure."

We waited until the guard left the dock and disappeared around the Customs building, then took up our act. It went fine, Harry making a quick check of the boat and starting the engine. I'd cast off the bow line and the spring, and was bending over the stern line when a slug hit the cabin bulkhead as a pistol shot popped. "Hey, take it easy," Harry growled. "She's taken enough damage already."

"It wasn't me; it was him," I said. A man had burst out of the shadows, running along the dock toward us, pistol in hand. He fired another shot. Good luck hitting anything, firing on the run. I unwound the line off the cleat, threw it in a pile on the cockpit floor and jumped into the boat. Harry gunned it away from the dock. I took the silencer off my gun, flipped off the safety and fired a shot back at the wharf for effect. And then we were beyond pistol range.

"Who was that, the guard?" Harry asked. "I thought he'd gone."

"Some other guy, coming from the other direction. I told you people were after me."

"Do they have boats? They going to follow us?"

"For all I know, they have ICBMs and stealth bombers. It's a big and varied band of brothers."

"We'll take the Caribbean side of the islands and skirt around St. Lucia and St. Vincent," Harry said. "On the lee side it's calmer. You can spell me on the helm for a while once we reach open water. You're hungry, there's food in the galley, stuff in cans and packages, nothin' fancy. Beer in the ice box, warm by now. Take it easy, relax. If you want anything," he concluded, "just whistle."

Off the island, we rode in a fresh breeze and a three-foot swell. Taking it on the quarter, it wasn't bad. A bright moon rose, getting close to full, fading the lesser stars out of the night sky. It laid a lustrous path across the water toward the east and backlit the Pitons as we passed St. Lucia. We ran along at a good clip for several hours and were breasting St. Vincent Island when we heard a boat off our port bow. Harry cut back the engine, and we listened as the sound drew nearer. "I don't like it," he said. "I had them on the radar. They come out of Kingstown and picked us up. Take the wheel." He went below and came up with a rifle. "Okay, bring it back up to 15 knots." When I advanced the throttle, a searchlight flashed on about 100 yards away and began sweeping its beam. Couldn't make out the other boat, just saw their light. "It's not Coastal Patrol," Harry said. "That light's too close to the water. It's private, something fast, I think. They'll spot us in a second." He stepped out into the cockpit and shot the rifle, a lever-action shark gun, from the hip. He handled it deftly, firing three shots, operating the lever one-handed by flipping the rifle up and catching it after the ejects for the first two. The searchlight went out. Whether he hit it or they just turned it off, I couldn't say. At that range, with a one-armed shooter firing a rifle free-handed, I'd bet on the latter. "Alter course 15 points to starboard," he breathed. "That's to the right," he added. I did so. He went toward the stern and opened the engine hatch, returned to the cabin a moment later with a tommy gun. "I had it stashed there for a another job," he explained. "I guess Customs didn't search too well, or they'd have confiscated it. What a fucking mess that was," he mused. "Blood all over the gunwales. Last time I ever haul Cubans. Live and learn. You know how to handle automatic weapons?" he asked me. I allowed as how I did. "This has a 50 round drum," he said. "The range isn't much better than a .45 automatic, but that's good enough if they close up to board us. Alter course 15 points to port and hold that heading. I'll ride shotgun with the rifle, but be ready to grab the Thompson and let 'em have it if they approach."

We rode on for a spell. "Oh shit," Harry said. "They're still out there, creeping up on us. Listen..." he cut the throttle and we heard the other boat astern off our port quarter. "Could you take care of it? It's awkward for me, a tommy gun."

"What do you want me to do?"

"Just fire a burst in their direction. Nobody sticks around after that."

I'd never used a vintage tommy gun. Interesting. Aiming low, I let a few rounds go—BapBapBapBapBapBapBap! Me and Machine Gun Kelly. It was a piece suitable for mobsters—simple and brutal. You could clear out an alley with one of those, but give me an M-16 for jungle work any day.

Harry estimated right. The other boat trailed off behind us for us for a while and finally called it a night. My various pursuers seemed to be professionals, not psychopathic serial murderers like the villains in crime thriller books. They wanted my books and disks, but not badly enough to take on automatic weapons in the dark. And so we continued on our way. No other suspicious boats showed up on Harry's radar. Along about dawn he pointed to a dark outline just visible against the sunrise sky and said it was Mustique. I didn't see how he could tell it from all the other islands out there. I put on my black clothes and stowed my shoes. I'd signed over t-cheques to cover the trip. My signature would alert the world when he cashed them at a bank, but I asked him to put that off for a day or two. I hoped to be somewhere far away by the time the word got around.

He eased the boat into a quiet bay on the north coast of Mustique. An easterly breeze sent catspaw ripples skittering across the smooth surface in the early morning calm. The air was cool and crisp, the sea smell pure. Sea birds had started their daybreak activities. We crept along until the bow touched bottom. "It's up to your waist," he told me. "There's no sand bar or drop-off here. You can wade straight in up the beach." I slipped over the side into the warm water. He handed me my backpack and I balanced it atop my head. "Good luck to you, Jake," he said.

"Good luck to you, Harry," I retorted. He'd need more of it than I did. All I had to do was figure out a way back to Malibu unharmed. Whereas he had to continue living his mess of a life.

Harry backed off the ground, swung his boat around and headed her back out. And I launched my amphibious assault on Mustique Island.

MANY RIVERS TO CROSS

A HARD SAND BOTTOM SLOPED GENTLY UP TO THE WATER'S EDGE, with no surf and no surprises. I sloshed ashore on a crescent of bay, maybe a half mile point to point. I crept up to the embankment and took a cautious look beyond. No nearby buildings, nothing stirring on shore but a big grey-green iguana staring back at me. I went back down on the sand and stripped off my clothes. My night-black outfit hadn't been necessary and certainly wouldn't be a good idea now. I let the air dry my body, then put on the most subdued tourist duds in my pack. Desert boots would do for footwear, and my Panama hat should be right in fashion. I rearranged everything back into my duffle bag, which had more room. But out in public, I'd be just another vacationer out for an early morning stroll. Who would tote a black duffle bag on an early morning stroll? I stashed it in a spot I'd easily locate but undetectable to anyone but professional trackers, and set out.

I'd come ashore on an undeveloped stretch of land. Off to my left, I saw trees planted in rows, some kind of orchard or plantation. Otherwise, the terrain was Caribbean island scrub—brush, cacti, low trees. I bushwhacked west and came upon a paved road. I went to my right. It looped around, bringing me to a posh resort compound, Cotton House Hotel, fronting on the sea. A slow-turning windmill stuck up above palm trees and low, colonial-style buildings. Unlike Club Med, it wasn't overflowing with youthful energy unleashed by the break of day, in fact, it showed little activity at all. I continued around the loop, passing some substantial houses, and it joined back into a road going south. A half mile beyond the junction, I found the end of a short-takeoff airstrip running cross-wise on the island. It looked well-maintained, but I couldn't make out much by way of terminal or support buildings along the tarmac. Obviously no major airlines used Mustique as an international hub.

I walked through a little settlement and presently came upon a larger bay bending toward the south. Several yachts and a couple big catamarans lolled at anchor, people moving about on them, enjoying morning coffee. A restaurant, Basil's, sat up on stilts over the water. I saw working boats and buildings in a cove at the northern end, and from an outcrop a jetty with docking facilities and a loading area reached out to boat-depth water. I continued further. The main road veered toward the center of the island and walking further I came upon what Harry Morgan had been talking about. The better parts along the shore resembled outskirts of Santa Barbara, but the middle of Mustique was as though Beverly Hills had been picked up and dropped here, and then supersized: bungalows (spacious), villas (elegant), and compounds (extensive). As I walked along, I found that the east coast of the island remained mostly undeveloped. The British upper crust didn't fancy surfing, so they preferred the more subdued lee side of the island. In Los Angeles, the wealthy paid dearly to build shoulder-to-shoulder along any stretch of beach front, whereas the Mustique shoreline boasted few of the island's big dwellings. But then, Southern California had millions more people within driving distance and relatively little available waterfront. Having to fly thousands of miles to your holiday pad dictated a different scheme of development.

In less than two hours, I'd scouted what there was of Mustique to see. The scant number of businesses offered not the standard tropical tourist array of souvenir shops, vacation clothing boutiques, smoothie stands and tiki bars, but rather existed for the regulars. Some shops provided everyday necessities for the locals—food, clothing and the like, but most catered to the British toffs who owned island property and the seasonal sojourners. Many properties seemed self-contained, no doubt with live-in cooks, gardeners and servants. At this early hour, none of the upscale shops had yet opened, so I made my way to the cove with the working boats. Indig housing here was distinctly better than what I'd seen on other islands. I found a café putting out breakfast for the local working class. Most customers were West Indians, but they were hospitable enough to a strange Anglo man, and everyone spoke good English. I found a table, sat down to chow and was soon conversing over coffee with some fellows seated nearby. They knew I hadn't come off one of the anchored boats but didn't question me closely.

What I wanted was intel about Mustique, and like people the world over they were eager to tell an amiable stranger what harmless information they knew about their home town. No ferry service connected Mustique to other islands; the jetty was for boats bringing supplies. A man might possibly get a ride on a supply boat. Most everybody on the island worked for the Mustique Company, which for all practical purposes ran the island for the benefit of the property owners. The palatial, landscaped villas and compounds belonged to Queens, Princesses, Earls, Dukes and Lords, as well as captains of industry, commerce, finance and sources of income best left unprobed. I later learned that some acquaintances, Sir Mick Jagger and Sir Paul McCartney, bought in when they could afford it, but that was years later than it would have done me any good. The winter season, which saw the bulk of visitors, was several weeks from commencing. Most villa owners let out their properties, at least for part of the season. The Mustique Company arranged rentals and provided security.

Following breakfast, I located the Mustique Company office

and told the receptionist I wished to inquire about renting a villa for the coming season. She put me in the hands of an assistant manager, one of whose job qualifications must have been that BBC accent designed to keep commoners in their proper place. My explanation of arriving in a passing yacht probably didn't fool him for a minute, but I had Malibu and Pacific Palisades bona fides, and I dropped enough Hollywood names and international sojourns to keep alive his skeptical hopes. With disdainful reserve, he explained that the season verged on commencing, and several excellent villas were still available. Owners preferred seasonal leases, but some could consider monthly stays. Generally a property came with full support staff. I pressed him for details, and he showed me pictures of several listed properties and their locations. I told him I would very definitely be getting back to him after the conclusion of my yachting holiday. He dubiously passed me his card and some sales literature and ushered me out.

I came away from the Mustique Company with what I wanted —a line on vacant villas where I could crash for a night or two. I plainly couldn't check into Cotton House, the only hotel on Mustique. I needed an anonymous refuge where I could call a time out and spend some time thinking. Because, as I reconned this rarified, exclusive little tropical paradise, I realized that I had thoroughly screwed myself by coming here. Ever since that fateful morning in George Town I'd been winging it, grabbing at floating straws, plunging ahead with inadequate intel. So far, I'd gotten away with it and managed to reach Mustique, safe and secure for the moment. But, now what? The island received no scheduled air service nor regular boat rides to other islands. However I contrived to reach another destination I'd need a passport, and I couldn't obtain one here. I was stuck with no crowd to blend into and no backup. Quite the contrary, I was an alien to an exclusive tribe highly resistant to outsiders. The only Brit I knew who might have clout on Mustique was Maggie Thatcher. So I could ring her up, explain the situation and enlist her help? Sure, and then I'd flap my arms and fly home to Malibu.

One possibility would be to call Evanston again and see if he could arrange a pickup or something. Even if I could find a phone, that would take time, and how long was I going to stay out of trouble on this tight little island, where everybody knew everybody and everything that went on? They might not have a secret police force, but with most everybody employed by the Mustique Company, they didn't need one. Anything untoward or out of place would reach the people who mattered. So far I may not have attracted much notice—just another American wandered ashore from a yacht—but if I stayed in circulation as the day's business progressed, I'd be noticed; if I were still visible tomorrow they'd be wondering about me, and beyond that they'd be demanding answers.

I walked back down the road and into the heart of the island, armed with a list of places the rental agent said were immediately available. The best prospects clustered on the southern side of the airstrip. One on my list had an obscured guest house across a large formal garden from its mansion. From concealment I observed it for an hour. No activity. I checked out several other piles in the neighborhood. Crashing a main house was a no-go as servants would probably be on site. That guest house was my target.

I returned to the settlement on the road above Britannia Bay, as the bay with the jetty was called and hit a provisioner's shop for enough portable food—sausage, cheese, bread, fresh fruit, bottled beer—to last a couple meals. I had to inconspicuously kill time until dark, so I bought a canvas tote, carried everything a couple hundred yards through the brush over to a beach, and took a leisurely lunch in the shade of some coconut palms. A downright pleasant way to while away a balmy afternoon were I not wracking my brain for an escape plan. Mustique's beaches did not teem with day-trippers. A few people came, strolled the shingle, splashed a bit in the shallows, went their way. If anyone noticed me, they didn't let on.

As the sun dropped toward the horizon, I rose from my reverie and headed back up the road to where I'd left my duffle. It hadn't been disturbed. I shouldered the strap and retraced one more time the road toward Britannia Bay. Shortly after I passed the little settlement, I took a side road in toward the villas. I located the one with the guest house and came at it through the vegetation behind it, using garden features and the guest house itself as a blind to avoid detection from the main manse. Unless spies lurked in the surrounding cover, no one saw me as I tested the back door. It was not locked. On an island controlled by one company, with no way for miscreants to get on or off easily, burglary didn't pose a serious threat. Or it could mean that the building was in use. I stowed my duffle and tote of food in one of the two bedrooms and positioned myself where I could keep an eye on movement between the two buildings. Nothing much happened. After dark, a light went on in a rear window on the ground floor of the main house. And then another, toward the other end of the ground floor. The kitchen? Servants' quarters? Electricity must come from generators on the properties—I hadn't seen any central power plants or transmission lines anywhere in my walk. Would they send juice to an unoccupied outbuilding?

No sign of any activity. I had the place to myself. I broke dinner out of my tote bag—a big step down from the Club Med buffet. On the other hand, I had a far superior room. So I sat in the dark and ate and thought and analyzed. Where had I gone wrong?

On Grand Cayman? I should have waited for the "African American" with the Uzi and given him the suitcase? I should have run up to my room and gathered my gear? I should have declined to fly out with Clyde Driffter?

On Cuba? I should have stayed behind with Vesco? I shouldn't have traded gunfire with the black chopper?

On Jamaica? After wasting those three thugs, I should have returned to the U.S. Embassy and explained how I'd arrived there, what I was carrying and how I'd come by it?

In Haiti? I should have waited patiently in my locked room in the Consulate, not knowing why they'd locked me in, or what they had in mind?

In Santo Domingo? I should have tried to work something out rather than head for Puerto Rico?

On Puerto Rico? I should have gone to the U.S. authorities, after the U.S. authorities previously had tried to nab me?

By the time I got to Sint Maarten I clearly couldn't go back, with pursuers on the alert everywhere I'd previously been. So moving down the chain of islands to St. Barts and Martinique was my only option, though every step took me further from home.

Reviewing the past couple weeks, I decided I hadn't really fucked everything up. My only misstep was taking the job in the first place, and from that point the situation was fucked up, no matter how I played it. I'd wound up on Mustique, safe in a little tropical garden spot for the time being. But now that I had the time finally to think my next step through... I couldn't come up with one. I couldn't parse out a pattern. It was a dead end. The U.S. had no presence here. It was an island privately owned by the British Ultra Class. What they'd make of me, I couldn't guess. No doubt they had ties to MI6. What story could I give *them*?

I couldn't help but flash on Clyde Driffter's final words: "A man alone ain't got no bloody fucking chance."

It was getting late, and I'd been on my feet out in the sun all day after a sleep-short night before. My mind was getting foggy, fading out. Tomorrow, I'd be thinking more clearly. I took off my shoes and lay down on the bed in the room I'd chosen.

A little later, I snapped awake at the sound of the front door opening. I heard tinkly giggles and deeper chuckles draw nearer. The door swung open, and a light flashed on. A young local couple, I guessed a maid and a yard boy had in mind some off-duty fun and games. The Caribbean has a reputation for being slow moving, but her hand came out of the front of his pants, and his hand out from under her top, at warp speed. She hid her face in her apron, and he flicked the light off. "So sorry, sah! Please excuse us." And they scampered back out the door. Young lovers hoping to share a tender moment in the privacy of the guest house. Sorry, I spoiled it, but at least I bet they'd not be reporting it to the owners right away. I could move on tomorrow, bright and early, but for now I could sleep.

A tapping on the front door of the guest house awakened me in the grey dawn light. Now what? I weighed the options. Couldn't very well shoot my way out. Slip out the back and head into the brush? With no way off the island, they'd get me soon enough. Might as well just answer the damned door and see what's up. To my surprise, it was a dignified colored man in a neatly ironed, tropical weight white uniform, holding a silver tray of food and tableware. "The master thought you might appreciate some breakfast, sir," he said, extending it toward me. I stepped up to receive it, and a crouching man darted out from behind the door jamb. Tea cups, scones and clotted cream went flying as he rose up underneath the tray and jabbed something into my neck.

And that was that.

* * *

I CAME TO, LYING ON A SOFT BED IN A TASTEFULLY APPOINTED room all by myself. It reminded me of something... the last time something like that happened was... oh yes, when I reawakened after Soh Soon knocked me out in the Khmer Rouge's Tuol Sleng torture chamber. Well, this had to be more hopeful. The Brits hadn't established a world empire by playing patty-cake, but they wouldn't likely be adding me to a pile of corpses.

"Hello? Anybody home?" I barked. The door opened and... stocky build, broad Slavic face, straw-colored hair... "Grotesqcu! What are you doing here?"

"The usual, Jake," said Emil Grotesqcu, crack KGB agent. "Following you around. The key question is, what are *you* doing *here*? We're still trying to figure it out. I'd have thought you'd be on Grenada by now."

"Always keep 'em guessing," I replied. Grenada? The hell's that about? "Was it your guys that stuck me in neck? Where did you take me?"

"Those lust-crazed servants reported you. The Mustique Company figured rounding you up in the morning would be soon enough as you were stuck on the island. They saw no point wasting a night's sleep over you; they'd set the hounds out after breakfast. No telling how long you'd be tied up here if that happened, so there was no time to spare."

"There never is," I agreed. "So what happened? Where are we?"

"In a safe house. One of our useful British idiots lets us Friends of the People use it when we need a base in this region. After my men incapacitated you, we loaded you in his Land Rover and brought you here. You're fine, nobody's going to bother you now. We'll send you forward this evening. Couldn't you at least give me a hint what you're up to down here? We initially figured it must be something dire and desperate for the CIA to team you up with DRAGONFLY, but why all the rigamarole, we wondered? I mean, why didn't you just turn that suitcase over to the CIA station in the U.S. Embassy in Jamaica? The chaos and destruction you left in your wake... staging that dogfight with the CIA helicopter... you're lucky somebody didn't get killed. Well, initially we assumed the purpose was to confuse us, and you did have us going there for a while. It was all our network could manage, keeping track of you."

"I'm not working for the CIA."

"Of course not. Wink wink nudge nudge say no more," he chortled. "But Driffter, after the crash—that threw us for a loop."

"Yeah? How so?"

"He made his way to Grand Cayman and took some document files back to BCCI, claiming he'd retrieved them and demanding a reward. He kept yammering about $230,000, and finally they wrote him a loan for that amount that he'll not have to repay. Costs them nothing, they'll just post a loss of money that never existed anyhow. Fractional reserve banking, the Devil's own invention. I wish we could claim credit for the force that's going to take your economic system to eventual ruin, but your financial masters instituted it all by themselves before we even seized power in 1917. So my analysts next explored the possibility that Drifter was just a distraction, that there must be more to all this than meets the eye."

"They worked that out, did they?"

"You led us on a merry chase, eluding all those thugs. It looked like it was genuine. Finally we realized that it *was* genuine."

"Who were they, anyway?"

"Quite a rogues' gallery. On Jamaica you killed three minions of a Ukrainian sex trafficking ring (explains the CZ 75) and then eluded some Arabs in Kingston. That plane from Grand Cayman was BCCI thugs. The Contras sent the man who visited you in the Trianon Hotel, and the ones in Santo Domingo were Columbians. The boat you encountered off Puerto Rico, that was Manuel Noriega's men, Panamanians. That was a clever stunt you pulled in the Puerto Rico airport—several of your pursuers landed in the hospital after that free-for-all. The men tracking you at the Saint Martin airport were South African arms smugglers. I felt a little bad about winging the policeman."

"It was you that shot that guy?"

"I calculated it was the best way to break up the pursuit. If I'd shot one of the South Africans, they'd just have taken off, and the police would have kept after you. Shooting the officer was more likely to touch off a gunfight. It worked as I'd hoped. Operatives of the Palestine Liberation Organization met you in the airport at St. Barts—loved the way you threw them off the track. I wonder how Clark Clifford's henchmen are going to describe their mission when they report in. The fellow who shot at you in Martinique harbor was from the Chicago mob. Off St. Vincent it could have been Iranians or the Mossad, or maybe Nigerians—several groups had staked out that island, but it was dark, we couldn't tell who was in the boat. I don't know why I bother worrying about you— you handled it all with your usual aplomb."

"Why thank you. I was afraid I'd been getting stale."

"Not in the least. Same old Jake."

"Those people after me around Ochos Rios, who were they?"

"Ganga gangsters? Cubans? I don't know. Castro was pretty annoyed about that MIG. I suppose he'll expect us to replace it. But the fax of your passport photo didn't start circulating right away. Our own people didn't pick up your trail until you dropped in on the American Consulate in Kingston. You probably never noticed them. You certainly faked them out with that sailing excursion ploy, though—sheer brilliance. Had them in a dither until the St. Barts airport. I was surprised your CIA went to the trouble and expense of setting it up, but it worked like a charm. And Club Med? That New York slut...? What a hoot!"

"Just another wayward soul in search of love and acceptance in an indifferent world," I said. "Let's not judge harshly. One thing I wonder about is, these thugs on my trail have been going easy. I didn't get the feeling they wanted to take me out."

"No, I don't think they did. Most of them had a vague apprehension that you just might be a CIA agent—killing you could bring them a lot of trouble. Besides, it wasn't you, it was the ledgers they were after, and from what I've seen of the ledgers, they pose no dire threats to anyone's operations or cash flows. BCCI's clients want those materials so as to avoid embarrassment and inconvenience—tax evasion investigations, patterns of past transactions, money trails, evidence useful to political enemies—data that in the hands of the wrong people might bring a little trouble. Taking you out was a last resort, not worth the risk. Of course, that occurred to us late in the game. By the time you landed here on Mustique, we were working on another theory. Maybe your adventures weren't a series of decoys and obfuscations at all. Maybe your assignment was ill-starred from the outset. Maybe Driffter wasn't part of it after all, and you hadn't intended to end up on Jamaica."

"That was never in my marching orders, I can assure you."

"So we back-analyzed the pattern of your movements, and it became clear that you were heading in the direction of Grenada all along. When you moved south from St. Barts the day after the coup, that confirmed our suspicions because soon thereafter my service alerted me to a major U.S. military operation afoot. So we concluded your objective all along had been Grenada for some kind of supportive activity, but you had to reach it clandestinely. However, something must have gone wrong because Mustique turned out to be a dead end for you. You had no hope of arriving on Grenada in time, so I thought I'd better step in and lend a hand.

"You see, Jake," he continued, "we—the two us, I mean—have a serious problem. Two problems, really. I was able to make excuses about how you absconded with that satchel of our money in Belfast. Ultimately, it only caused a minor inconvenience as some other Irish Republican gang ponied up for the arms shipment. Russia lost nothing on the deal, and your ripping us off bolstered the case for my continued attention to you. But if you don't make your rendezvous tonight and carry out your mission, that's going to blemish the reputation of Jake Fonko, Superspy, and if my bosses conclude you're no longer a primary threat and lose interest in you, my cushy job is done for. They'll downgrade your case and put me back to subverting restive Muslim movements in our collection of Stans—a corner of the world noteworthy for dust, filth and flies. That's problem number one, but I think I've got that one covered. I'll deliver you to Grenada on schedule.

"The other problem is, it's all very well for you to be a CIA superstar, but as far as my service can tell, you've bested me at every turn. I'll admit I'm partly to blame for that because of the exaggerations I build into my after-action reports to pump up your reputation. If I don't come through on this assignment, though, they just may decide I'm not up to the job and assign someone else to it. Already things are being whispered. So you've got to let me win one this time, Jake."

"Do you have something in mind?"

"Those ledgers and disks from the Bank of Credit and Commerce International in your backpack would be of great interest to my service. We've had our eye on BCCI since its inception, though we use them from time to time. Those materials could provide a lot of valuable intel on various criminal and subversive networks around the world. So while you were unconscious, I took the liberty of photographing the ledger pages and duplicating the disks. I hope that's all right?"

I gave his proposition a quick mull-over. Since I wasn't working for the CIA, and since the stuff from BCCI was secrets neither from the U.S. nor any other government, nor related to any U.S. government operation, they were public property, sort of. I hadn't stolen them, they'd just dropped into my hands, mine to dispose of any way I saw fit—finders keepers, no harm no foul. "Patriotic duty" had nothing to do with it, and while Todd Sonarr may have thought I owed him something for springing me from The Maze Prison in Belfast, I thought I owed the CIA bupkis for how they'd wrecked my army career.

I was tempted to just turn the whole lot over to Grotesqcu, post a "To Whom it may Concern" notice and let the Forces of Evil chase *him* for a while, but I saw angles to it that I could work. If I kept the original ledgers and disks, it would maintain the illusion that I was on a CIA assignment, and they still had value as bargaining chips. Letting Emil copy everything seemed only fair, since he'd rescued me, and I had to admit that his dogged devotion to my case over the years had gotten me out of more than one impending game ender. I had an interest in keeping him in business. If that BCCI stuff would boost his cred in the KGB, it worked in my favor too. He was the best backup I could ask for. The guy was a wizard.

"Okay," I sighed with resignation. "I'm boxed in with no way out. But this has to be buried—deep cover, eyes only, strictest need to know. I don't want to face fifty years in Leavenworth on a treason rap."

"Not to worry, Jake," he said. "How many of our spies has that ever happened to? For decades a number of your countrymen have quietly helped us out while faithfully doing their jobs, and all but a few freely walk the streets today. I can see benefits from this all the way around. You deliver product to the CIA. I return home with a trophy, the only man ever to count coup on Jake Fonko. My service can benefit from more insight into the networks and cash flows of the world's scoundrels, and I doubt there's anything about your CIA on those disks that we don't know already. Depending what's there, you may even be in for a hefty payday. You can count on the KGB to give money for value."

"Enjoy them in good health," I chirped.

"I thought you'd see it that way," he said, looking altogether pleased. "You must be famished by now. Let's have a bite to eat. Our host here has a most excellent Island chef from St. Barts— French and Caribbean fusion. I know there are cases of The Widow, as the Brits call Veuve Clicquot champagne, down in the cellar. We'll pop open a bottle, and I'll belatedly toast your birthday. Thirty five years, isn't it? The prime of a man's life. And then we'll be on our way."

It touched my heart. Somebody remembered. In the helter-skelter of the last couple weeks, even I'd forgotten. October 23rd, yesterday. "The years roll on, Emil," I said. "Gone before you realize it." But a little dark cloud crept in. I'd just turned 35, and what did I have to show for it? An interesting life, free and easy, pretty much doing as I pleased, comfortable and exciting with glamorous interludes (punctuated by occasions of terror and danger, of course). But no real roots, no solid accomplishments, no permanent fixtures, no legacy, no family, building toward nothing. Did those 35 years add up to anything worthwhile, or was I on track for a fool's existence?

We dined on the verandah. Grotesqcu fired the Widow's cork out into the garden and filled our flutes. We raised them, touched them with a clink, and soon I was distracted from further dour reflections.

But I did wonder if there'd be a card from Dana Wehrli waiting in my mail, if I ever got home.

* * *

NIGHT FALLS ABRUPTLY IN THE TROPICS. THE SUN SLIDES BELOW the horizon as an intact disk—boom. We finished off the bubbly and Grotesqcu led me out to the Land Rover. The driver—the man with the tray this morning—drove us to the jetty, where two Cigarette speedboats were moored. Four men who'd been standing around smoking, gathered beside them. Three climbed into the forward boat, and Grotesqcu, I and the other man stepped aboard the other.

"The other boat will lead," Emil said as he took the skipper's seat and started the motors. "We'll follow along with no lights. We'll have you there within an hour."

"Where?" I asked.

"Oh, come on, Jake," he said. "Don't play dumb. Grenada, of course."

"Of course."

The other man cast off the lines, and we pulled away into the bay. We reached open water and Grotesqcu put us on a plane, screaming along at 50 knots behind the lead boat's rooster tail. Cigarettes—a class of boats nicknamed from their role in smuggling them in bygone days—are designed for speed and nothing else. No amenities, no comfort, no embellishments. Torpedo-sleek foredeck and streamlined hull account for most of the 40 or so foot length. Massive engines take up the stern, and in between there's an open cockpit with a skipper's chair and leatherette bucket seats for a few passengers. Getting from one place to another? You bet. Where you want to be? Only if you're a hardcore speed junkie. Emil was having a ball.

We followed the lead boat to the east and then took a southerly course, skirting around the Grenadines to windward, and the going got rough. The winds had quieted a little, but the ocean swell persisted, coming off our bow quarter. Grotesqcu handled the boat expertly, but at that speed every other wave we hit sent us airborne, jarring my kidneys and rattling my teeth when we landed . We flew along in the dark, far enough windward to avoid shoals and reefs, but God help us if we ran into floating debris. The full moon rose, setting the sea to port side a-shimmer, but didn't throw enough light to show any land to our starboard. A few glimmers sparkled here and there, suggesting a large island a few miles distant. An hour or so passed, and then the boats slowed down and dropped off the plane. "Jake, go below. There are clothes for you to change into," Grotesqcu instructed.

"What's up?" I asked.

"You're going to join some people. You'll want to blend in."

The cabin didn't provide much elbow room, and headroom enough only for dwarves. I found a stack of clothes on one of the forward bunks. A well-used work shirt. Soiled coveralls. What the hell? I put them on, stuffed my own clothes in the duffle and returned to the cockpit. A light flashed on shore. The third man in the boat answered it with a spotlight. The lead boat angled toward the shore signal, us trailing in behind. We pulled alongside what appeared to be a construction wharf—rough wood bulkhead, creosoted pilings, a concrete surface, cranes and heavy equipment, illuminated by lights hung on poles. We tossed our lines to some men waiting for us on the wharf, who cleated them fast. I climbed ashore on legs shaky from the rough ride, duffle in hand.

"Here you are, Point Salines. We made good time," said Grotesqcu. "I think everything will be fine. You'll be all rested and ready to go for tomorrow."

Tomorrow?

A man came over, a Latino dressed as I was. "Jake, this is Desi."

"Buenos noches, Senor Zhake," Desi said with a wide smile.

"He speaks English, don't worry," said Grotesqcu. "He'll take care of you, get you squared away. Well, Jake, this was an assignment I appreciate, a great improvement over Cambodia and Iran, better even than Belfast, and surely superior to other venues where the KGB could have sent me. I could get used to this lifestyle, especially come winter. What a couple of weeks! Too bad we couldn't slow down and enjoy it a bit. I do have to wonder why my masters are so bent on subverting your system. Seems to me we'd be better off emulating it. Oh well..." He extended his hand and we shook. "Ciao, Jake," he said. "Much obliged for the BCCI materials. You can wrap your business up now. Do the right thing tomorrow, and everything will turn out rosy for all concerned. Somebody should award you frequent flyer miles for all the international air travel you provoked," he added with a chuckle.

Too bad I couldn't ask him to lay out what the "right thing tomorrow" might be. "Thanks for rescue and the ride, Emil," I said. "Take care of yourself." As if he needed any encouragement. He hopped back into the Cigarette and resumed the helm, eager to fire it up and roar away. Men cast off lines, the idling engines purred to life, and the two boats rumbled away into the darkness. I heard them throttle up to full power, and within a minute the roar faded away to the south.

So I'm now on Grenada. And therefore? Desi flashed a wide smile and motioned me to follow him. It was a quiet night, nothing much happening. He led me onto what under the bright tropical moonlight appeared to be a large airstrip under construction.

GOVERNMENT BOOTS

WE WALKED OVER SMOOTH CONCRETE; WE WALKED OVER STONE ballast; we walked over lanes of bare dirt, all stretching into the moonlit distance. We walked around bulldozers, earth movers, skip loaders, backhoes, cranes, cement mixers and asphalt machines. Desi told me he was foreman on a grading crew. More important than that was his position as barracks political officer. I told him Grotesqcu brought me to Grenada because I was an American secret undercover agent for the Russian KGB with special instructions, and I asked him to bring me up to speed on the local situation so that I could complete my plans. He explained that Cuban construction crews had been imported to the southern tip of Grenada to build a modern airport with a landing strip of 2,700 meters. The old airport had a bad location and was too short for the big jet planes that the gringos ricos like to fly on. The Grenadian government saw it as a way to attract tourist dollars and development to the island. British money backed it, Grenada being a former colony that still maintained ties. Cuba sent construction workers, plus doctors, teachers and technicians, part of their goodwill program to foster friendships with other islands in the region.

We approached some large, temporary buildings along the

construction site. Shirtless men milling around outside paid me no attention beyond curious glances. Aromas of spicy food mingled with sweat and grease hit me. I heard loud voices, laughter and salsa music. He opened a door and we entered a big, low-ceilinged barracks housing a raucous assembly in a haze of cigar smoke which ceiling fans did little to disperse. Dinnertime had ended, evening relaxation had begun. Men at tables played cards and dominos. Over to the side, a string combo worked out a Latin number with an upbeat rhythm. Other tables hosted animated discussions. Some men sat contentedly smoking cigars or nursing beers. The assemblage comprised mostly men older than me, working stiffs. Away from their own impoverished island, they must be having the time of their lives down there. All they needed was women. I wondered how much of their pay Castro allowed them to keep.

Desi showed me to a far corner bunk, and I stowed my kit. He offered me food. I wasn't hungry after my birthday feast on Mustique, but I was grateful for a beer in the muggy, close room. I stayed out of the way and presently the evening wound down and the crowd readied for bed. They were working men. They'd worked hard all day. Tomorrow they'd be working hard again.

I followed their routine, tagging along at the rear ends of washroom queues and deflecting any conversations with nods, smiles and grunts. We were all in bed and lights out soon after 2200.

And I still didn't have a clue about tomorrow.

* * *

THE NEXT MORNING I AWAKENED WITH THE THOUGHT THAT FOR an airstrip under construction, Port Salines sure had a lot of air traffic. The sound of automatic weapons fire snapped me to attention. My watch said a little after 0530. I threw my coveralls on over my shorts and slipped my running shoes onto my bare feet. A pandemonium was developing as the crew in the barracks came out of their slumbers. I threaded my way through roiling men to a door and slipped outside. Staying close to the wall, I found a spot that afforded a view of the airstrip. Two low-flying AC-130 Spectre Gunships circled Port Salines in their wide-ranging, port-side combat loops. Some green tracer streaked up toward one from a machine gun emplacement off to the side, and the lizard-green Spectre opened up on it with its autocannons. No more tracer.

Black shapes in the distance grew into Hercules transport planes, the same airframe as the Spectres, but without the port-side armament. At first it looked like they might be in a landing descent pattern... but with all the clutter on the incomplete runway, how could they? They roared in over Port Salines at 500 feet spewing black objects, and chutes opened instantaneously. Nobody chutes into a live fire zone from 500 feet but the Rangers, my old outfit. Holy shit. We were under full-scale assault by U.S. Army Rangers.

I went back into the barracks, by that time a-buzz like a knocked-over beehive, and surveyed my pot-bellied, coveralled co-workers. Several separate clusters of men listened to impassioned harangues by men brandishing AK-47s. The rest sat at tables, or lined up for coffee and gruel, or wandered around looking distressed. I located Desi in one of the crowds and beckoned to him. He excused himself from his group and came over. "What's going on here?" I demanded firmly. "What are those men saying?" I waved my hand in the direction of two of the groups, implying that I meant them all.

"It is different leaders, trying to take control," he said. "We have crews of combat construction engineers, and their officers try to organize a resistance. Other groups are Communist party men. They don't want the military guys to take over, but Revolutionary Army is very powerful in Cuba. So the party men try to persuade the men to follow their leadership, rather than the army's. Most of the men do not want to fight with the Americanos at all. They know they will lose and many will be killed and hurt. They came here for the work. But every Cuban man must take military training, so they fear they will be forced to fight the Americanos, no matter who seizes the leadership."

Meanwhile the Rangers were converging on us, and the gunships circled overhead suppressing any signs of opposition. Good luck resisting that. "This is all happening according to my plan," I confided. "This is why the Russian KGB sent me to Point Salines."

"Tell me your plan, Senor Zhake. I stand ready to implement it."

"This apparent attack is simply a probe," I said. "The Americanos sent in a weak unit to test us. If we resist them here at Point Salines, they will land overwhelming forces all over the island. But if we let them think they have won, the Americanos will be lulled into false consciousness. Then, while their guard is down, we will launch a successful counterattack."

Some men at the window were shouting excitedly. "The Americanos are advancing along the airstrip," Desi translated for me. Several men with AK-47s bolted outside to engage the Rangers. They got a few rounds off before they were cut down.

"Enough," I said. "You are the political officer. Tell the others to desist. Have some men shoot guns out the doors. The Americans will shoot back. After that, we wait a little. Then, when they draw closer, we wave a white flag. We will have shown honor defending Cuba, and we will draw them into our trap."

Desi drew a pistol from his pocket and fired three shots at the ceiling. Having gained their attention, he told the men my plan and urged them to follow it. It was total bullshit and probably every man knew it, but it worked because no one really lusted for a firefight with the American army, and any excuse not to would do. Orders from Russia? Sure, let's obey! All looked relieved except a few army hotspurs. Those, Desi selected to fire their weapons and thus uphold Cuban honor while being careful not to kill any Americanos. They did their duty, and an answering fusillade perforated the walls. The men hit the deck, but not before several got winged.

A few minutes later, Desi waved a white dishcloth on a broom handle out a window, and then everybody settled down to wait.

Everybody but me, that is. I hustled back to my bunk, threw off my construction gang clothes, donned my civvies and combed my hair. I chucked the CZ 75 under somebody else's bunk. And I retreated to a storage closet, keeping an eye on the situation through the cracked door opening.

Presently flash-bang grenades came through two windows. After the blasts, all the doors flew open and crouching Rangers burst in, M-16s leveled at belly height. The work crews, hands raised, gladly let themselves be frisked and sorted out for processing. When the barracks was secured, I shoved the closet door open, staggered out, and, hands high in the air, proclaimed, "Thank God you've come. I'm an American. They've been holding me hostage!"

* * *

S<small>ERGEANT</small> G<small>RANGER TOOK CHARGE OF ME</small>.

"Do you have any proof you're American?" he asked.

"They confiscated my passport, but they left me my California Driver's License. Will that do?"

"Let me see it," he said. I fished it out of my wallet and gave it to him. He studied it. He compared the picture with my face. "You're from Malibu, Mr. Fonko? I've never been out there. Is that like in the Gidget movies?"

"Not very much," I said. "Who's your commanding officer?"

"I'm not authorized to disclose information, Mr. Fonko."

"I was in the Rangers myself. Did a tour in Nam in 69-70 with the Lurps, a Sergeant in Company B, 75th Rangers."

Ranger Granger brightened up. "The Lurps? That must have been some kind of action. Major Wallace tells stories about it."

"Major Wallace? Is that Henry Wallace? (Granger nodded "yes.") We were team leaders together. Is he involved in this operation?"

"He's the battalion XO, but he won't be here until we can land planes on the runway. They're working on that now. Come see." We went outside. Soldiers had taken over bulldozers and were using them to shove other equipment out of the way. By 0740 they'd cleared a usable stretch of airstrip, and supply planes soon arrived. Though officially in Sergeant Granger's custody, he let me wander around as he had more urgent tasks at hand. I enjoyed watching the troops go about their business. Damn but they were good, as sharp an outfit as ever. I missed it. To this day I think I could have gone far in the military, had not Todd Sonarr and his CIA shenanigans fucked up my career.

A number of supply planes landed before Sgt. Granger told me Major Wallace was on the ground. By that time I'd convinced him that enough of my story was genuine. He carried my note to field headquarters and returned with a reply: "Major Wallace said it would be a little while, but you're to wait, Mr. Fonko."

"That's fine. Meantime, where can a man get some chow around here?"

He directed me to a field kitchen. Nowadays, they ate better in the field than we used to out in the boonies. Then he escorted me back to the barracks. After about an hour, Granger returned with a ramrod straight soldier sporting black embroidered oak leafs on his camo uniform, along with a name strip, "Wallace." The senior officer stopped and stony-faced, looked me up and down carefully. I was on the verge of rising to greet him when he declared, "Sergeant, put this traitor in irons! Now!"

After a long pause, Henry burst out in loud laughter. "Jake, I wish you could have seen your face just then." He strode over and clasped my hand. "Too long a time, buddy," he said, then turned to Granger. "That will be all, Sergeant." Granger left us.

"Henry, what's going on here?" I asked.

"Operation Urgent Fury. Almost spur of the moment. There was a Marxist coup on October 19, deposing the president, Maurice Bishop. The population rose up and called a general strike. Riots broke out, and Bishop's supporters tried to spring him from jail. The revolutionaries shot Bishop and others in his faction, soldiers massacred people on the street, and President Reagan decided enough was enough. He'd been concerned that the Russians and Cubans are building this airstrip as a forward operating base, at a location too critical for Caribbean shipping to let that stand. And he felt that we should protect hundreds of American students going to medical school on Grenada. So, in no more than a week's time, we organized this attack. They deployed us out of Hunter Army Airfield in Georgia and brought the 2nd Battalion from Fort Lewis, Washington."

"Just here at Point Salines?"

"The Rangers, yes. Marines and SEALS had an amphibious landing on Grand Anse near the capital, and there was a landing at the airport up the coast. The 82nd Airborne will be coming in here a little later. We'll land a force of something like 8,000 in all, mostly Americans but a few token foreign personnel. I gather the other operations met resistance from the Grenadian Army, such as it is. Cubans and Russians reportedly were firing mortars out of the Russian Embassy. In fact, we had to chopper a squad from the 1st battalion over to Grand Anse to bail some of our guys out of a jam. The Point Salines airstrip was the critical phase, and it went smoother than anyone had dared hope."

"That's the Rangers for you," I said.

"The same old story, Jake. The higher-ups issue FUBAR battle plans, and the Rangers make them work. At least we had our logistics people involved in the planning. Believe me, that helped a lot. So," he said, "what the hell are *you* doing here?"

"You wouldn't believe me if I told you, but I'll tell you anyhow."

* * *

I RELATED MOST OF MY ADVENTURES, GIVING HIM A LOT OF chuckles. He sort of believed some of it. The thing is, we hadn't seen one another since 1975, before my military career went SNAFU, so we had a lot of catching up to do. His big brother,

Sarge, had been advising me from time to time and filled him in on some aspects of my post-military doings, but enough of it was Classified that the pieces didn't fit. Henry accepted that, and he marveled at my civilian exploits. He'd gone on to OCS after our LRRP tour and, not having Todd Sonarr to bollix everything up, had risen to Major. Not only that, "You're a Daddy now?"

"A little boy and a bigger girl. An uncle, too."

"Don't tell me Sarge got married?"

"Go forth and multiply, as the Good Book says. Two sons, so far." Out came the pictures. Wives good looking, kids cute. "How about you, Jake?"

"Mmmm... went forth some, no multiplication to show for it. So is Sarge still in the Service?"

"Forever. He got assigned to Korea for a while, did him good. Stateside made him antsy, no side business possibilities. All kinds of fiddles for him over in Asia. Same old Sarge. 'Pay up or pay otherwise,' that motto of his."

Henry being a battalion XO in the midst of a combat operation, we both understood that he had more important tasks at hand than jawing with me. Before he went, I asked him if he had any liaison with the CIA. "More than we ever needed or desired, Jake. That same old story too."

"True that," I said. "But I need to talk to somebody from there. Could you put me in touch?"

What a stroke of luck. To one Ranger, another's word was always good, and Henry and I were as close as any. Having him there meant I wouldn't be facing uncomfortable hours with professional interrogators—none of whom would rest until they got to the truth of the matter, and any fable I made up would have been more believable than the truth. Henry endorsed my story that I was just a hapless tourist who happened to be in the wrong place at the wrong time. He later told me about a Cuban they'd captured named "Desi" who'd been ranting that an American secret KGB agent had ordered them not to fight because it was part of a Russian strategy. I assured him that, being locked in a closet, I knew nothing about it, but probably it was just more Commie lies.

* * *

BY THE END OF THAT DAY POINT SALINES AIRSTRIP WAS FULLY secure, and 800 troops from the 82nd landed and deployed to the north. Machine gun fire killed one Ranger in the initial landing foray, and four others were shot en route to rescue American students when they lost their way in their gun jeep and blundered into an ambush, but in general casualties in the operation were light. Their haul of Cuban construction workers from my barracks numbered about 200. The Rangers turned their custody over to a contingent of the Caribbean Peacekeeping Force that arrived later that day—an international unit assembled from around the region to deflect accusations of American Imperialism.

The Rangers arranged a cot and meals for me. I insisted on seeing the CIA guy before I left Grenada, but he wasn't expected for a day or two. I hung around with nothing to do except stay out of the way. On my third day Grenada was considered under control, and the CIA liaison flew in. As the U.S. Force was anxious to send me on my way, they put me early on his schedule. Sterling Steadfast, I'll call him, met me in some makeshift quarters. About my age and overweight, he clearly spent his time in an office, not out in the field. He already looked wilted in his business suit and tie. Unlike the CIA eager beavers I'd known in the past, he seemed tired and dispirited. "Pleased to meet you, Mr. Fonko. They pre-alerted me to your interest in a meeting. I made some inquiries, and it seems you've something of a reputation around Langley, though no one had any details they could impart. What's on your mind?"

"I came across something that might be useful to the CIA. Is intel gathering part of your job?"

"Jake, if I may call you Jake, I would be delighted to gather any and all intel available. Though at this point some people may be doubting that was ever in my job description. You wouldn't believe the complaints and second-guessing we're getting left and right about faulty intel for this operation. Didn't alert the troops to the presence of a second campus. Misestimated enemy troop deployment. Didn't do this. Fucked up that. As if anybody could produce a detailed assessment for a five-pronged military assault in a week's time. It's CYA all the way, as usual. We've been beavering away for years down here, focused on subverting Leftist influences—economic sanctions, disinformation, funneling money to the opposition, engineering support from neighboring islands—you were in intel, you know the drill. Then out of the blue, they gave us one week to gather and supply the intel for an air and amphibious assault on a sovereign island nation, with the top brass insisting on iron-tight secrecy and a compartmentalized planning process—the old 'element of surprise' ploy. Well, that's the way to ensure a functional information flow for sure, guys. Communications and force coordination were a tangle from the outset, but of course that's the CIA's fault too. So, yes, I'd love to gather some intel to take back with me, some nugget to redeem ourselves. What are you offering?"

"Bank records. You've heard of Bank of Credit and Commerce International? Is that of interest to the CIA?"

"BCCI? The Bank of Crooks and Criminals. You've got something on them? You bet we're interested."

I unzipped my duffle, displaying my wares. "These seem to be ledger books for the last several years, entries in English and Urdu."

"Urdu?"

"Pakistanis run the bank. It's their language. Here, take a look." I extracted the 1982 ledger and passed it to him.

"Pakistanis? Running BCCI? Sonofabitch. That explains some things..." He opened it to a random page and looked it over. "I'm not a banker or an accountant, of course, but this looks... hmmmm." He flipped to another page. "Let me see the one for 1981." I took 1982 back and gave him the other. "These are day-by-day, month-by-month?" He opened it about two thirds of the way through—August or so—slowly ran his finger down the entries for several pages, then stopped. "Bingo," he muttered with a chuckle. He closed the book. "Okay, definitely interested. What else?"

"Computer disks from BCCI. A dozen of them. I don't know what's on them."

"You've got records and data from the crookedest bank in the world, for the past several years? Do you know the kinds of clients they have?"

"I've an inkling, yes."

"You've heard the phrase, follow the money? This material could give us a line on the activities and money flows of a number of groups and activities we track. How did you come in possession of this?"

"I took it from a KGB agent." Technically true. Grotesqcu was the last man to handle the stuff. "That's all I can disclose," I added regretfully.

Steadfast shook his head side to side. "Awesome. I can see why your name circulates around Langley. Tell me, are you on a government assignment here?"

"If I told you the answer to that question, I'd have to kill you," I joked. "Consider me just a private citizen doing his part to help the cause. As far as anyone's concerned, I'm stranded down here in need of a little help."

"I'm not authorized to disburse funds," Steadfast cautioned. "Tell you what. Let me get on the horn to my office at Langley and see what they say. Can you wait a few minutes?" I could, and he went away.

He returned in a half hour. "Okay, Jake, I think we can make a deal here. What do you want in exchange for your BCCI materials? I can't outright offer you money, but maybe there's something we can do for you?"

By then I was grateful just to get out from under their curse. "I need two simple things." I said. "First, I need a replacement passport, and second, a ride back to the States." Then I had a thought.

"Make that three simple things. Make sure that Todd Sonarr in your agency hears about this. In fact, I'll give you a message to relay to him."

"I know of Mr. Sonarr. What's the message?"

"Describe what I delivered to you and tell him Jake Fonko wants to know if that makes us even now."

YOU CAN GET IT IF YOU REALLY WANT

So many loose ends to tie up in this tangled yarn...

Sterling Steadfast arranged to fly me back to Washington DC with some State Department staff who'd come down to make an assessment and incidentally spend a few days doing the Caribbean on OPM. They expedited the passport process, so getting my new one took only a day. The photo turned out well, I thought. Apparently, whatever APB went out on me after I escaped the Haiti Consulate lockup had been rescinded. The CIA put me up overnight and sprang for a ticket on a commercial flight from DC to LA the next day, economy class. I was sleeping in my own bed by the start of November. With little expectation of success, I called my hotel in George Town to see about the stuff I'd left there. Much to my surprise, they'd left my room undisturbed, since I'd never checked out. Not being fully booked, they'd let room charges continue to rack up against my American Express card in hopes that they'd eventually be covered. I settled the bill, and they sent my gear to me, including my SIG Sauer. My passport had gone missing, but I had a new one. All's well enough that ends well enough, as the Bard sort of said.

* * *

As for Grenada. The Reagan administration desperately wanted to put a win up on the board, particularly after the bombing of the Marine barracks in Lebanon so recently. They touted Operation Urgent Fury as a stunning success, and in some ways it was. We came in fast and completed the job with dispatch. As battles go, bloodshed was slight. Americans—19 killed, 113 wounded: Cubans—25 killed, 59 wounded: Grenadian forces—45 killed, 358 wounded, plus around 25 civilians died. Grenadians were cool with the outcome as most didn't cotton to the Marxist revolution any more than our State Department did.

What we accomplished was up for debate. The American version claimed we'd stopped the Russians and Cubans from setting up a military foothold, a forward operating base threatening the Caribbean shipping lanes and Venezuelan oil. We justified this view by insisting that the size of the runway and the numerous fuel storage tanks were way beyond necessary for commercial flights. We claimed also that our forces captured a warehouse stacked floor to ceiling with Soviet arms and explosives, "enough to take out half the island had it been detonated." Counterclaims had it that the airstrip was never intended for anything but commercial flights and that the arms cache was simply a Grenadian army storehouse, greatly exaggerated in our report. Castro released a personnel roster making a plausible case that the Cubans had very little military presence there. Nor was it clear that the American students actually faced serious danger at the time.

Of course, there's no way to know where things would have gone had we not invaded. In any case, they completed the Point Salines airport and named it after the martyred president, Maurice Bishop. Grenada, one more little paradise in that long chain of tropical garden spots, subsequently enjoyed a much expanded tourist trade and established a lively bare boat chartering base.

* * *

ON THE MATTER OF BANK OF CREDIT AND COMMERCE International: In 1988 American Customs Agents arrested five BCCI bankers in Tampa, Florida, plus other bankers and some narcotics traffickers in London and elsewhere on money laundering charges. BCCI ultimately pleaded guilty. An audit by Price Waterhouse in 1990 found a hole of at least $1.7 billion in the bank's accounts. A second audit revealed that BCCI illegally held controlling shares in First American Bank, an insertion of its tentacles into the U.S. banking system. BCCI bought their shares from Clark Clifford and partner Robert Altman, who as officers of First American had vociferously promoted BCCI's interests, giving them jointly a profit of $30 million on the sale. Then Manhattan District Attorney Robert Morgenthau took up the BCCI case, the beginning of BCCI's demise. In 1991, a New York grand jury indicted the bank and its two principal officers for fraud, bribery, grand larceny and money laundering. The Federal Reserve Board fined BCCI $200 million for illegally acquiring control of three prominent U.S. banks: First American, National Bank of Georgia (with the assistance of former Carter administration officials) and Miami's CenTrust Savings. At the end of the year, BCCI entered another guilty plea and agreed to forfeit $550 million.

Two BCCI principals were indicted by Manhattan grand juries in 1992, as were Clark Clifford and Robert Altman. The latter two stoutly denied wrongdoing, claiming they'd been deceived along with the Federal Reserve Board. In other words, they weren't dishonest, just stupid—a shabby excuse for a high-powered lawyer who had once been a shining star and premier fixer of Democrat politics, including a hitch as Lyndon Johnson's Secretary of Defense. After Clifford underwent quadruple bypass heart surgery and a heart attack shortly thereafter, a New York judge dropped the state charges against him, citing his age (85) and deteriorating health. Altman was subsequently acquitted after a four-month trial in New York. The two agreed to forfeit $5 million to settle Federal

Reserve Board charges that they knew BCCI owned First American and had lied about it to bank inspectors. Later Clifford and Altman settled the last of the civil lawsuits stemming from the BCCI scandal by giving up their claims to $18.5 million in legal fees and First American stock.

BCCI's collapse was the world's largest financial debacle to that date, crashing from assets of $8.5 billion to $0. The extent of American political corruption sustaining it was deemed too wide and deep ever to be fully known. Not that America's politicians were necessarily desperate to have the story of BCCI corruption fully known. Some critics even alleged that it had been under the protection of the CIA, that it had assisted the CIA in numerous covert operations, and that the CIA may have been instrumental in its getting established in the first place. No wonder Sterling Steadfast so eagerly took up my offer.

It appears Robert Vesco was on to something.

* * *

SPEAKING OF ROBERT VESCO: BY THE TIME CLYDE DRIFFTER and I met him on Cuba, his star had flamed out, its cinders tumbling earthward. Whatever else he might have been pursuing in Castro's paradise, he was charged with drug smuggling six years later. He came up with a scheme to run clinical tests of a drug supposed to boost immunity, with the support of the Cuban government. It came to naught. In the 1990s the Cuban government indicted him for fraud and illicit economic activity and acts prejudicial to the economic plans and contracts of the state—suggesting that the Cuban justice system was more direct and straightforward than ours. Sentenced to 13 years in prison, Robert Vesco died of lung cancer two years before he was scheduled for release.

Another case of brilliant mind and formidable talent squandered.

* * *

AND ABOUT JAKE FONKO: I LANDED AT LAX INTACT IN MIND and body. Sadder? Not really. Wiser? I wouldn't be surprised. Poorer? Not by a penny. Even after I covered Evanston's loan and paid off my American Express charges, my advance on the fee for the original job pretty much broke me even for my adventures. So, worst case, I landed back where I started. More assignments would come along. I'd have to put off new wheels for a while, but I could live with my Vette a little longer. Then it dawned on me—as two week vacations in the Caribbean go, I could have done a lot worse. I toured one of the world's choice regions, saw new places, learned about sailboat cruising and never lacked for interesting things to do. Looking back, I rather enjoyed it.

I drove down to Pacific Palisades a few days after I got back to check in with Mom and Evanston. I soon lost Mom with my tale—when I mentioned my flight over the Virgin Islands, she fixated on the vacation a canasta club buddy had taken on St. Thomas Island ("They drive on the wrong side of the road. Evanston, you will have to take special care when we go there.") and tuned out. But Evanston took it in raptly, particularly the BCCI aspects. That was years before their shit hit the fan, and his ears perked up at possibilities of massive billable hours for his international law firm. He asked a lot of specific questions, a few of which I could answer, and he chuckled at the context in which Clark Clifford's name came up. No love lost there. He also mentioned some buzz circulating around his network about the Cuban MIG I'd brought down and the intel I'd delivered to the Company. Two more gold stars on my covert resume, he thought. "Jake," he sighed, "I really appreciate those business cards and that address book you took off Clark Clifford's boys, but I only wish to God you'd saved out just one of those floppy disks for me."

Not long after that a letter with a Russian stamp came in the mail. The note inside, on a sheet of paper with a logo I recognized, said: "Congratulations, Jake. It couldn't have happened to a more deserving man. The goods were pure gold." Below these few words was a "Г", a Russian "G." Okay, Grotesqcu sent the note. But what happening was he referring to? What goods? I guessed that meant the BCCI stuff—what else could it be? The rest of it, I couldn't fathom.

Mystery solved a few days later. Another letter arrived, this in a fine parchment envelope embossed with the return address of one the major American philanthropic foundations—I'd best not name it here. The gist of the letter, on similar parchment with a similar embossed letterhead, was:

Dear Mr. Fonko:

Our board of overseers occasionally sees fit to make unpublicized awards to individuals we recognize as having made significant contributions to the cause of World Peace. We believe your recent accomplishments qualify as such a contribution, and we are pleased to award you the enclosed honorarium in appreciation of your outstanding achievement. This award will not be publicly announced, nor is there any accompanying certificate or other formal token of recognition. We caution you not to seek press coverage or any other public celebration or other mention of this award, as in that event we would regretfully be forced to publicly repudiate it and to take forceful steps to ensure the return of our emolument.

With sincerest thanks and etc., etc., etc.

Also in the envelope, I found a check in six figures. Whether it was coincidence or irony, I can't say, but it was drawn on First American Bank. Okay, I got the message: take the money, zip your lip and run like a thief.

That solved the wheels problem but revived the wheels dilemma. I spent some time checking out Vettes, Porches, Maseratis and the like. Then I realized—sports cars are fun but damned inconvenient. Time to grow up. I needed more cargo capacity.

Widening my search, I checked out sport utility vehicles, SUVs. Jeep Cherokees caught my eye. A test drive convinced me, and I traded my Corvette in on a 4-door wagon with a heavy-duty roof rack.

And then what? I heard reports of snow in the Rockies. Snowboarding was catching on, something I could get into. The kitty was flush enough for a few months vacation. I'd just had a taste of the tropics. Why not be a snow-bum for a while? Must be something like a surf-bum, only colder. Cheyenne, Wyoming, wasn't far from the Tetons and the Colorado ski towns. I bet Dana Wehrli would take to snowboarding, or at least to hanging out in ski resorts on her days off. (Yes, her birthday card was in my pile of mail when I got home.) We could write it off as weather-babe field trips. LA sporting goods stores offered a poor selection of snowboards. Too early in the season, too far from the action. No problem, I'd pick one up in Cheyenne.

As I made arrangements to take off for Wyoming, another note, postmarked Langley, VA, but with no return address, arrived. The plain index card inside said, in plain block letters:

"Jake—we're even up."

A check drawn on the U.S. Treasury accompanied the note. I don't want to sound ungrateful; it was a decent amount of money but a little embarrassing. Judging from my own experience, it was plain why the KGB had an easier time recruiting spies than the CIA did.

Not that I was some kind of spy, of course. It did strike me, though, that if word got out that I was being paid by both the CIA and the KGB, my career as a freelance whatever might henceforth face complications.

THE END

EDITOR'S AFTERWORD (AMENDED)

Some controversies arose following the release of the previous book in the series, *Fonko's Errand Go Boom*, which must be addressed. Colleagues in the English Literature Department called my attention to several passages in the book that, they claimed, were direct quotes from James Joyce's classic book, *Ulysses*, and they showed me corresponding passages, four of them, in the two books to prove their case. As you know, my arrangement with my publisher entailed my turning over to them my raw materials compiled from Jake Fonko's recounting and my further research, analysis and interpretations, upon which they assume subsequent responsibility for producing publishable versions of his exploits.

As it turned out, one of their editorial assistants holds a graduate degree in English Literature. Her MA thesis has an interesting story behind it. It seems she started college aiming at a degree in speech therapy, a sop to her parents, who, paying her tuition, stipulated she choose a major that would result in a job upon graduation. However, the scientific aspects of speech therapy soon bored her, and she switched her major to English Lit. She qualified for a modest scholarship, which mollified her parents and encouraged her to continue in that field. The topic of her MA thesis reflected her bifurcated background: "James Joyce: Modernist Genius or Asperger Sufferer?" So the assignment on *Fonko's Errand Go Boom* was right down her alley, and in several instances she took it upon herself to improve, shall we say, the materials provided to her. She also slipped in an allusion to Irish playwright Samuel Beckett.

But she resolutely denied abridging Mr. Fonko's excursion through the streets of Dublin, and he, too, claimed that he followed the route exactly as described, similar though it may seem to Leopold Bloom's famously fateful day. I asked him if he had ever read *Ulysses*, and he said no, but admitted he had seen the movie. "Kirk Douglas was great," he said.

So I avow innocence of plagiarism, and I contend that no harm was done. In fact, I rather liked her little embellishments, and I intend some day to read *Ulysses* myself. As for the rest of the book, my back-checking came up with no reason to doubt that his recounting of his Belfast adventures was, as always, a true and factual account. My calls to Mr. Steven Spielberg seeking confirmation that he did indeed feature Mr. Fonko's DeLorean sportscar in *Back to the Future* went unreturned. And George Chutney had carried out Mrs. Thatcher's instructions to the extent that no trace of Jake Fonko remains in Northern Ireland (exactly as Jake had described). Everything else, as best as I could determine, reflected the facts, as unlikely as some of them may seem. To give just one example, that Barbra Streisand would crawl into a movie theater under the box office turnstile might strain anyone's credulity. However, my research assistant, Dr. Bertha Sikorski, turned up an article about the Malibu Theater in the *Wall Street Journal* that reported an occasion on which Ms. Streisand did exactly that. The article did not mention Jake Fonko being present, but why should it have?

* * *

Controversies erupted concerning the present book, *Fonko in the Sun*, that are not so easily passed over. Immediately upon the book's release, I was deluged with irate, sometimes apoplectic telephone calls, letters and emails from scholars and critics all across the nation. The gist of the complaints was that the book abounds with quotations, plots, scenes, characters and allusions stolen from a spectrum of literature and cinema, in particular the works of Ernest Hemingway (*To Have and Have Not*, *The Old Man and the Sea*), Graham Greene (*Our Man in Havana*, *The Comedians*), Ian Fleming (*Dr. No*), Harry Belafonte (*The Banana Boat Song*), a snippet from *West Side Story*, among others. Especially egregious, many claim, was the book's opening scene, a barroom shootout reproduced almost word for word from *To Have and Have Not*.

I will admit that my review of the book's pre-release draft was cursory. I had just received the turndown of my application for a position in the history department at Western North Dakota Normal College. Shortly thereafter, Sallye, my wife of many years, left me to pursue her bliss as a potter at a commune in New Mexico. I was depressed and distracted and for that reason paid only perfunctory attention to my scholarly work, including the final review of the forthcoming book. The uproar brought me back into focus, and, returning to *Fonko in the Sun*, I was appalled by what I found. The critics were only too correct. How could such a travesty have happened?

My publisher launched a thorough investigation and promptly reported back. The editors assigned to winnowing through my materials and compiling them into a publishable book had decided that Mr. Fonko's account here and there contained gaps or lacked detail or, given the helter-skelter nature of his adventures, even continuity. As it happened, when Mr. Fonko and I were transcribing that part of his recollections, my interest in the Caribbean Islands was aroused. I had never been there and was taken with his descriptions of that exotic setting, so I read widely and deeply (for example, the works noted above) and included along with the transcriptions copious notes, references and ancillary materials. In an effort to produce a more coherent and readable book, the editors folded some of my reference notes and ancillary materials directly into the narrative. WITH NO PROPER ATTRIBUTIONS!

By the time this scandal came to light, it was too late to withdraw, or even revise, *Fonko in the Sun*. However, my publisher allowed me to amend the Afterword I had prepared, so as to address these extremely sensitive and serious issues. I sincerely apologize for all problems and authorial lapses, and I promise followers of Mr. Fonko's exploits and adventures that I will in the future diligently endeavor to make certain such will never happen again. And let me assure everyone that, apart from these editorial derelictions, *Fonko in the Sun* is, like the previous Jake Fonko memoirs, a true and factual account.

In light of my recent personal vicissitudes, I am now planning a two-week sojourn at the Club Med on Martinique Island. I think it may be just what the doctor ordered, in a manner of speaking, to repair my shattered sensibilities. I may even ask Dr. Sikorski if a little break might appeal to her. Her thus far unsuccessful quest for a full-time post in the current employment situation has been deeply dispiriting, she tells me.

B. Hesse Pflingger, PhD
Professor of Contemporary History
California State University, Cucamonga

INDIA / THE PHILIPPINES 1984 - 1986

FONKO BOLO

A JAKE FONKO ADVENTURE
B. HESSE PFLINGGER

TRIGGER WARNING

The following text may contain content some readers may find offensive, disgusting, hurtful, humiliating, nauseating, revolting, disorienting, frustrating, threatening, distressful, confusing and/or self-esteem-diminishing, including but not limited to: (1) thoughts, phrases, words, code words, penumbras, emanations, dog whistles, implications, omissions, graphic representations, memes and/or microaggressions that may be interpreted as threatening, traumatizing, judgmentalist, sexist, racist, ageist, genderist, ableist, heightist, weightest, ideologist, religionist, philosophist, speciesist, climateist, militarist, capitalist, corporatist, consumerist or promoting of guns, violence, social injustice, unwanted sexual invasions, or environmentally unfriendly or unsound behavior related to nutrition or personal health and safety of oneself or others; (2) stereotypes of persons, places, races, nationalities, regions, eras, lifestyles, continents, ethnic affiliations, political movements and/or unspecified animate and inanimate objects; and (3) facts and/or narratives that may be contradictory of, or contrary to, or deviant from, facts, counter-narratives, beliefs, fantasies and/or conceits that a reader may find comforting, reassuring or fulfilling.

Aside from that, this book is safe, informative and enjoyable for anyone to read.

PRELUDE TO THE STORY

EAST IS EAST AND WEST IS WEST, AND NEVER THE TWAIN SHALL meet, said Rudyard Kipling famously. I'm from the West. I met the East. Damn near killed me, more than once. Considering the adventures I've had in The East—Vietnam, Cambodia, India, China, Tibet, Japan, North Korea—I'm like a modern-day Marco Polo. After what I went through in the Philippines, they might well call me "Fonko Bolo."

* * *

WE'LL GET TO THAT PRESENTLY. FIRST, LET'S BRING MY STORY UP to date. After the fourth time it happened, I began considering the possibility that waking up in strange places, wondering where I was and how I got there, might be an occupational hazard for freelance whatevers like myself. I came to, on a rude charpoy—a thin pad supported by crisscrossed cords in a wood frame—wearing only a dhoti, one of those Mahatma Gandhi diapers. I was scratched, slashed and bruised, aching in every part of my abused carcass. My left wrist and right ankle didn't seem to be working well. The cords of the charpoy bit deeply into my savaged flesh through the filthy, tattered pad. Though it was stifling hot I couldn't stop shivering. I raised my head up through the pain and looked around. I lay in a dimly-lit room crammed with men of all ages suffering every form of distress, disability, disease and desperation. It reeked to high heaven.

Next to me a husk of a man on a torn, stained mattress pad drooled and gurgled. He was emaciated, his bare ribcage covered with open sores and lesions, his arms and legs reduced to bones and tendons tightly encased by distressed black skin. Several wounds fed a little puddle of blood and pus on the pad beside him. He writhed in agony yet nevertheless sported a beatific smile.

"Having a good day there, friend?" I asked. "They dope you up pretty good?"

"Dope?" he replied in a sing-songy Indian lilt.

"Pain-killing drugs," I said.

"Oh no, they have given me no medications, nothing to ease my pain."

"Taking good care of you, though?"

"Oh yes, very good care. They bring me thin rice gruel and tepid water. They clean up my soil and issue a fresh garment every now and then. Just the other day a barber came and shaved us men here."

"And that makes you smile so widely?"

"I have never slept in a proper bed in my entire life," he said. "They found me lying on a rubbish heap, helpless and hopeless, where I had collapsed while searching for scraps to eat, and brought me here. They assure me now I will die like a human being, beautifully."

Well, there's something to be said for that, but where the hell was I? I said, "Hello." Nothing. I repeated it louder.

A small woman in a white nun's habit floated quietly in and approached my bunk. "Why are you making all this commotion?" she asked solicitously. She also had that Indian lilt to her English.

"I'm sorry. I just want to know where I am."

"You are in the hospice of our Missionary in Calcutta, India," she said.

"Aren't hospices where they take people who are dying?"

"Yes. That is true. You speak strangely. You are not of this country?"

"No, I'm an American, and as far as I know, I am not dying."

She seemed flustered. "There must be some mistake. We brought you here because you seemed to be dying."

"I'm pretty banged up, that's for sure. I think I have a broken wrist and a broken ankle. I could use a drink of water. I'm very thirsty."

"Of course," she said. "I'll bring you some water straightaway. It would be good if you talked to Mother. I will summon her."

"Mother …?"

"Yes. She will know what to do. Your situation is not what we thought, and I am at a loss. She will know. I'll return directly." And she floated ghost-like away out the door. Presently she returned with a glass in her hand, accompanied by a short, bent, ancient Sister with downcast eyes wearing a white habit with a blue border.

"I am Mother," said the older woman softly. "Or you can call me Ma. How are you feeling today?" (I'll call her "Mother" here— her humbleness dictated avoiding personal publicity so I'll not elaborate on that)

The younger nun offered me the glass. I took it in my right hand, but propping myself up on my left arm was very painful. The water tasted warm and putrid, but it was water, which I needed badly. If it gave me dysentery how much worse off would I be? Not enough to notice. "I've had better days," I replied.

"Every day is a blessing from Jesus," Mother assured me. "Our bad ones bring us closer to His suffering. And, you see, He has already relieved your distress. When we first found you our hopes were not high. How did you come to be lying, dying in a gutter of the worst slum in Calcutta?"

"That's a long story, but the immediate cause was that I gave a $100 bill to a beggar."

"My goodness. Why did you do that?"

"A, er, friend requested that I do so, on his behalf. He told me that a Calcutta beggar once saved his life, and that was his way of repaying the kindness."

"Yes, a kindness multiplies many times. So how did that lead to your distress?" She had that quality of seeming to giving me her rapt and undivided attention, as if I was the most important person in the world—a knack also characteristic of top-notch politicians, salesmen and con artists.

"I couldn't tell one beggar from another, there being so many and all so miserable. So I picked out one at random. He accepted the bill, looked at it and exclaimed loudly, 'A Benjamin! This man gave me a Benjamin!' Other beggars rose from their perches and came over to look. More appeared from the shadows, from alleyways, from under doorstoops, seemingly materializing from nowhere, until a large crowd of clamoring derelicts had gathered, me at the center of it. 'A Benjamin!' all were exclaiming. They passed it from hand to hand, until one wizened old fellow, apparently a leader of sorts, examined it closely through thick glasses. 'This bill is false!' he shouted, and crowd's mood of awe and amazement turned into a wave of anger. How could a Calcutta beggar identify a counterfeit U. S. $100 bill?"

"Those slumdogs know their currencies," Mother assured me. "They cannot afford not to, being desperately poor ... the great majority, anyway. Please continue. What happened next?"

"That's the last thing I remember."

"Those poor men felt disappointed and, worse than that, betrayed. To raise their spirits and then dash them like that! That is why they gave you such a going-over. It is sad that they did not honor the spirit of love and charity that accompanied your gift, but so few feel appreciation for good intentions. Sorry to say, it is the way of the world. Some of our Sisters found you lying there among the garbage in the street, stripped naked, unconscious and abandoned. Thinking you were a dying untouchable, they borrowed a wheelbarrow and brought you here. We cleaned you up a little, covered you for decency sake and installed you in the hospice. I am pleased that you recovered, but your situation is somewhat irregular. What shall we do, I wonder?"

"Let me suggest we start by putting casts on my wrist and ankle, and dosing me with antiseptics and antibiotics?"

"I am sorry, Mr...?"

"Fonko. Jake Fonko. Please call me Jake."

"I am sorry, Jake, but our Mission does not function as a hospital. We dedicate ourselves to ministering to the spiritual needs of the world's poorest and most forlorn, and they number in legions. Here in Calcutta six million people live in wretched mud and straw shanties, and a half million live on the sidewalks—they cannot even afford wretched shanties. No, we cannot hope to cure the world's material ills, so we do not try. Rather, to the world's forlorn and abandoned we dispense love and spiritual solace, spreading the message that even in their poverty, pain and misery, no matter how dire, Jesus loves each and every one, enfolding their suffering unto His own. We have Missions all over the world, including in your own country. We minister to AIDs victims in New York City and drug addicts in Washington D.C., for example. You may find it hard to believe, but America, despite its lavish wealth, desperately needs our help. Spiritual poverty is mankind's biggest curse of all, and your country has that like few others."

"Could you contact the American consulate on my behalf?"

"Though we have many dealings with America, we have never had an American, er, guest in our hospice before. I am known at the consulate, and I will send a message, and we will see what can be done. What would you like the message to say?"

I gave her my name and the contact numbers for Mom and Evanston, and Dad, back in Los Angeles, with the request that the consulate send word of my whereabouts and situation. "Could someone from the consulate come here to talk to me?" I asked.

"They might send someone eventually, but they have never

shown much enthusiasm for venturing into this district, except for ceremonial occasions and photo opportunities. Anything else?"

"A little something to eat, perhaps? And put some splints on my broken bones?"

"One of the Sisters will attend to it," she said. She put her hand atop my head with affectionate pressure (aggravating lumps and bruises and open scalp wounds) and admonished me to feel Jesus's love. Noticing my wince, she soothed, "We believe that every stab of pain is a kiss from Jesus." Please in your prayers beseech Him to stop kissing me, I didn't say. She gave me a wide, sincere smile and left me to my thoughts.

My first thought: Why on Earth did Emil Grotesqcu have me give a Calcutta beggar a counterfeit Benjamin?

* * *

THEY MOVED ME OUT OF THE HOSPICE INTO A RECOVERY ROOM of sorts, a place whose clientele had reasonable hopes of postponing their meeting with Jesus for a decent interval. They supplied me with a threadbare cotton pajama bottom and a shirt of stitched-together old flour sacks. The visiting barber scraped away the beard I'd sprouted over the past six months. It had helped blend me into the Indian masses, but I was so glad to be rid of that itchy tangle that I didn't begrudge the lacerations his dull razor added to my already torn up hide. The Sisters brought me some sticks and rags, with which we fashioned field-dressing splints on my broken appendages. I had a few fractured ribs, too, but all you can do about those is endure the pain for six weeks, and with no analgesics, not even an aspirin, endure it I did. They'd swabbed me down with the same untreated water they use for washing clothes, floors and latrines, with the result that my wounds were festering, not healing. The food was at least better than what they'd given me in Tuol Sleng, the Khmer Rouge's torture chamber, I'll give them credit for that.

Mother came around again to see how I was getting along. Better, I assured her, and I gave her sincere thanks for her help.

"Tell me, Jake, how did you come to be in India in the first place?" she asked. "Perhaps you had some business here?"

JAKE'S STORY OF THE AMRITSAR MASSACRE

"I work as a consultant," I explained. "People hire me for advice, or for services, having to do with a variety of situations. My background is military intelligence, so often I'm employed in matters of security. I was approached last year by a man who claimed to represent the Indian government. He wanted to hire me to make assessments of preparedness of the Indian military for anti-insurgency and anti-terrorist defense ..."

"There is so much violence and ill-will in this world," Mother sighed.

"True, unfortunately. The man's credentials seemed legitimate, and the assignment he outlined seemed within my capabilities, so I agreed to come to India and explore how I could help, with the understanding that a larger assignment would follow if my talents suited the situation.

"I flew into New Delhi in June, and from there took a small plane to Amritsar, in the Punjab region, where my contact met me. We discussed the situation, that region being one of great potential conflict, lying near the border with Pakistan. He told me that ever since the partition in 1948 in which Hindus streamed east and Muslims west, slaughtering each other by the millions as they passed, bad blood has threatened to erupt into war, so I was to advise the intelligence service on how to thwart guerilla attacks. Their headquarters, he confided, was in a most secure fortress, into which I would enter in strictest secrecy, as the program I was to advise was ultra-confidential. He had me change into a uniform, assuring me that it was of a branch of his service and my wearing it was a matter of security, as anyone seeing an American involved would have cause to investigate. Early in the morning we approached an extensive, ornate building in Amritsar. There seemed to be an unusually large number of armed troops in the vicinity, which he explained as standard public safety precautions in border areas. The tanks I noticed in the side streets he explained as being on maneuvers.

"He gave me a cloak to wear over my uniform. We crept in through a side door, and he took me through dark corridors and obscure passages. The men I saw in the building all wore turbans and heavy beards. There seemed to be a lot of religious décor and artwork. He led me through a door that opened onto a walkway leading to a dazzling gold-covered building at the center of a large reflecting pool. That was the headquarters, he told me. His orders were to remain out of sight, so I was to go to the headquarters alone. To gain entrance I should stand in the middle of the walkway and shout the passwords, *banchut* and *matachut*..."

"Those are very naughty words," Mother tut-tutted.

(Sister-fucker and mother-fucker, respectively, I learned later)

"The whole set-up seemed fishy to me, but he removed my cloak with reassurances, and I did as instructed. And all of a sudden guys with turbans and beards popped up and started shooting at me from every direction. Instantly, a rattling cascade of gunfire erupted outside the compound in answer. I had nowhere to run, so I dove into the pool. It was shallower than it looked, and I hit my head on the bottom, which momentarily stunned me, and ..."

Just then the racket of a commotion broke out in the reception area, shouts and screams and sounds of breakage. Mother shuffled out and I hobbled along in her wake. A man was running amok, knocking people around, smashing glassware, pounding furniture. A weaselly little fellow, his left leg was cut off at mid-calf and his left eye was scar tissue. He maintained astounding balance on his serviceable leg, the crutch with which he walked made an excellent weapon, and lack of depth perception didn't hinder his accuracy with it. With two younger Sisters at her side Mother strode up to him and stared him into temporary quiescence. "May I help you?" she asked softly. "Jesus loves you. We Sisters love you."

The man glanced about furtively. Mother moved in closer. From her bent-over sub-five-foot height she reached up and placed one of her large, wrinkled hands atop his head, beaming an embracing smile. His one good eye held as much evil lust as any other man's two did, and its glint indicated an intention to avail himself of Sisterly affection. I watched him edge over toward Sister Shalimar, the younger and more comely of Mother's two accomplices. As his hand snaked down toward the hem of her habit, preparatory to sliding up inside it, I intercepted it with my good hand and, clamping a come-along hold on him, administered enough of Jesus's kisses that he quietly wilted and sat down on the floor.

"Mother's hands are so soothing," Sister Shalimar gushed.

"You poor man," said Mother. "What brings you to our Mission? How ever did you descend to this sorry state of desperation and violence?"

"Let me tell you my story," said the man.

THE POOR MAN'S STORY

"When I was a little lad I enjoyed a happy home. My younger sister, Lakshmi, and I basked in our mother's sweet and ever-flowing love. Father was a stern but upright man and well thought of in our village. He was kind to my sister and me. He must not have inherited these traits from his mother, however, because she became jealous of his affection for our mum and one day doused her with kerosene from the cooker and burnt her to death before our horrified eyes. This happenstance completely undid father. He became listless and ineffectual, neglectful of both family and village duties. Eventually he took to drinking to excess, which caused him to beat me and my sister viciously. Finally it became too much to bear, so one day I laced his spirits with wood alcohol, blinding him and sending him insane. Not long after that he stumbled into a latrine and drowned.

"A kindly merchant in the village took us orphans into his home and undertook to raise us as his own children. However, after several comfortable and contented years a most terrible thing happened. My little sister, at the age of eleven, took it upon herself to seduce me, wiggling her cute little bottom before me, showing succulent little toes and enticing ankles from under her sari, smiling at me in invitation all too plain to see. Finally I was lured to caress her, and she then made her evil intentions clear by resisting and fighting my advances, all too aware that doing so would only inflame my passion the more. In fact, I had to beat her unconscious before I succumbed to her wiles and had my way with her.

"The merchant, returning home that evening, found her in a tearful state of collapse. He pressed her for an explanation and, believing the lies she told to cover her sinful behavior, he thrashed me mercilessly and cast me from his premises. I bundled up my meager belongings and left, taking with me also the money I had found hidden in a little chest behind the collection of pornographic artwork on his shelf. Being young and inexperienced I fell in with unsavory companions and soon my funds had dissipated. I cast about for a way to earn my crust and was taken up by a man who managed an organization of beggars. The usual practice in India is for beggars to affect disguises for sympathy—false wounds, fake injuries, feigned mental impairment and so forth. My master was of the opinion that genuine deformities opened the gates of compassion wider, so he cut off my foot and blinded my one eye and, once the wounds healed, set me up on a busy corner in a well-to-do section of this city. In fact my injuries, not to mention my outspoken anguish at having sustained them, worked wondrously well, and soon I was raking in more revenue than any other of his crew. Then I received a letter from my beloved sister, which told a story of profound sadness...

THE POOR MAN'S SISTER'S STORY

"Oh my dear brother," said her letter, "I have written this secretly and sent it in hopes of its reaching you, persuading one of my customers to post it in return for providing him extraordinary services (I pray he honors the bargain we made). I am in deepest despair and have nowhere else to turn. After you left, our merchant benefactor, reflecting that once the end of the loaf is cut off no one notices a few subsequent slices, took up having his way with me. Inspired by his collection of vile pornographic art, his disgusting demands became insatiable. However, spies working on behalf of his rivals in the village observed his taking liberties with me and spread the word. Rather than admitting to his sins he denounced me as a whore and sold me to a brothel located near an army encampment. As I was young and pretty, soon my favors were in great demand every Saturday night, not to mention on holidays, which as you know occur with great frequency, reflecting as they do the variety of religions in our nation. It has reached the point where many nights I get only an hour of sleep between one evening's onslaught of lustful soldiers and the next morning's resumption of my loathsome duties to service the townspeople. I am exhausted and at wit's end. The brothel keeper tells me that my freedom can be bought for 50,000 rupees. Please, please, please save me from these dreadful nights. Signed, your loving sister, Lakshmi"

"Needless to say, her letter ripped my heartstrings loose from their moorings. What could I do? What choice did I have? Thinking to redeem her and thus rescue her from the consequences of her depravity and set her back on an honorable path, I started holding back from my daily takings. However, my master soon caught on. Not sympathetic in the least to my altruistic program, he beat me bloody and cast me out into the street with naught but the rags on my back.

"What could I, crippled, half-blind and destitute, do then? A man must live, after all. I sought honest employment to the point of starvation, but being impaired with no one willing to testify to my good character, my efforts turned up fruitless. Grasping the last straw, I joined a band of dacoits who specialized in snatching purses and picking pockets. My role was to lag behind the snatcher and, if a victim gave chase, to trip him up with my crutch. This proved a lucrative occupation until one day the police took notice and began a program of surveillance on me. I ask you, have the police such a right as that to interfere with a poor man's living? Not even an hour ago I noticed the hounds of the state on my trail, so to evade their persecutions I steeled myself to prevail upon your charity to those in dire need.

"And that is my tale of woe," he concluded.

"Talk about sad," sighed Sister Shalimar.

"You poor, poor man," said Mother. "Jesus loves you, you know. He never forgets the poor, the suffering or the desolate. He resides in them through all eternity. We offer sanctuary to the oppressed, but we cannot provide you lodgings here. Come, share a meal with us. You will see in action the love of Christian charity, perhaps leading you to the first steps toward a productive and compassionate life here on Earth, and salvation in the Hereafter. Please accept this prayer card, with my blessing. Follow me."

"A thousand thank yous, Mother," said the poor man, stuffing the prayer card into a grimy pocket. "I am grateful beyond words for your benevolent offer to assuage my woes."

As they started toward the food tables I put a hand on Sister Shalimar's shoulder and held her back. "Keep an eye on everything not nailed down," I whispered.

"Goodness resides in all God's creatures," she replied quietly.

That evening the dishwashing crew found their utensil count short a few items.

So I never did finish telling Mother how the KGB had set me up, hoping the CIA would be blamed for provoking the civil war that was sure to result in the wake of a massacre at the Amritsar Golden Temple of the Sikhs, to which the Indian army had brought tanks and artillery to dislodge the Sikh rebels who'd taken control of the Temple and were demanding a separatist Sikh state. All hell subsequently broke loose across that benighted country, and me in the thick of it. But that's a story for another time…

* * *

I'D BEEN AT MOTHER'S MISSION THREE DAYS, HELPING WHERE I could and watching the Sisters go about their business. A humble lot, they washed their white habits in buckets of water, brushed their teeth with ashes from the kitchen stove, had no personal possessions, lived in as severe poverty as their clientele. They taught the slum children to read and had the girls learn typing as a means of finding work. Many of the Sisters had come to the Mission as children and found a permanent occupation there. They worked hard and accomplished great good.

As I lay on my charpoy—now outfitted with a slightly more comfortable pad—concerned that my wounds were not healing and wondering what to do next, Mother approached. "How are you feeling today, Jake?" she asked.

"Not much better," I admitted. "I really think I'd benefit from more advanced medical care."

"It is in Jesus's hands," she said. "We do the very best we can, but medicine is not our specialty. We did send word to the American consulate, and we expect we will be hearing from them. Until we do, there is no place we can send you. But listen. I noticed how you assisted me in calming down our recent visitor, and I very much appreciate it, as he was not responsive to my gentle ministrations. Certainly you saved Sister Shalimar some embarrassment. I was wondering if, while you are staying with us, you might help us by, um, insuring that the better angels of our visitors emerge, as you did with that poor man, should the need arise again."

"Sure," I said. "And let me know if there is any other way in which I can lend a helping hand."

"So much to be done," she sighed. "So many are in need…"

"How did you come to this line of work, Mother?" I asked. "I understand you hail from Albania. That is quite a distance from here."

"It is a long story..." she began.

MOTHER'S STORY

"I was born many years ago, in the city of Skopje, in the region of Macedonia that was at that time Serbia, then became Albania. My father was a prosperous merchant and entrepreneur, as well as active in politics. He was a learned man and spoke Albanian, Turk, Italian, French and Serbo-Croatian. My mother was active in the Roman Catholic Church. We lived well, in a happy, upright home. Following the Great War my father made a trip to Belgrade for a political conclave. He returned home sick and hemorrhaging, and soon died, we suspect of poisoning by his political enemies. Then his erstwhile Italian partner seized the assets of their business, leaving the surviving family virtually penniless.

"Despite our poverty my mother was always charitable. 'Never eat a single mouthful unless you are sharing it with others,' was one of her tenets. She saved for the poor and cared for the destitute. So I learned charity and service to the less fortunate right from the cradle. I learned about suffering also from tales told by people from the nearby villages. One old woman told me a story that affected me deeply, which I remember clearly to this day..."

THE OLD WOMAN'S STORY

"My family originated in a village high in mountains not too distant from here,' the old woman told me. "My village has a tradition going back centuries, and it contains lessons for us all. Long, long ago a Serbian army came to the village and demanded that the villagers surrender. The men of the village, being proud and warlike, refused. The Serbian delegation became overbearing in their demands, so the villagers killed a couple of them. The Serbians therefore surrounded the village and laid siege to it. The village men thought nothing of it because, being atop a hill, it was easily defended by armed men.

"However, in their pride the men overlooked that the village had not provided for an extended siege, nor, with the Serbs controlling the roads, could they procure food or other essential goods. Soon the village larders were emptied of ready food. Next the village ate their reserves, then their seeds. They ate their livestock, then their dogs and cats. With the cats gone, rats multiplied, so the villagers ate the rats. Meanwhile the Serbian army camped down the hill, singing, drinking, carousing ...waiting.

"After all the rats, mice and other vermin were gone, the villagers ate their shoes and their harnesses. They sucked the glue from book bindings. Parents gave their infants sips of their own blood to sustain their little lives. Starvation seemed inevitable. The villager elders in desperation formulated a final, hideous plan: To save the village, each woman would sacrifice one buttock which, stewed with tree leaves and thistles, would maintain the village one more day while all prayed for deliverance. Looking ahead, they concluded that it was best to spare the prettiest women (most of whom were wives of village elders) until the very end in the interests of re-populating the village when the siege lifted. This plan greatly distressed the village women, of course, but all faced certain starvation unless they made this sacrifice. The plan commenced, and the village resisted the siege for two more agonizing months.

"Then their prayers were answered. The Turkish army marched in from the other direction and in short order routed the Serbs, who had grown fat and complacent and lost their fighting spirit while awaiting the village surrender. A cheer rose up from the villagers, but alas their joy was short lived.

"The Turks entered the village and were aghast at what they found—a rabble of walking skeletons and infirm women. Seeing no value in claiming it, they beheaded all the men (including the village elders, despite their tearful pleas that the village depended on their leadership), collected the children to be sold into slavery and took the pretty, unmarked women with them for their seraglios. All that remained were old, misshapen and ugly women, each missing a buttock. The future of the village seemed foreclosed. But then human nature took a hand. Men began coming from surrounding villages with food and assistance, and, being the beasts they are, demanded as payment the only thing a poor woman has to offer. Within a few years the village had regained much of its former population, and within 15 years the young were marrying and having children and the village was back on its feet. But the villagers learned a valuable lesson from that terrible time. Henceforth the village extended its welcome and hospitality to any and every army that came along, and opened markets to supply their provisions, with the result that the village over the years prospered and grew rich.

"'That was centuries ago, yet to this day the village holds an annual festival in remembrance of their day of deliverance. The women wear black and walk with a limp. They serve a feast of rump roast, barbecued rat and fricasseed shoe tongues—though it's said the latter really are rabbit and strips of sowbelly."

* * *

"THERE ARE MANY STORIES LIKE THAT WHERE I COME FROM," Mother said, "because that land has always known trouble and strife. But that particular story taught me important lessons. Never give up hope. In sacrifice there is salvation. Be kind, welcoming and charitable to all you encounter. And also it turned me off on the idea of getting involved with men.

"By age 13 I had found my calling in religion and charitable works. I resolved to go where suffering was greatest and compassion was needed most. As tragic and pathetic as my homeland may be, India was far worse. I arrived in Calcutta in 1929. The poverty of India was appalling. I came upon a woman dying on the street in front of a hospital. I took her inside but they would not admit her because she had no money, and so she died in the street. My work was cut out for me. In the beginning we nuns were so poor that we had to beg for food, but God always provided what we needed. And we had many laughs along the way. One time I thoughtlessly assigned the same pair of sandals to three different Sisters, each of whom needed to wear them immediately. I still chuckle over that one..."

"My Missionary received the blessing of Pope Pius XII in 1950, and from that time on we have grown and extended our charity to many nations all over the world. We rejoice in our work, and from it I have established a philosophy of life. It goes like this:

"Life is an opportunity, avail it

Life is a beauty, admire it

Life is bliss, taste it

Life is a..."

Sister Nefertiti arrived at my bedside. "Mother, someone is at the door whom you must talk to."

Mother rose from my bedside, "Excuse me a moment, Jake," she said. She followed Sister Nefertiti out the door, then returned a few minutes later. "Jake, it seems you have a visitor, a Miss Wehrli."

Dana! In my hour of need! "Please show her in," I said. "I would be very happy to see her."

"Tell me about her," said Mother.

"Not a lot to tell," I said. "She's a dear friend, a girl friend. I've known her for years; we grew up together. She works for ABC television now, producing news documentaries."

"A producer for an American television network, you say?"

"The last I heard, she was involved in their weekly feature program, *20/20*."

Mother turned to Sister Nefertiti. "Sister, perhaps you could find some way to tidy up Jake's appearance for his visitor?" She got a knowing nod in reply. "Jake, you go with Sister Nefertiti. It won't take a minute. Meanwhile, I'll keep your visitor entertained."

Sister Nefertiti led me down a corridor to an unmarked door and ushered me in. It featured racks of clothing, as well as a washstand and sink with several 10-gallon carboys of clear water on the floor beside it. "First let's clean you up a bit," she said. She shucked me out of my pajamas and flour-sack shirt. With more strength than I thought she had, she hefted a carboy and glopped water into the sink, then grabbed a jug of bleach from the cabinet beneath it and dumped in a generous amount. "We don't indulge in such treatments as a rule, but rules are made to be broken, you know," she chirped. She sponged me clean, the disinfectant wracking me with numerous Jesus-kisses. After the swab-down she took me to a rack of men's clothing. "Let's see what we have here," she muttered. "Even with your weight loss, you're larger than most men we get..." She pulled out a pair of worn, khaki pajama bottoms that fit well enough. Next a madras-cloth shirt, not too faded. Finally a presentable pair of slippers. "There, that's better," she cooed as she ran a comb through my tangled hair (more Jesus-kisses). "Let's go greet your guest."

Dana was perched on a wood chair in a little parlor below a photograph of Mother and Pope John Paul II, chatting with Mother. Blond. Tanned. Radiant. "Whirlybird!" I exclaimed.

She turned to greet me and went wide-eyed. "Jake! I don't hear anything from you for six months, and now *this*? What have they done to you? You look terrible!" Her teacup and saucer clattered down on the little wooden table before her.

You should have seen the other guy, I didn't say. "It's a longer story than I can relate right now. Dana, you are a genuine vision of paradise." I took a painful step toward her.

"Hasn't the consulate sent anyone? I phoned them direct, right after your mother called me."

"Haven't heard a word."

"We'll see about that! Jake, fond hellos will have to wait. I have to do some things, and there is no time to waste!" And she sprang up and dashed out of the room.

"A charming but impetuous girl," Mother observed.

* * *

Two hours later two white-clad orderlies burst into my ward. They piled me on a gurney and rumbled me through the halls and out the door into a waiting U. S. government van. Sirens a-wail, we bullied our way through Calcutta congestion to the American compound. They rolled me into an isolation ward, doused me with industrial-strength disinfectants, pumped me full of antibiotics and every inoculation imaginable, put plaster casts on my wrist and ankle and shot me full of morphine. As I drifted off to dreamland, I entertained the comforting notion that I had a chance of getting out of this mess alive.

* * *

The next morning found me in less pain and better spirits though a little woozy. I got some food down and was able to make it to the john all right. I awoke from the next night's deep sleep with fever abated and no more shakes. My wounds showed signs of healing. My appetite had returned. I needed morphine no longer, just a little OxyContin.

My third morning in the isolation ward I was propped up on pillows enjoying a hot cup of coffee when a man in his forties wearing a suit, white shirt and striped tie rapped on the door jamb and stepped in. Well-groomed and earnest, he had "paper pusher" written all over him. "Good morning, Mr. Fonko," he said in an over-friendly voice. "I'm Payne D'Arse (we'll call him—I don't want to derail his career by mentioning his real name) from the American consulate. How are you feeling today?"

"Better than I've felt for a long time. I actually think I'm on the mend."

"Your lab tests came back, and they look good. You've nothing contagious or incurable. It was a near thing, though. You arrived here in frightful shape. It's fortunate your friend, Ms. Wehrli, alerted us to your situation. Naturally we rushed right over. Can't neglect an American citizen in dire distress, no sir."

"I appreciate it, I surely do," I said. "I didn't fit the profile of the Missionary's usual customer list very well, and they weren't geared up for my particular situation." Truth be told, their treatment was making everything worse, except possibly my spiritual ennoblement. Her approach may work for the locals, but my immune system was way behind the curve for what it faced in Calcutta.

"Over the last couple days we've looked into your case. It seems the Indian authorities were eager to get hold of you. They'd issued a number of APBs and warrants for your arrest: The massacre at the Amritsar Golden Temple. The jailbreaks. The train derailment. The stolen armored car (we were going to return it). Numerous charges of defrauding innkeepers. Simian assault (I *hate* those monkeys!). The cattle stampede (we intended to eat only one of them, but the herd spooked). The unfortunate fracas at the Chinese border. The riot in Calcutta. Indecent exposure at the Aligaut Temple (it was *her* idea to try that *Kama Sutra* position, not mine). The houseboat incident in Srinigar. The mayhem in Uttar Pradesh (that was the Bandit Queen, not me). The hijacked army transport plane. The aborted bombing attempt of the Taj Mahal. (no, dammit, we *prevented* it!) The altercation with the constables in New Delhi. Indira Gandhi's assassination (we arrived too late to stop it)..."

"Listen, I can explain..."

"*But*," he continued, "Ms. Wehrli hinted that you might have been on a covert assignment, so I took the matter to our chief of station. He asked his colleagues at Langley a few questions, got a few answers, met with his counterpart in Indian Intelligence, and I'm happy to say they worked it out to everyone's satisfaction, and all is copacetic. As far as the records reflect, Jake Fonko has never set foot in India."

"I'm relieved to hear that, Mr. D'Arse." I only wished it were true. "Can you tell me what's my prognosis? When do I get out of here?"

"Call me Payne, please. They'll be moving you out of isolation a little later today, but they recommend you stay in hospital a few days longer, at least until the open wounds have all closed up. They'll put a walking cast on your ankle, and you should be good to go in a week or two."

"When will I be able to have visitors?"

"Tomorrow morning. I'll personally notify Ms. Wehrli. By the way, when you next see her, you'll put in a good word for us? Our service, I mean? The way we've seen to your needs?"

The hell's *that* about? "Sure, Payne—blue ribbon right down the line, I'll tell her," I assured him.

* * *

I LUXURIATED THROUGH MY FIRST NIGHT IN A PRIVATE ROOM IN the recovery ward, woke up much refreshed. The nurse cleared my breakfast dishes away, visiting hours commenced and Dana popped up at my door on the dot.

"Oh, Jake," she sighed. She rushed over, knelt at my bedside, gently put her hands on me where it didn't hurt and planted warm kisses on spots that weren't bandaged or scabbed over. "It broke my heart to see you the other day," she said. "I had worried about you ever since you left for India, and then to see you looking all beat up was such a shock. Sorry I ran off like that, but I was so pissed off at the people in the consulate! They assured me on the phone they'd take care of you, and they hadn't done one single thing. I made my driver take me straight over there and stormed into the consul's office. I gave him my ABC-TV business card and told him I came to Calcutta on an assignment for *20/20*. We were considering doing an exposé of incompetence and malfeasance in America's Foreign Service outposts, I said, and I wanted to sound him out on the concept and any examples of it he knew of. However, the friend I'd told them about over the phone was in serious trouble at a Missionary in the slums, and I couldn't get on with my assignment until I knew my friend was seen to.

"Well, I might as well have set a bomb off under his chair. He jumped up, ran down the hall, shouted some orders. Went somewhere else and shouted some other orders. Then he came back, picked up his phone and shouted at someone else. Then he apologized until I thought he'd fall down and cry, told me help was on the way, and after that he poured drinks and we had a nice chat about how diligently the Foreign Service attends to its duties and responsibilities. He assured me we wouldn't find enough of that kind of material to fill out a *20/20* segment. Ha ha! Your mother sure had that bunch pegged."

Let me backtrack a little. I'd given the consulate the numbers for Mom and Evanston, and Dad. I thought Evanston, my lawyer stepfather, or my journalist father, would know what to do. However, it was Mom who moved the mountain. She'd been indifferent to Dana Wehrli ever since high school and my surfing days. After I streaked Dana's engagement shower in college, Mom had written her off her A-list permanently. However, last year Mom saw Dana's name among the credits after a *20/20* exposé of fat farms. Mom has never wavered from her core values—Status, Image and Appearances—and from that moment on she spoke of Dana as her "future daughter-in-law."

Mom also possesses an unerring instinct for the Levers of Power. Immediately after the consulate's call she dialed Dana, made a few suggestions and offered to underwrite an emergency trip to Calcutta. Et voila!

I congratulated Dana on her presence of mind and her quick action, thanking her with sincerest gratitude. She asked about my sojourn in India, and I gave her a rough outline, saying that the entire story would emerge in the fullness of time. "Thanks to you, Dana, I've been doing fine the last few days. They tell me I can go home in a week or two. How's your schedule look?"

"I explained the situation to my boss. All my productions are under control, so he told me to use as much vacation time as I needed ... and to keep my eyes open for program leads. That Mother lady, for example. We could do a program about her, I bet. The work she's doing here, alleviating everybody's misery, that's a hot topic these days. Or maybe a feature on those amazing Hindu temples—all those weird little statues of gods tangled up together, Walt Disney should eat his heart out. They even have one with an elephant's head on a man's body. I'll stick around until you're free to leave, Jake, but, boy, that can't come soon enough for me."

"Calcutta hasn't been showing you a good time?"

She rolled her eyes. "Let me tell you about it," she said.

DANA WEHRLI'S STORY

"I've never been in a worse place than this in my whole life," she began. "I thought Watts and East LA were the bottom, but oooh no! They should send all those people over here, show them how good they have it, maybe they'd quit rioting. I don't know where they ever got the idea for that musical. *Oh Calcutta!* must mean some other Calcutta, certainly not this one.

"I took a room in the Oberoi Grand, and that's okay, sort of like the Beverly Hills Hotel once you get inside. Retro elegance, you know. But the service guys are creepy, you'd think they'd never seen a blonde before, and they have a hand out for a tip for every little thing. I slept okay, and the next morning I thought I'd do some shopping. There's so much exotic stuff here, and much better quality than Pier One. The gold shops have 22 carat, and the prices make American jewelry stores seem like a bad joke. The concierge tried to steer me to the hotel boutiques, but they have the same ones on Rodeo Drive, big deal. Finally he told me about a government craft emporium that has things from all the Indian states—can you beat that? They have states in India too—but the cab driver didn't know where it was. So I got out and tried another cab driver. He said he'd take me, but when we got there it was on a crummy side street, and somebody had painted "Government Craft Store" on the wall. So I told him to take me back to the Oberoi.

"I got a city map and located the government emporium, and it turned out it was just two blocks down the road! The cab drivers must have known that—the crooks. So I went out on the street and nearly died from the air. It's worse than anything in L.A., and the smell, you must have noticed that yourself. The streets were jam-packed with every kind of vehicle I ever saw—cars, bikes, mopeds, rickshaws, donkey carts, and these big cows just poking along, blocking everything. Old, filthy buses and trollies crept along with people hanging all over outside because they were jammed full inside. And this in the nice part of town!

"I had to walk two blocks to the store, but they were long blocks, and brother, the crowds on those sidewalks! Big families waddling along six abreast and hogging the whole pavement, men brushing against me and worse, women giving me the look, all kinds of filthy creeps loitering and staring. When I stopped or paused peddlers converged on me, beggars too, little kids tugging on my shirt. Some woman even tried to hand me her baby. It's like New York City—if you keep moving and look pissed off, people leave you be. I found the shop, you didn't have to bargain, and they had some darling things, I'll show you when you get out of here. Some of their fabrics are really beautiful, but I don't see myself wearing a sari. (Dana, you'd look stunning wearing a trash bag, I thought.)

"That was pretty much my day. Sitars are from India, and the Beatles used one to good effect, so I thought after dinner I'd go to a club and catch some sitar music. Wrong! I didn't find any clubs I'd want to go into alone. I didn't even feel safe out on the street, all those creeps with beards and turbans loitering round, staring at me. Anyhow, I had nine hours of jetlag to deal with, so I gave it up and went to bed early.

"The next day the weather was okay, so I thought I'd walk around and see what's what. There's a big park across the street, and that would have been okay, except that shabby little men kept pointing out things and then asking for money. They don't have public toilets, so people were peeing in the bushes. The whole country is a public toilet, I think. I found a restaurant for lunch that looked clean enough. I like chicken tandoori, so I ordered some, and it was even better than that Indian restaurant in Santa Monica we go to. The way people wander around here, anybody goes anywhere, and while I was eating, this strange man came up to my table. He had a sort of sheet draped over him, which could have used a good bleaching, and he had this scraggly grey beard and wild grey hair. He looked like the gurus the rock stars hang around with. He also looked like he could use a square meal. He wasn't really bothering me, just staring. After he stood there a while I asked him, "Are you a guru?"

"Thank you for asking," he said. "I am a holy man of sorts, I suppose some might call me a guru. I see you are enjoying a platter of chicken. Around the whole world, all peoples enjoy chicken. Hindus cannot take beef. Muslims cannot take the meat of pigs. Neither can the Jews, nor can they eat some creatures of the sea. But everyone can take chicken. There is fable that explains why that is. Would you like me to relate it?'

What the heck, he was being nice. "Sure," I said. "Tell me your fable."

THE GURU'S FABLE OF THE CHICKEN

"Back in the Oldest of Old Times," he began, "before the Days before the Days, when the World yet rested upon the back of the Elephant that stood upon the back of the Turtle that swam in the Sea of Eternity, a churlish Chicken found himself alone in a vast and empty land.

"What's a guy supposed to do out here?" he wondered. "There's gotta be some rules, or some boss, or a traffic cop, or a tour guide, or an instruction manual, or *something*. They can't just expect a fellow to figure it all out for himself. I mean, where do you start?" So he thought and thought about it for a minute or two and decided that, since there was nothing for it where he stood, he'd better start walking.

The Chicken walked forever and not quite a day, until he reached a sandy desert wherein a group of men dressed in flowing robes and headdress stood among oil wells and Cadillac limousines. "Yo, who's in charge around here?" he asked them.

"Be it known that we are humble slaves of Allah, whose words were revealed by the Prophet, peace be upon Him, in the Holy Quran," came the reply.

"Well, where do I connect with this guy, Allah?" the Chicken inquired.

The men shuddered and recoiled. "Be it known, infidel," their leader admonished him, "that there is no god but Allah, the Infinite, and Muhammad is his Prophet. Peace be upon Him," he added. "Therefore venture beyond the horizon calling his name, and surely he will speak to thee."

The Chicken set off, calling out for Allah every now and then, but he never could quite reach the horizon, nor Allah either. Finally, his breath and body nearly exhausted, he desperately beseeched, "Allah, Allah, Allah, I really gotta talk to you!"

At once a whirlwind rose from the arid desert sands and approached him. "What do you want of me?" an ethereal voice commanded from the swirl.

"Hey, it's about time you showed up," exclaimed the Chicken. "Listen, I need some advice. I'm new in this world. What's the skinny, anyhow? Some guys with towels on their heads told me you could help."

"Follow the Five Pillars of Islam faithfully, and you will be transported to a paradise of succulent fruit, sweets, sparkling streams of clear water and an endless supply of beautiful virgins," the whirlwind assured him.

"Virgins?" said the Chicken with a leer. "All right, chicks galore! And I suppose a guy can make a pig of himself, you old dog?"

"Pig?! Dog?!" roared the whirlwind. "Begone, you wretched little beast, and my curses be upon you!"

"Hey, just a minute!" the Chicken exclaimed, but the whirlwind had already dissolved into the clear desert air. "Well, geez..." sighed the Chicken. "Nothing to do but keep on walkin'." So he resumed his trek and crossed more desert forever and not quite a day, until he happened upon a group of men with bushy beards, ringlet curls and beanie caps adorning their solemn skulls, standing before a high wall, wailing.

"Mornin', gents," said the Chicken. "Maybe you can give a stranger a little helping hand? I'm looking for guidance."

"Jehovah is our true guide," one of the men informed him. "We have been Chosen to follow His Laws, and His Laws only."

"Sounds good to me," said the Chicken. "Where do I find this Jehovah?"

"Seek him in the desert," said one of the men.

"On a hilltop, that's my advice," said another.

"Don't listen to them. A cave, that's the ticket," said another.

As the men argued about the best way to find Jehovah the Chicken wandered off and soon came to a mount, which a passerby told him was named Sinai. To get a better view the Chicken climbed the mount, whereupon a voice boomed out, "What, you want more Commandments? Ten weren't enough?"

"Just tell me what gives, that's all," said the Chicken. "I'm having trouble figuring the world out, and somebody's gotta know the answer."

"Have I got a deal for you," said the voice. Whereupon it commenced reciting the Torah, Chapter and Verse.

Along about the begats, the Chicken chimed in, "Hey, how much more of this do I have to listen to? I mean, you've already started repeating some of these stories."

"We have only barely begun. My Laws are many, and each and every one must be obeyed to the letter. And the Laws are not the end of it, because to understand and follow them properly requires deep, careful, endless study and contemplation."

"You gotta be kiddin'," said the Chicken. "Well, okay, get on with it."

About halfway through Numbers the Chicken wearily interjected, "So, after all this washing and purifying, and all those sacrifices and observances, and the rest of this mumbo jumbo, what's in it for me? Any virgins, or fruits, or sparkling streams?"

"Well, maybe a little milk and honey," said the voice. "That's about it."

"Seems to me, these priests of yours have a sweet racket going," observed the Chicken. "Everybody else works by the sweat of his brow, and they rake off 10%."

"Get off my mountain, you schmendrick!" bellowed the voice. "And be assured, my curse will follow you, and your children, and their children! And their kids too!"

"Sheesh," sighed the Chicken. And so he descended from Mount Sinai and resumed his trek. Not even halfway to forever he found himself along the shores of an inland sea, where a multitude had gathered. A man in flowing white robes, His head adorned by a golden halo, was distributing loaves and fishes to His followers.

"Well, this free lunch is all right," thought the Chicken as he munched away. "And this guy looks like he might have something to impart." Wiping his beak on his wing, he approached the man and said, "Hey pal, I blew into town a little late today. What have you been telling this lot?"

"Blessed are the poor and the meek," the man pronounced. "Turn the other cheek. Store up not the treasures of this world."

"Sounds to me like three E-Z steps to being a loser," commented the Chicken.

"Each has his cross to bear," answered the man, "and you can henceforth count on that going double for the likes of you." Whereupon He resumed handing out loaves and fishes to the multitude.

The Chicken reflected that he'd found no enlightenment in these sandy desert wastes, and that furthermore obviously nobody was ever going to get rich around there. He resolved to try his luck elsewhere and directed his steps toward the East.

Forever and not quite a day later, he found himself in a lush, steaming jungle, where he came upon a golden giant with voluminous ears, seated with his legs arranged in what appeared to the Chicken a very painful posture indeed. "What guidance can you give to a tired and lonely traveler?" the Chicken asked.

The golden giant serenely raised a gentle hand in blessing and intoned, "Rid yourself of all earthly desires. That is the way to Nirvana, the truest bliss."

"Let me get this straight," said the Chicken. "I shouldn't want wine, women, song and a Porsche? And that's supposed to make me blissful?"

"The One True Way to Enlightenment," the golden giant assured him. "It works for me."

"Here's my version of enlightenment," the Chicken declaimed. "I've rid myself of desire for your Nirvana."

The golden giant sat up abruptly. "Ordinarily I teach gentleness toward all living things. But I'm teaching no one to be gentle toward you, you bum. Beat it!"

On the Chicken slogged, and after forever and not quite a day he found himself atop a lofty mountain peak looking out over the entire world. Sitting before him was a wizened old man in a loincloth. "You seek guidance, pilgrim?" inquired the man.

"Well, that's what I've been doing, lo these many moons," lamented the Chicken, "but everybody I ask just hands me a line of bullshit."

"I was going to advise you to perfect your karma by earning merit so that in later incarnations you can free yourself from eternal suffering on the onerous Wheel of Existence," said the old man sadly. "However, you have insulted the sacred Hindu cow. Therefore go your miserable way with no blessings from me. You'll never be anything but a chicken."

And thus the Chicken traveled hither and yon, and to and fro, and north, south, east and west, across the Seven Seas to the Four Corners and back, seeking guidance from any and all. And without exception insulting each and every god and holy man he encountered.

Some gods protect the lowly pig. Some gods protect the noble cow. Some gods protect humble creatures of the sea. Many and sundry animals fall under the divine protection of the diverse gods.

But because of his churlishness, the hapless Chicken is not only permitted, but welcomed, on every table across the wide, wide world.

* * *

"Well, that explains everything," I told him. "Thank you. I enjoyed your story."

"Just so," he said with a little bow, his hands together prayer-style, like they do. "I am pleased my story amused you, Memsahib. By the way," he added. "I don't suppose you could spare one of those drumsticks?"

* * *

"The next day I thought I'd come to the hospital and check up on you, so I got into one of those crummy little Indian cabs. However, after a few blocks I realized that the driver was going in the wrong direction. 'Hey,' I said. 'The hospital is the other way.'

"He held up a tourist guide opened to an ad for a carpet store. 'My cousin owns this shop,' he said. 'He has excellent rugs and most reasonable prices. I thought we could stop there first.'

"Absolutely not!" I shouted at him. "Take me to the hospital! Now!" He turned at the next corner, and I think he really did mean to head back to the hospital, but at the next intersection we came to this long column of dingy, grim-faced little men marching along, blocking all traffic.

"Oh dear," the driver sighed. "The sewer workers' union is staging another demonstration. The Communists must have incited them again." He started nudging the car into the line, but they wouldn't make way for him, and pretty soon we were surrounded by pissed-off Communists marching by, me sitting in the middle of it like Sheena, Queen of the Jungle. I thought they'd start rocking the cab or stoning it or something, but eventually he managed to squeeze his way through the line and eventually brought me to the hospital. But they told me you couldn't have visitors until today. So I hung it up, went back to the Oberoi, had a couple gin and tonics, and that was it for yesterday. Anyhow, I needed the sleep, so I napped through the afternoon.

"So, that's been my time in glorious Calcutta. What a godawful grim place this is! Utterly a city without joy. Such unhappiness. And the men are such jerks. I thought it was just the Indians that come to Los Angeles, but it's all of them. I cannot wait to go home!"

* * *

DANA SPENT EVERY DAY WITH ME, WHILE MY WOUNDS HEALED and my sickness subsided. Sooner than I'd hoped, the docs cleared me for takeoff, and Dana and I arranged our flight home. My passport had strayed somewhere in the Indian hinterlands, and Payne D'Arse smoothed the way by expediting my new one—my second in two years. The photo this time would cause any conscientious customs clerk to double-check the "no entry" roster. I was in no shape to comb Calcutta for clothing in a style I liked, so Dana rounded up an outfit for me to fly home in from the boutiques in her hotel. The day before departure we paid a visit to Mother to thank her for saving my life.

"Think nothing of it, Jake," she said. "We served you out of the spirit of pure Christian charity. I am overjoyed that you recovered from your distress so thoroughly. Certainly you have your friend, Miss Wehrli, to thank, and I hope as well as the humble efforts of me and the Sisters."

"I would like to make a contribution to your Missionary," I said. "How does it work? Do I send the check to you here?"

"No, Jake, send no money. It would only cause difficulty," Mother said.

"But couldn't you use some money for medicines, or food, or a better water supply? I see so many things here that could be improved with just a little money."

"You do not understand our philosophy, Jake. We do not see poverty and suffering as afflictions. We see them as blessings, as ennobling, for Christ lived in poverty and suffering, and by emulating Him in our daily lives and our ministrations it brings us closer to His true spirit. We dress as the poorest, we eat as the poorest, we live as the poorest. When Sisters travel to Missions in other lands they carry only as much belongings as will fit in a plain cardboard box. So the poor whom we serve know that we are truly humble, and thus they find our help easier to accept."

"I know people who have contributed substantial amounts to your Missionaries. May I ask what you do with their money?"

"It is an embarrassment to admit this, but we don't know what to do with it, so we deposit it in the bank, hoping that Christ will some day reveal His plans for it. Oh, we need a little money, of course, for travel and so forth, and the Bank of Credit and Commerce International is very handy for that, as they have offices in all the poor countries where we work."

"Your money is on deposit in BCCI?"

"Yes. It is operated by some nice gentlemen in Pakistan. We feel that being of a kindred race they understand us, and with the bank situated in one of the world's poorest countries, we are helping the poor even with our bank deposits."

I told Mother about my recent encounter with BCCI. By the conclusion of my story her normally downcast eyes were flashing, and she said, "Hmmm. This is news to me. Thank you, Jake. Your information is contribution enough. I will have our accountants make some calls this very afternoon to some people they know at the Vatican Bank in Rome. Christ Himself had differences with money changers, you know," she added. So I couldn't contribute money, but at least I contributed my services as her bouncer for a few days, as well as a little timely financial counseling. Considering what finally happened to BCCI, I may have saved her Missionary millions of dollars.

From each according to his abilities, they say. We do what we can.

* * *

AND THUS IT HAPPENED THAT I OWED MY LIFE TO TWO GREAT women. Mother rescued me from a squalid death in a Calcutta gutter. And Dana Wehrli rescued me from Mother. I don't mean to make light of Mother's efforts. Her Missionary accomplishes considerable good the world over, and many honors and accolades have been bestowed on her and her organization. But a recipient has to be suffering total immersion in the depths of abject despair and misery to appreciate her ministrations fully. Sadly, all too many such people remain with us. For those of you not among them, my advice is: Do your utmost to avoid getting yourself into a situation where what Mother's Missionary will do for you amounts to an improvement.

I personally had no lust for salvation or spiritual ennoblement just then. My fondest desire was to get back home to my beach pad and resume normal life in Malibu, California, U. S. of A., that best of all possible worlds.

INTRODUCTION TO THE STORY

As you might imagine, returning home after an unscheduled, abrupt, incommunicado absence of six months required some adjustments. There was of course the obvious matter of recuperating from injuries and diseases incurred from my near-death experience in a Calcutta gutter. My fevers and shakes progressed to feeling wrung out and finally to energy and spirits revived. Wounds healed up, bruises and lumps faded away. The casts graced my wrist and ankle for another few weeks, and my broken ribs still ached, but I could get around. Too bad it didn't result from doing something heroic, rather than from a beggars' riot over a counterfeit one hundred dollar bill. Not the kind of feat to impress a sports bar full of beer-besotted buddies with. Especially since I didn't think I'd better mention the involvement of Emil Grotesqcu, my perennial KGB shadow.

Straightening out practical details kept me busy without requiring much physical activity. Having paid no bills for six months, things were shut off—phone, electricity, gas, water. I had to replace a refrigerator and the rotted food that filled it; also called in a plumber to set dried-out seals and connections right. My Cherokee went to the shop for refitting as well. After my mail overwhelmed the box at the end of the driveway the post office took to storing it, filling most of a mail bag with bills, catalogs, grocery store fliers and solicitations for donations (UCLA expelled me my sophomore year, yet they still pursue me—I wouldn't have been surprised if one of their fundraisers reached me while I languished in that Lucknow dungeon). The telephone answering machine had long since hit storage capacity. At least the landscaping hadn't gone out of control—not much happens to sand, oleander bushes, sea apples and cacti over six months.

By the time my casts came off I'd pretty much gotten on top of everything. Mail sorted, letters answered, clients re-contacted, bills paid, normal life resuming. Fortunately my absence occurred after I'd sent in my tax returns, one thing I gratefully did not have to resolve. Also fortunately, my investment portfolio on autopilot had grown enough to cover my expenses. Yes indeedy, long term T-Notes at 10% are a fine investment, and the Reagan 1980s stock market revival was underway.

JAKE'S STORY OF THE AMRITSAR MASSACRE, CONTINUED

All in all, it was the worst six months of my life (Cambodia had it beat as a harrowing experience, but took less time). I hit the water in the Amritsar Golden Temple pool with nothing on me but my wallet and standard men's pocket equipage. I thank my stars the guys shooting at me were hysterical religious fanatics, not trained military. Despite being stunned when I banged my head I managed to keep below the surface of the murky water and swim away from the gunfire without being hit. I surfaced, got my bearings and a deep breath, plunged back underwater and swam further to a spot by an open doorway in the building through which I'd entered the complex. I lunged up out of the pool and scuffled my way inside against the flow of the crowd flocking to see what all the hubbub was about. Typically Asian, every man was eager to be first in line, so they paid me no attention as I squeezed toward the back of the crush. The gunfire outside increased in volume and frequency.

Mortar rounds began landing around the building. The surge of gawkers reversed field and became a raging stampede of safety-seekers. Bucking the tide of panic, I threw elbows, knocked turbaned men over, ducked incoming lead and found a hidey-hole to calm down, gather my thoughts and formulate a plan.

My plan—get the hell out of here! The troops I'd seen massed outside were laying siege to the Golden Temple. The sodden clothes on my back were an Indian army uniform—it got me a pass with one side of the fray but made me a target for the other. I found a doorway fronting a street with cover enough that I could make a break for it. I dodged my way through street pandemonium to the skirmish line, where I paused to rally a team of Indian regulars with wild arm waving and urgent, incoherent commands. That focused their attention on riddling the building with enthusiastic and totally ineffective fire, and they paid me no mind as I passed behind them and worked my way to the rear.

Amritsar is relatively small compared to major centers like New Delhi, Calcutta and Mumbai, and though shabby by Western standards it is as well kept as Indian cities get. That owes to its predominately Sikh population—a rule of thumb in India, I was to learn, is "if you want something done competently, ask a Sikh to do it." In quieter times Amritsar would have been a nice place to visit, but Sikh extremists had holed up in the Golden Temple. The Indian Army arrived in force and set up positions, poised to attack at first provocation. Which I unwittingly provided, and it was now a live-fire war zone resounding with explosions, rattling machine guns, the fully panoply of noise and stinks of battle. I threaded my way through the narrow streets of the roiling city to my hotel. The desk clerk said he'd never heard of me and refused to give me the key to my room. I went around behind the building, negotiating my way through an alleyway clogged with dustbins, trash piles, discarded junk and tangles of parked bicycles. I rock-climbed up the back wall via windowsills, ledges and rusty drainpipe to the window of my third-floor room and burgled my way in. To my dismay, the room had been ransacked and all my stuff stolen.

Several sets of determined footsteps came pounding up the stairs, so I bailed out the window and clambered back down to the cluttered alleyway, dropping from above the ground floor onto a trash heap I'd previously noted comprised mostly cardboard boxes and soft-looking garbage.

I'm getting a little old for urban acrobatics—and believe me, the reality of it ain't like spy-thriller rooftop chase scenes—but I alighted without spraining anything and scurried away. Once again I found myself stranded in the middle of an unholy mess with no passport, no kit, no weapon, no support, very little money and nary a clue. Indians tend to be taller than other Asian nationalities, so I at least wouldn't be standing a head taller than everyone else around me. It was a population I could blend into, fortunate because I soon found myself a fugitive sought by Sikh militants, Muslim terrorists, gangsters and departments of the Indian government including, but not limited to, the Army, the secret police and civil authorities. This in a vast, impoverished and hostile country I knew next to nothing about, whose inhabitants mostly spoke languages that I didn't. Just what I deserved for placing my trust in swarthy strangers.

That incident became known as the Massacre at the Amritsar Golden Temple. A thousand Sikh rebels were slaughtered, more or less, and a larger number of civilians, touching off bloody riots and insurrections across the country, including the assassination of Premier Indira Gandhi by her Sikh bodyguards. Talk about misplacing your trust.

By that time starving hungry, I grabbed a naan and helping of curry from a street vendor who was happy to be overpaid with an American dollar. I found an unassuming, cheap hotel on an out of the way street, where I sponged myself off (full en suite bath being not included). My clothes had dried out but were droopy and bedraggled. In any event, I wouldn't fare well wearing a bottle-green Army uniform amidst running gun battles in the streets. I skulked around until I found a clothing shop, where I got an off-white, loose blouse with a Nehru collar and grey pajama bottoms like the Indian men wear (in contrast to the neon-colored, spangled saris the women flaunt). I replaced my leather shoes, ruined from my impromptu swim, with sturdy work shoes that could cover ground. Back in my room I opened the window and rubbed my new duds around on the outside wall to grime them up for the sake of camouflage, gave the shoes a good scuffing, and then turned in for some desperately need sleep. In the middle of the night I awoke with shits and shakes, maybe from the food, maybe from bugs I picked up from my plunge in "the pool of nectar," as "Amritsar" translates to. Recovery took another day, by which time the scrape I got when I hit bottom with my forehead in the Amritsar Temple pool had become inflamed.

I set about searching for a route home from Punjab, but unidentified pursuers I soon found on my trail introduced new complications. My money ran out fast, leaving me scrounging food, shelter and transportation in any way I could. Periodically I sampled the menu of fevers and festering diseases that India so abundantly provides. My off-again on-again partnership with Emil Groteqcu turned out to be both a blessing and a curse. All in all, a classic misadventure—the gods were against me on that one, for sure.

Love it or hate it, you'll never forget it, they say about India. How true that is. I saw some gorgeous scenery and spectacular art there, not to mention some of the world's most beautiful women. Was amazed by exotic architecture straight out of oriental fantasies. On a few occasions when I wasn't scrambling for a mouthful of anything digestible I tasted flavors I'd never have imagined—hot, sweet, tangy, savory and spicy all in one glorious rush (just because food is brown, don't turn it down). Strangers displayed extraordinary generosity and kindness (and not just Mother and her Missionary). Nevertheless, the poverty, the desperation and the meanness of the place stick with me. So many, many miserable people. And for most of six months, me trapped among their numbers and sharing their squalor.

I'd been had. The questions were: How? And why?

I later compared notes with Pat Swayze, who starred in *City of Joy*. Supposedly set in those same Calcutta slums, nobody from Hollywood would go within 8.000 miles of them. The set designers built a brand new, sanitized slum for the movie shoot. I recounted to him my own India adventures, good for some hearty laughs when we weren't wincing.

My tour there was in 1985. I hear that since then things have improved, with money being made in high-tech ventures, people manning outsourced call centers, modernized agriculture now feeding the country closer to adequately and so forth. But they've also added hundreds of millions more Indians. Maybe economic progress has gotten ahead of population growth, but with one of the world's highest birthrates the race against poverty stays close. I haven't been back lately to see for myself, but I note that emigration is still very popular there.

Oh well. Win some, lose some. There was half a year's lost income to make up, so I got back to work, picking up mundane delivery jobs, security consulting, celebrity escorting and the like, nothing major. It paid the bills and kept me close to home, which was good, because it also kept me in touch with Dana Wehrli.

We'd been keeping close company up until I left on my disastrous assignment in India, and after she flew over and rescued me, even closer. To update that: I spent the winter of 1983/84 in Cheyenne, Wyoming, where she worked at the ABC station as local weather-babe. A role designed for her, and vice-versa, she thrived on it. The locals had never before been so glued to the morning weather reports. When we could, we did getaways at ski resorts, where I tried my hand at snowboarding. It was close enough to surfing that I got into it pretty quickly. Not all Rockies resorts welcomed it, especially not Aspen, but you can't keep a good concept down, and one weekend we found snowboarders messing around with something they now call "half-pipe," doing stunts back and forth between opposed ridges of snow. It became an Olympic Sport, of course, but in the winter of 1984 few had ever heard of anything like it. Guys flying into the air and turning spins and somersaults on snow-going surfboards? Gnarly!

Dana was intrigued, so she cajoled a cameraman from the station to come along with us and shoot some footage. One of my wipeouts provided comic relief—it's a sport you want to take up in your teens, not at age 35. She got an editor to shape it into a newsbite for her weather segment one morning, and other ABC affiliates picked it up. Audiences responded enthusiastically, so her boss assigned her to produce a short subject on half-pipe snowboarding, which ABC aired on *Wide World of Sports*. Turned out, she had a flair for production and direction, and coupled with her captivating on-air presence, one thing led to another. She wound up back in Los Angeles in the ABC production unit assigned to human interest features. And then she hit the Big Time: *20/20* snapped her up. Sure worked for me in Calcutta.

As I said, we'd been keeping closer company, but no serious consideration of marriage. With my free-lance career, such as it was, and the demands of TV feature production on her, our lives didn't mesh in any kind of daily routine. Plus I declined moving from Malibu, whereas Dana had no time for long commuting so needed to live near her studio. We each had a king-sized bed, and we spent as much time together as we could in the context of our mutual chaotic arrangements. We were happy enough with it.

And then came that fateful knock on my door on that sunny autumn afternoon in 1985. Opportunity? No. It was Todd Sonarr, my former CIA boss who sent me on that doomed mission in the closing days of the war (as recounted in the first of Professor Pflingger's books, *Jake Fonko MIA*).

Strictly speaking, Sonarr didn't actually knock; he poked the buzzer on the back door by the parking apron. Considering that he ruined my Army career and damned near got me killed in Cambodia, you can understand why my reaction when I saw him standing there was muted. "Todd? What the hell are *you* doing here?"

"Hey there, Jake," he said. "Long time no see. I was in the

neighborhood, thought I'd drop by and see how an old friend is getting along these days."

Huh? In the neighborhood? Old friend? My internal bullshit detectors lit up like the Las Vegas strip. "Just strolling through Malibu, were you?"

"Well, you know ... you going to invite me in, or just stare at me through the screen door?"

What could I say? I opened the door and stepped back. He swung the screen door wide and came in. He was still beefy, a few pounds more so than when I'd last seen him in 1975. A receding hairline encroached into his crewcut, and what remained of it showed grey. Hardly a glimmer of his former gung-ho intensity remained; in fact, he looked tired and defeated.

"Let's go in here," I said, leading him to the living room. "Have a seat. Get you something to drink?"

"Scotch if you have it. Anything else if you don't. Don't be stingy. Throw a little ice in it." He looked out the picture window at the rollers crashing on the beach. "Nice view you got here. Man, you're living the life, aren't you just! Oh, hey," he exclaimed. "That is some carpet!"

He meant my superfine Naheen, that token of gratitude from Razi Q'ereshi. "A souvenir from Iran," I replied over my shoulder as I went to the bar. I poured him a tumbler of Chivas Regal, took a couple fingers myself, plopped in some ice and took a seat across the room from him. He savored an initial sip of scotch. "You look good, Jake. Keeping yourself in shape. I understand you went through a bad patch in India recently?"

"Let's just say they provided me with a prolonged refresher course in Survival, Escape, Resistance and Evasion. Not as tough as Ranger training. So, what's up?" I asked. "Still going great guns with the Company?"

TODD SONARR'S STORY

Todd took a big swallow from his glass and relief spread through his face. He sat silently for a moment, then took another big swallow. After a long pause he said, "Not exactly great guns, Jake." Another pause. Then he drained his glass. "Not great at all. Any chance of a refill?" he asked, tentatively.

What the heck? "Sure." Remembering how he and his CIA buddies used to swill it down, I poured the tumbler full and returned it to him. He grabbed it and swigged a third of it. Some things never change.

That braced him. He sat up straighter. "It's been a rough decade," he said. "That mole hunt I involved you in, all that trouble and turmoil, and nothing ever came of it. Just a false lead, but it was the straw that broke Angleton's career; had to resign in disgrace. Damned near got me canned, too, but with some fancy footwork I managed to dodge that bullet. And then the Church Committee shafted the Company but good. Everything went down the crapper after they got through with their investigation. Oh, prohibiting CIA assassinations of foreign leaders was well-advised, I suppose. Looking back, they usually caused more trouble than they were worth. Having Ngo Dinh Diem bumped off was the root of our troubles in Nam, for example. But Congress went too far, gutted the Company, slashed our funding, put us under the microscope. That was the worst. How are you supposed to run covert ops with a gaggle of Senators looking over your shoulder? Every Congressional staff has young hotshot aides determined to Make a Difference, so the goddamned oversight committee leaks like a geezer with a shot prostate. You were there in the last of the good old days. You'd never recognize the place now."

"Todd, I was never in the CIA. I was an officer in Army Intelligence, on loan."

"Right," he said. He gulped the last of his Chivas. "Whatever. The Church Committee started us downhill," he continued. "Then Jimmy Carter took over. That fucking hillbilly peanut farmer finished us off, but good. He appointed a fellow Navy guy, Stansfield Turner, as director. A technocrat like Carter, they both favored gadgets over human intelligence, shrank what networks we still had. Shifted the mission from protecting America to promoting human rights. Human rights! Some of our enemies aren't even human! Promoting their rights? The hell's the point of *that*?

"So then we had that Iranian disaster, the Islamic Revolution. Naturally the CIA gets all the blame, but Carter wouldn't let us do anything that might offend or upset the Shah, wouldn't let us probe the opposition, so our intel was crappy. I think you might know a little about all that mess. Then Carter set us to undermining Apartheid in South Africa. Sure, life wasn't a picnic for the indigs, but who thinks the place will be better off when they take over? He had us trying to subvert the Soviets with cultural exchanges, underground presses, radio broadcasts, support for dissidents. No harm in it, but not enough to tip the scales against those bloody-minded bastards. Boycott the Olympics? Yeah, that sure showed'em!

"When Reagan came in he appointed Bill Casey as director, and things looked up. Casey was a protégé of Bill Donovan back in the OSS. Reagan was a Cold Warrior, dedicated to beating the Commies, not containing them. Casey got the budget restored, and he restaffed with 2,000 new officers. The Company got more active, set about doing something to root the Commies out of Central America. Went after Muammar Gaddafi in Libya in '81. Supplied Egyptian-made arms to the rebels in Afghanistan ..."

"So what's the problem?" I asked. "Sounds like you're back in business."

"Two problems. The new officers turned out mostly to be 'yuppie spies,' more interested in their retirement plans than in going to the mat to protect Americans, better at infighting and obstruction than intel work. Casey figured John McMahon as too cautious for a chief of clandestine services and replaced him with Max Hugel, an obnoxious runt who wore a rug. Hugel was a campaign fundraiser and former used car salesman, absolutely clueless about the CIA. The covert ops guys rebelled and applied their talents against him, forced him out in two months, the first of a series of lackluster appointments that came and went. Finally got a man with balls in that slot, Clair George ..."

"Todd, I just asked how things were going at the CIA by way of making conversation. Why this extended tale of woe?"

"I'm coming to that. It concerns you. Be patient. I came out here for a specific purpose."

Concerns *me*? Specific purpose? Shit. He looked expectantly from his empty tumbler to me, but I wasn't going to turn him into a menace on the Pacific Coast Highway by passing him more scotch. "How about if I make us some coffee?" I asked. Keeping him awake was imperative. I wanted him to leave my pad and drive away ASAP, not flake out on my couch. Unfortunately, ASAP didn't seem likely to come any time soon.

"Sure, okay, coffee's okay," he said, disappointedly. I took our tumblers into the kitchen, unlimbered the coffee gear and got a strong blend brewing while Sonarr continued his story. "So the Company was chaotic and disorganized, but with Reagan in the White House at least we seemed pointed in the right direction. Protect American interests, beat the Commies. Not that the two goals always coincided, but you don't always know that at the time you make the decisions.

"Now, covert ops is about the only thing I've ever had a talent for, hard as it may be for you to believe that I have any talent at all for that. So I stuck with it through thick and thin and four years of shitty missions, and after Bill Casey took over and we weathered Max Hugel it seemed things were looking brighter. In 1981 Bill Haig announced that international terrorism would replace human rights as Issue Number One, and that the Ruskies were behind the international terror. That approach was more to my liking, but I wound up in bad news assignments nevertheless. Israel invaded Lebanon in 1982, so they sent me there, where we backed, as it belatedly became clear, the most unpopular group available,

Maronite Christians. Fortunately I was out in the field the day they blew up the U.S. Embassy 1983. Killed 63 people, including Bob Ames, the CIA chief of station, a long-time friend. A few months later they blew up the marine barracks by the airport, and Reagan pulled out of Lebanon entirely.

"But by that time I'd been hauled into planning the Grenada invasion. Spur of the moment, rush-rush-rush, with water-tight compartmentalized security. Of course we botched some of it—what else? The only bright point was the assault on Point Salines airstrip. Rangers saved my ass, and the intel you delivered kept our part of it from being a total loss.

"Came 1984, and Reagan's skivvies were in a wad. The Lebanese had kidnapped 14 Americans in Beirut, including our station chief, Bill Buckley, and were holding them hostage. They even sent us a tape of Buckley being tortured, which Bill Casey played for Reagan. So guess who they sent in to sort that out? Yours truly. There was no way for an American who couldn't speak the various languages to penetrate the Hezbollah networks, of course, and, par for the course in the Middle East, our paid informants weren't worth shit. The CIA couldn't find, let alone rescue, the hostages the Lebanese were holding. Mission failed, they recalled me, and now I get wind that they're working on some kind of arms deals with the Iranians, who are fighting a war with Iraq. Iran controls Hezbollah, so we're hoping they can tease out the hostages. Good luck with that.

"Meantime, Congress outlawed funding for our operations in Central America, and I'm afraid that's where they'll send me next. Casey's committed to backing the Contras and throwing out the Sandinistas, but who knows where he's going to dig up the dollars to do that?

"To top it all off, our Soviet network has been wrapped up, reviving suspicions that there's a mole in the works after all, fingering our agents. Believe it or not, some in the Company now are hinting that I'm to blame, for giving up on my search too soon.

"Sad to say, the only gold star I've gotten since Nam was when word circulated around Langley that you'd gotten tipped off on the Russian Afghanistan invasion from a KGB mole you were running. I let it be known that I was your case officer, and…"

"What?! You told people at Langley I still work for the CIA?"

"I said I 'was' your case officer. Left it ambiguous what the meaning of 'was' was. When we were in Nam I was, you know. Calm down, Jake. I told only a few people, top secret, need to know."

"Todd, why did you show up here? Get to the point!"

"Okay, okay, I'm coming to that. Now, I report to Steele Bosserman (not his real name: I can't divulge names of covert ops personnel), close to the top in the clandestine section. He recently took a fact-finder to Asia, and on his return he called me into his office, shut the door and told me something he'd learned."

STEELE BOSSERMAN'S STORY

"It seems he'd done a very hush-hush situation assessment of Asian nations to determine what, if any, looming emergencies the CIA might have to address. 'Todd,' he said, 'the Philippines are key to our presence in the Far East. A major shitstorm is brewing there but nobody sees the gathering clouds. Okay, South Korea's under control. Our troops keep the Commies north of the 38th in line. Singapore's rock-solid. Nam, Laos and Cambodia, they're sideshows right now. The Reds took over and are staying in place, have their hands full just recovering from the wars. In Red China we're already doing as much as we can, there's even some reason for hope there. Malaysia and Indonesia, no troubles on the horizon. Japan a non-issue.

"'But look here…' and he got up and went over to a world map on the wall. 'The Philippines. More than 7,000 islands stretching from Indonesia in the south, to Taiwan in the north, controlling two of the world's most important seaways. We maintain major military bases there, the Navy in Subic Bay, the Air Force at Clark

Air Base—critical operations, essential for sustaining our influence in the western Pacific. And it's on the verge of toppling.'

"Really?" I said. "This is the first I've heard of that. Not that I'm an expert on Asian relations ...'

"'It's not widely known, Todd, but the Commies are conniving to overthrow the president, Ferdinand Marcos. He's been a staunch American ally ever since World War Two, the staunchest. He was a war hero, you know, led the guerrillas after MacArthur departed, gave the Japs fits. The most decorated soldier in that theater. He entered politics after the war and has been President since 1965. No Asian political leader has been more steadfast ... or effective ... in standing shoulder to shoulder with America. And he's made great strides modernizing his country—Manila abounds with showcase developments. That new Cultural Center of theirs would be a crown jewel anywhere in the developed world.

"'What I learned on my tour is that Marcos and his government face a dire threat. A Communist insurgency, the New People's Army, is gaining strength throughout the islands, and they're planning to make a decisive move soon, subvert elections, install their own puppets and seize control. Once the Philippines go Red, we're done for in the western Pacific. We're playing catch-up ball and it's bottom of the ninth.'

"How did you find about this?" I asked him.

"The old fashioned way—shoe leather and big ears. I talked to all the people who matter there—the generals, the politicos, newspaper publishers, industrialists, bankers, you name it. General Ver, Marcos's right hand man, arranged for an aerial recon, spent a whole day flying me around, surveying the terrain. Beautiful tropical islands, but the poverty and misery would break your heart. Some of the finest folks in the world, but poor, desperately poor. Even from the air you could tell the threat was palpable. Few cities in Asia have slums as bad as Manila and the other Filipino cities. And you know what slums in Third World cities represent—festering petri dishes of social discontent, nurseries of dissatisfaction, resentment and rage, ideal breeding grounds for Commie agitation."

"Where does the CIA fit in?" I asked him. "What actions can we take? What assets do we have on the ground?"

"That's the hell of it," he replied. "We don't have any presence in the Philippines to speak of. They're an ally, after all. Doesn't look good to station spooks among our allies. But dammit, the Philippines cry out for our aid and assistance. They're crying out for our help. We're honor-bound to take an active part, but—and I can't stress this too strongly—it can't look like the help is coming from the CIA. We have to do this thing very, very dark."

Uh oh. "So let me guess, Todd ... Bosserman then went on to propose some kind of covert operation to help Marcos fend off this New People's Army?"

"I can see you haven't lost your old intel instincts, Jake. That's exactly what he went on to do. He outlined a plan for slipping in a highly-qualified special agent under deep cover to thwart the insurgents, the same kind of work Ed Lansdale did so well in Indochina. Couldn't send in someone from the Company, because it would be impossible to get Congressional approval and funding. In fact, if Congress got wind of it, some liberal hotshot would almost certainly leak it, blow the cover and scotch the whole thing. No sir—the Company has to stay at arm's length, and somebody else's arm at that."

"By any chance, did the names of any particular highly-qualified candidates for this mission come up?"

"As a matter of fact, one did. It seems that in a vague sort of way you enjoy quite a reputation around Langley, Jake. The details of what you did in Cambodia remain deeply buried, of course, but our people have the impression that you've been real busy since you uprooted Clyde Drifter and outfoxed the Khmer Rouge. Shepherded the Shah out of Iran. Ferreted that Afghani invasion tip. Derailed a Russian gun-running op in Belfast. Shot down one of Castro's MIGs. Got the goods on Bank of Credit and Commerce International. Steele and I couldn't come up with any other of our private contractors that came close to your quals."

"Okay, I get it. Let's cut to the chase. Let me spell it out for you, Todd. N O space W A Y space P E R I O D."

"I figured that might be your initial reaction, Jake, before you thought it through. Here's how it will go. You won't be on the CIA payroll, not on *any* government payroll. We'll pay you out of an unaudited slush fund, straight cash, used bills of various denominations, no receipts. It'll be like finding $50,000 on the street, with no witnesses. Plus expenses, of course. We'll give you air-tight cover and an unassailable legend, and we'll have assets covering you like brown on chocolate. The Philippines is a peaceful country, law-and-order reign. Marcos has the place buttoned up. What could go wrong?"

"Judging from past performance, just about everything conceivable plus stuff no sane person could imagine. When Murphy formulated his famous Law, I think he was looking over your shoulder."

"Well, I must say that's an unkind thing to say, after all I've done for you."

"Just about got me killed, wrecked my Army career ... what else?"

"You think you'd be better off if you'd stayed in the Army? I did you a favor, getting you RIF'd and setting you up in business. Look around you, this Malibu beach pad, a gentleman surf bum lifestyle the whole world aspires to. Compare what you've been doing for the last 10 years to what it would have been like, cooling your heels in a peacetime army. You're complaining?"

"Todd, I am not going to throw in with another of your hare-brained, off-the-books CIA fiascos. End of discussion."

"Oh well. At least you gave me a fair hearing. If you've made up your mind and set it in concrete, what can I say? By the way, a couple things have come up recently that I need to discuss with you. Seems your name was mentioned in some on-going investigations, and... "

"Investigations? What about?"

"Well, embezzlement, for one. When you mustered out of the Army, some dimwit clerk inadvertently cut you a check for ten times the actual amount of pay you were owed. Rather than return it, as an honest man would have done, you cashed it and kept it."

"You said nobody would say anything."

"Jake, I have never advised anyone to steal money from the United States government."

"Oh, for Chrissake. The government's going to prosecute me for that?"

"You never can tell."

"I'll pay it back."

"Also there's a matter of accepting bribes from foreign interests while performing government work ..."

"What on earth are you talking about?"

"That bag of uncut diamonds Old Man Poon gave you while you were on mission in Cambodia. If that wasn't a bribe, I don't know what is."

"I don't think you could prove it."

"Oh, maybe not, but we could try. Might have to call Sarge Wallace in for testimony, seeing as how he fenced them for you. I'd sure hate to put old Sarge in a tough spot like that, having to choose between being a stand-up guy and losing his pension. Even if we couldn't prove anything, you'd be tied up in court for a while. Pretty expensive, legal defense. It saddens me, to think of a man like Sarge out on the bricks."

"I'll take my chances."

"Impersonating a CIA officer is a very serious federal offense, too. People who do that can go to jail for a long time."

"I've never impersonated a CIA officer. I never even *was* one."

"A lot of people in high places around the world have the impression you're a deep-cover covert op with the CIA. *We* never said you were, and there's no records of it in our personnel files. Who else but you would lead people to believe that? Shit, even the

KGB thinks you're in the CIA. That's pretty convincing proof that you've been telling tales."

"Todd, I'm not going into the Philippines for the CIA. Final. The end."

"Not to mention your directing hostile gunfire at a U. S. Service helicopter off Jamaica."

"They fired first. Anyway, nobody got hurt."

"And then there's the statutory rape charge."

"What??!! I've never bonked any San Quentin quail, not even back in my college days."

"What about that Chinese girl you were banging in Phnom Penh? The one you brought to Bangkok. We have videotapes from the Oriental Hotel. A teenager, wasn't she?"

"Todd, that was in another country, and besides, she's now director of her father's electronics division. She said she was eighteen."

"She may well have been. I'm sure there'd be no problem if she'd bring a birth certificate to court for evidence. Probably get the charges dismissed. Might even be past the statute of limitations, don't know if that applies. I'll bet a federal court would straighten it out pretty quickly; all she'd have to do is come over and testify. Though she'd probably be embarrassed by our tapes—pretty steamy stuff. Her daddy would be fit to be tied, I'd think. Probably livid with outrage, and you know how ruthless those Hong Kong tai pans can be when provoked. With his resources, no telling what grief he might bring down on you if you involved his daughter in a rape trial."

"Todd, you came all the way out here to rope me into a CIA project, and now you're trying to blackmail me. You must be really desperate. Tell me the truth, just this one time. What's up?"

"Oh, just my career, that's all. No big deal to you, I'm sure."

"You're a federal bureaucrat. Can't you ride it out a few more years and collect your pension?"

"I'm a political appointee, serving 'at the pleasure of,' and I'm far enough from being retirement-eligible that if they canned me now I'd lose it all. So then what, I start over again as a gofer for one of the private military contractors, if they'd even look at a middle-aged, washed-out CIA op? The way things stand, I'd probably wind up as a mall cop. I said I didn't have many gold stars. Well, if you want to know the whole truth, I've collected a passel of black uglies as well. When Reagan directed us to go after Gaddafi it was my bright idea to supply Stinger anti-aircraft missiles to rebels in Chad, which borders on Libya. I thought they could use 'em against Gaddafi's air force. Then a bunch of those missiles went missing. Turned out our so-called allies also were getting backing from Saddam Hussein. James Baker sent a memo down demanding to know who had the insane idea of sending advanced ordnance to a bunch of wild-ass desert Arabs who were beholden to one of our leading enemies. He found my signature on the recommendation.

"Those bombings in Lebanon happened on my watch: why didn't we see them coming, people wanted to know. You want fun, go up in front of a Senate closed-door committee hearing and try to explain why the millions we'd been paying for HumInt in Lebanon had been wasted on crooks, liars and double agents that never told us anything useful, usually just disinformation for the benefit of their own factions. Then they sent me to Central America. We had some insurgency manuals in comic-book format that we'd captured in Nam, how to take control of a village, stuff like that. I thought maybe they'd be good training materials for the peasants rebelling against the Sandinistas, so I had them translated, reproduced and distributed. Next thing I knew, they were calling for my scalp for passing out Commie propaganda the Sandinistas could use against our guys.

"So you can appreciate why nobody's got my back after that litany of fuckups. I've got to produce something pretty good, pretty quick, or I'm on the bench. Or out the door. At present they have me involved with logistical support in Afghanistan, coordinating supplies for the rebels, but that's going down the crapper. The Soviet Hind gunships slaughter them in the mountain passes, so the flow of supplies is down to a trickle. The outcome's still iffy there, and a lot of CIA people are involved. If Afghanistan comes up aces, others will take whatever credit. If it goes to shit, they assigned me to that mission with a 'Kick Me' sign on my ass and guess who'll take the rap?

"When Steele Bosserman came in with his report on the Philippines, I saw a glimmer of hope. Here's a chance to do well by doing good, I thought. C'mon, Jake, for old time's sake help me out, what say?"

"Todd, for old time's sake I should shoot you in the balls and then bury you alive."

"Jake, this Philippines caper is a sure thing. It can't go wrong. Reagan's behind Marcos 100%. He's long admired him as a man, and the guy's a war hero, for Chrissake. Reagan publicly declared that to throw him to the wolves would confront America with a Communist power in the Pacific. This is strictly on the QT, but here's some inside dope. The word's leaked out that Marcos will soon announce a special election to demonstrate how the Filipinos stand behind him, and all we have to do is go over there and keep the Commies from stealing it. Marcos stays in power, Reagan's happy, and I don't lose my job. I need this, I really do. Afghanistan's the only thing I have going, and I'm grasping at the last straw here."

"Maybe there's something you could do, Todd. Those Stinger missiles you mentioned. Seems to me they'd be just the thing to combat the Russian gunships. They attack close to the ground, and they aren't very fast. Those passes are at high altitudes, so the Hinds would be struggling in thin air. What better targets for shoulder-launched heat-seekers? Sitting ducks for Stingers."

"What's to prevent another debacle like happened in Chad?"

"Better controls and monitoring? Instead of just passing them out wholesale, distribute them one at a time to trusted tribesmen and have our advisors keep close tabs?"

"Hmmm. That's an interesting idea. Might work. I'll look into that, maybe run it by some people. Meantime, don't reject my proposition too hastily. Take a little time, give it due consideration. Could be easy money for just a couple months' work. The Philippines are not a hot zone, you know, not a situation teeming with hostiles. The New People's Army isn't actually an effective armed force, more like a dangerous political opposition group. You'd be doing subversion, not a shooting war." He checked his watch. "My goodness, how time does fly," he said. "Gotta run, got a plane to catch back to D.C. Thanks for your time, Jake. Good to see you again after all these years. Think about my offer. I'll be in touch."

My switch from booze to coffee had rendered him fit to drive, and our discussion seemed to have lifted his spirits. He decisively rose to his feet, I walked him to the back door, and he strode briskly out to his rental car. He climbed in, backed it out onto Malibu Drive, shot me a thumbs-up and took off toward the Pacific Coast Highway, next stop LAX.

I returned to my living room and admired my priceless Naheen carpet, a memento from my gig with the Shah in Iran. I sauntered out onto my deck, eased onto one of the lounge chairs and settled back into the comfy, sun-warmed pad. I shaded my eyes against the glare to follow for a few minutes the long Pacific swell as it rolled in, mounded up, toppled over and crashed foamy over the sand. I took a deep inhale of crisp, kelpy sea breeze. I got up, leaned on the railing and gazed down at a bevy of bikinied girls stretched out on bright beach towels, having an animated discussion while soaking up the dwindling afternoon autumn rays. I tracked a couple of young surfers bobbing on their boards down the way, frantically paddling and mounting up to catch what they hoped was The Big One. Newbies, making progress on their technique on five-footers, every now and then riding one in with no wipeout. It wasn't too late in the day to get my own board out...

I thought about all the stuff I'd done since my CIA assignment in 1975. I thought about the items in my souvenir drawer: Black pajamas and red ball point pen from the Khmer Rouge. The uncut diamond from Mr. Poon. The Patek Phillippe wrist watch from the Shah. The DeLorean DMC-12 Maggie Thatcher sent me that I'd passed along to Steve Spielberg. I thought about Dana Wehrli.

Life after my Cambodia horror story had been good, I had to admit, better than good. The only thing I truly missed about my Ranger career was the action, and our military hadn't been involved in much of that post-Nam. The Grenada invasion briefly took me back to my military days and reminded me what it was like, but I saw as much U. S. military action during that short week as most Rangers had seen anywhere, post-Nam. On the other hand, my free-lancing had taken me into interesting action a-plenty.

Dammit, the sonofabitch had a point. Ten years existing as an officer in the shrunken, scaled-back peacetime Army, devoting my energies to politicking my way to the next promotion, would have sent me mental.

I suddenly had an inkling how the water must feel when it swirls away down a drain.

The Beginning of the Story

The bills were laid out on the desk, three discrete stacks of used $20, $50 and $100 bills in paper-taped packets. It made a sizeable heap, thanks to the smaller denominations. All in hundreds it wouldn't have made much of an impression. "Everything's there, $80,000, Jake," said my lawyer/step-father, Evanston. "We counted it. Old bills, untraceable, at least by conventional methods. I suppose they could use radioactive markers or DNA, but I doubt they did."

"Did they follow the procedure we stipulated?" I asked him.

"To the letter. A messenger wearing a hoodie. fake nose-mustache-and-glasses, and gloves came into the lobby, placed the suitcase in the elevator, poked the button for the floor above this one, and left, exchanging no words or other communication with anyone. We had a temp worker, wearing gloves, go up the stairs and get it from the elevator, take it out of sight of the security cameras and transfer it into a mailbag. He sent the suitcase down the elevator back to the lobby and took the mailbag to the stairwell, where he kicked it down to our floor. Another temp worker, wearing gloves and a hoodie, fetched it back here. Are you sure you aren't overdoing your precautions?"

"Evanston, you know as well as I do the workings of the CIA. I don't want to give anybody a link between me, this money and the CIA. Especially I don't want Todd Sonarr to be able to prove I received this money from him. There's a million ways that could be used against me, so I've insisted on oral agreements and instructions all along. I have enough misgivings about taking on this assignment as it is."

EVANSTON'S LAWYER STORY

"This reminds me of one of those lawyer jokes that make the rounds," said Evanston. "A lawyer is having a drink in a bar with an older colleague, and he says, 'You've been in this business a long time. I've got an ethical dilemma. Maybe you can help me sort it out.'

'Describe the situation, and we'll see,' says the other guy.

'It was like this. I was sitting alone in my office late last night when this stranger bursts in. "People I know have worked with you, and they say you're trustworthy," the man says. "I've got one million dollars in untraceable bills in this briefcase. I want you to hold it for me overnight. Nobody knows I have it, and nobody knows I've been here. I'll come get it in the morning, and I'll pay you a thousand dollars for doing this."

'So I agreed, stowed the briefcase in my closet and returned to my work. Then I heard a horn, a screech of brakes and a loud thud outside. I looked out the window, and there was the guy who was just in the office, run over by a truck and sprawled out on the street, dead.'

'Okay. So what's your ethical dilemma?'

'Should I tell my partners?'

"But, speaking of ethics, Jake, you've got this boodle of untraceable money here. Like I've told you in the past..."

"You can't always be honest, but you must always to be legal," I recited. "Don't worry. I'll declare it as income and pay the taxes. I just don't want anybody to be able to connect me with the CIA. Including the CIA."

* * *

YES, I'D SIGNED ONTO TODD SONARR'S SCHEME TO COVERTLY help Ferdinand Marcos stay in power. A major motive was money, of course, as I had some deficits to cover, but big gigs like this one are few and far between, and the word gets around. For the sake of my so-called career, I couldn't pass it up, despite my aversion to the CIA. Before I accepted the assignment I researched the Philippines as best I could, and it seemed a safe enough way to rehabilitate my crippled coffers, so I worked him up from his initial offer. According to the best public sources, on the face of it the Philippines is an allied country in good standing. They don't seem to be facing an armed insurrection or a religious revolution. A contested election, yes, but they have a long history of those, and the country has been reasonably law-and-orderly for the past 20 years. I didn't have a dog in that fight, so what the hell?

Sonarr didn't want me to be seen at Langley, or anywhere around DC, so in early October he flew me back to New York City for a final briefing. I'd caught an early non-stop from LAX so arrived in late afternoon. As instructed, I took a cab from JFK to the Plaza Hotel in Manhattan and asked at the desk for Mr. Gladstone. "Yes, he's expecting you, sir," said the clerk. He gave me the room number and up I went.

Sonarr answered my rap on the door. He poked his head out the doorway and looked up and down the hall, "Nobody out there. Good. Come in, Jake," he said, stepping aside, "come on in." I did. He then shut the door quickly but quietly. It was a posh suite, could have passed for the display window of an upscale antique shop. He ushered me into the sitting area. "Get you a drink?" he offered.

"I could use some refreshment after eight hours in transit, sure."

He motioned me to an armchair that one of the French Louis might have sat in, then filled two glasses with ice and Glenfiddich, his quaff of choice. Handing me one, he plonked down on the tufted, buttery leather loveseat facing me. "Confusion to the enemy," he said, hoisting his glass. I did likewise. "Jake, I am delighted that you chose to join our team for this mission. A great relief to all concerned."

"After giving it some thought, it seemed like maybe I could help you out. Depending on what it is that you want done, of course. Now that I'm on board, how about telling me what I'm supposed to do."

"Like I told you previously, we want to make sure that the Commies don't steal the upcoming election from Ferdinand Marcos. We want to keep the Philippines firmly in our camp."

"Okay, but what do you want me to do, specifically?"

"If we knew that, specifically, we'd just send somebody from the Company in to do it. I'm sending you over there because you have a knack for getting to the crux of difficult situations and then resolving them."

"You mean I just go in there cold, and in a couple weeks I sort out a contested election taking place across 7,000 islands? Todd, I hope you haven't been reading that CIA legend you fabricated for me. I'm not a superspy, and you know it."

"Jake, I know exactly what you are and what you can do, and I'm confident you can do this. Above all, I know that I can count on you, when the chips are down, to do the right thing."

"Fill me in on what you have in mind, and we'll see. What cover are you sending me in under? What resources will I have? What back-up?"

"You're going in as an investment banker and loan syndicator, a director and vice president of Thermite Holdings, a very private banking concern. We'll use your old Cambodian a.k.a., Jack Philco. I've updated the documents. You will have credible credentials and an office here in New York, and I, Stokes Gladstone, president and managing director, will personally vouch for you. You will have a bank account you can draw on and an unlimited credit card. We will lay groundwork for you before you reach Manila. You'll assess the situation, formulate some strategy, then get back to me. At that point, if it looks like a go, we'll disclose your role to Marcos, and you will work with him, with the back-up of the Filipino army and secret service."

"Why not just tell Marcos about me from the outset??"

"Ummm ... Ferdinand Marcos is a staunch ally of the United States, but we have reason to believe that he is not always forthcoming. Steele Bosserman and I thought it would be best if you did your own fact-finding at first. And that's the beauty of your cover. The Philippine government is desperate for loans. You'll be treated like royalty. You can ask any questions you want, and they'll fall all over themselves to accommodate you. Not that you can necessarily trust their answers, but with your intel background that shouldn't be a problem."

"Suppose they ask *me* questions? I don't know anything about investment banking."

"You don't have to tell them anything. Bankers are the most discreet folks in the world. You're sizing *them* up, not vice versa. Cards close to your vest. Mysterious smiles and nods. Loose lips sink ships. And if they make any inquiries, your office here will back you all the way. So you pump them for all the information you can get, and in return you tell them nothing."

"What about coaching and costuming for the role?"

"Got that covered. We have good contacts in the big banking houses, and one of our guys will give you a tour and tutorial. As for costuming, the New York clothiers all are stocking winter fashions, so I've arranged for a tailor to outfit you with some tropical weight banker togs. You'll have a room here in the Plaza for as long as the suits and the coaching take. It's the kind of place high-powered investment bankers stay. Then you fly out to LA, get yourself straightened out and your affairs in order, and off you go to Manila.

What we'll do is put you up in a hotel in L.A., logical for a New York banker headed to Asia, just in case anybody in Manila does some back-checking. You can drive from there over to Malibu to take care of things."

Sonarr had finished his drink. I'd barely begun mine. "Get you a refill, top you up?" he offered. Negative. He rose and went to the bar to pour himself one.

"Todd," I said to his back, "I still don't understand the urgency here. We've got a lot of allies in Asia—Japan, Taiwan, Singapore, Australia. A big presence in Guam, thousands of troops stationed in South Korea. What makes the Philippines so crucial?"

"Jake, few people appreciate the gravity of this situation. When the Commies took over Cam Ranh Bay in Nam, Subic and Clark became the most important American overseas bases. We're paying $900 million a year in rents on those two bases, not to mention about twice that much in related expenditures. The Philippine government doesn't want to see those hard currency revenues go away, and we sure as hell can't lose those bases. You're participating in a potential game changer here. If the Commies win this one, we lose control of the western Pacific, and everybody's toast."

* * *

SO I SPENT SEVERAL DAYS IN NEW YORK CITY. THE WEATHER was early-autumn crisp and clear, the leaves in Central Park just starting to turn—a pretty view from my room. I went in for initial measurements at the tailor, picked out luxurious light-weight linen and wool fabrics, and settled on conservative but form-flattering styles. The suits required two fitting sessions, but the tailors, Hong Kong Chinese, worked quickly. I dropped by Barney's and Paul Stuart's for shirts, ties and shoes that, they assured me, were what investment bankers in the Philippines sported that season. Should I ever have serious business dealings around LA, with that haberdashery I'd knock their socks off.

I spent one morning with Sonarr's contact at one of the major investment banks, we'll call him Rumford Rightway. He was a few years older than me, neither pudgy nor trim, and though his hair showed no grey, his hairline was in early stages of retreat. The picture windows in his corner office faced north and east, providing a 50-something floor view of Manhattan Island reaching away from Wall Street, the skyscrapers sharply outlined in the clear sunlight, reflections off the windows intense enough to give you a tan. On the other side, the port and river ran busy with commerce, and I could make out airliners swooping in on the approach path to JFK out on Long Island.

Apparently I wasn't the first CIA operative to use "banker" as cover, because Rumford had a chalk-talk all prepared. He earnestly explained investment banking, a way different kind of deal from the black money legerdemain of Bank of Credit and Commerce International (or so I thought at the time—I had a lot to learn). Essentially it consists of assembling and organizing large and complex financial transactions, facilitating mergers and other corporate reorganizations, and acting as a broker or financial adviser for institutional clients. I'd be posing as a loan syndicator, which he told me involves bringing together consortiums of lending institutions for extremely large loans, for example to sovereign governments. In this case, the Philippine government would be under the impression I was going to get a bunch of big banks like Rumford's together to lend them mountains of money. The Filipino officials would take great pains to impress me that the principal was safe and would be fully paid back with interest in timely fashion. They would heap reports and reams of data on me, Rumford said, and would escort me on field trips and fact-finding jaunts. They would answer all my questions, though not necessarily with the unvarnished truth.

Rumford had a sheet of banking vocabulary—"fiduciary," "collateral," "market making," "debt-to-equity ratio," "risk management," "asset-backed securities," "sovereign debt," "rocket scientists" (financial, not NASA), "portfolio insurance," "derivatives" and the like. We went over those, and by then it was lunchtime. He took me up to the executive dining room one floor below the penthouse, where we enjoyed a panoramic view of the New York metro area and ate sumptuously. Not a bad life those high-powered investment bankers led, if you didn't mind spending 60 hours every week in an office, chained to a desk with your head full of figures representing huge amounts of other people's money. It's probably even worse now, with 24/7 on-call through wireless gadgetry.

After lunch he gave me a pop quiz on vocabulary by way of review, added a few helpful hints on the etiquette of the world of high finance, gave me a list of bank names to drop, and bade me farewell and good luck. From movies like *Wall Street* many people have the impression that people like Rumford Rightway are voracious, unprincipled greed machines who, when they aren't doing lines of coke and orgies with hookers, screw hapless old geezers out of their IRAs and rape the nest eggs of innocent widows and orphans. Maybe some traders are like that, maybe some bucket shop operators. From what I saw during my day at the bank, your typical investment banker was a competent, conscientious person with a good head for numbers, slaving away at a pressure-ridden job in a competitive field. Unimaginable amounts of money flow through their offices, which they never touch but only experience as many-digit, fleeting figures on a computer screen. They hope to do their jobs well enough that some of those flickering numbers will wend their way to their year-end bonuses, making what struck me as a dull and stressful life worthwhile for them.

On the plus side, nobody tries to kill them.

* * *

I BOUGHT SUITABLE LUGGAGE, PACKED IT WITH MY NEW wardrobe, and was on my way back west five days after I arrived. My "bank" flew me out to L.A. in a private Gulfstream jet and limo'd me to the Bonaventure Hotel. I hadn't set foot there since I was a bit player in an FBI surveillance tape of John DeLorean's drug schemes. Nothing needed doing in Los Angeles proper, so after I got settled into my room I rented a BMW 535 to get over to Malibu and make preparations from my trip. I left my new duds in the room, figuring nobody would be tailing me, because at this point Jack Philco, New York investment banker, was not a person of interest. Any back-check would find what counted on paper—the flight plan, the hotel, the rental car. First order of business was to retrieve my Cherokee from LAX long term parking. My screenwriter neighbor was stuck on a script and thought driving down the coast with somebody in my line of work would be a good chance to sound out some ideas. I don't know what he got out of our conversation, but a few scenes in *Lethal Weapon* did look familiar.

I stayed in my beach pad a few days, setting it straight for an absence of four months—the estimate Todd Sonarr had given me. Dana was in town, so we made the most of that. I dropped in on Mom and Evanston in Pacific Palisades to say goodbye. Mom was as usual thrilled that I was going on some kind of secret mission, something to brag to her canasta buddies about. Evanston had some last minute thoughts to impart.

"I like your cover, Jake," he said. "If you play your role right, nobody's going to risk getting on the wrong side of a potential lender. The thing is, when you command that amount of money, there's a lot at stake for the borrowers. Look out for every trick in the book to get the loans. They can't strong-arm you, but bribes and blackmail can't be counted out."

"But I don't have any money to loan them."

"That's the other thing. If they find that out before you complete your mission, whatever it is, you'll be dead in the water ... maybe even literally, depending on your mission. It has something to do with Marcos?"

"I can't tell you that."

"It's a safe guess—in the Philippines, *everything* has to do with Marcos."

"He's that far-reaching?"

"Marcos reaches into every corner of everything in the Philippines, and not only there. His wife, too. They have large property holdings in Hawaii, California, New York, and other places, I'm sure. I don't think she's the brains of the outfit, but watch your back around her. To say she can be a bitch on wheels is a gross understatement. Over the years clients doing business with that pair have come out either rich or bloodied. And not always sure why it went the one way or the other."

Packing for the trip didn't take long, just a suitcase-worth. The banker clothes I'd be officially wearing were at the Bonaventure, so from home I threw things that might otherwise come in handy into my Gucci satchel from Iran. A rough outdoor outfit. Night-black kit. Sturdy running shoes. Field gear. And my silencer-fitted SIG Sauer. Dana stayed over in Malibu my last night in town. It was too late in the year to sit out on the beach in the evening chill, so we doused the living room lights and gazed through the picture window at the breakers phosphorescing in the moonlight.

"Jake, be careful this time," she said. "You had a close call in India. We'd just about given you up for lost."

"Don't worry," I told her. "That was a cosmic sucker punch. I never had a hint all that grief was coming down, and I still haven't figured it out. This time I've an idea what I'm getting into."

"You once explained to me what kind of jobs you do, and I scolded you because I couldn't get with the violence. I understand it better now. Whatever you have to do to stay safe, do it, do it, do it," she murmured.

"I always do, Whirlybird."

Breakers crashing into blue-white fire. Flutes of champagne. A gorgeous blonde in my arms. A soft king-size bed down the hall. The kind of send-off that makes a man sorry to leave.

But early the next morning I left for Manila anyhow.

First stop was the Bonaventure, to pick up my stuff and check out. I had some time to kill before my flight, so I dialed up Sarge Wallace, still stationed in South Korea. As wise in the ways of Asia as anyone I knew, I figured he might have some useful dope on the Philippines. Luck was with me, he was on base near the phone. "Jake, my main man!" he exclaimed when I identified myself. "It's been too long. I heared some things about you from Henry, of course. He said you'd smoothed the way for that Grenada invasion."

"No, not me. It was the Rangers all the way," I replied.

"What? You ain't callin' Major Henry Wallace, my kid brother, a liar, is you? You be careful there; he's the white sheep of the family." This with his growling chuckle.

"I'm calling him a good friend and a top notch soldier. Man, it did my heart good to see those guys come in there, brought back fond memories. Figure me as an innocent bystander to the action and let it go at that. How's life in South Korea?"

"You know how it is with a peacetime Army life, Jake. Training, upgrading, treading water. Can't complain. Got some little businesses going to fill my off duty hours. Brought the family over. They're counting the days back to stateside. Say, what are you up to these days, Jake?"

Sarge, as you may recall, was my mentor, guide and protector during that Saigon/Cambodia fiasco in 1975. He was the quintessential Master Sergeant, those guys who make the Army function, and therefore my go-to guy for any questions concerning the military. Sarge also ran side businesses from time to time, gold trading, tax assistance for the men, go-between where parties needed bringing together. Nothing illegal, nor even very shady, but that aspect made Sarge also my go-to guy for questions concerning the seamy side of life. And that was why I had him on the phone. "I was wondering what you could tell me about the Philippines," I said.

"Never been stationed there, that's mostly Navy and Air Force at them bases, but I've heard some things. Why are you askin'? Some job you're takin' on?"

"I'm heading over there on an assignment, yeah."

"This ain't for the CIA again, is it?"

"I can't answer that question."

"Okay, you answered it. Does that Todd Sonarr have anything to do with it?"

"Can't answer that either."

"Okay, I got the picture. What do you want to know?"

"General lay of the land, pitfalls to avoid, danger zones, intel not in the tourist guides."

"Lemme ask you this: Which side are you on?"

"The current government, Marcos."

"Okay. Marcos is a U. S. ally, but he's also crooked as a hunch-backed sidewinder. And that wife of his, Imelda, is as mean as one. They be rakin' in money with both hands, any way they can get it. He controls everything, and things happens to people that get in his way. Or her way. Jake, why you keep gettin' into these situations? That Shah in Iran, John DeLorean, that BCCI bank, now this. I ain't sayin' Marcos compares with the Khmer Rouge, but..."

"Bad news, he is?"

"Bad as they come. But being a U.S. ally, not much word of it gets out to the public. How much our government knows about it, I can't say. Probably plenty, but they don't want to badmouth a staunch ally, you know. Listen to me, Jake, you're one of the best, you can handle yourself, but you just take care now. Keep both eyes open, and one of 'em on your backtrail. And don't forget that CIA in your backtrail."

Sarge's perennial advice, always apt, and I only wish I could always follow it. Okay, I've been warned by One Who Knows. Maybe I didn't fully realize what I was getting into after all. But I still had the assignment. We chit-chatted a bit longer, and then I rang off. Time to drive to LAX for my flight to Manila.

* * *

My first surprise of the gig came when I arrived at the First Class counter for my United Airlines flight to Manila, to be told my reservation had been canceled. Before I could ramp up into high dudgeon a slightly built man in a dark business suit appeared beside me. He was Asian, with a roundish face. "I hope you will not mind, Mr. Philco," he said softly. "My name is Dominguez. My government dispatched me to welcome and assist you. President Marcos took the liberty of extending his hospitality by bringing you to our lovely country via our flagship carrier, Philippine Airlines."

Now what? "I suppose one way's as good as the other, Mr. Dominguez," I said. Generally true among foreign flagship carriers in those days, but this was a little creepy. "I appreciate your president's concern and generosity."

"Oh, you'll be pleased by PAL, I assure you," he said. "If you will come with me. My aides will see to your luggage." Two somewhat larger, business-suited men stepped over and put my bags on a cart. Mr. Dominguez guided me back out through the lobby doors to a waiting limousine, which ferried me around the LAX perimeter road to the International Terminal. He led me past a lineup of exotically-named airlines to the PAL counter, where a petite Asian clerk in a crisp uniform checked me in and sent my bags down the belt. I had misgivings about what a luggage search would come up with, but it was out of my hands now. Mr. Dominguez and his helpers shepherded me through security and exit procedures, waited with me for the boarding call, then bade me a pleasant journey as I entered the tunnel. No need to go into details of the flight, which spanned the Pacific Ocean over a period of too many hours. Suffice to say that they'd put me in the best cabin a 747 offered, and the comely flight attendants showered every possible attention short of mile-high club on me. I'd never flown so luxuriously before. Creepy aspects aside, I can't say I minded the airline swap at all.

My seat was sufficiently large, comfortable and private that I caught decent sleep en route. We arrived in Manila after dark, so I couldn't get much of a look at the place as we came in—blackness fronting a clutch of bright lights, a dimmer surround stretching quite a distance, and beyond that more blackness. My seating qualified me to be an early de-planer. A squad of several slight and several husky, business-suited Filipinos awaited me as I emerged into a modern, gleaming concourse. They greeted me with gracious enthusiasm, collected my passport and customs forms, then led me straight to an equally well-appointed lobby, and from there to a Mercedes sedan sitting at the curb. No passport lines for visiting investment bankers? I'd been looking forward to getting my freshly forged but expertly weathered "Jack Philco" passport stamped for the Philippines, adding to the numerous stamps for Switzerland, Belgium, the United Kingdom and other countries where I'd traveled for banking business.

They led me through the glass doors, and I got my first taste of Manila as heavy, steamy air enveloped me, pretty much the same as in Nam and Thailand, and this in the dry season. My tropical weight suit wasn't nearly tropical-weight enough. My banker's wardrobe included short-sleeved shirts, which I'd be make sure to put on whenever I couldn't take refuge in air-conditioning. Which, to my relief, the limo had. Porters brought my bags out and loaded them in the trunk, and the driver whisked us over broad boulevards through light, late-night traffic to my next surprise. "I'm booked at the Intercontinental Hotel," I protested, as the limo pulled up at the portal of the Manila Hotel.

"President Marcos thought you would be better accommodated here," my greeter said, "so we took the liberty..." You can't tell much at first glance by night, but the floodlit façade of the building looked austere and faded. The uniformed doorman ushered me out of the car and through a revolving door, and it was like cutting open a kiwi fruit. That grey exterior contained a sprawling, elegant lobby of arcades, plush armchairs and glittering chandeliers. My greeter returned my documents, said a few words to the desk clerk, and before I knew it a bellman had conveyed me into a very fine suite of rooms that didn't reach Plaza-level luxury but came close enough. The bellman stowed my bags and refused my tip. I checked my luggage. It showed no signs of having been tampered with. Was I being paranoid? Why would they surveil an incoming investment banker? I undressed, showered, tossed aside the throw-pillows and hit the rack.

Killing me with kindness? No, Manila had other methods, should the need arise.

* * *

DEEP SLEEP CARRIED ME THROUGH THE NIGHT TO MID-MORNING, when bright sunlight intruding around the drapes finally roused me. I made a cup of coffee from the set-up on the sideboard, munched a starfruit from the welcome basket, cleaned up and went down for an early lunch. Sleep schedule was one adjustment to jet-lag, and meal schedule was another. The mental haziness inflicted by eight time zones of jet-lag takes a while to shake. You need to stay awake through the first day no matter what and go to bed at a normal hour. Todd Sonarr had given me a list of people to contact, and he told me I should touch base with the economic counselor at the U.S. Embassy. Plus there were several messages from Philippine government functionaries waiting for me when I got to the lobby. But it wouldn't do me any good to meet with people my first day in town while still befogged from a trans-Pacific flight.

After lunch I took a cab over to the Bank of America to get finances squared away. Sonarr had sent me off with a wad of cash and a thick envelope of travelers cheques. I verified that my account there was in good order and changed half the cash into Philippine pisos, leaving me with an even heavier wad of bills than I came in with. Nothing else needed immediate attention, so I went back to the Manila Hotel, stashed my dollars and t-cheques in the hotel safe, and set about reconning my new base of operations. By light of day it had plenty of charm. My room overlooked Manila Bay, a view that framed memorably colorful sunsets. The lobby sported shops as chic as any, anywhere. Sleek restaurants offered a variety of cuisines. The fitness center was well-equipped, and out back I found an inviting pool with a canopied bar, nestled among palms. I returned to the suite and made a surreptitious scan to locate cameras and bugs I suspected were there. Then I sat down at the desk in my suite to straighten out my paperwork. They'd got my passport stamped somewhere along the line and dealt with the rest of entry documentation as well. I sorted my messages, pulled out Sonarr's list and started on drafting a plan of attack to support my cover as a big-bucks loan syndicator. As my first step, I called the Embassy and made an appointment to see the economic counselor, I'll call him "Taunton Trustworth," the day after next—which actually was the day after that, as I'd flown over the International Dateline into tomorrow. Sound confusing? Blame it on jet-lag.

Then I assessed my list of various government figures I should talk to, also newspaper publishers and editors, college professors, bankers and businessmen. The pretext for the interviews was to sound out the economic climate in consideration of making loans, but what I'd really be doing was getting a handle on the election Sonarr assured me was imminent. I drafted a tentative plan, figuring maybe one meeting per day, no more than two, starting with key people and seeing where things snowballed from there. It was the tail end of October, giving me plenty of time before an election took place. What I could do to thwart the Communists remained to be seen. I assumed that after I reported to Sonarr and he disclosed my role to the government, I'd coordinate with the Filipino Army and the local police. And then I'd serve in an advisory capacity? What could I learn from interviewing people here, that the Filipino government didn't know already, I wondered?

I worked over my lists, then went down and got a tourist guide book and some brochures in the lobby. I took my reading out by the pool, found a seat at a little table in the shade and ordered a San Miguel, the local beer of note. Presently the clock said dinnertime, though my stomach was primed for breakfast. You can't let your stomach boss you around and hope to beat jet-lag, so I took a light dinner in the Chinese restaurant. Afterwards I returned to my room, extracted a little bottle of scotch from the minibar and forced myself to stay awake to 11 p.m. by exploring what Filipino television had to offer. News broadcasts. Chop-socky movies. Sports they don't play in America. Game shows even sillier than ours. And finally, mercifully, zzzzzzzzzzzz.

I rose late the next morning still feeling behind the curve. Rather than undertake serious work I opted for a day-long tour of Corregidor, that famous World War Two bastion. The boat ride across Manila Bay provided a refreshing breeze, and I've always liked being out on the water. My prior images of this setting came from a movie about PT Boats in the Philippines, *They Were Expendable,* which I later learned was filmed in Florida; but the look was close enough. The Rock, fortified and honeycombed with man-made tunnels and caverns, is impressive. The stats on the American defeat in 1942 shocked my post-Nam sensibilities—more than 20,000 American personnel were left behind to be captured by the Japanese and death-marched to murderous POW camps. What kind of outrage would the *New York Times* headline writers make of that in the present day?

My third morning in Manila I had the desk awaken me at a normal hour, and after breakfast I readied myself to see Taunton Trustworth. The American Embassy sat on the other side of Rizal Park, about a half mile away. On my own, in suitable clothes, I'd have walked it for the exercise, but an investment banker in suit and tie facing that muggy heat would naturally be driven. Wouldn't do to arrive sweaty! The doorman put me in a cab, and he, too, refused a tip, saying, "It has been seen to, Mr. Philco."

The U. S. Embassy commanded as fine a view of the Bay as the Manila Hotel's. It was a building in Federal style dating back to pre-World War Two, three solid, tree-shaded stories announced by a large, bronze placard by the gate. The driver dropped me off at the entrance. I presented myself to the receptionist, and after a short wait a clerk led me to the office of the economic counselor. Taunton Trustworth was standard issue foreign service, which is to say competent and seasoned by a series of shifting overseas assignments. He rose to welcome me, and then I took a seat opposite him at his desk. He perused my card and said, "I'm not familiar with Thermite Holdings, Mr. Philco."

"It's a closely-held, private concern based in New York," I said. "We don't command large assets ourselves or work much in the public eye, but rather serve as advisors and facilitators."

"And what is your interest in the Philippines?"

"Loan syndication. We are investigating the possibilities for assembling a consortium to float a loan to the Philippine government. My role is advance scout, to assess the situation."

Trustworth looked thoughtful as he weighed his next words. "We are not authorized to make invidious public statements concerning our host countries, Mr. Philco, but I would strongly advise you to exercise due diligence, *extremely* due diligence, before conducting business with the Marcos government. Do not be misled by the red carpet treatment. They do that for everyone whom they think might bring money their way."

"Our principals are risk-averse, let me assure you, and any loans would be structured according to that constraint. You're suggesting there might be problems?"

"Just a couple weeks ago President Reagan dispatched Senator Philip Laxalt of Nevada as a special envoy to look into unrest here. It seems opposition to the Marcos regime has been building ever since the assassination of Benigno Aquino and in the past months has reached troubling levels. Senator Laxalt was not pleased by what he observed, and apparently Marcos reciprocated that sentiment. After he left one of the Marcos newspapers was headlined, 'Good Riddance.' So yes, there might be problems."

"I've heard an election might take place soon."

"There are rumblings about that circulating, yes."

"Could Marcos be deposed? That would certainly raise cautions regarding a loan."

"No chance of an election resulting in that. No matter how the people vote, Marcos won't lose the election."

"Couldn't the opposition steal it?"

"Steal an election from Ferdinand Marcos? What a joke. Stalin famously observed that it's not the people who vote that count, it's the people who count the votes, and in Philippine elections, Marcos's gang collects the vote, counts it and reports it. An election would be just for show. No one of stature will run against him, and even if someone somehow got more votes on Election Day, Marcos would prevail in the end. His term runs until 1987, but with the current turmoil he might feel a need to demonstrate his support. He's under a lot of pressure right now."

"Very interesting and informative," I remarked. "We hadn't heard. It's a good thing I came to see for myself. "

"That's always wise, dealing with these, um, developing nations. Anything else I can do for you, Mr. Philco?"

"What about the New People's Army? I've heard that name mentioned. Are they a threat to Marcos?"

"A ragtag, disorganized bunch. They might raise a ruckus here and then, protests, demonstrations, maybe some guerilla skirmishes and ambushes out in the rural districts and so forth, but no, no serious threat. Anything else?"

"Not right now. You've been very helpful already, Mr. Trustworth. I thank you."

"Don't hesitate to call if I can be of further assistance. A pleasure meeting you. Good luck with your investigations. And be careful. An unwary visitor here can find himself in trouble."

I took a cab back to my hotel. Three days in town and already I gathered valuable intel. Like, who had Steele Bosserman been talking to? Taunton Trustworth saw no danger of the opposition winning an election from Marcos, nor saw the National People's Army any kind of serious threat. It was a clear-cut proposition: either the U. S. State Department had their heads up their butts, or the CIA did.

* * *

AFTER LUNCH I HIT THE EXERCISE ROOM HARD, THINKING THAT some physical fatigue would push me closer to jet-lag adjust. Afterwards I went out to the pool. It was empty enough for strenuous laps to the point of muscle-tax. I'd have no trouble getting to sleep that night. I found a table in the shade and sipped a couple San Miguels while I took stock of the beauties decorating the pool. Filipina women tend to be small, trim and of a soft beauty. Don't take my word for it. The Philippines have produced more Miss Universe finalists than most other countries.

Having accomplished what I'd set out to do, I drifted through the rest of the day, ate a full dinner and settled in my suite for the evening. I'd planned out the next day and had tuned the TV to a sepak takraw match, an amazing Southeast Asian sport, essentially teams playing volleyball with their feet. Around 9 o'clock, someone rapped gently on my door. I opened it to find one of those Filipina beauties gazing up at me. Well, not exactly Filipina—her softly filled-out face had western features, especially those striking ice-blue eyes. Her mane of loosely waved, brown-black hair definitely was indigenous, ditto her petite body, closely sheathed in lustrous tangerine silk. "Yes?" I inquired.

"Good evening, Mr. Philco, I am Luz," she said. "A friend sent me to pay you a visit. Men get lonely far from home. Welcome to Manila."

More government hospitality, "taking the liberty to"? Or a honey trap? I may be over-suspicious, but I thought I'd spotted a camera in the bedroom, and it takes an expert to locate all the bugs. "One moment," I said. I closed the door softly, slipped into my loafers, tossed my linen blazer on over my polo shirt and grabbed my room key. Rejoining Luz in the hallway, I said, "I'm happy you came. I was just getting ready to go downstairs for a drink. Would you like to join me?"

"Yes, I would enjoy that," she said. I guided her to the elevator. "How do you like Manila?" she asked by way of conversation.

"Very nice so far, but I've only been here three days."

"Yes, your friend said you had just arrived. You haven't seen much of the city then. Not all of it is nice, but you are in the best hotel."

We sat down at a remote table in the bar. She said a Coke would be fine (not a bar girl, or she would have ordered a champagne cocktail), and I ordered a gin and tonic. "Luz," I said. "Beautiful ladies don't usually come to my hotel rooms in strange cities my third night in town. You say a friend of mine sent you? What is my friend's name?"

"I was instructed not to tell you, it was to be an anonymous gift."

"I don't mean to insult you, but I imagine there must be some matter of money here?"

"Yes, it is a professional arrangement. I have already been paid. For you it is on the house, as they say."

"That was very thoughtful of my friend, but I don't think tonight is going to work out well for what he had in mind. You seem like a nice girl. Is this what you do for a living?"

"It is not quite what you think. I am an escort, not a street whore. Oh, I know I sometimes do what they do, but it's different."

It's always different, I thought. "You are very well spoken. You are a very striking woman. Tell me a little about yourself."

LUZ'S STORY

"I never intended to become an escort; I suppose few girls do, even here in the Philippines, but that is the way things have worked out. You see, I am of mixed race—American and Filipino. There are many thousands of us here, from the men at the military bases getting it on with the local ladies. I never knew my father. Filipinos are tolerant of racial mixes, for we have always had many races—native, Chinese, Spanish, American—but not to know your father is disgraceful. My mother tells me he was an American Marine, stationed at Subic Bay. His name was 'Lance' something..."

"Corporal?" I suggested.

"Yes, something like that, I think. Mum was very much in love with him, but then he was sent to another posting, and soon after that Mum discovered I was on the way. She never heard from him after that and told me that he had been killed in action. Her family took her back in, and the whole family raised me. Though we were poor, I enjoyed a happy childhood. I had no advantages, but I did well in the Catholic school and received scholarships, and in due time I earned a teaching credential. My grades were top notch, but considering my background, I could not hope for a plum assignment, of course. In fact I was fortunate: many girls with credentials cannot find teaching jobs at all. I took an assignment on a remote island teaching in a poor tribal school. It was hell. I could barely understand the local language, and the children were wild animals with no interest in learning anything. I was cut off from the city life I preferred, the pay was a pittance and the village men wouldn't leave me alone. Before my first year was out I broke my contract and returned to Manila. Because I broke my contract I had no prospects of another teaching job.

"Many Filipino girls with credentials who can't find work here hire out as maids in wealthier countries. A placement agency arranged for me to work as a maid for a Chinese family in Singapore. At first it seemed like a good situation, and it could have been far worse, for some agencies are nothing but fronts for sex trafficking. Singapore is a wealthy and pretty place: there are no slums at all. But the lady of the house treated me like a slave, ordering me to do petty and useless things even when I had already done all my duties—she wanted to get her money's worth, I suppose. The children were nice enough, but the husband soon had eyes for me. Not that he could come after me, because the wife wouldn't let me out of her sight. She would never leave me alone in the house for fear that I might steal something or make telephone calls to back home, so they dragged me along everywhere they went.

"Two years was enough of that kind of life. At the end of my contract I bought gold with my saved wages and returned to Manila, though I had no plans for making a living. My mother's aunt saw me soon after I arrived, and she exclaimed over my beauty. She operates a network of cultured, beautiful young girls whom she supplies as escorts. Yes, bedtime could be part of the service, but the main thing was that they are publicly presentable and companionable, as they are often hired as arm-candy, as they say. It took some getting used to, as I had to overcome my shyness, but now I enjoy my work. Generally the clientele are decent men —government officials, businessmen, wealthy foreigners. I am paid well for my time, and I inhabit a much better world than most teachers and maids do. I think I have several years before my beauty will begin to fade, and in that time, who knows, I may meet a big spender who takes a fancy to me. It happens. One can hope. Look at Evita Peron."

"A big spender?"

"Like in the Shirley MacLaine movie about the dancehall girls. Such a sad movie. But where they work, what can they expect? They will never meet big spenders there, renting themselves out for a dollar a dance, and not much more after hours. I think my situation is more favorable. Auntie assigns me only to big spenders, so it is just a matter of meeting the right one."

"I'm glad you came to see me, Luz," I said. "Tonight is not convenient, but perhaps we could get together again in a few days. I would very much like a tour of Manila, and I think you would be the perfect guide."

"I know the many sides of Manila very intimately, and I would be most happy to show them to you, Mr. Philco," she said. "It must be arranged through Auntie, of course." She pulled a little wallet from her purse and fished out a business card, which she handed me. "This is the number for you to call. Yes, I would like to guide you around Manila. And, by the way," she added with a coy smile, "I still owe you some services not yet rendered."

I rose and gave her hand a squeeze. "I'll leave you here. I'll be calling your aunt soon."

"Please do, I'd like that," she said with a smile.

The old Fonko charm? No, the poor deluded thing thought I

was a big spender. Never a dull moment in the exciting world of investment banking.

* * *

Stokes Gladstone, a.k.a. Todd Sonarr, had sent letters of introduction to contacts he thought would be worth talking to, so I had no trouble setting up appointments. The next morning I spent an hour with a couple of executives at the Philippine National Bank. They showed me charts, quoted me figures and loaded me with reports, all to the effect that a loan to the Philippine government would be as safe as houses, as secure as a mother's arms. After lunch I met with a member of the Monetary Board, the primary economic policy-making body in the Philippines. He extolled the country's bright prospects for the future, its financial stability and the unparalleled integrity of the government. In neither meeting did I get any hint of threat to the Marcos regime.

The day's meetings were upbeat and enthusiastic. At both meetings I heard great things the government would do with the loan to benefit the Filipino people. Probes I ventured about threats from opposition were brushed off like doughnut crumbs from a beat cop's shirt front. The glorious future of the Philippine nation, all my interviewees implied, sat right there in my checkbook, within easy reach of my Mont Blanc pen. The problem was, everybody seemed to be reciting lines from the same script.

The desk clerk gave me a message when I returned to the hotel. "Beth Romulo" had called, left a number and said it was urgent that I return the call. What kind of "urgent?" I wondered. I dialed her from the phone in my room. A woman with a local accent answered the phone. "Beth Romulo?" I asked.

"Un momento." And in just a moment, another woman picked up. "Hello, this is Beth Romulo." This one had a definitely American tone.

"This is Jack Philco. You left a message for me this afternoon."

"Yes, I did. Welcome to Manila, Mr. Philco. Imelda wanted me to call you. Seeing as how I'm a fellow American, she thought it would be better if I broke the ice. How are you finding our fair city?"

"I've been here only four days, but so far, so good. The people I've met have been very hospitable."

"That's the Filipino way, very welcoming, friendly people. That's why I'm calling. The Marcoses are most anxious to meet you. They're planning a little soiree for Saturday night, and Imelda is hoping you're free."

"I'm free and clear. That's great. I'd been wondering how to go about setting up a meeting. This will be a pleasure."

"As I understand the nature of your business here, the pleasure will be all theirs. It'll be for drinks and dinner, business attire, not formal. It would be best if I pick you up and fill you in on the way over."

"Fine. Why don't we have a drink here at the hotel first and get acquainted. What time will they be expecting me?"

"Ummm—they're on Filipino time."

"Which means...?"

"Any time you show up. But I think 7:30 would be right."

"So perhaps we could meet in the Manila Hotel lobby around 6:30 ... American time?"

"I'll be there. Looking forward to it. Until then."

"Yes, thank you. See you Saturday."

The name "Romulo" rang familiar. I sorted though some materials I'd picked up at the Embassy and located a Romulo, a very high ranking general in the Philippine Army. Also a very old one. The woman on the phone sounded young and American. But there must be a connection—she invited me to meet the Marcoses. How many Romulos at that level of society could there be? Todd Sonarr hadn't sent a letter directly to President Marcos, but any of several government officials who'd received them would have hastened to forward the excellent news of an American banker coming to loan them money. I'd have to bone up on my investment banking by

Friday and be primed for more than just casual chit chat. The Marcoses would be taking me very seriously.

The evening was young, and I'd had enough of languishing around the hotel. Manila's bright lights, the Ermita tourist district, lay on the other side of Rizal Park beyond the U. S. Embassy, only a klick away, a 15-minute walk. A sea breeze wafted in from the Bay, making the evening air lush rather than oppressively muggy, and I was back up to full energy. I stepped out through the portal and the doorman moved to wave a taxi over. "No cab, I'm just going over to check out the action down Roxas Boulevard. It's a nice night for a walk."

"I would strongly advise a cab, Mr. Philco," he said.

"'No problem, it isn't far, and I need to stretch my legs."

"Suit yourself, sir, but be careful."

I cut across lower Rizal Park, a broad, monument-festooned expanse lively with couples promenading along the walkways, children cavorting on the grass, and clusters of youths hanging out around obnoxiously loud boom-boxes. Further into the plaza to my left some kind of rally was in progress. I walked past the Embassy and turned up a side street to get to the nightlife on Pilar Street, which ran parallel to Roxas Boulevard, three blocks over. The street bordered a little park. At a point well-shielded from streetlights a pair of young men emerged from the shadows in the park and fell in behind me.

From behind a tree another young man stepped out in front of me, a revolver in his hand. "Your money and your watch, and we won't hurt you." His accomplices closed up quickly, flanking my back. Probably had knives. The few people who'd been on the street had drifted away from our developing tableau, leaving the four of us to sort it out on our own.

"You mean to rob me?" I asked, my hands up level with my face. The pistol looked like a .22, hardly heavy artillery. His buddies hadn't immobilized me. Amateurs.

"Shut up and hand it over," he snarled as best he could with a high-pitched juvenile voice.

"Okay, okay, okay," I said. "No problemo, my friend, right away, no problemo." I fumbled and fussed getting my wallet out, shuffling a little closer to him as I worked at it. I finally produced it and extended it part way in my hand. I stepped closer to pass it to him, and as he reached for it I dropped it on his right foot.

"Sorry," I said, and made a move to bend down for it, then quickly grabbed the wrist of his gun hand, stretching the arm out straight and giving it a hard whack from underneath with my other forearm, dislocating his elbow. The pistol fired as I ducked beneath his gun arm and backed into him, throwing him off balance. I flipped him forward over my back, slamming him hard onto the pavement in front of me, and fell on him with a knee into his stomach. I pinned his useless arm to the ground and ripped the gun from his hand. His reflexive gunshot had hit one of his buddies in the groin, who now stood there looking puzzled. The third guy glanced nervously from the one writhing on the ground, to the one with the bullet hole in him, to me now holding the pistol, then turned and took off, ducking into the nearest bushes. The final score: Fonko 3, punks 0.

Well, that put a damper on my festive mood. I pocketed the gun and called it a night. Had I worn cheaper clothes they'd probably not have bothered me, but my silk polo shirt, tailored trousers and Patek Philippe wristwatch advertised easy pickings. Too bad for the next guy they mug—if they persist in street crime, they'll be tougher customers in the future ... until they meet somebody even tougher. I walked back along Roxas Boulevard, well-lit with heavy traffic. As I passed through Rizal Park I slipped the revolver into an over-flowing trashcan. At the hotel entrance the doorman said, "Back so soon, Mr. Philco?"

"It was a more strenuous walk than I'd expected," I said. "Your advice was good. I'll take a cab next time I wish to sample the night life."

I went to the desk to get my key, and the clerk said, "Good evening, Mr. Philco. A gentleman just came calling for you. I told him you were out, and he said he would wait in the bar for a while. I believe he is still there."

"Did the gentleman leave his name?"

"Gutman, he told me. Kaspar Gutman."

What the hell is *this?* Am I supposed to deliver the Maltese falcon? First a mugging and then an encounter with a mysterious stranger. The life of an investment banker held more adventure than I'd ever dreamed possible.

The Second Part of the Story

I entered the bar and scanned around, and what else? Stocky build and a broad, unremarkable face topped with straw-blond hair —Emil Grotesqcu, my perennial KGB shadow, taking his ease on a stool at the bar. He was leaning back against it, amusedly surveying the chattery tete-a-tetes that occupied most of the tables. A tumbler a third filled with what I presumed to be vodka rocks sweated on a coaster beside his elbow. Other than being blatantly Eastern European he looked right at home in his short sleeved tropical shirt and cotton trousers. "Mr. Gutman, I presume?" I said.

"As I live and breath—Jack Philco!" he exclaimed. "It's been a long time. Last we met, as I recall, was in a Phnom Penh shop house back in, what was it, 1975?" He pumped my hand with enthusiasm. "A sight for sore eyes, yes indeed. It's been far too long. What say we go somewhere we can catch up on old times?"

"It's a nice night for an ocean-front stroll, if you don't mind the occasional mugging," I said. He nodded assent, stubbed out his cigarette and drained his drink, and we went through the lobby out into the evening. Again the doorman made to get me a cab, and again I waved him off. Once we were out of his earshot I said, "Kaspar Gutman?"

"I thought a Humphrey Bogart fan like you would get a kick out of that. *By Gad, sir, you are a character, that you are. There's never any telling what you'll say or do next, except that it's bound to be something astonishing,*" he said with a passable Sidney Greenstreet intonation.

"That's your cover name in Manila?"

"No, that was by way of a little titillation for a dear old friend. I'm at the Intercontinental Hotel, registered as Evgeny Grotelov, exporter of fine Russian vodka, here in Manila to drum up business. Since I'm here anyway, they expect me to peddle vodka. Russia needs the dollars. Matching Reagan's defense ramp-up is costing my government a lot of money, so budgets are tight for us." Then he veered serious. "Jake, I must apologize. It's been preying on my mind for months. What happened to you in Calcutta mortified me. I never intended that you should wind up a near-carcass requiring ICU treatment. It was just a prank gone terribly wrong, that's all it was. It was all my fault."

"I couldn't figure it out. I'm still at a loss. What was going on?"

EMIL GROTESQCU'S STORY

"You must remember that, after all that muss and fuss we endured criss-crossing India, we reached that train station and I persuaded you to head for Calcutta as your safest exit point? What I hadn't told you was that I'd gotten squared away with my people, and they'd arranged to extract me, which they did after we parted company. I figured you'd be okay once you arrived in Calcutta and talked to the American consulate, and I could use the Communists' political influence in Bengal to grease the skids with the local authorities. So I took the opportunity to pay you back for that elephant stampede in Cambodia—all in good fun, you understand. I gave you that bogus $100 bill and that cock-and-bull story about owing my life to a Calcutta beggar, thinking that when you bestowed it on one of them, the rest would follow you around like fruit flies behind a banana cart, pestering and pawing at you wherever you went for the rest of the day. I didn't foresee that one of them would spot the bill for a phony and the mob would riot."

"Why counterfeit money? I don't get it."

"We always use counterfeit American bills in Third-World countries. Why waste good hard currency on them? Usually there's no problem. We cover our expenses with it, and pretty soon the bills wind up in the hands of their corrupt rulers. They send them to Switzerland, where the bankers catch them, pluck them out and subtract them from their balances before they stash it in their numbered accounts. The despot won't live long enough to spend all the money he's stolen, so it makes no difference to him. In the end, nobody comes out a loser. "

"Russia prints phony U.S. currency. You spend it for stuff in a foreign country. A Swiss bank confiscates it and destroys it. So money that never existed buys real things and then disappears, and nobody loses? I don't follow the logic of that, and I'm supposed to be an investment banker," I said.

"Don't even try, Jake, don't take money too seriously. I mean, you should take it seriously in the sense that you always want to have enough of it, but don't try to understand it. Where does it come from? How much is it worth? Where does it go? How does it circulate? It's all a big con game predicated on faith. As long as everybody believes money is worth what the world's Central Bankers say it's worth, it is. Every now and then a Central Bank overplays its hand and spews out too much currency. The suckers lose confidence, the country ramps up the printing presses even higher to cover its escalating obligations and you get hyperinflation and economic collapse. But usually the system chugs along. Press any economist or finance guru far enough concerning the essence of money and he finally has to admit that it's basically a matter of faith. The experts, I mean. Your average economist doesn't have a clue, believes what they told him in university, and if you probe too deeply with them they'll take refuge in railing and ranting about gold reserves, exchange rates, scientifically-based monetary controls and the like."

"I'm glad to hear you didn't get me mob-stomped on purpose, anyhow."

"Jake, such a possibility never entered my mind—live and learn. As I've told you before, you're my iron rice bowl. I'm running a KGB desk devoted to thwarting Jake Fonko, CIA Super Agent. You've gotten me promotions. They've raised my budget on account of you. You've saved me from assignments on some terrible KGB missions. Well, the reports I submit to my superiors about your exploits are a factor. What you accomplished in Iran, Northern Ireland, Cambodia and Grenada was genuine, but I window-dressed it a bit to suit my own needs.

"I might as well come clean on that India fiasco," he continued. "The whole thing originated in KGB internal politics. I work in counter-intelligence, and we do our best to keep our activities in strictest secrecy. Now, there's an old Russian story about peasant Boris, who has a goat, and his neighbor, Igor, who doesn't. Igor finds a bottle, he rubs it, a genie appears, and he offers Igor one wish. Igor says, 'I wish Boris's goat would die.' So sadly typical of Russia at all levels. One of my rivals in counter-intelligence was jealous of my sinecure, because he couldn't figure one out for himself. He therefore went to someone he knew in the India section with a brilliant plan. He'd stolen a peek at the reports I'd written. He told them of legendary Jake Fonko, of how this CIA Super Operative had eluded the KGB for nearly a decade, how he had foiled us time and again. So his plan was to lure you to Amritsar, where frictions between the Sikhs and the government had worsened to the point that Sikh rebels had taken control of the Golden Temple. If we could get you to touch off a civil war, then our propaganda machine would go into high gear and paint the whole thing as resulting from CIA subversion of Indian political affairs.

"Your corpse was to be the evidence. After you left your hotel on that fateful day our operatives broke into your room and stole your belongings. As you'd gone there under your own name, they had all the proof they needed. You see the beauty of it? The India section scores a coup, the KGB pulls a thorn out of its side, and Boris's goat dies—I'd lose my cushy racket. The scheme unfolded as conceived until you made your break, slipped out of the Temple and escaped the trap. Then it was every man for himself. Only then did I learn of the plot. I sped straightaway to India to help you out of your jam. You led me on a merry chase before I caught up with you."

"With so many people pursuing me, I wasn't taking chances. But we barely got started when you wound up in that Gwalior jail."

"My rival's doing. He learned I'd high-tailed it to India and had his friend in the India section rat me out to Indian security as a Russian infiltrator. God, the filth of that cell! The rats weren't even the worst of it. I'd about given up hope when you broke in and sprang me."

"You can thank the Bandit Queen. We got word of a Russian in prison. She checked it out, determined it was you. Her gang took care of it. It wasn't the first jailbreak they'd pulled. Mostly I think they did it the old fashioned way, a few bucks to the guard. I thought your tipping them a Benjamin was a nice gesture."

"Are you sure she was *the* Bandit Queen? Phoolan Devi was in custody at that time."

"She said she was a bandit queen, and she commanded a gang of thugs. There might be more than one bandit queen in that screwed up country. Once we got you out, I was glad to get away from her. I mean, we had some fun trying out *Kama Sutra* positions, but the guys in her gang were real swine. Another thing I can't figure out—why didn't you try harder to get us out of there? You had cash and contacts. Wasn't there some way?"

"The situation was clogged up because of KGB office politics, and not only did you have no documents, but mine were left behind when you sprung me—and the Indians are sticklers about documents. Also, I hoped maybe you could do something noteworthy to clear your name and provide me with fodder for my after-action report. I thought we had a good one in Agra when we came across that Sikh plot to blow up the dome of the Taj Mahal, but then the police caught us as we were taking the explosives out of the space between the inner and outer masonry shells. They assumed we were putting them *in*, and from then on we were wanted for that, on top of everything else."

"What a disaster that was," I put in. "So close to getting clear, and then we had to backtrack with the Indian Army at our heels. I thought we'd at least found some breathing space in Srinigar among those lotus-eaters on the houseboats, but those floating carpet peddlers blew our cover to the Pakistani terrorists and we had to beat it."

"Sheer genius, rigging that sail with a bedsheet," Grotesqcu continued. "You got us all the way across the lake in the dead of night. Too bad we had to scuttle the houseboat to throw them off our tracks; it was an elegant piece of craftsmanship. Those harrowing weeks that ensued, scuffling our way from Kashmir to New Delhi! If we'd reached there in time to prevent Indira Gandhi's assassination, that might have gotten us clear, but just our luck to arrive a hair too late and get the blame for that, too. Thank goodness for the ineptitude of the Indian authorities, but it was a close call."

"Not so close, thanks to your hot-wiring that armored car."

"Nothing to it," Grotesqcu said. "It was a knock-off of a Russian make, and luckily the gas tank had enough fuel in it to reach the Chinese border. Then those sirens went off and the guards on both sides opened fire, and we had to abandon it and head back south. At times I feared we'd never manage to get home. If that flight crew hadn't left their transport plane unattended with engines idling for a tiffin break, we might still be lurching back and forth, dodging pursuers and living by our wits. I thought we'd made our way free, until Pakistan scrambled their jets and chased us back over the border."

"Oh well," I said, "here we are, hale, hearty and alive to tell the tale."

"And what a Munchausen-esque tale it turned out to be, "Grotesqcu marveled. "I doubt any fiction writer venturing to invent such an odyssey out of his imagination would have the genius to succeed."

"After my little war, all I wanted was to go home. But that's behind us, just water under the dam now. How about you? Things work out okay?"

"I'm sorry to say that my KGB rival met with an unfortunate fate. Someone blew up his apartment building—we usually blame Chechen terrorists for such happenstances—and, alas, he and all his family perished. The poor fellow was honored with a hero's burial. At that point my fortunes reversed. Office politics cleared up, freeing my department to smooth things over with the Indian authorities. That done, I could safely send you on your way. The whole episode was a gigantic cock-up, beginning to end, but at least we got out alive. So, what brings you to Manila, Jake?"

"You're a professional spy. Earn your pay and find out for yourself."

"Ha ha. I suppose you're going to deny as usual that you're here on CIA business?"

"No, I won't deny it."

"Now you're getting cagey. What was that you said earlier about occasional muggings?"

"Some punks jumped me on my way over to the bright lights and good times in the Ermita district, an annoyance, nothing more."

"Doesn't surprise me. Manila reeks with crime, from the streets all the way to the top."

"Does that open opportunities for the Communists?"

"Here? No, we've never had much luck; they lack the ambition even to aspire to Communism. How does that aphorism go? First the Spanish came to the Philippines and taught the natives to be lazy. Then the Chinese came and taught them to be corrupt. Then the Americans came and taught them to be spendthrift. Consequently, the masses have never risen to the level of a proletariat. There's a Communist Party of the Philippines, the CPP, and we have our usual people in the schools, the labor unions, the media and the intelligentsia, of course. A smattering of useful idiots here and there ..."

"What about the New People's Army? Aren't they on your side?"

"Our vaunted 'armed wing'? If you call World War Two

Garands and rusted Crag rifles 'arms'? Their numbers have grown since Marcos declared martial law in 1972, from maybe 1,000 then, up to more than 10.000 now. They're hardly in a position to overthrow Marcos. They stage sporadic hit-and-run raids out in the islands—this is a wild and wooly country—but Filipinos are notoriously hard to organize. When America thrashed the Spanish in 1898 they inherited the Philippines, up 'til then a Spanish colony. The Filipino rebels, led by General Emilio Aguinaldo, had the naive notion that independence from Spain meant independence for the Philippines, and disabusing them of that fantasy was a long, bloody struggle. At one point the Americans had 4,800 men stationed in the town of San Fernando. Aguinaldo surrounded the town with his entire force of 7,000, broke it up into small groups so as to avoid detection, and ordered all groups to converge on the town at three in the morning. They could have captured the entire American garrison at a single stroke, except that none of his commanders appreciated the point of simultaneous attack. They went in when they felt like it, some units not arriving until the battle was long over. Consequently after the first attack the Americans simply wiped out each group as they came in.

"Don't get me wrong—Filipinos can be brave and determined fighters. Your .45 automatic pistol was inspired by this country. The Filipino insurgents ambushed American patrols, charging at them from the bushes with their bolo knives and inflicting terrible damage before they were subdued. The army needed a side-arm that would stop a man in his tracks at close quarters, hence the Colt M1911."

We'd reached the waterfront and strolled a way down the Bayside. It was one of those languid tropical nights where the sea breeze stirred the muggy air enough to keep the heat from settling down over the land. Emil and I turned around and sauntered back, catching up on things, swapping notes on recent world events— Palestinian terrorists had just hijacked a cruise ship, the *Achille Lauro*, in the Mediterranean Sea and tossed an old man in a wheel chair overboard—an act disgusting even to a KGB agent. We passed packs of loitering young men, but they must have picked up lethalness vibes, for none paid us more than cursory attention. Back at my hotel's portal the doorman waved a cab over. Grotesqcu handed me a business card and said, "Mr. Philco, I hope I've made my case for Russian vodka. We perfected it, and the competition can't compare. I'll be in Manila for a while, so don't hesitate to ring me up if I can be of service."

"Thanks, Mr. Grotelov, I'll do that, and you know where to find me. Enjoyed the evening."

"By the way, Jack," he said under his breath, "I don't mean to meddle in your love life, but that girlfriend of yours, the blonde that flew to Calcutta for you? She's a keeper. Don't let that one get away. Ciao."

The doorman closed the cab door on him, and Grotesqcu took off. Damn. I was growing to like the sonofabitch.

The Filipinos were too lazy even to be Communists? What kind of threat was *that* to Marcos?

* * *

DURING THE NEXT TWO DAYS I INTERVIEWED A NEWSPAPER publisher, executives with the country's largest sugar company and an economics professor at the University of the Philippines. They covered the same dot-points I'd heard in my previous interviews: the future was bright, the economy was sound, the country was solidly behind Marcos, the population was content, the loans would bring the people jobs and much needed improvements, etc, etc, etc. The spiel didn't jibe with what I saw on the ground. Anti-Marcos demonstrations and posters? Street crime? A high-living elite and a piss-poor population? Granted, Manila had a first rate airport, a well-functioning seaport, a city center boasting modern buildings and a lot of conspicuous consumption. Granted, there were problems that an infusion of capital would help solve. But the place had an unsettling feeling to it. Were I here to loan anyone money, I'd be marking bond ratings down at a rapid rate, but I'd been sent to backstop the Marcos regime. I hoped getting to know them would clarify matters.

Saturday evening arrived. Sporting my most elegant business suit I went down to the lobby to meet Beth Romulo. At 6:30 precisely a Mercedes sedan pulled up at the portal. An Anglo woman got out. The doorman greeted her with familiarity and ushered her in, and her driver took the car away. I rose from my armchair and walked over to intercept her. "Beth Romulo?" I ventured. She was handsome and stylishly-dressed, I guessed 60-ish but carrying her age well. She fitted the voice I'd heard on the phone.

"Mr. Philco? Pleased to meet you," she said, extending a gloved hand in greeting.

"Should we go into the bar, or would you prefer to sit out here?" I asked.

"A stiff drink would suit me just fine," she said.

We found a table and a waiter took our orders. She wasn't kidding about that stiff drink—a double martini straight up. "Having a tough day?" I asked.

"Tough day, tough week, tough month, tough year. My husband, General Romulo, is very ill, probably terminally so. That's why he is not with me tonight. Imelda thought that you, a visiting American of great importance, would be a proper escort for me. So my husband, obviously, is on my mind. And then there's the disturbing business with Dr. Baccay yesterday."

"Found dead? I saw it mentioned in this morning's paper."

"Found murdered, with 19 stab wounds, but that won't be in the papers for a while, if ever. Also the papers didn't mention that he had recently disclosed to the press that Ferdinand Marcos had two kidney transplant operations, which Ferdinand had been keeping secret. It was not a coincidence. There are no coincidences in this country. It has put everyone on his guard."

"I'm sorry to hear about your husband, and I hope his situation is not dire."

"Thank you for the thought, but I'm afraid that it is. It's not as though it is some kind of tragedy. He's much older than I. It's what one expects and prepares for."

Our drinks arrived. She lifted hers and said, "Cheers."

"Cheers," I echoed, then added with a twinkle, "So tell me, Mrs. Romulo, what's a girl like you doing in a nice place like this?"

"A good question, to be sure," she replied. "Well, it's a long story…"

BETH ROMULO'S STORY

". . .but call me Beth, and I'll call you Jack, my escort for the evening, okay? I first met General Romulo in 1957 in New York City. I worked as a freelance journalist, and *Reader's Digest* assigned me to write an article about him. At the time he was both the Philippine Representative to the United Nations and also their United States Ambassador. He invited me to breakfast in New York City. Among other things, he had once been a reporter, and he structured the story he gave me in such a way that my article virtually wrote itself. Despite being several inches shorter than I, Romy was a very compelling man, dapper and fastidious. He wore custom-tailored clothing, even his pajamas, and maintained meticulous grooming. He could dominate a room simply through his self-assurance and charm. He and I were both married at the time; nevertheless we felt a mutual attraction. He was 20 years my senior, but he carried his age well and it made no difference to either of us.

"Fast forward 15 years, to 1972. He had survived a near-fatal auto accident in Manila and was back in New York City. *Reader's Digest* thought there might be another story there. I called for an appointment, and he invited me to a dinner he was hosting in honor of George and Barbara Bush, George being the U. S. Representative to the U. N. at that time. It was only then I learned that his wife, Virginia, had died four years previously, leaving Carlos a much sought-after widower. I'd become a widow myself in 1967. I began spending time with him and soon found out how revered he was in his native land—a general, a diplomat, by the end with 84 honorary degrees and nearly 200 special medals and decorations. He even served as President of the United Nations General Assembly. Oh, the man could speak! A real spellbinder. He had his difficult side, as men often do—present company excepted, I'm sure—but easily forgiven.

"I flew to Manila in 1973, as a guest of the government, to interview Ferdinand for a *Saturday Review* cover story, and *Ladies Home Journal* had asked me to write something about Imelda. I was in Manila three weeks, toward the end of which the General all but proposed marriage. He explained that an ambassador must get permission to marry a foreigner, which was impossible at that time, as Carlos was on a panel negotiating the renewal of leases for the American military bases. His marrying an American would have dubious implications. So I went back to New York to straighten things up there and returned here a few months later. He put me up in a suite in the Manila Hilton, and I was 'the girlfriend' until we married in 1978. By then everyone realized I was no threat to anyone, least of all their beloved General, so I was accepted in elite circles. Imelda, particularly, took to me—she's very much a romantic, as are Filipinas in general. And I've been here ever since, and...

". . . goodness—those martinis do loosen one's tongue! I hope I haven't bent your ear too far."

"I asked for it, didn't I? You mentioned Dr. Baccay. It sounded like there's a story behind it."

"Dr. Baccay was president of the Kidney Foundation of the Philippines, and he had revealed to the *Pittsburgh Press* that Marcos had two kidney transplant operations."

"And he was killed because of that?"

"Many suspect so. You see, Ferdinand Marcos aspires to be President forever, and he is something of a fitness nut. However, he also is a very sick man, with severe kidney disease. He kept his transplants secret, fearing that the people would not let him continue in office if they knew. A murder suspect was caught, and his motive supposedly was robbery. As usual. Though they had a difficult time asserting that in the case of Ninoy Aquino."

"Why so?"

"Because he was shot by government soldiers in front of witnesses as he stepped off a plane at the airport."

The time to depart soon arrived. Beth's car idled at the curb. The uniformed driver put us in, and we took off for Malacanang Palace, the Marcos's residence. It was about two miles away, sited on the banks of the Pasig River. En route she asked how my work was going.

"Not badly," I replied. "I'm here to investigate the possibilities of a syndicated loan to the government, and people have understandably been very helpful." I told her the list of interviews I'd had thus far. "One thing I wonder about," I said, "is that without exception they've told me pretty much the same thing. They present a good picture, but I'm surprised at the uniformity."

"You shouldn't be surprised. Marcos owns all those companies, and the newspaper publisher and the professor you talked to are in his pocket. They knew you were coming, and they were primed for it."

"He owns the bank, the telephone company and the sugar company?"

"Not necessarily 'owns.' Some, yes. Others he controls through the people he appoints. Marcos controls just about everything here—banks, sugar, coconuts, the telephone company, the television and radio stations, the newspapers. His cronies get rich, but beyond that the profits mostly flow to him and Imelda. A few years ago I wouldn't be telling you all this, but since the Aquino assassination the Philippines have been increasingly aboil. Situations are coming to a head, opposition is gaining support and Marcos feels under attack. I don't like any of it. My husband, throughout his long career in the highest levels of government, has never been party to the corruption, and that is one reason why he is so beloved by the people. We live well, that is true, but his integrity is unquestioned. Unlike most others in the elite."

Suddenly lights along the road blacked out. I looked around—few lights showed anywhere. "Now what?" I asked.

"Power outage. We have them every now and then. If you've been spending your evenings around your hotel you may not have noticed them. The Manila Hotel has a backup generator, as do other important buildings. Sometimes it's a fuel shortage—we have to import our oil and coal—and sometimes it's equipment breakdown. Sometimes, who knows? Sabotage? Work stoppage? It's not so bad here as it is on the other islands, where outages are simply part of the rhythm of life. In the better parts of Manila the government looks after its own."

The road followed the curve of the Pasig River, and presently we approached an oasis of bright lights. Two-storied and sprawling, with a complicated roofline, the Palace architecture fit no pattern I could identify. Mercedes sedans, Jaguars, Rolls-Royces, Cadillacs and other luxury rides were rolling up, disgorging Manila's elite, then shuttling over to parking areas. "Most of the guests have arrived," Beth remarked. "They don't want to miss any time at a free bar."

Uniformed butlers ushered us into a thronging, tropically-ornate reception area. The men I saw wore either fine business suits or medal-bedizened military uniforms. Their ladies augmented elegant evening gowns with cascades of pearls, diamonds and gold. I estimated around 50 people in the room. Not exactly a casual, drop-in evening. Several women circulating through the crowd wore identical, pure white gowns with odd, upthrust shoulders on the sleeves, and bright blue sashes around their midriffs. Highlights and pinpoints sprayed off the diamonds that covered them.

"Those women, they can't be household staff?" I asked Beth.

" Ha ha, no. They are Imelda's Blue Ladies," she answered. "Imelda has a large retinue of them, always on call. Most are the wives of men Ferdinand or Imelda made wealthy through business connections. Imelda will go nowhere without an entourage of them in tow. In return for their attendance she showers with them with jewelry and other gifts. And assists their husbands' pursuit of wealth, of course. For the Blue Ladies, having to be at Imelda's beck and call is a price they pay for the comfortable lives they lead."

"What's with the sleeves on those dresses?"

"They call them 'butterfly sleeves.' Very popular here. Filipina women think they enhance their beauty, as if they need any help. Come, I'll give you a quick tour and introduce you to people." The public areas of the Palace were elegant, as befits the residence of a head of state. Nowhere near the Shah's sumptuous opulence, but reaching. The Shah had 6,000 years of tradition behind him, plus fields of black-gold-spewing wells shoring up his wealth. Considering the economic development of the Philippines, Malacanang Palace's extravagance exceeded the call of vanity.

Beth led me down wide, chandelier-lit corridors, and we took peeks into dim meeting rooms, halls and salons. The other guests mostly congregated in the reception rooms where exotic, petite maids dispensed drinks and hors d'oeuvres from silver trays, so we had the rest of the place pretty much to ourselves. She explained that the Palace dated back to the early 19th century, the Spanish colonial period. After 1863 it had been the residence of the Spanish heads of government, and following them the American governors, the first civilian one being William Howard Taft before he became President and then Supreme Court Chief Justice. The building survived World War Two, serving as the Japanese headquarters, and since Independence it housed Philippine heads of state. The Marcoses had lived there since the 1960s.

Panels of lustrous dark tropical woods covered some walls. Display cases of artifacts, awards and trinkets of note lined others. I'm no art expert, but some paintings on public display looked like European masterpieces. Portraits of past rulers occupied a lot of wall space, including a surfeit of paintings and photographs of Ferdinand and Imelda. In their younger days Ferdinand was a handsome, vital man, and Imelda, with wide brown eyes and soft features in a heart-shaped face, was indisputably a knockout. "The hell's that?" I asked, pointing to a pair of large oils. One showed Ferdinand bare from the waist up, standing behind bushes in a jungle setting. The other showcased Imelda in a flowing gown posed before a dramatic sky, a wispy fog of yellows and green swirling before her.

"The Filipino Adam and Eve," Beth quipped. "Or maybe Adam and Venus. Nobody ever accused the Marcoses of having good taste."

We returned to the crowd, noisy with gossip, shop talk and good cheer. "Here's somebody you should meet," Beth said and steered me toward a short, pugnacious man in a ranking officer's uniform. "Fabian, this is Jack Philco, visiting from New York. I believe you've been told about him. Jack, this is General Fabian Ver."

"Pleased to meet you, sir," I said extending my hand.

He took it in a firm grip. "The pleasure is all mine. So you are a banker who might see his way to a loan for our government and are therefore doing some investigating?"

"That's why I'm here, yes sir," I said. Beth excused herself to fetch drinks.

"I did a little investigating of my own. I had an informative conversation with your Mr. Gladstone. But the odd thing is, asking around to other people in New York banking circles, I found no one who could tell me anything at all about your firm, Thermite Holdings."

"I'm not surprised. We are a very private concern, and the business we do with others is strictly confidential. It is to their credit that none would discuss it with you."

"Confidentiality is a virtue. We practice it here. We like to arrange financial matters out of the public eye. Funds pass from hand to hand in ways that might shrink from the light of publicity, for example considerations for friendly bankers."

"I wouldn't know about that, General Ver," I said.

"Of course not, of course not," he said with a sly smile and a little chuckle.

Beth rejoined us with champagne flutes in hand. Passing me one, she said, "We must move along, Jack. There are many people here you must talk to."

"Would you please excuse us, General Ver?" I said with a slight bow. "I am very glad to have made your acquaintance."

"I am sure we will be seeing more of each other, my friend," he said.

Away from him, I whispered to Beth, "That crook all but offered me a kickback."

"Why did it take him so long? That's why I wanted you to meet him, an example of the kind of people you're dealing with. Yes, he is a crook, and not necessarily the worst of the lot. He's a killer as well. He was Ferdinand's Chief of Staff, but he's currently on leave because he's under indictment for the murder of Ninoy Aquino. He's still in control of the National Intelligence and Security Authority."

"He doesn't show any sign of stress or strain."

"He's no reason to. Nothing's going to happen to him."

"Maybe you should tell me more about Ninoy Aquino."

"Definitely I should, and shall, but not here right now. Come along." And so I met more of Manila's A-List, the men generally enthusiastic banty roosters, the women diamond-draped little kittens and vixens, and all of the lot well-educated and full of themselves. Dinner seating put Beth and me among executives and government officials, nowhere near the Marcoses. Beth explained that I was only a visiting banker, not an emissary of state, so would not be invited to the head of the table, but Imelda had indicated that she definitely wanted to talk to me following dinner.

And so, after dessert was done, she did. "Mr. Philco, I welcome you to our lovely land. I understand you are here to assess the prospects for a large loan to the government, and I assure you that I will do everything in my power to help you with your work."

In the woman standing before me I recognized the young stunner of the photos I'd examined during my Palace tour. Now in her 50s, Imelda Marcos plainly had been a beauty not long ago. But

I recognized also something I'd seen in faded Hollywood starlets. Some women in their youth find they can get their way through beauty. But when they lose their beauty they do not lose their taste for getting their way and so develop other means, some not so nice. Imelda Marcos was one of those, and I wouldn't want to be trapped between her and a diamond bauble she coveted.

On the other hand, there were ways around those women. "Mrs. Marcos," I breathed, gently taking her hand and gazing into her eyes, "I immediately recognized you from the photos in the corridor. They were taken recently, no?"

"Oh, I'll bet you say that to all the girls," she giggled. "Please, call me Imelda."

"With pleasure, and to you I am Jack, of course." I could see from the corner of my eye Beth Romulo with difficulty holding back a guffaw.

"Are you enjoying your stay in the Manila Hotel, Jack?" Imelda asked. "It's one of my favorite places, so I arranged a little room for you. I sent a welcome woman as well."

"The Hotel is everything I could wish for, and the lady was charming. I thank you for your hospitality. Beth showed me around earlier. What a magnificent Palace this is, Imelda. No doubt it reflects the wealth of your lovely nation?"

"Yes, the Philippines are rich in resources and especially in our fine people. We wish to bring even more prosperity to our country, and that is why we need to borrow money, to build and improve these lovely islands for the future. So much promise to be awakened, so much wealth to be released."

"In my interviews the last few days I've heard much the same. Of course I'll have to make a close examination of the financial structure and assess available collateral."

"That's the reason why we held this party, Mr. Philco. So you could meet the people who matter in the Philippines. Now that you're here, I think we should talk about your mission here. Beth, could you excuse us? Go and mingle with your friends?"

"Certainly, Imelda," she said. "I'll collect you later, Jack."

"Let's get another drink, and then you come with me, Jack," Imelda said. We plucked flutes from a passing maid's tray, and Imelda led me through the still-lively crowd toward a portal. We went down a corridor and through a door into an office. "This is where I do my work," she said, shutting the door. "Please sit there," she said, waving toward a leather chair by a mahogany coffee table. She settled her still-shapely butt down on a couch on the other side.

"Jack, I can't tell you how important this loan your bank is considering is to the welfare of my country," she began. "There is unrest, which only more jobs, more education, better government services, will quell. How large a loan did your consortium have in mind?"

"Still being studied. I presume your monetary board will give me some figures as to your needs?"

"I'll make sure they do, as soon as you want."

"I'll be talking to your husband, the president about this also?"

"Of course. This very evening, in a little while. But I'm the one who will get this done, don't you worry."

"I hadn't realized. I might have known you would have a post in the government."

IMELDA'S STORY

She leaned forward and put on a knowing smile. "Not one post, but several. In addition to being First Lady, I currently serve as Governor of Metropolitan Manila and Minister of Human Settlements."

"All those duties must keep you running."

"They aren't even the half of it. Lately I've been investing property in New York City—the Crown Building, the Woolworth Building, the Herald Centre, and some others. Also properties in California, here in the Philippines, Hawaii. The Cultural Center was a project of mine, also. I'll take you on a tour. Ha ha, I've heard that people say I have an edifice complex—because of my fondness for buildings—edifices, you know.

"Plus, of course, my duties as the nation's hostess. Over the years the Pope has come to visit. Your President Ford. The Beatles, too, although they were rather rude. General Qaddafi from Libya, a very nice man. Mr. Khashoggi, from Arabia, a very influential man in influential circles. Van Cliburn, the world famous pianist, oh that man has magic in his fingers! And of course we attended the Shah's celebration in Persepolis in 1972, 2,500th anniversary of the Persian Empire—imagine that! Talk about glorious. Ever since then I've been more expansive in organizing spectacles here in the Philippines, though none like that, of course.

"And, of course, raising our children takes time and attention, not that I would trade them for anything. But it has not been all roses. In 1972 Ferdinand had to declare martial law, and later that year some man attacked me with a bolo knife, injuring my arm seriously. Lately more unrest has arisen, making for unpleasant days, and that is why this loan is so important. The funds will be spent to provide jobs and needed services to our citizens."

"One of my consortium's concerns is the security of the loan," I said, "but it sounds as though with all your properties and the assets I've observed since I've been here, collateral will be no problem?"

"Collateral?" she said. "You mean to back the loan in case of default?"

"Of course a default would be unthinkable, but nevertheless bankers are cautious folks, and they would insist on sufficient collateral. Which could certainly include future tax revenues, I might add."

"Of course, of course," she said. "Ferdinand and I would have it no other way. You will find our finances in excellent shape. As for this collateral you mention ... can you keep a confidence?"

"No one is more discreet than an investment banker."

"Have you ever heard of the Yamashita Horde?"

"I've heard stories, but I thought they were just that, stories."

"Oh no, not just stories, not at all! He was a Japanese general, Yamashita. He commanded the Japanese Army of Southeast Asia, as you may have heard. During the Occupation he looted Singapore, Malaysia, Indonesia, the Philippines of all the gold he could lay his greedy hands on. And do you know what he did with it? He had it melted into bars and brought it by ship to the Philippines, where he hid it. Billions in pure gold, imagine the wealth—beyond belief!"

"I'll bet," I said, and meant it, though in a different sense than she'd intended.

"Well, during World War Two Ferdinand stumbled across it while conducting his guerilla operations. It is the basis of our personal fortune, and we have barely tapped it. Wouldn't that be excellent collateral for these loans! Tons of pure gold bars!"

"As good as gold," I agreed.

Someone knocked on the door. "That would be the President," Imelda said. "He is not feeling well this evening, so he will just step in for a moment. Come in, dear," she spoke up to the door.

I hadn't gotten a good look at Ferdinand Marcos earlier in the evening, only saw him in bad light from across the reception room and from down the dinner table. He wore a spit-and-polish-spiffy military uniform sporting a chest full of medals so densely packed and colorful as to pass for a table of costume jewelry in a flea market. Despite that, he looked very sick. His face was bloated, his eyes were sunken above discolored bags, and he seemed to be bearing some degree of pain. It did not entirely eclipse his personal force—leadership and faded charisma showed through his distress. He reminded me of the Shah, another sick old despot. I rose to meet him. He shuffled in and offered me a hand, "I am pleased to meet you, Mr. Philco. Welcome to my country." He didn't have much grip, and he added, "You must excuse me, but I seem to have come down with a severe allergy this evening and am not my usual self." He eased himself down beside Imelda on the couch.

"I was telling Mr. Philco about your wartime exploits," she said, giving him an opening to a story he'd told many times, to many people.

FERDINAND'S STORY

"Imelda is shameless in the way she talks up my modest adventures to visitors," he said, anticipating the concept of "humblebrag" by a quarter century. "But yes, I think of myself primarily as a soldier who in his youth served the defense of his country, rather than a lawyer or a politician. It is true that I was top-notcher on the bar examination, scoring higher than everyone else who took it in 1939. And of course I have presided over the Philippines since being elected twenty years ago. But the Japanese invasion in World War Two provided my opportunity to make the contributions which give me the most pride..."

"Ferdinand is the most highly decorated soldier in Philippines history," Imelda interjected. I didn't doubt it. The number of medals fronting his chest left few available for anyone else.

"My future was still uncertain at that time," he continued. "My father in 1935 ran for re-election as assemblyman in our district at the northeastern tip of Luzon, this island. A rival won the vote, then chose to taunt my father's defeat, trying to humiliate him. The rival one night was shot and killed through his window. I was tried for that crime and convicted, the same year as my bar examination triumph. This coincidence of events gained press attention and made me something of a minor celebrity. Then a year later a judge overturned my conviction, again putting me on the front page of all the newspapers.

"In December of the next year the Japanese attacked the Philippines, simultaneously with their attacks on Pearl Harbor and Indochina. I had already enlisted in the Army as a third lieutenant, having heard the distant rumblings of impending war. I served with General MacArthur and saw him off when he evacuated by PT boat. Of course he was needed elsewhere, because America had to fight a war all across the Pacific region. But I repaired to Bataan to fight our last stand against the Japs—for which I received 12 Philippine medals for bravery and four American ones, including the Silver Star and the Distinguished Service Cross. My recommendation for the Congressional Medal of Honor was not honored, but what does one do?

"When Bataan surrendered I was taken prisoner, along with many others, and wound up in Fort Santiago, where my captors pronounced a death sentence on me. I managed to escape and fled to the hills, where I formed a guerilla group, Ang Manga Maharilka, with four other officers. We sailed to Mindanao in two boats. We conducted hit-and-run raids and smuggled radio equipment to Luzon for other guerilla units, and I for a time reported on Japanese troop strength of Bohol. Working with Colonel Fertig, I came to be in charge of two other guerilla units, the Nakar and Enriques groups, and operating in Luzon we harassed enemy supply lines and blew up three ships in the harbor, an action for which I received the Silver Star. I served as an advance scout with the famed Ghost Soldiers, whose raid rescued more than 500 prisoners, survivors of the infamous Bataan Death March, from a Japanese POW camp near the city of Cabanatuan, saving them from certain execution as the war drew to an end. When General MacArthur returned with his troops in the Philippines he promoted me by telephone to the rank of Major, lauding me as 'an Army of one man.'

"It was a harrowing four years, but I am proud to say that I served my people in their hour of need and was honored with 39 medals and decorations. After the war I actively entered politics, serving terms in our Congress and our Senate. The Philippine people hungered for effective, honest government, and so they elected me their President in 1965. One year later we signed the United Nations-sponsored International Covenant on Civil and Political Rights, another accomplishment of which I am proud. The people have seen fit to retain me as President ever since. Recently, as you may have heard, there has been unrest. That is a major reason that we were pleased to hear of the loan your bank is considering. An infusion of capital will enable us to install crucial infrastructure needed for economic development, as well as to improve services for our less fortunate citizens. Ummm ... how large a loan does your bank have in mind, if I may ask?"

"We've fixed some rough boundaries on the amount, but the final figure we propose will depend on my report. What size loan would enable your government to undertake those efforts?"

"It is a point of pride that we maintain our debt-service ratio at 20 percent on the amount we can borrow from abroad. But that pertains to long-term debt only; short-term debt is not included. So if we could create a debt structure comprising both long- and short-term debt, oh, perhaps a loan of, say two billion dollars...?"

I steeled myself not to blink. "Two billion, you say? I'm not sure our present consortium could come up with that amount, but if Philippine finances are sound and collateral is adequate, perhaps additional banks would join us. We had been thinking more in terms of around $500 million, but..."

Imelda looked pained. "We were hoping ... so much to be done..."

Ferdinand brightened up. "Mr. Philco, I can see that your investigations are far from completed. You have been here only a few days. After you have attained a more comprehensive view of our country, you will realize how much can be accomplished with a loan of the size we envisage. And how enriching for your consortium and all parties concerned that will be! Tomorrow I will make a speech over American television that will shock the world. And the day after that I will make arrangements for you to see the Philippines in the proper light. Now you will please excuse me, as my health is not at its best this evening, an old allergy came upon me, you know. Tomorrow will be a busy day, so I must get my rest. It was such a pleasure to meet you, Mr. Philco." He shuffled to the door, opened it and said something to an aide, who left. Ferdinand Marcos then faded off in the opposite direction. Imelda and I exchanged pleasantries for a minute or two, and Beth Romulo appeared at the doorway. "Are we ready to go, Jack?" she asked.

"Ferdinand sent word to meet you here. I should be getting back to my husband."

I rose and took Imelda's hand. "Imelda, I am so glad to have met you tonight," I said, giving her manicured paw a tender squeeze. "I hope it will not be the last time."

"We will have many more meetings, Jack, I can assure you," she said with a cat-at-the-canary smile. I backed out to the door, and Beth and I fled the scene.

* * *

"So, he told you all about his military exploits?"

"It sounded like a prepared speech. An Army of one man, for sure."

"All fanciful tales. My husband was there; in fact, he was General MacArthur's aide de camp. I've heard the real story, and it's not the one Ferdinand Marcos promulgates."

"So how does Marcos get away with the stories he tells?"

"Some who know the truth, such as my husband, are loyal to the Philippine government, and therefore to President Marcos, as long as he is in office. Others who know the truth also know what will happen to them if they mention it to anyone."

"Imelda seems fond of him."

"That's also for show. In fact she hardly pays attention to him at all, but goes her merry and profligate way. It's been like that for 20 years, ever since Dovie Beams. She was a third-rate American actress who came to Manila for a film shoot. Filipino men are notorious tomcats, and Ferdinand being no exception, the two of them soon fell into a torrid affair. Unlike Filipina girls, however, Dovie brought along a tape recorder, and when Ferdinand tired of her and made moves to cast her off, she went public with some very steamy sound effects. Filipina women are resigned to putting up with their husband's dalliances, but only if it is possible to ignore them. Imelda, publicly confronted with Dovie Beams, was humiliated and outraged, and she laid down the law—her way or the highway. In the ensuing years she has only extended her power and her influence. I think it's fair to say that at present she runs the country, not Ferdinand."

"I'd not dispute that, from what I saw. He remarked that he was going to make a speech on television tomorrow that will shock the world. Do you know anything about that?"

"I doubt the world will be shaken, but knowing Ferdinand, it's bound to be something astonishing," she said. "Stay tuned."

* * *

TWO BILLION DOLLARS? FIVE HUNDRED MILLION DOLLARS? What was I even talking about?

THE THIRD PART OF THE STORY

NEXT MORNING AFTER THE PARTY AT MALACANANG PALACE I went down to the lobby cafe for breakfast. I took my time, reading the morning paper over coffee following my Spanish omelet and rolls. As I passed the registration desk en route to the elevators the clerk called softly to me, beckoning me over, "Mr. Philco? A parcel arrived for you while you were in the café." He handed me a small, expensively wrapped package with an envelope affixed. In the elevator I opened the envelope and flicked out a folded piece of notepaper with an embossed gold logo. The message said: "Jack —such a pleasure meeting you last night. You will be seeing more of me, count on that. Imelda." My goodness, love letters so soon?

I shut the door to my room and prized off the giftwrap. Surprise, surprise, a brick of U.S. $100 bills—one hundred of them, by my reckoning. Love had nothing to do with it. The old Fonko charm never rated that much. It was a down payment on kickbacks to come. Little did Imelda Marcos suspect that I was bribery-proof, with no mega-loans or anything else of value to bestow in consideration. I hoped she wouldn't take it too hard when she found out. An ethical dilemma: should I turn the ten grand over to the CIA? I decided to use it for pin money, figuring it would save me trips to the bank when I needed pocket cash, which amounted to turning it over, for the time being anyway.

Marcos made his announcement live on American TV, on *This Week With David Brinkeley*. I'd no interest in hearing its bombastic entirety, but did want to collect the gist of it. A scan of the local TV channels found a news broadcast. They showed a clip of Ferdinand Marcos proclaiming that, to dispel unfounded notions circulating that the government was inept, he was calling for a snap election on January 17th to let all Filipinos express their confidence. His current term in office didn't expire for two more years, but subversive agitators were raising doubts that the people supported him, and he wanted to show the world how wrong they were. The newscaster proclaimed the speech, and the idea of the election, as a benevolent gesture and an endorsement of democracy, altogether a great thing for the proud nation, the Philippines. No surprise, since Marcos owned the station.

So Todd Sonarr was right, an election was in the offing, and my mission was on to help ensure that the opposition didn't steal it. From what I'd seen of the Philippines and the Marcos government so far, that didn't seem a major threat, but now I had something solid to focus my attention on. We'd soon see what turned up. No doubt I'd pick up useful information on the tour Marcos promised me. In the meantime, the conversation I'd had with Ferdinand and Imelda about the size of the loan had piqued my curiosity. It being Sunday morning and much of the population in church and the town pretty dead, I faced a quiet day. I planned to spend the afternoon in the pool and the fitness center, but there was time to dig through the financial data people had been showering me with at my interviews. It would provide some perspective, and in any event boning up would help me sound like I knew what I was doing, should anyone ask during the tour.

I'd had some basic financial training in the Army and some practical experience investing since then. I was passable with lower math, and I'd picked up a smattering of financial concepts from Rumford Rightway's briefing. This was before laptops with spreadsheet apps became common, so I drew out a grid on a sheet of paper. I listed a series of recent years across the columns, and down the rows I blocked out space for accounting categories—income, expenditures, debt, foreign aid, profits and losses and so forth. As I leafed through reports and sheets of data I'd collected from banks and businesses and government officials, I plugged numbers into their appropriate slots.

When I reached the bottom of my pile of paper I inspected my grid to see if any patterns emerged from the figures I'd jotted down. The picture was chaotic, but one pattern jumped out. Every year a gap showed between government revenues plus new debt, versus government expenditures. The government took in more than it spent, yet kept borrowing more money and receiving foreign aid. My jottings were a patchwork, far from official or rigorous, but the gaps were too large just to reflect missing data. I figured my exercise as a rough starting point, but that shortfall was curious. Governments usually spend more than they take in, not less. My grid showed surpluses, not deficits. Yet debt was building up. Where were the surpluses going? The CIA would have financial and economic reports on the Philippines, so I decided to call Todd tomorrow, which was to say late that night by Philippines time. I'd check in with him now that the election had been announced and also ask him to send me some recent economic data.

I returned from strenuous laps in the hotel pool to find a note slipped under my door. A Mr. Enrile had left a message to call him. I did so.

"Thank you for returning my call, Mr. Philco," he said. "I am Juan Enrile, the Minister of Defense. President Marcos asked me to call you and see about conducting you on a tour of our fair city. He was hoping you would be free to do that tomorrow."

"I am delighted that you are able to spare your valuable time for me. I've no plans for tomorrow that I can't postpone," I said. "What time shall we meet?"

"If you could set aside the whole day, that would be good, as I had in mind a comprehensive inspection. President Marcos stressed the importance of making you aware of our economic well-being, as well as our needs. Shall we say I pick you up at your hotel door at nine in the morning?"

"Nine would be fine."

"Good, I look forward to seeing you then," he said and hung up. Interesting. The Minister of Defense, on two days' notice, devoting a whole day to chauffeuring me around the town. Either he had a goldbrick job or Marcos was feeling a lot of pressure.

I spent the rest of the afternoon puttering around and in the evening took a cab over to the Ermita district to check out the action. It was a semi-shabby collection of restaurants, bars and sex shows mostly, sporting lots of neon and throngs of tourists and American Navy and Air Force guys—but no muggings this time. After a good Chinese dinner I took in one set of a fairly good local rock band, fended off the bar girls, then returned to the Manila Hotel. I figured Todd Sonarr would be on duty by nine a.m., so at 10 p.m. I placed a call to Thermite Holdings' home office. "I'd like to speak to Mr. Gladstone," I told the receptionist.

"I'll connect you," she said, and Todd picked up on the second ring. "Gladstone," he said.

"Stokes, this is Jack Philco in Manila, calling to touch base. Did you catch the announcement yesterday evening?"

"Yes, it's exactly as we anticipated. Short notice for an election, but he doesn't want to give the opposition a chance to get organized. How's it going over there?"

"So far, so good. I've talked to some well-connected people, met the Marcoses last night. Still getting grounded on the local scene. Enrile, the Minister of Defense, will show me around tomorrow, and that should yield a lot of useful information. So, now that the announcement's been made, anything special you want me to do?"

"For the time being, steady as she goes. I'm going to delay informing powerful parties of your mission there while you continue your assessment of the situation. That sound okay to you?"

"Sure. So far it doesn't look like anybody needs my help. The Marcos government seems to have things under control. There's one thing you could do for me, Stokes. I've been merging the facts and figures people here have provided, and there are big data gaps. If you have any recent reports on the Philippine economic and financial situation, could you send them out? I need more info to round out my picture."

"I'll check with our analysts. I'm sure they have what you need. Tell you what, I'll send it in care of the American Embassy. I arranged an assistant for you there, and you can pick it up from him in a couple days. Somebody you know—do you remember Kevin, from Phnom Penh?"

"Kevin? Give me a hint."

"The bicycle."

It came back—the hippie who was supposed to be my CIA backup before the Khmer Rouge ran everybody out of town. "Okay, rings a bell."

"He's there as a consultant in the economics section; he left here two days ago. I'll send what economic reports we have to him. Contact him in a couple days. (He gave me Kevin's last name, let's say it's 'Blank,' for security's sake) Sounds like you're on top of things. Sharpen your pencil on those figures. We need a solid assessment on the loan. Keep me in the loop." And he rang off. A guarded conversation in case anyone was listening in, but even between the lines it added up to nothing definite. I'd been sent to assist Marcos with his election. He'd announced it. My next move hinged on further instructions.

* * *

A Mercedes sedan pulled up at the Manila Hotel portal close enough to 0900 to attribute the delay to traffic, and the driver opened the door for Juan Ponce Enrile to step out and greet me. The Minister of Defense, at least, seemed not to operate on "Filipino time." "I am pleased to meet you, Mr. Philco," he said, with a manner more austere than the people I'd met at the Palace party. The man had gravity. "Please join me, and we will tour some of the sights of Metro Manila." He motioned me into the back seat of the car. I scooched over to make room for him, and the doorman closed us in.

As we pulled away and headed down the driveway Enrile said, "President Marcos thought I would be an appropriate tour guide. Although I am Minister of Defense right now, in the past I was Secretary of Finance and Secretary of Justice, as well as on the boards of the Philippine National Oil Company, the Philippine Coconut Authority and the Philippine National Bank. So I am well-qualified to explain to you many facets of the Philippine economic situation. I thought first we would drive through the Makati district, the heart of Philippine commercial activity, for an overview." Well-qualified he certainly was, but also it was becoming clear to me that a close clique controlled this country—a very few men held many important offices each.

The driver rolled us slowly through modest canyons of office buildings old and new in the Makati district. Enrile expounded on the ownership and functions of the chief ones, also pointing out various foreign embassies as we passed by them. I nodded sagely and posed investment-bankerish questions. Then we turned toward the waterfront, not far away.

"What's *that?*" I asked him, pointing to a vehicle crossing our bow as we waited at a traffic stop. It looked like a roving stainless steel diner that had been outfitted by Ken Kesey's Merrie Pranksters in one of their more acid-trippy moods.

"A jeepney. It's like a tram, public transportation. They are used throughout the Philippines. They follow specified routes and cost a pittance, so they are very popular with the people. Should you venture onto one, and I strongly advise you against doing that, you must hold your wallet in a safe place and keep your eyes open. Pickpockets abound on them, and you would be a prime target."

Manila Bay affords an excellent natural harbor, and its commercial port facilities were big and busy, if behind more developed, modern seaports like Singapore and Hamburg. Freighters of various flags took on cargoes of agricultural goods; hoists and cranes swung containers of manufactured goods onto wharfside stacks; and tankers piped petroleum products and chemicals to and from storage tanks. I commented that the port was outdated compared to others I'd seen around the world, and Enrile told me that was one of the critical reasons for needing loans—to modernize the Manila harbor facilities.

"It seems to me that, as busy a port as it is, private investors and sound management could turn a good profit here," I remarked. "Has the government made any effort to seek private money for upgrading the facilities?"

"It's a matter of retaining control," he said. "We want the port to remain in Filipino hands."

"How about the government surpluses? With proper structuring, the government could use those to improve the port and come out ahead on tax revenues."

"What government surpluses?" Enrile asked with surprise. "What are you talking about?"

"According to a spreadsheet I compiled from the data I have been gathering," I said, "as far as I could tell, every year the government takes in more than in spends."

"Oh no no no," he insisted. "There are no surpluses. Never. It is the idiosyncrasies of our accounting regulations that make it appear so. Loans are critical to our economy. As well as foreign aid. It has always been thus. We spend every centavo wisely, believe me. But come to think of it, your consortium could obviate the difficulty you raise by structuring the loan in tranches, with the shipyard tranch subordinated to the general domestic improvements tranch and carrying a variable interest rate pegged to annualized discounted forward gross revenues, indexed to the prior 60 day moving average of the piso/US dollar exchange rate and predicated on the current disbursement of the sinking fund ... would that be a possibility?"

Whatever he said. "We normally don't do them that way, Juan, but anything is possible. I'll propose your idea to the committee. I'm sure they will listen sympathetically."

"Oh, I know it is possible because the loan from the Sultan of Brunei was exactly of that nature. You must have reviewed our debt history...?"

"Yes, yes, we always do that, we research our loans very thoroughly. Maybe I was confusing it with the loan from the Bank of Japan." Hoping there had been one.

"Hmmm..." After an awkward pause he veered the discussion to other topics, leaving me wondering who was bullshitting whom the most.

We returned to the Makati district for a swank lunch at a swank rooftop restaurant where Enrile seemed to know everyone in sight on a first name basis. What with endless greet-and-chats and laid-back service, we weren't on the road until 2:30. For the afternoon phase of the tour we careered south of the city along country highways lined with tall palm trees and beyond them farms and plantations growing coconuts, rice, sugar cane and table vegetables. Sugar and coconut products were the major Philippine exports, he said, but their profitability suffered because of poor infrastructure, which the loan would help alleviate. We tooled past shacks pieced together of bamboo, weathered boards and rusty corrugated steel, as well as occasional battered ship containers converted to other uses by means of doors and windows crudely gouged out of their walls. The palm-shaded villages didn't amount to much out there, and towns we breezed through were squalid little slums where thatched roofs were popular. Skinny laborers hoed and chopped and toted and sweated beneath straw hats fending off the beating sun. We reached the shore of a big bay, the island's major fishing port. You couldn't mistake the smell. The boats, buildings, piers, processing plants and storage sheds made for quaint postcards of exotic tropical climes, but their commercial adequacy didn't impress. Here, too, the proposed loan would work economic wonders, Enrile assured me.

We'd passed my dinnertime but approached Filipino dinnertime by the time we re-entered Manila proper. Enrile insisted I join him for the evening meal, which I gladly did. Neither for lunch, nor for dinner, did he steer us to Filipino cuisine, I noted. Think about the last time you saw a Philippine eatery on restaurant row among the Italian, Chinese, Mexican, Indian, Thai, French and Japanese restaurants where you live. Hmmm, there wasn't any "last time"? There are reasons for that, principally that indig Filipino food is very bland. He took me to a steakhouse—well, more than just a run-of-the-mill steakhouse—and over a leisurely meal lubricated with a decent burgundy or three I learned more about Senor Enrile.

JUAN PONCE ENRILE'S STORY

Like others in the government here, Enrile had been well-trained in law, with a master's from Harvard. A few years younger than Marcos and Romulo, he'd not been as active during the War. After a stint as a practicing lawyer he entered politics, working for Marcos as he ascended the political ranks. By the time Marcos became president in 1965 Enrile was in the inner circle. He held several offices, and Marcos made him Defense Chief in 1972. An ambush of his car later that year gave Marcos a pretext for declaring martial law, which stayed in force for nine years. "Filipinos are enthusiastic gossips, and if they don't know the facts they are prone to inventing any fantastic yarn that fits the occasion and the audience," he told me. "If you talk to enough people you will eventually hear that the ambush was a staged assassination attempt as an excuse for martial law, so I might as well admit to you that it was," he said. "Shortly thereafter someone attacked Imelda with a bolo knife, and considering the severe injuries she sustained, no one has ever asserted that was faked at all. She was handing out awards at an outdoor ceremony and one of the awardees came at her. She instinctively crossed her arms in front of her chest, thereby averting being killed on the spot.

"Soon after that I got on the wrong side of Imelda," Enrile confided. "As Defense Chief I was responsible for enforcing the travel ban on political enemies. As it happened a mother wanted her daughter, who was married to an exiled rebel, to be allowed to come to have her baby born in the Philippines. That was against the law, so I refused permission. Imelda was outraged that I would enforce a law rather than bow to her whim, and she has never forgiven me. She even screamed at me, when others could hear, 'You are swell-headed! But I can tell you this—I am going to destroy you!' All because I did not humor one of her fancies. After that, she had me put under surveillance by General Ver's men, out of fear that I might be a threat to her ambitions. Last year I ran for assemblyman, and despite her active support for my opponent, I won the office. And it was Imelda's doing that Ver became the President's Chief of Staff over me, though while he is on trial for the Aquino murder he has temporarily stepped down. In her eyes I am a pariah, not that it matters much. After they killed Ninoy Aquino I've been gravitating toward the opposition in any event. She dares not attack me overtly, but I take care not to stand near open windows when Imelda is nearby.

"You may wonder why I'm telling you about internal political matters that would seem best to keep from outsiders. No doubt this excellent wine has loosened my tongue. But your bank is contemplating loans to the Philippine government, and it is only fair to warn you that not all is well with this government. I would be remiss to lead you into a false understanding of current conditions. The Philippines need the money desperately, yes, but perhaps it would be prudent not to float any big loans while Marcos and his wife remain in power."

"Marcos seemed confident enough when he announced the election on Sunday," I ventured. "Why would he hold an election two years before his term runs out?"

"Because he's not confident at all," said Enrile. "Opposition against him now runs more strongly than at any time in the past. Recently there has been talk in the Philippine Assembly about beginning impeachment proceedings against him. But you won't hear much about that because Marcos has been shutting down papers and broadcasting stations that he doesn't control, and he will shut down more of the opposition papers if they stray too far. You would learn more truth about the Philippines back home in the States than you'll hear in Manila. Your Senator Laxalt, for example, saw the situation clearly and has been spreading the truth to your newspapers. Those stories will not be reprinted in Manila, except by the underground press."

"Isn't Marcos taking a chance, then, standing for election?"

"On the contrary, he's holding the election to shore up his position. He'll buy it and rig it and steal it and miscount it as he has every other election he's ever run in. It isn't who casts the votes, but who counts the votes that matter, Stalin supposedly said. In the Philippines, Ferdinand Marcos counts the votes. The ones he doesn't burn, that is. He has crates of money that he will use to buy votes out in the islands, and when the votes are collected many of the ones against him will disappear. Disappearing them could amount to quite a task, as such votes will be very numerous in this election. When he's decided enough votes are in the bag he'll announce his victory, and his forces will rough up some of the opposition and throw some others in jail. And the reign of Ferdinand Marcos will roll on."

"There's no way the opposition could steal the election, then?"

"That is a most funny joke you make, Mr. Philco. Out-cheat Ferdinand Marcos in his own backyard? Satan himself could not accomplish that."

"Who will run against him?" I asked.

"No one of importance—the usual suspects, as they say in the movies. Though many Filipinos, perhaps the majority, oppose Marcos, he has made sure to keep the political opposition weak through bribery, intimidation, exile and jail terms. A few politicians here and there in the islands will mount token campaigns aimed at boosting their stock in their own districts. The opposition taken together is disorganized, underfunded and demoralized, with insufficient time or resources to mobilize voters. Their vote will be split among several candidates, which even if by some miracle the total surpassed Marcos would give none a winning margin. Sad to say for my country, but Ferdinand Marcos will once again coast to victory."

Enrile took me back to the Manila Hotel and let off at the door with these words: "Mr. Philco, I am delighted to have had the opportunity to conduct you on a tour of our capital city and to show what great benefits will flow from the loan your bank is considering. I hope the day was as informative for you as it was for me, and be assured that my office is always open to you. Call on me at any time I can be of service. By the way, my friends call me 'Johnny.' Oh, and a word to the wise. A genuine investment banker would have laughed me out of the car after my doubletalk about the shipyard tranch. You are very good, but be careful."

Oops. It's easy enough to fake your way through an hour or two meeting with people who have a set message to deliver, but giving someone as sharp as Enrile a whole day to poke and probe is asking for it. Who knows what all I unknowingly gave away? Still, his parting invitation sounded sincere, even though my investment banker act hadn't been entirely convincing. I hope he meant what he said about "friends."

My day with Juan Ponce Enrile enlightened me in some ways, puzzled me in others. Steele Bosserman and Todd Sonarr predicted correctly that an election was in the cards, but they were the only people I'd yet encountered who thought Ferdinand Marcos was in any danger of losing it. Also they numbered among the few people outside the regime who wanted him to stay in office. Enrile gave me a look at some highlights of Metro Manila, such as they were, but he'd carefully kept us moving fast on nice streets and main highways. I'd spent enough time among "real people" around the world to know that I hadn't seen much of them yet in the Philippines, excepting possibly the punks that jumped me my first night out on the town.

I needed a look at Manila's "real people." And who was going to lead me to them? I'd already lined up my guide.

* * *

Assuming that the nature of her business entailed wee small hours, I waited until late morning to go to a lobby pay phone and dial the number Luz gave me for her aunt. She picked up right away. "Yes?" a weary female voice answered.

"Good morning. A young woman named Luz gave me this number to call."

"Luz? Yes. And what can I do for you, please?" The voice brightened slightly but still sounded wrung out.

"Am I speaking to her aunt?"

"I am her aunt. And you are...?"

"Jack Philco. Luz paid me a visit a week ago."

"Was she satisfactory?"

"A most beautiful, charming young woman. Entirely satisfactory. That is why I am calling. I would like to see her again."

"I am delighted to hear that. I am very proud of Luz, my niece, you know. I will be happy to arrange another meeting. The person who engaged her for you instructed me to gratify your every desire."

"Very thoughtful," I said, "but this has nothing to do with that. I want to hire her as an escort for an entire day, and I would be paying her fee myself. I do not want to involve anyone else in this."

"We are discreet, Mr. Philco, on that you can rely. What day do you have in mind?"

"The day after tomorrow? Is she available?"

"I will make sure she is. She gave me a good report on you, Mr. Philco. She will call you at the hotel this evening to set up the arrangement. Say about eight o'clock?"

"Very good, but I think it would be better if she came in person. Could she meet me in the hotel bar?"

"That can be arranged, but it is more complicated. I cannot guarantee the exact time, but she will meet you there in mid evening. Will that do?"

"It will be fine. Much obliged, Miss…"

"Just call me 'Auntie'," she said and hung up.

So now I had a Mother in Calcutta and an Auntie in Manila. Some extended family.

* * *

I TOOK A VISIBLE TABLE IN THE BAR AT 2000 HOURS, AND LUZ appeared a nursed beer later. She glanced around, spotted me and came over. "Good evening, Mr. Philco," she said with an alluring smile.

"Hello, Luz," I said. "Sit. Can I order something for you?"

She daintily settled her little self into the chair beside me and edged it over, putting us thigh to thigh. "No," she said, "I have an assignment this evening, but I excused myself for a few minutes to run an important errand, assuring my client that when I returned I would be all his. I have to hurry right back, as he was very excited to see me. Auntie said you want me to give you the tour you mentioned the other night?"

"Yes, the day after tomorrow, if you can. I think we should take the whole day, as I want to see Manila from top to bottom and best to worst. Can you arrange for an inconspicuous car, one several years old with dents and scratches in the paint?"

"You mean like all the other the cars on the road? No problem."

"I'll need a place to change my clothes."

"My place, no problem."

"Good. Should I meet you at your place in the morning?"

"It will be better if I come in my car, and we'll take it to my place and go from there in the inconspicuous car."

"I like the way you think, Luz," I said. "Anything else I should do?"

"Shall I arrange for a gun?" she asked.

"Gun?"

"If you want a thorough tour of Manila, in some districts you wouldn't want to be the only man without one."

"I'll bring my own."

"That covers everything important. Anything else that arises, we can deal with it on the way. What time shall I arrive?"

"Nine in the morning?"

"Excellent, Mr. Philco. I'll see you then. Now I must be off. So we shouldn't be talking over the phone in your room, then?"

"Not about anything important," I said.

"You are a very wise man," she said. She got up, gave me a little squeeze and a warm peck on the cheek, and swayed away. Exceptional rear view.

* * *

I spent the next morning in the Makati commercial district interviewing the publisher of a Philippine business magazine. I took notes for show, but it was the same dog-and-pony routine I'd heard before, covering the glories of the Philippines, the stability of the government and the rosy future that a large loan would unleash. In other words, like everyone else I'd talked to, he was in Marcos's pocket. He treated me to another lavish lunch in a restaurant where everyone knew everyone else intimately, after which I bade him an appreciative good day and emerged on the steamy streets of business district Manila.

First I reconned a few boulevards and side streets to gather an impression of what Juan Q. Publico was wearing. Definitely not fashions from Barney's and Paul Stuart. My high-powered investment banker costume was posh even for the Makati district here, and mugger bait outside of it. Nor would the outdoor gear I'd brought along blend in to any surround we'd be passing through. A firm picture of mid-scale Manila dress in mind, I hiked over to the SM Mall along the EDSA (as the locals call E de los Santos Avenue). A gigantic enclosed shopping palace, the mall housed a collection of sleek stores and shops offering anything any Filipino might need or desire. It would have not looked out of place on the outskirts of any upscale American suburb. I had no trouble locating shirts, trousers and shoes that would blend me into the local flow.

That errand accomplished, I walked over to the Intercontinental Hotel, just a couple blocks away. It catered to the international business crowd, and my investment banker duds fit in better there. At the desk I asked for Evgeny Grotelov. He was out, the clerk informed me. I took a seat at the bar off the lobby and cooled down from my sun-broiled perambulations with a San Miguel. Grotesqcu didn't show by the time I finished it. I'd nothing urgent to see him about, so I took a cab back to the Manila Hotel figuring I'd catch up with him another time.

The civvies I bought were fresh and crisp, which wouldn't fit some places I wanted to see. Neither did I want to go out of investment banker character by wearing them around the Manila Hotel. I rolled up the shirt and pants I'd wear on the tour and carried them down, via the back staircase, to the fitness room, which, it still being business hours, sat empty. I changed into them and ran a brisk several miles on the treadmill, then engaged in a strenuous half hour on the machines. That took away the fresh off-the-rack look. I'd rough them up a little more at Luz's.

* * *

Luz showed up in a midnight blue Mercedes sedan, having dressed down from her usual elegance for the occasion. "It's Auntie's car," she explained. "She thought it would be more proper for an investment banker." I stuck my Gucci satchel in the back seat and climbed aboard. She deftly drove us through the morning traffic into a nicer section of the city and dove into the underground parking beneath a modern high rise. "That's my car over there,' she said, pointing to a shiny red, vintage Ford Mustang. A beat-up Toyota Corolla occupied the adjacent space. "Do you think that one would be okay for the tour?" she asked. "I borrowed it from a friend."

"Looks right to me," I said. We rode the elevator up to her place. It was a two-bedroom condo unit with a good view out to sea. She'd furnished it tastefully: the gal had style. "Where can I change my clothes, and then we'll get going?" I said. She pointed to a bedroom. I noticed a planter on her balcony. "I need to make some little adjustments," I said. I took my clothes from the satchel, stepped through the sliding glass door out to the balcony and scrambled a little dirt from the planter into the shirt to make it look worn. Then did the same with the pants.

Luz watched with interest. "You are a very unusual investment banker," she observed. "You brought your gun? May I see it?" I pulled it from the bag and passed it to her, and she inspected it while I slipped into the civvies. "A SIG Sauer? Like the commandos use? Not only an unusual investment banker, but also a well-armed one. You raise questions in my mind, but I'll not ask them."

"That's best," I said.

"If you are trying to look Filipino, come in here," Luz said, and she led me to the bathroom. "I'll fix your hair." She applied a little mousse and a comb, and I looked much less like an American investment banker. Then she took out a make-up kit. "Your natural face is in the right direction, but this will help," she said. She unlimbered some foundation and applied it lightly over my face, taking care to round out my cheeks. She stepped back, inspected her work and said, "That's better. From a distance no one can tell."

I checked the results in the mirror. "You do good work, Luz."

"In my line of work we have to know our cosmetics," she said.

We took the elevator back to the garage and mounted the Corolla. "Will I need to carry my gun everywhere?" I asked.

"I'll tell you when," she said. "For now leave it on the floor."

When we emerged onto the street she announced, "We'll start at the top and work our way down." Soon we were on the EDSA, heading for the Makati district.

"The topmost level of Manila is Forbes Park," she said. "It is a gated, heavily guarded community where government officials and big businessmen live. Ordinary people cannot enter, but I come here often enough that the gatemen know me. It would be helpful if you give him a twenty-dollar bill," she added. She turned off the EDSA to a side road and after a few twists and turns past lush landscaping stopped at to the lowered gate.

A uniformed, armed guard stepped out of the kiosk. "Holla, Luz," he said. "What, coming down in the world?"

"My Mustang's in the shop. They loaned me this wreck for the day. I want to show my cousin around Forbes, how the ricos live. He's from Cebu, never been to Manila." She slipped him my twenty, which promptly vanished as he ushered us in with a broad smile.

Shades of Beverly Hills and north Tehran. The lush lanes of Forbes Park revealed mini-palaces galore, sited on tropically landscaped spreads, sitting at the ends of spacious driveways. But in neither Los Angeles nor the rich side of Tehran did the ultra-wealthy live behind such heavily armed protection. Bodyguards, yes, but not the shotguns and machine pistols I noticed. Not only did we encounter a number of prowling patrol cars (which slowed down to scope us out), but some mansions had manned guard posts at the gates. "Is all this security necessary?" I asked.

"Kidnappings are a problem for the wealthy in the Philippines," she answered, "and our robbers are bold, skillful and ruthless. Fewer incidents happen where there are guards present."

We cruised a few more streets and I'd seen enough to grasp the gist. "What's our next stop?" I asked.

"What, you don't want to spend the rest of the day admiring how our upper crust enjoy the nation's money?" she chided. "I could point out which homes have Olympic- size swimming pools and who drives Rolls-Royces, if you'd like to know. We could drop by the country club and the polo field. No? (I shook my head) Well then, let's go see where their employees live."

We crossed the Pasig River to the San Miguel district, location of Malacanang Palace, and continued to Sampaloc, home of several universities. She drove by one that looked like many an American college campus—a mixture of well-kept traditional and modern buildings teeming with clean-cut, eager young people. And also a big mob of students gathered in what seemed to be the Main Quad, ranting and chanting and waving protest signs. "An anti-Marcos rally?" I asked.

"They have them all the time here," Luz said. "At other universities, too. The children from Forbes Park attend them. Even some of the wives do, and often their maids come along."

A facet of Manila life Enrile had neglected to show me.

Some adjacent residential sections sported bungalow housing as you might see in 1950s-ish Southern California suburbs, but other sections displayed shophouses and two-story apartment buildings intermixed with recent low-rises already edging toward shabby. Not so much landscaping in these areas, no posted guards, no sleek new cars, no driveways. A lot of churches, which, judging by their architecture and condition, had been around for a long time. Street life was lively in the shopping areas, mostly tidily-dressed women going about daily routines. "Who lives here?" I asked.

"Professional people—teachers, office workers, business people. You know, middle-class."

By American standards, lower middle-class, anyhow. Now I was seeing the upper reaches of Manila's "real people." From my reading I'd learned that of Manila's roughly five million people (about half the size of L.A.), half lived in slums. I asked to see some of those. "First, let's have some lunch," Luz suggested. "How about Chinese?"

"Not Filipino food?"

"If you insist..."

"Chinese is fine." The restaurant was a favorite of hers if a client wasn't springing for it, and I let her do the ordering. It beat what I was used to in Southern California, and the menu offered items you'd never see in your neighborhood take-out joint: chicken claws? shark fin soup? pork fat?

I prodded her along, not wanting to waste the day with another Filipino leisurely lunch. "Okay, okay," she said. "Such a hurry to see misery." Lunch downed, we headed out again. "Hold your pistol on your lap, never can tell. And keep your arm inside the car unless you want to lose that nice wristwatch at a traffic stop." I slipped it off and pocketed it. She took us into a neighborhood of shacks, tarpaper, rust, garbage and droopy banana plants, as bad as any I'd seen in Indochina or the Caribbean. Our beat-up Corolla quickly became the ritziest ride in sight. It was a busy place. Skinny, dirty little kids thronged the streets. Clusters of small, dark people—men in dirty shorts and singlets, women in thread-bare, faded dresses—eyed us suspiciously as they shambled about their business. Streets held markets of bamboo-and-canvas food vendor stalls. Shabby shops and dram houses interspersed the rusty tin and scrapwood shacks. Crude signs, gang-tags and random paint splotches of graffiti covered everything.

"Seen enough real people?" Luz asked. "I don't like to be here very long. Things can happen."

"Is this the worst slum in Manila?"

"By no means. There are plenty of worse ones. We are in one of the better slums. Most of these people own or rent their shacks, such as they are, and many work at menial jobs—laborers, cleaners and so forth. But youth gangs have territories here, and they can be troublesome. If we attract their attention they may try something. We have much that they want."

"Sure, I've seen enough of this," I said, a hair too late. Luz had slowed down to veer around a pig ambling across the street, and two boys suddenly jumped in front of us, causing her to slam on the brakes. Two others then stepped from the shade of a roof overhang and closed up behind us. More boys were assembling along the street's edge. One of the ones in front moved toward Luz's side of the car and motioned that she should roll her window down. If I got out and confronted them, no telling how large a force I'd be facing, and I had only the clip in the gun. The gangs probably shot each other up all the time, but they'd not cotton to an outsider horning in on the action.

So I jacked a round into the chamber, rolled my window down, leaned out and fired a round into the dirt by the foot of the guy on my side of the car. He made a big jump away, and I said, "Go, Luz." She did, grazing the one on her side with the fender as she spurted forward, knocking him on his ass. I fired two shots in the air as we pulled away and leaned on the horn, and people cleared a path. For good measure I lowered the gun and aimed it around at the people we passed. Dodging as fast as she could around litter, dogs, scruffy kids and other obstacles, she reached a wide lane and slewed around the corner. Luckily it was not a dead end. We'd stirred up a commotion, but no one was in hot pursuit. I suppose gunfire is common enough there that a couple shots wouldn't set the populace on red alert. After a few false starts Luz found her way back to a main road.

"You like our real people?" she asked.

"We have them in America, too," I said, though I couldn't think of any American slums this wasted. Watts was Easy Street compared to this.

"I have one other slum to show you, if you want to see Manila's worst example."

"I signed on for the whole tour," I said. "Bring'em on."

"Many of the poor are squatters," Liz explained. "A family puts a hut on an empty plot, and then other join them, and soon you have a neighborhood living on somebody's land. We are now going to Tondo. I have never been there myself, but everyone says it is the worst place in Manila. I will not drive the car into it, if there even are roads, so I hope you can satisfy your curiosity from a distance."

Luz consulted her map and went down some doubtful lanes, and presently we approached Tondo's border. One look and I didn't want to venture in either—distance was good. "Okay, stop here," I told her. It was as if some cosmic litterbug had strewn a square mile with trash and garbage, and then a bought-off judge had sentenced thousands of people to live in it. I could make out definitions of possibly habitable enclosures haphazardly stacked into the distance, in a jumble with barely coherent street patterns. Smoke from trash fires and cooking fires hung over the landscape, adding acridity to the rancid odor of rot. Emaciated, desperate-looking people stood, squatted or shuffled about, reviving Calcutta memories. When a clutch of them started moving in our direction with their hands outstretched I said, "Okay, seen enough." Luz eagerly put the car in gear, hung a U-ey and beat a smart retreat.

"How is it on the other islands?" I asked her as we headed back to her place.

"Manila is our richest city. There are some nice places in the Philippines, Boracay Island for example, but that is a resort, of course. Cities on Cebu, Mindanao, Leyte and so forth, are not as nice as Manila. Most people on the islands live in country villages. They are very poor, but life is perhaps better for them than for poor people in the city slums, where there is so much crime. Most Filipinos are poor, and the rich Filipinos live well apart from them. To tell the truth, I am surprised that our poor are interesting to an American investment banker, one who uses a commando gun so deftly. Certainly no rich Filipinos are interested in them."

* * *

BACK AT HER PLACE I SCRUBBED THE MAKE-UP OFF MY FACE AND resumed my banker costume. Luz at first declined payment for the day, but I insisted, so she computed an amount based on her standard escort rate, pretty reasonable by American standards. She said she wasn't busy that evening, and she could call it a night off, but I thought not. I'd had enough of Manila for one day, driving around in the humidity. I wanted a quick shower, some fresh clothes and a good night's sleep. She drove me back to my hotel in the Mercedes. "I hope the day was satisfactory," she said when we pulled up at the entrance.

"Exactly what I wanted," I said. "You were an excellent guide."

"I am so glad you think so. Will I be seeing you again?" she asked with expectant eyes (and what eyes they were!). "There is still paid-for service I haven't delivered."

"I haven't forgotten, Luz. Definitely you'll be seeing more of me." I leaned over and gave her a little kiss and a squeeze, and the doorman let me out.

I'd had two looks at Manila, the cheerleader tour, and the reality tour, and very different looks they were. I was already making further plans for Luz. Depending on how the next couple weeks shook out, I might need to visit some of the other islands, in the "reality" format.

* * *

When I picked up my key at the hotel the clerk plucked a note out of my box. "This man left a number for you to call," he said. "I think he was a little confused. First he asked to speak with Jake Fonko, but when I told him no one by that name is registered here, he said that he meant Jack Philco, which of course is you." So I took the telephone number from Mr. Kevin."

"Thank you," I said, pocketing the note. "Mr. Fonko works in our office also, and people often get our names confused." What kind of screwup is this? Didn't Sonarr put him in the loop?

I called Kevin the next morning. "Jack Philco here. I got your note yesterday when I got back. Some kind of mixup on the names?"

"Hi Mr. Fonko..."

"Philco!" I interjected.

"Right, *Philco*," he said. "Sorry about that. Jet lag still has me under its spell. That's a long flight over. Listen, Todd Sonarr..."

"Do you mean *Mr. Gladstone?*"

"Yeah, him, that's right. My slip. I got a package from him

today with instructions to forward it to you. When can you pick it up?"

"Sometime this afternoon okay?"

"Yeah, fine. I'm at the U.S. Embassy. The receptionist can direct you. About 2 p.m.? Man, it's been a long time. I'm looking forward to it." "Sure. See you at two."

That was annoying. He'd been with The Company 10 years now. You'd think he'd know better. No harm done, I hope, but I really didn't want my real name circulating in the Philippines.

I had a meeting with another Filipino Who Mattered in the morning, who gave me the standard spiel, and then busywork to fill the time until the meeting. The weather was temperate, so I put on my lightest weight suit and for the exercise walked to the Embassy. In short order I was in Kevin's office. His torso was a little heftier and his face had filled out since our Cambodia foray, but he hadn't lost the hint of sly "nobody can prove I did it" in his mien. They'd stuck him in small, back-corridor office with a desk, two chairs, a filing cabinet and not much else, especially not a window. He rose to greet me with enthusiasm. "Sorry about the phone slip-ups," he said, putting out his hand. "I've been looking forward to seeing you again ever since those days, Jake ... is it okay if I call you Jake?"

"No. Here I'm Jack, and let's keep it that way, just for the sake of drill."

"Right, Jack. I'm still Kevin. They didn't give me a code name for this op. In fact I'm not clear on the op. Todd ... Mr. Gladstone ... shipped me out here on short notice as back-up and/or liaison for some project you're doing. Now that I'm here, I suppose I'll get mission specifics?"

"I'm not clear on those myself, Kevin. Until I am, there's not much I can tell you. Gladstone didn't brief you, then?"

KEVIN BLANK'S STORY

"Not much. He wanted someone on the ground for you, and I was the man most available. Plus we'd worked together before. So I'm officially here as a consultant on rice agriculture—your old Cambodian scam, ha ha. But unofficially I'm going to have to make myself look busy until the situation clarifies. Maybe I'll waste some of their time at the Rice Institute in Los Banos, see what's shaking with rice these days. You don't happen to be in the market for a sidekick, do you?"

"No, I work alone," I said. "For the time being, I'm an investment banker, and as far as I know, they don't have sidekicks. I'll keep you in mind if I need a wingman. What have you been up to since Cambodia?"

"After the Khmer Rouge rolled the place up, Todd Sonarr took me back to Langley and put me through a training program. He must have told you how he found me—sprung me out of a Phnom Penh jail after a buddy and I hijacked a munitions ship. Saved my life, literally. I'd not have lasted 10 minutes after the Reds overran the place. I thought the CIA would be a good fit—you know, dirty tricks, covert ops—but the reality wasn't what I'd imagined. In the aftermath of Nam no high adventure—mostly it was paperwork, scaling back and staying out of the public eye, thanks to the Church committee. Of course my only qualification for field ops was that ship caper, and that was nothing professional, just a prank. Up until then I'd been an idealistic, overeducated hippie bum. I've been getting along and biding my time, hoping a career-mover will come along, maybe something to do with these terrorist air liner hijackings—they just clouted one in Athens. They assigned me to the field a couple times, minor roles in Honduras and Nicaragua. Just as well I didn't get too involved down there—that's going to be trouble when the word on the arms deals leaks out. I did a hitch in Lebanon, and what a mess that place is, spent some time in the West Berlin station. But mostly I read stuff, write stuff, talk about stuff and weight down a desk chair so it doesn't float away. Not like you. Sonarr updates me on your exploits from time to time. Man, you're living the life—Malibu pad, Corvette, working for the Shah."

"He keeps track of me?"

"He keeps track of a lot of things. That man is an operator's operator, in an arena pitting him against some of the best."

"Kevin, I wish I could assign you some exciting deeds to accomplish, but I'm spinning wheels myself so far. It looks like the situation is hotting up with this election, but for the time being, find some good books and don't wander around drunk in dark streets, is my advice while you're in Manila. You said a package had come for me?"

"Got it right here." He reached into a desk drawer and came up with a bulging government envelope. "There's no security designation on it, so I took a look, thinking I might get a leg up on the situation. Seems to be economic reports, pretty dry stuff."

Reading my mail? "That's what I asked for. I'm here as an investment banker, and it's the kind of information I need to support my cover. It's dry stuff all right, but I'm finding interesting things in it. Kevin, one thing you can do for me right now is, find out what you can about the upcoming election. Use your cover to contact officials. Sound out people you bump into, but exercise caution—Marcos has secret police. If you run across anything out of the ordinary, contact me immediately. Otherwise, I'll touch base with you from time to time, and I'll sure let you know when I need your help."

"I hope so. I'm getting tired of spinning my wheels, which has been my lot for the last 10 years."

"Always look on the sunny side," I said. "Okay, I need to get into these reports. Good seeing you again, Kevin. And remember, I'm Jack Philco until further notice."

Too bad Sonarr didn't give him something useful to do. Looking for excitement in Manila could be dangerous for an unwary man alone, and idle hands are ever the devil's workshop. Lord knows it was challenge enough to fill my own days in plausible ways. A genuine investment banker would in three weeks have gathered enough intel to make recommendations, but I had to string out my act in Manila until the election, two months away.

Whose date Ferdinand extended. January 17, it turned out, allowed too little time to prepare ballots and organize polling all over the islands, so he put it off until February 7. I followed the election news: minor opposition politicians declared their candidacies; speeches were made; issues were raised; government grants were suddenly allocated; big contracts were awarded; major public works projects were announced with great fanfare; cheer-led Marcos rallies were held; conscripted school moppets sang patriotic songs—and every once in a while someone was mysteriously beaten up, jailed on dubious pretexts or found dead. I continued conducting pointless interviews, and I worked over the figures in the CIA reports Sonarr sent me. There were major chasms between the Philippine data and the CIA data, but one pattern stayed solid: a lot of money went unaccounted for over the years.

On December 2 the inquiries into the August 21, 1983, assassination of Benigno Aquino concluded. Their conclusion: General Ver and the rest of the military were innocent of any involvement. Whereupon President Marcos reinstated General Ver as his Chief of Staff.

And on December 3, Benigno Aquino's widow, Corazon Aquino, declared her candidacy for President of the Philippines.

THE FOURTH PART OF THE STORY

GENERAL VER'S ACQUITTAL SET MANILA ABUZZ, AND CORAZON Aquino's announcement touched the place off. Prior to that several opposition candidates had declared candidacies and launched plodding, demoralized campaigns. Cory, as they called her, ignited electricity and excitement. Her husband had been a popular Filipino figure, and his murder still inflamed popular passion. Posters popped up on walls all over Manila, demonstrations and rallies raged, and the place erupted with enthusiastic conjecture and speculation. She was headlined in the opposition press but downplayed in the pro-Marcos ones. This certainly bore on my mission, but how I couldn't say, because I still didn't know what my mission was supposed to be.

A couple days later my phone rang, Stokes Gladstone calling from New York. "How's it going, Jack?" he asked.

"Tops, Stokes," I said. "I'm getting the picture, filling in the details and awaiting further instructions."

"Good. Listen, we've a big venture brewing with the Development Bank of Singapore, and we need you there for some crucial meetings, post haste. Fly to Singapore on Sunday, bring your sharpest pencil, and plan to stay for a week. You're booked at the

Shangri La Hotel. I'll brief you on the situation when you arrive, and you can hit the ground running bright and early Monday morning. Okay? Gotta ring off now. See you in Singapore."

Now what?

I cancelled appointments and other business I'd arranged for next week, sent a note to Kevin that I'd be going out of town, and reserved a seat first class on Singapore Airlines (nothing but the best for us investment bankers, don't you know). That call came just at the right time—I badly needed a break from Manila, and my cover act was wearing on me. Living a fake life takes a lot of psychic energy, even when it's your job. A thousand miles away I could unwind a little.

It was my first landing at the new Changi Airport, an eye-opener. Singapore had gone all out to create one of the grandest air terminals in the world. Spacious, elegant and meticulously maintained, it blossomed with planters of live orchids and offered the kinds of shops, restaurants and amenities any weary traveler might desire, including an incoming duty-free shop swarmed by returning Singaporeans (when I saw booze prices in town, I understood). Most important, it through-putted travel-befuddled crowds more efficiently than DisneyWorld ever dreamed of. In no time at all a cab from the orderly taxi queue, a new Japanese make, whizzed me to the Shangri La over clean, modern roads. Singapore cab drivers don't run scams on the tourists, they don't play loud music on the radio, nor do they expect tips. Very refreshing after a month in the Philippines.

The Shangri La Hotel was Singapore's best (at that time—since then some amazing ones have gone up). Modern towers loomed over a traditional, lush tropical garden accented by the two-dimensional travelers palms unique to that region. A note from Stokes Gladstone graced my box when I checked in. Once settled, I rang his room—no answer. For the sake of stretching my legs I explored my new habitat. Couldn't ask for better. I wandered out the front portal and down the drive to the street. Cars, new Japanese makes mixed with BMWs and Mercs, flowed by. No poor people were in sight. Nor did I see a single scrap of litter in the street.

I should explain about Singapore. If all you know about it is what you read in American newspapers, you may be worse than simply ignorant, you may be disinformed. The Singapore government, very conservative and upright, has never bent in the slightest toward American left-liberal political conceits. The *New York Times* and other media that follow its lead (most mainstream papers, magazines and networks) return the favor by printing mostly lies about the place. Contrary to what you may have read or seen, Singapore is not a police state, not even close. It is an island off the southern tip of the Malay Peninsula with an area and population about that of the city of Chicago. An orderly little pocket of prosperity peopled predominantly by Chinese, Singapore sits hemmed in by two countries—Malaysia and Indonesia—whose natives feel no fondness for Chinese, something to do with their work ethic and resulting success.

Various surveys and ratings peg Singapore as having one of the least corrupt governments in the world, as well as one of the freest economies, with a crime rate next to nothing. It's one of the world's busiest ports, with the world's best airline. It stands as a tribute to traditions laid down by the British Empire in the 18th and 19th centuries. Few other colonial powers left success stories behind them, but Britain's former colonies include Singapore, Australia, New Zealand, Canada and, oh yes, the U.S. of A. Don't even think about doing drugs, tagging a wall or dropping litter on the street in Singapore, but otherwise you're good to go anywhere, at any time, in perfect safety. But not in perfect comfort. It lies just above the Equator, and while the surrounding seas forestall a sauna bath climate, the humidity rarely flags, nor are many days spared rain somewhere on the island.

Todd Sonarr and I crossed paths when I returned to the lobby and he emerged from the bar togged out in tropical casual wear. "What say, Jake?" he greeted me. "Great place, hey? It's on track to become the most modern city in the world. Gives me hope for Asia, eventually."

"What I've seen is an improvement over Manila, that's for sure," I said. "What's going on? Did something come up?"

"Giving you a break. I know the strain of living a cover identity, so I got you off the stage for a week. It'll boost your cred, too—doing investment banking in Singapore, where a lot of the Asia action happens these days."

"I sure appreciate the break. Those interviews are getting harder to sit through sounding like I know what I'm doing, and I think their Minister of Defense saw through my cover."

"Enrile? Don't worry about him. He's his own man. Jake, we have some business to talk over, but take this as a well-deserved week of R and R, and I'll leave you alone to enjoy it. What do you want to do right now? Get a drink? Go for a bite to eat? It's a little late in the day for tourist attractions, and the weather won't suit for a long stroll around town for a few hours. Ever had a Singapore Sling?"

"Nope."

"Let me welcome you to Singapore, then. It's the first punch in your tourist ticket. Umm, no pun intended." And he guided me to the bar. As alcoholic beverages go, a Singapore Sling rates a step above a Shirley Temple. It's a sweet-sour fruit cooler with some gin in it, refreshing on a hot day, which I guess was the original idea. Sonarr had a double Glenfiddich.

Over our drinks I described what I'd been doing and Sonarr seemed satisfied. "You should have stayed with the movies, the way you carry out these roles. I like your economic analysis. Have you come up with any explanation for the gaps?"

"Marcos and his cronies must be siphoning some off, but still there's a lot of dough that's gone wandering. Sloppy accounting? Mismanagement? Inflated bidding and kickbacks? Why on earth does the CIA want to keep this bunch of crooks in power here?"

"We know they're crooks. But they're our crooks, as the saying goes—staunch allies, anti-Communists. And those military bases are critical. You really think Marcos has the election fixed?"

"All agree he's an old hand at rigging elections," I said. "Not that there's much enthusiasm for him, but everyone assumes he'll carry it off. I still don't see what help we can give him. He seems to have vote fraud down to a science."

"There's two months yet to go," Sonarr said. "In politics anything can happen. Keep abreast of developments."

"When are you going to blow my cover to Marcos?"

"Not yet. No need for it. When the time comes, I'll let you know."

"What's the deal with Kevin? I don't see how he fits in."

"As yet, he doesn't. But he's there for when you need him. You'll see."

"Is this your 'mushroom management' all over again? Keep me in the dark and feed me bullshit?"

"Jake, you've got to get over that. There were reasons why I ran the Cambodian op the way I did. After all is said and done, everything turned up aces, didn't it? I'm doing well in my career, you're doing well in yours. If that Malibu lifestyle is making you miserable, I can recommend a good headshrinker."

"I survived that Cambodia clusterfuck through no fault of yours," I said.

"Jake, I would never deny you credit for your role in our success. That's why you're on this mission. It's the first one that's come up worthy of your considerable talents."

"But you won't give me specifics?"

"Patience and fortitude, Jake. You'll see. How about some eats?"

"They fed me pretty well on the flight. Maybe a snack."

"It's time for another tourist ticket punch—a Singapore hawker centre. We'll go to Newton Circus, very popular with the locals. You can get whatever you want there."

We taxied over to the most amazing food extravaganza I'd ever seen—dozens of stalls each serving some exotic specialty, an outdoor mega food court. Singapore is a foodie paradise. In addition to Chinese, the population comprises Malays, Indonesians and Indians, and hawker centres offer the gamut. You wash it down with local beer or smoothies made of any combination of tropical fruits you can dream up, and top it off with ice kacang, a sno-cone concoction so indescribable that I won't even try (Google it).

So commenced my Singapore sojourn. As it happened, that was the only business Todd Sonarr had to discuss with me. The upshot: Everything's fine. Stay your course. Go with the flow. Await further instructions. I spent the rest of the week chilling out, so to speak, on that tidy little island, but the first thing I did was ring up Dana Wehrli in the morning, which was bedtime in Los Angeles.

"Oh, Jake, I've been waiting to hear from you," she said. "Is everything all right? Are they shooting at you or anything?"

"Manila's a dump, except the expensive parts. But no, I'm not in any kind of danger. I couldn't call you from there, in case the phones were tapped. Didn't want to blow my cover. I'm in Singapore right now, so I can call with no trouble."

"Singapore? Wow! If I could go shopping there for just one day ... have you seen the bird farm? People say it's great."

"I'll be here for a week. I'll definitely look into it. How about you? What are you up to these days?"

"You know, work work work. They're keeping me running full tilt. I did a segment on Roger Moore replacing Sean Connery as James Bond. Now we're putting together one about the Oscars— pretty blah lineup this year for best picture, but *Amadeus* looks good. Barbara Walters is so diva-ish, but Hugh Downs is a nice enough guy. So far he's kept his hands to himself, which sets him apart in TV land. They're sending one of the other *20/20* teams to the Philippines next month, seems that election is a very hot topic. All the papers and everything will be covering it. Do you know anything about that? Who's Corazon Aquino, some local beauty queen? Have you met Imelda Marcos?"

"I was introduced to Imelda a party at their palace," I said. "With the Manila glitterati and so forth."

"Wow, you get around! I wish I'd been there. But they're keeping me on domestic assignments for now. I've been angling for overseas stories, but everybody wants those. You just have to wait your turn. I don't know. The *Washington Post* called what we do 'candy cane journalism,' but we're holding our own in the ratings against *Knott's Landing* and *Hill Street Blues*. I still like it."

And so we passed a pleasant hour swapping trivia, assuring each other how much we missed each other and then ringing off.

And I picked up some useful intel: America was flooding the place with journalists? What was up that Sonarr wasn't telling me? The *International Herald Tribune* and the *Asian Wall Street Journal* gave the Philippines some coverage, but in Manila honest news was rare, and as an investment banker I couldn't very well go courting the opposition for inside info.

As for the rest of my Singapore week ... I cruised the boutiques and malls along Orchard Road and picked up a collection of mind-blowing batik shirts. You couldn't buy them in the U.S., something about an import-export tiff with Indonesia where they're made. The gold shops took some attitude adjustment. Bargain for jewelry? No in Tiffany's, but yes in Singapore. Once I got the hang of it I bought some 22 carat baubles for Mom, Dana and Dad's wife, Judy. I looked in vain for a bird farm, but the Jurong Bird Park and its exotic, to-be-seen-nowhere-else collection of feathered friends was well worth the visit. On Sentosa Island I saw the coastal artillery that, legend has it, were pointed the wrong way when the Japs invaded (actually, the problem was malfeasance by the British Command). I wandered through museum exhibits. Was intrigued by the various styles of Asian arts and crafts. Sampled the food at a bunch of hawker centres and became addicted to roti prata with an egg and hawker coffee (a meal in a glass) for breakfast. Rode all over the island on double-decker buses for cheap sight-see tours. Doesn't sound exciting? If you crave high adventure, skip Singapore. If raging hormones urge you toward wild times, join the Eurotrash in Bangkok.

* * *

I RETURNED TO MANILA RE-ENERGIZED, BUT I WAS NEARING THE end of the list of plausible interviews, and people posed impatient questions about progress and estimated resolution of the loan. I had to stall them off and also come up with other ways to simulate investment banking. Nor did my meeting with Sonarr help me fathom what I was doing so important as to justify the five-star vacation I'd been indulging in.

While I was off to Singapore General Romulo died. The papers, both pro-Marcos and the opposition press, covered it lavishly and reverently. He was a genuine national hero, and the whole population mourned him. Therefore I was surprised to get a call from Beth Romulo the day after I got back. "Beth, I was so sorry to hear about your husband," I said. "It happened while I was out of town. The Philippines will miss him. They need more such men right now."

"Thank you for the thought, Jack. It was a last-ditch try, and he didn't make it. They operated on his stomach, five hours of ugly surgery, and he never really recovered. Considering his age, there wasn't much hope going in, but you do what you can. And you move on, which I will in due course. But to the matter at hand, the reason for this call at this odd time is that someone wants to meet with you, and being a fellow American they thought I might be the best person to arrange it."

"I like meeting people. No hints who it is?"

"Not over the phone, but don't worry. Trust me, it will be well worth your while. What's your availability?"

"Clear calendar, at your party's convenience."

She set it up for the afternoon two days hence and gave me a Forbes Park address. I hired a Mercedes and driver on the appointed day, and the gateman was expecting us when we showed up. For the sake of good international relations I had the driver slip him a U.S. $20 bill, and we proceeded to our destination, a mid-range (for Forbes Park) bungalow that sprawled only to a modest degree (by Forbes Park standards) over a landscaped plot. My knock brought a small, matronly woman to the door. Well-dressed, with lighter, Eurasian coloring, she carried her 50ish age graciously, her youthful beauty by no means faded. "You are Mr. Philco?" she said, looking me up and down.

"Yes, Jack Philco. Beth Romulo said I was to meet someone here. She didn't give me any names."

"In the circumstances, that was prudent. Come with me, Mr. Philco." She led me from the foyer through a well-appointed living room to a lanai-like sitting room overlooking a swimming pool enclosed in a neat tropical garden. Hibiscus, bougainvillea, orchids and birds-of-paradise accented lush greenery with bright colors. "Sit," she said, indicating a floral-print easy chair. "Would you like some tea?"

"That would be nice," I said. She stepped to another door and said something through it, then returned. "You're friend of Beth's?" I asked.

"I've known the General for many years, and then Beth came along. We became acquainted on some trips we took with Imelda, and we hit it off. I was one of Imelda's Blue Ladies, you see. Beth and I became good friends."

"Beth pointed out some of Imelda's Blue Ladies at a Palace soiree. Sort of like hostesses. You say you 'were' a Blue Lady?"

THE BLUE LADY'S STORY

"Yes, until Imelda drummed me out. Fine with me. By the time our falling out occurred I was weary of the whole business, and my husband was established securely enough that Imelda's patronage no longer mattered. Oh, she can be vindictive, believe that, but she had so many things on her plate that she just banished me from her entourage and forgot that I'd ever been in it."

A petite maid with a darker, native complexion arrived with tea service on a mahogany tray. She set it on the coffee table and poured while we talked.

"Beth didn't tell me much about Blue Ladies. You mentioned trips. It's more than just hostessing at parties?"

"Oh, much, much more. It's unlimited, arbitrary indentured servitude. It's being subject to the iron whim of a self-centered diva. It's round-the-clock ass-kissing, if you'll pardon my crudity. Imelda, you see, came from a home financially deprived and beset with family discord. Consequently, she always lusted for luxury and at the same time craved adulation. She blossomed into a natural beauty, which by Filipina standards is very beautiful indeed, and finished runner-up for Miss Manila one year. That brought marriage to Ferdinand, which was one solution to her needs—the luxury side.

"Her Blue Ladies are a solution to her need for constant attention. They mostly are wives of businessmen and government cronies whom the Marcoses have enriched. To be a Blue Lady is an honor and an affirmation of status, but also it is an obligation. The uniform is a traditional *ternos* dress with butterfly sleeves in pure white with a 'Marcos blue' sash. But that is subject to change according to her whim, which is not always in best taste, nor appropriate to the setting. For her audience with Pope Paul she was miffed to learn that only Catholic Queens could wear white, and that she must wear black with long sleeves. When he visited Manila she had us all arranged in a reception line, dressed in white with white parasols, to make her point and rub it in as he stepped off his plane. On other trips she dressed us in outfits quite out of keeping with the occasion, simply because they appealed to her at the moment.

"In addition to serving as hostesses at Malacanang Palace, and at the other palace she built at Olot, she always hauls along Blue Ladies in her traveling entourage, which could number as high as 100. One might think that free trips to luxury hotels in famous cities are a treat, but more often than not they were an ordeal. On short notice a few of us are called and expected to drop everything, pack and be off. Imelda has no consideration for anyone's comfort but her own, so we were left to scramble for our own luggage and crammed into the cheapest rooms in those nice hotels. Sometimes she would present us with jewelry or watches or other expensive items that caught her eye. Other times she left us in the lurch to make our own arrangements back to Manila as she leapt at some freshly presented opportunity to party somewhere else. On a flight back from India once she kept us all awake with her interminable chatter, though we'd had only two hours sleep, until finally Beth quietly suggested to Ferdinand that Imelda might want to get some sleep so as to look her best when we arrived. We all loved Beth for getting us that break.

"And then there were the shopping sprees. She'd descend on the most expensive shops in New York, Paris, London, Rome, anywhere we were, buying anything and everything that struck her fancy. She'd see shoes she liked and order a dozen pairs in different colors, likewise with gowns, jewelry, scarfs, fur coats—for the Philippines??!—anything at all. Often as not, we'd then be expected to tote it back to the hotel for her."

"You said you used to be a Blue Lady," I observed. "There's a retirement program?"

"No," she said, "you offend her in some small way and instantly you're persona non grata. My sin was, I demurred from going on one of her New York trips because it would mean missing my 25th wedding anniversary celebration, which had been long planned and arranged. That was the last call I got from Imelda. But at least she didn't insist on my returning the jewelry she'd given me, as she has demanded of others. Oh, I enjoyed the travel and the prestige at first, but by the time we parted ways I was glad to be rid of that greedy sow. It is probably too much to hope for, but maybe come February the Philippines will be rid of the both of them.

"She has simply become too full of herself. When she attended the Shah of Iran's glorious celebration in Persepolis she noticed a number of women wearing crowns, so she put on one of her diamond tiaras. Then she was told only queens could wear crowns there, so what did she do but turn it around and wear it backwards in her hair! No one could tell *her* not to wear her diamonds! There was the time, coming back from Rome, she discovered there was no cheese on the plane for her snacks, so she ordered the plane to return to the airport for some paltry amount of cheese.

"And everywhere, she sings, sings, sings! She has a nice soprano voice and knows every Filipina love song ever written. In her early days, Ferdinand was moving up the political ladder and she would sing at his rallies very charmingly. Now, wherever she is, if there are musicians performing she will contrive to take over the microphone and sing, not so charmingly. I think she truly believes that people enjoy it, when they are just enduring it because of her position."

"From what I've been finding out, many of the people around here (I gestured with a sweep of my arm) owe their prosperity to connections with Marcos," I said.

"True," she admitted, "but enough is enough. Trade is not doing as well as it might, and the government has become ever more grasping and oppressive. There is more opposition to him in Makati than appears on the surface."

"Is that why you wanted to meet with me, to talk about Marcos and the economy?" I asked.

She straightened, surprised. "Oh, goodness no," she said, flustered. "You got me started on a topic that still rankles, and my motor mouth went into high gear. I'm not the one you are to meet, I'm just providing a venue for the sake of discretion. She's waiting at the next door neighbor's house. Let's go over there before you set me off again."

We exited through a sliding glass door, skirted the sparkling pool, slipped through a break in a hedge and continued across a manicured stretch of Bermuda grass to another glass-fronted lanai room. My Blue Lady hostess tapped on the door, and a tiny woman with big glasses came to the door and slid it open for us. "Cory," said the ex-Blue Lady, "this is Mr. Jack Philco. Mr. Philco, may I present Corazon Aquino."

* * *

I'd seen news photos of Cory Aquino. Her front-page impression was the squirrely girl who sat in the front row and always had her hand in the air—with the right answer every time. Up close she was a tiny, intense little bird, one that wouldn't let an early worm get away. Her features combined Chinese with Filipina, blending the skin tones but sidestepping the essential beauty of either influence. She greeted me with a friendly smile that gave her a pleasant look. "I am pleased to meet you, Mr. Philco," she said. "It was recommended that I talk with you."

"The pleasure is all mine, Mrs. Aquino," I said. "I've heard so much about you."

"Would it be all right to call you Jack?" she asked. "And you to call me Cory?"

"Of course. What can I do for you? Who recommended that we meet?"

"That I cannot tell you, and he wasn't clear on the content of our meeting, either. Tell me, what are you doing here in Manila?"

"I represent a bank that is assembling a consortium interested in making a large loan to the Philippines."

"I see. How large a loan is being considered?"

"Not settled yet. Several hundred million dollars, possibly."

"You are aware of the unsettled state of affairs here, I take it?"

"Unstable, seems the current condition."

"Just so. May I ask if you have examined the current economic situation in the Philippines?"

"I've interviewed a number of people, been taken on a tour by Mr. Enrile and done some analysis of financial data and statistics."

"I see. What are your conclusions, if I may ask?"

Her intensity was contagious, as was her forthrightness. "It looks fishy to me. Particularly, it seems there are large sums that go unaccounted for every year, and everyone I talk to gives me the same canned speech."

"Good for you. I'm surprised you figured it out, the way the government cooks the books. Not everyone is as forthright as you. The sums go unaccounted for because Marcos and his cronies steal them. You get the same talk because you have been steered to people in the regime's pocket. Do you think your bank will approve the loan?"

"Remains to be seen." I said. "I haven't yet submitted my report. Now you tell me something—your declaring candidacy for the president came as a surprise to many. How is your campaign coming along?"

"It may have been presented as a surprise by the Marcos-controlled papers," she said, "but the fact is that we have gathered over a million signatures on petitions backing me. We have many people working on my behalf, but it is not emphasized in the news because Marcos suppresses it."

"You filed for the election the day after General Ver was acquitted, I noticed."

"That was the last straw!" she spat. "They had the whole assassination on video, and the idea that those beasts could just walk off scot free, I couldn't just let that go by. Let me tell you about my late husband…"

CORAZON AQUINO'S STORY

"Right from the earliest days, Benigno Aquino—Ninoy, everybody called him—represented the strongest and most effective opposition to Marcos. He came from a wealthy, landowning family. While still a teenager he became a war correspondent for the *Manila Times* and won a government award for his reporting in the Korean War. He took up law at the University of the Philippines and a few years after that successfully negotiated the surrender of the Huk communist rebels. For that he was awarded his second Philippine Legion of Honor. He then entered politics and became mayor of

Concepcion at the age of 22. His political career progressed to the point where at age 34 he became the youngest elected senator in the country's history.

"That occurred soon after Marcos became president, and Ninoy was his most vehement critic. He called out Imelda for her extravagant Cultural Center, labeling her a megalomaniac with a penchant to captivate. He warned that Marcos was trying to impose a garrison state. This of course made him a marked man. When Marcos declared martial law based on trumped-up pretexts, Ninoy was immediately arrested and imprisoned on charges of murder, illegal possession of firearms and subversion, linking him with the New People's Army and a Communist insurgency. He was kept in solitary confinement much of the time, finally resorting to a 40-day hunger strike. Several months later he was convicted by the Military Commission and sentenced to death by firing squad. The injustice of this provoked a world-wide outrage.

"However, the sentence could not be carried out because Ninoy had a heart attack in prison and was permitted to go to the United States for treatment. That being successful, and to recover the family finances that lay in ruins, he toured the U.S. giving speeches in freedom rallies.

"In 1983 word reached him that the Philippines' political situation was deteriorating, and his allies in the Liberal Party felt strongly he could help bring about the country's return to democracy. He called for Marcos to step down, for the good of the nation. He was advised to wear a bullet-proof vest for his return, which—foolishly, I think—he announced en route. Now, Ferdinand Marcos is a very superstitious man, and a soothsayer warned him that if Ninoy set foot on Philippine soil, Marcos would fall. Therefore, as Ninoy came down the steps from his China Airline flight a single shot hit him in the head before he alit on the tarmac. And then someone shot nearby Rolando Galman, whom the authorities immediately claimed to be 'the lone Communist gunman.' Some seconds later a squad of men stormed out of an Aviation Security Command van and pumped Galman's body full of additional bullets. The whole incident was recorded on film, and the delay of the security men proved it was a staged event gone wrong.

"The assassination was on front pages everywhere in the world except in the Marcos-controlled press here. Nevertheless, Filipinos immediately staged demonstrations and called for Marcos's resignation or impeachment. The country was in turmoil, which Marcos answered with further repression. When local business leaders publicly criticized Marcos's record on human rights, he ordered 33 of them charged with 'economic sabotage.' More than two million people lined the streets for Ninoy's funeral, and again the Marcos press ignored it, the only coverage being the Church-sponsored station, Radio Veritas.

"The outcry was strong enough to provoke a commission charged with investigating the assassination. The majority concluded that Ninoy and Galman were shot by someone in his security detail, which had been provided by Marcos. Finally, in February this year, 26 military and security men were indicted and put on trial for the assassination plot, including General Ver. As announced on December 2, all were acquitted, and that was just too much for everybody. When Ninoy returned to the Philippines in 1983 it was despite his forebodings, because he was dedicated to helping his people, and they killed him in plain sight and left his corpse lying there. And then this slap in the face! I declared my candidacy the next day after they let Ver off."

"I can certainly see why," I said. "How has your campaign been going?"

"Better than you'd take from the local press and television," she said. "I have a strong following on the larger islands, and probably the smaller ones too, though they don't amount to many votes. I think I'll do all right here on Luzon, too. It isn't that I won't have enough votes to win. I know I will. I have run political campaigns before. It's what Ferdinand will do to thwart me that's the obstacle."

"I've heard he cheats."

"I don't know that he's ever won an election honestly. Stuffing ballot boxes is only a part of it. His people remove opposition voters from the registration rolls, or move their names to other precincts without informing them. They throw away opposition votes without counting them or simply steal the ballot boxes. Out in the rural districts popular opposition candidates have been gunned down or their campaign workers beaten. On Mindanao they tell me that even the trees, rocks and monkeys vote for Mr. Marcos. My government sources report that right now the Treasury is printing money to send around to buy votes and influence. He does it every election. One time he overdid it and bankrupted the nation's economy."

"It's odd to be meeting you and talking about this here in Forbes Park. We're surrounded by Marcos supporters, aren't we?"

"On the contrary, when Benigno was murdered, Makati was ground zero for outrage and protest demonstrations. Here more than anywhere, because people in this district have a vital interest in such matters. Most of these people would dearly love to see Imelda's backside disappearing into the distance."

"I wish there were some way I could help," I said.

"You are not a citizen, so you cannot get involved. But one thing, please don't loan him any money."

* * *

I CHATTED WITH CORY AQUINO A WHILE LONGER ABOUT THE Philippines, about her background, about her vision, about her perspective on the situation. She was a very sharp woman, and despite my mission I couldn't help but root for her. I came away up more puzzled than ever. There was no way she could steal the election from Marcos. There wasn't even any way for her to win it fair and square.

Then the next day I got a call from Luz. "Mr. Philco," she said, "I wonder if I could impose on you a little. I of course report on my assignments to Auntie, and from what I have told her, she has taken an interest in you. I wonder if you could spare a little time from your busy schedule to meet with her?"

I was fast becoming Manila's favorite drop-in guest. An invite to shoot the shit with my call girl's madam? Is that a move up in the world, or a step down? Considering the nature of her clientele, she might provide intel from a different angle, so I didn't spend any time deciding. "Sure, I'd be delighted," I said. "Give me a time and place." The time was convenient, early afternoon the next day, but the place surprised me: another address in Forbes Park.

Same Mercedes, same driver, same U.S. $20 to the gate man. Today took us to a different part of town, though not much different in look from the rest. We stopped before a modern one-story home, lots of straight lines and glass, under a canted flat roof. The large leaves of well-tended banana plants softened the stark architecture and provided privacy from the road. A uniformed maid answered my ring and invited me in: "You are Mr. Philco? Come with me."

She ushered me to a room off the living area, an office with filing cabinets, work surfaces, bookshelves, several telephones and a shriveled, monkey-faced old crone facing me from a motorized wheel chair. The chair was top of the line, fitted with so many features that I wouldn't have been surprised to see her fly away in it. She wore a lush silk gown and was so bejeweled that you'd need polarized shades to look at her in bright sunlight. "Do not be alarmed," she said in a weary voice I recognized. "I'm not contagious. Please do sit down."

I eased myself onto a rattan, cushioned chair. "It's not that, of course," I said. "Coming into a house like this, you are not what one expects to see. You are Luz's aunt?"

"Yes, I am Auntie. I am glad you were able to come talk to me. Luz's report on your excursion with her aroused my interest. It is possible I may be able to help you, and rest assured, I have no intention of harming you. At first glance my appearance is a shock to people, so don't feel you have to apologize for your reaction. After you have heard my tale, you will understand. Life has treated me harshly. I rose to meet the challenge, but my current repulsive state, poorly concealed by all these trappings, is the price one pays."

AUNTIE'S TALE

"My misfortune began at the commencement of young womanhood. All women desire beauty, but it can be an evil curse in the wrong circumstances. I was the prettiest girl in my village at the age of 15. That same year the Japs invaded the Philippines. As ill-luck would have it, we were directly in the path of their advance from Linguyen Gulf to Manila. As the Jap army moved through our villages they kidnapped young women for use as comfort women for the troops. If our parents objected, the Japs bayonetted them before our eyes—not even spending a bullet on them. You can imagine our despair at that. No point in resisting, no thought of escape, no hope at all. The lucky ones were the ugly girls, who were left behind.

"The soldiers were preoccupied for the time being with slaughtering my countrymen and capturing our land, so we were not immediately put to the intended use. As we trailed along with the troops I flaunted my youthful charms and attracted the eye of one of the leading officers in the unit. He requisitioned me as his exclusive punchboard and took me under his protection. It was a reprieve from the worst fate facing me, but still I was brokenhearted and dared not complain nor even show distress. It is the world's most demanding school of acting, but I mastered what I needed to do despite my silent tears. I counted my blessings that I did not share the plight of the other girls, who served as public toilets for those depraved little beasts. Once the Jap conquest was complete and permanent garrisons set up, they were on continuous call for hours on end, every day, for the pleasures of those disgusting apes with their bathtub-stopper little dinkies. It ruined them for life; some girls want so far as to disfigure themselves or commit suicide rather than continue.

"I at least had some privacy and time off. I pleased my protector and busied myself in his quarters to enhance his comfort, which I hoped would cement his attachment to me. I succeeded in that, and when he was promoted to Imperial Army Headquarters in Manila he took me along. He delighted in buying me clothes and jewelry to enhance my beauty, and he enjoyed showing me off in the base social life, such as it was. Not only that, but I made myself useful and soon was given run of the camp. This enabled me to observe many comings and goings, of both Japs and their Filipino collaborators.

"When the Americans returned and threw the Japs out, I was judged to be a collaborator myself because I had avoided suffering; other comfort women who had not had my luck were only too eager to denounce me to the post-war examiners. They threw me in jail for several years—paying for my sins, as if any of it was my intention or I got any fun out of it. In addition to the standard maltreatment of Philippine prisons I was repeatedly raped by guards who revenged themselves on the Japs by the pleasures they stole from me. It was there I caught the diseases and afflictions that destroyed my looks and turned me into the wreck you see before you. Say what you will, the Japs at least adhered to standards of personal hygiene.

"By the time they released me I had reached my 20s and was already ruined both physically and socially. However, not ruined mentally. My brain functioned perfectly well, and I reasoned that, since powerful men are all the same the world over, there will always be a market for the temporary affections of beautiful women. I had learned something about organization and business from my contact with the military and the black marketers in Manila (for where do you think I procured delicacies and treats for my protector?). Former black marketers and undetected collaborators were succeeding in post-War Manila and rising to political power, and I knew many of them, so it was easy enough to build a client list. With Marcos, corrupt wealth and easy money became plentiful. As for girls, village poverty drives them by droves into my welcoming arms, and I weed out all but the most exquisitely beautiful and charming and put them through finishing school.

The results of years of dedicated toil and effort you see before you —this house, my baubles, all of it. What I am wearing is nothing. I can show you jewels, fine clothing, that even Imelda Marcos would envy. One might ask whether it was worth it. All I can say is, life dealt me a rotten hand, and I played my cards as well as anyone could." This last observation with a resigned shrug.

The spoils of war—every war. What do you say after a story like that? Where do you even *look*? In her eyes? At her hands? At the ceiling? At the floor? Out the window?

"I know what you are thinking, Mr. Philco," she said, "and do not let your thoughts be troubled. It happened. It could have been worse. I survived it, prospered and have reconciled myself to the past. Let us turn to present matters. I asked you to come see me because of Luz's reports. I have served many visiting bankers and businessmen from America, and you are very different from the others. The questions you asked Luz and the places you had her show you tipped me off, but insisting on paying for it yourself, that was the final clue. No American businessman ever turned down Imelda Marcos's freebies. So I think you may have other interests in Manila than making loans to Ferdinand Marcos. I do not wish to pry too deeply, but I was wondering if there is some way I could help you."

"I take it your opinion of Ferdinand Marcos is not very high?" I asked.

She shook her head slowly and coughed out a bitter laugh. "My opinion of that viper? Have you met him?"

"Only briefly. Mostly he told me about his war exploits."

"Oh yes, his famous war exploits. He has lived on those lies now for 40 years. I will bet he was wearing his chest full of medals. He bought every single one of them and conjured his commendations and awards out of thin air and whole cloth. His chief war exploit was running a very profitable black market operation. With my own eyes I saw him wearing a Japanese uniform, more than once. Whether he betrayed his own countrymen who were fighting for Philippine freedom, I do not know, but I do know that no battlefield ever benefited from his heroics. His heroics were confined to as many bedrooms he could breach. I will not say whether he ever saw the inside of mine, not to protect his reputation, but to protect mine. By the time he married Imelda he'd had several mistresses and fathered a dozen children ... whom Imelda refuses to acknowledge.

"Except that he is now too sick to be a tomcat, nothing has changed," she continued. "He still lives on lies and crooked dealings. Look, look here." She maneuvered her chair over to a desk, picked up a little packet, rolled back and stretched out a claw to hand it to me. It was a little sheaf of crisp new currency.

"He's up to his old tricks, printing money to buy another election," she said. "A government official paid one of my girls with these. Look at the serial numbers."

I did. They were the same on all eight bills.

"Ferdinand must be getting demented," she said. "Or desperate. He knows whom to bribe, whom to promise and whom to threaten, but he's never been this amateurish before. It's a disgrace. So, Mr. Philco, I do not know what your true business here is, but if it has anything to do with ridding us of that weasel and his greedy wife, I know of things I could do to help."

And me sent here by the CIA to help Marcos stay in office? "Auntie, as you know, we investment bankers are very discreet, every bit as much as you are. I certainly appreciate your offer of help, and I will keep it in mind. Luz has been very helpful to me already."

"She is a good girl," said Auntie. "I pray she will soon be able to leave this business. I have done my best to spare her the worst of it. She probably told you that she dreams of marrying a big spender. Having met you, I do not think you are that man, but perhaps you and I can trade favors nevertheless. I must bid you goodbye now, Mr. Philco. I have other business to take care of, and my energy is low these days. It was a pleasure to meet you, and feel free to call on me at any time." With that she poked a button on the arm of her chair and the maid stepped into the room. "Please show Mr. Philco out," she said.

* * *

I'D BEEN MEETING MORE PEOPLE LATELY THAN A WALMART door-geezer, but the next meet-and-greet I would gladly have passed up, had I any choice. They banged on my door just as I buttoning my shirt to go down to breakfast. It was six Filipinos, taller and bulkier than typical, dressed in sharp suits and designer shades. Their attitude didn't suggest law enforcement; rather, they came on like they *were* the law, and they barged into my room like they owned it, which in a sense they did. "Mr. Philco," said the thug in charge, "Imelda would like to talk to you. Right now. You must come with us."

How could I refuse? Three of them escorted me away, while the other three stayed behind to toss my room.

THE FIFTH PART OF THE STORY

One thing I've observed about beautiful women's faces: When they're happy, they're very, very pretty, but when they're infuriated, they can be butt ugly. Whether it's the contrast that shocks, or something about facial structure that shifts with mood, I can't say—maybe a plastic surgeon can give you an answer to that one.

Now, when the once-beautiful woman is 20 years past her prime, in addition is a raging control freak, and on top of that is white hot irate ... you can imagine what confronted me when my three thugs frog-marched me into Imelda Marcos's livid presence.

"Mr. Philco," she screeched. "I demand to know what the hell is going on here!"

"I'd like to know the same thing myself," I countered. "These goons dragged me out of the Manila Hotel before I even had breakfast. What's the big idea?"

"These goons are my brother, Kokoy, and some of his assistants. I dispatched them to bring you in to answer some very serious questions."

"And these questions are ...?"

"Just exactly what is your mission here in the Philippines?"

"Investigating the possibilities of a loan to your government, as I've said all along."

"So you said, but it was a lie all along. You were sent here by the CIA, and I want to know why."

Oops! "That's preposterous. Wherever did you get that idea?"

"From a source in the CIA, that's where."

"He's an imposter."

"I don't think so. He told me you were here to assist us with the election, as if we need any help! Listen, Mr. Jack Philco or whatever your real name is—your purpose for being here is of little importance, I just don't like being deceived by people who come here under false pretenses. Frankly, I'd rather you were truly here to make us a loan. We need the money more than we need CIA meddling. The CIA shoveled millions of dollars into the 1984 elections to subvert us, and the opposition beat my party by 14 to 7 *in my own district*. To help my party I even resigned from the Executive Committee, since everybody hated me when I had to hold things together after the unfortunate assassination. The CIA stuck their oar in, as they so often do, and cheated the people's will.

"So you tell your CIA bosses to stay out of this election. We do not need their help, if that is their aim. And if they are thinking of backing the opposition, tell them we will crush Mrs. Corazon Aquino, no matter what the CIA does. No one will vote for her, because she does not understand Filipino femininity. What our people want in a woman is beauty and a feeling of love, and that pathetic little mouse has no understanding of either beauty or of love. Have you seen her, for goodness sake? She's just a crude little woman without makeup or manicure. At least she ought to wear contact lenses! What experience has she had in politics, or government, any kind of experience? How could anyone vote for her, when she is neither beautiful nor competent? Ferdinand will win in a landslide, because Filipinos want to be ruled by a strongman, not by some owl-faced little mouse!

"And I'll tell you another thing. Benigno Aquino's wealthy father, the sugar cane king, was executed after the war. And do you know why? He was convicted of treason, because while Ferdinand and Romulo and other heroes were suffering in the jungle and fighting for Filipino freedom, he collaborated with the Japs. So all these people are raising a fuss about the son of a proven traitor who got what he deserved, and on top of that fussing about his ugly wife!

"Mr. Philco, you are no longer of any interest to us. Stay away from me and Ferdinand, and keep out of our election. If we catch you interfering in any way, you will regret it." She turned to her brother. "Kokoy, take this lying meddler back where you found him."

Which they did, with dispatch and none too gently.

I returned to find my room visibly mussed over, though not totally vandalized. I doubt that they found anything incriminating, as the only papers and documents there reflected investment banking and Philippine government propaganda. I couldn't tell if they'd picked the lock on my Gucci bag. I'd think some of the gear I'd brought might raise suspicions, but everything was still present, even my SIG. The only thing missing from the room was the 22 carat gold jewelry for Mom, Dana and Judy I'd bought in Singapore.

Notwithstanding that it would be late evening in New York, I went straight to a lobby pay phone and dialed up Thermite Holdings. "This is Jack Philco. Put me through to Stokes Gladstone," I barked.

"Yes sir, Mr. Philco," the operator said, and it was done.

"Hello, Jack, what's up?" said Todd Sonarr.

"I thought you were going to alert me before you disclosed my mission to certain parties."

"So I am. The time hasn't yet arrived. Why? Something happen?"

"This morning a certain First Lady had her goons haul me to the Palace to chew me out about some preposterous yarn that I'd been sent by the CIA. I cannot imagine who would have spread such a ridiculous rumor."

"Not me."

"Who else is party to our business besides you and me?"

"It's very tightly buttoned up. Just my superior and your contact."

And the light bulb over my head flashed on! "Okay. I'll look into that. Now that the situation is out in the open, any change in plans?"

"Steady as she goes, Jack. You're doing fine. Don't worry too much about said First Lady. She blames everything that goes wrong on the CIA. Nobody pays any attention to it. I'll relay any changes in plans to you as they arise. Roger and out." And he hung up. Changes in plans? What plans?

I next dialed Kevin Blank at the U. S. Embassy and told him to wait right there, that I'd be coming to see him in a few minutes. Then I went into the café and downed the breakfast that Imelda's brother and his buddies had so rudely interrupted. When I reached his office he was sitting at his skimpy desk pretending to read some policy manual, furtive and visibly agitated.

"Kevin, my man," I said brightly. "I thought it would be useful to get a briefing from you on what you've accomplished since the last time we met."

"Just what you said, Jack. I went out and talked to people."

"And how did that go?"

"Pretty well. I found out that most Filipinos don't like Marcos very much, and since the assassination they're less afraid to say so."

"Interesting. So you just talked to people on the street? Develop any good government sources?"

"Well ... I struck up a conversation with a Filipino guy in a bar in Ermita. He was well dressed and sounded like he had good connections pretty high up. I thought a little booze might loosen his tongue, so I stood a few rounds, and we hit it off pretty well. When we parted company he said he'd get back to me."

"Sounds promising. So ...?"

"So two days later he phoned me here and said some people in the government would like to talk with me, and he'd send a car.

Would you believe it, this Mercedes—not a fucking car pool Ford—came to the Embassy and took me right to Malacanang Palace!"

"Don't keep me in suspense. He took you in to meet Imelda Marcos?"

"Yes, he did." Kevin was shifting his eyes rapidly side to side and squirming all the more.

"Okay, Kevin," I said sternly. "How did she worm it out of you?"

He did some mental shuffles and back-stepping, then he abruptly straightened up in his chair and leaned toward me with a little fire in his eyes. "Jake, let me tell you something. When I met you in Cambodia, you were a hero to me. The things you did—just awesome! I wanted to join The Company and be a spook too, just like you. So I joined The Company, and it's turned out as boring as it could be. Nine years of pointless meetings, writing reports about nothing, foreign assignments that have me wasting my time trying to get intel out of lying assholes and killing time in two-bit hotels, and all that for a crappy G-10 salary. Meantime you're getting the Shah out of Iran, having firefights with the Irish Republican Army, busting up a Russian gun-running op, bringing in the Grenada invasion, shooting down a Cuban MIG, all that stuff you do, all the while living in a Malibu beach pad and getting rich in the process. For chrissakes, look at us right here. You're in a suite in the Manila Hotel with an open tab, and I'm in a three-star on a per diem, having to account for every fucking dime.

"Well, goddammit, there I am in that super palace, talking to one of the richest, most glamorous women in the world. Okay, when I loosened that guy's tongue, maybe I loosened mine a little too, and said some things out of school, and he passed the word along. Imelda up and offers me half a year's salary in cash on the spot for what I can tell her about you. So I tell her the CIA sent you to help them win their election, that's all. I didn't even blow your cover by telling her your real name. What's the harm?"

So—now *I'm* Boris's goat? "We don't yet know what's the harm," I said. "Some of her goons hauled me in for a grilling while their buddies ransacked my hotel room. Whether there's more harm coming remains to be seen."

"What's she going to do about it? You're an American citizen with Agency backing. You're here to help them. Big deal. Nothing the great Jake Fonko can't deal with."

"You don't know the Marcoses," I said. "Well, the cat's out of the bag, and I'll have to deal with it. I'll pass the word to Langley that I'm not going to be using you for backup any longer, and I'll let them sort out the rest of it." With that I got up from my chair and left the room.

I was in a quandary. Todd Sonarr hired me to keep the opposition from stealing the election from Ferdinand Marcos. It was now clear that not only could that not happen, but Marcos was on track to lose the election big time, deservedly, and then steal it himself. I've always done my duty, but I had no duty to Ferdinand and Imelda—they were exactly what I've always sided against. Nevertheless I'd taken on the mission. I was trembling, because I had to decide between two things, I recognized that. I thought hard for a minute, breath abated, and then decided: All right, then, if it comes to it, I'll go to Leavenworth.

But maybe I wouldn't. I wasn't in the service, so they'd probably send me somewhere else—Allenwood maybe? But the way I'd set the arrangement up, nobody could prove I worked for the CIA, nor did any written mission specs exist, so they couldn't nail me for dereliction. Maybe nobody would even notice, or if I succeeded maybe they'd seal it away to avoid embarrassment. It was worth the gamble. I'd do what I could to help oust the Marcos regime. First task at hand: with Kevin out of the picture I'd need some other backup, and I wanted the best. I rang up the Intercontinental Hotel on a lobby pay phone to see if Evgeny Grotelov was around.

* * *

"Too bad I'm not working on commission," Grotesqcu

mused. "Selling Russian vodka in this place is child's play. I'm doing okay on kickbacks, though—I'll take home a stash of hard currency. Considering where the KGB was going to send me, I'm sitting pretty here in Manila. I have you to thank for that, of course." We were sitting under some palms by the Intercontinental Hotel swimming pool having coffee, an innocent meeting of a Russian vodka salesman and an American banker in the interests of fostering international trade.

"What mission did you dodge?" I asked.

"Afghanistan. It's going crazy there. The goat-fuckers are shooting down our Hinds with American Stinger missiles, quite disrupting our military operations. The ragheads control the mountain passes now, and our escalating losses are starting to cause dissension at home. We may have to throw in the towel, another round lost in the Great Game. Jake, there's a rumor about that you had something to do with the Stingers."

"I might have suggested it to somebody a while back."

"Splendid, splendid. I can take that to the bank. You're more of a threat to my country than anyone had ever imagined. I'll use that to justify adding another analyst to my staff. So you're throwing in with Cory Aquino, you say? What do they call it — 'going rogue'?"

"Anything to put it to the Marcoses. You must have had some experience with crooked elections, being Russian."

"Not in Russia. We don't have elections there, just affirmations. But I've meddled here and there in other countries' elections, yes. Nothing like the situation here. You're aiming to steal an election from Ferdinand Marcos? I admire your ambition. If you could get control of the polling places, that always helps. The trouble is, there are so many islands. Impossible to organize that. Maybe the New People's Army?"

"Aren't they your guys?"

"Hardly. Marcos says they're Communists, but except for propaganda purposes we wouldn't touch them wearing hazmat gear. Maybe you can get some of them to mount an insurrection and draw government troops away from snatching ballot boxes, though I wouldn't hold out much hope."

"Well, it's a starting point," I reflected. "There's only three weeks until the election, not much time, but if they have forces already in place that could be coordinated, that's a possibility."

So I was off to check out the NPA situation on the islands. I figured, considering the tight time frame, I'd do a make it or break it trip to recon a major island and estimate the possibilities. I recalled from Todd Sonarr's visit in Malibu that Steele Bosserman deemed the NPA a dire threat to Marcos. For all I knew, the New People's Army was already poised and primed for action all across the archipelago. The problem was, I'd had no experience in political insurgency. The Long Range Reconnaissance Patrols didn't work with indigs. That was a Green Beret specialty. The CIA did that too, but I wasn't ever really in the CIA. So I'd need a guide, someone with local savvy that I could trust. Who else but Luz?

Auntie put me in touch with her, and she was willing to take off with me on short notice for a couple days. Next to Luzon, Mindanao is the key Philippine island. Insurrections brewed down there—Muslims, the NPA, pissed-off peons ... so maybe I could locate people willing to go up against Marcos. I put on my civvies for the trip and packed along outdoor and night gear, just in case. Luz called ahead to someone she knew who could help us, and we flew to Mindanao the next day. We landed at the Davao airport, a shabby affair emblazoned with Marcos banners and posters, and I let Luz do the talking. She'd dressed down for the trip, just a casual cotton dress, but even so was her usual stunning little self, so we got good service from every male we encountered. The airport cabs made a sorry lineup, and the taxi queue was every man's elbows for himself. But the jostlers made way for Luz, and we secured one that looked ready for the scrapyard crusher. The driver took us to what passed for the central district of the city using what passed for the scenic route. Davao was the main city on the island, but there was little to recommend it. Marcos banners festooned the streets. Fewer up for Aquino.

First we took rooms in Davao's best hotel, such as it was. Her friend's office was in one of the more presentable buildings a few blocks away. He was a local political honcho whom she'd met in Manila—I didn't inquire in what circumstances, but his eyes certainly lit up when we walked in. Our meeting with him was, from his point of view, disappointingly brief. She explained that we wanted to meet with someone in the New People's Army. From his matter-of-fact reaction, you'd think people dropping in to find the NPA was a daily occurrence. The NPA wasn't so much in the city, he explained. The fighters hung out in the hills. He wrote down a name and told her we'd find him in a certain village, in the general store. We returned to the hotel, and I put on some duds suitable for going in-country. At the curb we flagged down a cab. Luz told the driver what we wanted, and he was all for it—bigger business than what usually climbed into his hack, for U.S. dollars. And also it meant Luz would be riding in his cab for a long time.

Outside the city the view improved, though the place would benefit from Adopt-a-Highway. It was my first field trip away from Metro Manila, and what I saw on our flight and on our drive impressed me. Aside from big swaths clear-cut across hillsides by overzealous loggers, the Philippines are beautiful islands. In contrast to the hard-edged, spectacular scenery of the California coast and the Sierras, they enjoy the quiet, serene beauty of tropical Asia—soft rain forests, shimmering rice paddies stepping up terraced slopes, tea-colored rivers and streams sliding through lush green valleys. We passed by farms and coconut plantations, the smaller ones squalid third-world affairs, then followed a narrow, winding road through forest up into some foothills.

Presently we reached our target village, which amounted to several hundred yards of roadside shops and market stalls, with a school, a government building and a police station situated around a little square off to the side. Several larger homes fronted the main drag, bunched together apart from the many smaller, shabbier ones. Toward the far end of town I spotted the modest minarets of a small mosque. Dirt lanes led off the paved road, along which the rest of the residents lived in various grades of shacks and hovels. The town was in a carnival mood. Small, sunbrowned people milled along the street or squatted in the shade of palms and banana plants. Kids scampered among chickens, dogs, pigs and other denizens of rural life.

Our driver stopped before a cinderblock general store doing brisk business, with a tangle of bicycles, mopeds and motorcycles parked out front. Women, some of them wearing floral headscarves, pawed through racks of bright new clothing and picked over displays of baubles. Customers paraded in and out the door. We told our driver to park up the road and wait, and climbed out of the car. With a few hundred meters of elevation, the air wasn't as moistly heavy as down by the sea but was tropical enough to put a damper on exertion. The bright red paint on the store's metal door was dimmed by accumulating grime, faded by harsh sunlight and undermined by rust. I swung it open, and Luz and I went into the store's sporadically lit, cluttered interior. Women chattered as they stuffed items into string bags and gathered at the counter, where an antique cash register popped up tags to show transactions with the traditional "ka-ching." The men in the shop favored the liquor department, and several carried liter bottles of Russian vodka in hand.

A portly, genial man with Spanish coloring and thick, salt and pepper hair sat back of the counter keeping an eye on his clerks. Luz ascertained that he was the name her friend had given us. "Looks like business is good today," I remarked. "A holiday or something?"

"The government men came yesterday passing out money for the election and taking down Corazon Aquino's signs," he said. "Always good for business."

"They do this for every election?"

"No, just for the Marcos ones. What can I do for you?" he asked. He looked eager to do whatever he could for Luz.

She deferred to me. "I need to talk to someone about the New People's Army," I said.

"Why would you want to do that? You're an American. How come an American wants to talk to the NPA? Are you a reporter or something?"

"I'm interested to find out how they stand on the Marcos government."

"Oh, I can tell you that," he said. "They hate Ferdinand Marcos. Imelda, too. The whole government they hate."

"Did they do anything to interfere with the government people yesterday?"

"No, they lined up for their money, like everybody else. Nobody turns down government money."

"Are they actually an army?" I asked.

"Not really an army, but they are all around. They help people, that's what they do. If some landowner or somebody in the government treats somebody here badly, or if something is stolen, like somebody's water buffalo, maybe they'll pay a visit and straighten things out. Last year they shot a police chief in a village because he was cheating the villagers. And there was that ambush of government troops, too. Got a bunch of them. Not an army, though, the NPA. More like guerillas, you know."

"Are there a lot of them around here? How many, about?"

"Well ... not easy to say. Sometimes more, sometimes not so many."

"Is there somebody in the NPA here in the village I could to talk to?"

"They aren't around much in the daytime. They do their business mostly at night. But I can tell you where to find someone, their chief, he lives down the first lane you come to on the right. It's a white house, you can't miss it. Ask for Bonofacio. Tell him Carlos said it was okay."

"Oh, did we get your name wrong?" Luz said.

"No, you had the right name. 'Carlos', it's sort of a code."

We thanked him and had the cab driver take us down the lane. It was narrow and lined with bushes, stands of bamboos and trash. Teenybopper-aged kids hung out along the roadside. "Early warning system," Luz remarked. We went by a hundred yards of hovels until we reached a larger one painted white.

"This must be the place," I said. I told the cab driver to wait, we got out, and I rapped on the door. "Bonofacio in here?" I asked.

A voice inside said something I couldn't understand, and Luz said something I couldn't understand. The native language, Tagalog. "Tell him who we are," she whispered. "He speaks English a little."

"We're visitors," I said. "We want to talk to Bonofacio about the NPA. Carlos sent us."

"What Carlos?" the voice asked.

"Carlos from the store in town," I said.

There was a shuffling inside and the door opened. A small young man peered through the crack, looking us up and down with eyes a little woozy, at Luz more than me. His color and facial structure were more native than Spanish, and he wore a dirty singlet and droopy off-white shorts. "Okay, I'm Bonofacio," he said. "Come in."

We entered a living room of sorts, which also was a kitchen and dining room, possibly even a bedroom, but at least wasn't a bathroom. Three similar young men squatted in a circle in the middle of the floor, with playing cards in their hands and a half empty bottle of Russian vodka and a scatter of small money on the floor before them.

"What about the NPA?" he said. "You're not from the government, are you?"

"No, I'm a visitor to the Philippines. I want to find out something about NPA plans for the election."

"Plans for an election?" He looked at his buddies for clarification. Shrugs and head shakes. "What election?" he asked me.

"Marcos is running for president. Corazon Aquino is running against him. Next month."

Oh, that one," he said. "What do you want to know?"

"Can we sit down?" I asked, indicating some unoccupied chairs at the room's table.

"Sure, yeah, sit." We did. Luz spoke to him in Tagalog. "I get it," he said. "I'm the local NPA leader, yeah. The New People's Army is strong about that election. We'll guard the ballot box. The government won't try anything. They know better."

"They were here yesterday, Carlos told us."

"Yeah, the usual. They always give people money, say vote for Ferdinand. Promise things will be good if he wins, warn people not to vote for Aquino or they'll find out."

"You were there when they came?"

"Oh, sure. You never turn down government money. But that don't mean anything. We're against Marcos. We'll be out there on voting day."

"The NPA's a battle-ready outfit, then?" I posed.

THE GUERILLA CHIEF'S ACCOUNT

The group on the ground looked at him expectantly. Apparently not all could speak English. He said a few words in Tagalog, waved them off and joined us at the table. They folded his hand and continued their card game. "We don't do drills or have uniforms or that stuff, we're irregulars. But yeah, we're ready for anything. When something comes up we come together and do a raid—hit hard and run away, live to fight another day, like they say. When the government was pushing our farmers for bribes to let them cart their crops to market we set up a roadblock down the hill and chased them away. There's an insurgent area further up the road, and when the troops try to stop food shipments from reaching the people, we ambush them, shoot them up, they go away. We raided their headquarters in Magpet Town and stole some of their weapons, grenades, other stuff..."

"Do you coordinate with NPA on the other islands?" I asked. If the NPA worked in concert across the islands, even on short notice maybe effective opposition could be mounted.

"Coordinate? What's that?"

"It's when you have joint operations. Say you want to attack government positions at the same time, or trade intelligence, or send some people to help out some NPA on another island."

"Joint operations? Why we want to do that stuff, man? This here is our territory. Here, around this village, we take care of things. The other islands, that's their territory."

"If you don't mind my asking, how many NPA do you have in this area?"

He looked at Luz quizzically. She nodded okay. "A couple dozen. More if we need them. Like I said, it's not like the real army. Guys join us when they have a beef with the government, let it go when things are better. When something comes up, you can always count on enough showing up. They're not afraid of Marcos."

"How are things right now?"

"So-so ...you know..." He eyeballed me skeptically, puzzling out what was my angle. I was about to explain that I wanted to organize some resistance to stop Marcos election fraud when we heard a commotion outside, youthful yammering in the native language. "Oh shit," he muttered. He barked something in Tagalog his buddies. They all lurched up and bustled to the back rooms of the shack. We heard our cab take off down the road in a gravel scrunching hurry.

"The children just warned them that a government truck with troops is headed this way," Luz said.

"That's all we need," I said to Luz. "Let's beat it. I thought I saw some trees behind the house. What do you think?"

"Plenty of places to hide in these villages," she said. "We should go out the back." Good advice, but then the boys surged back into the room carrying an assortment of armament—a beat-up tommy gun, two old World War Two Garand rifles, a mismatched pair of revolvers. I heard a truck pull to a stop about 50 yards up the road. I peeped through a window to see men in brown uniforms spill out. They shouted something, then raised their rifles, and a fusillade of gunfire filled the silence. I pulled Luz to the floor as bullets ripped into the shack up at the roofline, sending dust and palm-frond thatch debris fluttering toward the floor through bars of sunlight. The boys fired some rounds out the windows, not in the direction of the truck. There was more shouting in Tagalog from the truck. "The soldier wants to know what the American is doing here," Luz translated.

Bonofacio turned to me. "You an American?"

"Canadian," I said.

Bonofacio yelled something back in Tagalog. "He said they didn't see any Americans," Luz relayed. Some more bullets from the truck perforated the wall, too high to hit anyone. The NPA shot some more bullets out the windows. Another shout in Tagalog from the truck. "He says there's a big reward for the American, but he has to be alive. Won't pay if he's dead," Luz said. That was reassuring, a little. Doors slammed. The truck revved its motor and from the window I watched it back and turn around. It left, and Bonofacio stepped outside to see it off.

"Why the truck follow you up here?" he asked, annoyed.

"I wasn't aware that he did. I never saw him behind us. Somebody must have tipped him off."

"They always leave us alone. You brought us trouble, man."

The leader got the attention of his crew and said something to them. Luz and I got up from the floor, and the guy with the tommy gun covered us. "He said maybe they should turn you in for the ransom, maybe they'll pay something for a Canadian," Luz whispered.

"It's time we left," I whispered back. "Thank you for your hospitality, but it's time we got going," I said genially. "I'll go out and find our taxi." We made a move toward the door, and the two rifles came up in our direction.

"You should stick around a while," said Bonofacio, motioning me back. "I'll get you a beer. You too," he said to Luz. He pulled a couple bottles of a local brew out of the top case of a fresh stack of them in the kitchen. Next to it on the floor sat a Russian vodka empty. He church-keyed the bottles and handed us warm beers, foam gushing out and dripping down over his hands.

Luz took hers with thanks and had a swig. After a moment she remarked, "My, it's getting hot in here." She parked her beer on the table, undid the top three buttons on her bodice and waved the lapels out back and forth from her chest. All attention in the room riveted on Luz. I edged nearer to the guy with the tommy gun. "I hope you don't mind if I sit down," she said. "I am really roasting." She took one of the kitchen chairs. Facing the boys, she spread her knees wide apart and began flapping her dress up and down over her bare thighs. Nobody noticed until it was too late that I'd headlocked the tommy gun guy and wrested his piece away.

"If you men don't mind, we'll be going now," I said, shoving him aside and pointing the tommy in the others' direction. "Luz, could you get the pistols?" While she did that I collected the two rusty Garands. We backed out the front door, tossed their arms into the bushes and quickmarched down the lane toward the village. "I'll leave your gun at the store," I shouted back.

"I don't think we can count on the New People's Army for help," I said as we walked along. "They're Keystone Kommandos."

"Keystone Kommandos? What is that?"

"Fuck-ups."

"I could have told you that, but I didn't know what you wanted from them. It's better that you saw for yourself. And who knows, maybe you could have figured some way for them to help."

"If they're all like that, there's no hope. Well, it was an idea. I'll have to think of something else."

It was getting late in the day, with long shadows stretching before us as we came to the paved road through town. Our cabbie from Davao had taken off for safer parts. Luz scanned around and pointed to a jeepney—one of those diner/jukeboxes on wheels—stopped by the general store. "It's loading passengers. Let's see where it's going." Just our luck, it was headed down the hill to Davao, and he threw two people off and made room for us when I said we had U.S. dollars. We stopped in to leave the gun with "Carlos." He registered surprise at seeing us come in, but he thanked me for the gun and set it down behind the counter. None of the customers paid any attention to us.

So I endured a cramped ride back, serenaded by blaring Filipino rock music all the way. Going "to Davao" did not mean door-to-door service. It's a sprawling collection of slum districts, and we were the only passengers headed downtown. The driver held out for extra bucks to deliver us to the hotel. We arrived after dark and well past dinnertime, famished after a discouraging day. The nearest chow available was Filipino food. It's not that it's inedible, just not very interesting. Afterwards I thought a stroll around town would be good for a leg stretch, but two blocks were plenty. It wasn't that downtown Davao was totally terrible, just not very interesting. We retreated to our hotel without enthusiasm. It's not that it was a shabby fleabag—it even had running hot water—just not very interesting.

I'd long since given up on the day. Luz had her arm linked with mine, and as we rode up in the elevator she snuggled closer. "I hope your trip wasn't wasted, Jack," she murmured.

"Well, at least it resolved one issue," I said. "I've seen enough here. We'll return to Manila first thing tomorrow. I'll have to come up with another plan pretty quick." We reached our floor and stepped out of the elevator.

"I will help you any way I can," she whispered. After a pause, she said, "You haven't forgotten, have you, that I still owe you some services from our first meeting?"

Now, *that* was interesting. A memory of Dana, so far away, passed through my mind. She'd told me, whatever I had to do to stay safe, to do it. And then the hotel lights blacked out, a power outage. Who knew what evils lurked in the darkness of sinister Davao? Luz said she'd help me. Better safe than sorry. We groped our way down the hall to my room.

* * *

WE ARRIVED BACK IN MANILA THE NEXT AFTERNOON WITH

nothing useful to show for the trip and plenty to discourage me. Hardly more than two weeks remained before the election. The city rattled with rallies, demonstrations, marches and speeches, with the audiences for Aquino's campaign the more animated and vociferous, at least until Marcos's goons showed up. Uniformed army and police deployed conspicuously. Marcos-blue signs, banners and posters four-walled the city, and Imelda sang her heart out. The media Marcos controlled—high-circulation newspapers and the TV stations—blared out endorsement. Cory didn't have the media coverage, and her yellow signs and posters tended to disappear soon after they went up, but she personally was here, there and everywhere, rallying supporters not only on Luzon, but on the other major islands—Cebu, Panay, Bohol. She was staunchly Catholic, as were most Filipinos, so she didn't spend a lot of energy on Mindanao with its heavy helping of Muslims.

Apparently with all the distractions it slipped Imelda's mind to cancel her hospitality, for I still occupied my nice suite at the Manila Hotel and nobody pestered me about bills. I was straightening out matters of business in my room the day after we returned when my phone rang. "Mr. Philco? Johnny Enrile here. How are you today? Did you have a nice vacation on Mindanao?"

"I've been to worse places," I said. How did he know about my trip?

"Then you have my sympathy," he said, with mirth in his voice. "Listen, we have things to talk about. Could you spare a few minutes this afternoon? I'll give you another tour of Manila."

His Mercedes arrived at the hotel at 1500 hours. I got in and we rolled away. "So my guided tour of Metro Manila was not sufficient?" he remarked once we got settled. "You took another tour shortly thereafter, and more lately one to Mindanao?"

"Investment bankers must check out every angle," I said. "So, you think I need another tour?"

He chuckled. "Yes, indeed. A visiting banker cannot see too much. So tell me, how are the deliberations over that formidable loan progressing?"

"Personally, I wouldn't loan Marcos a dime," I said.

"Yes, I sensed a lack of sympathy for our President from the outset. You are not alone in that, of course. May I ask what you really came to Manila for?"

"You can ask, but I'm not at leave to tell you. What I can tell you is that I have a good deal of sympathy for Mrs. Aquino. Does she have any chance of winning the election?"

'I think it is a certainty that she will win the most votes cast. It is even more certain that she will not be our next president."

"My impression, too. I've heard how Marcos conducts elections. And nothing can be done?"

"What is your interest in this? Are you acting on some U. S. government policy?"

"Purely personal," I said. "The traditional American penchant for underdogs and righteous causes, plus also I hate phony war heroes and I'm not too fond of arrogant bitchy women."

"Whomever can you mean?" he said with mock ignorance. "So, your trip to Mindanao had something to do with this sympathy?"

"I wanted to get a look at the New People's Army out in the field, see if they could do Corazon Aquino any good."

"Hopeless, aren't they? Maybe as many as 10,000 of them across all the islands, a rabble of ragtag, disorganized dreamers and troublemakers."

"Does Corazon have any organization behind her? Who are her supporters?"

"The university crowd—students and faculty. The uncorrupted portion of the business community. The international do-good crowd. *The New York Times*. Just about every Filipino not profiting from government corruption. They are devoted and enthusiastic, but they are Filipinos, and therefore not very organized. But Marcos is. If you're really serious about this, I suggest you try Cardinal Sin."

"Thanks for the offer, but I try to stay on the straight and narrow."

"Ha ha, you do have a sense of humor, Jack," he said. "Cardinal

Sin is the Archbishop of Manila. Sin is his name, though not his game, ha ha. The Church is strongly behind Corazon, and it is very well organized, as such things go in the Philippines. He might have some ideas for you. Yes, go see him. He's at the Manila Cathedral in the old section of town, the Intramuros district. If you like, I'll give him a call and set up a meeting."

"Yes, I'd appreciate that," I said. Enrile gave me some particulars, and then we went on to other topics. I couldn't figure out his agenda. He was Minister of Defense and had other government connections besides, but I didn't feel he'd be likely to rat me out to Marcos. Unless he saw profit in it.

The purpose of the tour wasn't an actual tour, of course. Enrile wanted to talk with me out of view of prying eyes. The driver took us nowhere in particular and dropped me off when Enrile had what he'd come after.

* * *

THUS I FOUND MYSELF STANDING BEFORE MANILA'S CATHEDRAL at Cabildo corner Beaterio, and an imposing Romanesque pile it was, replete with towers, cupolas and ornate bronze portals. The guidebook said it dated back to 1571, at the onset of Spanish colonization. Over the centuries it had been destroyed by earthquakes, World War Two and sundry other disasters, and restored every time. The most recent re-no occurred in the 1950s, and they did a fine job of making it look as old as new. It reminded me of George Washington's personal axe, now a valuable antique, and it has had only five replacement heads and seven new handles since his times.

Which is all very interesting, but my directions specified meeting him at the church vestry, not the Cathedral itself. I figured Cardinal Sin didn't operate on Filipino time, so at the scheduled hour of two p.m. I poked the vestry doorbell button. Light footsteps approached the door, and a small, grey-haired Filipina in a plain brown dress opened it. "Yes?" she said.

"I have an appointment to see Cardinal Sin," I said. "Jack Philco."

"Yes, Mr. Philco, follow me. He is expecting you."

She led me down a short hallway to a plain office. The bespectacled, stocky little man seated behind a desk rose to meet me. He wore a black shirt and trousers, not full church vestments. "Welcome to the House of Sin, Mr. Philco," he said with a gracious smile. He rose and came around the desk, extending his hand in greeting. He had a firm grip. He motioned me toward a nearby upholstered, upright chair, and he settled into a matching one. He was nearing 60, I estimated, and had a roundish Chinese face. He asked the woman to bring coffee, and she left us. "I was very distressed upon hearing the news of the Challenger disaster," he said. "Losing those astronauts and that school teacher, what a terrible tragedy."

"I saw the news on TV but know nothing about it beyond that," I said. "It's the largest failure to date in America's space program and a major setback for NASA."

"I'm not a scientist, so I do not understand the scientific purposes of the space station program."

"To tell the truth, neither do I," I said. "I think there may have been a public relations motive behind including the school teacher, which makes the situation even more tragic, I think."

"It is too soon after the event to indulge in cynicism," Sin said, "but there is something to what you say. Well, your time must be valuable, Mr. Philco, so to the point. Johnny Enrile told me it would be worthwhile to talk to you, but he wasn't specific as to why."

"I'm not sure either, but he thought we might share an interest in the upcoming election."

"You are an American banker, according to Johnny. Is there some financial dimension to our political situation you wish to explore?"

"How confidentially are we talking here?" I asked.

"Well, it's not as though we're in the confessional, which is absolutely confidential, but you can rest assured that, short of acting to prevent a crime, I won't be blabbing anything you tell me to anyone."

"To begin with, I'm not an American banker."

"Johnny intimated as much. He also mentioned that you are a sharp observer of Philippine affairs."

"My cover story is that I am here to assess the possibilities of a large loan to the government, which would give me access to people in power. But those who sent me were concerned that the upcoming election might be subverted and stolen from Marcos…"

Sin was gently laughing. "That's a good one," he said, "stealing an election from Ferdinand Marcos, ha ha. Continue, please."

"So I came quickly to realize as I went through the motions of being a banker. It didn't take long to figure out that despite Marcos's efforts, Corazon Aquino is very likely to win, in which case Marcos will cheat her out of it." "Johnny was correct; you are an astute observer. It sounds like you have changed your orientation …?"

"It was never made clear what I was supposed to do concerning the election in the first place, but having become familiar with Ferdinand and Imelda Marcos, and Corazon Aquino, it seems that the only thing I can do in good conscience is help Mrs. Aquino in any way I can."

"You are turning coat on your employer?"

"It's a complicated story. The short answer is yes, but don't worry about that. Perhaps you can tell me something of your own position here, Cardinal? I've seen your name around, of course, and the Marcos papers paint you as a subversive and a troublemaker, indicating that Marcos is afraid of you?"

CARDINAL SIN'S CONFESSION

"I'm certainly among the staunch opposition to the Marcos regime, but the rest of what you say is a matter of viewpoint. I consider myself a humble servant of God, reluctantly situated as the leader of his flock here in the Philippines, but giving the mission my best effort. The Catholic Church is very strong in my country. Something like 70 percent of Filipinos consider themselves Catholic, and most of them take their religion seriously. This you may find strange, coming from America. You see, Christianity is expanding throughout the world, particularly in Asia, Africa and Latin America. But in the Western, Caucasian nations not so much. The Faith is dying among the younger generation in Europe. America retains some religious fervor, but American Catholics campaign for liberalization and are indignant that Rome does not accommodate them, not grasping that they are only a minority among the world's faithful.

"Here in the Philippines the Church constitutes the major organized opposition to Marcos, and we are strong enough that he cannot move against us at whim. So instead he tries to bribe us into friendship and co-opt our support. Imelda tries also, with piety, cajolery and especially contributions, but with little success to show for it. Ferdinand himself approached me to serve on his special commission to investigate the Aquino assassination, and I turned him down. He was after my imprimatur on their proceedings, and I wanted no part of that whitewash. His position has become increasingly unstable since that incident. People more overtly speak out against him, whereas before they were afraid to. We saw spirited demonstrations in protest; first the well-to-do women took to the streets and then their husbands joined them, and then the broader populations found their voices. When Marcos called this special election to shore up the fiction of his support, it was I who persuaded Cory Aquino to run against him. She, I thought, had the strongest moral qualifications to publicly oppose him."

"I met her," I said. "A very impressive woman."

"Unlike the typical Filipina, she's not afraid to speak her mind in public. In a debate Marcos mocked that she lacked the experience to be president. Her rejoinder was, and I quote: 'I concede that I cannot match Mr. Marcos when it comes to experience. I admit that I have no experience in cheating, stealing, lying, or assassinating political opponents.' That drew an ovation, I can tell you."

"Imelda Marcos was dismissive of Corazon," I said.

"Imelda, Imelda ... that arrogant, greedy woman. I'm sure she bragged to you about her properties in New York City and elsewhere. She fancies herself a businesswoman, but her real expertise is mining. This is mine, she declares, and that is mine, and that is mine, ha ha."

"I brought something up with Johnny Enrile and he ducked it. Maybe you can help me out. I did some analysis of Philippine finances, and it was unmistakable that every year government revenues exceeded expenditures by substantial amounts, with the differences not accounted for."

"You're sure you're not a banker?" Sin said. "Your analysis confirms what my sources in the government tell me. According to unreleased figures, the Central Bank has been exaggerating its reserves all along, in 1984 by $1.5 billion more than they truly hold. More shocking is that our foreign debt has grown steadily and now stands at well above $30 billion. Clearly huge amounts of these moneys go astray in the maelstrom of Marcos corruption, but exact figures are impossible to get. It's something that he cannot blame on the Communists, about the only thing. In the wake of the assassination I publicly accused him of wanton extravagance, of spending precious and borrowed dollars in an orgy of waste and ostentation here and abroad. His reply to that was that an unholy alliance, a clergy-bourgeois clique, was bent on toppling his administration. As well as the Communists, of course. He relies on a Filipino trait, as our people have a short memory for unpleasantness and are forgiving by nature. And, of course, most Filipinos are poor and resentful toward the upper classes."

"So can anything be done to have Mrs. Aquino win, if she gets the votes?"

"I do not know. Marcos is bankrupting the country, spreading the Treasury's money around to buy votes. That probably won't win it for him, as Filipinos are fickle and forgetful, and don't stay bought. But then his people will run the election and count the ballots and announce the results. There is no way to prevent that. It will evoke a strong reaction, demonstrations in the streets, denunciations, outcries and so forth, but we have had those before and they always petered out. The newspapers and TV will back him up, since he controls them. If only we could circulate some of the American papers. The *New York Times* just published an expose of his supposed war record, and a paper in San Jose, California, reported on the Marcos real estate holdings in America. Such stories would have an impact, but they will not appear here in any visible way."

"Why did the previous demonstrations fail to produce results?"

"No organization, just passion. People gather and listen to speeches and shout and cheer, but then they go home. It helps that Salvador Laurel has joined Corazon as a running mate, as he has considerable organizational skills, but I fear that won't be sufficient."

"Can't the Church organize them?"

"I'm reluctant to do that. From the pulpit we will preach in favor of law and honest government, and against oppression and corruption, but if we advocated political action, that would give Marcos excuses to move against us. If he succeeded in stealing this election, he would have grounds to exile me to some barren island."

"In the U.S. we had demonstrations in the 1960s and '70s, Power to the People was their slogan," I said. "They were influential enough to force Lyndon Johnson not to seek a second term. Could something like that work here?"

"Power to the People ... hmmm," he said. "That's an idea. But we are 7,000 islands—2.000 of them inhabited—and Filipinos are very individualistic. Even if we rallied large numbers here in Manila, I'm at a loss as to how we'd organize the whole country in a way to depose Marcos."

We concluded our meeting in agreement on Marcos and the

election, but lacking any action plan. Cardinal Sin impressed me. He was a savvy man, exuding integrity, with lot of force lurking behind his genial manner. We definitely shared the same page. The crux of the matter was organization. Getting the population riled up and out in the streets was easy enough, but how would that lead to Marcos's ouster? After leaving Cardinal Sin I thought back to America's student demonstrators—the SDS, the Weathermen, the Chicago Seven, the campus sit-ins and teach-ins, the riots and disruptions, the folk singers, the March on Washington ...How were they organized?

The solution dawned on me.

* * *

"I saw your product in a village in the hills above Davao," I remarked to Emil Grotesqcu. "It was flying off the shelves in the little general store there." We rode on the canopied veranda deck of the Corregidor cruise boat, catching the sea breeze. I'd called Evgeny Grotelov and told him I wouldn't be available Saturday because I was taking the afternoon Corregidor tour. Coincidentally, he'd showed up for it too.

"My bosses anticipated modest sales, so they dispatched a shipment of a few hundred cases to peddle when I arrived. When I got the orders, they'd send more. But then this election was declared, and they immediately rushed a container of vodka down from Vladivostok. Much to the consternation of the local drunks, who had to endure short rations for several weeks. Marcos employed his usual tactic of flooding the country with money, and what are these people going to spend it on? I sold the lot out in no time."

"Seems like your bosses are savvy businessmen."

"Russians have a history of being canny traders, yes."

"Isn't there a contradiction, what with Russia having a Communist system?"

"There would be, if anybody took that ideology seriously any more. Our leaders don't give a fig about Communism, Lenin and all that Marxist rubbish our schools teach. It's about power and their jobs. Our people at the top live luxuriously, and they'll say and do whatever is necessary to keep it that way. Orwell was spot on with his *Animal Farm* fable. It's interesting how our two countries use consumption to control their populations. In my country they keep the masses from fomenting trouble by making them spend their time searching the shops and standing in long, slow lines for inferior versions of the necessities of life. In your country, they keep the population docile by assuring them they're the freest people in the world and showering them with baubles and vulgar distractions. And in both places life at the top floats along. So, how's investment banking going these days?"

"With all this election turmoil, that's temporarily on hold pending the outcome," I said. "From what I hear, Aquino will probably win the vote, but Marcos will steal the election and stay in office."

"So it appears."

"There will be demonstrations and protests, a lot of sound and fury, but because of lack of an organized opposition, it won't go anywhere."

"That's an astute summary," Grotesque said.

"So, I wonder," I said, "what your useful idiots are up to these days?"

THE STORY'S CONCLUSION

A PASSING RAIN SQUALL CHASED THE TOURISTS BACK INSIDE THE cabin, so we had the canopied upper deck of the tour boat to ourselves. Even so we spoke in lowered voices. "I'm having trouble getting my head around this," said Emil Grotesqcu. His usual air of cynical self-assurance had been temporarily disabled. "You're seriously telling me that you never were a CIA superagent, ever?"

"The Nam-Cambodia thing was a charade," I said. "Todd Sonarr created and managed my legend solely for the purpose of coaxing a rise out of the KGB."

"He did a hell of a job, I'll give him that. When I finally puzzled out your identity after months of analysis, I really thought I was on to something."

"You were, and you weren't. From Sonarr's point of view it was a bust. He was working with James Angleton, hoping to use a leak to smoke out a mole in the CIA. But the legend he created for me got leaked to the KGB by some other means entirely. That mole hunt of Angleton's finally went up in smoke."

"So when you denied that you were in Iran, and Belfast, and the Caribbean, and India, on CIA business …?"

"I really wasn't. I work free-lance, and other people hired me."

"But you say this time you're here in the Philippines on behalf of the CIA?"

"Now you've got it!"

"Got it? I don't even know what I'm talking about! Why the CIA this time, but not the others?"

"Todd Sonarr showed up at my door with a sob story. And a big paycheck. The job seemed harmless enough, so I thought I'd help him out."

"A sob story? Todd Sonarr?"

"He said his career was a wreck from a series of screw-ups he'd been involved in, and that keeping the opposition from stealing the election away from Marcos was his only hope of saving his ass."

"What screw-ups?" Grotesqcu asked. I recited the ones I could remember. Then it was his turn to spring a surprise: "Our counter-intelligence people maintain a dossier on Mr. Sonarr," he said, "and I can assure you that he did not screw up any of the missions you mentioned. On the contrary, he's one of the slickest operators in the CIA. I wouldn't be surprised if he winds up director someday."

"Then I'm as baffled as you are," I said. "I don't understand why he wanted me on this mission; I've never even understood the mission. He never gave me marching orders. Where did he ever get the idea that someone might steal an election from Marcos? He tells me to keep up the good work and stay the course ... but what's the work? What's the course?"

"I have some sorting out to do here," said Grotesqcu. "Over the last 10 years I've built a cushy sinecure in the KGB on the premise of countering Jake Fonko, CIA superspy. And now you tell me you aren't one. But you did all the things you did. And through the hallowed halls of Langley your reputation echoes *sub rosa*. So you really could be a superspy, and maybe what you're telling me *now* is subterfuge. But if you really aren't, and my service finds out, being relieved of my job is the very best I could hope for." He thought about it. "Jake, you might even be telling me the truth.

But for the sake of my sanity and my job security, I'm going to pretend that I never heard a word of this and let this hall of mirrors we inhabit take care of the rest. Okay?"

"If it keeps you employed and out of trouble, it's fine with me. I'd miss you if they took you off my case. But, how about this? What if I'm running a CIA con to divert scarce KGB resources into a blind alley?"

"Dastardly!" he spat with a chuckle. "That'll keep my staff busy, getting to the bottom of that."

"But on the other hand, why should I believe your cockamamie yarn about setting up your own KGB department to keep tabs on me, when you might just be using me in some way or setting me up for something in the future?"

"There's no reason why you should take me at my word. Since I'm in the KGB, you'd be foolish to do so. If I'm in the KGB, of course. I could show you ID, but you never know, it might be forged ... Maybe you're a sleeper?" he asked hopefully.

"Negative," I said, "and there we are. Since neither of us knows what's really going on here, let's shrug it off and return to the matter we were discussing before you asked me to explain my interest in the election. I think if a few things fall right, we can come out with some win-wins here. It's clear that the Filipinos would be better off without Marcos. If Cory Aquino captures the vote, I'd like to help her secure the presidency. That's where your useful idiots would come in—organizing demonstrations, diverting the Marcos forces, creating an anti-Marcos popular movement that the rest of the opposition can rally around. Getting Marcos to leave will probably take some maneuvering on the inside, but I have contacts and maybe I can push things in the right direction. That's my win—Marcos gets shitcanned. If your useful idiots succeed, you can claim that you thwarted my CIA mission to keep Marcos in office. That's your win—you countered Jake Fonko, superspy. Cory Aquino has the public behind her, so if she becomes president, that's the Filipinos' win, and hers also."

"What about the CIA's agenda?"

"Four out of five ain't bad," I said.

"I can contact some people and set things in motion," Grotesqcu said. "Do you have a plan in mind?"

"We'll have to play it as things unfold. The next move depends on how the election goes. Best case: Aquino wins outright, Marcos steps aside, and they won't have to do much at all. Keep your guys on low profile until after Election Day. Marcos is trying to link Aquino to the Communists, and we don't want to give him that kind of ammunition until the votes are in."

We stood under the lee side of the canopy, so few raindrops reached us, and soon the squall passed. Our conversation was over, and we acted like we'd reached the point of boring each other. Grotesqcu nodded a polite "good day" and wandered back into the cabin to get a beer. I stayed topside, appreciating the cooling breeze. We landed on Corregidor and took the tour separately, with no further contact for the rest of the trip. Until the election results were known, there was nothing further for us to do.

* * *

As Election Day drew near Manila teemed with Americans. An unruly mob of journalists—estimates reached 1000—arrived to cover the election, most of them hoping for a shooting war to break out. Some media played the election in a horse-race format, like they do American election campaigns. Others used a more Hollywood-style approach, a morality play template with, thanks to Imelda, some soap opera mixed in. The situation was more tangled than that, of course, but except for the "prestige press," reporters fitted it whichever model had worked for them in the past.

And not only news and TV crews clogged the hotels and bars. Marcos had such confidence in his victory and the righteousness of his cause that he invited observers from the four corners of the globe to monitor the election. President Reagan sent a group that included Richard Lugar (head of the Senate Foreign Relations Committee) and Admiral Robert Long (former Commander in Chief of the Pacific Command). A local volunteer group called NAMFREL—The National Movement for Free Elections—took upon itself the task of bringing to light voting fraud and other irregularities.

Among the visiting firemen a carnival atmosphere prevailed. One night I wound up at a raucous American Club bash. I recognized a few faces from the Manila Hotel and hither and yon in my wanderings. I spotted Beth Romulo, whom I hadn't seen since the do at Malacanang Palace. She was in animated discussion with a husky man with a shaggy shock of brown hair falling over his brow. She noticed me and beckoned me over. "Jack, meet a fellow American, P. J. O'Rourke. *Rolling Stone* magazine sent him to cover the election. We were swapping notes, comparing journalism in my heyday—the Edward R. Murrow era—with the present gonzo version a la Hunter Thompson. I contend we've lost something, and Mr. O'Rourke says it's a living."

O'Rourke, half in the bag, extended a friendly hand. "Jack claims he's an investment banker here to loan money to Marcos," Beth continued. "Not everyone in Manila buys that yarn. Some doubts pervade the Palace, I hear. Oh, excuse me, boys. I see someone over there I simply must say hello to. Nice meeting you, P. J.—good luck with your story. I'll see you later, Jack."

"So you're an international man of mystery, eh?" said O'Rourke with a wink-wink nudge-nudge intonation, but revealing a newshound curiosity.

"Didn't you used to write stuff for *National Lampoon*?" I asked him.

"Guilty as charged," he said.

"It was good. That mag really cracked us up back in the 70s. Everything was fair game. Come to think of it, I've seen your stuff here and there. Seems more conservative than I'd expect from an Ivy League humor jockey."

P. J. O'ROURKE'S STORY

"I came to regret the follies of my youth," he said. "What can I say? At Harvard in the late '60s and early '70s, shit, at just about every college in America, it was chic to be a radical, and college kids are herd animals. Rampaging with the peaceniks was a great way to meet easy girls, and for guys facing the draft, it offered vain hopes of heading off that prospect."

"You were drafted, then?"

"No, I dodged it, got a sympathetic doc to certify me as mentally unsuited. Which I think I actually was, and the Army psychiatrist who interviewed me agreed, but anyhow, I floated through the sex/drugs/rock and roll era in the usual haze. What's that they say, 'If you can remember the '60s, you weren't participating.' I notice your look. No, casting back over my misspent youth, I'm not proud of it. One anti-war demonstration I was in, some clean-cut guy punched me in the nose, just decked me, for being a hairy peace creep. When later I sobered up it occurred to me that, because I ducked out, some other guy had to go in the place I would have occupied. I sincerely hope he was the guy who punched me, and I'm glad he came back okay."

"You're here to cover the election, then?"

"Yeah, I'm trying to drum up a *Rolling Stone* slant on it, find some hip angle or uncover some salacious slime underneath a rock. Mostly, I drummed the trip up for a pretext to make a junket to the Philippines. I fell in love with the place when I was nine years old. My dad was a chief petty officer in a Naval Construction Battalion, the famous Sea-Bees. He'd been a salesman but always wanted to be an engineer, and for a couple years he was one, building docks, warehouses, barracks here. You ask around, the Filipinos still remember the CBs fondly. They were about the only people that ever could get anything done here. I saw his photos of palm trees, and warships, and sailors and natives—to a nine-year old boy it looked like paradise on earth."

"Does it meet your expectations?"

"No, but I've only been here a few days, and so far I haven't seen anything outside Makati and Ermita. Manila's the biggest city, and it's full of modern buildings Marcos put up, though I've gotten a glimpse of some pretty rotten-looking slums. I'd think the other islands would be closer to the tropical paradise vision, as I hear they're poor and undeveloped. Have you seen much beyond Luzon?"

"Only Mindanao, for two days."

"Tropical paradise-ish at all?"

"Tropical, not any kind of paradise. More like piss-poor rural, but they do have a lot of coconut palms down there, if that's your idea of exotic. The biggest city on the island is Davao. You say you've seen some slums in Manila? All cities have slums, but Davao *is* slums."

"Good line," he said. "See any subversives there? I've heard Mindanao is crawling with Commies, Muslims, the New People's Army...?"

"What I saw of the NPA couldn't subvert anything."

He paused to let that digest, then tried a different tack. "You're in the Philippines to do banking, Beth said?"

"Sounding out the possibilities for loans to the government."

"How's it look, if you don't mind my asking?"

Why should I mind him asking? It wasn't as though I was a banker. "I personally wouldn't lend Marcos a dime," I said.

"Any prediction for the election?"

"It looks like Cory's going to win it, and Marcos is going to steal it," I said. "If he loses the vote he'll claim it was because of the Communists."

"That's the consensus," O'Rourke agreed. "Say, if you'd excuse me, there's some writers over there I need to touch base with. The mainstream press is playing it up as 'The Thrilla in Manila.' In this Corner: Ferdinand Marcos the Bad Guy, a ruthless dictator. In That Corner: Cory Aquino the Humble Heroine, she of the God-fearing iron will. In The Center of the Ring: Imelda Marcos the Femme Fatale, the flamboyant, attention-grabbing ex-beauty queen. Those guys have been out canvassing in the streets, maybe picked up some off-beat thread worth following. Journalism's an incestuous business, you know."

"So I've heard," I said. "I'll be looking for your story in *Rolling Stone*."

I jawed with a few more people, gathered some useful intel, which I'd need if Emil and I had a hope of warding off election theft. Before long I was hearing the same things over and over again and washing it down with more San Miguel than my capacity. Called it a night, hoping that the International Man of Mystery wasn't a thread the journo-pack deemed fit to follow.

I caught a cab back to the Manila Hotel, weaved through what seemed like a lot of police presence parked out front, and stepped into my room to find it already occupied by Imelda's brother, Kokoy, and his five sharp-suited buddies. They took their ease on every chair in the suite, with Kokoy sprawled across the bed I'd looked forward to crashing into. "Good evening, Mr. Philco," Kokoy said with a smirk. "Out carousing with your meddlesome countrymen, were you?" Kokoy kept his place, but the other five thugs rose and moved to closely surround me.

"I was hoping you guys would drop in again," I said. "You owe me some gold trinkets."

"Oh, has something gone missing from your room?" Kokoy said with a contemptuous grin. "You should be careful in Manila. Thieves lurk everywhere, even in our premier hotels. Unwary foreign visitors often have problems with thieves, I am sorry to say. You should have reported any missing items to the police at the time, and they would have found the thief for you. We will do what we can to help now that you have brought it to our attention, but chances of retrieving your missing items are slight at this late date. The thief has no doubt already disposed of them. But we're wasting time. To the business at hand. My sister wants to see you again, immediately, so we have come to fetch you. Let's go." He sat up and drew an automatic pistol from a shoulder holster, and his buddies closed up around me.

They marched me down through the lobby to a pair of Mercedes sedans waiting out front, along with a police escort. With sirens a-wail and lights a-flash, our drive to Malacanang Palace took no time at all. I'll give Kokoy and his boys this: for lazy, insouciant Filipinos, they were pretty damned efficient. They took me straight to Imelda's office, where she sat imperiously behind her desk. "Take a seat, Mr. Philco," she commanded, pointing to a chair across from her. "Kokoy, send your men away. You stay here. Sit there," she said, indicating the couch by the coffee table. The goon squad left the room, closing the door behind them.

"To what do I owe the pleasure of this summons?" I asked. At least she wasn't fuming angry this time.

"You said you had come to Manila to help Ferdinand win his election," she said. "May I ask what you have been doing to help since the campaign began?"

" I said that I'm here to assess the possibilities of a syndicated loan to your government," I replied with as much indignation as I could muster. "Your faulty information came from some obscure government clerk whom I'd never met and whose motives for spreading lies escape me. Having your goons drag me to the Palace for these unwarranted interrogations does not raise your government's credit rating," I added with a huff.

"Your government shipped my informant back to the States immediately after he spilled your beans, proving to me that he told the truth. Which is more than I can say for you. Tell me this: what were you doing on Mindanao recently? Surely poking around the New People's Army cannot have anything to do with syndicated loans. Why did you visit our enemy, Cardinal Sin?"

"Simply performing due diligence, Mrs. Marcos," I replied calmly and formally — we'd long since dropped "Imelda" and

"Jack". "Cardinal Sin provided me with perspectives on the stability of the Philippine economy. My investigation of the NPA reassured me that your government faces no serious threat of an insurrection."

"Glib answers," she grunted, but with waning dudgeon. "You haven't been doing anything to help us with the election, then?"

"I've seen no evidence that Ferdinand won't win it with ease," I said. "Even if that were my job, what would be the need?"

"Yes, that is so," she said. "All indications are that Ferdinand will win handily, despite the great amount of effort the American government is exerting to defeat him." She hesitated. "It is very saddening," she went on. "And also very annoying. We're hounded at all hours by your obnoxious news reporters, all looking to dig up something with which to further embarrass us. Your politicians come and accuse us of every kind of corruption and thievery, despite that we invited observers from all over the world to monitor the election. All along Ferdinand has been a most steadfast ally of the United States, right from the beginning with his assistance to General MacArthur. Is this how your country repays its friends?"

Thinking back on things we'd done with regard to Vietnam and Iran, it was a more astute question than she might realize, but I wasn't about to debate geopolitics. "Mrs. Marcos, I'm just an investment banker, a numbers guy, strictly dealing with dollars and cents. I must confess that my government's foreign policies have always been a mystery to me." The first true thing I'd said.

"Well . . ." She paused uncertainly. "After the election is over, we will need your loan more urgently than ever. To repair the damage done to our stability by Corazon Aquino and her lackeys, and to repay the Filipino people for their loyalty. I hope nothing has happened to dim our prospects for a loan from your bank?"

"I can promise you that once Ferdinand's tenure in office is secured, your government will receive not one penny less." Another true thing.

"Thank you, Mr. Philco, I feel much relieved," she said. "These are unsettling times, but Ferdinand and I hope and pray for the best. God willing, he will breeze to a win on Election Day and life will return to normal. Kokoy, please return Mr. Philco to his hotel."

Which he did, with grudging courtesy and great self-restraint to not rough me up on the way out. He dispatched me in one of the Merc sedans, no police escort this time. In my absence a maid had tidied up my room, leaving the bed with no sign of having been disheveled by night visitors.

* * *

ON FEBRUARY 5 MARCOS AND CORY AQUINO HAD ANOTHER American TV face-off, this time on ABC's "Nightline," Ted Koppel moderating. I heard a crew from *20/20* was on the ground in Manila, but Dana wasn't with them. One more day of rallies and demonstrations passed, and then it was Election Day. In Manila Filipinos mobbed the polls, particularly in the more upscale districts. As for the other islands, who knew? NAMFREL dispatched volunteers, most of them priests and nuns but including a population cross-section, to watch polling places all over the country. Rumors of obstruction and intimidation buzzed around, but Filipinos love to gossip, making it up if they're short on facts, so facts were scarce. Finally the polls closed and the frenetic day ended, leaving nothing to do but wait. Unlike elections in America these days, where the statisticians call the outcomes even before the machine curtains close after the last vote is cast, it would be days before all votes were collected from rural districts and the out islands. Marcos controlled the airwaves, precluding any possibility of an accurate idea of the voting. NAMFREL made their own quick counts, while the government insisted on waiting for the election commission's results. NAMFREL's provincial coordinators convened in Manila to compare personal accounts, and on the basis of that, the Catholic bishops denounced the election as a fraud unparalleled in Philippine history and wrote a letter to that effect. Imelda Marcos pounded on the door of the bishops' headquarters at two in the morning, pleading that they not release the letter, but they did anyhow on February 13.

Despite that, on February 15 the National Assembly declared Marcos the winner and President for six more years. From a lobby pay phone I immediately dialed up the Intercontinental Hotel and was connected with Evgeny Grotelov. "The balloon's gone up," I said. "We'd better get rolling."

"We have people on Corazon's staff. I'll make a call and get them started. There are some standard tactics we can use in this situation. Let's put our heads together tomorrow morning."

We met the next morning for breakfast in the lobby café of my hotel. It was so jammed and buzzing that nobody took note of us. "This should be a piece of cake, compared to the October Revolution," said Emil Grotesqcu. "This time we have the people, the church, the press and world opinion staunchly behind us. Didn't lose a war, nobody starving in the streets. All Marcos has is his office, his money and his corrupt supporters, and once they realize nothing much will change with a new administration, they'll drop him. I'm not sure how much he can rely on the Police and the Army; there's a lot of disaffection in the ranks."

"Isn't Cory Aquino going to reform the government?" I said.

"She claims she'd like to, but you can revamp an entrenched system just so far. Considering how much the Marcoses steal, getting their hands out of the till will be a vast improvement for Filipinos."

"So, what do we have to work with?" I asked.

"A couple of my people serve on the staffs of the inner circle. None has real power, but they're good sources to tap for inside information. There are quite a number in the unions and the schools. They're good for organizing and logistics, spreading the word, bringing out the mob. Several in the press. And even a few on Cory's team, though she may not realize it. We've no one in the Church, naturally, but often our goals and theirs coincide, and if we aren't too obvious they won't reject our help—Liberation Theology being one example."

"What do your useful idiots get out of this, anyhow?" I asked. "The Communists have them everywhere. What's in it for them?"

"That warm glow of Making a Difference, of being part of something more important and bigger then themselves," Grotesqcu said. "And for some of them, the possibility of gaining power over others, since they have so much less of their own than they'd like. Have you ever wondered why, despite our actual record on human rights and the blood on our hands, the Nazis are the universal Bad Guys and not us? The Nazis proclaimed themselves the Master Race—excluding everybody else—and set about conquering *lebensraum* and getting inconvenient populations out of the way. If you examine the facts, we didn't do much very different. But here's the key: right from the beginning we spread our arms wide in welcome. Workers of the World Unite! The Brotherhood of Man! Equality! From each according to his abilities, to each according to his needs! Cast off your chains, overthrow your oppressors! What could be nobler? Was Christ's preaching very different? If things never quite worked out accordingly, we at least went in with the best of intentions, and, *if we only try harder*, maybe next time ... That's good enough for people who in their hearts feel they amount to so much less than their aspirations. At Least We Meant Well."

"At bottom," he continued, "people who long to Make a Difference are just egoists like everybody else, but with a streak of smug knowingness. Really, what difference can they make against the flow of history? They'd make a bigger difference if they just did their jobs more diligently and tended to their families, but that's too mundane for the romantic idealists. So as long as we frame our program to achieve power for an idealistic end—Social Justice!—we'll always have a certain number eager to pitch in. That's what makes this campaign so easy. They won't be at odds with anybody except The Enemy. What a glorious thrill to be numbered among a righteous, triumphant mob! But in the end, that thrill is all they'll get. Filipinos have no use for Communism. Meet the new government, same as the old government. And we Friends of the People will soldier on, as disappointed, earnest dissenters."

"Cory called for this mass rally today at Luneta, following the bishops' reading of the letter yesterday morning," I said. "That's drawing quite a crowd."

"It's a start," he said. "My people guided her to calling for a boycott of products that Marcos controls—Coca Cola, San Miguel beer and the papers he owns. Readership of the *Times Journal* and the *Express* has dropped already. I don't think Coke and beer will suffer much, but threat of a boycott scares corporations. We'll have to get demonstrations out on the streets, with a good slogan. What was that one from the New Left in the 1960s?"

"Power to the People."

"Never accomplished much in America—the public understood that as far as the people protesting were concerned, *they* were the enemy. Wouldn't work here either, because the issue is installing Cory Aquino, not overthrowing the government."

"How about 'People Power'? Like, the people use their power to rid themselves of Marcos."

He considered it. "That'll work," he said. "I'll have the printers' union start turning out placards and posters and flyers. You're sure you're not a fellow traveler? No, you're too smart for that."

There was nothing more to do, so we walked over to Rizal Park to see how Cory's rally was going. The government reported only a few thousand people attended. Aquino supporters claimed a crowd of three million. The true number, I can't say, but I'd not seen that many jubilant people thronging the streets since the Ayatollah returned to Tehran.

Of all the resident foreign ambassadors, only the Russian congratulated Marcos on his victory. To avoid further embarrassment, Marcos canceled the elaborate inaugural he'd planned and instead announced a peaceful inaugural ceremony at Malacanang Palace to which, however, no diplomats were invited. Ronald Reagan made an off-the-cuff remark that there was probably cheating on both sides, provoking widespread criticism and a hasty State Department backpedal that he'd misspoke. Envoy Philip Habbib was dispatched to assess the situation. Three days after Cory's rally the U. S. Senate passed a resolution declaring the Philippine election fraudulent.

The People Power movement gained momentum quickly, but the Marcos faction was not fading away. Aquino's backers made an effort to reach compromises, but Imelda offered not an inch to her enemies. Figuring Luz to be my best source inside the regime, I'd asked her to keep her ears open and let me know if she heard anything important. She didn't let me down. She came to the Manila Hotel dressed for a date and was sent straight to my room. "Jack, I was with one of the men on General Ver's staff, and he gloated about how they are going to turn the election around. They will first set bombs and fires around the islands and blame it on the Communists. That will give them a reason to declare a state of emergency and impose martial law. Then they will arrest all the opposition leaders and call out the troops to subdue the demonstrators. My friend boasted of jailing 10,000 enemies."

"Johnny Enrile is Minister of Defense. Can they call out the troops without his okay?"

"Ver's group plans to seize him first thing."

"And when will this happen?"

"In the next day or two."

"I'd better alert Enrile right away."

Luz looked at me with a coy little smile. "Surely you have time to reward a faithful assistant before you go rushing off to duty?" she asked.

It's a tenet of good management: take care of your people. Of course I had time. Honey traps be damned! I slipped her a fistful of Imelda's cash, too.

* * *

ENRILE TOOK MY CALL, AND 20 MINUTES LATER OUT FRONT OF

the hotel I ducked through a light sprinkle and climbed into the back seat of his Mercedes with him. "I don't have all the details, but here's what I heard," and I repeated what Luz told me.

"It's the same stunt they pulled in 1972," he said. "That fake assassination was my part in that, and I've regretted it ever since. I figured I'd be on the hit list this time, and I suspected something was up when they arrested Bobby Ongpin's security men. Thanks to your tip, I think I can head this off. Ver doesn't know it, but the Army's no longer in his pocket. I command some troops, General Ramos will throw in with me, and I think my security forces are a match for Ver's."

"So you can pre-empt him?"

"He has the capability of wiping us out if he moves fast, but he's never been much of a military man. I think we can hold him off."

Enrile talked to Ver and, certain of his ground, called a press conference at which he and Ramos announced their defection, that they were no longer part of the Marcos government. Asked if he would go to the Palace to negotiate with Marcos, Enrile said it would be like going inside a prison camp. Another reporter asked if he would support Corazon Aquino. "I am morally convinced it was Mrs. Aquino who was elected by the Filipino people," he declared.

In answer, Marcos held a press conference shown on all TV channels. Before he could get a word in, Imelda told the newsmen that she'd had her eye on Enrile all along. "I told my husband way back in 1972 to watch out, it might be Johnny who will kill you," she declared. Marcos, in turn, paraded Imelda's personal chief security officer, Captain Morales, out, denounced him of being a leader of the coup, and after he "confessed" had him escorted away, leaving Imelda in tears.

From that point on, events moved quickly. Cory Aquino decamped to Cebu Island to organize civil disobedience. Enrile's forces took over Camp Aguinaldo to the north of the city, while the government's troops mustered around the Palace. All over

Manila people overflowed the streets. Word went out that Camp Aguinaldo needed food, and Filipinos flocked there, the poor bringing rice and the well-off toting large pots of meat and fish stew. Demonstrations erupted everywhere. Cardinal Sin stationed nuns at the forefronts, knowing that this prevented the army from using force against them, Filipinos being highly respectful of the Church. Battle tanks rumbling down the street clanked to a halt when they reached the cordon of little white-clad nuns kneeling and saying rosaries. Even an attack force of 10 heavily-armed landing vehicles carrying three battalions of marines was cowed by a resolute civilian crowd on EDSA: "We could have plowed right over them," said their commander, General Tadiar, "But I didn't want to be known as the Butcher of Ottigas Avenue."

General Ramos was headquartered at Camp Crame, adjacently to the west of Aguinaldo. He reached his field commanders with a simple message: join us here if you can. If not, stay neutral. Civilians flocked to join him, many bringing food and mattresses so they could camp on the grounds. Word spread that General Ver had ordered a full-scale attack on the Camp, with artillery and armored columns massing in position. Then a civilian spotted black-clad Rangers creeping toward the perimeter and honked his car horn. Exposed, the Rangers scampered back to their lines. Just before dawn trucks of soldiers drew up to the protesters surrounding the camp and fired tear gas. At sunrise a flight of Sikorsky gunships swooped over the horizon and converged over Camp Crame. They carried enough armament to wipe out the crowd, but to everyone's surprise and relief they hovered in over the camp airfield and lowered to the ground. Pilots, crews and soldiers jumped out waving white flags. Their leader, Colonel Sotelo, had opted to defect, and in addition to the five gunships he brought along two rescue ships, a utility ship and 15 combat pilots. Upon hearing that General Ver was going to launch an air attack, three of the gunships were dispatched to destroy Ver's force on the ground. Interviewed by reporters as a cheering crowd pressed in, Colonel Sotelo explained, "I have not really done much in my life, and for once I wanted to make a decision for my country."

On February 25, instead of Marcos's announced peaceful inauguration, an army helicopter gunship flew in over Malacanang Palace, hovered there, then fired six rockets. Five landed harmlessly in the garden, and one shattered the windows in Imelda's bedroom. The rumor circulated that Marcos had fled the Palace, so Manila was deeply disappointed to see him appear on Channel 6. At that point General Ramos ordered his troops out to seize the Marcos TV and radio stations. In retaliation, Marcos ordered the air force to bomb Camp Crame. Several fighter jets overflew it, but dropped no bombs. The pilots blamed poor visibility.

The rocket attack on the Palace tipped the scales, for it brought home to Ferdinand Marcos that he could be killed. He held another TV news conference where he maintained that the situation was under control, and that he would be issuing an ultimatum to the rebels. However, in truth there was nothing he could do without slaughtering his own people. Imelda, too demurred. "If we wipe them out," she was heard to remark, "what will happen to our assets in the U.S.?"

President Reagan had a cable sent to Manila stating that it was time for Marcos to prepare for a government transition and offering him safe haven and medical care in the U.S. Later Reagan went on radio and TV to say: "Any attempt to resolve the military crisis by force would surely result in bloodshed and casualties, further polarizing Philippine society and doing untold damage to the relationship between our governments." He went on to caution against government factions attacking one another, as President Marcos had pledged to refrain from initiating violence. And he all but ordered Marcos to abdicate in favor of Corazon Aquino. Marcos called Senator Laxalt to negotiate an exit strategy and discovered that the only strategy open to him was to exit.

The next day, little yellow-clad Corazon Aquino was inaugurated as President of the Philippines, to the huzzahs of throngs in the streets. Ferdinand Marcos remained hunkered in the Palace, searching for straws to grasp but finding none left. That evening three U.S. Air Force H-3 choppers ferried Ferdinand and Imelda Marcos and their party of 87 to Clark Air Force base. He did his reluctant best to exit with dignity and a "they never laid a glove on me" mien, all but declaring "I Shall Return."

Despite the amount of military hardware deployed, battle casualties were slight. The People Power Revolution was (mostly) peaceful because at heart Filipinos are a (mostly) peaceful people.

* * *

When Cory's inauguration ceremony was over the task I'd set for myself was finished—I'd helped keep Marcos from stealing the election. With luck I wouldn't be clapped in irons for dereliction of duty, or whatever the CIA did to punish operatives who went rogue. Then it was party time, everyone unwinding from what had been a fraught couple of weeks. I bumped into Beth Romulo one last time, who told me friends had, because of her government connections, advised her to return to the States until things quieted down. "Not on your life," she declared. "It was my first revolution, and I wouldn't have missed it for the world." We toasted the good fortune of the Philippines. "You weren't really here to make loans, were you, Jack?" she asked.

"Well, I sure won't be making any now," was my reply.

One bothersome issue cropped up. With Imelda out of power my line of credit at the Manila Hotel was gone with the trade winds. The management presented me with a bill for three months of their hospitality, and an eye-opener it was. It was too formidable to put on a credit card, but fortunately my CIA bank account had enough balance to cover it, with some left over. I called Dana Wehrli—no need for tradecraft now—to tell her I'd be arriving home in a couple days and was delighted to hear that she was delighted. I was treating myself to a San Miguel (boycott ended!) after some laps in the pool, when a waiter told me I had a phone call. It was Todd Sonarr ...er, Stokes Gladstone. Shit! My Day of Reckoning was now at hand.

"Jack," he said, "good to hear your voice."

"Thanks, Stokes," I said. "What can I do for you?"

"I just want to congratulate you on a job well done. Mission accomplished. Time to return to home base, no need to linger in Manila any longer. Settle up your affairs. Keep the change."

BUT STORIES NEVER CONCLUDE

Todd Sonarr's last words:
"Just wanted to congratulate you on a job well done. Mission accomplished. Time to return to home base, no need to linger in Manila any longer. Settle up your affairs. Keep the change."

My reply:
"Uh, right," I said. "Umm... thanks. Anything else?"
"Details later. Take care." And he hung up.

Did I hear him right? Mission accomplished? What mission? Job well done? What job? Keep the change? What change?

Mine not to reason why. I deduced that the residue in the bank account after I covered expenses was mine to pocket. Plus I still had some of Imelda's bribe. A bonus on top of my fee. But the rest I couldn't fathom at all. Unless the call was a feint to lull me into a false sense of confidence, which I wouldn't put past him, at least I might not be arrested when I deplaned in LAX.

As I puzzled over it, the waiter brought me another phone call. This one was Luz. "Jack," she said, "Auntie would like very much to talk with you. It is most urgent. Can you come see her this afternoon?"

I could, and shortly thereafter my driver pulled up in front of her Forbes Park mini-mansion. I told him to wait. The maid escorted me into a bedroom this time, and there was Auntie, buried in a heap of lacy pillows that propped her up, surrounded by medical paraphernalia, looking like she was at death's door. Which, it turned out, she was. Luz sat on a chair beside the bed in solace mode.

THE REST OF AUNTIE'S STORY

"So good of you to come see an old dying whore, Mr. Philco," she said, still able to muster a mischievous little smile. "Luz has kept me advised of your goings-on. You are the only man I have met that I think I can trust—certainly my Filipino male friends do not qualify—so there is something I must tell you. I have been dying for a while now, but I feel the end will come soon. Therefore I wish to entrust you with an important secret. But you must first promise to honor a dying woman's last wish."

"I promise, if it is in my power to do so."

"That's all anyone can promise," she said. She had a hard time breathing, and speaking took most of the energy she had left. "I told you something of my past, but not all. You see, my Jap protector was second in command to General Yamashita. You perhaps have heard stories and rumors about Yamashita's fabulous gold hoard?"

"From Ferdinand Marcos himself," I said.

"Oh, that filthy liar," she spat, coming back to life just a little. "That is how he explains his great wealth—he didn't steal it, he found Yamashita's gold. I know for a fact that story isn't true. Because I know its location. Let me explain. My protector was given the task of hiding the gold, because Yamashita wanted it for his own, perhaps to buy his way into a position of power after Japan won the war. He searched the Philippines for a suitable hiding place, finally settling on a deserted island, an extinct volcano. He loaded the gold on a barge and carefully selected several aides, who conscripted some natives from a distant island to do the work. They stored the gold in a cavern in a lava field, leaving no traces of their activity. On the way back they killed all the native workers and threw them into the sea for the sharks to dispose of.

"When the Americans came to re-conquer the Philippines, a bombing raid scored a lucky hit on my protector's headquarters building and killed him and all his aides. He'd given me gold trinkets and dropped hints about Yamashita's gold, so upon his death I immediately scoured his files and belongings and found a map hidden away, which I am sure leads to the treasure. General Yamashita was captured by the Americans, tried for war crimes and executed, carrying his secret to the grave, if he ever even knew the location. My protector was a devious, greedy man, and he may have kept it to himself or misled Yamashita.

"But what was a used-up comfort woman to do with an important secret like that? A billion dollars of gold, and whom could I trust? So I carefully guarded that map for all these years, until Luz brought you here."

"It's an amazing story, all right," I said. "A map is the only proof you have?"

"Luz, show him," she said. Luz went to a sideboard, opened a drawer and drew something out. She came back and handed it to me, a small, very heavy golden Buddha statue. "There are others. I've given them to Luz. That is for you to keep. Now, here is the promise I ask of you. Collect that treasure. Keep half. Give the other half to Luz. That's all. A simple thing."

"Here's what I'll promise. I'll call in a friend who specializes in salvaging treasures, and we'll follow the directions on your map. If we find the gold, and if we can claim it, I will certainly give Luz half the proceeds of the operation."

"Ha! Spoken like a banker," Auntie said. "Done. Luz, get the map." Luz pulled out a filing cabinet drawer, groped underneath it and came out with a plastic folder that had been taped to the underside. She brought it to me. I examined it through the plastic, a chart of islands, with coordinates given, and one of them indicated. It appeared to be in tangle of small islands on the Pacific side of the Bicol region in southeast Luzon. Some Japanese writing, with arrows, suggested directions.

"This will take a little time, Auntie," I said.

"You have plenty of time. I don't. I thank you, Mr. Philco. I trust you to keep your promise."

"I will do my level best. God bless," and I leaned down and gave her a kiss on the forehead. She smiled.

Luz took me to the door. "May I ask how you will proceed with this project?" she asked.

"It's not as simple as Auntie said. I'll have to contact my friend, and if he agrees, we'll return to the Philippines, go to the islands on the map and see if the gold really is there. If we locate it, then we'll have to consult with the authorities. If we get their permission, we'll collect the gold and convert it to cash. And believe me, you'll get your half, if there's a half to get."

"This will take time, then? How much time?" "Several months, I estimate."

"You will be returning to the States in the meantime?"

"Yes, in a day or two."

"I don't suppose you would take me with you?"

"No," I said, and I explained why not as delicately and tenderly as I could.

* * *

So I arrived back at LAX a couple days later, with a billion or so potential dollars worth of map in my luggage. Next step was to contact old surfing buddy "Wild Blue Under" (a.k.a. Scott Brentfield), who'd made a career of salvaging sunken treasure. But more of that later.

Many threads of this yarn remain to be tied up.

Ferdinand and Imelda Marcos finally ended up in one of their several Hawaiian properties, a mansion on landscaped grounds in Honolulu. Financial post-mortems revealed the extent of the Marcos corruption. Or perhaps I should say "suggested it", as the full scope may never be known. Someone in Manila calculated that from his government service between 1966 and 1986, Ferdinand Marcos earned a total of $372,000, an opulent living for the Philippines. Probably came with a pension, too. American politicians often retire richer than their career-long public servant salaries, but Lyndon Johnson and "Lady Bird's radio stations" was peanuts compared to the Marcos boodle.

The daily take from Philippine businesses the Marcoses owned or controlled required a "money room" in Malacanang Palace where it was accumulated and distributed. In 1983 alone, $278,000,000 was moved out of the money room to foreign accounts. A World Bank Report stated that, between 1978 to 1982, $3.1 billion of foreign loans failed to reach their specified beneficiaries (and we were going to lend this guy money?). Following his departure, a Commission on Good Government formed to investigate his finances. The net value of Marcos real estate holdings uncovered in New York, California, Texas, London, Australia and Canada came to $622,389,000, and no doubt holdings at other locations remained unaccounted for. Three of Imelda's personal bank accounts totaled to $37,900,000. Listed investments ran to $500,000,000, and gold bullion to $300,000,000. During the weeks running up to the 1986 election, Marcos transferred $100,000,000 from the Treasury to personal Swiss bank accounts while he bankrupted the country buying votes.

How did Ferdinand and Imelda do it? Through the connivance of corrupted cronies both in the Philippines and abroad, coupled with numbered bank accounts, shell companies, multi-tiered ownerships, kickbacks from foreign corporations and bald-faced theft. Estimates reached as high as $30 billion that the Marcoses cost the Philippines, of which they may have reserved $10 billion for themselves—at the 1985 value of the U.S. dollar—making him not only one of the richest men in the world, but in the running for Most Corrupt Politician of All Time. When all this was revealed, where did the American press focus its attention? On an aspect that readers of *People Magazine* could grasp: Imelda's collection of 3,000 pairs of shoes. Of course, had the media been fully diligent, some prominent Americans might have suffered embarrassment from their relationships with the Marcoses. Beth Romulo pegged it right that journalism had declined since her day. Or maybe the same integrity continued on, but the style degenerated. It wasn't, after all, the first time our press gave deep corruption a wink and a nod.

A variety of chronic diseases finally caught up with Ferdinand Marcos, who died three years later in Honolulu. Corazon Aquino allowed Imelda to return to the Philippines in 1991, and the day after she arrived the authorities arrested her for tax fraud and corruption. In 1993 she was found guilty and sentenced to prison, just one of 100 or so cases involving $350,000,000 allegedly held by the Marcos family in Swiss banks. She appealed and not only avoided prison but in 1995 won election as a congresswoman of Leyte, collecting twice the votes of her opponent. She stayed active in politics, as well as actively defending herself in court, well past the turn of the century, needless to say living quite comfortably.

That's the Philippines for you. Or perhaps it's the Way of the World.

Beth Day Romulo remained in the Philippines, a country she truly loved, and continued writing, eventually authoring 28 books, including *Inside the Palace*, which detailed the Marcos saga from Beth's insider perspective.

P. J. O'Rourke returned to the Philippines one year later, assigned by *Rolling Stone Magazine* to write a piece on how Corazon Aquino had improved the Philippines and changed Philippine politics. His article, "The Post-Marcos Philippines—Life in the Archipelago After One Year of Justice, Democracy and Things Like That," came to this conclusion: not a hell of a lot. He did find the nation's Communists greatly miffed that they'd never been given any role in the government, despite their efforts on Cory's behalf. The same thing happened to them in Iran when Khomeini took over. You'd think they'd learn.

Speaking of Communists, **Evgeny Grotelov** had already checked out of the Intercontinental Hotel by the time I called to say goodbye. I'd see Grotesqcu again the next time I went on an overseas assignment, no doubt.

Luz and I kept in touch pending my quest for Yamashita's hoard. I'll anticipate the finale of this tale by reporting that she landed her big spender, a high official in the Philippine government. Thanks to prior, er, contacts, with many of his colleagues, she enjoyed numerous fond friendships and reigned as the toast of Manila for a number of years. After which she lived, as far as I know, happily ever after.

Langley recalled **Kevin Blank** to base immediately after I mentioned my problem with him to Todd Sonarr. Several years later the police caught him burglarizing houses in the Langley vicinity during his CIA lunch hours. They found his Alexandria apartment full of stolen articles and trinkets, little of it especially valuable. Apparently he'd been doing B and E out of boredom. The CIA fired him, and I haven't heard of him since. His tragedy, I think, lay in the failure of the CIA to utilize his true talents.

Todd Sonarr showed up at my Malibu door six weeks after I returned home. "Jake, my man," he said brightly, in much better spirits than he'd shown the last time he dropped in. "I was passing through the area, thought I'd come by and see how you're holding up."

"Getting along okay," I said. "None the worse for wear."

"Quite a ride, the Philippines," he said, as I led him into the living room. "Man, that carpet! Blows me away each time I see it." I didn't wait for him to ask, but went to the liquor shelf and pulled the scotch down.

I got a Dos Equis for myself and handed him his drink. He raised it and said, "Here's to democracy and free elections!" And guffawed out loud. "Jake, I didn't really just drop in, you know, casual-like. I owe you a debriefing on your Philippine mission, and I came out here to pay up."

"Todd, I'd settle for just finding out what the mission was."

"Well, yes, that's part of what I wanted to discuss with you. You went rogue on me, I know that. What you didn't know is, you were *supposed* to go rogue."

"Huh?"

"Everybody in the U.S. Government, and I mean *everybody*, wanted Marcos out of there. So they came to us. Marcos had a habit of publicly blaming the CIA for everything that got fucked up in the Philippines, when the plain fact was that we never had much presence there. So how would it look if we sent someone in to help depose the president of an allied country who was a dedicated anti-Communist and one of our staunchest supporters—that is, except when he was stealing us blind? We couldn't do that. Instead, I sent you in, ostensibly to help him, knowing that once you got a good look at that crook and his bitch of a wife you couldn't in good conscience do it. Worked like a charm."

"I was *supposed* to throw in with Corazon Aquino?"

"What any man of integrity and decent standards would do, but not everyone in our employ has the balls to do it. But here's the thigh-slapper, the crowning irony of the caper. Our Senate denounced the election, and Cory Aquino was declared the winner, before all the votes came in from the other islands and were properly counted. The initial tally of the final collected ballots had Marcos winning by over a million votes. Then the National Assembly and NAMFREL went through them with a fine-toothed comb, discounting whatever fraud they could find. And Reagan didn't misspeak; all concerned did their share of cheating. At the end of the day, Marcos still won by more than 700,000 votes. He bought those votes with the public's money, of course, but it's not like he was the first politician ever to stay in power that way. The Democrats did the same with their Great Society, though it's going to take Americans a couple more decades to cotton on to the full tab for that."

Then he broke out a wide, delighted grin. "Don't you get it, Jake? You helped Corazon Aquino steal the election from Ferdinand Marcos—exactly what you were assigned to prevent. Ha ha, and they said it couldn't be done!"

"That was okay?"

"Okay? Jake, it was a royal flush. It was a grand slam. Steele Bosserman and I couldn't have planned it better. Another question. We were aware of a lot of Communist activity, especially after the vote. How about counter-espionage? Did you get any sense of KGB presence?"

Where did *this* come from? "Now that you mention it, there was a suspicious guy lurking around, more often than you'd expect from sheer coincidence. He reminded me of that schlub from the Polish Mission in Saigon, 'Mickey Mouse,' we code-named him. Plain-faced, stocky, with straw-colored hair—looked sort of like him, but I couldn't be certain."

"I was afraid of that. I don't want to disturb you, but I think the Ruskies have you under surveillance, maybe have from way back when. There's only one thing to do. I'll assign a man to the case. Count on us, we've got your back."

So I'm a one-man spook employment agency? Emil Grotesqcu expands his staff to thwart me. Todd Sonarr adds a guy to thwart Grotesqcu thwarting me? I'll never walk alone. Todd was right about the irony. Rogue CIA and KGB covert operatives conspired to steal an election from Ferdinand Marcos (with an assist from the United States Senate)? You can't make this stuff up. "Look, Todd," I said, "there's no need for that. I don't work for the CIA, never did, never will. This was a one-off consulting gig."

"Of course, of course. Don't sweat it, we have your back anyhow."

Whatever that was supposed to mean. But by the time he left I felt more congenial toward him than I'd expected.

A few days later my phone rang, and I picked it up to hear a voice familiar to millions of Americans. "I'd like to speak to Mr. Jake Fonko?"

"Speaking," I replied.

"Mr. Fonko, this is President Reagan. I'm calling to congratulate you by telephone, because I can't do it in public. I'm not supposed to know this, but I hear you received an award from our Central Intelligence Agency for outstanding clandestine service. I think they call them 'jockstrap awards,' because you can't wear them where anyone can see them."

"I am deeply honored by your call, Mr. President, but that was 10 years ago that I got that award. I haven't done anything outstanding lately."

"Modesty becomes a man, but the award I'm not supposed to know about was issued just yesterday, for your work in keeping the Philippine presidential election honest. Another thing I'm not supposed to know is that you're one of the few ever to receive a second one."

That threw me for a loop, because I hadn't really done much, nor had Grotesqcu. We could claim credit for a few tweaks and nudges, but essentially it was a homegrown uprising, not even a genuine revolution, just a stolen election and a swap of people at the top of an established and pretty corrupt system. All I could figure is that Todd Sonarr coveted another gold star by his name and I was a sort of reverse-patsy, the opposite of a fall-guy. It was his operation, and it turned out as everyone wanted, quickly and cleanly, with no unpleasant after-taste. So he maxed out the kudos he could grab, including recommending me for a citation. Despite my wandering off the reservation I wound up accomplishing exactly the desired result with no collateral damage, without blowing my cover (Kevin did that). Compared to real heroes maybe I earned my pay but I sure didn't do anything worth a commendation. Not that I'd turn it down. I knew exactly what my lawyer-stepfather Evanston would say when I told him: "That's good, Jake. I advise you to raise your rates."

The CIA held ceremonies for those awards, but Sonarr didn't notify me. He hadn't invited me to the ceremony for the first award either. Just as well. I'd enter the CIA's Langley headquarters only at gunpoint.

* * *

Scott Brentfield, Dana Wehrli and I plowed toward our destiny through placid island waters off Luzon's southeastern coast. We lucked out with the weather and were enjoying a bright and not oppressively humid day of late spring tropical bliss, mild breezes rippling cats' paws across the sea's blue surface. Our treasure hunt was on.

Wild Blue Under (Scott's surf-gang handle) and I had put our heads together and scoped out the possibilities. He studied the most detailed charts he could find, compared them to Auntie's map, and pinpointed our island. It lay in the vicinity of the waters where the "Tin Can Sailors" held off a superior Japanese fleet in one of history's great naval upsets. He checked with Philippine authorities on laws regarding salvaging treasure. Providing we met certain conditions, we'd keep a decent slice of what we found. He scrounged up what information he could on the Yamashita hoard, applied his 10 years' experience in treasure salvage to the available intel and decided it was worth a little time and expense to take a look. I fronted the bread.

Dana had some vacation days coming and a light schedule just then, so she came along for the adventure. Bowled over by the little gold Buddha I gave her, she thought a treasure hunt story would make a great *20/20* segment. She brought along a mini-cam for some footage to take back to her studio. I looked forward to being a billionaire, or at least very, very rich, with my one-quarter share of the loot (Luz, Scott and me splitting the take). I was happy for Luz, too. If the need arose, I'd tell Dana more about our thus-far unidentified Filipino partner.

We hired a trawler out of a fishing port an easy day's round trip from the island. The boat smelled like leftover shrimp, but what the heck? The skipper, a weathered Filipino of indeterminate age, came with the boat and handled it expertly. The plan was to land and scout the terrain following the directions we'd had translated from the original Japanese. If we found evidence of the gold, Dana would film enough to establish bona fides and we'd quietly return to Manila and set the salvage operation in motion. If this turned up a fool's errand, Scott would put the trip to good use by checking into other sunken salvage possibilities around the islands, as the Spanish had lost a number of treasure ships in Philippine waters over the centuries. Dana and I would write it off as a nice tropical getaway.

Which it was, whatever the outcome. She'd stripped down to her swimsuit, bent on deepening her tan. Lying back on a cushion, with arms behind her neck and big sunglasses peering from the shadow of a broad-brimmed straw hat, she looked posed for a Club Med ad shoot. Scott and I sat up on the bridge with the skipper, who didn't say much and asked no questions. "We're going along here," Scott said, pointing on the chart to a channel behind a narrow island that stretched about eight miles. "When we round this point here, our island should be visible on the horizon."

Sure enough, when we passed the point I made out a little pimple poking above the horizon line. It seemed to be smoking. "You're sure that's the one?" I asked.

Scott checked Auntie's map against the chart again. "Yeah, you see? There's this island here ... (he pointed to an island on the map and on the chart, and then to one off to port) ... and there's this one here ... and off over there, there's this one. So the one ahead, that's the one marked on your map. I wonder what that smoke is...? I thought you said it was uninhabited."

"Dana?" I called down to the cabin. "You want to come up and see our island?" She stirred from her cushion, adjusted her swimsuit, slipped on a loose cotton shirt and climbed the steps to the bridge.

"Can I use those binoculars?" she said. I handed them to her. She raised them to her face, adjusted the focus and peered ahead.

"It's shaped like a triangle," she said, "doesn't seem to be much of anything on it. There's smoke coming out of the top."

Scott took the binocs. "That smoke is picking up. When we get closer I'll be better able to tell what's going on. With that shape it's gotta be volcanic. That checks out with your old gal's story. Sometimes they smoke."

We could see the island more clearly as we approached to three miles. It was about the size of Catalina Island on the north side of the Isthmus, a volcanic cone shape with a chopped-off peak. The smoke had increased drastically and was now gushing dirty clouds up into the blue sky above sprigs of flame. Dana took a look through the glass and exclaimed, "There's stuff flowing over the edge and out of cracks in the sides! Is lava bright red?"

I grabbed the glass and looked for myself. True—lava flowed like crazy, smoke and flame spurted wildly. "This is not encouraging," I muttered. Then we saw a big gout of stuff blasted skyward, accompanied by a huge cloud of smoke. Fifteen seconds later the sound of the explosion reached the boat.

"Holy shit!" exclaimed Scott. "It's a volcano eruption! I thought this one was supposed to be extinct."

"Well, the map was in Japanese," I said. "Maybe there was a problem with the translation."

"Oh my god," shrieked Dana. "This is awesome! This would make such a news bite! Where's a camera crew when you need them?!" She scampered down to the deck, pulled out her mini-cam and brought it back to the bridge. Lava flows now touched the sea, sending up clouds of steam.

The skipper plowed on.

"You're sure that's our island?" I asked Scott. We laid out the map and the chart and checked again. There was no doubt. The little peak spewed out another volley of smoke and flame. The eruption's roar reached us quicker than last time—10 seconds, two miles away. After a moment things splashed in the water around us. A pebble landed on the bridge. Scott and I looked at one another, then peered at our island. The skipper peered at the island too, then looked plaintively to me, to Scott.

We proceeded further, and our treasure island spewed another, bigger burst. "Take us back to port," Scott told the skipper, and the man spun the wheel, much relieved. The boat followed a tight semi-circle and straightened out 180 degrees off the previous course. Seven seconds passed and we heard the latest explosion come from astern.

"Can't we go in a little closer?" Dana pleaded as she captured the spectacle with her camera. "We're too far away for my zoom to bring in any detail. This is like Saint Helen's. We'll never get to see anything like this again. I need more footage. I need more detail." Then debris from that last explosion rained down all over the place and a chunk of still-molten lava the size of a grapefruit hurtled in and pulverized the cushion where she'd been catching rays a few minutes ago. She gasped, considered that for a moment and said, "Whoa, scratch that last request, guys!"

I told the skipper to put the throttles to the red lines, and he happily complied. Scott and I clambered down to stomp out the flames spreading on the cushion. Dana caught it all on tape. Back in Los Angeles, *20/20* programming executives reviewed her volcano eruption footage, decided there was no story worth airing, and spiked her proposal.

THE END

EDITOR'S AFTERWORD

You may have noticed the "Trigger Warning" preceding the text of this book. I regret having included it, but I had no choice in the matter. Following publication of *Fonko in the Sun*, one of my students, a winsome if highly strung young lady, approached me after class in an agitated state. It seems she'd read the book and was upset by Jake Fonko's encounter with the assassins on Jamaica Island. "He shot three blind men!" she lamented.

"But they intended to kill him," I reminded her. "It was self-defense."

"They were blind! How did they know who it was? Maybe they meant to kill somebody else. Maybe it was all a mistake. What if they were innocent?"

"But they were pointing their guns at him. There was some reason to believe they were faking their blindness."

"That doesn't mean he should just kill them like that. Couldn't he have shot the guns out of their hands?"

"But he didn't have a gun until he subdued one of them," I reminded her.

With that she burst into tears and fled the classroom. I thought that was the end of it, but the next day I got a stern phone call from Mellowdee Coxbawm, an Assistant Associate Dean in the Office of Student Succor and Solace, whom I would characterize as Nurse Ratchid wearing a smiley-face mask. I wound up spending a very uneasy two hours discussing the incident with Dean Coxbawm (she insists on the honorific, though she holds only an M.A. degree in Womyn's Studies). She adamantly asserted that my student's upset was not to be countenanced. My final justification was that Jake Fonko may not have done the action in question at all, that my publisher's editors may have slipped in material from Ian Fleming's James Bond adventure, *Dr. No.* (as explained in the afterword of *Fonko in the Sun*).

Dean Coxbawm was having none of it. "If that's the case, in the future be more judicious in what you plagiarize," she hissed. She insisted that all my future books contain Trigger Warnings. This is a recent practice some universities have adopted, intended to alert victimized students to material that might cause them emotional upset. So there you are. I would have posted a Trigger Warning about the Trigger Warning, but Dean Coxbawm seemed bereft of a sense of humor, and I dread spending more time in her presence.

Mr. Fonko fared far better in the Philippines than he did in India, which nearly cost him his life. Perhaps a future installment of his Saga will relate his foray in the Jewel in the Crown (as the British Raj fondly nicknamed it) in its entirety. But the editors attempting to compile that book from my notes were baffled by the complexity of the story and the incoherence of Mr. Fonko's narrative. Deprivation, distress and desperation clouded his mind and his memory, at times to the point of hallucination. Perhaps at some later date…

Mr. Fonko's only regret about his Philippine adventure was the outcome of his treasure hunt. The expedition never did reach the island, which in any case had been obliterated when the volcano awoke from its dormancy. "Between that Swiss bank account whose number I don't know, and Yamashita's hoard buried under a mountain of lava, I'd have been pretty well off," he sighed.

Dr. Bertha Sikorski and I have obtained access to Mr. Edward

Snowden's recently disclosed voluminous cache of secret government materials. What a treasure trove of contemporary history it is! Our diligent search so far has turned up not one single mention of Jake Fonko, which to my mind confirms the veracity of his stories. Obviously, his exploits were so top secret that the CIA successfully prevented any mention of them whatsoever from appearing even in the most closely held government documents. Thus I harbor no doubts that these books contain true and factual accounts.

B. Hesse Pflingger, Ph.D.
Professor of Contemporary History
California State University, Cucamonga

KUWAIT / IRAQ 1990 – 1991

THE MOTHER OF ALL FONKOS

A JAKE FONKO ADVENTURE
B. HESSE PFLINGGER

HOORAY FOR HOLLYWOOD

SATURDAY, JULY 21 & SUNDAY, JULY 22, 1990

> He who meddles
> in a quarrel not his own
> is like one who grabs
> a passing dog by the ears

It was a sweet gesture by Dana Wehrli, my main squeeze. After seeing me return home from my gigs safe and sound, time after time (umm, except from India), she'd finally quit fretting and developed a sense of humor about my profession as a free-lance whatever. When I came back intact from my eight-month Kuwait debacle she presented me with that motto, done in the style of a needlepoint sampler, elegantly framed and nicely gift-wrapped, at a welcome home party she threw, and it drew a big laugh from the assembled.

She must have commissioned it custom-made, because I've never seen anything like it for sale or on display, and a beautiful piece of craftsmanship it is. Lord knows it applied to many of my past misadventures, and it was apt for what landed on me in Kuwait. I went there on what seemed to be an innocent-sounding intel assignment and wound up at both ends of that fracas, barely escaping with my life from the bloody "Highway of Death" during the Iraqi retreat.

If that's what grabbing passing dogs by the ears is like, I'll henceforth give peripatetic pooches a wide berth. However, a couple months in Saddam Hussein's dungeons under the TLC of his psycho son, Uday, ultimately made Operation Desert Storm my own quarrel, up close and personal.

* * *

TO RECAP: MY PHILIPPINE ASSIGNMENT—HELPING CORAZON Aquino steal the election from Ferdinand Marcos (see *Fonko Bolo*) —left me in good shape despite missing out on Yamashita's hoard of stolen gold. Not only did it net a solid paycheck but that caper ratcheted my cred for international intrigues up several tiers. My second CIA "jockstrap award" just iced the cake. Those are supposed to be deeply hidden secrets, of course (you can wear the medal only on your jockstrap is The Company in-joke). But word leaks out to Those In The Know, a roster that includes Very Important People all around the world, some of whom need help of a certain nature from time to time.

Not that I hire out for wet work, nor do I do the bread-and-butter jobs that Hollywood P.I.s like Tony Pellicano thrive on— sanitizing crime scenes, retrieving drugged-out actors and wayward actresses, digging up dirt for divorce cases, breaking studio contracts, and so forth. Oh, I get my hands dirty enough, but after 1986 I could be pickier about jobs I took on and could ask top dollar for my services with a straight face.

Previously, I'd shepherded celebrities and executives through situations they feared posed danger. I'd made deliveries of valuable objects and questionable items. I'd sold advice on security to corporations and overseas concerns. I'd put my Ranger experience to good use for foreign military clients. And I was always happy to take on intel jobs, my old Army specialty, when they came up. Things like that. My foray in Colombia with the drug cartels that included a harrowing traverse of Panama's Darien Jungle and culminated in my persuading Manny Noriega to give himself up got a little out of control (an interesting story for some other time). But the Philippines job elevated me to the lofty reaches of international consultant/advisor.

What kind of work is that? They say about consultants: *He'll borrow your watch, tell you what time it is, then keep the watch.* They also say about consultants: *A consultant is just an ordinary man 50 miles away from home.* And another thing they say about consultants is: *He's smart enough to tell you how to run your business, but too smart to start a business of his own.*

There's some truth in those sayings.

For example, a corporate or government honcho may hire a consultant to endorse a decision he's already made. The consultant's task is not to conjure up a genius business plan. Rather, he's supposed to figure out what the decision is, and then present an arrangement of the facts of the matter framed in such a way that naysayers in the picture accept that they'd be better off going along with it. Not to mention the added bonus that everybody gets if the decision turns out all wrong: "Don't blame me. That's what our highly-paid consultant advised."

Or the consultant conducts an investigation on some delicate matter. He may not be any smarter or better informed than insiders, but coming from the outside he can present findings, ideas, conclusions and recommendations that insiders endorse but wouldn't dare voice for fear of career immolation.

It's nice work if you can get it, and I was getting more of it through 1987, '88 and '89. Don't take me wrong. I wasn't running some kind of con job on the world. I delivered as much value for money as anybody in my line of work. What had happened over the years was that, starting with my ill-starred stint for the Central Intelligence Agency—our beloved CIA—in the closing days of the Vietnam War, penumbras and emanations surrounding my adventures had created an impression of deep-cover involvements in international espionage intrigues at the very highest levels. I steadfastly denied it, but in that hall of mirrors my denials only bolstered the impression that the rumors and whisperings must be true. The fact that the Russian KGB had a section devoted to thwarting me boosted my legend further. Emil Grotesqcu, the KGB agent in charge of their Fonko Desk, had every reason to maintain the fiction, as his own job security depended on promoting me as a formidable foe. It worked just fine for me and only a fool would argue with it.

Meantime, life at my beach pad on the Malibu shore continued copacetic, a flow of balmy days, lush living and celeb parties. Our nearest brush with local excitement happened in 1989, when the Malibu Chamber of Commerce appointed Marty Sheen Honorary Mayor of Malibu, a ceremonial position. He surprised everyone by immediately issuing a unilateral proclamation: "I hereby declare Malibu a nuclear-free zone, a sanctuary for aliens and the homeless, and a protected environment for all life, wild and tame." Then busloads of homeless bums arrived to take him up on the offer. It wasn't long before The Malibu Inn marquee featured a counter-proclamation: "Dump Martin Sheen." You can always count on outraged money to trump harebrained idealism, and the situation was soon straightened out. Was that political experience crucial to landing him the role of "President Bartlett" on *The West Wing*? I'm nobody to question anyone else's cred.

Sad to say, 1989 didn't go well for Dana Wehrli. She continued producing successful shows for ABC-TV, but clawing her way up the corporate ladder came with supersized stress. The docs discovered that her father, whom she loved dearly, had prostate cancer at a terminal stage. And she gave her lower back a painful and lingering wrench trying for a dig during a beach volleyball game at a surf rat reunion party in my front yard (alas, my old gang isn't getting younger).

Her resulting menu of pain-killers, uppers and downers reached the extent that she knew every clerk at every pharmacy within twenty miles by their first names. Until she found herself hooked on Vicodin. Dana's no fool. When she realized she had a drug problem she arranged a leave of absence from ABC and checked into a new clinic in town, *Promises*. A luxe rehab center up in the hills with an enviable ocean vista, it came to boast a distinguished alumni roster: Charlie Sheen, Robert Downey Jr., and Ben Affleck, among others. They did good work, but it took time.

With Dana at *Promises* and focused on getting straightened out, I was left temporarily on my lonesome. My workload hit a light patch, and with time on my hands one sunny afternoon I drove down Pacific Coast Highway to check out the action around Marina del Rey. For those unfamiliar, it's a seaside residential complex on the Los Angeles coast. Apartments, condos, townhouses, what have you, centered around the unifying theme of a sprawling marina stocked with big sailboats and cabin cruisers that rarely left their slips. Off-site party pads, most of them. I dropped into a beachside bar, not special enough to burden you with a detailed description—fishnet draped around the faux-distressed rafters, simulated hatch-covers for tables, mounted sailfish, the place where young up-and-comers and wannabes gather for TGIF Happy Hours. You've all been at that bar or one of its kin.

The ratio was better than the typical singles bar five-guys-for-every-gal and pretty soon I was chatting up a pert little California-tanned brunette. She looked lively and seemed welcoming. The mating ritual in those places was like contract bridge, bid and counter bid in breezy small-talk, play your hand and woe betide the dummy. After preliminaries I opened with "What's your sign?"—one of the standards back in those days.

"Slippery when wet," she said with a mischievous smile. I've used that one myself, but from her it suggested playfulness.

"Mine is 'Danger—Animal Crossing,'" I countered with a stage-leer, and we took off from there. She was DeeDee, a stewardess with Pacific Southwest Airlines, and as the "Coffee, Tea or Me" era hadn't entirely faded away, one job qualification was comeliness. She lived with another stewardess in one of those apartment blocks in the Marina. I suggested we go somewhere else, and she was for that.

"What would you like to do?" I asked. We'd filled up on bar munchies enough that the prospect of dinner didn't entice.

"My roommate's away. Why don't we go over to my place?" she suggested.

"And what would we do there?"

"Well..." she said. "Are you into kinky sex?" That was out of the blue, for sure, but DeeDee didn't seem depraved. Whatever kinkiness she might come up with wouldn't likely go amok.

"Try anything once," I said enthusiastically. "Tell you what, let's make a party out of it. Is there a liquor store around here?" There was, and I was feeling flush just then. We went in and came out with a magnum of cold *Dom Perignon* champagne. Then over to Marina del Rey. Sports cars and muscle wagons crammed the parking areas, so we wound up in a space far-removed from her pad. She took me by the hand and led me over and in. Your typical bachelorette digs, no need for detailed description. Imagine a mid-scale motel room with a little extra frou-frou.

"Okay, we're here," I said. "What do you have in mind?"

Confronted with the reality of her offer, she flushed and fished for words. "Gee, I don't know, it was just something clever to say. *Cosmopolitan* has these articles about things to try... let me think." She thought a little. "I know, why don't you tie me up? That's kinky, isn't it?"

"Tie you up?"

"You know, strip me and tie me to the bedposts." I didn't know, but what the heck? I shucked off her clothes and she lay back, and I bound her wrists and her ankles to the bedposts with some belts and scarves we'd dug up out of her dresser. Not "dangerous prisoner" tight, of course, but immobilizing enough.

"You okay with this?" I asked.

"Actually, it's sort of exciting," she said. "What's gonna happen next, you know?" Surveying her spread out there, I could see the situation had possibilities.

Then I remembered that cold bottle of champagne. We'd left it in the Cherokee, and it was a hot summer afternoon. "Just a minute," I said. "I'll run down and get the champagne and put it in the fridge. Otherwise it'll be too warm, and when we open it we'll look like a winning World Series team in the locker room celebration. I'll be back in a sec. In the meantime, get your mind fired up for some wild, insane sex. You are in my power, heh heh heh."

"Hurry back," she said.

I jogged over to the car, collected the bottle and started back, only to realize that I'd not noted her door number. There were scores of doors, and all the places looked alike. I wasn't even sure which block it was in. Now what to do? Start knocking on random doors? Find the security office and have them look up DeeDee (if that was really her name, and she'd never given me her last one)? And if by chance they located her they'd open the door to find a naked women tied up on her bed... and what are *you* doing here, mister?

What to do but beat it for home and hope for the best (I'd not given my last name either, thank God—at least they couldn't track me down). For the next two weeks I searched through the *L.A. Times* each morning for stories about stewardesses found tortured and starved to death in their Marina del Rey apartments, and APBs out for the perp. But no such stories turned up, nor did TV news report anything like that. Finally I added it to my long list of Things I Wish I'd Never Done and put it out of my mind.

So, some months later Dana was back as good as new (and she being the quintessence of California blonde beach-bunniness, that's mighty good indeed!). We were approaching the portals of a steakhouse in Santa Monica when who should come out but DeeDee, on the arm of a dude who looked like, whatever he did for a living, it paid well. She stopped and looked me up and down. Recognition beamed across her face. She gave me a grin and a wink and chirped, "Kink-eee!"

"What was that about?" Dana asked after DeeDee and dude had passed out of earshot.

"It's L. A." I said with a puzzled shoulder-shrug. "Who knows?"

* * *

One Saturday evening in July Eddie Lipschitz (Edward LeGrande to his Tinseltown peers) took me along to a big Beverly Hills bash celebrating a studio mega-merger... or maybe it was a mega-spin-off, Eddie wasn't clear on that. Anyhow, the point of the party wasn't the point: as usual it was all about schmoozing. Some of those Hollywood parties Eddie took me to had a more than passing kinship to Walgreen's—lineups of crystal bowls offering a buffet-style rainbow of pills, and guests gulping them by the fistful hoping some new kind of buzz would kick in. Not to mention the cocaine lines. This soiree could have been catered by Merck, Pfizer and Lilly together, for all that was on offer. Myself, I avoid recreational pharmaceuticals; too much risk for someone in my line of work.

An old Indian chief once was asked why he didn't drink firewater like the braves in his tribe did. "I have to deal with the White Man," he replied. "Why would I want to make myself stupid?" Likewise me with pills, lines and tokes: I have to deal with crooks, assassins and spies. Why would I want to make myself crazy?

Stoners floating along in their own exclusive worlds bore the hell out of us on the outside, and I was feeling out of the flow. I hit the bar for another Dos Equis when a couple of guys weaved over to me. They'd been sampling the goodies—that was obvious.

One of them, once-athletic but now saggy around the jowls, exclaimed to his buddy, a sun-bleached, leather-tanned, wiry guy, "I told you it was him! Meet my old compadre, Max Rummage." He meant me. "God damn, Max, long time no see. When was the last time? Doing stunt work for *Waterworld*, wasn't it? Man, what an all-time clusterfuck that shoot was, hey? We were in that bunch of bad guys on jet-skis," he asided to his pal. "Nobody can handle a jet-ski like Max Rummage! Remember when ya saved my life? One of the rehearsals went way wrong. My ski turned turtle and started sinking, and Max dove down and pulled me off it."

Then back at me, "How's life in Topanga Canyon these days, Max?"

"Pretty good, from what I hear, but I live in Malibu," I told him.

"Coming up in the world, are you? Or down, as the case, topographically, may be," he chortled. "You dyed your hair, Max? You was a carrot-top last I saw you."

"Well, you know…"

He looked me up and down. "Hey, are you shrinking, or am I getting bigger?" he said. "Seems to me you were above six feet, weren't you?"

"Must be the lighting in here," I said.

"Man, the times Max and I had. Remember that costume gal, Cindy Whatshername? Nobody could give head like good old Cindy Whatshername."

This was getting out of hand. "Look, friend," I said, "I think there's some mistake. I'm not Max Rummage. I'm Jake Fonko."

He put a gleeful elbow in his friend's ribs. "Didn't I tell ya Max was a hoot?" he exclaimed. "The sonofagun even changed his name!"

With that I excused myself and wandered away through the jabbering throng. It's L. A., I thought. Who knows?

In the atrium by the indoor pool I found Eddie talking to a sharply-dressed, swarthy man. He spotted me and waved me over. "Jake," he said, "here's somebody you need to meet. Jake Fonko, shake hands with Mr. Fawaz…? Al Sabah…? Did I get the pronunciations right?"

"Close enough, Mr. Edward," he said with a smile. He turned to me and extended a hand. "Mr. Jake, I am delighted to meet you."

"The pleasure is all mine, Mr.… . Sabah?"

"My countrymen customarily use the honorific with the first name, so Mr. Fawaz will be fine for now."

"He's a prince from Kuwait," Eddie put in.

Well he could have been. He was slender, about my height (5' 10") and several years older, with a handsome face that would have looked even better without the Cuban-gigolo mustache and the patch of short chin whiskers. His dark-olive complexion and closely-trimmed brown-black mop reminded me of the folks I'd tangled with on my Iranian gig. "You're a long way from home," I said. "What brings you to Los Angeles?"

"Various business on behalf of my government. In fact, one assignment is to see about hiring you to perform a service for my government. I was going to try and contact you tomorrow. Knowing of your Hollywood connections, I mentioned your name to several people here, and I was referred to Mr. Edward, and it is my good fortune to find you in attendance."

"Eddie and I go back a long way," I said. "What is the nature of the service you have in mind?"

"Now is neither the time nor the place to discuss it. If you could meet me at my hotel, that would be best. I'm staying at the Beverly Wilshire. I apologize for the short notice, but if it is not inconvenient, could you meet me there tomorrow at, say, two in the afternoon?"

Kuwait + Prince + Beverly Wilshire = Money. "Could we make that a little later, say 3:15? I can juggle my schedule to be available after that."

"3:15 it will be, Mr. Jake. I look forward to seeing you then. Ask at the desk for me. Now, I see someone else I must talk to, if you will excuse me...?" and he smoothly slipped away through buzzing clumps of movie biz thrusters, hangers-on and desperados to join a clump of sober-looking finance guys in the next room.

"You think he's legit?" I asked Eddie.

"If that suit cost him less than $3,000, I'm out of touch with Savile Row. Either he's what he says, or he's a damn good actor and I'll get him under contract for my next wog flick. He'd make a hell of a Palestinian terrorist."

* * *

So in the morning I went for a three-mile run along the

surf line, splashing through the backwash, and after lunch took care of things around the house until two in the afternoon. Then I donned a tropical-weight business suit left from when I posed as an investment banker in the Philippines, slipped my Patek Philippe wristwatch on and set out for Beverly Hills.

It was one more gorgeous July day in southern California, a sunny Sunday, so I took the long, scenic route, Sunset Boulevard through the hills. By that hour everybody was where they wanted to be, so traffic was tolerable. Looping through the sinuous road curves awash with the pungent smell of sage and chaparral made me rue having dumped my convertible Vette in favor of the Cherokee. I hit my destination with time to spare, so I parked at a mall near UCLA and strolled around for a few minutes. Being summer, there wasn't much student traffic, but the Westwood wives and bachelorettes going about their weekend shopping were pleasant enough to mingle with. At 1514 hours I turned the car over to the Beverly Wilshire valet.

The desk clerk put me through to Mr. Fawaz, who directed me to his room. He answered my knock with an invitation to come in, and as I entered he rose from his seat at the desk. He'd dressed more casually than he had for last night's party, but the duds on him were every bit as pricey. "Mr. Jake," he said with a welcoming smile, "how good of you to come. It is a pleasure to see you again. I am glad you were able to make time for me on such short notice, as there is some urgency in the matter I need to discuss with you."

"No problem, Mr. Fawaz," I assured him. "A couple phone calls took care of it." He occupied a suite of rooms, well-appointed it goes without saying. "My friend, Mr. LeGrande, mentioned that you are a prince in Kuwait. Should I be addressing you as 'your highness' or something like that?"

"Oh no," he said. "No need for that at all. Arab princes are a dime a dozen, as your saying goes. We are sons of ruling tribes, that is all. We don't go around kissing sleeping beauties or slaying dragons. We're lucky if we even have legitimate jobs. Many of my cousins have little to do in life except luxuriate. Did you have a pleasant drive over from Malibu?" he asked. "My sources told me you have a beach house there."

"Yes, I took Sunset through the hills, a more scenic ride than the freeways."

"Isn't it just so! I sometimes regret that I have not the leisure time to experience the pleasures of driving around California, as my Maserati would surely be up to it. The climate and the natural beauty here are objects of envy for anyone from my region of the world."

"You visit California often then?"

"From time to time. Kuwait has many interests in America, and so I am called to New York, Washington DC, Texas...but California is my favorite destination. I took the liberty of having room service lay out some refreshments. Would you like anything? Please help yourself."

He indicted a trolley laden with fruit, biscuits, cookies, and drinks—coffee, iced tea and assorted carafes of juice, nothing alcoholic. I took a nut-festooned cookie, poured a cup of coffee to wash it down with, and we moved to a sitting area. Middle East etiquette, I have learned in my travels, dictates that one does not launch into business immediately upon convening, nor does the guest bring it up. So we sipped and nibbled and small-talked about his travels, my home in Malibu, the California weather, the prospects of the Dodgers that year, the latest BMW models, current happenings in Kuwait, a rundown on his family and, of course, current dish on Hollywood stars. Being in no particular hurry, I appreciated the chance to sound him out.

Finally he got around to his agenda. "Your name is known to some of my associates from your work with the late Shah, peace be upon him," he said.

"I wish I could have done more to help him," I said.

"He was a good man, the Shah," said Mr. Fawaz. "Not like those fanatics who deposed him. You aided him more than most. Many others turned their backs and a blind eye to his plight, out of fear of that *shaytan* Khomeini. Also, I gather that you have considerable experience in international finance."

"I'd hardly call it considerable," I demurred.

"Plus an exemplary record in covert espionage work, our intelligence specialists tell me. So my ministry sent me to investigate whether you might be able to help us with a certain task."

"Describe the task, and we'll see," I said.

"Kuwait, as you may know, is a small country with considerable petroleum reserves," he began. "Among the most extensive in the world, in fact. Our oil fields bring in vast amounts of money, so much that we sometimes have trouble figuring out what to do with it. We are not like some other Arab nations, where a few lavish in unimaginable riches while the many remain impoverished. Since we are small we can provide many comforts for all our citizens, yet we invest most of our revenues with an eye toward the future—our oil fields, large as they are, won't produce forever. But we have been blessed with wealth only for a few decades, barely a generation in fact, and so we have scant history of experience in managing large scale financial matters. Sometimes the lessons we learn about wealth cost us dearly.

"You may have heard of our stock market debacle just a few years ago. We instituted an unofficial, over-the counter stock exchange, Souk al-Manakh, listing 45 companies in Arab nations around the Gulf. The *Quran* forbids gambling, with good reason, because soon our people had caught the scent of easy riches and piled money into stocks with a vengeance. With huge and hungry sums chasing a small number of stocks, well, you can imagine the result. Naïve plungers punted in their cash and, making some profits in the initial rush, then started trading with post-dated checks, counting on their holdings rising enough to cover the checks when they came due. The prices of stocks ramped up and up and up, more than 300%, until the Biggest Fool arrived and the whole enterprise collapsed in ruin. Ultimately, government investigators discovered that there were 29,000 checks, totaling 27 billion dinars, or about $91 billion, outstanding. It was a sobering experience.

"Subsequently we have taken pains to diversify, investing in solid assets rather than chasing paper wealth. One avenue we've followed is buying foreign businesses. Recently the Kuwaiti Investment Office in London reported that they'd identified promising Spanish businesses, and apparently billions of dollars have gone into dozens of those enterprises, comprising chemicals, food, and real estate among others. However, it is not clear how much was spent in Spain, nor into what businesses, nor whether all the funds were legitimately invested. One Spanish man, Javier de la Rosa, has particularly come under suspicion as having diverted assets in his own favor. Managers of the Investment Office claim he victimized them, but their own innocence in the situation has come into question.

"So, what I have come here to ask you is: Would you be available to help my ministry get to the bottom of this situation?"

"As you describe the situation, it sounds like a job for lawyers and accountants," I said.

"In America it well might be, but Kuwait does not have the same rules of law, nor have we strictly followed accountancy procedures and standards, nor even routine financial controls for that matter. What we need is a man who can ferret out information, including if necessary by means of interrogation, in a variety of settings and countries. Once that man obtains the requisite information, we can then engage the lawyers and accountants to settle the details. The thing is, Kuwait is a closely-knit country, an intricate fabric woven of family and tribal loyalties. Therefore you as an outsider could conduct investigations and make inquiries that would be delicate in the extreme for a native Kuwaiti to conduct. And there is the fact that the situation involves not only Kuwait, but three different countries, which speaks to your wide range of experience."

Once again, my international rep was strides far ahead of reality. My "financial expertise" consisted of fencing stolen books from

BCCI, the notorious Bank of Credit and Commerce International, and impersonating an investment banker for the benefit of Ferdinand and Imelda Marcos. No doubt whispers about my deep cover CIA exploits, fictitious as they were, had reached Kuwait. But it was true that I navigate easily in foreign countries as long as somebody in the vicinity spoke English, and most people of importance did. Plus intel was my training, though some of the field interrogation methods we'd used in Nam couldn't very well be applied in civilized settings... if the Middle East was civilized, a proposition some disputed.

I saw no compelling reasons to throw away a chance at a gig for the government of a wealthy Arab sheikdom. "I could be available for such a project, depending on a few things. When would you want me to begin?"

"As soon as possible, as time is of the essence. With these sums of money at stake, principals who sensed an impending investigation could disappear on short notice, so we need the element of surprise in our favor. Could you come to Kuwait, say, by the end of this week?"

"May we broach the matter of remuneration? This would be a consulting project, so I would have to bill you at consulting rates..."

"Mr. Jake, set your mind at ease. Kuwait can afford the best, which is why I have contacted you in the first place. And we naturally expect to pay for the best. How does... ?" He suggested a figure large enough that I'd have gone to Kuwait for it by yesterday if necessary.

We sketched out a travel schedule and a rough plan of attack. I'd jet out from LAX, spend several weeks on the project shuttling among Kuwait, Spain and London conducting interviews, inspecting businesses and examining records. Then I'd report my findings to Mr. Fawaz. Ever since my India misadventure I've kept my life prepped for short-notice jaunts of indeterminate length, with people I can click in to look after the house and mail, cover bills and so forth. I'd have to cancel a couple of short-term jobs and postpone some others, but none was a drastic disruption. There was enough time to bid Dana Wehrli a fond good-bye. And I'd be able to put in a few hours at the library researching some background on Kuwait. The situation was as much a "go" as most of my work.

"By the way," said Mr. Fawaz as he took me to the door, "when you pack you should bring along, in addition to business and everyday attire, some clothing suitable for outdoor adventures."

"What kind of adventures?" I asked.

"Hunting. We Arabs are very keen on hunting, you know. We may find time for a hunting expedition. You needn't bring firearms, of course. We can supply anything in that line you need."

"What would we hunt?"

"Oh, many things. The barren sections of my country harbor all manner of wild beasts. You'll see when you get there. It's desert land, of course, and this time of year is very hot. Keep that in mind when you assemble your kit."

* * *

THE DAY WAS STILL YOUNG, AND IT WAS STILL GORGEOUS, so I took Sunset back to the beach. It was on that section of Sunset where it merges with Beverly Glen—I'd pulled to a stop at the light where the two roads part company when—WHAM! Some jerk rear-ended me. It was a Cadillac, I saw in the rear view mirror, and the driver was getting out. I got out too and went back to survey the damage. He'd crumpled my rear bumper in pretty badly. I noted some damage to the body beyond that, and he'd wiped out the rear lights on the passenger side.

The other driver, hands on hips and looking exasperated, surveyed the front end damage he'd incurred. He drove an older, forest-green Seville in classic-car condition. He turned to me and said, "I'll need the name of your insurance company so I can file a claim, and I'd like to see your driver's license."

"Excuse me, friend," I said, "but you rear-ended me. I'll be the one filing the claim here."

"I can see how you might interpret the situation in that way," he said, "and I sympathize deeply. I can appreciate that you are very upset about this, as any average person would be, and you have every right to be. You may not be thinking clearly right now. That often happens at accident scenes. People get disorientated and they look for someone else to blame." The guy resembled Ted Danson from back in the *Cheers* days. He wore new Ralph Lauren workout togs with expensive running shoes to match, and he sported a deep sunlamp tan.

"I'm thinking perfectly clearly right now," I said. "I was at a dead stop, and you ploughed into the back of my car."

"Are you sure you weren't backing up?" he asked solicitously. "People with automatic transmissions often do that unconsciously. It's nothing to be ashamed of."

"No, I definitely was not backing up. Are you crazy? I'd have had to be going 10 miles per hour to cause that damage." I looked back at his car. Another man sat on the passenger side. He was large, but he had a friendly face.

The other driver looked grievously affronted, as though I'd slapped him upside the head with a dead halibut. "Please!" he said. "We do NOT use the C-word! Why are you being so hostile? There's no reason to be so hostile. Are you sure your bumper wasn't damaged already? See here," he said, stooping down and pointing at a scratch. "This looks old. I wouldn't be surprised if this was there before."

"There wasn't a scratch on the car before you hit it," I said. "Now, if you'll be so kind as to give me your particulars and the name of your insurance company... just a sec." I went back to my car to get something to write on. He followed me, and when I turned to him he was affecting a semi-karate stance.

Gimme a break. I took a decisive step right up to him, and he relaxed and backed away a pace. "Look," he said, "if you submit this claim, my company may raise my rates or even cancel me.

Why don't we just call it even—no harm, no foul? My car's as damaged as yours. See how we're blocking traffic. We're annoying all these drivers, keeping them from going about their business. You don't want to be thoughtless like that, do you? Let's just go away and forget this ever happened."

"You're the party at fault, and my car sustained quite a bit of damage. What your insurance company does is no concern of mine, as long as they cover the damage. Look, either give me the information, or I'll take your license number down and report you as a hit and run."

"There you go, being hostile again," he said. "Everybody is so ego-involved these days." He looked down at the Patek Philippe on my wrist and snickered, "It's not that you can't afford it."

I'd had enough. I copied down his license plate number, then went around to the passenger side of his car and tapped on the window. The other guy rolled it down.

"Yes?" he said.

"Your friend is being recalcitrant. I'd hate to do it, but if I have to report him as a hit and run, I'll need your name and contact info as a witness."

"Sure," he said. He fished out his wallet, extracted a card and handed it to me. He was an L.A. homicide detective. "Don't worry. It won't come to that. He gets like this occasionally, but he's essentially a sympathetic, caring person." He opened the door, got out and stood up. He was a bear of a man, but seemed a strangely motherly one. "It's not working," he said to the driver. "Just give him the info, and let's get going."

The driver huffed over, pulled his wallet out of a side pocket in his workout pants and showed me his driver's license. I copied down the number, his name and contact info. "If you're going to be such an anal-retentive...here," and he handed me a business card. "Will this do?"

"It's fine, we're good," I said. I gave him my name, address and insurance company. "Thank you. Sorry it happened."

"Don't mention it," he sniffed. "I hope it makes you feel good about yourself." We got in our cars. The light was red, so as I sat there I looked at his card. He was a... "forensic psychologist"? The hell's *that*? Oh well, I thought, it's L.A. Who knows?

The light turned green. I continued down Sunset. He'd been in the wrong lane so he waited for a break in the turn lane, then continued south on Beverly Glen. My car drove all right, but the bodywork wouldn't come cheap. The bump might have even totaled the car for what insurance would cover. If so it would be a good excuse to upgrade the Cherokee. I was getting tired of it anyhow.

ARABIAN NIGHTS

MONDAY, JULY 23, TO THURSDAY, JULY 26, 1990

THE SCHEDULE FAWAZ LAID OUT LEFT ME LITTLE PREP TIME. The next morning, I called my insurance agent. He told me to get an estimate from a body shop. The nearest one was in Santa Monica, and that errand absorbed half the day. The news was not good. As I'd feared, the car was actuarially totaled, so I'd have to sink some of my own money into it to get it fully repaired, if I wanted to keep it. It was drivable for the time being, so I put that decision off for when I returned in three or four weeks. I spent the afternoon rearranging my looming schedule. No bodyguarding or escorting jobs needed to be canceled. A couple things could be put on ice for the duration I'd be away, and that left one that I could put to bed before I left town if I hit it hard. I did, and by midevening, I'd squared it with the client.

Tuesday morning I spent a couple hours in the library boning up on Kuwait. The basics were simple enough. It was a small Arab country situated on the northwestern tip of the Persian Gulf, pinched between Iraq to the north and Saudi Arabia to the south. The population was around 2,000,000, the majority of them foreigners. Kuwaitis enjoyed free education and health care, as well as housing subsidies and other benefits and allowances. The foreigners, apparently, did the dirty work. Oil money paid for it all. As Fawaz had said, Kuwait had vast petroleum reserves and they pumped a lot. That accounted for the bulk of their economy. Kuwait had no industries or agriculture to speak of; they exported oil and imported everything they needed, except dates.

The government was essentially a monarchy headed by an Emir of the Al Sabah tribe. The country had previously been a province of the Ottoman Empire, and following World War I it became a British protectorate. Their oil business boomed in the '50s, and in 1961 Kuwait achieved independence from Britain. I combed back issues of *The Economist* for the scoop on the current situation.

Kuwait didn't appear much in the news—just some mentions in stories about the international oil business, some disputes with Iraq about their mutual border and about alleged poaching from Iraqi oil fields. Generally it seemed that Kuwaitis kept to themselves, a little country that was prosperous, peaceful and caused no trouble for anybody. Life in the Gulf region had been relatively quiet since Saddam Hussein claimed victory in the Iran/Iraq war in August '88. Except for the horrendously hot summer weather in the Gulf it wouldn't be a burdensome assignment, I concluded. Some travel, some interviews, some sleuthing, then present my findings and come home. I spent Tuesday afternoon scurrying around making arrangements for my place to be looked after for the month I'd be away and running through my departure checklist.

Dana Wehrli came by around dinnertime for our last night together for several weeks. By now it had become a ritual: a nice dinner and drinks, a jog on the beach in good weather or else a movie at the Malibu Theater. Capped off by long goodbye kisses, both good night and good morning. But that evening she was subdued, a definite contrast with her usual perkiness. She'd graduated from *Promises* a few weeks previously, and that experience still affected her.

"It really got me thinking," she said. "I'd been taking those meds, and the next thing I knew I was letting everything go while

I frantically tried to find doctors who would prescribe me more pills. I even did some street buys. Scary. You have no control of your life any more and you get paranoid, afraid they'll arrest you or something. I knew I couldn't go on like that, so I checked in to *Promises*. They detox you first thing. That's kind of rough but they handle it well, and the detox isn't the most important part of the treatment anyhow. They put you through a lot of counseling and therapy, getting at why you got addicted, what's going on in your life to lead to that, what you can do to avoid it in the future. They do groups. Man, I thought I had troubles until I heard some other people's stories."

"Did they come to any conclusions?"

"They're not that definite. They want you to figure it out for yourself, so you'll accept it better. What I realized is, as much as I like being a producer, that job at ABC was driving me crazy. I'd hung around there too long until I was a total burnout."

"How so?"

"It's a one hour weekly time slot that has to be filled, okay? And it's a sort-of news show. There's all this pressure to come up with new and timely material, scoops if possible, week after week after week. Then you have to meet the deadlines, and they're iron-clad—no network will tolerate empty air, and they hate to re-run stuff. You have to rush everything, cut corners, pass up potentially good material, leave stuff out, cram the story into the time slot they give you, and then the executives and the lawyers swoop in and dictate last minute changes, which you have to readjust the whole segment for. And everything has to fit with their politically correct politics, which you have to intuit, as they'll never tell you outright what's bugging their butts that week. And of course you're competing with all the other producers for airtime so you can get promotions and raises and better assignments. That means a lot of politicking and in-fighting among the staff in addition to everything else."

"It'd drive *me* crazy, no doubt," I said. "What are you thinking of doing about it? Did *Promises* give you any plan of action?"

"They don't tell you, you tell them. What I figured out I have to do is change jobs. I'm a good producer, everybody agrees on that. I talked to Eddie about it. His production company doesn't have any openings right now, but he said he'd put in a good word for me with some indie outfits. Indie companies are involved in most of Hollywood's films these days, so there's a lot going on. I'd have to learn the movie business, but I think my TV experience would translate pretty well. The work schedules wouldn't pull me in so many directions at once. I'd have more time to stay focused and do a better job. I've been at ABC way too long, and at the very least this would be a welcome change of scene."

"I'm sure you'd do great. Red carpet, here she comes. Any time frame in mind?"

"I've had one interview, and it seemed promising. I'm working on a couple more. Who knows? Maybe by the time you come back in a month I'll be launched on a whole new career."

"That would be two things for us to celebrate," I said, and I told her how much they were paying me.

"Wow!" she said. "Who do you have to kill for that much money?"

"Whirlybird, you know I don't kill people for a living."

"Just saying... this Kuwait place has a lot of money?"

"More than they know what to do with."

"I'll drink to that," she said. She poured the last of the champagne into our flutes. It still had a little fizz. "Here's to having more money than you know what to do with. May it be our fate!" We clinked glasses, drained them and decided we'd stayed up late enough for a going-away evening.

* * *

MY FLIGHT TO KUWAIT CITY LEFT THE NEXT DAY, WEDNESDAY afternoon, arriving me there late Thursday. Fawaz during our Sunday meeting suggested a hop on a private Kuwaiti jet leaving that same day. It would have been the most convenient option and no doubt promised sheer luxury, but I turned it down. As kind as his offer was, I told him apologetically, if I were going to investigate high-level financial mischief I'd best arrive anonymously and keep a low profile. I reminded him of the element of surprise angle he'd mentioned, and that was the convincer. He had me booked on Lufthansa, first class all the way. I faced nineteen hours in transit over eleven time zones, but at least I'd ride in comfort. I'd be wigged out for a few days after I got there, after which I'd dig into the serious work.

Wednesday morning I checked with my bank first thing. Funds had been wired to my account, an amount I would have hesitated to ask for, and that was just the upfront. I was beginning to wonder if they expected more than I could deliver. Well, I'd do my best. They couldn't very well ask for the down payment back, and even if that was all I got, it was enough. I finished up getting packed and arranging last minute things, humming a happy tune. At noon I had a cab run me down to LAX.

* * *

Nothing much to say about a Lufthansa flight. If I'm destined to spend most of a day in airplanes it's my conveyance of choice. As usual, things went right, nothing went wrong, and first class was comfy enough that I arrived in Kuwait City reasonably well-rested but way out of tune with the clocks.

Fawaz was waiting for me by the gate with a couple helpers, and they led me through the spacious, modern concourse. The terminal seemed oddly busy, some families in traditional Arab robes and niqabs, some in western garb, bustling to departure gates. Crowds teemed around ticket counters, men urgently pushing and nudging and imploring while their wives rode herd on their broods while guarding high-piled luggage carts.

"A lot of activity for this time of night," I remarked.

"Well, you know how it is, vacation time and everybody wants to get away for the weekend," Fawaz said.

He had the juice to steer me around the usual customs and passport control routines. "Don't worry, it's taken care of," he assured me. "My assistant will clear your passport with the authorities and return it to you later. My car is out here. My men will see to your bags." We stepped through the glass doors into searing heat. "Over here," he said, and we went straight to a silver BMW 535 sedan parked right out front. "Keeping with the idea of a low profile, I brought a car that wouldn't be conspicuous."

We got in—thank goodness he'd left it running with the air conditioner going—and he spurted away from the curb into the traffic. Like in most less-developed parts of the world, drivers in Kuwait either were fast and aggressive, or they never got where they'd hoped to go. Until we reached the main road, that is. There we bogged down among a mass of luxe cars, in which his ride was indeed low profile, small potatoes compared to the Rollses, Bentleys, Cadillacs, Mercs, Jaguar sedans, Land Rovers, Maseratis, Ferraris and Lamborghinis.

We came out of the airport at least moving along. The jam on the other side of the road was bent on crowding into it. Heading southbound toward town the cars and vans, many of them heaped with dunnage, crawled along. Traffic going in our direction wasn't nearly as heavy.

"I've arranged for you the customary one month business visa," he said. "That should suffice for the assignment at hand. It can be extended if necessary, of course."

"Why so much traffic south?" I asked.

"It's vacation season," he said breezily. "Kuwaitis like to go on desert treks. I booked rooms for you at the Hilton Hotel. It's a favorite of visiting VIPS. It overlooks the Bay with a nice water view, and it's close to the U.S. Embassy. It's a little distant from the business center, but you'll have a car and driver at your disposal at all hours."

It was late evening by the time we arrived at the Hilton Hotel. I'd eaten plenty on the plane, and what I now longed for was a snooze. He checked me in at the desk, and before the porter took me up he said, "You should take it easy at first, get yourself settled. Serious business we can commence soon enough. The important thing is to get a good night's rest. Some matters have unexpectedly arisen, so I will be unable to join you tomorrow. Instead, I've arranged for you a tour of Kuwait City in the morning. It will give you your bearings. Whenever you're ready, tell the desk and they'll summon your car."

The Hilton was a five-star joint, elegant in an overstuffed sort of way. My rooms were spacious and comfortable, really more space than I needed. The sofa had an abundance of throw pillows, and the windows were heavily draped. The carved coffee table sat atop a small (cheap) oriental rug. They'd put me on the city side of the building affording a fine view of Kuwait Bay, the ocean view as promised, though there wasn't much to view at night besides the distant lights of a number of boats heading out around the point. Down below, people still lounged by the floodlit outside pool. Otherwise I couldn't make out much in the dark.

I slept okay, considering that my internal clocks were eleven hours out of synch. I woke up way too early but felt rested enough. I cleaned up and dressed, then did some exploring until the restaurant opened its breakfast buffet. The buffet catered to every man from every land: congee for Asians, dates and rolls for Arabs, eggs and pancakes for Americans (handy hint for visitors to the Middle East—don't expect too much from the beef bacon).

It was already too hot to cross the highway and go for a run along the shoreline, and too early to start my tour, so I got a copy of the *Arab Times*, one of the English language papers, and looked for clues to the local scene over a second cup of coffee. An odd, tense vibe reverberated through the place. Men bent heads together over their tables talking rapidly in hushed tones, giving their worry beads a workout. A number gulped their breakfasts and hurried out. Those lined up at the checkout desk seemed unusually fidgety. I felt that vibe when I arrived at the airport, too. There was nothing in the paper to suggest anything amiss, however. But then most of the international news was gleaned from British wire services, and I didn't doubt that the Al Sabah's gate-kept the local skinny to ensure the news got no one out of joint.

Around 0900 hours I asked the concierge about my car and driver. It had all been arranged, I was told. Could he be there in a half hour? He could and would, I was assured. I returned to my room and readied myself, throwing on the lightest weight clothes I'd brought (and believe me, we don't customarily dress for that kind of heat in Malibu), then went down to finish my paper in the lobby. At 0930 a bright-eyed and bushy-bearded young Arab man in a khaki military uniform approached me and asked, "Excuse me, sir. Are you Mr. Jake?"

"That I am. Are you my driver?"

"Yes sir," he said. "Mr. Fawaz asked me to conduct you around Kuwait City. I am Lieutenant Haroun Asad Al Sabah."

"I'm pleased to meet you, Mr... . Haroun?" He nodded. "Are you then related to Mr. Fawaz?"

"Yes, distantly. We are members of the Al Sabah family, and it is rather large. Please come with me, Mr. Jake." He led me outside, where the temperature had already reached 100F (forecasted to top 115F later). A doorman opened the passenger door of a new Mercedes Benz E-class sedan. "If you have any specific interests or things you specially wish to see, please let me know," Haroun said genially after we'd settled in.

"It's my first day in town," I said. "Perhaps Mr. Fawaz told you things he thought I should see?"

"He had no specific plan but thought familiarizing you with the city would be to your benefit. As we are now on Arabian Gulf Street perhaps we should continue along it, passing by the Kuwait Towers, and then the road will take us into the city center."

The road was several lanes wide and in excellent condition. He drove slowly and deliberately, ensuring that I got a good look. Not that he could have gone much faster. Traffic was heavy, particularly with a number of heavily-laden cars going south. Mostly what I saw, until we reached the towers, were luxe hotels and a vast amount of calm blue water. Several big cruisers hugged the coast heading south, a continuation of the previous night's parade I'd noted. The numerous trees in view were date palms. The vaunted Towers thrust upward on a point of parkland demarcating Kuwait Bay on the east coast from the harbor along the north coast that lay at a right angle. From a distance, they resembled three large artichokes impaled on 600-foot-high white ice picks. I asked Mr. Haroun what they did, and he explained that they had a restaurant in one green globe, an observation deck in another and some water storage capacity, but mostly they were supposed to symbolize modern Kuwait. He drove out to the seaward edge of the park and stopped the car. "What do you think about that island?" he asked, pointing out to sea.

A low island lay about five miles off shore. "What about the island?" I asked.

"Failaka Island. It has ruins on it, ancient Greek, they say. Thousands of years ago, before the Arabs settled here. I imagine they came for the pearls. Before oil, Kuwait's main export was pearls... until the Japanese introduced cultured pearls, which cut drastically into the market for natural pearls. Would you say the island has a good location? For defending the harbor, I mean."

"Excellent for that. A few big guns could keep any ship out."

"Yes, it would require some big guns," he sighed. He backed the car out of the parking space and resumed the tour. We rounded the bend and the city skyline rose up to meet us. There were more modern glass-façade high rises than I'd expected, some still under construction and topped with building cranes. "Our national bird," Mr. Haroun quipped. He proceeded slowly through the central district streets, pointing out the Foreign Ministry, the National Assembly Building, the Stock Exchange--starkly modern buildings all. "Over next to the Municipal Park is our covered souk," he remarked. "A marketplace, quite extensive. One can buy anything there except gold. The nearby gold souk is where the gold sellers do their business."

"The souk seems much newer and more orderly than the Tehran Bazaar," I remarked.

"I have never been to Tehran, but I hear their Bazaar is quite large and comprehensive, and also very much older. Arab souks are much the same from one city to the next, I imagine. Hawkers doing business. If you should happen to shop there, never accept the seller's asking price. He will think you a fool if you do. Kuwait City is, of course, a small place compared to Tehran." *And has a worse climate*, I was thinking. Not only had the temperature surpassed 110F, but it was steamy humid. Tehran, at nearly a mile in the air, was sheer bliss by comparison. He drove by the Grand Mosque and Seif Palace of the Emir. He found a spot where the road veered close to the shore, and he pulled over and stopped. "What is your impression of the beach?" he asked.

It was narrow, and the strand was pebbly. There was no surf. "Not bad as city beaches go," I said. "It would be a good respite from the heat. I'm sure the Kuwaitis enjoy it." There were, in fact, very few people down there in the water, just a few kids splashing. The adults were well-covered up and sitting in the shade of umbrellas, catching no rays whatsoever.

"Do you think troops could land here? Coming in from the sea, I mean."

An odd question. Amphib landings were the Marines' specialty; the Rangers rarely attacked that way. "It seems a little spare for a beachhead," I said. "A few could land, but not a large force."

"Would it be hard to defend?"

"On the one hand, there's no cover on the beach, so an invading force would be easy targets until they got across this road. But there's also no cover for defenders to dig in. You'd need artillery and air superiority to do an adequate job."

He nodded glumly and pulled away. We left the clean and modern city center, continued around the bay past the commercial harbor and approached an industrialized area. It seemed mostly to be oil storage tanks, petroleum refineries and miles of pipeline. "These are some of our oil facilities," he said. "There are other such centers down the coast. We don't ship so much crude as we do higher value petroleum products, such as refined oil, gasoline, jet fuel and so forth. More profitable, you know. It looks rather vulnerable, wouldn't you say?" he added wistfully.

"Very," I agreed. Any attack would turn it instantly into an inferno, but why was he concerned about it?

We stayed there for a few minutes, and then he started away. "I wish I could show you our desalination plants. We have some of the world's most sophisticated desalination equipment. Our lives depend on it. As any desert Bedouin can tell you, water is more precious than oil. But they are a little up the coast and out of our range today."

"Kuwait has no ground water?"

"Believe me, we've looked and looked, and we haven't found much. Oil is what we have under the ground, not water. But at least we can use the oil to run the desalination plants. That would be hideously expensive, had we not such a plentitude of oil. It used to be that all our water was supplied by boat. This is a great improvement over that plan. Well, that about does it for the business side of Kuwait. Let's take a break for lunch, and after that I will take you around to show you where the people live."

He steered us to a posh restaurant where he knew everybody we encountered. However, we took a leisurely meal in a private booth, where he filled me in with facts and figures about his country. Nothing came up in any way related to the job I was brought there to do. I passed it off as that practice of the Arab culture not to brook business hastily. Of course it was possible he was not party to anything about the investigation at all.

At half past two p.m. we started off again. "It is customary to take a nap in the heat of the day, but I want to complete our tour and get you back to your hotel. It's not a big city, so it won't take much longer." As he drove he explained that most of the foreign workers lived in apartment blocks designated for them, but most Kuwaiti citizens lived in private villas. The various ethnic groups had their own districts—it created better harmony, he said. So the

Filipinos tended to cluster together, likewise the Palestinians, the Indians, the Bangladeshis, and so forth. He pointed out some of the respective apartment districts as we encountered them. "Most of these foreign people are here to do menial work," he said. "Cleaning, gardening, maids and nannies, nurses and such, work that Kuwaitis disdain or lack the training to do. Each group has its own ways, and we are tolerant of other faiths so long as they do not impose themselves on the Faithful."

"Their quarters look adequate enough," I said. "Does Kuwait have any slum districts?"

"None to speak of," he said. "Oh, the menial workers do not live luxuriously, by any means, but many of them nevertheless make enough money to remit a good portion home to their families. And while they stay here they live in great comfort compared to their home countries. So they come here to work, by preference. We would not allow indigent foreigners to remain. As it is, there are considerably more foreigners here than Kuwaiti citizens. It's an interesting question: would the foreigners act on Kuwait's behalf in a time of strife, I wonder?"

"Native sons generally are more loyal than outsiders, I've observed."

His face went a little grim. "I suppose that's so," he said. He crossed over into a residential district. "Now you see typical Kuwaiti villas. You cannot see much, actually, as most of them present plain faces to the world." He meant high, bare concrete or stone walls topped by broken glass and interrupted only by large gates. "Do not be fooled by this appearance. Inside those walls may be luxurious palaces, as high as three stories. We find it is best to present a humble face to the outside world."

There wasn't much to see in the villa districts—concrete walls aren't especially scenic. The districts had minareted mosques aplenty and also shopping areas, mostly enclosed, their parking lots filled with shiny new cars. Even the Arab districts were segregated, as Sunnis and Shiites get along better throughout the Arab world if they are kept apart, he noted.

There wasn't much life on the streets, not surprising in that heat. Traffic on the boulevards was heavy, and among the housing districts congested. I saw a number of heavily laden cars, vans and SUVs emerge from villa gates and head toward the south, the menial help securing the gates behind them.

He was right: the city was not large. A couple more hours of slow touring exhausted the possibilities of the residential districts. Mr. Haroun took to a major, modern road, Highway 6, or Sixth Ring Road. It passed the airport, which seemed very busy for a city that size. Planes took off at a steady pace. Planes sat loading passengers at every boarding gate. Incoming planes lined up on the tarmac waiting for departure gates to clear.

We were on the outskirts of town, but it was not like other cities' outskirts. Kuwait City had no suburbs in our sense of the word, with lawns, driveways and school yards. And whereas most large cities in undeveloped countries bleed off into the boondocks with shabby commercial strips and sporadic shacks and hovels, Kuwait City had fairly abrupt boundaries. To the right along the highway sat businesses and residential complexes—walled villas in various shades of brown, ornamented predominantly by palm trees. To our left lay flat, limitless, barren plains. The bulk of the traffic, heavily laden cars and trucks interspersed with convoys of army trucks and haulers, headed west. We drove several miles on the highway to a cloverleaf intersection where almost all the traffic, except the army vehicles, took the Highway 70 exit and went south.

We continued along Highway 6 to Selayel Resort, where Mr. Haroun proposed we take some afternoon refreshment. It was an oasis graced with modern buildings, greenery, large reflecting pools of water and at least one elegant restaurant. What I really craved was a cold Dos Equis or three, but Kuwait being a strictly Muslim country, a tall fruit smoothie and some pastry had to do. It was a welcome relief after several hours in the car. Afterwards we traveled a little further along to another cloverleaf intersection. Mr. Haroun took the north exit and joined Highway 80, another modern highway with three lanes in both directions. Unlike downtown Kuwait City the traffic was light; few other vehicles besides military convoys took Highway 80 north. After a mile or so he found a convenient place to pull over and stopped.

"This is the highway to Basrah, in Iraq," he said. "Beyond here there is nothing much to see." There wasn't much to see right there. To the west flat, barren, arid plains stretched toward ruler-straight horizons that promised no delights beyond. There was a line of low hills off in the distance to the northeast.

"Are those mountains in Kuwait?" I asked.

"What you are looking at is Mutla ridge, our highest point, all of 300 meters."

"Your country is basically flat, then. It's odd there's no other traffic on the Basrah road than military vehicles," I remarked.

"Maybe they're having exercises at J-One Army Base at Sulaibikhat or something," he said. "And I guess no one else wants to go to Basrah right now. There's nothing much between here and the Iraq border except oil fields and some farms."

"How far is the border?"

"From here, perhaps 60 kilometers," he replied. "This fine highway was originally built as a token of friendship with Iraq," he added. "It never sees much traffic. Iraq is not a welcoming place." He threw a U-ey and headed the other way back toward the city.

"I noticed that many civilian cars turned south on Highway 70. That leads to Saudi Arabia?"

"Yes, that is true." He did not further elaborate. "Well, that's pretty much the extent of Kuwait, Mr. Jake. You've seen it all," Mr. Haroun concluded. "What do you think of our fair city, Mr. Jake?"

"Most impressive. It is without a doubt one of the most modern, prosperous and well-tended cities I've visited."

"We are proud of what we have accomplished in such a short period of time. Two generations ago very little of this existed, and our people lived in mud-walled houses much less fine." He paused. "I wish to ask your opinion about something, Mr. Jake. Would Kuwait City be easily conquered by an outside invader?"

Why was he asking me such a question? "Mr. Haroun, you must understand that my military training and experience was as a combat soldier, specifically in jungle warfare. I've no familiarity with urban combat or desert warfare. An honest answer to your question would depend on many factors—your defenses, the nature of the invader and his forces, and so forth. Is there some reason why you bring up this question? If I knew what was on your mind, I could perhaps form a better answer."

"Just wondering, that is all," he said. "Well, let's get you back to your hotel." Soon we were back in the crush of cars and commercial traffic, and it took a while to reach the Hilton. By then the sun had set, and my jet-lagged carcass shrieked for Z's. We'd long exceeded my internal bed time. My fondest desire was to grab a bite to eat and crash.

Mr. Haroun pulled to a stop at the front door and waved away the attendant who'd hurried over to usher us in. "I hope you found our tour informative, Mr. Jake," he said.

"Very informative, indeed. I'm looking forward to spending more time in your sumptuous city when my work here commences."

"That will be very soon, I'm sure. Mr. Fawaz was tied up today but he looks forward to seeing you tomorrow. He will send a driver to collect you at five o'clock in the morning, if that is all right with you. And by the way, he suggests that you will be more comfortable if you wear clothing suitable for being out in the country."

I thanked him again for the tour and he drove away, leaving me standing there wondering: five a.m. for a drive in the country?

FRIDAY, JULY 27, TO WEDNESDAY, AUGUST 1, 1990

I waited in the hotel lobby at 0500 hours togged out for a jaunt in the countryside, such as it was. From what I'd seen of it yesterday Kuwait didn't boast much jaunt-worthy countryside. The hot buffet hadn't yet been laid, but I managed to round up enough coffee, dates and rolls to fuel me for a while. Mr. Fawaz showed up within a few minutes. He wore a military uniform today, mid-level officer.

"Good morning, Mr. Jake," he said brightly. I hope you slept well last night."

I said I had, though I hadn't really.

"Good," he said. "Did your tour with Mr. Haroun go well?"

"Yes it did," I said. "He was very thorough and informative. He covered your city from one end to the other. Very impressive, I must say."

"Yes, we have tried our utmost to do right for our people with our oil revenues. Today I will show you some other aspects of our nation that cannot be conveniently seen by automobile. I apologize for the early hour, but as you will see, some variety of wildlife are best observed before the world has fully awakened."

He guided me outside to the curb, to a military vehicle with cop lights and sirens above the windshield. The sun was just rising in a crystal clear sky, a few stars still twinkling at the opposite horizon. The early morning gloom had only begun to disperse, but the temperature already challenged 90F. We took the back seat and he instructed the driver to get under way.

Traffic was light so we were able to speed down Highway 51. A short way beyond the International Airport we went through a major cloverleaf interchange and abruptly our six-lane highway became a country road with fewer lanes but still well paved. We proceeded south about 20 miles through flat, mostly desolate terrain populated by oil derricks along one stretch. We came to a large compound with military length runways, Ahmed Ali Jaber Air Force Base. The driver pulled out on the tarmac and rolled to a stop beside an attack helicopter, a French *Gazelle*, rotors lazily turning. The pilot and another military man stood by.

Fawaz and I got out and approached the chopper. "Mr. Jake, meet Colonel Aarzam of the Kuwait Army, and our pilot, Major Nmir. Gentlemen, this is Mr. Jake Fonko, who has come from America to assist us." We shook hands all around. "Let's not tarry," said Fawaz. "We've no time to spare. Element of surprise, you know," he quipped to me.

We climbed aboard and donned flight helmets. I couldn't fathom what this had to do with my assignment to investigate financial irregularities in Spain; all would be made clear, no doubt. We lifted up, tilted northward and took off over the city, flying fast. Rather than follow the highway toward Basrah, the pilot took us easterly out across a stretch of bay. After a time we flew low past a big field of oil wells, then followed a course between farmlands along Mutla Ridge to our left, and what looked like marshland to our right. At a point where a large inlet flowed into the marsh, Fawaz remarked, "Now we have reached the Iraqi border." To the pilot he said, "Go three more miles north. Then take us up to 1500 meters and turn west, paralleling the border."

We sped along, coming out of the rising sun, and I spotted something on the horizon at two o'clock. As we drew nearer, I could see a large troop encampment spread out across the desert. Did I say *large*? It soon was revealed to be *huge*. Fawaz handed me some binoculars.

The camps were still waking up and stirring about, but it was clear these were battle-ready units. They had tanks. Hundreds of tanks, and some mobile artillery. And a shitload of APCs—armored personnel carriers. We passed over a small town and found more troops and tanks positioned on the other side. I estimated at least four divisions, about 80,000 men, in a line several miles long, poised not far above the border crossing of Highway 80. Oddly there were a number of large, articulated cargo trucks—in the U.S. we'd call them "big rigs"—scattered around the rear areas. Hauling what kinds of cargo?

Fawaz said something to the pilot in Arabic, and he turned us abruptly south toward Kuwait and upped our speed. "We'd best clear out of here before they scramble something after us," Fawaz remarked to me. In a minute we'd re-crossed the border, and after passing over another large oil field Major Nmir set us down on the edge of a forward Army outpost. Compared to what I'd just witnessed, it seemed more like a Boy Scout Jamboree campout, with perhaps a couple platoons on site. The camp looked neat, maybe a little too neat. It had been set up recently and could be quickly disassembled and evacuated. The three of us took our helmets off and climbed down to the ground. "Well, Mr. Jake," said Fawaz, "what do you think?"

"Think about what? If you mean the army we just saw, I'd say Kuwait is facing big trouble ahead. That's at least four divisions lined up a couple miles across the border, and they look ready to fight."

"Actually, our intelligence people say it's five divisions—about 100,000 men—including Republican Guards…the Iraqi equivalent of your Airborne Divisions."

"How long have they been there?"

"They've been establishing the camp for several weeks, but

once the facilities were in place, the numbers ran up rapidly and then stabilized at present strength in the last few days."

"Has Iraq been threatening war lately?"

"Iraq has perennial complaints against Kuwait, but they have issued no threats or declarations pertaining to these troops here, no. In fact their diplomats assure us that their country means Kuwait no harm."

"Perhaps it's just a big war game, but I'm not aware of any instances in which that kind of troop concentration didn't soon attack."

"My government fears so too, despite all the reassurances. So what would you advise us to do?"

"Do you mean you want my off-hand opinion?"

"Oh no," said Mr. Fawaz. "We need your considered opinion, after careful analysis. That is why we brought you here."

"I agreed to come here to investigate some financial irregularities between Kuwaiti investors and Spanish investments."

"So you were told. When I talked to you in Los Angeles I was not authorized to mention the military situation, for security reasons. The world at large still does not know anything about it. And we feared that you'd never agree to come if we told you at the outset we were in danger of being invaded by Iraq. But surely you must have suspected something when you saw the deposit in your account? Why on earth would we pay you that much for a job that could be done as well by a team of ordinary accountants and lawyers?"

"But if you'd approached me straightforwardly, I'd have told you that I'm not qualified to give you that sort of military advice."

"Come now, Mr. Jake. Your modesty is commendable, but when we saw that this Iraqi troop build-up was in earnest our intelligence specialists asked their colleagues in allied nations for recommendations. Your name came up in more places than any other. Such a reputation cannot be undeserved."

If you only knew, I thought. "Look," I said. "For several years I was an officer in army intelligence. I served a hitch in Nam with the Rangers in the Long Range Reconnaissance Patrols. I had a brief assignment on loan to the Central Intelligence Agency. But I've had no experience in strategic planning. Small unit tactics in jungle warfare is where my expertise lies."

"Yes, of course," Fawaz said. "And that will come in handy too. Now, what kinds of preparations would you advise? Considering the force buildup across the border, it appears we have very little time to get a defense in place."

"Look...oh, what the hell. Okay, first of all what kinds of armed forces does Kuwait have?"

"All Kuwaiti men—citizens, I mean—have military training, and between ages 18 and 30 they are in the reserves. So theoretically that's perhaps as many as 100,000 men we could call on. Especially if some of the foreigners volunteer."

"If they're well-equipped that's not a bad start, if there was adequate time. The foreigners would have to be trained. How quickly can your regulars and reserves be mustered?"

"I'm afraid it's not even that simple," Fawaz said. "Many Kuwaiti men in the reserves are out of shape. Another problem is their training, which I fear can be desultory. Our professional soldiers are very good, but our young men do not always take their service seriously. They are sons of the wealthy, after all. Many of them live in luxury and do not even work. Few if any of our soldiers have ever been in a real battle, or even a real fight, in their lives. And then many of those theoretically eligible are currently out of the country—on vacation, studying abroad, and what have you. Nor do we have adequate equipment on hand at short notice to engage in a full-scale shooting war."

"So what size operational army are we looking at?"

"Optimistically, 17,000 in total, and like any army, most of them are not combat arms."

Facing 100,000 troops battle-hardened by the recent war with Iran, positioned less than an hour from where we stood. "What does your air force look like?"

"We have 24 *Gazelle* attack helicopters, several of which are requisitioned to the police. For interceptors we have 34 *Mirage* fighter jets. For ground support we have several dozen Douglas *Skyhawk* attack jets."

"And they are operational?"

"No, not all of them. Most, maybe. The pilots are well-trained but not battle-tested."

"What about armor?"

"Of main battle tanks, we have fifteen World War II M-48AB Patton tanks. Also we have more than 200 BMP-3 infantry fighting vehicles from the Soviet Union. We have on order 200 M-84s from Yugoslavia, but unfortunately, only four have yet been delivered."

"If I may ask, what battle plan did your military have in mind when they structured their forces?"

"We are a small country," said Mr. Fawaz. "Our thinking was that we should be able to hold off an attack long enough to give allied nations time to bring in sufficient men and arms. We never anticipated attacking any other nation, nor withstanding a powerful invader on our own."

"Okay," I said. "Let me sit down with some of your military planners and see what kind of defensive strategy we can devise."

The heavily loaded traffic on the roads and the big cruisers off the coast, all heading south, now made sense. Word of the border build-up was leaking out, and in-the-know Kuwaitis were leaking out too. And so I followed the Kuwaiti military doctrine. Comparing what I saw massed across the border to Kuwaiti defense forces available, clearly the Kuwait army had the survival chances of a crippled anchovy in a shark feeding frenzy. Therefore my personal strategy was to buy some time while I came up with a way out of this mess.

* * *

THE CHOPPER WHISKED US BACK TO KUWAIT CITY, DROPPING US off on a helipad, and Fawaz returned me to my hotel by mid-morning, leaving me able to catch the breakfast I'd missed earlier. It was Friday, the Muslim Holy Day, so most everything in town, including government offices, was closed while the Faithful did their duties at mosque. Therefore I intended to spend the rest of the day gathering my thoughts, I told him when he dropped me off. My first thought was to pay a pronto visit to the U.S. Embassy to find out their take on the situation.

After breakfast I strolled around the hotel lobby and out to the swimming pool overlooking the Bay. No one was using it, and I hadn't had any exercise in the last several days, so I returned to my room and put on my swim trunks. The pool was warm and the blazing sun had brought the air temperature up toward 110F. My dip was anything but refreshing, but I swam hard laps to the point of exhaustion and then lay on a chaise in the shade until I dried off. That didn't take long.

Returning to my room, I found a petite Asian maid tidying up the bed. Her facial features looked familiar. "Excuse me," I said.

She left off tidying and turned around, "Yes sir?" she said.

"Are you by any chance from the Philippines?"

"Why, yes I am. How did you know?"

"I spent some time there, and the Filipinas have a distinctive look. Very beautiful ladies. What part of the Philippines do you hail from?"

"The city of Manila. Are you familiar with it?"

"It was where I spent most of my time. Are you one of the Filipinas with a teaching degree who couldn't find work there?"

"How did you know about us? Yes, that is my situation."

"I knew a woman, her name was Luz, who worked for a time as a housemaid in Singapore." I'd thought it best not go into Luz's subsequent career, but not to worry.

"Oh, was that the same Luz, the escort woman who married the minister? She is very famous."

"I believe it was. She told me that being a housemaid in Singapore was not easy work. How is your job here?"

"Thankfully, my job here is better than that, though several of the managers have trouble keeping their hands to themselves. There are many Filipinas employed here as housemaids and nannies in Kuwaiti homes, and it is much worse here than in Singapore. Here they are often treated as nothing more than slaves. Employers confiscate their passports, work them all day long with no time off and withhold their pay. The men of the households use them as concubines, and the women beat and abuse them in retaliation. And there is nothing they can do about it, as foreigners have no rights here. Here in the Hilton Hotel I have long working hours but otherwise am free to go about town in my time off, and there is a workers' union to look out for us, a little at least."

"I gather there are a lot of foreigners here in Kuwait?"

"I believe the foreigners somewhat outnumber the Kuwaitis. In addition to maids and nurses from the Philippines, many Palestinians and Bangladeshis come here to work as laborers and cleaners. Also nurses and menials and shop clerks from India. Kuwaitis will not do those kinds of jobs. Because of the oil money they do not have to, and often families spoil the little boys and little girls rotten. So it suits them to bring in poor foreigners to do the necessary work. Oh, it is not that bad a place. It is well-managed and clean. Compared to other places the pay is adequate, so we can send money home to our families. I'll not complain, as this is better than my prospects in the Philippines. There is nothing like Philippine poverty in Kuwait, and also very little crime. I count my blessings."

"As well we all should," I replied. I went into the other room and read a copy of *The Financial Times* I'd picked up in the lobby while she finished her work. I found nothing at all in it about the army across the border.

After Christabel (I gathered from her name tag) had tidied the room to perfection I put on some street clothes and went down to see what's what at the Embassy, located across the road. I'd presumed our Embassy would keep to a normal American working schedule, but I walked over to find it shut tight. Friday was the Muslim Holy Day, and our Embassy adhered to the local workweek, Sunday through Thursday. At least they followed standard American working hours, 8:00 a.m. to 4:30 p.m. Great—another two days, at least, to get a clue.

Now that I'd been Shanghaied into being a military strategic advisor, I thought another tour was in order, analyzing Kuwait City through different eyes. It being Holy Day, no Muslims worked, so a young Indian man, Raghu by name, drove the Merc today. I told him what I had in mind and we were on our way. Traffic was lighter than usual, which was good because he drove as recklessly as third-world people tend to do. As a first destination I told Raghu to drive me over to the Grand Souk—might as well take a look. "I can take you there, sir," he said, "but everything is closed right now. A few shops and food stalls will open later in the day."

"All right. I'll tell you what, just drive me around slowly through the city center. I'll tell if I want to stop anyplace."

"Very good, sir," he said, and around city center we cruised. It had an entirely different aspect from the tour yesterday. Then it was a gleaming, ultra-modern city on the edge of the desert. Now it was a potential invasion target. What could that horde massed across the border do here? Hundreds of tanks roaming through broad avenues in a modern city supported by infantry could do plenty. The glass-sheathed high-rise office buildings looked pathetically fragile.

We drove back and forth for a while, and then I directed Raghu to follow Highway 6 out of the city. When we reached Highway 80, we went north a few miles. I had him stop, and I got out of the car and walked out onto the bare ground.

Forget any images of desert you may have picked up from *Lawrence of Arabia* or *The English Patient*. This was no expanse of sensuous, drifting sand dunes. This ground was flat as a pool table, pebble-strewn, firm and bereft of vegetation. Tanks and personnel carriers could stream into Kuwait City down that six lane highway at cruising speed. Nor did any terrain features suitable for defensive positions present themselves. The only cover I saw on our chopper trip was oil fields and farm plots. Say the Kuwaitis positioned their tank force in ambush below Mutla Ridge, concealed among date palm orchards. Fifteen obsolete Patton tanks in the hands of amateurs spring out to challenge 300 Russian T-72s run by veterans? They might as well just lay spike strips across the road, for all the difference it would make.

Shit. Mission Im-bleeping-possible.

I wanted no part of this impending tragedy. There was simply no useful advice I could give them, from any angle. I couldn't even fake anything. Come tomorrow I would get my passport from Fawaz, resign my commission and join the mob leaving town. Back in L.A. I'd return their money, less a bit for a few days' time and uncovered expenses. So long, it's been good to know you.

I climbed back into the Merc and told Raghu to return me to the hotel.

* * *

BRIGHT AND EARLY THE NEXT MORNING I GOT A CALL FROM Fawaz. "Good morning, Mr. Jake. I hope you had a good night's sleep?" he said. "For we have a big day ahead of us. When you have breakfasted, have your driver bring you to the Ministries Complex. He will escort you to the meeting venue." And before I could reply, he hung up.

It would be just the place to tender my resignation, I thought. Get all the paperwork done in one stop. I took my time at breakfast, cleaned up, donned a business suit and went down to the lobby desk to call up my driver. The desk clerk told me he was waiting for me, and I turned to find Mr. Haroun at my elbow. "Good morning, Mr. Jake," he said. "Mr. Fawaz told me that you took a trip across the border on Thursday and that it was very revealing. An emergency conference has been called to discuss that issue. If you would come this way, I'll take you directly there."

"Who will be at this conference?"

"The leading ministers and generals, other high officials,

perhaps even the Emir himself. There is much urgency and concern, as you may well imagine."

He took me to the Merc and efficiently negotiated the heavy traffic into the city center. As we passed the airport I saw that it was as busy as ever. Government trucks and packed private cars were still heading south.

The Ministries Complex was a large block of modern, concrete office buildings of five stories. He descended into an underground parking garage and took a reserved space by a bank of elevators. We rode one up and got off in a spacious but austere office corridor, mercifully air conditioned. The place was bustling-busy with men in robes and men in business suits. In the offices we passed, women—some with headscarves, some without—worked at typewriters, telephones and filing cabinets. He guided me to a door, knocked and then opened it and motioned me in. Around an arrangement of polished conference tables sat a couple dozen men. They ranged from middle-aged to white-beard elderly, and divided among medal-bedecked military uniforms, a few finely-tailored western suits, and mostly dishadasha robes and white head dress. A chairman, flanked by several others, sat behind a lectern.

Mr. Fawaz rose from one of the padded leather swivel chairs and came to us at the door. "Good morning, Mr. Jake. Good to see you. As you can see, this is a very important meeting. All the ministers are here, most of the top generals, and also leaders of the business community. Come." All eyes in the room followed me. He led me to an empty chair next to his and announced something to the group in Arabic. Most of the men nodded approval, and some smiled. "I introduced you as an intelligence specialist I have brought from America. They are familiar with your credentials, so there is no need to mention them right now. This is a conference to discuss the matter at the border, which as you know needs our full and immediate attention. Your role here today is to observe and listen. No one expects you to render any judgments or express any opinions. That will come at a later time. For now, listen and learn."

He pulled out the chair for me, and I took it. What choice did I have? I could hardly stand up and resign in a language most of them probably did not understand. An orderly set a cup of coffee and a fine china dish of sweet rolls down in front of me. The discussion was in Arabic, which left me out. It ranged from thoughtful and deliberate to animated and heated, with much massaging of worry beads around the table. Everyone had his say, and Fawaz whispered translations as it went on. And on. And on.

The topic of the morning was the nature of the threat across the border. Some expressed great concern. Others questioned the accuracy of reports on the size and nature of the force. Others delved into the politics of the situation. Rather than Q and A, it was more serial bloviating, and much of it Fawaz didn't bother to translate for me at all. Eventually we reached the lunch hour and the meeting was adjourned to be continued. Fawaz took me to the canteen in the building, explaining what had gone on as we walked. "There have been a number of meetings among the various groups, but this is the first one where representatives of all the key groups have gathered. Nothing much will get settled in the early stages. It is more a matter of everyone placing his markers and offering his viewpoint. It's almost ritualistic."

"Mr. Fawaz," I said. "I have given this matter much thought, and I don't see how I can be of any help to your country. The facts of the matter are plain enough for everyone to see; and let me be frank about it. An overwhelming invasion force is poised on your border. Your own military forces could hardly slow them down, and there is not time for allied support to arrive with any effect. The only possible solution lies in negotiations with Saddam Hussein, and the intricacies of that are far beyond my capabilities. I have no alternative but to resign from this job, go back to the U.S. and return your money."

"But Mr. Jake, there you prove your value to us. You speak the plain truth. I agree with you one hundred percent, but I could not say anything like what you told me in front of the men in that room. They would have my head. Listen to me. Sit in the meetings and pay attention. Soon the mission that has brought you to Kuwait will unfold before you."

"I will come to your meeting tomorrow and perhaps the next day, but if I don't by then clearly see my way to contribute something substantive, I will in good conscience have to resign the job."

* * *

THE NEXT MORNING, I CALLED THE U.S. EMBASSY AS SOON AS they opened. It took a while to get through to them owing to their being swamped, the receptionist claimed. The soonest appointment I could get to see anyone was tomorrow, Monday, with an underling Foreign Service Officer. It was a start. I gave the clerk my name and passport number (off the photocopy I always pack along), figuring maybe he'd check me out in advance to save some time. I wanted to find out what our government knew about the situation and also if there were any American evacs I could hitch a ride on. I'd had an early breakfast and taken a half hour to work out on some machines in the fitness center, so as soon as I completed the call I threw on a suit and had Mr. Haroun take me to today's meeting.

The guys around the table looked pretty much the same as on Sunday, with the exception of one man to whom all paid deference. As I took my seat next to Fawaz, he whispered, "The Emir is sitting in today. I'll introduce you later."

The meeting droned on in Arabic, sounding pretty much like yesterday. One of the generals opened it with a statement and then a general question. Commentary then bounced from one man to another. Each made long, emotional declarations. "What's up today?" I asked Fawaz during a coffee break.

"The general posed the question of leadership in the defense against Iraq. The men around the table represent the most powerful families in Kuwait. The Emir represents the Al Sabah family, obviously. In addition there is an Al Kharafi of the retailing family. The Al Bahar family controls shipping. The Al Sagar family has a strong presence in oil and petrochemicals, the Al Sayer family in trading and transportation, the Al Ghunaims in real estate, and so on."

"Okay, so what's the issue? They all sound like they're in earnest."

"It's a matter of face. All the families have sons in the military, so they are volunteering their sons to lead the most dangerous missions."

"That's suicidal. Any defense put up against an onslaught by the Iraqi force we saw will be wiped out in a minute."

"They all know that, and none expects the army brass to take them up on it. But it is part of the culture. Everything is about the honor of one's family, one's clan, one's tribe. So they forthrightly offer up their sons."

"Considering the urgency of the matter, isn't this wasting valuable time?"

"The men at the table don't think so."

And so went the rest of the day. When the meeting broke up, as nearly as I could figure nothing had been decided or accomplished. Meetings were the same the whole world over. Exiting the room I guided Fawaz away from the others.

"Mr. Fawaz," I said. "I need my passport. I'm going to pay a visit to our Embassy tomorrow morning to see what I can find out from the U.S. point of view (I didn't mention the part about evacuation), and I'll need the passport for identification."

"No problem, Mr. Jake. You'll have your passport in all good time. What did you think of the meeting? Are you gaining insight into the matter?"

"As you translated it for me it made no sense at all. Why was the Emir here today? He didn't say much of anything?"

"He came to underscore the importance of the problem and to observe first hand the proceedings. Of course the important decisions and arrangements will be made privately, as they always are, but it is necessary for him to be on hand for the public expressions by the various factions, which are made for his benefit. It also is important for you to observe our way of doing things. Time is getting short and the situation grows ever more urgent. We will be expecting your recommendations on Wednesday morning."

"Shouldn't I then be getting together with some military strategists and planners? Assess troop and equipment readiness, look at dispositions of forces and so forth?"

"No, no—that's taken care of. You'll see. Come as soon as you can tomorrow after your visit to your Embassy and stay alert. Trust in Allah. Come with me now. I'll introduce you to the Emir." And so I met Sheik Jaber Al Ahmad Al Sabah. Middle aged, he glowed with authority. He spoke English fluently, having been educated abroad. Our conversation was brief, as he obviously had pressing duties. He clearly recognized the dire situation facing his country and showed concern yet remained upbeat. He thanked me for being there to help and encouraged my efforts. He had a kindly face and a gracious smile. The Emir seemed as capable a leader as any I'd met. He left me feeling that I must do my best for embattled Kuwait.

* * *

I STROLLED OVER ACROSS THE ROAD TO THE U.S. EMBASSY FOR my morning appointment. The place was swamped with visa-seekers, most of them foreign workers. The Kuwaitis weren't alone in contracting the skedaddle bug. I sat waiting for about twenty minutes and then a harassed-looking paper-shuffler came out of an office and approached me.

"Mr. Jake Fonko?" he asked. I nodded. "I'm Ernest Toyler (we'll call him: I don't want to embarrass private citizens unnecessarily). Pleased to meet you. Come this way. I'm afraid I can't spare you much time. You can see how busy we are this morning. Inundated with people who want to leave here." He closed his office door behind us, and we took seats. "What can I do for you?"

"Two things. Let's tackle them one at a time. I'm working as an advisor to the Kuwaiti government on the Iraq invasion threat, and I would like to know whatever you can tell me about the situation here from the American point of view."

"Who is your contact man in the Kuwaiti government, if I may ask?"

"Fawaz Al Sabbah."

"Hmmm... I think he may be one of their top intelligence people. Okay, what makes you think there's an imminent threat of invasion?" he asked.

"Fawaz took me up in a chopper and gave me a good look at the Iraqi troop buildup along the border at Highway 80."

"Really? And you think it's that bad?"

"Five divisions. Four hundred tanks. Yes, it's that bad."

"Holy shit. Excuse me. From what I've learned of your background, I'll take your word for it. Our own intelligence has been sketchy about it to date. What, if I may ask, is your position vis-à-vis the Kuwaitis?"

"They expect me to render advice on dealing with the threat."

"Here's what I can tell you, Mr. Fonko. On July 25 our ambassador in Iraq, Ms. April Glaspie, met with Saddam Hussein. She expressed our concerns about the troop buildup on the border and told him that America wants better relations with Iraq. She told him that we have no opinion one way or the other about these perennial border disputes they have. But we at State are hoping he got the message that invading Kuwait would not further good relations with the U.S. For that matter, it would not be good relations with other Arab nations. Arab countries don't invade other Arab countries. It isn't done."

"Nations don't usually mass 100,000 combat troops on another's border without the intention of using them. It's rather extravagant for a bluff."

"The Iraqi ambassador to the U.S. in D.C. has been reassuring State that they have no hostile intentions here, but, yes, I take your point. You've seen it, whereas none of our people stateside have, so it's possible they're underestimating the threat. I imagine the CIA has been monitoring it, probably Defense Intelligence too. They probably have satellite photos, but if so they haven't shared them with Foggy Bottom. That makes the horde storming in here for visas more understandable—news and rumors must be raging throughout the city. We've observed that more cars than usual have been crossing the border into Saudi Arabia lately. There's a load of anxiety about it in all quarters but no definite news or positions. Well, that's all I can tell you about that."

"Let me ask you this: Suppose the Iraqi army moves into Kuwait City. What could the U.S. do about it?"

"Here in Kuwait all we have on the ground is a small Marine security detachment for the Embassy, capable of moderate crowd control at best. The nearest U.S. force of any size is on Diego Garcia, 3,000 miles away in the Indian Ocean. So the short answer to your question is: damned little. But according to our diplomats an invasion is still unlikely, so nothing has been done about arranging a military intervention. What was the other thing you needed?"

"I'd like to leave Kuwait myself, ASAP. Do you have any plan for evacuating Americans? Or, barring that, could you give me any help in arranging a flight out? I don't think I'd stand much of a chance against the crush in the airport on my own."

"There are only about 180 Americans in Kuwait right now and we've not seen any need to evacuate them yet. As for arranging a flight out, I'll keep my ears open and let you know if I hear anything. That's all I can do right now. We've got plenty on our plate just now, as you may have noticed."

"Sure, I understand," I said. "Thank you for your time, and good luck." I got up and left his office. He had enough to do without showing me to the door.

My visit didn't much help with either of the matters I came about. Apparently, the State Department wasn't too concerned about the troop concentration. I hoped they knew something I didn't know, but I'd seen plenty of cause for concern. An invasion loomed, was my estimation, and the only variable in question was the timing.

Haroun took me to the Ministry Complex, where I crept into the meeting already in progress and took my seat next to Fawaz. He was happy to see me, but few of the others took any notice. He explained to me that today they were discussing some of the points at issue between Kuwait and Iraq, each man contributing his own perspectives to each bone of contention.

Fawaz translated the gist of every statement—typically they were long, drawn out and verbose, and do those Arab waves with their hands—as the meeting droned on. By the end of the day, no matters of military defense at all had been discussed. I sure hoped some deliberations and decisions were being carried out somewhere in private, because nothing useful had happened in three days of meetings of the cream of the Kuwaiti ruling class.

As he walked me out, Fawaz said, "So, Mr. Jake, now you have the picture. We are expecting your recommendations first thing tomorrow morning."

"But nothing has happened in the meetings I've sat in on to give me any basis for recommendations. I haven't had a single discussion with any of your military leaders, and military matters haven't been broached in any of these meetings. I haven't been given substantive information about available defensive forces. I know nothing about your activation procedures. I haven't even seen a topo map of Kuwait. I can't possibly recommend anything."

"You underestimate yourself, Mr. Jake," he said reassuringly. "You have seen what you need to know. Think about it. Well, here we have Mr. Haroun to take you back to the hotel. I look forward to seeing you tomorrow morning. Please be early, if you can. Inshallah."

* * *

Needless to say, my head was spinning. Allah's will seemed to dictate that I would make a fool of myself in front of Kuwait's leading citizens, who would then have my hands cut off for stealing their money. Yet Fawaz was confident I could deliver, if I would think about what I'd seen in the meetings.

Okay. First and foremost, they seemed to be slow-walking. They were in no hurry to decide anything. Because... they very well knew the situation was too hideous to contemplate. Second, all the foremost families, clans, factions and interests were present. I wasn't expected to resolve their disputes. They wanted me to advise them to do something that all of them wanted to do. Third, face was paramount. None of them wanted to lose face in front of the others.

Think about it, Mr. Jake.

What was it that consultants did?

Long pause.

Bingo!

* * *

The next morning I showed up as others were just starting to arrive at the conference room. Fawaz was there already and greeted me warmly. "Did you sleep well, Mr. Jake?" he said. "Your jet lag must be fading by now. You look good. There will be some preliminaries for the meeting as usual, but after that you are first on the agenda."

"I look forward to it," I said. "My remarks are brief and right to the point. I hope they are not expecting a long speech."

"By no means. Speak the plain truth and all will be well."

"I'll deliver my recommendations in English. Is that all right?"

"Excellent. Most here speak English. For those who don't, translators are at hand."

We took our places and waited as the remainder of participants filed in. When the seats had filled the chairman called the meeting to order and, as Fawaz had said, saw to a bunch of preliminaries. Then, Show Time! Fawaz escorted me to the podium, switched the microphone on and introduced me in Arabic, getting approving nods and smiles. He backed away and left me in the spotlight.

I looked around the room to engage eye contact, with an especially friendly smile toward the Emir. Then... here goes nothing!

"Honored Emir," I began. "Distinguished leaders of Kuwait. Mr. Fawaz has entrusted me with the task of offering some ideas and suggestions in regard to the unfortunate situation along your northern border. He personally took me on a helicopter inspection tour to witness the situation with my own eyes. On the basis of what I saw there, I will now share with you my thoughts on the subject. Some of what I say may displease some in this room, but be assured I speak with deepest respect as a loyal friend and servant.

"What I witnessed across your border is a formidable army, brought there by the Iraqi *shaytan*, Saddam Hussein. I will not mislead you. It is an army of 100,000 hardened soldiers, with 400 battle tanks and artillery battalions. They lie 40 miles from your beautiful city. I know of no situation in which an army that large and combat-ready has not been sent into battle. As they have no need to fear an attack by Kuwait, those troops can have been brought there for one purpose only—to invade your innocent and friendly country."

Most of the men in the room received the news calmly. I was telling them nothing they didn't know very well already.

"Sunday I heard spokesmen for your honorable families offer their sons as leaders in the defense against the Iraqi aggressors. That is laudable and to be commended. But... should the Iraqi forces storm across the border your sons would be slaughtered to no avail. Kuwaiti armed forces as they presently stand have no hope of turning back the Iraqi tide, or even of delaying them long enough to make a difference. If Saddam Hussein is bent on taking Kuwait, your sons cannot prevent it.

"So here is my summation: From a military standpoint the immediate situation is hopeless. My advice is to safeguard and preserve what you can of your military materiel and prepare to evacuate as many of your leading people as possible. Kuwait has billions of dollars of overseas reserves, so a government in exile can easily be supported for as long as it takes for your allies to expel the invaders. And that time will not be long in coming, for you can rest assured that the Western, petroleum-dependent nations will not allow such a catastrophe as Saddam Hussein controlling half of the Gulf's oil fields to stand.

"It would be insanity to needlessly sacrifice your beloved sons in a doomed defensive mission. Rather, they better should be kept out of harm's way in readiness to return and rebuild your beloved country once the Iraqi devils are expelled. Of course some of them must stay behind to look after your families' interests. For those loyal Kuwaiti sons remaining, arms and ammunition should be distributed immediately so that they may carry on resistance against the invaders.

"For the time being, Kuwait should use every diplomatic means to avert, or at least delay, an attack by Iraq, while praying to Allah that Saddam Hussein will recognize the error of his ways and abandon his evil scheme. But waste no time in preparing for an evacuation in the event of an attack. Should the Iraqi troops move across the border, seek safe havens abroad where you can bide your time until they are defeated and sent back where they came from.

"I thank you gentlemen for allowing me to express my humble opinions. I hope I have been of service to you."

I made a little bow, then stepped back away from the lectern. I saw no visible audience reaction aside from a little cessation on the worry beads.

"No need for us to remain. These men have much to discuss among themselves. Your job is done. Let's go get some coffee," said Fawaz as he rose, put a hand on my elbow and guided me out into the hallway. He closed the door and exclaimed, "Brilliant, Mr. Jake. I knew you'd come through."

"It wasn't much. I just advised them to do what all of them really wanted to do, and gave them public permission to get on with it. I don't see anything further I can do here, so I really think I should be getting back to Los Angeles."

"Quite right," said Fawaz. "Excellent. You've earned every

penny of your fee. Ha ha, half their sons are on vacation in Paris, London, Monaco and Dubai already, as are the rest of the elite families, as Kuwaitis who can afford it always leave during the hot months. The rest have been packing for evacuation for days. I'll get working on your journey home. I think I can put you on a Kuwait Airlines plane heading out of here on Thursday, the day after tomorrow. That will give you one more day to enjoy Kuwait City now that your job is completed. I have to get back in the meeting. You have provided an action plan, so my job now is to help get everything in motion. Thank you again, Mr. Jake. You were magnificent."

* * *

Mid-morning the next day Fawaz called to tell me everything was arranged. He would personally pick me up at 0930 hours to deliver me to the airport. A Kuwait Airlines non-scheduled flight would take me First Class to Paris, where I could either catch a connection to Los Angeles or stay for a few days to enjoy myself as their guest if I wished. He'd bring my papers and passport, and after he saw me off he'd tell the bank to wire the balance of my fee to my account.

So I had the rest of Wednesday to myself. With the pressure off, I decided to take a closer look at the town. The desk told me Mr. Haroun was assigned to other duties, so Raghu drove me to the city center. First stop was the Grand Souk. It was like a Walmart wet dream—huge, filled with every type of goods anyone could ever want, and teeming with desperate, rich customers. Although it was completely covered and sun-shaded, unfortunately it also opened to the outside hot, muggy air. The crowd seemed about equally divided into Kuwaitis in traditional robes (white for the men, black for the women), and foreigners in more westernized garb, jeans especially. Reflecting the generally apprehensive atmosphere in town, many of them stocked up on necessities. I didn't need anything by way of household goods, Arabian art or souvenir trinkets, but it was entertaining enough to roam around soaking up exotic sights, sounds (Arab music) and smells... excepting one area where the sewage system apparently had broken down.

For lunch I grabbed a mystery meat burger at a local fast food joint, Hungry Bunny, and ate it in air-conditioned comfort. I then had Raghu guide me over to the gold souk. It reminded me of the gold shops in Singapore, but it held shimmering displays of necklaces, rings, bangles, bracelets, barrettes, broaches, pins, pendants, charms and bars of bullion vaster by orders of magnitude. Those Arabs do love their gold. And today they hurriedly bought up large amounts of it. Made sense, since it was a proven safe store of wealth in times of trouble. I managed to elbow my way through the crush to buy a few trinkets for Dana—gold jewelry showed up well against her blonde ponytail and tan. The guidebooks said Kuwait had some museums, but the descriptions didn't appeal. For all its wealth and modernity there wasn't much interesting for a foreigner to do in Kuwait. Even having a drink somewhere posed a challenge.

I went back to the hotel, swam some laps in the pool, lounged around. Read the papers. Evening came and I packed my things up. Called Dana, told her I'd be home earlier than planned, filled her in on the latest. Watched CNN on the TV through a news cycle, didn't learn anything. But that's typical.

Overseas CNN showed selected foreign news with an American spin, played exotic music at the station breaks, and called itself "international." The news on the local English-language channel, KTV2, was odd. It showed Kuwaiti dignitaries coming and going, here and there, but had no commentary, just some semi-classical background music. I went to bed looking forward to boarding that plane. First class, Fawaz said. Thinking about the past week, it turned out to be some of the easiest money I'd ever made. And a few days R and R in Paris? That's the ticket! Oh nine thirty hours couldn't come soon enough.

THURSDAY, AUGUST 2, 1990

I was enjoying a goofily pleasant dream that featured me tap-dancing to "Begin the Beguine" with Fred Astaire and Eleanor Powell in a black-and-white Busby Berkeley stage setting when I snapped awake to what I realized was the rattle of heavy machine-gun fire. The clock showed 6:28. I bounced out of bed and parted the window drapes.

A rising orange sun still hung low in the sky, but I could see enough to get the picture. Flames and billows of black smoke rose in several parts of the city center. It was two klicks away, so I couldn't tell what was burning. A tank, swiveling its turret, moved along a shadowy section of First Ring Road down below that was visible from my room. I saw it loose a machine-gun burst at something.

No doubt tanks roved along Arabian Gulf Street on the other side of the hotel as well. That was closer, so the gunfire that woke me up probably came from there. Attack choppers buzzed around through the downtown high-rise buildings. It looked like one fired a rocket. I checked out the airport. No air traffic, just more attack choppers hovering and darting like fire-spitting dragonflies.

Shit. The Iraqis had attacked. *There goes my R & R in Paris.*

I couldn't see any troops moving around on the streets below my window. A few cars passed on the Ring Road, despite the tank—brave drivers. Or clueless. Apparently most of the action was downtown and around the harbor. The east side of the city wasn't an immediately critical military objective. Troops would arrive in numbers soon enough. I saw another tank on First Ring Road roll out from behind a building.

I cleaned up and dressed—electricity and water still functioned, a good sign. At least I wouldn't have to walk down all those stairs to get breakfast. I looked out the window again—more smoke plumes rose among the high-rises. I saw an explosion. Waited a few seconds, didn't hear it. The double-glazed windows killed the sound. Then I did hear an explosion echoing up, a cannon report, probably a tank down below firing at something. I got no sense of any military opposition mounted against the Iraqis.

My flight home wouldn't be happening for a while, damn the luck. It made sense for the Iraqis to shut down the airport first thing. When it would reopen for civilian flights remained to be seen, and when it did they would control it.

I turned on the TV and scanned the news channels, but it was too soon for accurate, let alone comprehensive, coverage. I had a better chance of getting the skinny in the lobby. I rode the elevator down along with a clutch of anxiously chatty fellow guests to find the place abuzz with people in various states of dress and panic. I hadn't seen much of my fellow guests in between my comings and goings, and it turned out to be quite a mix. Voluble Europeans in business suits. Ululating Arabs in robes and headdress. Outspoken Americans in expensive polo shirts asserting their rights. Restrained but obviously frightened Asians. A regular United Nations convention. And the hotel management anxiously trying to forestall a potential uprising. I noted several stern, berobed Arab men standing around on the side, closely monitoring the crowd.

No one knew much at that early hour. The Iraqis crossed the border at 2 a.m., roared down Highway 80 and streamed straight into the center of the city, was the consensus. J-One Army Base put up some resistance, but the main force bypassed them and secured the harbor, the airport and government buildings. City center already swarmed with Iraqi troops. They brooked no interference, shot first and didn't ask questions later. The lobby crowd pressed the desk with distraught questions about immediate dangers and ways out of Kuwait City, but the management spokesmen could tell them little. I went toward the front door to take a look outside, and two of those stern Arab men intercepted me and motioned me back to the lobby.

It was too early in the game for the invasion to disrupt the hotel's operations, so the restaurant had opened its lavish breakfast buffet on time. I filled a platter and took a small table. A waiter poured me some strong local coffee. As if I needed a wake-up jolt. Diners around me huddled together in close, nervous conferences. I took stock of my situation. The Iraqi force I'd seen over the border was sufficient to overwhelm the Kuwaiti military, and they'd already pretty much done it. There was no chance I'd be getting on a flight out any time soon. The Hilton Hotel was as safe as anywhere, as it had no military value. Typically, invading forces house their honchos in the best accommodations available, so the Iraqis had good reason to keep it functioning. As for me personally, much depended on the stance of Iraq vis-à-vis America. If we were a declared enemy I was too visible there to last long once the Iraqis checked the registry.

So let's see:

Personal equipage: No weapons. Enough money if my credit cards worked. Some traveler's cheques but very little local cash if they didn't. Six changes of haute-business clothes—half of it suitable for European climates—and two weeks of shirts and underwear, plus the outdoors duds I'd brought as advised. I neither speak nor read the local language, but many locals speak English.

Contacts and back-up: Fawaz, who I'm sure had heeded my advice at first opportunity. Ernest Toyler at the U.S. Embassy. Christabel, my Filipina maid. Raghu, my Indian driver. Even if Fawaz were still in town, he'd given me no contact numbers, and as I'd worked strictly under his control and would be leaving soon, I knew no one in the government but him. My passport resided at Fawaz's intelligence ministry (which Iraqi intelligence operatives probably were rifling through already) leaving me with no documentation but a photocopy of it and my California driver's license; and Arabs were sticklers for documents. It had never occurred to me to bring along one of my fake passports.

Situation assessment: (1) I'm on my own. (2) I'm fucked.

* * *

I RETURNED TO MY ROOM AFTER BREAKFAST. IT WAS MID-evening in Los Angeles so I tried to call Dana Wehrli to let her know I'd be delayed. The phone worked, but it was no dice getting an out-of-country line. The Iraqis most likely had seized the telecommunications building. I parted the drapes and surveyed the unfolding catastrophe. More smoke rose from the city center. Uniformed soldiers now wandered around on the streets below in gangs, apparently without defined missions. As I watched, a couple of them probed a parked BMW sedan, trying the doors. One smashed the driver's window with his rifle, opened the door from the inside and scrambled in, the other hovering raptly. Presently he emerged with the car's radio in his triumphant hands—useless to him, but he must have totally destroyed the dashboard in getting it. After an animated debate between the two he tossed his trophy onto the street, and they sauntered away to find a shady spot.

There was still no local TV news, and what came through from Dubai told nothing informative. I had a better chance of learning something useful in the lobby, so I went back down. Despite Iraqi soldiers and tanks roaming around in our vicinity the Hilton Hotel had not yet brooked any damage. While the help went about their business as best they could, the guests who weren't mobbing the desk milled around in a daze. At least it wasn't like the fall of Phnom Penh in 1975 when the Khmer Rouge took over, ordered everybody out of town, and mowed down anybody who objected. The recollection gave me comfort. I'd survived that—no way could this be worse.

I started chats with several of the westerners who looked like they might have a clue. None did. Like me, most were transients with no access at that moment to their local contacts. The Iraqi force concentrated on securing downtown and the harbor. The Hilton Hotel sat several klicks distant from the day's main action, which except for the explosions and smoke clouds, was beyond our view. With no news to be had and no one venturing out on the streets, hard facts were scarce. One of the men behind the desk caught my eye and motioned me over with a nod of his head. As I approached him, he indicated I should follow him.

He led me into the manager's office, closed the door and motioned for me to sit. "Mr. Fonko," he said, "it goes without saying how sorry I am for this inconvenience, as I know you planned to leave this morning."

"No need to apologize. It was hardly your fault."

"True, but one does feel sympathy. Since you are a guest of the Al Sabah family, as well as an American, there are some things I need to tell you. Reports are that members of the Al Sabah family, as well as other high-ranking officials, evacuated before the Iraqis arrived. Rest assured that charges for your room and other services will be covered by the prior arrangement for the foreseeable future."

"I appreciate that," I said.

"Think nothing of it. Al Sabah credit is always good in Kuwait. As for your American status, it is highly likely that America is considered to be an enemy of Iraq, and if your President Bush protests the invasion, that is a certainty. So I must warn you that several days ago a number of highly-placed Iraqi officials took rooms here in the Hilton Hotel, obviously in anticipation of today's invasion. In fact I saw two of them turn you away from venturing outside earlier in the day. Inevitably they will examine our register book, so be careful. Especially, watch what you say over the telephone. I understand they already have seized control of the ministry of information and the telephone office."

"Thank you for the warnings. Is there anywhere I can get news of what's happening right now?

"Not yet. It's too early. The invasion took us by surprise, and the world at large is just now hearing about these unfortunate events, with few details or even facts yet known. The invasion has not even been mentioned on television news yet, and I doubt you'll get any semblance of truth about it when Kuwaiti TV channels resume broadcasting. My sources tell me the Iraqis crossed the border at two o'clock last night and reached here four hours later. They met little opposition, seized control of the airport, and bypassed the military base at Jahra to take the harbor and the central district. They are inflicting considerable damage there, and already have begun looting the shops."

"Do you anticipate trouble here in the Hotel?"

"One hopes not. This hotel is not a military objective, and as I said, a number of their people are staying here, so I imagine they will want to keep it in good condition. I'm sure more of their people will arrive wanting rooms, but until the soldiers impose their presence on us we will try to function as usual."

"Utilities are operational and supplies are sufficient, then?"

"For the time being, Inshallah."

I got up to leave. "Thank you very much for taking the trouble to inform me," I said. "Let's hope it will all be over with soon."

"Alas, I fear not. Bismallah, Mr. Fonko."

Iraqi brass in the building, and me listed in the register as an American guest of the Al Sabah family. *Action plan*: Low profile. Blend in. Butt out at earliest opportunity.

The hotel had the usual array of boutiques, so I scuttled over there while there still was stock left, keeping to what cover the lobby crowd offered. The shops had opened for business. They featured European fashions, some pretty sharp stuff. I bought a couple outfits that looked serviceable and low-maintenance and wouldn't stand out too much. I put it on my hotel tab. The desk changed some T-cheques into local dinars, so I was set for street money. I'd come with only one hat, part of my outdoorsy kit, never thinking I'd have to spend much time under the Arabian sun. Now it looked like I might be on the run some, and if so I'd need head cover, also some means of carrying water. The boutiques had nothing suitable, but possibly after things calmed down I could find something in the shops across the road. If the Iraqis were clouting parked BMWs for their audios, it would be a while before they got around to looting haberdasheries. Or so I assumed.

 I retreated to my room and reviewed my face. My complexion could pass for local, face shape not too bad. My hair was dark enough if I oiled it a bit. In a couple days my beard would be thick enough to affect a van dyke with a pencil mustache. Then I could pass for a local, possibly in western wear and certainly in a robe and headdress.

 I dialed the number of the U.S. Embassy and got a busy signal, meaning either they were swamped or their service had been cut off. The rest of the day was all about killing time, watching out the window, seeking information and re-dialing the U.S. Embassy. Finally my call got picked up by a harried clerk. He could tell me nothing. They could do nothing about my passport today. They were officially closed right now. They'd be open next on Sunday, operating business hours as usual. I made an appointment to see Ernest Toyler that morning. "Stay indoors for the time being and keep your head down. If you have a radio follow what BBC is reporting. Check back with us for further instructions," the clerk advised and rang off.

SUNDAY, AUGUST 5, TO FRIDAY, AUGUST 10, 1990

Not much happened to me personally the next couple days, though plenty happened elsewhere all over town. I swam in the hotel pool and worked out in the fitness room. I listened to the BBC news on a neighbor's shortwave radio. What else could I do, with no passport, no mission, no outside contacts and no firm notion of the situation?

My window gave me a grandstand view of the destruction of downtown Kuwait City. Waning old smoke plumes wafted upward among the glittering high rise towers, and new explosions and black billows erupted. Several buildings showed damage visible even from two klicks distance. Attack choppers flitted here and there strafing things and occasionally launching a rocket or two. Down on the roads nearby, more tanks rumbled along, convoying up and down Arabian Gulf Street and probing the wider side streets. Rag-tag Iraqi troops meandered around and loafed in the shade beneath overhangs, when they weren't breaking into shops and stripping them bare. I saw a couple of them enter into the lobby of the Hilton, only to be shooed away by the Iraqi bigwigs staying here. More Iraqi bigwigs arrived every day.

Some visiting Brits with better local connections than mine

talked about joining a convoy and making a break through the desert across the Saudi border. I guess they must have done it, because I didn't see them the next day or thereafter. Out of curiosity I stepped out of the lobby and walked around the neighborhood for a look-see. A brace of rumpled Iraqi grunts sitting in the shade of some palm trees eye-balled me for a minute, then went back to comparing the wristwatches they'd stolen.

Outside in the open, the sounds of war came through clearer—explosions nearer and farther, occasional machine gun fire, small arms popping and pinging. I toured only a few blocks, curiosity not being enough motivation for a longer walkabout in 110F heat. I needed to do some shopping, but shops in the vicinity were closed. Those lacking rattle-down steel shutters displayed smashed windows and empty shelves. The shuttered ones stayed intact for the time being, having so far withstood Iraqi attempts to breach. Civilian car traffic moved on the streets now, though nowhere approaching the jams I'd seen on the roads when I arrived. The Hilton Hotel functioned more or less normally, and I was under no immediate threat so saw no point in pushing my luck. I stayed indoors and kept my head down, like the U.S. Embassy and the BBC exhorted.

Sunday morning, I readied up for my scheduled appointment at the Embassy. It sat across the street overlooking the Bay, a short enough walk to be endurable even in that heat. I reached the palm tree shaded Embassy compound gate without incident. I explained to the Marine guard my appointment with Ernest Toyler. He verified it over his walkie-talkie and waved me in. The crowd today numbered somewhat fewer than the pre-invasion mob, but was sizeable enough to keep the place jumping. I checked in with the receptionist, who indicated a sitting area where I should wait.

After fifteen minutes, an anguished middle-aged couple emerged from Toyler's office, he leading the way as he assured them that everything would be fine. After ushering them out the portal he came over to me. "Good morning, Mr. Fonko. Sorry for the delay. Come into my office, please."

We seated ourselves on opposite sides of his desk. "Sorry I can't offer you coffee, but as you may imagine, we're swamped, simply going out of our minds, and can't do all the usual niceties."

"That's fine," I said. "Understandable. You've a good location here. Looks like a nice beach down below."

"It's our private beach. Unfortunately our women can't sunbathe on it. When they do, Kuwaiti men passing by on water skis wave their peckers at them. Their subtle hint about Muslim dress codes, I suppose, or maybe an expression of their opinion of western women. You say you have a problem with your passport?"

"When I arrived my Kuwaiti employer took it to attend to entry formalities and hasn't yet returned it. Now I have no way to reach him, if he's even still in Kuwait."

"Your employer here was Fawaz Al Sabah, you told me? Fawaz Al Sabah is in Kuwaiti Intelligence. He probably evacuated with the rest of them. It seems the CIA gave them a four-hour heads up when the invasion commenced, and much of the government took off for Saudi Arabia in the country's fleet of helicopters in the dead of night. Made good sense. In the circumstances it'd have been suicidal for them to stay and fight. Evacuated some fighter planes as well. A lot of their air force was caught on the ground and destroyed by Iraqi choppers and tanks. It appears to have been a well-planned and well-executed operation."

"So, can you issue me a new passport, or at least some temporary documents?"

"Of course. Do you happen to have any suitable photos?"

"Could you use this?" I pulled out my photocopy. It was fairly clean.

"No, we'd have to Xerox it, and the copies would be too grainy. We have a photographer here. I'll have him take the shots. We can have it ready for you by tomorrow, if that's okay."

"It will do. I'm not going anywhere that I know of. Tell me, are there any plans for an American evacuation?"

"Not at present. There aren't that many Americans here, and

they aren't in immediate danger. The Iraqis shut down the airport, so they can't leave anyhow."

"What about overland, to Saudi Arabia?"

"Chancy. The Iraqis patrol the border and sometimes arrest people trying to cross and confiscate their vehicles. The road south is not as good as the ones in Kuwait City, so cars going off it risk getting stuck in the sand. For the time being it's best to stay put. The Iraqis are brutalizing the locals, but they've kept their hands off westerners so far."

"The news has been spotty. Do you know of any developments back home?"

"Needless to say, the U.S. is very upset about it. It seems that the day before the invasion the Iraqi ambassador told an assistant Secretary of State that they were not going to move against anybody. Like the Japanese and Pearl Harbor all over again. Not that Iraq attacked the U.S., of course. President Bush hit the fan, as well you can imagine, and I understand he is taking it up with the United Nations pronto. Baker and Shevardnadze issued a joint American/Russian statement condemning the invasion and calling for an arms embargo. Most members of the Arab League condemned the invasion. Saddam claims that the troops came into Kuwait only to support a native revolt against the ruling family, and that they will leave as soon as the new government is stabilized. He expects the world to believe that? The man is barking mad."

"Barking mad may be an understatement. I can't imagine this army will be leaving any time soon."

"Obviously they mean to stay. They've made sure not to damage the power and desalination plants, and they're keeping the workers running them. They destroyed the Ministry of Information building and TV stations the minute they reached town and seized control of the newspapers."

"Sounds to me like a full-scale takeover. Well, thank you, Mr. Toyler. I won't take up any more of your time. I can pick up my passport tomorrow, then?"

"Come in the afternoon. The receptionist will help you." He picked up the phone and called the man who took pictures. He told me how to find him. I thanked him for his help and went and had it done.

I returned to the hotel and had a cup of coffee. I decided I needed a better idea of what was happening in the city. From the window in my room civilian traffic seemed to be moving. If one were cautious, the danger might not be great. I went down to the lobby and asked the concierge to summon my driver. The concierge questioned my wisdom, but I pressed upon him some urgent business in town. He got on his phone and a few minutes later Raghu, my Indian driver, appeared.

"Are you up for a tour around the city?" I asked him.

"If it is necessary, certainly, sir," he said.

"It is. Let's go."

I followed him down to the parking garage, and he led me to a well-used Chevrolet. "The Iraqi soldiers sometimes stop the nicer cars and steal them," he explained apologetically.

"Nothing wrong with American iron," I observed, though I don't think he understood the reference.

The car ran all right. We emerged on the street out front. He turned left and drove gingerly along Arabian Gulf Street. "Best not make eye contact with the Iraqis," he warned me. "One shouldn't attract their attention."

Point taken. I noted a number of burnt-out cars standing along the curb. Others sat on blocks, their wheels missing. Where there were no cars, as often as not a scattering of window glass glittered on the pavement. The Iraqis had been beavering away.

"I think we can manage this," he said. "Traffic is coming and going. Ordinary people are going about their business. The Iraqis want them to keep the city operating."

He followed Arabian Gulf Street around the point. I noted holes in one of the Kuwait Towers pylons as we passed. Apparently some hotspur tanker had tried to shoot it down. Inasmuch as the towers held a major amount of the city's water supply, I hope he got a good dressing-down by his senior officers. Several big motor cruisers lay grounded on rocks outside the downtown marina. Iraqi thieves found out the hard way that running them isn't as simple as it looks in the movies.

Traffic was light but smashed cars sat hither and yon. Raghu took a main road past the Great Souk, now a shambles thronged with looters. I could only imagine what a time they'd had at the gold souk.

Ambling among the high rises we saw buildings cannon-blasted to shambles. Fires blazed here and there, unattended. Facades showed bullet holes and fractured windows. We passed soldiers loading pickup trucks with the contents of stores—shoe stores, furniture stores, appliance stores, electronics stores, even a Kids R Us. Battered taxicabs, driven down from Basrah or Baghdad, were taking on stolen cargo. Clumps of discarded loot—didn't meet the soldiers' high standards, I guess—obstructed the streets. Out front of a shoe store the street was cluttered with empty shoe boxes and scattered running shoes. I saw a squabble among soldiers, probably over who called "dibs" first, coming to blows. A cemetery in town had received piles of recent fly-flocked corpses, with no burial details yet assigned. In the ambient heat that would be hard duty.

The sights were altogether sickening, but at least it was an improvement over what I'd seen in Cambodia. The Iraqis came out of the traditional soldier mold—killing people and breaking things—though they over-indulged the looting. Whereas the Khmer Rouge was like a low-tech neutron bomb. They killed the people but left the buildings intact.

I told Raghu to head back to the hotel. "I've seen enough. Nothing good can happen to us, driving around like this," I remarked.

"Truly, sir." He aimed us back at Arabian Gulf Street, a less distressing route than continuing through the city streets. "I have been hearing stories," he said hesitantly.

"Stories?"

"Yes sir, from my friend who owns a shop. I wonder whether they can be credited."

"Depends on the stories. What have you heard?"

'Yesterday some Iraqi soldiers paid his shop a visit. He sells ladies' clothing. The soldiers were collecting dresses to steal, and he overheard one of them claim he and his mates had happened upon a compound where Indian nurses at the hospital live. He boasted that it was better than a brothel, because you could do as many as you liked and didn't have to pay them. Can such a story be true?"

"I'm afraid it might be."

"But these are educated Indian women of higher caste. That is not their way at all."

"Unfortunately, it is the way of the Iraqi soldiers."

"It is very distressing, sir," he said sadly.

Yes, it was. One hundred thousand hungry, illiterate soldiers had been turned loose with no discipline in a wealthy, defenseless town. This promised no happy ending.

* * *

I picked up my passport at the Embassy the next day without trouble. I appreciated their promptness. It was my third passport in six years; I ought to be getting bonus points. Ernest Toyler told me he'd heard word that Saudi Arabia now feared the Iraqi invasion would extend to their northern oil fields, so they had requested American troops. That was a first. Muslim nations had never welcomed an infidel military presence before. It was bound to ignite controversy among Arab nations, but I couldn't blame the Saudis. Against Saddam's million-man army his Saudi brothers wouldn't stand a chance.

Smoke plumes still rose from the city center, though fewer as time went on. During the moments when I wasn't in either a building or a car I was still hearing gunfire, most of it some distance away from the Hilton. The Iraqis imposed a curfew on the city, seven p.m. to seven a.m. Rumor had it they'd done so because they were meeting armed resistance in the form of night raids. I doubted that a curfew would hinder that. If anything it would abet them by clearing the streets of civilians.

Tuesday's TV news from Dubai confirmed the Saudi's request for American troops and reported that George Bush was wasting no time with what they were calling "Desert Shield." CNN showed Army transport planes taking off from American bases and landing on desert strips. No way to tell whether it was live coverage or stock footage, but either way it portended relief. Also they reported a U.N. trade embargo against Iraq as long as their army occupied Kuwait. I wondered how that would affect Kuwait. Fresh produce had largely diminished in the restaurant offerings—most of that was imported and the port was shut down—but otherwise the food and service remained pretty much as before.

What the heck, life in the Hilton Hotel wafted on. It was a welcome contrast from the dangers and privations I remembered of post-collapse Phnom Penh.

* * *

ON THURSDAY MORNING, CNN REPORTED THAT SADDAM Hussein had announced the annexation of Kuwait by Iraq. The oil fields were absorbed into Basrah, and Kuwait City was to be an additional province. They broadcasted excerpts from President Bush's address in answer, a forceful statement that it will not stand, that sounded like he meant it.

Christabel, the Filipina maid, intercepted me as I came out of the coffee shop after lunch. "Mr. Fonko, I thought it best to warn you," she said, much agitated. "Several Iraqi soldiers and two of the Iraqi guests came to your room while I was cleaning it, looking for you. I think they may be there still."

Shit. If an enemy patrol came probing in the jungle I'd know what to do. But in a five-star hotel? Where do you position the claymores? "What did the soldiers look like?" I asked. "Were they well-dressed, or dirty and rumpled?"

"Very clean. They had nice uniforms and wore red berets."

Republican Guards. "I guess I'd better stay out of sight until they go away," I said. "Do you know of someplace I could wait where guests do not go?"

"I think the staff quarters will do. Come with me." She led me to a stairwell and from there to an unmarked door. Behind it was an extensive but cramped dormitory setup, definitely not five-star. "You can stay in the sitting room," she said. "I'll let you know when they've gone."

So I twiddled my thumbs there for an hour or so, watching maids, cleaners, laundrymen, bellhops and busboys bustle in and out. The range of nationalities covered several continents—in addition to Filipinos, also Thais, Bangladeshis, Indians, Pakistanis, Palestinians, Egyptians and a European or two. Christabel returned and said, "They went away and the soldiers left the building. So if you want to come out, your room is empty now."

"Thank you, Christabel. I'll have to take precautions from now on."

"As we all do. Mr. Fonko, those soldiers looked at me in a very disgusting way, grinning and leering and hungry-eyed. One of them said Arab women were haram, but the foreign women are halal. Does that mean what I think?"

"Haram means forbidden, like pork. Halal means permissible. Applied to women, I fear you are correct."

"Then the stories I hear are true, that they are raping Filipina women when they find them?"

"I've heard similar stories, and from what I've seen I wouldn't doubt them."

"So far I have been safe here in the hotel, but the Iraqi soldiers come more frequently all the time, and I wonder if my safety will continue. What is it about these Arabs? How can they think like that? 'Haram' and 'halal'? Aren't Filipinas women too? No wonder they abuse their housemaids. They don't think we're even human.

I've heard word that the Philippine Embassy is sheltering Filipina women and plans to evacuate them. Do you think I would be safer there?"

"If you can join an evacuation and get away from Kuwait, I think that would definitely be safer, yes."

"I will look into that, then," she said. "Thank you." She ushered me back to the stairwell, and I returned to my room. Nothing seemed to be missing.

* * *

THE NEXT MORNING CHRISTABEL CAME IN AS SHE MADE HER round of duties. She closed the door and said, "Mr. Fonko, I have discussed with my manager about the situation. He says he understands and will return my passport if I want to take refuge in the Philippine Embassy. The hotel will not pay me the money they owe because I will be breaking my contract, but I think leaving Kuwait is most important right now."

"I can give you some money," I said.

"That is very kind of you," she said, "but I have money saved, so it is not a problem. What I most need is transport to the Embassy. It is a distance from here and it is not easy to get a taxi. And maybe not safe."

"I can get a car and driver, so I'd be happy to take you there. When do you want to go?"

"I'll pack my things. Perhaps in one hour?"

"Sure. I'll arrange for the car."

And so an hour later Christabel and I joined Raghu in the parking garage. I opened the rear door of the Chevrolet and she slid in with her suitcase. I took the passenger seat in the front. Raghu had a general idea where the Embassy was, and he drove slowly and deliberately past tanks, soldiers, smashed cars and shattered buildings. Wreckage blocked one road entirely, so he detoured into a side street. Street signs had been removed and he soon lost his way. He found an intersection he recognized and turned into a narrow lane that would get us back on track. We went by clumps of Iraqi soldiers lolling in the shade as he picked his way through scattered debris. Just before we reached the intersection, two roughneck Iraqi soldiers stepped out from the shade of a shop overhang and with rifles pointed at us waved him to a stop. I imagine they originally intended a shakedown for a little baksheesh, but then one of them spotted Christabel. He threw open the rear door, grabbed her arm and jerked her out onto the street. The two of them appraised her with bright, animated eyes. They had a brief argument in Arabic over who got firsts. The one in possession prevailed and put his rifle down while the other one stood there covering us.

Then he got the bright idea to make the infidel watch the proceedings. He motioned me out of the car with his gun barrel. There I stood, hands in the air, while his buddy proceeded to rip little Christabel's bodice open and grab her breasts. She screamed and he clamped his hand over her mouth and started dragging her to the shelter of the overhang, where their sleeping pads lay. The other soldier was so transfixed by the scene that he took his eyes off the car. Unfortunately for him, he was standing in front of it, and suddenly Raghu floored it and ran right over him. I took the opportunity to spring over and grab the other guy in a headlock from the rear. Reluctant to let go of Christabel, he didn't put up much of a fight. I wrestled him off her, smashed a forearm hard in his face, threw him to the ground and dropped a knee into his throat.

Raghu had quietly gotten out of the car and picked up the discarded rifle. He inspected it, chambered a round and shot the man I'd just dispatched in the head. Then he squatted down, lined up a shot at the man under the car and killed him too. "That's two of the bastards, anyhow," he muttered.

Some of the soldiers down the street stirred and started in our direction, though with the temperature above 110F they weren't double-timing. "Let's get out of here," I suggested. We all climbed back in and Raghu sped off around the corner. I heard shots echoing off the storefronts behind us, but he got us away without taking any rounds.

Christabel worked at restoring her garments and her composure in the back seat. "Thank you, Raghu, Mr. Fonko," she murmured.

"Any time," I said.

I heard her mutter, "I can't get away from these animals soon enough."

Raghu found his way again and soon brought us up to the gate of the Philippine Embassy. Sited in a district of apartment blocks and streets of walled villas, it was a sand-hued, desert fortress-like pile with arched windows set in bare walls with rounded corners. Christabel was back in presentable shape, shaken but stirred by the thought of sanctuary. A brief discussion with the guards got her admitted. She turned and blew us kisses, then disappeared inside. To a safer place soon, I hoped.

As we drove away I remarked, "Raghu, you handled that rather smoothly."

"I was infantry-trained," he said. "I saw action at Amritsar and subsequently in quelling all the terrible uprisings that followed. These Iraqis troops are amateurs, nothing but thugs. Someone should exterminate the brutes," he added.

I thought the better of swapping reminisces of Amritsar, considering that I'd sort of touched off that whole bloody mess.

MONDAY, AUGUST 13, TO THURSDAY, AUGUST 16, 1990

THE IRAQIS SEALED THE BORDER ON THE 13TH. THANKS TO heeding the CYA advice of the U.S. State Department to stay indoors and keep my head down, I missed any opportunity to join a convoy evacuating to Saudi Arabia. Big mistake, that. Not that I'd had much opportunity to convoy out. Talk flowed around the Hilton Hotel about driving south to safety, but mostly it was just talk because none of the guests had cars, and who would rent a car out for that particular trip? The few with connections to make a break for it, mainly Brits, issued me no invitations. The Iraqis controlled the airport and harbor, foreclosing the only other means of escape. So the rest of us sat tight, if anxiously.

International opposition to the invasion picked up momentum. The Arab League voted to commit troops to the buildup in Saudi Arabia, and the first Egyptian and Syrian units joined the Americans. Saddam Hussein issued a proclamation that Iraq might withdraw from Kuwait if Israel withdrew from its occupied territories in Palestine, Syria and Lebanon, knowing full well that he'd never have to cough up on that offer.

For me, time passed and that's about all. I worked on keeping exercised, monitored TV and BBC radio, combed what foreign newspapers I could find for news, and watched the destruction and looting from my window as it continued. After Christabel's heads up about the Iraqis on my scent, I kept both eyes open and one of them on my backtrail, my buddy Sarge's perennial advice. I found spaces where I could hang out away from view and moved from one to another throughout the day. If they wanted me, they'd have to track me down.

So you can imagine my reaction when a be-robed Arab suddenly popped in as I was reading a two-day-old *International Herald Tribune* in one of my hidey-holes, an idle conference room. Bosnia-Herzegovina had recently declared independence, and as it was the region of my ancestors, speculation over that development interested me (never even imagining that I'd be caught up in that mess all too soon). The Arab entered alone with hands visible and no weapon, not an immediate threat but I hoped getting out of there wouldn't come to a brawl.

"Mr. Jake?" he said. I looked more closely. Bright eyes. Bushy beard. It was Lieutenant Haroun Asad Al Sabah, my erstwhile tour guide, out of uniform.

"Mr. Haroun?" I said. "What brings you here? I'd have thought you'd evacuated with the rest of the Al Sabah family."

"The entire family did not evacuate, by any means. Many of us stayed behind. Ha ha, I almost didn't recognize you with that beard. But we shouldn't talk in a public place like this. One can never tell who listens in. Can we go to your room?"

I was agreeable, and there we went. Haroun closed the door saying, "Individual rooms at the Hilton Hotel are not bugged, except the ones where the Iraqis are staying. Mr. Jake, it is so good to see you again," he said, giving me a big hug. "It appears you are all right then."

"Except for the fact that I should have been in Los Angeles two weeks ago, I suppose I'm all right. Bored, as you might imagine, but the hotel is taking good care of me. What brings you here?"

"Several things. First and foremost I came to warn you of great danger. Iraqi intelligence seized our headquarters and took control of our archives and records. Soon enough they found your file, and my sources tell me they are most anxious to locate you."

"I was told some Republican Guards showed up in my room while I was out."

"Lucky for you, the warning. Rest assured they will return."

"They may have already. I've been taking evasive action."

"I would have expected no less from you. Let me bring you up to date on the situation, and then I will broach other matters at hand. I must apologize for having left you in the lurch, but the attack took us by surprise and left us scrambling to maintain control. The timing, I mean. Everybody knew Saddam would attack. However we never expected such an exquisitely executed blitzkrieg. Not only did his army attack from the north, but commando units converged on the city by sea and air. Our military people customarily sleep at home and report to base for duty, so the Iraqis timed their arrival at Kuwait City to beat our soldiers to the punch, as you say. Those on their way to base discovered Iraqis blocking their routes and had no choice but to turn tail. Many had to shed their uniforms and skulk home in their underwear, knowing they'd be killed on the spot otherwise."

"That's why J-One base put up no resistance?"

"Some Kuwaiti troops did assault J-One, and the Kuwaiti troops already on duty managed to fight the attackers to a stand-off for a time. A few of our other units fought bravely to little avail. The main Iraqi force bypassed the J-One base and went straight to Shuwaikh Port. You see, the Iraqis had a dock of their own there, for landing supplies for the Iraq/Iran war. After the war the dock remained with an Iraqi complement to tend it, who in the event served as spies. The advanced guard of the Iraqi force went straightaway to that dock, and from there they were led very efficiently by their countrymen to key points in the city. Kuwait City was taken before we knew what hit us. Some of our tanks were en route to J-One on tank carriers, but they were captured by the Iraqis before they could engage in the battle."

"I heard that the government fled before the Iraqis arrived."

"Yes, many did, Mr. Jake. Your CIA alerted them when the Iraqis moved across the border. Preparations had been made, so they had time to assemble and depart. They took the fleet of attack helicopters with them, seeing no point having them destroyed in futile combat."

"Sad to say, but that was for the best. I hope they will be able to return home soon. What about those left behind?"

"It is not good, Mr. Jake. Clearly Saddam's aim is to absorb Kuwait as another province of Iraq. The Iraqis leveled the Emir's Palace—bombed it and burnt the entire compound to the ground, women, children and all; and the Emir's younger brother died defending it. They are destroying all the public records—driver's licenses, deeds, birth certificates, everything that was on computers. First thing, they looted all the banks, stole the country's gold reserves, and they continue to steal everything else in sight! Many sixteen-wheel articulated transport trucks accompanied the invasion force, which they immediately commenced loading with factory machinery, new automobiles from dealers' showrooms, spare parts... everything! And now private cars, vans, trucks and taxicabs arrive from Bagdad and Basrah to steal more. They raided the hospitals and made everybody go home, then stole all the medicines and equipment. They loosed the animals in the zoo and used them for target practice! When they have finished I fear nothing of the former Kuwait will remain."

"It's a terrible tragedy, that's sure. So, you said there were reasons you came, besides to warn me?"

"Yes. I hope you will forgive my skipping over the niceties of Arab business etiquette, but there is no time to waste on chit-chat, so like you Americans I will not beat around the bush and come straight to the point."

"Which is...?"

"I am asking if you would be so kind as to assist us, Mr. Jake."

"Assist who? Doing what?"

"The Kuwaiti resistance. Kuwaitis are organizing resistance

units to guard homes, protect families, secure food supplies and keep essential services operating. So far the Iraqis have mostly confined their depredations to the city center, key facilities and public utilities. They have not as yet stormed into the residential districts. They know they would be at a disadvantage, being sniped at from rooftops and behind thick walls, with their tanks easy prey for Molotov cocktails in the narrow streets. Our units attack by night and increasingly the Iraqis dread the nights. But lately troops have been released from the Iranian border and brought to Kuwait. Their numbers grow considerably, and obviously their next move is to loot the residential blocks. "

"Who is left in Kuwait? What size force do you have?"

"Let me explain about Kuwait, Mr. Jake. Before the invasion there were approximately 800,000 native Kuwaiti citizens—that is, of the original Arab tribes around whom the country formed. Already large numbers have become refugees elsewhere, close to half perhaps. The Iraqis have been seizing our men of fighting age and either killing them or putting them in prison, so that means fewer numbers. Before the Iraqis came we were a minority in our own country, only about 27% of the total population. As you have seen, foreigners do most of the work here. They numbered nearly a half million Palestinians, and several hundred thousand each of Egyptians, Indians, Pakistanis, Bangladeshis and Sri Lankans. Plus one hundred thousand of Filipinos and Thais. Most of them still remain and the Iraqis are keeping them in their usual employments to run the city. It is unfortunate but true that Kuwait can survive without the Kuwaitis. We just gave orders to the foreign workers and paid them with our oil money. Anyone can do that, you know. Many of our men are sent overseas for education, but they aren't inclined to sully themselves in practical occupations. They expect to be proprietors and bosses."

"The foreign workers aren't so against the invasion, then?"

"It is very bad for those not Muslim, because the Iraqi soldiers have been given leave to have their way with their women, and the men they regard as inferior dogs. The Thais are fighting back.

They include along with their workers men with military experience, for the sake of security for their own people, you see. Arabs look down on Asians and Africans because they are godless peoples, so the Thais protect their own, and they have lately taken to assassinating Iraqi soldiers. This disturbs me, that infidels are killing Arabs. And on our own soil."

"Perhaps they are defending the honor of their women?" I suggested.

"What honor?" he huffily replied. "I've been to Bangkok. Their women are all whores." I thought it best not to argue the point. "But with the Palestinians it is different," he continued. "They are Arab brothers, so they have been welcomed here, for we Kuwaitis respect and sympathize with their plight regarding the Israelis. But many of them resent Kuwaitis because, despite our contributions to their cause, they feel we do not sufficiently share our wealth nor pay them enough for their work here. That son of a she-pig, Arafat, endorsed Saddam's invasion, and many of the Palestinians here actually rejoiced in his victory. The fact that Palestinians occupy many high managerial positions in our corporations, banks, industries, merchandising, education, and power and transportation companies further complicates matters, for Kuwait would collapse without the Palestinians. Certainly the Iraqis could not run the place themselves. So how can we now trust the Palestinians? They are everywhere in Kuwait City, and I am sure many act as spies and operatives for the Iraqis."

"As much as I would like to help you I do not see how I would fit into your operations."

"Oh Mr. Jake, again you are too modest. I have seen your record regarding combat, intelligence and espionage. We would welcome your leadership with great enthusiasm."

"And I'd be doing this from the hotel here?"

"Oh no, oh no. You will come to stay with me in an Al Sabah villa. We conduct operations from there. My cousin Salah Melik Al-Sabah is heading the group."

"And you are well supplied?"

"Every villa that remains occupied had stockpiled provisions, and the food shops are still operating in any case. Kuwait, being import-constrained, has months of foodstuffs in storage to avoid shortages in the event of disruptions. As for weapons, the armories were opened to us before the Iraqis arrived. We secured the guns and ammunition before they fell into their hands. We can hold out for quite some time, I think."

"Can I have some time to think your offer over?"

"Of course, of course, Mr. Jake." He wrote a phone number down on the telephone note pad and gave it to me. "Call this number and say you wish to speak, nothing more, no names. I will come here immediately upon hearing from you."

There was no more to discuss. I took him to the door, thanked him for his visit and bade him goodbye with a promise to consider his offer.

* * *

So, the next day I considered it. An interesting proposition, indeed. *Fonko of Kuwait* ?? I was learning that Kuwait, though prosperous and orderly, was a snake pit of cross-purposes and mutual hatreds. Nobody deserved an invasion like the one in progress, but the 27% of actual Kuwaitis—collectively a smug, stingy, overbearing and condescending lot—presided over unhappy campers outnumbering them by three to one. I counted myself on the Kuwaitis' side but couldn't help but sympathize with some of the others. My best interests still lay in getting away and letting the Kuwaitis, George Bush, the United Nations and Saddam Hussein sort it out among themselves. Clearly the buildup of Desert Shield forces beyond the border increasingly posed a threat to Saddam.

I hesitated to throw in with Haroun and his merry band. Aside from my brief encounter with the Khmer Rouge I'd had no experience in urban warfare, one of the nastiest kinds of warfare there is —block by block, building by building, room by room, with little cover and plenty of concealment. I was bored and wouldn't have minded a little action, but launching an escapade just to relieve boredom often as not brings more trouble than it's worth. As long as I could keep dodging snooping Iraqis it seemed my best chances for safely getting back to Malibu lay in sitting tight at the Hilton Hotel while our diplomats negotiated.

The following day Saddam Hussein announced that henceforth foreigners were forbidden to leave Kuwait.

I packed my luggage that night, and first thing the next morning I dialed the number Haroun gave me. "I want to speak," I said when the other end picked up, then replaced the phone in its cradle.

* * *

HAROUN WAS AS GOOD AS HIS WORD. HE SHOWED UP AT MY door thirty minutes later with a bundle under his arm.

"Mr. Jake," he said, "I am very glad you saw the wisdom of my offer."

"You can thank Saddam for that," I said. "I didn't like the sound of forbidding foreigners to leave. Whatever comes next won't be pleasant. Yes, I'll help you out, but in exchange I want you to arrange passage for me out of Kuwait."

"It is a fair exchange. Kuwaitis continue to evacuate, some through the desert to Saudi Arabia, and others through Iraq to Jordan and Egypt. So good, let's be off. I suggest you change your clothes first. It will make our exit easier." He unfurled his bundle onto the bed. It was an everyday Arab robe and headdress, plus a pair of Arab slippers.

"You want me to wear this?"

"Yes, please. The hotel is under surveillance so a disguise is advisable. Take off everything but your underwear and slip into this." He looked me up and down. "The beard is an excellent idea, but if I may offer a suggestion, we can trim it so as to look more Arabian."

We went into the bathroom and he showed me where to lather it up. He directed me to contour it here and there, and after I toweled off the guy in the mirror could have been cast in a *Raiders of the Lost Ark* bazaar crowd scene. Putting the robe on was a revelation. Hollywood desert movies give the impression that Arab robes are grimy tent substitutes, but the better sort are woven of fine fabrics and feel like elegant bathrobes. He adjusted my head scarf and fitted the head band, and I put on the slippers. "Where do I put my pocket stuff?" I asked.

"Arab men carry pouches," he said. "For now, put it in your flight bag. You can transport it under the robe." I made to get my luggage. "No, it is unseemly for an Arab man to carry something himself," he admonished. "I'll have a servant bring it down." He barked something in Arabic into the phone and soon a bellboy appeared at the door. Haroun barked more Arabic and we left the room, the bellboy toting my gear behind us. We paraded through the lobby and out to the entrance curb to a waiting luxe-model Jeep. The robe was surprisingly comfortable in the 110F heat. It didn't cling and allowed for ample air circulation. Climbing into the car was awkward with all the folds of cloth to keep track of, but I got it sorted out.

Haroun's villa sat deep in the Hawalli district on a narrow, nondescript street. The driver stopped before a security gate in a high cement wall and tooted a code. The gate opened and we entered, passing by two guards with submachine guns, into a compound of several buildings standing among well-tended, palm-shaded gardens. The scope of it was much larger than it appeared from the street; the wall blocked the view effectively. We stopped at the entrance of the main building, three tall stories with an imposing facade. "Come in, Mr. Jake," he said. "Some others of our unit are staying here as well. I'll introduce you and then show you your quarters."

We passed from an ornate foyer through a short hallway to as sumptuous a salon as I'd ever seen, surpassing the wildest fantasies of Hollywood set designers. Carpets like I'd bought during my Iran gig covered polished marble floors. Heavy silk drapes accented double-glazed picture windows on opposite walls. Fine European tables and casual chairs sat among cushion-laden sofas and settees. Air conditioning kept the place comfy-cool. One thing was clear—it's good to be a member of an oil-sheikdom's ruling family.

Several men sat around the room. They rose to greet me, and Haroun introduced us—another Al Sabah, an Al Bahar, an Al Sayer, and an Al Segar or two—the very sons the men in the conference had extolled so enthusiastically. Another man in the group, whose name did not fit the Kuwaiti template, Nasr Abu Khattab, was a Palestinian highly placed in one of their businesses. Their ages ranged from twenties to thirties, and they looked physically fit. A couple wore Arab robes, the others western clothes. They were grave but welcoming. "Mr. Haroun has told us of your exploits," Mamoon Al Bahar said. "We welcome your assistance."

Another man stepped forward and offered his hand. "I am Salah Melik Al-Sabah, Mr. Jake," he said. "Welcome to my family's villa. Most of my family have retired to safer places from which to plan and arrange the return of Kuwait to its rightful citizens. I stayed behind to organize resistance to the Iraqis. Fawaz Al Sabah told us of your experience and expertise in unconventional warfare and advised us to contact you if you were still in Kuwait. He thought your assistance would be invaluable to our cause."

"Mr. Haroun honored me with his invitation," I replied. "I will do what I can to help you." Salah summoned a servant, gave instructions, and the servant soon returned with a serving cart of coffee, tea and fruit drinks. We all took seats and tentatively got acquainted. They represented families that lived in that district, many of whose members had gone into exile. They had stayed in Kuwait City to protect their family villas from looters and vandalism and also to fight the Iraqis. After preliminary chit-chat about the weather, distant world events and the mystery of Michael Jackson (they'd seen his "New Generation" Pepsi ad and couldn't fathom his appeal), the talk turned to Kuwait. It was discouraging, one said, because more Iraqis arrived every day, each batch worse than the previous ones. When they had finished with their desecration of the city center they would inevitably progress to looting the residences.

"We know we Kuwaitis can't defeat them by ourselves," Ghanem Al Segar admitted. "We only hope to forestall and harass them until the forces gathering at the Saudi border drive them out."

"It may be many months," observed Salah Al Sabah. "The logistics of such an operation forming from distant nations are formidable."

"What do you think about that, Mr. Jake?" asked Haroun.

"I agree with Mr. Salah that the buildup may take months," I said. "But once they have prepared you can rely that the force will be overwhelming. President Bush will not take half-measures. To change the subject, can someone give me an idea of the kind of resistance your unit engages in, how you go about it?"

Salah was the leader and he took my question. "The Iraqis swarm over everything during the day, so we go forth after dark when they are timid. What we do depends on the circumstances. We sometimes run messages and deliver things to other units. We stand guard duty. We are working on setting up ambushes and establishing snipers. That is where you can help us, as our military training did not cover this kind of warfare. The Kuwaiti government in exile has sent word that they will pay 20,000 dinars—about 60,000 American dollars—for each assassination of an Iraqi soldier, so that is an additional incentive for us. Of course if Iraqis approached any of our villas we would defend them to the death with arms. No Arab can abide someone forcing his way into his home unbidden."

I stood up and moved to a clear area on the big carpet. "I don't know how Kuwaitis run night operations, but American Rangers rely on stealth, concealment and rapid movement. I appreciate this robe Mr. Haroun has loaned me, but I don't see how I could be of much help dressed in this way."

"What do you mean, Mr. Jake?" Haroun asked.

"Are any of you trained in the martial arts, hand-to-hand fighting?" I asked, sweeping the room with a glance. A couple had been. I asked the more fit-looking one, Kadar Al Sayer, to join me and assume a fighting stance. I tried a few moves on him, tried a few holds, and it was as I'd feared. From my side, folds of cloth impeded every move I made. From his side, he easily faked me out and left me grabbing fabric rather than solid wrists, and punching an empty bag rather than flesh and bone. "It's hopeless," I said. "How do you people fight in these get ups?"

Salah said, "From a distance, with a rifle. Up close, with a knife in the guts. If we have to do such things. Preferably we'd rather pay somebody to do it. It's not a cowboy movie, Mr. Jake. Arabs do not customarily fight with fists."

"Actually neither do Rangers. We have other means of physical fighting. And I can't do them if I'm dressed like this. I brought no clothing suitable for night ops. Is there some way I could get some loose fitting western clothing, in black?"

"Of course." He summoned a servant and dispatched him out of the room. Presently he returned with a man holding a tape measure. "This is our tailor," Mr. Salah said. "Tell him what you want, and you will have it by nightfall." The tailor took my specs and my measurements, then left. "After dinner we'll see about arms," said Mr. Salah.

Thus went my induction into the Kuwaiti resistance.

* * *

FOLLOWING A SUMPTUOUS DINNER THE TAILOR PRESENTED HIS work: a black silk, loose-fitting dojo suit that covered my arms and legs. Perfect. A servant brought an assortment of running shoes. I found a pair that fit and we rounded up some blacking to adapt them for night duty. I picked out a side arm—no SIG Sauers so a Beretta would do—strapped on a holster and we were ready to roll.

Salah explained that we had no specific mission that night so would patrol the neighborhood for a while. He wanted to see how

I approached the work. We mounted up in a Land Rover pickup, me riding in the cab with Salah and two others with submachine guns in the bed. At first it seemed like a college prank, for we drove slowly along under a bright half-crescent moon, our own lights off, stopping to take down street signs. "To confuse the Iraqis," Salah explained. "You will notice also that villas have removed their numbers. When they finally assault our district we want to hinder them in every way possible."

There wasn't much action out and about that night. There was the curfew, of course, but the Iraqis stayed in too. As we cruised down one of the main streets I saw street signs on the other side. "Should we go over and get those?" I asked.

"That's a Shiite block," Salah said. "Let them take care of their own. No problem" he reassured me, "they hate Saddam even more than we do."

We passed a shopping complex and I noticed some movement in the shadows. "Is that worth checking out?" I asked.

"My friends in back are not trained in that kind of warfare. They could shoot at it, but that is not a good idea if there is no obvious threat."

What the heck, might as well earn my pay. "I'll tell you what. Drive around behind the shops. I'll hop out, then you drive slowly back around to the front. By then I should have found out what's going on."

Salah slowed down in the back street and I quietly left the car. I crept back through the shadows to where I'd detected movement and spotted my man planted in the doorway of a food store. I stepped out with pistol drawn and said, "You there!" He wasted no time, springing up and bolting around the corner of the building before I could react. I holstered the pistol and sprinted after him, slowing down as I approached the end of the building. I took a quick step out past the corner and retracted it instantly. A figure lunged with arms outstretched and, missing his target, stumbled into the building across the breezeway. I bum-rushed him, sending him sprawling with me atop. He had surprisingly good moves, but I out-muscled him to submission. "Speak English?" I asked.

"English yes. Falang?"

"Falang yes. American."

"I am Thai," he said. "Friend. No fight, ok? No fight."

"No fight ok." I let him go and we got up and dusted ourselves off. "What are you doing here?" I asked.

"Thai friends have this shop. They live upstairs with wives and daughters. Iraq soldiers rape Thai ladies, kill their men. Kuwaitis give us no help. So we protect our own." He bent over and retrieved something from the ground.

"What do you have there?"

"Garrote. For killing Iraq soldiers. Quiet and quick." He showed me a long, fine wire with wood handles at each end. Loop it around someone's throat, pull hard and that's that for him—as he'd tried to do with me.

"Piano wire?"

"Guitar string. Falang friend give me, bPaulo Kennedy from Al-Muthanna Block. You know he?"

"No, never had the pleasure. I've only been in Kuwait a few days, don't know any other falangs. What are those on the ends?"

"Broomstick for handles."

"That's a pretty neat rig. Any luck so far?"

"I've done eight, trying for ten. Iraqis are easy. Soldiers are idiots, Republican Guards only average."

"Where'd you learn this stuff?" I asked.

"Thai Rangers, served on Chinese border."

"American Ranger myself, LRRP in Nam."

"Paint face guys?"

"Same same."

"Some U.S. Rangers come to Thailand, give us training. Good outfit. Tough men."

Haroun showed up at the curb out front. Nothing more to do here. "My ride's arrived. Good hunting."

"You too, Falang."

I reported the incident to Salah. "That isn't right, foreigners killing Arabs on our soil," he said.

"He's doing God's work," I said.

"There is no God but Allah," he huffed. "Do the Thais and Filipinos and Indians think they have a monopoly on revenge? The Iraqis rape Kuwaiti girls, too, some not even ten years old, and women of all ages, even white-haired grandmothers. They make their husbands and fathers and sons watch, then they slaughter them all afterwards and leave them there in their own blood. And I'll tell you something else. You don't want to fall into their hands. I've heard what happens when they catch our men—electroshock. Cut out tongues. Gouge out eyes. Cut off manhood. I hope every Iraqi is welcomed by Shaytan through the gates of Hell to burn in the eternal fire. They disgrace Islam."

* * *

My foray with the Thai Ranger highlighted the evening's action. We dodged a couple Iraqi army vehicles by slipping into alleyways. If they spotted us, they weren't hot to pursue the matter. We returned to the villa around midnight.

"How about some refreshments?" Salah suggested. No dissents. Hydration was an unrelenting issue in that climate. He had a servant bring in tea, coffee, and an array of cold soft drinks and fruit juices, plus an assortment of nibblies.

"After action in Nam we'd always knock back a few beers," I remarked. "Same the whole world over, I guess."

"Beers, you say? Would you prefer a beer?"

"I wouldn't mind at all, but isn't this a Muslim country?"

He summoned a servant and gave him an instruction. "One of my uncles was at one time assigned a diplomatic task in Brussels, Belgium. Everyone extolled the wonders of Belgium beer. He finally took a taste out of curiosity, and it pleased him. My uncle was a devout man and he knew very well the Quran's strictures on alcohol, so he looked into the nature of these beers. He found the ingredients to be grains, hops, some flavorings and water. There was no alcohol listed in the ingredients. So he reasoned, 'If alcohol somehow appears in these beers it must be Allah's will, and who am I to question Allah's will?' When he returned to Kuwait he contrived to bring a supply with him."

Presently a servant appeared with a cold bottle of some variety of Trappist beer and a crystal goblet. It lived up to its reputation.

SUNDAY, AUGUST 26, 1990

OUR LITTLE RESISTANCE CELL SOLDIERED ALONG. IT WAS definitely a man's world. Other women lived in the compound, but we guests rarely saw them and then only foreign servants. Al Sabah women stayed out of our sight. In those early days of the Iraqi occupation the resistance still coalesced, shifted and developed, feeling its way, testing its capabilities and discovering its weaknesses. The latter outweighed the former, as we were up against an overwhelming, well-armed and ruthless enemy.

Our group mostly patrolled our district, delivered materiel, ferried people around, relayed messages, and stood guard duty—low-level logistical support, basically. The Iraqis plastered posters and billboards featuring Saddam Hussein all over Kuwait City, and we tore them down or defaced them. We had a few shootouts when we were called to support other units in emergencies, but overall we didn't rack up many bodies. We rarely encountered Iraqi incursions into our territory on our regular patrols. Just as well we didn't get into serious firefights, as I was twenty years past my Nam combat tour and about an order of magnitude out of shape for the rigors of close fighting. There are sound reasons why we send 19-year-old men to fight our wars.

One night after a regular patrol set out Kadar Al Sayer and I decided to try our luck with some freelancing by way of a training exercise for him. We crept through side streets and alleyways to a police station in a neighboring residential block where we found a couple Iraqi soldiers listlessly sitting on chairs out front, standing guard. I maneuvered us into a shadowy gap between buildings across the street. It afforded good cover and an escape route, and brought us close enough for clear shots. We took them out with simultaneous short bursts and scurried away cleanly. Salah had an Arab's lax sense of discipline. He didn't mind at all that we'd gone it alone and rejoiced to hear of our success. His patrol had again come up empty.

On August 16, the U.S. announced a blockade of Iraq, closing off imports—legal ones, anyhow. There's always a black market and backdoor deals, but at least the blockade ran the costs of incoming goods and materiel up. That plus the force buildup across the Saudi border provoked Saddam to place American hostages (about 2,000 Americans were in Baghdad) at key military and infrastructure sites, making them human targets for any missiles or bombs we might send in. TV news featured a particularly obnoxious clip of Saddam Hussein, togged out in a western business suit and tie, acting the beaming, walrus-mustached uncle with five-year-old Stuart Lockwood. He asked Stuart if he was getting enough corn-flakes and milk, and Stuart grimly nodded yes. Saddam ruffled Stuart's hair affectionately and a military aide patted his neck. Stuart with arms crossed inched away from them, and Saddam recognized it as bad optics and moved on to other topics. By August 23 Saddam realized his hostage trick had aroused not fear or respect around the world but only disgust, so called it off.

On August 24 Iraqi troops surrounded the 27 Embassies still open in Kuwait, the U.S. Embassy among them. Apparently the idea was to intimidate them to close up shop without a confrontation that could lead to war. The Iraqis cut off their electricity and water, but most of the Embassies stood their ground. Meanwhile the Iraqi troops continued their determined destruction of

Kuwait. And allied forces continued their buildup across the border.

We were all sitting around whiling away the time after dinner one evening, biding time until patrolling duties commenced. A couple of the others had developed a liking for Belgian beer and we were feeling mellow. Someone asked Nasr Abu Khattab why he left Palestine and settled in Kuwait.

"My friends, there is a long and strange story behind that," Nasr said.

"We've time to listen," said Salah, our host. "Tell us your story, please."

Nasr was a handsome devil in his mid-thirties. "Very well," said he. "Now, as you are aware, much of the world holds the impression from years of news accounts that the people of Palestine are poor refugees. That is not the case at all. There are many wealthy Palestinians. My father is such a man, the richest man in his village. I am his eldest son. I was the apple of his eye and destined to inherit great wealth when I reached a certain age. When I was twenty years old I fell deeply in love with the most beautiful girl for many miles around, and she with me, and so it came to pass that plans were laid for our marriage.

"In celebration of the upcoming wedding my father held a lavish party, to which all the leading people in the village were invited. The party had just finished a sumptuous feast and had settled down to hear speeches and tributes when, to my great shame and embarrassment, sitting at the head table in front of all the guests I let loose a thunderous fart.

"The room's cheerful chatter came to an instant halt, then after a second resumed again as if nothing had happened. I sat there with a blank expression on my face for a couple minutes, then excused myself to my bride-to-be, rose from my seat and left the room with great dignity. I went out and got into my car, drove it to my house, packed some things and drove out of town. I drove through Jordan and thought, 'No, it's too near to home.' So I continued on to Iraq. I didn't like the look of the place, too many poor people and under the thumb of Saddam Hussein. So I continued on to Kuwait, a prosperous place where I sensed I could make my fortune. I found a position with one of the Al Sayer family's trading concerns. The work suited me and on the strength of my talents I rose steadily in the firm..."

"It's true," put in Kadar Al Sayer. "He's become our trusted director of trading now."

"But you had such a promising future in your village," said Mamoon Al Bahar. "Why didn't you return there? It is natural that a man should remain true to his family and tribe."

"Yes I wholeheartedly agree," said Nasr. "I share those feelings too, and after ten years in Kuwait, having secured my fortune, I made inquiries. I learned that my bride-to-be had never married and still pined for me. So I drove back there to assess the possibilities of returning. When I arrived in my village I stopped in a café for a cool drink to refresh myself. Near my table sat a man and his young son, and I overheard their conversation. The boy asked his father, 'When was I born?'

"The father replied, 'My son, you were born in the very same month that Nasr Asad Khattab farted at his wedding feast, just two days later.'

"I had become a date in my tribe's lore, and for that reason I could never again live in that village. So I got back in my car and returned to Kuwait where, I must tell you, life has been bountiful for me ever since, Inshallah."

"Nasr, my friend, perhaps you can answer a question that has been long troubling me," put in Haroun Al Sabah. "We Kuwaitis have all along been steadfast supporters of the Palestinian cause against the accursed Israelis. We have taken in their refugees and given them employment. We have contributed billions of dinars to help them. We without fail vote in their favor at the United Nations. Yet Arafat, their leader, and many of his followers have rejoiced in Saddam's victory. Can you explain this contradiction?"

Nasr thought for a moment. "Perhaps there is no contradiction. Recall that we all are descendants of desert tribes. Has there ever been a desert tribe that did not feel whatever good fortune befell them was theirs by right as a gift from Allah? So we feel gratitude toward Allah, not toward the instruments of his will. And has there ever been a desert tribe that felt the neighboring tribe did not have more camels than they needed? Iraq's incursion into Kuwait is but a modern raid, not for camels but for oil fields."

"Ah, it is so, it is so," sighed Salah Al Sabah. "This story of yours reminds me of a tale of another man who traveled in pursuit of wealth and his good fortune. It seems that in a time several generations ago, the Emir went on a hunting trip in the desert..."

"Do you mean Emir Sheik Jaber Al Ahmad Al Sabah, our ruler in exile...?" asked Kadar Al Sayer.

"No, this happened many years ago in simpler times, when the Emir still lived in a mud-brick palace. On this hunting trip he killed a gazelle and left his retinue to clean it. While doing so a man came out of the desert on an ass. Not recognizing the Emir, he stopped to observe him at his task. After a time the Emir asked him, 'Where are you going?'

'To see the Emir,' the man replied. 'I have an early crop of the finest cucumbers, and I mean to sell them to the Emir, who is known for his munificence.'

'And what do you expect to get of him?' the Emir asked.

'One thousand dinars.'

'And if the Emir says that is too much...?'

'Then I will say five hundred dinars.'

'Supposing he says five hundred is too much?'

'Then three hundred.'

'And if still he says that is too much?'

'Then two hundred.'

"And so it went until finally the man said, 'If I quote him thirty dinars and he will not accept that, then I will get back on my ass and return to my people, disappointed and empty handed.'

The Emir laughed and bade the man farewell. He returned home to his palace and told his chamberlain that if a man with cucumbers came to the door, to admit him. Presently the man arrived, was brought in, and did not recognize the Emir as the man he had met in the desert. He explained his mission, and the Emir asked, 'How much do you want for your cucumbers?'

'One thousand dinars,' said the man.

'Preposterous. That is far too much.'

'Then five hundred.'

'For those cucumbers? Impossible.'

'Three hundred, then.'

'Do you take me for a fool?'

"And so it went until the man reached thirty dinars. When the Emir again declined, the man exclaimed, 'By Allah, I will not go lower than thirty. The man I met in the desert assuredly brought me bad luck. I will return to my people with my cucumbers. My ass is tied up at the door and ready to depart.'

"Then the Emir laughed until he fell on his back. He instructed his chamberlain to take the cucumbers and give the man a thousand dinars, plus five hundred, plus three hundred—in all, two thousand one hundred and eighty dinars—and to leave the ass where it was. Thus we learn not only of the generosity of that Emir, but also of his fine sense of humor."

"Speaking of generosity," said Siyaf Al Segar, "My family has passed a tale through the generations about a certain ancestor, Hatim, who died and was buried on a certain mountaintop at whose foot ran a stream of pure water. One time the King of Himyar came into that valley, and when he came to that stream and stopped to water his camels he heard wailing and keening. He was told it came from the tomb of Hatim, which had two stone girls with disheveled hair adorning it. So he jestingly said, "O Hatim, we are thy guests this night and we are lank with hunger.'

"Sleep overcame him, but he awoke in affright, crying out, 'Help, O Arabs, look to my beast!' His she-camel was struggling and struck down, so they stabbed her throat, then roasted her flesh and ate. They asked him what had happened, and he replied that Hatim had come to him in a dream and cried, 'Thou comest to us and we have nothing by us, so he smote my camel with a sword.' And when I awoke she was already dead. The King mounted the beast of one of his companions, and the man rode behind him. Midday they saw a man coming toward them mounted on a camel, leading another camel. The King asked him who he was, and the man replied, 'I am Adi, son of Hatim. Where is the King of Himyar?'

'I am he,' said the King.

'My father, Hatim, last night came to me in a dream and said that the King of Himyar sought the guest-rite of me and I had naught to give him, so I slaughtered his she-camel that he might eat. So take him a she-camel to ride, for in my grave I have nothing.'

"Thus we may marvel at the generosity of Hatim, both alive and dead, and at the marvelous ways of Allah," Siyaf concluded.

"Speaking of dreams," said Mamoon Al Bahar, "my family tells a story, they swear it is true, of a man my grandfather knew who became rich again through a dream."

"I have many dreams but am not rich yet," observed Kadar Al Sayer.

"Ha, says he who drives a BMW 7 Series," scoffed Nasr Abu Khattab. "Your dreams are about fucking Sharon Stone, most likely."

"It is my father's BMW, not mine," protested Kadar.

"Nevertheless, relate your story, Mamoon" said Nasr.

"Certainly. It seems many years ago this wealthy man, in truth made of money, launched some unfortunate business ventures and lost all his substance. He became so destitute that he had to earn his living by hiring out for hard labor. One night, dejected and heavy hearted, he lay down to sleep, and in a dream a Speaker came to him and said, 'Thy fortune is in Cairo. Go there and seek it.'

"The man journeyed to Cairo. But when he arrived, night overtook him and he lay down to sleep in a mosque. By decree of Allah the Almighty some bandits entered the mosque and made their way from there to an adjoining house. The owner of the house was wakened by the noise of the thieves and cried out, and the Chief of Police and his officers quickly came. They found no one there but the man asleep in the mosque, so they beat him with palm fronds until nigh to death and cast him into jail. After three days the Chief asked him what he was doing in Cairo.

'In a dream I was told my fortune lay here,' said the man, 'so I came here to seek it.'

"The Chief of Police laughed at him. 'I've never met such a fool as you, to travel all this way because of something in a dream. I myself have several times been told in a dream of a house in your city, in such a district and of such a fashion, in whose garden sits a fountain, under which a great fortune is buried. But never would I be so stupid as to consider traveling to your city because of those dreams.' He gave the man some money and told him to go home, forget the dreams and get back to work.

"The man returned home. Realizing that the home described in the Chief's dreams was his own, he set to digging beneath his fountain and soon uncovered a great treasure, by which his lost wealth was restored in full. So we see that Allah may speak to us in dreams, and that only the foolish do not heed them."

"How about you, Mr. Jake?" asked Haroun. "Americans must have many stories to tell that would astound and amaze us."

You can't even begin to imagine what I could tell you about Hollywood, I thought. I combed my memories... the tale of my pig-smuggling Serbian great-grandfather wouldn't be appropriate... winding up in the Rangers because of streaking Dana Wehrli's engagement shower would make no more sense to them than it did to me in retrospect... "Here is a story that may interest you," I began. "At one time when I fought in Vietnam my unit was stationed at an outpost in the jungles of a certain province. We were a reconnaissance patrol, assigned to search out Viet Cong activity in the area. The soldiers we joined told us this story. Some time before we came, two field operatives from our Central Intelligence Agency, the CIA, arrived at this camp, Kevin and Kurt. They explained that they had come to get some hands-on experience in the field so they would have a better idea how to interpret the reports we sent in.

We rangers never liked to have CIA operatives around, as they usually just caused trouble and inconvenience. But these guys seemed sincerely interested to learn what jungle warfare was all about, and they were so green that the Rangers felt sorry for them and decided to help them. They'd already determined that there were no VC's close by so they gave them M-16s and bush hats, warned them about avoiding the claymore mines around the perimeter and pointed them down a trail known to be safe.

Two hours went by and then came a call on the radio. It was Kurt screaming: "May Day! May Day! Help! Help! SOS! SOS!!" They answered the call, and Kurt, panic-stricken, shrieked, "We've got a big problem here! We came to a bend in the trail, and we thought we heard something up ahead, so we dived into the brush for cover. Kevin tripped and fell down and his rifle went off. Shot himself in the chest. He's just lying there. I think he's dead."

The radio operator said, "Calm down, Kurt, calm down. Here's your situation. You are in no danger. There are no Charlies in your area. Depending on your location we can reach you on foot with help in less than an hour, or maybe even call in a medevac chopper if you've got an LZ nearby. What action we take depends on the exact status of Kevin. So the first thing to do is, you go and make sure he's dead."

There was a silence over the radio, and then they heard "Bang Bang." And then Kurt came back on and said, "Okay, done it. Now what?"

Through the laughter, Haroun asked, "Are your CIA operatives really that foolish?"

"It's a story that makes the rounds among the Rangers. Probably it is not strictly true…but sometimes you do have to wonder."

KISMET

TUESDAY, SEPTEMBER 25, TO SATURDAY, SEPTEMBER 29, 1990

THE IRAQIS HAD ROLLED IN WELL OVER A MONTH AGO, AND since then the situation had only fallen even further apart. Kuwaiti resistance fighters, however determined and steadfast some of them may have been, amounted to an annoyance to the invaders, no real threat or obstruction. And when it came to actual combat the Iraqis had by far the upper hand.

Urban warfare is a painstaking, dangerous, fraught and frustrating kind of fighting. Your team infiltrates a building. Then you advance floor by floor and room by room, some guys covering from around the corner, other guys busting a hole in the door or the wall and tossing in flashbang grenades. Then you storm in with weapons at the ready, having no idea whether you'll be facing stunned enemies, a terrified family or an empty room. Or booby traps. Then repeat. And repeat.

That's textbook urban warfare the way the U.S. Army does it. The Iraqis figured out a shortcut to all that. If a building came into question they just rolled a tank up and fired a few cannon rounds into it, demolishing said building and the people in it. The result was that Kuwait City became progressively wrecked as the weeks went on. More women, and not just halal ones, were raped. More shops and dwellings were looted. All photos and other images of the Al Sabah ruling family were torn down and destroyed. The Iraqis toppled monuments and leveled civic buildings. Parks became trash pits, garbage dumps and makeshift cemeteries. Having forced the abdication of nearly half the Kuwaitis, Saddam now sent thousands of Iraqi families down to occupy vacated villas.

On September 23 Saddam had issued a threat to attack Israel, Saudi Arabia's oil fields, and other Gulf States, if the U.N. economic embargo continued to strangle Iraq. Clearly he felt pressured and we feared that might lead to further hardships for Kuwait. Taking stock of my personal situation, it seemed a good time to butt out. My role in the Kuwaiti guerilla force was winding down. Our cell found fewer missions to pursue, and our patrols of the neighborhood seemed to be yielding little benefit besides giving us a sense of fighting back. Iraqi soldiers rarely ventured into our territory. In the early days I'd done some combat training of our little band, but there isn't much desert Arabs don't already instinctively know about ambushes and hit-and-run tactics, so my teaching efforts reached diminishing returns.

I took up the question of getting out of Kuwait with Salah, and he saw my point. "Mr. Jake, we appreciate what you have done for us, but this is our fight, not yours. If you think it best to return to your own people I can understand that, and I'll see what can be arranged. There is a problem, though. Foreigners aren't being allowed to leave, and in any case you're a marked man. I gather the Iraqis actively seek you. To leave Kuwait you would have to make your way across the desert to the American lines in Saudi Arabia. In peaceful times that is not a difficult journey, but with the Iraqis patrolling the border and the road south it has become dangerous and perhaps arduous, as you will have to cross barren, unmarked desert. Without proper equipment and guidance you would be doomed. Give me a little time to consider this. I'll let you know."

The next day he came to me and said, "Mr. Jake, Mamoon Al Bahar has received word that his family in exile desperately needs his help. He has a large Jeep vehicle suitable for a cross-country desert traverse and he is a skilled driver. He thinks the two of you could set out in the early morning the day after Holy Day, Saturday, four days from now. To evade Iraqi border patrols you would take a western route across the desert beyond Al Wafrah until you cross the border, then drive southeast to intercept Highway 662. It isn't a very long distance but it would be slow going. Once on the road you should easily reach Khafji on the Arabian coast before nightfall. It is a hazardous trip, but many parties have made it successfully."

"I'm game," I said. "Let me know what I can do to help between now and then."

Mostly the next few days consisted of routine gear maintenance, guard duty and prep for the trek. On paper it didn't look too bad, maybe 200 miles maximum. If all went well and we could average 20 miles per hour, we'd meet Salah's estimate with ease. The night before setting out we loaded the Jeep with gas and water. My own gear didn't take much space. Mamoon was carting out family stuff.

We left Salah's villa at seven a.m. on the nose, at the lift of curfew. Why risk a stop by Iraqi patrols? We headed south on Highway 306 past Sabah Al Ahmad Air Base (now used by Iraqi planes), talking our way through one check point with a good story and a little baksheesh and skirting another using back lanes. Where 306 petered out we set off cross-country. The terrain was flat and fairly firm and the Jeep handled it well. We passed a number of abandoned cars including some Mercs and a Cadillac, plus vans and light trucks here and there, and a lot of scattered belongings. Everything had been well picked over, leaving only junk and scraps cluttering the sandy waste. "Not everybody makes it," Mamoon said. "Get stuck in the sand out here by yourself and you've had it. These fancy air-conditioned cars become your coffin. I heard about one American who tried to escape to Saudi Arabia in his BMW 6-series before they shut off the border. Along the way he veered off the road and dug his wheels into the sand, and the people he convoyed with kept right on going, abandoning him. Some Bedouins stopped to help and only dug him in deeper. He managed to hitch a ride back to Kuwait City. The Bedouins returned later, unstuck the car and made off with it. Sixty thousand bucks worth of car!"

By the time we cleared the Saudi border the sun was high enough to bring the air up above 100F. We traveled ten miles further south, then turned easterly to catch highway 662. I spotted a black dot on the horizon and pointed it out to Mamoon. "Oh shit," he said. "Something's coming, and it's not going to be good news. We're too far from the American lines yet." The dot danced and wiggled in the heat waves rising from the ground. Fascinated, I watched it grow and shrink and shimmer, floating above the flat, barren desert. Then it started forming into a shape, though I couldn't make out what. Suddenly a hail of tracer bullets dug up the sand fifty yards ahead of us. Mamoon slowed down. The black, shifting blob rose in the air above ground interference and became an attack helicopter, closing in on us.

There was no use trying to evade it so Mamoon stopped the car. The chopper, a Russian model, circled around stirring up gritty clouds of dust. We had submachine guns in the car, but the chopper set down with us in his sights, the rotor turning at hover speed. If we fired on them as they got out, those machine guns would turn us to grease. If we took off in the car, they'd just rise, follow us and turn us to grease. Any evasive action we might try, we'd wind up as grease.

Two Iraqi Republican Guards climbed down and, AK-47s leveled at us, advanced. Ten yards away they stopped and motioned us out of the car. We came out slowly, hands in the air. One of them walked forward to us. "Your papers, please," he said.

"Sir, we are now in Saudi Arabia," said Mamoon. "We do not have to obey your orders."

"Considering that we have you at our mercy I think you would be wise to comply. Your papers, please."

Nothing for it but to hand over our papers. They examined them, and one turned to me. "You are Mr. Jake Fonko, then? This photo does not show the beard, but the other man is definitely not Mr. Fonko."

"Yes, I'm Fonko," I said.

"'You will come with us, please." The other Guard stepped forward and patted me down for weapons. Finding me clean, the one in charge said, "You have some belongings in the car? Get them." I went over and dug my gear out of the Jeep, and they motioned me toward the chopper. "Mr. Al Bahar, you are free to go. We apologize for the inconvenience. If you continue in your present direction you will reach the American lines in two hours." The Iraqi returned his papers.

They loaded me into the rear compartment of the chopper, where a couple Iraqi army officers sat waiting. The pilot hit the throttle and we lifted off. I looked down. Mamoon had gotten into the Jeep and started in the direction we'd been going. The pilot rotated the chopper around, drew a bead and, laughing, hosed down Mamoon with his cannon. Then he raised us aloft and took a northwesterly course at a fast clip, leaving behind a heap of wreckage sending flames and black smoke into the clear desert air —my friend Mamoon's coffin .

"What's going on here?" I asked. "You were looking for me specifically. How did you locate me out here in the desert?"

"From the tracking device in your vehicle," one of the officers said. "We've been seeking you since we found your file in the Kuwaiti Intelligence Department, but you evaded us at the Hilton Hotel. Our agent reported that you joined Salah Al Sabah's group, and we've had you under surveillance ever since. Our orders were to take you alive and in good condition, and this was our first opportunity to do so with certainty. We didn't, after all, want to risk your life by storming the villa, or by attacking your patrols on their fool's errands. We bided our time until an opportunity presented itself. So here you are. And now we can safely move in and wipe out the Salah group."

The cartoon lightbulb flashed above my head. That fucking

Palestinian! No wonder Iraqis were so scarce when he knew we were going on patrol.

"What now?" I asked.

"Next stop is Baghdad. Make yourself comfortable."

* * *

We flew fast over a lot of empty desert. The pilot put down at an Iraqi air base for a fuel top-up. While the ground crew took care of it my captors gave me coffee and sweet rolls and let me hit the john. We continued over more desert, then farm fields and orchards, villages, small towns and a big river. I asked questions of the officers overseeing me, but they wouldn't tell me anything.

Presently we reached the outskirts of a large city. Our low altitude flight didn't afford a panoramic view of it, but I could estimate from what I saw on the horizon that it was major—must be Baghdad. We soon touched down at a sprawling airfield, an Iraqi Air Force base by all appearances. As the rotors wound down an armed guard came out to receive me. We de-coptered and they escorted me directly to their equivalent of a brig. "You will stay here for the time being, until arrangements are made," one of the officers informed me. The guard led me to a barred cell. As jails go, it wasn't the worst I'd been in. I had the cell to myself. The pad on the bunk didn't show blood or any other kinds of stains. The toilet bucket had been hosed clean. You accepted cockroaches as part of the service. If there were rats, they had the decency to keep out of sight. At dusk a military guard brought me a bowl of stew—Lamb? Goat?—some bread and some coffee. Tastier than most prison chow I'd eaten. Luxe accommodations.

And then night fell. I recalled Salah's warning about falling into their hands. How soon would the electroshocking, eye-gouging and de-manhooding get under way? Nothing for me to do there but wait and wonder.

TUESDAY, OCTOBER 2, 1990

As jails go the present hospitality wasn't bad. They treated me respectfully and served me decent food. After searching my luggage and stealing the baubles I'd bought for Dana at the gold souk they brought the suitcases to my cell, allowing me changes of underwear and sox.

It was boring, of course—jail always is. I remembered a character in the book, *Catch 22*, Lieutenant Dunbar. His theory of life extension held that you should seek boredom because it made the passage of time seem slower. He'd have cherished a sentence in my Iraqi brig. But at least I wasn't under duress or immediate threat. The hospitable treatment puzzled me after the stories I'd heard about Iraqis prisoner policies, but count my blessings.

The third morning after I arrived the jailers brought a bucket of water, a towel and a little bar of soap, and told me to get cleaned up. I'd gotten pretty rank in that steaming, open-air cell, and did so gladly. The guard indicated I should wear one of my business suits, which I took to mean I'd be meeting important parties in a safe setting. Who ever heard of putting a $1700 suit on someone whose tongue you intended to cut out? Just imagine the cleaning bill!

A short while later armed guards unlocked my cell door, gathered up my gear and marched me out to a personnel carrier. We all climbed in and took off. After a forty minute drive along a litter-strewn road through scrubby desert, marginal farm fields, squalid villages, military posts and poor peasants on every hand, we entered a decent-looking suburban area and then arrived at a lavish palace set back in landscaped grounds. A stately man in a white robe and headdress came out to meet my guards and me as we emerged from the car into the hot sun.

"Mr. Jake Fonko?" he said. I nodded yes. "Please come with me." To my guards he said, "Wait here. Food and drink will be brought to you." To me he said, "Saddam regrets the delay, but he had many matters to attend to before he could make time for a proper meeting. I hope you haven't eaten yet, as his Excellency likes to see guests enjoy his hospitality." He led me into an elegant salon. A sprawling Persian carpet (expensive) lay over a deeply polished, parquetted wood floor. Florid tapestries decorated the walls. Couches, easy chairs, coffee tables and intricately carved sideboards sat around the periphery, and a glittering chandelier topped it all off. He guided me to a door over on the side, pulled it open and ushered me into a spacious, high-ceilinged office room with desk, bookcases, worktables and electronics in one area and meeting space in another.

Saddam Hussein, clad today in a be-medaled military uniform, sat on an expansive leather couch before a low table laden with platters and trays of food. A servant poured me out a cup of coffee and indicated I take a seat on a cushioned armchair opposite Saddam.

"Greetings, Mr. Fonko," said Saddam. He started off surprisingly soft-spoken that morning. History's dictators have tended toward the pipsqueak side—Napoleon, Stalin, Arafat and Tito, were under 5' 6"—but Saddam looked over six feet tall and bulky. "I am sorry I couldn't see you sooner but urgent matters interfered, as you might imagine with all that is going on these days. I thought it best to detain you behind bars in the interim for your own protection. I hope you weren't mistreated?"

"As far as being in a jail cell for three days goes, I can't complain," I replied. He seemed to be in a "fellow soldier" mood. As long as we kept it on that level maybe this wouldn't be as bad as I'd feared.

"When my intelligence people first informed me you were in Kuwait I worried about what trouble you might cause us. We put you under surveillance as soon as I heard, but it was only when you tried to cross the desert that we could safely take you into custody."

How the hell does a foreigner address a Third World dictator? Your Excellency? Your Highness? Your Eminence? Screw it: I wasn't feeling very honorific just then. "I don't understand this at all, " I said. "What interest do you have in me? I came to Kuwait on a consulting assignment, then got caught up in the events of your invasion. I was all set to leave Kuwait on August 2 and would happily have done so had your troops not shut the airport down."

"Yes, I accept that your covert status would dictate evasions and denials, and I don't blame you for that. Iraq employs spies too, so I know the routines. But you were working for Fawaz Al Sabah of Kuwaiti Intelligence. What more proof do I need? I've been aware of Jake Fonko for some time now. You first came to my attention during my war with Iran. My army had won a particularly difficult battle by stampeding a troop of boys over a minefield in front of the Iranian gun emplacements, and following it up with a massed bayonet charge. Afterwards, one of my spies reported that the Ayatollah, upon hearing the news, screamed, 'That devil Fonko must be behind this!' Of course we won the battle by dint of my superior military leadership, but the Ayatollah's remark intrigued me, and I set some intelligence specialists to look into it. They probed and asked around and came up with amazing stories of your secret exploits and espionage."

"Whatever you've heard about me in intelligence circles is

greatly exaggerated. I've done nothing to merit a personal interview like this."

"You are too modest, Mr. Fonko. I'm satisfied that the reports I've seen are accurate. The action on Grenada. Toppling Ferdinand Marcos. Rescuing the Shah. The question is, now that I have you here, what is to be done with you? I think we will have to find out what your role in this war is and what you know of American strategy behind their buildup across the border. Working for the Al Sabah interests, obviously you were brought to Kuwait to prevent the rebel government we support from gaining control of the country. I think also you will be a good bargaining chip. What is your Central Intelligence Agency willing to give me, to get their superspy back, I wonder? I foresee interesting negotiations ahead."

"They won't give you much, considering that I don't work for them."

"Of course not, of course not," he said with a knowing smile. "Some of our allies are interested in you too, and we may reap some benefits from that. Say, are you hungry? I told the prison to treat you well but even their best is far from acceptable. Please take a plate and see if you can find something fit to eat on the buffet."

I was hungry, he had that right at least. The feast laid out before us was sumptuous, top of the line Middle Eastern eats—couscous, savory stews, warm bread, skewered kabobs with spicy marinades, preserved and fresh fruits, sweet cakes and delicate pastries. I'd had few better meals anywhere. He wolfed a heaping assortment of delicacies and refilled his plate before I'd finished my first helping. "I can see you enjoy our humble fare?" he asked. My mouth full, I nodded enthusiastic agreement. "What do you think of our invasion?" he asked, chomping away.

"I wasn't an on-the-ground observer but from what I saw and heard from a mile away on the other side of town, it was very well executed."

"It should have been. We planned and prepared for it carefully."

"What I don't understand," I said, "is why Iraq invaded Kuwait in the first place."

"You haven't spent much time in Arab nations, or you would understand."

"I spent a number of months in Iran at the end of the Shah's reign."

"Iranians are not Arabs; they are Persians. Though I suppose in some ways not very different from us. The Shah," he mused. "We had our differences but he wasn't a bad man, not at all like the deranged fanatics that overthrew him. You see, we Arabs—Iraqis, Kuwaitis, Egyptians, Palestinians, the Gulf States, northern Africans—we are brothers. And like brothers in a family we love one another with all our hearts but nevertheless have fights over this and that from time to time.

"To Iraq Kuwait is like a younger brother to whom the parents give everything. Iraq—Mesopotamia in olden times—is the site of the first civilization on Earth, the Sumerians, inventors of cuneiform writing. Some say even the garden of Adam and Eve was located here, in the region of Basrah. Whereas only a few generations ago the Kuwaitis were nothing but nomadic desert tribes, and roaming in not much of a desert either. When the Turks were defeated in the Great War the Europeans divided up the Ottoman Empire to suit their own purposes. They set Kuwait apart for its strategic position, denying Iraq a decent Gulf port, allotting to us instead just one river outlet and some swamps. For all our size, we have less than twenty miles of shoreline. How can we, as an oil exporting nation, prosper if we have no port?

"Kuwaitis number fewer than one million, whereas Iraqis are twenty times that many. Many Iraqis are poor, as you may have noticed on your ride over here. After the westerners discovered oil the Kuwaitis became rich beyond imagining. Now they bring foreigners in several times their own number and pay them to do their work, while they themselves bask in lives of ease and luxury. A tiny country and a big country side-by-side, and they have equally large oil reserves. It is all part of Allah's plan, of course, but it is hard for us humans to overlook the unfairness. And perhaps it is Allah's will that the unfairness should be ended. Do they have enough, those Kuwaitis? No, even despite their blessings they ignore OPEC quotas on oil production, selling more than their allotted share and thereby bringing the price down for the rest of us. And if that is not enough, while we were fighting Iran the Kuwaitis moved the border three miles north so they could steal oil from our Rumaila oil field. They might as well steal gold from our treasury."

"I was given to believe that Kuwait has been generous in their support of their Arab brothers," I put in.

"Oh, you mean the Palestinians? Yes, Kuwait pledges its support of their cause and donates money to help the refugees. They bring Palestinians into Kuwait to work and make money to send home, where they find out how well the Kuwaitis live and how cheaply they pay. This creates envy and resentments. It is no accident that Palestinians take our side, not the Kuwaiti's. You are going to also point out that they supported us in the war against Iran? Save your breath. We sacrificed a million of our sons, and how many Kuwaiti sons died in that war? As for money, it's true that Kuwait supplied money to us, billions of dinars—but it was *loans*. Iraq lies in financial ruin from ten years of war with the Iranian devils, which we fought on behalf of our Arab brothers to keep the Iranians' vile notions of Islamic Fundamentalism from spreading to our own lands, and now Kuwait wants us to repay it, while they invest their billions of stolen oil wealth in infidel businesses? Some generosity!

"We are doing our little brothers, the Kuwaitis, a great service. We are bringing them under the protection of a stronger nation. As part of Iraq their ports will expand, enjoy greater trade and make more money. Poor, jobless Arab brothers will go to do the work that foreigners from Asia now do, whom we will return to their own lands where they belong. Kuwait's northern oil fields will become part of Basrah, and Kuwait City itself will be a separate province of Iraq. It is tragic that the Kuwaitis do not see the blessing of our coming in its true light. Instead they put up a resistance such that we had to cause pain and suffering to overcome it. It is necessary for us to obliterate all vestiges of the corruption, greed and profligacy of the former ruling family, the Al Sabah. Atop the rubble we will build a new and better place for our little brothers. In time they will come to appreciate the gift we give them."

It seemed the wrong time to mention wholesale destruction, rape, murder and looting. "As I said, I didn't see much of the actual fighting. The U.S. Embassy issued a warning for Americans to stay indoors and I followed their instructions, pending finding some way to return to America."

"Of course, of course. The Arab robe we found in your luggage, the black garments and the beard you have grown, had nothing whatsoever to do with clandestine activities, I am certain. And your work with the Kuwaiti resistance was of no account at all. I have my people in Kuwait getting to the bottom of all that. One thing that puzzles me, though. Why are the Americans massing troops along the southern border? We aren't going to invade Saudi Arabia. "

"I think the U.S. objects to your invasion of a country to seize control of such a large oil reserve. We have an interest in keeping petroleum flowing freely from this region."

"That is absurd! Do they think we would not sell them as much oil as Kuwait did? We have no quarrel with the U.S., and I thought when your ambassador gave us the go-ahead they had no quarrel with us. And now the Germans and Japanese, and even some of our Arab brothers have taken their side! "

"Our ambassador gave you the go-ahead? I hadn't heard about that."

"Certainly," Saddam said. "It was public and is well-known. In a meeting, face-to-face, Ambassador Glaspie assured me that the U.S. wouldn't take sides in our border disputes. And now they're massing troops in Saudi Arabia because of our border dispute. Not very trustworthy on her part, I'd say, but what can one expect from a woman in a position of power? And your president Bush has frozen all the money Iraq had deposited in American banks. What right has he to do that with our sovereign money?"

"I haven't read Ambassador Glaspie's statement. I imagine President Bush thinks that the recent invasion amounts to more than just a border dispute."

"If there's a misunderstanding I'm sure we can straighten it out diplomatically. Fears of an invasion of Saudi Arabia are misplaced, I can assure you from the bottom of my heart. Our only intention is to restore Kuwait into its rightful place in the Arab scheme of things. Well, Mr. Fonko, I have enjoyed our chat, and I look forward to future meetings. Though I must say that I am a little disappointed. From what I had heard of you, I was expecting to meet a more formidable adversary. But they say that still waters run deep, so we shall see, we shall see. Now if you will excuse me, I must see to a number of weighty and urgent matters, as you may understand..." There was a harsh knock on the door. "Come in," he said.

Did I mention that Saddam was large and imposing? The man who strode in was taller by half a head and just as bulky. He resembled Saddam facially but looked in much better shape.

"Mr. Fonko, this is my son, Uday," Saddam said. I couldn't help but think that his name sounded like pig-latin for something your neighbor's dog would leave on your lawn. From the look of him he'd have a promising future as a bouncer in a biker bar. The dudes would behave themselves, for sure. He swaggered in with the sneering arrogance of a spoiled brat who had more money than he could spend and could get away with any mischief that caught his fancy. "I hope you won't mind," said Saddam, "but it wouldn't do to have you running around Baghdad unsecured. We'll be housing you at Abu Ghraib Prison for the time being. Uday will escort you there. Do not worry. Whatever you may have heard about Abu Ghraib, I can assure you that you will be treated with all due respect. Should we want to use you as a bargaining chip with your CIA we would want to have you in tip-top condition, after all.

Uday, please see him out. Be gentle. Mr. Fonko is an honored guest. As well as money in the bank."

Uday looked me over like a cat looks over a cornered mouse. I hoped he was an obedient son. He took a firm grip on my left arm above the elbow and wrenched me toward the door.

A LONG STRETCH OF DAYS IN OCTOBER AND NOVEMBER, 1990

WERE I TO TAKE UP PENNING REVIEWS OF THE WORLD'S dungeons for TripAdvisor, I'd award Abu Ghraib a high mark. On a scale of 1 to 5 they all rate 0, of course, but I'd give Abu Ghraib five 0's compared to others I've spent time in—The Maze in Belfast, Gasr Prison in Tehran, Tuol Sleng in Phnom Penh, and assorted pestholes in India. Of course that stellar rating reflects the red carpet hospitality Abu Ghraib accorded me. I had a cell all to myself in a ground-level block. It featured an actual mattress pad, a chair and even a ceramic crapper. They fed me the same food the guards ate (and a miserable life those bastards led), they let me wear my own clothes, and they even helped me live up to Muslim standards of hygiene (somewhat short of Malibu's). I had American money, good for coaxing favors, goodies and laundry service from my guards. The guards were a piss-poor lot, so it went a long way.

Saddam lived up to his word about keeping me in good condition as a bargaining chip, and about keeping his sadistic son, Uday, at a distance. Judging from the screams and groans I heard coming through the floor from the basement cell blocks, not everyone enjoyed the same Club Med Baghdad experience that I did. On his visits, Uday eyed me as though he'd be happy to make me their equal in every way but behaved himself, under protest.

As I mentioned, jail stays are boring, and the longer you're there, the boringer they get. Rehabilitation and job training not having a high priority—no priority at all, in fact—Abu Ghraib lacked a prison library. The only reading matter at hand was a collection of grimy, tattered porn mags hoarded by the prison staff, which they lent out for a consideration. Dutch and Scandinavian porn outdid our own offerings graphically by a long way, but they contained no readable content. Over the weeks I read everything those estimable American journals, *Hustler* and *Playboy*, had to offer. By the time my sojourn ended, I felt all primed for oral exams on "The Playboy Philosophy" (umm... I probably could come up with better wording there). Some of the interviews actually were interesting—Jimmy Carter "lusted in his heart"? What a jerk that man was. The interviews whose continuity wasn't interrupted by torn-out pages were interesting, at least.

They let me out for exercise occasionally, and the climate in Baghdad was marginally more conducive to physical exertion than Kuwait's. In my cell I did calisthenics and isometrics. Fellow prisoners kept their distance, knowing that whatever they said to me could and would be used against them. One day the guards installed a fresh inmate into an adjoining cell (the previous occupant having been taken out and shot). He was Iraqi, a lively old fellow with a gleam in his eye. He wore a once-white robe that had spent a lot of time on the streets and sported a soiled Haji topper.

The guards roughly threw him into his cell. After they locked the door and left he gathered himself up and got his bearings. He explored the cell and then beyond it. When his gaze found me, he looked me up and down with curiosity. Finally he spoke up. "I'll take a wild guess. You're an American."

"What makes you think that?" I said.

"Your manner, your mien, your modus operandi. Dauntless, optimistic, ambitious, adventurous. Typical Yankee."

"You could tell all that in ten minutes?"

"That and much, much more. What is your name, if I may ask?"

"Jake Fonko."

He put his chin in his hand and pondered the floor, muttering, "Fonko... Fonko... that's a poser..." Then he brightened up. "I have it! Entrust the job to Fonko / How far could anything wrong go? But Jake! Now there's a glittering gold mine, a poetic plentitude, a coruscating cornucopia of rhyme. Jake: rhymes with ache, awake, bake, break, betake, cake, daybreak, drake, fake, flake, lake, make, mistake, opaque, quake, rake, sake, shake, snake, steak, take, wake. Make no mistake / Jake / Took the cake / At the clambake / By the lake. That's just off the top of my head, you understand. I could do ten times better had I pen and paper."

"I take it that you are a poet?"

"Ah, I see you are an observant man. Yes, I am Haj the poet, and I know it. Ha ha ha."

"They put poets in jail in Baghdad?"

"There is more to it than that, but it's a long story."

"We've got all the time in the world. Tell me."

"If you insist."

"Oh, I do, I do."

"Very well," he said as he settled back on his bunk. "It started when my daughter, Marsinah, and I came to Baghdad in quest of a better life. She fell under the spell of Baghdad's glamor and excitement..."

"Are you talking about the same Baghdad we're in right now?"

"Compared to the impoverished dung heap of a village from which we emanated, it's the bright lights and the Great White Way, let me assure you. Well, she soon was coveting baubles, bangles and beads. To realize her dreams I needed money, so I took to selling rhymes on the street..."

"I can't imagine you'd get much for Jake/Flake/Snake."

"No, not for those. But my top-of-the-line rhymes command premium prices. How about Rhinoceros/Prepocerous? Or Platinum/Flatten 'em? Parsley/Gharsley, no need to discount that one.

Pinafore/Din Afore, another top shelf item. Nantucket/Bucket... whatever a 'Nantucket' is."

"And those are rhymes you made up yourself?"

"Not precisely by myself, no, not exactly. In addition to originally-composed rhymes I also deal in previously-owned rhymes. With guarantees that they not only rhyme, they scan. And for a further consideration I also offer instruction on expressing them to best advantage. Gesticulate! That's the ticket! Arms in the air, fingers here and there, hands flying everywhere. But to continue, so my daughter, Marsinah, happened to fall in love with the Caliph and he with her..."

"They have a Caliph in Baghdad?"

"In a manner of speaking. If they had Caliphs the lad would definitely be one. A man of Caliph-like caliber, there's no denying. In the meantime I had, owing to a case of mistaken identity, inadvertently acquired a reputation as a seer who could bestow and remove curses. So a bandit chief had me kidnapped to relieve him of a curse he thought I had put on him years ago. Truthfully I have no such power and feared for my life, but through the fortunate intercession of Allah the curse was lifted, and he rewarded me with 100 pieces of gold. So I hurried back to the bazaar to find Marsinah. However, I fell afoul of the local Wazir..."

"They have Wazirs in Baghdad?"

"He was very Wazir-ish, a black-hearted devil of the finest water, you bet he was. He identified my gold as having been stolen, so he had me thrown into this wretched cell, as you see. Now my daughter is adrift and at the mercy of this wicked city, and I am helpless to save her."

"Do you have any idea what to do?"

"I can only place my trust in all-seeing, all-powerful Allah. Fate, Jake my friend, Kismet. We fight it in vain. What will happen, will happen according to Allah's will. All is written. I feel confident that something has been written in my favor and it will turn up soon. One thing I'll say, that Wazir has one hot wife, and when I get free I'd happily make her a widow to get her off to a secluded desert oasis."

"I wish you the best of luck,' I said.

We had more conversations like this during the next couple weeks, and then the guards came and took him away. To a lunatic asylum, most likely.

* * *

THE DAYS PASSED GRUDGINGLY. UDAY DROPPED IN occasionally to check on me but didn't do more than shove me around a little, much as he'd have liked to crank it up. Word reached me that Saddam had decreed foreigners were now permitted to leave Kuwait. If only I'd been able to hang around. Screams and moans continued filtering up from the basement dungeons, but I'd gotten used to it so slept through most nights. Then in early November I had another visitor. Imagine my surprise when the guards took me from my cell to an interrogation room. There he sat behind a beaten deal table, stocky with straw-colored hair and a plain European face, looking older and a little subdued compared to the last time I'd seen him.

"Grotesqcu! What are you doing here?" I whispered.

"This is Mr. Fonko?" he asked the guards. Their senior man nodded. "Good. Leave me alone with him." They left the room and closed the door. "The room's bugged," he said under his breath. "Sit down," he said gruffly. I did so. "As you know, your President Bush has announced an immediate, large increase in his troop deployments to Saudi Arabia, obviously much more extensive than needed for simple border defense. President Hussein is very concerned about this development. Inasmuch as you were on an American espionage mission to Kuwait, he needs to find out what you know about Kuwaiti defense strategy and any looming invasion plans. I am an espionage specialist with the Russian KGB, brought here to interrogate you. I will tell you truthfully right now that if you simply disclose everything you know, things will go much better for you"

"That's easy," I said. "I don't know anything about defense strategies or any forthcoming invasion plans. I went to Kuwait on a consulting job having to do with suspected international financial irregularities. The morning I was scheduled to leave, the Iraqi army invaded Kuwait, leaving me stuck there. I've never had any involvement with American force deployments."

"So you say. As a trained CIA spy it's expected that you would deny any knowledge. I've been through this sort of thing many, many times before, and I've seen it all. We could talk and talk, and go around and around, but President Hussein is anxious to find out what you know, and he wants it in a hurry. I am authorized to use any methods I see fit to get the information, and I should warn you that my methods range from unpleasant to ruinous. Really, it's best for all concerned if you just say what you know."

"Honestly, I know nothing."

"I respect your dedication and forbearance, but you have been warned." He got up, opened the door, leaned out and said something in Arabic. The guards came in and escorted me out, Grotesqcu right behind me. He said something to the leader and they took us to the exercise area and left us there.

"Good to see you again, Jake," said Emil Grotesqcu, crack KGB agent and sometime sidekick. "I told the guards I need to assess your physical condition to see how much torture you can survive. Walk around briskly with me for a while. They can't listen to us out here. You're looking good, all things considered."

"Hard as it is to believe, they've treated me well," I said. "Not that I ever wanted to spend a month in an Iraqi prison. I haven't even had a chance to call home. Nobody in California has any idea what happened to me."

"I can place a call to Miss Wehrli, if that would help."

"Indeed it would, and I'd be grateful. What are you doing here, Emil?"

"I've been greatly concerned ever since I learned you'd been captured by the Iraqis, knowing what they're capable of. Apparently Saddam considers you some kind of solid gold prize, giving him a lot of bargaining power with the U.S. government if need be. He was going to keep you until deals could be made, spy swaps, concessions, whatever. But this troop deployment has him beside himself—he never in a million years thought Saudi Arabia would allow American troops on Muslim soil and certainly not so many. He bought your superspy reputation to the extent that he's sure you went to Kuwait to carry out George Bush's plans, and he wants to know what they are. Usually he turns interrogations of this level over to Uday and his aides. Their methods not only get prisoners to tell everything they know, but before they expire even to squeak out things they didn't know they knew. Needless to say, having them do that to you is not in my best interests. I'd lose my meal ticket, and with the shaky state of things in Russia these days I can't afford to take any chances of that happening.

"Russia is a staunch ally of Saddam's, insomuch as he can have allies," he continued, "so I used my position as the KGB's top Fonko expert to convince their people to let me handle the interrogation. Interrogate you I must, but trust me on this. Better me than Uday."

"You can question me all you want, but really I don't know anything."

"Not good enough, Jake. I've got to give them something plausible and they expect you to resist, so I've got to use methods."

"You mean rip out my fingernails and hotwire my dick?"

"Uday would love to do that, with a little tooth extraction thrown in. We're more sophisticated. We use drugs these days. After subjecting prisoners to sleep deprivation, abuse and neglect, of course—have to get them in the proper frame of mind, you know. Not that it's any more humane. Some of our stuff leaves our, umm, clients mentally destroyed forever afterward. Sorry, old friend, but rest assured you're in good hands and just endure it. Well, I've had long enough to assess your health and resistance. Mustn't tarry or they'll suspect something. Back to your cell, and it'll be rough for a week or two, and then all will turn out well. Relatively speaking. You'll see."

* * *

So, that very afternoon a squad of Iraqi soldiers stormed into my cell. Grabbed me. Frog-marched me down stairs. Threw me into a damp, filthy isolation cell. Turned bright lights on and left them on. Had to sleep on the concrete floor in a putrid puddle. No shit bucket in the cell. Short rations of stale bread and rancid water.

Ranger survival training all over again.

After an indeterminate length of time they came and got me—dragged me, handcuffed, to a shower room. Stripped me and scrubbed me down with soap, tepid water and a very stiff bristle brush. Slipped a hospital gown on me and dragged / marched me up to a brightly-lit interrogation ward resembling an ER holding room in a cheap hospital. Strapped me down on a gurney.

Somebody stuck an IV needle in my arm and taped it firmly in place. Then Emil Grotesqcu came into the room in a white lab coat, carrying a thick attaché case. He set it down on a nearby table, pulled out a bottle and attached it to the IV line. "This won't hurt a bit, Mr. Fonko," he said. "I'm just sending you off to slumberland for a little while. How are you feeling today?"

"Never better," I snarled.

"That's the spirit. Always look on the sunny side." He hung the IV bottle up on one of those racks they use and opened a valve. A colored liquid seeped down the transparent line. When it reached the needle in my arm he looked at his wristwatch for a short interval, then said, "Mr. Fonko, I'd like you to count from 100 backwards, please."

I said, "Go fuck your..."

* * *

I woke up on an almost comfortable pad in a clean room feeling pretty good, certainly better than before he knocked me out. I needed the sleep.

"Anybody here?" I said. An Iraqi guard came into the room. "Speak English?" I asked.

"Little," he replied.

"How about something to drink?" I asked.

"Sure thing." He went out and said a few words to another guard, who left. The first guy went away and returned with a little bottle of pomegranate juice. It wasn't cold, but it hit the spot nevertheless. He returned to sitting outside the door and I lay back and gathered my thoughts, which seemed to be normal as far as I could tell. I still wore the hospital gown and had no idea where my things were. Presently the other guard returned and brought Emil Grotesqcu in.

"How's my sleepy-time boy?" he asked.

"Reasonable," I said. "What did you put into me?"

"A substance that's alleviated nearly as many ills as all the other modern drugs combined," he said. "It's called 'placebo.' Plus some sedative to knock you out and enough sodium pentothal to get you babbling. You've been out for a long time."

"So how'd I do?"

"Well enough. I asked you about America's military strategy and you gave me plenty of information that I can report to Saddam. What did you mean when you said, 'Grab 'em by the nose and then kick 'em in the ass'? Is that some kind of American martial arts?"

"No, it was one of Patton's dictums in World War II. The idea is that you divide your force in two. The smaller group engages the enemy's force with a frontal assault, and a bigger group goes around his flank and rolls him up from the rear. Patton innovated a lot of armored mobility tactics."

"Splendid. Saddam will love hearing about that—top secret stuff for sure. What was all that business about coordinated land, sea and air strikes, and ground game, wide-outs, throwing the big bomb? You mentioned the importance of flexible, mobile deployments. You also went on and on about air-supplied logistics, packaging supplies for parachute drops and so forth."

"I was out like a light. I don't remember a thing I said. What you mention sounds like stuff I learned in officers' training twenty years ago, mixed in with football game TV commentary."

"Whatever it was, there was enough of it that I can write an engrossing report on what my interrogation extracted from Jake Fonko, the CIA superspy. I'll convince Saddam that I siphoned out everything you know and he'll leave you alone for the time being."

"Fine by me, but what happens next?"

"I think I can move you out of Abu Ghraib. I'll tell Saddam that my drugs rendered you harmless and recommend that you be put under house arrest somewhere else. To keep you presentable as a bargaining chip, I'll tell him. Whatever he comes up with has got to be an improvement over Abu Ghraib. You'll have more privacy, and then we can plot how to get you out and back home."

* * *

GROTESQCU'S ATTEMPT TO SPRING ME FROM ABU GHRAIB FELL short, but he managed an upgrade to a nicer cell that even came with a barred-window view of outdoors—a non-scenic corner of the prison grounds plus some sky beyond. As autumn had progressed the temperature and humidity dropped, so it verged on being comfortable, some days even California-like. Guards were no longer posted nearby and pretty much left me alone unless I called them. Soon after they installed me in my new digs Emil came by with a bottle of Russian vodka, premium quality. He smoothed it over with the guards by presenting them with a bottle of the same. In gratitude they brought us a bottle of fruit juice for mixers. While they got roaring drunk we sipped warm ersatz screwdrivers and caught up on things. The conversation mostly centered on him, since his KGB group kept him current on my doings.

"That business in the Philippines finally worked out well from my point of view. The way I framed it, you exploited my Communist network to steal the election from Ferdinand Marcos, then turned around and stole the government from the Communists. Just what the KGB would expect from a CIA superspy. The tricky part came in finessing it so that your triumph didn't reflect badly on me. They bought my fictional account and upped my budget so that my group could keep a closer eye on you. 'We daren't let Fonko get away with something like this again!' I told them."

"I guess the Colombian drug cartel thing was easier for you to manage?"

"Once we got you through the Darien Jungle into Panama. It was touch and go for a while, but you handled it with your usual aplomb."

"You arrived in Baghdad in the nick of time," I said. "How'd you work that out?"

"Russia is an Iraqi ally. They're a major customer for our arms industry, and they rely on us for support and intelligence. Your name is well known enough that word soon reached me of your capture in Kuwait City. I asserted my prerogative over your case and justified an emergency trip. I shudder to think what might have happened if Uday had been put in charge of the interrogation. So far, so good, but the situation is developing in troublesome ways."

"I haven't heard any news for more than a month. What's happening?"

"The buildup of forces in Saudi Arabia continues apace," said Grotesqcu. "That announcement on November 8 about increasing troop deployments has Saddam spooked. The American presence there already is vast, but the general scope is not widely appreciated. Our satellites have identified infrastructure and logistics rapidly building up there—airstrips, housing, storage—which we estimate is precursor to at least 200,000 American troops coming soon, not to mention coalition forces from European and Arab countries. Carrier groups already lay in the Red Sea and the Persian Gulf, and more will be on station by the time hostilities break out. No country puts that much military force in motion without intending to use it. We haven't disclosed the full story to Saddam yet. He still doesn't accept the possibility that the Saudis would let Americans attack an Arab brother from their own soil. He'll find out soon enough."

"Are you here in Baghdad for a while?"

"For as long as you are, which gives me every incentive to move you out ASAP. How I do hate these Middle East countries! The weather and the grime and the squalor aren't even the worst of it. These wogs are simply insufferable. As polite as funeral directors to your face, and as mean as wolverines when they can get away with it. Take Saddam. He was as charming as a haute society hostess when he interviewed you. But a few years ago when the war with Iran was going badly the Minister of Health suggested he step down temporarily. Saddam personally shot him outside the chamber of the Revolutionary Command Council where they were meeting, then had him chopped up and delivered to his wife in a canvas bag. Uday's a chip off the old block, and his troops follow their commander's example.

"What they've been doing in Kuwait borders on insanity," he continued, "and that flows from Saddam's barbarian psychopathy as well. There's always been looting of conquered countries. The Louvre is full of paintings and statuary Napoleon brought back from his victories, and Hitler's collection of stolen art is well known. But the Iraqis have stolen everything from everywhere and carted it back home, from gutting factories and hospitals to trinkets and children's games from private villas. They dismantled Entertainment City, a big amusement park, and brought its carousels, miniature trains and even its chairs to Baghdad. Bah! Nickels and dimes and pennies! Though I suppose one can admire their attention to details. By the time the U.S. forces push them out there will be nothing left of Kuwait that was."

"The Iraqis had already pretty well stripped the place by the time I left," I said. "Nobody deserves what happened to Kuwait. As far as Arabs go, the Kuwaitis treated me well enough, all things considered. But they hired me to come there in the first place under false pretenses, come to think of it. What about you? How are things in Moscow these days? We haven't talked much since the Iron Curtain came down in Europe."

"Precarious situation. Very precarious. Those numbskulls in Oslo just awarded Mikhail Gorbachev the Nobel Peace Prize, anointing him to join Yasser Arafat, Henry Kissinger and Le Duc Tho in their harebrained Pantheon. I'm surprised they didn't give Peace Prizes to Neville Chamberlain and Vidkun Quisling, and Benedict Arnold too, posthumously. Your damned Ronald Reagan and his 'Mr. Gorbachev, tear down this wall.' And then it came down overnight, uniting East and West Germany much to everyone's surprise, and Gorbachev peeped not once.

"But there is such a delicious irony to it. In the 1960s our useful idiots at your universities formed the vanguard, led the revolution, waged the good war, and fought the good fight. Power to the people! Free speech! Equality! Off the pigs! Make love not war! Give peace a chance! All the usual rubbish we've always spouted, except that this time your students actually believed it! They succeeded in crippling your universities, but in doing so they brought about the collapse of the Soviet Empire. How did they manage that, one might ask? By frightening California voters into electing Ronald Reagan governor. They kept up the agitation and next thing you know, Reagan's sitting in your White House. Then he gets together with that Thatcher witch, and the curtain comes down. There's an object lesson in all this: Never rely on idiots."

"So you think this will spill over into Russia?"

"How can it not?" he said. "The arms race with your country is driving our economy to the wall, and on top of that you've exported your inflation to us. It won't be long before our former allies to our west join NATO. Without them to exploit our system is done for."

"How about the KGB? They'll keep that going, won't they?"

"Russia can't get along without secret police, but who says it necessarily must be the KGB? Russia is full of big fists just itching to occupy the seat of power and not all of them are fond of my organization. One ray of hope is a fellow named Vladimir Putin, an up-and-comer out of the KGB. But his rise is a long shot and who knows if he'd keep the KGB intact, or continue to support a Jake Fonko operation?"

"I'd hate to see you taken off my case,' I said. "If there's anything I can do to help, let me know."

"That's gracious of you, Jake," he said. "I'll surely tell you if something comes up. For the time being I'll just keep my head above water and see how long I stay afloat. I have nightmares about winding up on a trawler off Hawaii electronically monitoring financial transactions between the U.S. and Asia. By the way," he added, "I did place a call to your friend, Miss Wehrli. You never told her about me, did you?"

"I thought it best to keep our relationship under wraps. I get a lot of benefit out of it too, and I'd hate to have word leak out."

"Yes, that's best. She's a charming girl as you well know. I couldn't tell her much, certainly not where you are right now, but I assured her that you were fine and will be here for a while. She asked about taking care of your house. I told her you'd appreciate it if she'd look in from time to time and make sure things are okay. I hope that was right?"

"Much obliged. She has a key."

"She told me to tell you she has a new job and can't wait to tell you all about it. I told her it might be few weeks yet. The Iraqis are still letting foreigners leave Kuwait. If I can contrive to smuggle you down there, that's a possibility. Not much chance of getting you out through Baghdad with the tight surveillance they have on you, but I'll try. In not too long a time this is no place we will want to be. Those American troops across the border from Kuwait mean serious business."

DECEMBER 8, 1990 TO JANUARY 17, 1991

Emil Grotesqcu dropped in from time to time to keep me up to date on world events. I enjoyed the company but after my interrogation it was mostly one boring day after another—me a gilded bird in a cage. Until he came in with disturbing information. "The U.S. evacuated their Kuwaiti Embassy yesterday," he told me. "All Americans who wanted to leave have left now. This in the wake of the U.N. Security Council authorizing the use of force."

"Sounds like they're clearing the decks for invasion," I said.

"Yes it does, and here's some other bad news. Saddam received an official report from his intelligence people in Kuwait. According to them, you masterminded the escape of the Al Sabah family. You were organizing the Kuwaiti resistance movement. None of this came out in my interrogation, so now he has his doubts about me. He wants a re-do to find out what else you know."

"Same routine as last time?"

"He wants to go further. I'll forestall him as best I can and I'll shape the interrogation around what he wants to find out, but you're going to have to come up with new material."

"I can't tell you what I don't know," I said.

"I could skip the drugs and we could fake the whole thing. You were in the movies. You could babble out a prepared script that might satisfy him."

"I'm not that good an actor. I was only an extra in Hollywood, not a star of stage and screen. They never gave me speaking parts. You'll have to do the drugs, and we'll hope for the best."

So we repeated the softening-up process, the IV drip and whatever theatrics Grotesqcu performed while I was knocked out. A few days later he returned looking discouraged. "Not good, Jake, not good at all," he said. "Saddam's swallowed the tales of your espionage prowess so he expects more out of these interrogations. You babbled something about meetings with the Kuwaiti leadership, but it made no sense at all. Saddam is not impressed with my methods. He's going to interview you again, personally. I needn't mention that the both of us are in grave danger right now. Damn it, Jake, couldn't you at least have made something up for me?"

"I don't pretend to be a pharmacist, but don't they call sodium pentothal 'truth serum'?"

"Yes, but... Oh well, do your best with him."

* * *

A COUPLE DAYS LATER SADDAM HIMSELF CAME INTO MY CELL block, along with Uday and a couple of towering, stone-faced Republican Guards. Saddam carried some file folders and Uday packed a truncheon. One of the Guards unlocked my door and they escorted me to an interrogation room. It was bare save for two chairs and a well-worn wood table. Saddam and Uday seated themselves in the two chairs behind the table, leaving me standing in front of it. The Guards stood at attention right alongside me. Oozing hostility, Uday eased back, hoisting his big feet up on the table, the soles of his shoes in my face—an Arab sign of emphatic disrespect. Saddam placed his file folders on the table, opened one and sifted through some papers.

Saddam was not in his charming-host persona today. "Mr. Fonko, our KGB associate has interrogated you two times. Neither time did he uncover the secret information that I am firmly convinced you harbor. I suppose, owing to your espionage training, you were able to resist disclosing secrets but every man has his breaking point, and I am sure that so far we have not approached yours." *You're close enough*, I thought. "The last American hostages left Iraq few days ago. Holding them no longer served my purposes. The two sides are gearing up for war and I promise you it will be the mother of all battles. It will pit my combat-hardened army and invincible Republican Guards, fighting on their own soil and equipped with the latest Russian tanks, against an inexperienced and poorly organized coalition of forces thrown together in an unfamiliar part of the world.

"I would like you to explain further what the interrogations have disclosed, and if you do not satisfy me we will have to move on to harsher methods." He picked up a sheaf from the table and read it. "This business about grabbing the nose and kicking the ass —how would that apply to Kuwait?"

"The best frontal assault on Kuwait City would be an amphibious invasion, coming in around Failaka Island," I said. "That's grabbing the nose. Kicking the ass means an attack from the rear. The idea is to occupy the army in one direction, then hit it at its weakest point, which would be the border with Saudi Arabia. Or in a broader scope, attack Kuwait from Saudi Arabia, and then sweep into Iraq from Turkey and capture Baghdad from the north, the kick in the ass."

"I told you we should fortify the beaches and the seashore," put in Uday. "We should mine the approaches to the bay too. The landing boats would never get in, and if they try we could sink them all."

Saddam knitted his brow in thought. He returned to his papers. "Hmmm," he said. "You went on and on about armored mobility. That means...?"

I couldn't believe he was focusing on this stuff, all of which had been well known since World War II. "U.S. Army doctrine relies on movement of troops and armor, not static fronts."

"Ground game... wide-outs... the big bomb? This is some kind of Pentagon terminology?"

"Yes. Ground game means a grinding war of attrition. Wide-outs are flanking attacks from distant bases. The big bomb means a decisive blow." My bullshit generators were getting a lot of exercise today.

Saddam sat thinking. Uday glared at me. "You may fancy me a backward dictator of a so-called Third World country, Mr. Fonko," Saddam said slowly and deliberately, "but let me assure you that governing a fractious nation in the Middle East requires a subtle, analytic mind. What I detect here is a double-cross strategy. You tell me the truth thinking that I naturally will assume that you lie. But I am going to jump you one square further on the board and take what you are telling me as the truth. So that is a beginning. We can adjust our defenses in light of what you have disclosed. We'll need to further fortify the border with Saudi Arabia—lay mines, set up trench networks and so forth against the kick in the ass," he remarked to Uday.

"We could flood the coast with Kuwaiti petroleum," put in Uday. "Then set the sea on fire when the Americans try to land."

"That's an idea," said Saddam. He returned to me: "This is more helpful, Mr. Fonko, but there is much more that you know, that we need to find out. For example, the organization of the Kuwaiti resistance and the names of its key leaders. We will have to neutralize them so that they cannot act as a fifth column and cause trouble in the event of an invasion by the Americans. I gather the Americans have some new high-technology weapons they may deploy. The newspapers discuss them in general terms, but we need detailed specifications and capabilities, which you surely must know."

"Sorry to contradict you," I said, "but I spent only a few days with a small group of Kuwaitis who were protecting their neighborhood. I know nothing of any organized Kuwaiti resistance force. As for high-tech weapons you've read about in the newspapers, I haven't even seen the newspaper stories. You know more about that than I do."

"You expect me to believe you?" Saddam scoffed. "A top CIA agent serving as a mere neighborhood watchman? Who knows nothing about current military weaponry? I will let you examine your thoughts and your position, and give you one more chance to be forthcoming. If you are not, further interrogations will take place, which I hope will not have to go so far as to compromise your value as a bargaining chip. Uday, let us give him a taste. Mr. Fonko, sit down on the floor." I did so. He nodded at the Guards. They unceremoniously bent down, grabbed my ankles, jerked my feet up in the air and wrenched off my shoes. My efforts to squirm out went nowhere.

Uday swung his feet off the table, got up, came around and without warning gave me some sharp whacks across the soles of my feet with his nightstick. Youch! That hurt like hell! He could do it all day and it would leave no mark on my body. If that was a taste, I didn't want to think about full servings. The Guards dropped me to the floor, grabbed me above the elbows, yanked me upright, and trundled me out the door.

* * *

I DIDN'T FULLY RECOVER FROM THE PAINFUL LIMP BACK TO MY cell for a couple days. Grotesqcu had heard about the incident and dropped in to sympathize.

"Is Uday Hussein the sadistic bully he seems to be?" I asked him.

"No, actually he's much worse," said Grotesqcu. "He positively delights in torturing prisoners to the point of death and beyond. He's said to have an actual iron maiden in his chambers, and he uses it on people who displease him. He crashes parties, picks out pretty women, takes them home and rapes them. A real boy scout, as you Americans would say."

"And he's going to interrogate me?"

"He'd like to. I'll put them off as best I can, but he's trying to convince Saddam that his methods are better than mine. I had an idea. How about if we concoct intelligence that I can say I tortured out of you. Stall them for as long as possible and see how things develop."

So we put our heads together and dreamed up all kinds of fantasies. Missiles that could be directed to house addresses. Bombs that could be dropped and guided by laser through building windows. Planes that radar couldn't detect. We described it in great detail, operational specs, performance data and all. Grotesqcu threw in some stuff he remembered from a U.S. Army publication, *Field Manual 100-5*, that had made the rounds in the KGB, describing the "AirLand Battle." It was post-Vietnam doctrine conjectured for World War III describing airstrikes to isolate the battlefield by cutting off reinforcements and supply lines. It wasn't classified, in fact was standard material in our War College, but it sounded impressive. Grotesqcu wrote it all up as the results of advanced interrogations and passed them along to Saddam.

Saddam was intrigued but not satisfied, and Uday started visiting my cell more frequently. He was still on Saddam's leash but straining at it. He roughed me up right to the line he was told not to exceed. I pushed back right up to the line that would provoke him to exceed his line. I definitely did not want to take that brute on in a context that gave him a chance—he was too big and too tough. Even if I won there'd be a price to pay. I wanted to fight him on my own terms, preferably from behind, in the dark, with something hard and heavy in my hand.

Grotesqcu kept me informed of events in the outside world. On January 15 George Bush set a deadline for diplomatic negotiations on Iraq withdrawing from Kuwait. Two nights later explosions awakened me. I looked out the cell window upon a scene like a distant Fourth of July festival. My view was limited and downtown Baghdad was many miles away, but I could make out tracer streaming upwards from several points closer to Abu Ghraib. The sky in the direction of Baghdad took on an orange glow from fiery explosions that I glimpsed erupting, though I couldn't hear them. There must have been military targets around Abu Ghraib, judging by loud bursts nearby, some of them close enough to shake the air in my cell. Jets screamed overhead, heading into the city to the accompaniment of wailing prison sirens. Surface-to-air missiles flew up from the outskirts of town, apparently not hitting anything.

The air attack kept on through the night and into the next day. Toward noon, Emil Grotesqcu dropped by in a cheerful mood. "Hi ho, Jake," he exclaimed, waving an unopened bottle of vodka. "Enjoy the night's display? I thought we might toast the onset of the Mother of All Battles."

"I couldn't see much from here. It looked like a comprehensive attack. Any damage assessment?"

"A lot of the Iraqi Air Force was destroyed on the ground. The Ministry of Defense took a big hit, as did a number of other strategic targets—bases, storage tanks, factories and so forth. Seems your team used a particularly devilish tactic—when Iraqi fire-control tried to track the incoming jets for targeting, other jets sent radar-seeking missiles at them. Pretty soon the ground crews were launching their SAMs blind. Either that or turn on their radar and get instantly wiped out. U.S. planes struck all over Iraq with surprising accuracy and limited collateral damage. They're keeping it up this morning. Big missiles are coming in near ground level and heading straight for specific targets. It's almost as if that pack of lies we sent to Saddam had some truth in it. Where are your glasses? It's time we bent our elbows."

It was a little early in the day for me, but what the heck? I poured two shots and we raised them. "Confusion to the enemy... provided he's not us," declared Grotesqcu. "In a way, this war is all about excess."

"How do you mean?"

"In Saddam's case, he has excess soldiers. He'd been waging war with Iran for ten years, and now that's over. That left his economy a basket case, stone broke and deeply in debt, such that he hasn't paid his soldiers in months. So what does he do with hundreds of thousands of hardened and battle-weary troops? If he demobilizes them he's got a country full of unemployed, armed and seasoned fighters who are rightly outraged about how he's dealt with them. No police he could muster could stop them if they decided to organize and demand what he owes them. On his doorstep sits a rich and defenseless neighbor. What better solution than to send his excess soldiers to sack the place and collect what they want?"

"Okay," I said, "from Saddam's point of view it's a way of deflecting a potential insurrection, as well as discharging billions of dollars of debt and clasping huge oil wealth to his bosom. What excess is on our side?"

"Weapons. Reagan's arms buildup in the 1980s left America with a profusion of tanks, planes, bombs, missiles, you name it. The point was to thwart Russian expansion and challenge our hegemony of Eastern Europe. Then suddenly the Iron Curtain comes down and the Fulda Gap is on your side of the fence. No longer any need for all the stockpiles of arms in West Germany. In the meantime your Silicon Valley geniuses have been turning out a new generation of high tech weapons beyond imagining—laser-guided bombs, GPS guided missiles, stealth aircraft designs and who knows what all else? I'm not saying that Bush entered into this war just to pare down his arsenal and test his new toys. But when the opportunity arose they were just sitting there. From a dollars and cents standpoint it's going to be a cheap war. The money's been spent already out of Reagan's budget, and there'll be no need to rebuild to the same level after this is over. Have your war and a peace dividend to boot."

Food for thought. We'd finished our drinks—Grotesqcu downed his in one slug, Russian style, and I'd sipped mine empty. I'd picked up the bottle to pour another round when Uday Hussein came storming down the hall and into my cell, red-faced and panting. "Fonko, my father wants to see you! Right now!" he sputtered.

His right fist clenched, he grabbed my shoulder with his left and gave me a jarring shake.

"Now wait a minute," Grotesqcu blurted, giving Uday a sharp shove in the back.

Uday let me go and whirled around, looming over Grotesqcu. "Listen, you worthless Russian bastard," he snarled, "you've fucked this up from the beginning, you and your sophisticated interrogation techniques. I'm taking charge of this prisoner, and from now on we interrogate him *my* way!"

Grotesqcu backed away a step, putting his weight on his rear foot and adjusting into a ready-to-fight stance. Considering the size differential it was a heroic gesture, but regardless of his martial arts skills he had doubtful chances in the impending brawl, especially when the guards joined in. I stood behind Uday with something heavy and hard—a nearly full bottle of vodka—in hand. It wasn't dark, my third specification, but you can't always have it all your way. Bottles in movie bar fights explode on people's skulls because they use candy bottles. Not the bottle in my hand—it was solid glass. I laid it upside Uday's temple with a full-arm swing, and he collapsed in a big heap.

"Good move," said Grotesqcu, "but now what?"

"Obviously, we've got to get out of here. Let's take care of him first." I checked his pulse, and he still had one. We pulled his shirt off him and ripped it in half up the back (hated to waste a $200 shirt like that). We tied his wrists behind his back with one half and tied his ankles firmly together with the other. Then we muscled him up on my bunk. We stuffed my washcloth into his mouth, knotted his socks together and looped them around his face to secure the gag. As a final touch, we covered as much of him as we could with the cell blanket.

"Any idea where we can go?" I asked.

"I'm staying at the Russian Embassy," he said. "I can put you up. Saddam can't bother you there."

"Are you kidding? You told me I'm on the KGB's Most Wanted

list, and you want me to walk into a Russian Embassy fronting for a spy station?"

"Good point. If they took you out of circulation I'd lose my cushy job. So, what do you suggest?"

"Do they let Arabs in there?"

"The place is swarming with the buggers. They do all the menial tasks."

"Okay. I've got a full Arab outfit from Kuwait in my kit. Take me in as an Arab."

"Under what pretext?"

"You'll think of something on the way. Let's go."

"Get changed, Jake. I'll go fix it with the guards."

He scurried out of the cell. By the time he returned, I was robed and head-dressed. I'd not completely shaved off my beard and mustache, and that rounded out the disguise. He looked shocked when he saw me. "Amazing," he said. "You'd have fooled me if I didn't know you. Get your bags and follow me. I have a car and driver waiting out front. I gave the guards a Benjamin to look the other way while an Arab friend and I left the premises. For that amount I believe they'd carry us to the curb on their shoulders."

Too bad for those guards when Uday came to.

I threw everything into my kit and we strode out the front door. As we approached his car I asked him, "Have you figured out our story yet?"

"I've always fancied having an Arab lackey. Come along, Abdul, and mind you don't damage my luggage."

MONDAY, JANUARY 18, TO SATURDAY, FEBRUARY 23, 1991

WITH THE U.S. EMBASSY IN BAGHDAD SHUT DOWN, THE Russian Embassy was my only safe refuge. It commanded a compound in Baghdad which I was confident wasn't listed on Allied targeting schedules. My safety there depended on successfully playing the most challenging role in my so-called acting career —an Arab errand boy who spoke neither Arabic nor Russian, living among Russians, most of whom couldn't speak Arabic but many of whom could speak my native tongue, English. Grotesqcu drilled me in some useful Russian phrases: *da, ser* for "yes sir," *nyet, ser* for "no sir", *spasibo, ser* for "thank you, sir", and *ya ne ponimayu, ser* for "I don't understand sir." He taught them to me with an Arabic accent.

By then I'd been around Arabs enough that I could mimic their attitude toward us infidels—oily obsequiousness anchored to a bedrock of smoldering resentment—sufficiently to get by. I scooped my food out of my bowl with my right hand, did not use toilet paper, and dutifully hit the prayer rug five times each day as signaled by ululations from the minarets of nearby mosques. The prayers were an annoyance until I realized that at least it was a little exercise, so I made the most of them with some stretching and isometrics. Being congenitally allergic to work, Arabs avoid exerting themselves unduly, one reason why slavery has always been popular with them. Therefore I couldn't show too much energy, but I did my best to keep in trim.

The cover story Grotesqcu put about was that when the American attacks began demolishing Baghdad I'd cornered him on the street and begged him to let me work for food and shelter. The shelter they gave me amounted to a closet in a storage building, and the food I got was bleak and grudging. To be fair, rations were short all over Baghdad by that time, thanks to the embargo—not that my Russian hosts stinted on themselves. At least Ramadan hadn't yet begun, so I got a couple skimpy meals a day.

In return for their miserly largesse I adopted the Arab penchants for passive resistance and non-work ethic. We coexisted according to the Iraqi equivalent of the Russian dictum, "we pretend to work, and they pretend to pay us." Grotesqcu, in keeping with the spirit of the situation, hounded and berated me and complained to his buddies about my sloth and incompetence. It played out so convincingly with the Russians that one particularly obnoxious slob offered me ten dinars for a blowjob, making his offer in well-practiced pantomime. I backed away from him bowing with hands clasped prayer-style, shaking my head and babbling "ya ne ponimayu, ser". Grotesqcu got a hearty laugh out of it. My propositioner, a senior diplomatic attaché, was a standing joke around the Embassy as a loser who couldn't make out in a whorehouse with a fistful of American fifties. I steered clear of him after that, and after the word got around he kept a proper distance.

My Kuwaiti outfit fooled the Russians, who didn't much know one wog from another and despised them all equally. The other Arabs who worked around the compound had sharper eyes and posed a different problem. They spotted me for a phony from the git-go, but they couldn't fathom what kind of phony I was, and I kept them guessing. All but a few cooks and house servants lived outside the compound. The crews of gardeners, cleaners and gofers trooped dutifully in from their hovels for work in the morning and left at dusk. I was the only Arab in the compound that wore a robe and headdress. The rest wore western-style pants and shirt and sweaters, or beige pajamas and tunics. Plus my clothing was of a finer quality fabric than all but a few of the local Arabs could afford. The minions knew there was money behind it, and if I was rich what was I doing running errands for the hated infidels? To up my Muslim cred I made sure some of them saw me at prayer but otherwise I snubbed them with haughty Middle Eastern disdain as I shuffled around the grounds schlepping small items pointlessly from one place to another. As much as possible I skulked out of sight in my closet.

Grotesqcu and I were able to converse freely as long as nobody heard me speak English. The Russian Embassy, basically a nest of spies, kept very well-informed, so I was able finally to catch up on events. It had taken Saddam no time at all to retaliate for the initial wave of Allied air strikes on Baghdad. The very next day he launched some Russian Scuds into Israel, a country that had taken no part in the battle. He assumed they, being Middle Eastern hot heads, would retaliate in turn and sic a jet attack on Iraq. Most Arab nations hated Israel, Egypt ostensibly being one exception. Saddam's plan was that Israeli retaliation would trigger his Arab brothers to ditch their partnership with the U.S. and band together with him in defeating the infidel devils who were, as everyone knew, in thrall to International Jewry.

American air strikes continued relentlessly, and now that I was at Ground Zero it was a spectacle to behold. Baghdad rang with explosions throughout day and night, and acrid smoke clouded the air. Ineffectual Iraqi anti-aircraft fire decorated the night sky with fearsome fireworks. Even with the publicly announced timetable the American air attack had achieved total tactical surprise. The onslaught was as well-coordinated as a philharmonic symphony orchestra. Wild Weasels in F-4s swooped in and knocked out ground radar with their HARM missiles. F-15 Eagles, F-16 Fighting Falcons and carrier-launched F-18 Hornets followed, guiding "smart bombs" via lasers and TV literally down smokestacks and through windows. Tomahawk missiles left ships in the Red Sea, followed below-the-radar GPS-directed routes at airliner speeds and took out specific buildings. Outside the cities, B-52 bombers plastered Iraqi troops, bunkers and tank concentrations with 750 lb free-fall bombs. French Jaguar fighters hit Iraqi air bases around Kuwait City, and British Tornados ripped up Iraqi airfields with runway-cratering bombs.

Saddam's legions sat helpless and hapless against the annihilation. Of his air force of 700 jets that weren't destroyed on the ground, 19 were shot down in the air (against 0 of the allied planes), and none ever attacked American ground targets. The Iraqi air force preserved 147 of their planes by evacuating them to Iran. The whereabouts of the remaining planes remained a mystery —apparently secreted out of harm's way pending better days—but they never saw combat. Saddam was reduced to gloating that misguided bombs had obliterated a powdered milk factory and killed 400 civilians in a bomb shelter. He felt sure these "propaganda victories" would discredit the attacks and swing world sympathy in his favor, so he took pains to give CNN on-site coverage with full access to the atrocities. Anchor Peter Arnett had stayed behind in Baghdad, braving incoming Tomahawks to bring the story to the world audience. His problem was that if he told too much truth he would be thrown out of Iraq. Just one of the difficulties inherent in reporting on-the-scene news about dictators.

Saddam continued firing Scuds into Israel, but to his dismay the Israelis sucked it up. Rather than letting them shoot back, Bush installed Patriot missile batteries that were reasonably effective in shooting down incoming Scuds before they did damage. The Scud attacks caused Israelis concern, anguish and inconvenience—they feared poison gas warheads, so they sealed their homes and hunkered down in gasmasks—but overall had little effect. Saddam's forty-odd Scuds that landed there scored only four civilian deaths and 200 casualties, while damaging 4,000 buildings.

Of the Scuds Saddam fired into Saudi Arabia, one got lucky during the 100-Hour War and hit a U.S. barracks in Dhahran, killing 28 soldiers and wounding 89. The main effect of the Scuds was to divert too many air sorties to seeking out mobile Scud launch sites rather than hitting more important targets. The Iraqis proved talented at camouflage, causing our flyers to waste a lot of ammo and expensive flying time chasing mockups and fiberglass replicas around the vast Iraqi desert.

Day by day the pounding took its toll on Baghdad. The city lay blacked out at night, not that it helped much against infrared sensors and AWACS-borne radar. Road travel was restricted amid all the shooting, but thanks to the smart weapons haphazard collateral damage in the city was relatively light. Power outages became frequent and then general as the bombs took out utilities stations, shutting most of the city down for days while Iraqi technicians labored to get things going again. The Russian Embassy had its own generators, so we had juice for what mattered and lights until bedtime.

From my place and point of view it was all a great sound-and-light show, and it couldn't have happened to more deserving guys.

But the longer I remained stuck there, sooner or later something was bound to blow my cover. It's one thing to be in five takes of a ten minute crowd shot in a Hollywood sound studio. It's quite another to live a double role day in and day out in tight quarters among two different sets of enemies. Nor was it a piece of cake for Grotesqcu: He had to maintain the pretense, which meant finding ways to keep me busy and sequestering me away from the prying eyes of the other Arabs lurking around. He told me that rumors circulated concerning our sexual proclivities, which helped maintain the mystery and kept Russians and Arabs alike at a wary distance.

No one beats an Arab at sneakiness. I had reason to believe they were snooping in my room but didn't catch anyone at it until one afternoon while on my make-work rounds. I noticed garden clippers dropped outside the door of the storage building where I stayed, at some distance away from the nearest bushes. I picked them up, eased silently inside and crept to my closet. One of the grounds crew, a creepy little lizard who I'd noticed previously stalking my comings and goings, was hunched over on his knees furtively pawing through my goods. He'd left the door open and was so engrossed in his search that he didn't hear me approach. I grabbed him by an ankle and yanked him back, banging his face on the cement floor. I dropped the clippers and flipped him over on his back with a hard landing, then hauled his trousers down. Holding him flat with a knee on his stomach, I put the clipper blades around his family jewelry and stared long and hard into his terrified eyes. I put my finger to my lips and zipped it across them. I closed the clippers a little tighter and looked at him quizzically signaling "you gonna keep quiet?" He got my drift and nodded in enthusiastic, semi-hysterical agreement. I climbed off him with an additional shove in the stomach, let him get himself together and launched him out the door with a hearty kick in the ass that sent him tumbling onto the walkway. I didn't see him around the compound after that, and he must have spread the word, because I found no signs of snooping after that day.

* * *

I WAS IN A BOX. RUSSIAN PLANES CAME AND WENT AT THE Baghdad airport when it was operable, but they flew non-stop to Russia and I couldn't take that route. Kuwait City presented no easy way out as long as Iraq controlled it. Otherwise, Iraq bordered on Syria and Iran—unsafe havens for a fugitive American spy. So I sweated out my stay in the Russian Embassy while Bush's campaign rolled inexorably on, impatiently waiting for something to turn up in my favor.

"Saddam's army is being dismembered," Grotesqcu told me. "The Iraqis excel at desert concealment, and they've been hiding troops in underground bunkers and tanks under camouflage, but with all those planes in the air all Saddam can do is slow down the losses. Reports we've received have it that army morale is dismal and desertions are rife. The Americans have moved two battleships, the *Wisconsin* and the *Missouri*, into position off Kuwait within range of their guns. Iraqi casualties already approximate 20,000 killed and 60,000 wounded. It's only a matter of time before Saddam goes down."

"I agree, but then what?" I said. "Bush isn't going to liberate Iraq. He's been sticking to the U.N. guidelines and resolutions, which don't authorize Allied troops to occupy territory across the border. So Saddam throws in the towel and retreats back home and then what? My best hope is to get back to Kuwait City. When the Americans reclaim it, figuring a way out will be easy."

"That makes sense to me," he said. "The timing will be tricky, though. Leave here too soon and you'll find yourself in the middle of an increasingly desperate Iraqi occupation. Leave too late and you'll be fighting your way through a desperate mob of beaten soldiers hell-bent on getting home."

We got word that Iraq emptied Kuwaiti oil storage tanks into the Gulf. The spill, 126 million gallons of crude oil, was the largest in history, covering 350 square miles of water and stretching far enough to threaten Arabian desalination plants. Unless it was a screwup or Saddam was just being barbaric, the only reason I could see for this was to forestall an amphibious attack. But it happened way too soon, and anyway, an amphib invasion never figured in the campaign. American troops were pursuing a massive AirLand assault, and the Air part of it had just about finished. By mid-February 50,000 air sorties had softened Saddam's armed forces to the consistency of oatmeal.

One day Grotesqcu brought me the news that Saddam had made an offer to withdraw from Kuwait. "That's it, then?" I said.

"Not by a long way. He attached conditions. American forces must first leave the region. Israel must abandon their occupied territories. And all countries who took part in the war must contribute to rebuilding what they destroyed."

"That's *not* it, then. The man's insane if he thinks Bush will agree to that."

"He doesn't think so for a minute. It's a time-honored technique from the souks: Make a ridiculous opening offer that you can bargain back from. It apparently hasn't dawned on him that Americans don't like to bargain. 'Here's my price, it's fair, and take it or leave it,' is their approach. But the fact that Saddam's making an offer at all is a clear sign that we've reached the endgame."

* * *

A few days later Grotesqcu told me that Saddam announced he would unconditionally withdraw from Kuwait in agreement with an eight-point plan that Gorbachev had put forward. Among other points the plan stipulated that the U.N. must lift its sanctions once two-thirds of Iraqi troops had left, and that all resolutions be lifted once withdrawal was complete.

"Why should Bush agree to anything but his own terms at this point?" I asked.

"He shouldn't," said Grotesqcu, "and he won't. Let's get ready. Our chance draws nigh."

Our escape entailed some tricky mechanics. Our only way to Kuwait City was by car, a trip of nearly 400 miles over war-ravaged roads jam-packed with military congestion. We might be able to make it as far as Basrah on one tank of gas, depending on our vehicle, but we'd have to refuel somewhere to go all the way. Grotesqcu could slide through the checkpoints, since Iraq give their Russian allies immunity and free passage. I posed the problem: Go as an Arab? Or as an Iraqi civilian, perhaps a businessman or government official? Or in an Iraqi military uniform, in which case I might be pressed into other duties at a checkpoint until they found out I couldn't speak Arabic? We decided to send me out in civvies, which meant hiding them under my Arab robes until we cleared Baghdad. Next issue: what kind of wheels? I reasoned that an ordinary car would give us the best odds. American planes seeking ground targets seemed to be under orders to avoid civilian casualties, so they'd be more likely to hit a military vehicle on the road. If Grotesqcu traveled as a civilian also, a military vehicle would be out of character. Then there was provisioning, weapons, money, documents and all the other details of sneaking 400 miles through an active war zone in alien territory. Don't believe what you've seen in the thriller movies—you don't just get your instructions, drop in and heroically save the world. The real-life spy business takes a lot of effort and pre-planning.

On February 22 Bush announced that to end the war and avoid a ground offensive, Saddam must publicly agree to the allied coalition's terms of disengagement and commence an unconditional exit of Kuwait by noon EST, February 23. His terms, needless to say, differed from Saddam's and Gorbachev's, including: Complete withdrawal within a week. Facilitate the Kuwait government's return. Release all prisoners within two days. Remove all explosives from oil fields. And provide maps of all mines. That's my offer. Take it or leave it.

"That's our cue," Grotesqcu announced. "Trim your beard to civilian contours and assemble your gear. We leave at daybreak Sunday."

TO HELL AND BACK

SUNDAY, FEBRUARY 24, TO MONDAY, FEBRUARY 25, 1991

A HALF HOUR BEFORE DAYBREAK GROTESQCU ORDERED ABDUL, his faithful Arab gofer, to load the car, which turned out to be a midnight blue Mercedes 420SEL sedan.

"Hide in plain sight—it never fails. The Iraqi army stole it right out of a Kuwait dealer's showroom," he explained, "so in a sense we'll be returning it to its rightful owners." How he managed to procure things like that, I have never been able to fathom—he'd have been a hell of a supply sergeant—but not mine to question.

I stowed our kits in the trunk. As I swung the door open to enter the passenger side he came up to me carrying a heavy gym bag. He unzipped it and pulled out an Uzi.

"Stick this under your seat," he said, shoving it in my hand. "It's got a full clip. Just in case. You've used them before?"

"In training, not in combat," I said. "It's an effective piece at close range."

"Let's be off," he said. He went back around, got in, slid another Uzi from the bag under his seat and tossed the bag over his shoulder into the back. "Not a moment to lose."

Our plan was to take Highway 97 west past the airport and Abu Ghraib, catch Highway 1, the main north-south road, then follow it down to pick up Highway 80 into Kuwait City. There were a number of other routes to Basrah, our pivot point, and we'd debated that one against the alternatives. It was the most straightforward but would be the most heavily traveled and also most subject to Allied attack. Some lesser roads closer to the Tigris River might have been a little shorter in miles but possibly longer in time. A more southwesterly route would range us far out into desert, possibly getting us entangled in military positions. The distance of our ride compared to that between Los Angeles and San Francisco, which used to take around eight hours. We'd no idea what awaited us but figured we'd be lucky to make Kuwait City in one calendar day.

"What's our backstory?" I asked as Grotesqcu pulled us away from the Russian Embassy. "It takes a little time to get in character."

"Two backstories. I told my Russian colleagues that I'd just received word CIA superspy Jake Fonko escaped from Abu Ghraib prison and was heading toward the Kuwaiti border. I had an idea which route he took so we intend to head him off and bring him in. Once we get out of town, you and I are Scud engineers ordered to do urgent flightpath reprogramming. I'm from the Russian Scud factory and you are my Iraqi counterpart. To whomever asks, the Scud installation we're seeking is located 50 kilometers down the road, and our orders are to get there ASAP."

Traffic through Baghdad was subdued, thanks to three weeks of continuing aerial bombardment. The lack of widespread devastation surprised me. Various government buildings and military sites were obliterated, but residential areas and shopping districts stood relatively unscathed. Compared to what I'd seen of Kuwait City before I left, the demolition in Baghdad might have passed for normal urban renewal. Post-World-War-II Berlin it wasn't.

As we approached the junction with Highway 1 Grotesqcu found a sheltered spot to pull over. I got out, shed my Arab robe and headdress and stuffed them in the trunk with our stuff. Now I traveled in expensive business casuals. We merged onto the highway heading south and found it bustling with military hardware—trucks, tanks, and personnel carriers—pressing in both directions. Saddam had disregarded Bush's deadline and now girded his army for a desperate last-ditch defense. Traffic was heavy during daytime. Their infrared signatures made vehicles sitting ducks for the jets after dark, so traveling in daylight was easier and no more dangerous. The Iraqis calculated that enough traffic would elude our ravaging jets to make it worthwhile. Not that many escaped. Signs of Allied kills decorated the road: blackened former tanks pulled aside, wrecked convoys (some still smoking) heaped on the verge, stretches of patched pavement and craters that the repair crews hadn't yet tackled.

"This could be dangerous, you know," Grotesqcu observed. "The Allies are going to ramp it up now that Saddam's in default."

"Our pilots have excellent eyesight, so let's hope Bush hasn't changed his rules of engagement about not targeting civilians. Keep your distance from anything military we come to, and let's hope for the best."

The first part of our trip took us through farmland that reminded me of California's Central Valley south of Stockton, though on a smaller and poorer scale. Both deserts bloomed thanks to irrigation, but our Central Valley lies under mechanized Big Ag cultivation, while peasants do most of the farming in Iraq's Fertile Crescent. Dates and cotton seemed to be popular crops. It was a welcome contrast to the flat, barren desert land of Kuwait. But thank goodness we were making the drive in February in warm, dry weather rather than through blistering summer heat in the 110s.

Highway 80 was basically good road: except for war damage we'd have breezed along. Bomb craters, wrecks and lumbering semis and tank transporters slowed us down, keeping our average speed under 30 miles per hour, not including checkpoint stops. Grotesqcu's cover story and paperwork got us through those with no arguments. He carefully hung back behind military convoys until he caught a break in traffic, then whipped around them as fast as we could go, leaving them behind. U.S. jets streaked overhead throughout the morning. Now and then one came in low with an ear-splitting shriek en route to a target up ahead or to our rear. Unnerving. You never get used to it. We came upon the results of attacks ahead while they still flamed. Waiting for wrecked trucks and tanks to be shoved out of the way accounted for much of our delays.

Cultivated countryside dwindled to desert south of Diwaniyah. It had taken us four hours to reach there from the Embassy and we were well due for a break. Grotesqcu pulled off the main highway and hunted up a functioning marketplace. He'd laid in some field rations, but you always eat fresh where you can, saving the canned stuff for emergencies. The stretch of Highway 1 south to Nasiriyah traversed less cultivated and sometimes barren land for another 120 miles. Heavier military traffic and more frequent air raids slowed us down more than in the morning, leaving us crossing the broad, slow-flowing Euphrates River toward dusk. Abruptly we found ourselves in palm-tree lined marshland.

"This is the region of the Marsh Arabs I've heard about?" I asked.

"We're on the southern edge of it. The Tigris and Euphrates Rivers come together at Basrah. This is nothing compared to the swamps closer to the Iranian border. It's a completely different mode of life and a thorn in Saddam's side."

"The Sunni / Shiite thing?"

"Essentially. Saddam's ruling Ba'ath Party is Sunni, as is Saudi Arabia, but Shiites are the majority in Iraq and feel kinship with Iran, also Shiite. It's a schism throughout the Arab world, like your Protestants and Catholics, or our Stalinists and Trotskyites. In every case the doctrinal differences amount to little. Here it's not really a battle to the death over who succeeded Muhammad, but like the other schisms about who's going to be on top. Power struggles pure and simple."

Straddling the river, Nasiriyah was a full-fledged city with a modern business district and some broad boulevards. But as darkness fell the city stayed dark. "Your jets have been knocking out power plants all over Iraq," Grotesqcu observed. "Hearing it reported in the news it may seem like just one of those things, but you'd better hope it never happens to America. These people modernized recently enough that they still can struggle along at a more primitive level. If some enemy disabled 90% of the power generation where you come from, your way of life would be doomed."

We drove around town until we found a marketplace operating by kerosene lanterns and gas generators. It teemed with families whose houses no longer had power and couldn't cook. Fortunately we weren't the only well-dressed civilians there, nor were we in the only expensive car, so except for being infidels we didn't stand out too much. What with all the chaos and lawlessness about, we thought the safest procedure was for Grotesqcu to fetch the food from a food stall. I sat waiting in the car, Uzi at the ready between my legs. The locals paid us only glancing attention as we ate the kabobs and rice he'd bought. A number of Iraqi soldiers were mixed in the crowd. They looked lost, desperate, dirty and armed, and some of them took an interest in our car. We stared them down if they came too close, figuring they'd not try anything in the midst of the marketplace crowd.

"We've five or six more hours, minimum, to reach Kuwait City," said Grotesqcu. "What do you think?"

"We'd be driving in the dark, and night vision detectors can't tell that we're civilians. What say we put up here for the night and get an early start?"

"Makes sense," he concluded. "With the war on and the power out, there's no way we're going to find an operating hotel with rooms for infidels. I'll hunt up a secluded spot where we can sleep in the car. We're near the university. They're usually pretty quiet settings." He circled around the university grounds until he found a parking lot with a smattering of cars in it next to some darkened buildings. "How about this?"

"Looks as good as anywhere," I said. Night had long since

fallen, the time approaching ten p.m. He took a spot distant from other cars with clear access to the road and shut off the engine. "One sleep and one stand watch?" I suggested.

"Suits me," he said. "How about I sleep first? I've been driving all day, and in these conditions it's wearying. Wake me up in four hours?" He laid his seat back as far as it would go and soon was out. I sat there with my Uzi in my lap. As the evening progressed two cars left the lot. Another car rolled slowly through, paused nearby us, and then drove on. It didn't seem to be an official vehicle, so I paid it little attention. I nudged Grotesqcu awake at 0200 hours.

"Thanks, Jake," he said. He straightened his seat up and fished his Uzi out. I put my seat back down and dozed off.

"Up and at 'em, Jake," he said a little while later. It was still dark outside. I snapped awake and reached for my gun. "A couple men came creeping into the lot, and they're right alongside us," he whispered. I made them out in the gloom. One came over close, peered inside and banged hard on the driver's window. Grotesqcu said something in Arabic, and the man barked an answer. "He wants us to get out of the car. He's in an army uniform, but it doesn't seem to be an official bust. I think they just want to steal the car. He has an assault rifle. There's one other man, standing behind him."

Grotesqcu pushed his door open, holding his Uzi below the window and then behind his back as he swiveled out of his bucket seat. I flicked off the safety off mine and climbed out my side of the car keeping it low behind me. We had our visitor outgunned two to one, and an Uzi beats an AK-47 at close quarters, but where would a shootout in this setting lead? We'd come in during the dark and never got a good look at our surroundings. For all I knew we'd parked across the street from the town police station. The guy gave Grotesqcu a shove and held out his hand. He must have been asking for the keys, because Grotesqcu said something and pointed at the ignition switch. He elbowed Grotesqcu out of the way and took his eyes off him for a fatal moment. The Uzi came up and the soldier found a new hole in his skull. As he toppled over Grotesqcu covered the other guy before he could raise his weapon. I went over, took his rifle and threw it aside. He was thuggish-looking, in his 20s, walrus-mustached and like his buddy togged in a reekingly foul army uniform. And at the sight of what had just happened to his pal, scared shitless.

"Can't leave him here to tell the tale," Grotesqcu remarked as he put a couple slugs in the man's face. The poor bastards were just too anxious to show up back home with a trophy for their trouble. "We have to clear out of here before anyone comes to investigate," he said. "It's four a.m. and nobody's about, but the shots may have wakened somebody up." We got back in the car and he drove a distance with lights off, then turned them on and scouted around until he found another secluded spot. "Finish your nap, Jake," he said. "I'll keep an eye out."

Morning came without further incident. In daylight Nasiriyah wasn't a bad little city. It had its Middle Eastern squalor, of course, but also some green areas and nicer districts. As Iraqi towns went, decent enough. Not being heavily military, it seemed not to have taken much damage, though losing power was quite enough, thank you. We drove into the central district and found a businessman-grade restaurant where we could fit in. We got breakfast—oven-baked sweet rolls, dates and coffee—and cleaned up a little. All around us conversations buzzed and worry beads rattled. Grotesqcu listened in and told me, "It's on the radio this morning. Saddam just gave the order to withdraw from Kuwait."

"Our timing's pretty good, then," I said. "We're arriving right on schedule. They go out, and we go in."

"If only. Intact, retreating armies that have just been humiliated aren't pleasant company to be driving through."

"Say, I've been smelling burning oil since we crossed the Euphrates. Did you notice that?"

"Yes, and it's growing stronger. I'd heard that the Iraqis set fire to some of the Kuwaiti oil wells to create smoke screens against the jet attacks. I don't see how that would deter radar, but it might hinder laser beams and free-fall bombing."

We finished breakfast and after a long search found a station selling gas out of a tank truck (petrol station pumps, being electrical, didn't work) and topped up our tank. The proprietor may have gloated about how much he gouged us for fifteen gallons of gas, as long as he didn't find out that the U.S. $100 bill Grotesqcu paid him with was counterfeit. Back on the road we left the greenery of the Euphrates and found ourselves once again crossing arid desert. We made fair time down Highway 8 south of town, although northbound military traffic had picked up and we saw more evidence of jet strikes. At our intended junction with Highway 1 we hit a wall—northbound traffic was jammed and now pretty much took up both sides of the road. It was the vanguard of the evacuation, and congestion would only thicken. Highway 8 so far had less northbound traffic and southbound was relatively clear—no reinforcements headed into Kuwait now. According to the map 8 more or less paralleled 1 all the way to the Basrah connection and then continued east beyond where Highway 1 dipped south. We figured we could pick up 1 then, so stuck with 8, driving across desert from that point. The two highways veered closer together from time to time, and we could see Highway 1 traffic getting slower and heavier. American jet harassment of Highway 8 increased, but we avoided getting hit.

* * *

WE COVERED 100 MILES IN A LITTLE OVER THREE HOURS. It wasn't as bad as other drives I've taken in war-ravaged countries, for example crossing Cambodia in a beat-up VW. Compared to that we rode today in regal style. We passed by the heaving derricks of the vast Rumaila oil field. The sky grew visibly heavier with oil smoke the further southeast we drove, but it wasn't emanating from Rumaila.

We reached our intersection with Highway 1 just short of Az

Zubayr to find that no civilian traffic was allowed south on 1. We had no choice but to continue east on Highway 8. Attack jets buzzed around seeking targets as retreating traffic thickened. Past Az Zubayr, roadblocks shunted us up into Basrah, ensnarling us in a creeping traffic jam. Basrah was a huge city, Iraq's second largest, with over a million in population, and the place swirled in turmoil. It had been Saddam's military headquarters for the Kuwait invasion. Now troops and vehicles had overrun it, grateful to be out of Kuwait but desperate for coherent instructions, eager to clear out of Basrah and seeking every possible exit. We sought to find refuge in a quieter suburb where the local gentry lived and our Mercedes wouldn't seem out of place and invite a carjacking. Power was spotty in Basrah, but we still had a little daylight. We found a marketplace where we could get coffee and something to eat, and took stock of our situation.

"It'll be at a snail's pace from here on," I said.

"We've no chance at all on Highway 80," said Grotesqcu. "It's the most direct road out of Kuwait, and the bulk of the retreating army will be on it, slouching their way north. What we could try is follow 8 to a lesser road, 26, going south to Um Qasr at the border. That's Iraq's main port, in fact its only port, the terminus for Highway 1. Highway 26 will have some traffic, but probably not as bad as 1. From there the road continues south around Bubiyan Island, then connects with 801 along Kuwait Bay and into Kuwait City. There's no way we can reach Kuwait City tonight—the going's too slow. But if we can find a place to put up in Um Qasr overnight we ought to make Kuwait City by midday tomorrow."

"Well, let's try that and hope for the best," I said.

Famous last words.

TUESDAY, FEBRUARY 26, 1991

We finally reached Um Qasr later than we'd thought, and we'd thought we'd be plenty late. The going got slower, and the oil smoke grew thicker as we neared the Kuwaiti border. Um Qasr, being Iraq's only entry port, had been hit hard by the jets. Docks, loading equipment and storage buildings lay in still-smoldering ruins, and we saw collateral damage aplenty. Grotesqcu didn't even look for a market place. He parked in an open storage area with good visibility all around. An Iraqi came out of a shed on the periphery and asked our business. Grotesqcu said we'd like to park there overnight and handed him a bunch of dinars. He counted them, thanked us profusely and went away. We pissed behind a big heap of rubble, then broke out some food he'd brought along and washed it down with bottled water. We slept soundly with no disturbances.

We rose at daybreak next morning and downed some more canned stuff. With an early start we hoped to cover the ground to Kuwait City by noon, which was more time than it took Saddam's tanks to arrive. Today it was my turn at the wheel. "One problem I foresee," I said as we careered along, "is that my passport went missing at Abu Ghraib. The staff took it when I checked in, or maybe the guards ripped it off. They took off with my wristwatch too, so why not the passport? An American passport's worth its weight in gold around here."

"No problem," Grotesqcu said as he unbuttoned his shirt and reached inside. He pulled something out of a hidden interior pocket and handed it to me. It was an American passport...mine! Not exactly mine, for it had to be a forgery, but a very good one. It showed years of use and had all the proper stamps in it, plus a few more besides.

"Where'd this come from?" I asked.

"The KGB forges passports all the time; no one can beat the quality. Owing to past experience—you've been separated from your passport how many times lately?—I thought I'd bring it along just in case. I've used it several times myself, with a different photo, naturally. You'd be surprised at some of the shit you've pulled around the world in recent years. Adds to your legend, ha ha."

Our planning seemed well-founded. The Kuwait border wasn't far south of the city. The land to the east and south was mostly empty, and it hadn't figured much in the invasion. Exiting traffic didn't seem heavy, but smoke in the air was. Border control let us through based on our western passports, our elegant appearance and another of Grotesqcu's counterfeit Benjamins. Relatively few vehicles headed south on Highway 801, compared to those coming north. As we neared the Sabriyah Oil Field the oil smoke got worse. We passed it several miles to the east and could make out leaping columns of flame throwing off big black clouds. We heard a series of explosions and saw new flames and billows burst forth. The skies filled with a smudgy black blanket.

If you've ever wondered why petroleum fires spew all that black smoke, here's the thing: Petroleum is a mixture hydrocarbon molecules—hydrogen atoms attached along chains of carbon atoms. Combusting in open air, the hydrogen atoms burn off first. Burning hydrogen does not make a flame. The flames you see are glowing carbon particles before they completely combust. But it takes heat to ignite carbon, so a lot of the carbon does not burn but goes off as pure carbon—soot.

You may have recently read in "climate change" news reports about a "blanket of carbon dioxide" trapping heat with a greenhouse effect. The fact is that CO_2 amounts to only 0.03% of the atmosphere—300 CO_2 molecules interspersed throughout one million molecules of mostly nitrogen, partly oxygen. Picture one Cheerio in a box of corn flakes. Some blanket! What we witnessed as we drove along Highway 801 was a literal blanket of pure carbon, and an evil mess it was. The Iraqis were blowing up Kuwaiti oil wells on their way out, creating a genuine ecological disaster for spite.

The Merc was a pleasure to drive, and we weren't bucking so much military traffic. Compared to yesterday we made good time. The road took us southwesterly and swung us past a big military encampment in the process of frantically hauling total ass. This installation didn't show up on any maps and was a complication we couldn't have foreseen. As far as we could tell, the Iraqis had dug in and fortified the north side of Kuwait Bay to defend against the amphibious assault Uday Hussein was certain would spearhead any American invasion. Judging from the armor and artillery on the way out, had it happened that way the Iraqis would have been in the catbird seat—until the jets and the battleships zeroed in on them. Now they were salvaging what they could of a bad tactical decision and hoping to get it back to Iraq. The shortest way out was overland to Highway 80, so I imagine that vehicles operable on bare ground followed dirt tracks out. We gritted our teeth as we merged in with departing Iraqi vehicles taking the long way by highway. We tried not to bother them, and they were in too urgent a hurry to bother with us. A number of officers were exiting in liberated Kuwaiti luxe cars, so our Merc didn't look too out of place in the big parade.

Our serious troubles began when we approached the junction with Highway 80 near Jahra. Movement slowed to a crawl as Iraq-bound traffic on 801 met the mob streaming frantically out of

Kuwait City. It was clear that we would have no chance of going south on Highway 80. We inched along with the jam, discussing what to do next. Soldiers on foot clamored around the vehicles seeking rides—they faced a long walk to the border. They climbed atop tanks and squeezed into trucks that could make room for them. Many toted packs of booty, making it difficult to hitch a ride on vehicles already stuffed with looted Kuwaiti goods.

Movement ceased and we sat idling. A pair of red-bereted Republican Guards who'd been riding on an adjacent tank hopped off with their packs and walked over to us. One of them rapped on my window. He carried a submachine gun, so I thought it best to pay attention to him. I rolled down the window and he said something in Arabic. I shrugged my shoulders and pointed to Grotesqcu. The soldier went around the front of the car and spoke to Grotesqcu. They had a polite conversation, and then the two men opened the back doors of the Merc, dumped their packs on the seat and got in.

"What's going on?" I whispered.

"He asked where we were going. I told him Kuwait City. He told me, no, we're all going to Basrah. He had a submachine pointed at me. So I graciously bade them enter."

"And...?"

"Unless we come up with a better idea quick, we're going to join the crush on Highway 80 going north."

I could see in the rearview mirror that our two guests were greatly pleased. Despite being cramped by their packs they eased back on the seat, fingered the soft leather and positively sighed. It's a hard fate, after all, retreating to piss-poor Iraq after luxuriating in other people's wealth for seven months. They'd faced a hot, clanking ride on top of that tank. Our happening along was a great windfall. One of them jabbered something. Grotesqcu jabbered back, and the soldier laughed. "What was that about?" I asked.

"He said you should go faster. I told him you would as soon as

Saddam Hussein sends us a magic carpet to get us over all the cars in our way. He thought that was funny."

"Always leave 'em laughing," I said. Just like on our freeways, once the merge onto Highway 80 got smoothed out the traffic moved along steadily if slowly. It being a big military convoy with a lot of stolen cars and Kuwaiti buses thrown in, the vehicles spread out across all six lanes and maintained decent space among them. Transporting 100,000 troops and their baggage train up a highway on short notice is a massive operation, and they weren't handling it badly. It was not a moving parking lot like the Hollywood Freeway morning rush hour (and wouldn't it be something if L.A. drivers carried automatic weapons!). Any vehicle that faltered was shoved off to the side of the road and left there so as not to impede the flow. One of our passengers dug a bottle of cognac out of his pack, took a swig and passed it around. The other guy dug out some chocolate and offered us some. They meant no harm, just wanted us to drive them home... until we crossed the border and they'd shoot us and steal the car. For the time being they were enjoying their chauffeured ride with the infidels. It was embarrassing, a Ranger and a *Spetsnaz*-trained KGB agent at the mercy of a couple Iraqi grunts, but they had the drop on us.

We'd been creeping north for about two hours. We passed blazing oil wells to our left, towering flares belching writhing black soot skywards, and more explosions lit the horizon at intervals. Mutla Ridge rose up ahead. I had Grotesqcu ask our passengers if they had any water. A bottle appeared and I took a few swallows. Then the traffic ahead of us came to a stop. I braked to a halt as well. Now what? Now nothing. We sat there, and sat there, and sat there. I got out of the car for a look around. I saw a fighter jet swooping overhead, and I got back into the car.

"Emil, do you remember those kites in India, the birds?"

"Yes, what about them?"

"You remember how they'd each circle around, riding the thermals, searching for something to eat? And when one found a dead cow he'd dive down on it, and the other kites, who'd been keeping an eye on each other, would quickly converge to share in the feast?"

"Clever birds, yes. So...?"

"Our fighter jets do the same. If one finds a target-rich environment, he's soon joined by a lot of others. Have you ever been in a kill sack?"

"You mean one of those situations in which the enemy force is shunted into an easily-targeted concentration? Jake, you won't meet many people who have been in a kill sack. After all, the name implies..."

"We're in one right now." As if to put an exclamation point on it, a jet came down from behind and roared by on a strafing run. Fortunately we sat off to the far left side, because his cannons took out a couple lanes of trucks and armored personnel carriers, and he hit a tank with the rocket he fired as he pulled up. More explosions rocked the road fore and aft, jolting our passengers out of their reverie. Well-trained troops, they piled out of the car to assess the situation. A well-trained espionage operative, Grotesqcu immediately ducked down and snatched up his Uzi.

"We're dead meat if we stay here," I said. Up ahead I saw rockets flash down and then explosions erupt. From the sound delay I judged the range about 1200 yards.

"What do you suggest?"

"Wait until the next run, then I'll find a gap and take off into the desert." I wasn't the first to think of that ploy. Cars and trucks on both sides were scattering and making a run for it. Vehicles with machine guns or anti-aircraft unlimbered and their gunners scanned for incoming while their drivers dodged around corpses and flaming debris. Smoke from the oil fields gave us a little cover. The planes didn't enjoy a clear field of fire with unobstructed visibility. More jets flashed across the sky above us. The kites were converging fast.

A half mile behind us a salvo of free-fall bombs made a hell of a racket but exploded off to the side of the caravan. That was close enough for me. There was no curb or barrier along the road, so I gunned it onto what looked like a firm surface, then let it roll slower and carefully guided it away from the road. Our ex-passengers were otherwise occupied and didn't notice our departure. We got maybe 500 yards before I hit a soft spot and got stuck. "No point trying to go farther," I said. "Let's grab our gear and clear out."

"Where to?"

"Further away from the road, further away from the car. No pilot is going to target two guys sitting out on the sand with those juicy trucks and tanks lined up there all pretty like that." We'd come to a halt on the upslope of the ridge. Looking back down, the traffic jam extended for miles, and the jets were plastering it with gay abandon. We trudged another half mile with our gear and plunked down all by ourselves in the middle of nowhere. Further from the road and nearer to the oil wells, we were under thicker smoke—a little better cover, and I wanted every advantage I could get.

"I've heard so much about your air force, but I've never actually seen it in action up close like this," said Grotesqcu. "It's amazing. It's awesome. It's magnificent."

"Just goes to show what you can accomplish with air supremacy," I said.

"No wonder your military doctrine insists on it."

"Some of these are carrier jets. It helps to be able to deliver them to the battlefield."

As the flyboys chewed 'em up we heard explosions behind us further out in the desert. Beyond the horizon flashes flared through the black smoke and more black smoke joined the oily blanket. The attack lasted ten hours, well into the night, and we had nothing better to do than sit there and watch the rockets and cluster bombs take their toll. We were far enough away from the road that we couldn't hear the screams of the wounded, of which there must have been plenty.

The weather was mild, but the acrid clouds from burning oil wells kept it from being pleasant. Our food and water were good for a day or two. Coping with the aftermath of the attack preoccupied the Iraqis. They remained intent on reaching Basrah, so they didn't make any effort to track down the infidels that had hotfooted it, if they'd even noticed us leaving. We kept a low profile and at nearly a mile away from the road weren't visible to them. By two days later, the Iraqis had salvaged what they could and vacated Highway 80. We trooped back over to the road and surveyed the damage. Lots of bodies and parts thereof. Vehicles shattered, wrecked and smoldering. Looted items of all descriptions great and small—BMWs, children's dresses, TV sets, window draperies—lay strewn all over, like someone had detonated a Walmart, including the parking lot, out there in the desert. Bedouins would soon arrive to salvage what they could, and what a time they would have.

The media later dubbed it "the Turkey Shoot" or the "Highway of Death." You might think that an onslaught like that would leave nothing alive, but most men on the ground survived it. The death toll was later estimated at around 600 out of as many as 10,000 present on site. Professional sympathizers carped that we had overdone it by savaging an enemy while he was beaten and leaving the battlefield. Others more savvy pointed out that Saddam had never surrendered, which would have given his troops some Geneva rights, and there was nothing in military ethics against attacking an enemy in retreat. I'm sure no Kuwaiti shed one single tear for any of them.

Eventually an American Marine unit rolled in, and I hailed them. A sergeant came over and asked us to identify ourselves. "I'm Jake Fonko from Malibu, California," I said as I handed him my fake passport. "I was a consultant to the Kuwaiti government. The Iraqis captured the two of us when they invaded the city. They were taking us back to Baghdad as hostages. We got away when the air attack started. Man, am I glad to see you guys."

"I've heard of Malibu, great place. Bay Watch, Pamela Anderson, right? I'm from North Carolina, myself. We have some good beaches too. And some pretty fine young ladies. You guys are okay now. We'll get you back to Kuwait City ASAP. Some of our vehicles will be heading down there soon. You have some ID, sir?" he asked Grotesqcu.

"Yes sir," he answered with a flat Midwestern accent. "Got it right here." He unbuttoned his shirt, reached inside to his hidden pocket and came out with an American passport. He handed it over, saying, "I'm Earl Groton from Des Moines, Iowa. I work with Jake."

THEREAFTER

The Marines carted us to their base, where the formalities of being captured on a battlefield delayed our return to Kuwait City. My Ranger history smoothed the process and saved a little time. Grotesqcu and I cleaned up, and I got rid of my beard. We knocked back some sorely missed beers and lounged around between interrogations and examinations for a couple days.

When we finally rode into the city what I saw sickened me. The Iraqis had done a fair amount of damage by the time they'd nabbed me, but during the ensuing six months they'd trashed the city to the point of desecration. Every monument, every public building, every indicator of Kuwaiti culture and the Al Sabah family had been obliterated. They'd stripped shops, businesses, office buildings, hospitals and private residences bare to the walls of everything moveable and stolen it clean away. How, I wondered, would Kuwait ever recover from this?

In a heap of rubble like that, billeting was doubtful. Our Marine driver had heard that the Iraqi brass had stayed in the Hilton Hotel so it, along with a couple luxe hotels in the city center, had been spared major damage. Being the only home I'd ever known here I had him take us there. With Kuwaitis now returning to restart the government and setting about salvaging what they could I figured the Hilton would be jammed, but I hoped that for old times' sake they could find space in a corner for us. Departing Iraqis had done a little mischief to the entrance and the facade but the lobby seemed not too much worse for wear.

The manager from before was busy behind the marble reception counter. When he noticed us approaching he broke out a big smile. "Mr. Fonko!" he exclaimed. "How good to see you again. We were very concerned about your disappearance and wondered what had happened to you."

"It's a long story, but I spent a little time in Baghdad."

"How ghastly! But now you're back and praise Allah for that. You'll find your rooms in order. Having not checked out we thought it best to keep them ready for your return."

"You held that suite for me all these months?"

"Yes sir. Actually it was not registered in your name. The Al Sabah family engaged the room, and since they gave us no further instructions we thought it best to keep it available for you. It is not unusual, sir. A number of Kuwaitis have rooms here that they maintain perpetually in case a need for, er, privacy arises unexpectedly. I'll have a porter show you to your rooms."

Thus after all the chaos, destruction and woe, Emil Grotesqcu and I landed in a suite in the Hilton Hotel. Everything worked—hot water, phone service and all. He racked out on the sofa bed for a couple days, then said to me, "Jake, old friend, it's been an interesting adventure, as always, but now that your threat to Russia's interests has been neutralized I must move on. The airport is working again and my agency has arranged a flight out for me."

"Thanks for your help, Emil," I said. "I'd have been in big trouble in Baghdad if you hadn't showed up."

"You in trouble? What about *me*? I was just protecting my investment. I shudder to think where I'd be if the redoubtable Jake Fonko weren't causing the KGB headaches all over the world. My immediate task will be to conjure up a yarn about your role in thwarting Saddam Hussein and putting a spanner in Russia's plans.

You've given me plenty of material, and I'm sure I can come up with a good one. Rest assured nobody is going to knock you off the top of the KGB's Most Wanted list. I'll enjoy this ride we're on as long as it lasts, but I'm very concerned about the course of events. Your President Reagan viewed the Cold War not as a matter of containment but as 'We win. You lose.' He was right, and we've lost. That being the case, my career is up in the air. But we shall see. Russia will always need spies and secret police."

We shook hands. "Take care of yourself, Emil," I said.

"You too, Jake Fonko." He left and I was sorry to part company. I didn't have many better friends in the world. If he was a friend. Or was it, as he kept insisting, simply a matter of keeping his cushy job with the Russian KGB going? With Grotesqcu I could never be sure of anything. What the heck—with enemies like that, who needs friends?

I spent the next several days working on a flight out of Kuwait but it wasn't easy, especially with the U.S. Embassy still inoperative. One afternoon I sat reading a newspaper over a coffee in the restaurant when someone said my name. I looked up into the face of Fawaz Al Sabah. "Mr. Fawaz," I said, standing to greet him. "You're back home now?"

"Yes, we all returned as soon as possible, but my home is, alas, not as it used to be. So much to do and where does one begin? You're looking well, and that pleases me. When you and Mamoon Al Bahar didn't show up in Saudi Arabia as expected we all naturally were deeply concerned. Later his corpse was found in the wreckage of his car and we deduced the rest. I'm sure you have a long story to tell and I look forward to hearing it in total. But I have an interesting story myself that you should hear immediately. It seems that one of our resistance groups captured an Iraqi officer of some influence. They of course sought to find out what they could about Iraqi defense positions around Kuwait so they could relay it to the Americans. Before he expired he told our interrogators that Saddam had gotten the American battle plan from you, something about 'grasp them by the nose and kick them from behind.' So the Iraqis were heavily fortifying the approaches to the harbor and the border between Kuwait and Saudi Arabia. What a masterpiece of misdirection you pulled on them. You led them to a totally wasted effort and a state of unpreparedness. Not having any planes in the air, the Iraqis had no idea that the U.S. Army deployed 50 miles to the west along the Iraq border. When the war began, cavalry, airborne assault, mechanized infantry and armored units made massive, unhindered sweeps north into Iraq reaching as far as the Euphrates River. Then they pivoted east and swept across Iraq into Kuwait.

"Meanwhile, Saudi and Pan-Arab task forces, supported by U.S. Marine units, bulldozed their way through Iraqi barriers and entrenchments along the coast and to the west—it was thought best that Arab troops should be the ones to liberate Kuwait City itself. Rather than mounting a to-the-death defense, Iraqi soldiers surrendered en masse as soon as they saw American armored bulldozers approaching their trenches. The few that didn't jump out and wave white flags were buried alive.

"So you see, even as a captive of Saddam Hussein, you helped Kuwait. You completely misled them and disrupted their planning. We all know how the Iraqis treat prisoners. How did you withstand the torture?"

"With a little help from my friends," I said.

"As modest as ever, Mr. Fonko! I won't even ask about the aid you rendered to my cousin Salah Melik and his resistance unit. He's already told me the whole story. In any event, when I heard you had returned to the Hilton Hotel I hastened over to greet and thank you. In case you had concerns I also wish to reassure you that the remainder of your fee has been deposited in your account, and I hope you don't mind that I added a little more in appreciation of services later rendered."

"I don't mind at all," I said. "Thank you very much."

"Think nothing of it. After such a long absence you must be anxious to return home. The airport is now operational and

Kuwait Airline flights are resuming. How soon do you want to leave?"

"Tomorrow?"

"Consider it done. I'll put you on a flight to Paris. My secretary will send you the ticket and the details. There's plenty of time to take care of that. I'd like to hear your story now." He summoned a waiter and ordered two coffees. I put my brain in high gear, arranging events so as not to mention Emil Grotesqcu's role. The yarn I spun for Fawaz had a distant relationship to reality and made me out as more heroic than I was. That's been the essence of Jake Fonko's legend all along.

* * *

MY FORGED PASSPORT, BEING A FAITHFUL DUPLICATE OF MY REAL one, got me by, and I flew out of Kuwait City the next afternoon. I changed planes in Paris and headed directly to Los Angeles. So concluded my Kuwaiti consulting gig, eight months after it commenced. The finale to the saga happened in a relative eyeblink. The "One-Hundred-Hour War"—or as Saddam proclaimed it, "The Mother of All Battles"—lasted from February 24 to 28. The preparatory air bombardment of course shortened the decisive engagement considerably. By the time U.S. ground forces moved across the Iraq border under the command of General "Stormin' Norman" Schwarzkopf, the Iraqi Air Force was out of the picture and their army already was blooded, reeling and staggering.

Some perspectives:

Iraq losses in that war have never been accurately tallied. Estimates ranged from 22,000 deaths to several hundred thousand. American losses totaled 376 throughout the entire campaign, including accidents.

In the largest tank engagement since the Nazis and the Russians had at it in the World War II Battle at Kursk, U.S. and British forces engaged the Republican Guards' armor. The Iraqis lost more than 200 tanks, the Americans none. Part of the difference was in their cannons. U.S. tanks had longer range, so they retreated beyond where Iraqi guns could reach them, then knocked them off at will. Having attack helicopters, fighter jets and laser-guided anti-tank rockets didn't hurt our cause either.

According to our Environmental Protection Agency, Iraqi forces, beginning on January 16, blew up more than 700 oil wells, refineries and storage tanks. At its peak this incinerated six million barrels of petroleum per day as well as dirtying the desert skies with vast clouds of noxious black soot reaching as far away as India (and let's not forget all that nasty CO_2!). Red Adair, Safety Boss and other American oil well fire experts were brought in. Experts estimated two to five years to complete the job. In fact, thanks to good old American know-how all fires were out by November, 1991, most of them extinguished with sea water channeled through repurposed oil pipelines.

The cost to **Kuwait** was immense, of course. Iraqis killed more than 1,000 Kuwaiti civilians and another 600 or so went missing. Their country was wrecked—buildings, infrastructure, power and desalination plants, you name it. However, it is amazing what a country of fewer than a million citizens with $100,000,000,000 stashed in overseas banks and investments can accomplish. By the time I told the story to Professor Pflingger, Kuwait City was rebuilt, bustling and basking in prosperity once again. With one caveat—desert treks are discouraged owing to the landmines the Iraqis spread around and never disclosed. Because of the collaboration of Palestinians with the Iraqis, in the aftermath Kuwait threw most of them out, leaving perhaps one tenth as many as before the war. Their places were filled by workers from other countries as well as by native Kuwaitis who appreciated having something worthwhile to do with themselves.

Saddam Hussein's defeat did not change his ways, despite Iraq's shattered infrastructure and decimated military force. The United Nations imposed myriad sanctions on post-war Iraq, which Saddam ignored and violated from the start. His troops fired missiles at American planes patrolling the no-fly zone. He embezzled the funds from petroleum sales meant to relieve the suffering of his people and spent them instead on arms and palaces. President Bush, thinking to take advantage of Saddam's weakness, encouraged the Kurds and the Swamp Arabs to rise up against him. Too bad for them that the U.S. didn't back up their nudging with sufficient arms and support. The Iraqi army no longer had the capability to invade its neighbors, but they had no trouble crushing the two rebellions. To underscore the point Saddam dug canals that drained the coastal swamps to a fraction of their previous area. This, plus the oil field fires and the oil spill he released, qualified Saddam Hussein as one of history's greatest environmental criminals, among other dubious titles. Funny how little support the Sierra Club and the Friends of the Earth gave to this and the next war against Saddam. And where were their Baghdad protests and lawsuits? Hello?

Thirteen years later the U.S. fought another war with Saddam Hussein. Like in the first Gulf War President Bush (W., that is) dispatched his army quickly and efficiently. Son Uday was killed in a Mosul shootout. American troops pulled Saddam out of the spider hole where he had been hiding. He was tried, convicted and hanged for war crimes by the Iraqi government several years later.

Some critics faulted **George H. W. Bush** for not going all the way to Baghdad and deposing Saddam Hussein. But Bush played it by the book all the way, and the U.N. authorized his coalition only to remove the Iraqis from Kuwait. This our side did, delivering the first clear-cut American military win in nearly 50 years more efficiently and humanely than any other modern war. Unfortunately his 90% approval rating did not last long enough to win him re-election. A mild economic recession gave the Democrats a campaign issue, and they pounded away with "It's the economy, stupid." H. Ross Perot entered the race and split the vote, enabling Bill Clinton to win with 43% of the popular vote. Clinton won again four years later with less than 50% of the vote. To this day, despite his impeachment and disbarment, his sexual predations (with the abetment of wife Hillary) and a record of unaddressed allegations of corruption, the media tout him as a "popular president."

Abu Ghraib prison came into the spotlight in the aftermath of the Second Gulf War. Photos of "atrocities" showed American guards humiliating Iraqi prisoners of war. Intended to embarrass and blunt the popularity (90% approval) of President George W. Bush, who had just won two of the quickest and cleanest victories in U.S. military history, Democrat-sympathetic news outlets spread Abu Ghraib photos long, far and wide. From what I saw there, Saddam's prisoners would have paid good money to wear dog collars and pose for silly pictures in place of what his jailers inflicted on them.

The **American public** was treated to a cartoonish war. Smart bomb through the window—KA-BOOM! Tomahawks launched from a missile cruiser—FLASH! WHOOSH! Oh oh, Scud! Yea, Patriot! ZISS! BOOM! AHHHH! Tanks across the desert. LOOK AT 'EM GO! This was in part because of the military's media relations policies. The American commanders in Iraq had been junior officers in Vietnam, where they learned to view the media as the enemy. They weren't about to let THAT happen to them again. For Desert Storm they grouped the media people into pools and herded them to what the military wanted them to see.

But war coverage has always been sanitized. Warfare has been described as endless boredom punctuated by moments of sheer terror. The media will not air boredom, and the terror part is frightening: It hurts, is deafeningly loud, smells bad and leaves blood and body parts strewn all over everywhere. Showing those realities on TV would be obscene. We've never been allowed to see the people jumping off the World Trade Center on 9/11. Trust our media to tell us the stories that are best for us to hear and smother the ones that aren't.

When **our troops** arrived home from Desert Storm they were cheered, welcomed and praised, unlike after Vietnam. They won their war and good for them. They earned the praise they got. But the main difference between now and Nam was that it was an all-volunteer army this time, with no crowds of draft-shy college boys and their girlfriends doing everything possible to spare themselves that fate, even to the point of abusing and spitting at our men and women serving their country in uniform.

* * *

I'D TALKED TO DANA WEHRLI ON THE PHONE, LETTING HER know I was all right and would be coming home soon. When I learned my flight schedule from Fawaz I called her again and arranged for her to pick me up at LAX. The hell with R and R in Paris, I wanted to get back to Malibu! Thanks to First Class the entire route I arrived well rested and reasonably presentable. Dana was waiting as I came out of customs, blonde, tanned and glowing as usual, and she planted eight months' worth of missed kisses on me right then and there. She saw my two suitcases and looked dismayed. "What's the trouble?" I asked.

"I don't think they'll fit in my new car," she said. "It's kind of little."

We thought about it and hit upon the idea of having a cabbie drive them up to Malibu and leave them at my house. I got some cash at an ATM and paid the cabbie in advance, and he took off. Dana led me to short-term parking. "See?" she said. "We might have gotten one of them in the trunk, but not both." It was a red Alfa Romeo Spider, the same model Dustin Hoffman drove down 101 in *The Graduate*.

"Don't sweat it," I said. "Let's get home."

"That's another thing I need to tell you about," she said as we climbed in. "There are some things a little different now."

"There's a problem with my house?" "No, no, your house is fine, just great, don't worry about that." She started the car, pulled out and went to the exit. Out on the road, she continued. "I better start at the beginning. It's because I quit ABC and got this new job. It's with a production company, 'Roadkill Films.' It's named that because we travel all over and shoot location footage for the studios. They started me out on backdrops, establishing shots, backscreen projections, scenery and so forth. Like when people are driving in a car, and you see the road from through the rear window behind them? Or on a train, and you see passing scenery through the window? We shoot the stuff you see out the window. We do it for less money than the studio could."

We were out on the road by then. It was a snappy little car and she drove it with verve. "Sounds like interesting work."

"Oh it really is. I've already produced footage for *Boyz N the Hood* and *Thelma and Louise*. Boy, the southwest—that's some place! The Grand Canyon, you know? But the best part is, I'm learning about the film industry. At ABC all I did was shoot news stories. I'd scramble to get them wrapped, and then somebody would edit them to fit the story the executives wanted to tell, cut them to size and they'd go on the air. And then I'd do it again, and again, and again. Now I'm getting into film editing and sound mixing and process shots and everything. I never realized! I should have quit ABC years ago. I thought I was a producer because I could get projects done, but I knew next to nothing about the technical side."

She went on and on about her job. During a pause I remarked that the job must pay well, considering the car she drove. "Oh, it pays okay," she said, "but what happened was that my father died while you were away and he left me something in his will."

"I'm sorry to hear that," I said. "He was a good man, and I know how much you loved him."

"Yes, it was sad. But dying of cancer, it's awful... by the end it was a relief to everyone, especially him."

"So what's different about my house?" I asked. We were breezing up Pacific Coast Highway now. Unfortunately it was an overcast day in March so we couldn't bask in the full sunbathed California convertible experience.

"I was coming to that. For the ABC Job I had to live out near Burbank, but Roadkill is in West Hollywood, which is much nearer to Malibu. After a few days I realized that commuting from Burbank to Hollywood would be a grind I didn't need. So I looked around for a place where I could live closer to work. I have a lot of friends around Hollywood, of course, but it seemed like it would be lonely moving into a new apartment just like that. I looked at a few and checked out some condos but I didn't have a lot of time for house hunting and I needed to do something about the situation soon, so I moved out of my apartment and sort of, well, you know, like moved into your house? Only temporarily! I mean just until I can find a suitable place of my own. When your friend I talked to on the phone said you wanted me to take care of your house I flashed that I could take better care of it if I was living right there in it... so I sort of temporarily moved in. I felt alone after Dad's passing and being there in a familiar place with your things and so forth, well, it was comforting, like your spirit was there with me."

"I'm always happy to help out a girlfriend in distress," I said. "So, what's different about it?"

"We're almost there. Maybe it's better if I show you." A couple more miles to the intersection, then along Malibu Road and Dana turned into my driveway. My banged-up Cherokee sat on the apron out of the way. She poked a button on the sun visor and the garage door rolled up. "Hey, when did that happen?" I said.

"I thought I should protect my paint job in your garage and this made getting in so much more convenient, so I had it put in as a sort of homecoming present for you," she said.

We got out and went into the laundry room through the garage entrance. It seemed more cluttered than I remembered. Upstairs I found my kitchen chairs and tables were in new places. "You moved my furniture?"

"Only a little, so things wouldn't be in the way. Just a sec." She went to the fridge and came back with an open bottle of Dos Equis. "I know you like these, so I put a case of them in the fridge," she said, handing it to me.

"You've got that right," I said. She sure did. "What else did you do?"

"I had to rearrange the closets a little to hold my things. I hope that's all right."

We went into my bedroom. Her oversized chest of drawers was crowded into the corner along the wall. She'd scooched the bed over to make room for it. Another nightstand sat on the opposite side of the bed from mine, topped with a digital clock-radio and assorted bedroom items. I slid open the wardrobe to find it stuffed with dresses, blouses, skirts, coats, jackets, slacks and the rest. "Where's *my* stuff?" I asked.

"Your everyday clothes I put in the closet. I moved your outdoors things to the closet in the other room. It wasn't full, so I fitted most of it in there."

I checked the bedroom closet. It was less than half the size of the wardrobe and held my suits, shirts, slacks and jackets only under duress. I dreaded to see what she'd done to my bathroom so put off that part of the inspection.

I went to check out the second bedroom, my office/den. I'd stowed guns, athletic gear, guy odds and ends in that closet. The gear was still there but all my outdoors and sports clothes were draped over and around it. A couple chairs and her dining room table filled out the space. Her typewriter and some papers and pens and stuff sat neatly on it. "I needed a place to do my work," she said apologetically. I examined it more closely. She'd been laying out shooting schedules. She hadn't disturbed the mess I'd left on my desk and filing cabinet.

I must have looked pained, because she sheepishly said, "Jake, if you don't like it, I can fix it back like it was."

"Anything else?" I asked.

"No, that's about it. While you were gone I tidied the place up but I didn't throw anything out." I looked around. Except for my work area the house was neat as a Green Beret barracks. We went to the living room. The view of the Pacific Ocean out the picture window was as fine as ever. She'd fitted her bookcase and books in an empty slot against a wall. It wasn't in the way and actually added a little class to the room. I had to admit she had good taste in furniture.

"Where's the rest of your stuff?" I asked. "Downstairs in the rec room?"

"In storage. I didn't want to crowd your place up—I really like the way you have it—but I needed a few things here." She steered me to the dining room. "I paid your bills and kept track of everything while you were gone. I threw away all the junk mail, and the rest of your mail's stacked on the dining room table. There's one item I'm curious about. A messenger delivered it a few days ago. I signed for it. This one here."

She picked an envelope off the top of a pile. It was a parchment-like material, stamped with a Kuwaiti official seal. Ripping it open would have been trouble so I went into the kitchen (totally shipshape), got a paring knife (some new utensils in the drawer) and slit it open. I fished out a folded note and a check for $60,000 drawn on a Saudi Arabian bank. The note, handwritten, read: "Dear Mr. Jake. Here is your share of the reward for the incident at the police station. With gratitude and thanks, Salah Melik Al Sabah."

That got me curious. "Dana, did a bank statement come recently?"

"They're all in that pile on the right. The last one came two days ago."

I grabbed it and slit the envelope. I opened the statement to the deposits column. There was only one, a wire deposit a week ago. Whoa! I checked the account balance. Holy shit!

"Jake, you look surprised," Dana said.

"I just came home to find out I have more money than I know what to do with."

"Wow!" she said delightedly. "My toast came true! Do you remember? I said, Here's to having more money than you know what to do with. May it be our fate."

"Fate! Kismet! You better be careful about your toasts in the future. You have amazing powers."

"Jake, I didn't know if you'd arrive home hungry, but I got some steaks and things and a bottle of champagne to celebrate. I put charcoal in the grill and that's ready to go. And I got something else for you. Come see." We went back to the bedroom, and she turned the spread on the king size. "The sheets you had were kind of worn and ratty so I got these and put them on. They're 800 thread count." They had an exotic floral pattern. The Garden of Eden popped into my mind: Adam and Eve dwelt in a similar tropical lushness, no doubt. After eight Eve-less months I felt Adam-like stirrings down below. I reached out and ran my fingers over the surface. We'd need belaying lines to keep from sliding off onto the floor, but I was game. "I hope it's okay," she was saying, "my moving in and changing things around? If you want it's just temporary until I find a place of my own. I'm fine with that, really. You don't mind, do you?"

I put my hands around that firm, slender waist. I sat her down on the bed, then toppled her over and lay down beside her. "Whirlybird, I don't mind it in the least." I heard the taxicab pull up in the driveway and the car door open. The way Dana drove her Alfa I'm not surprised we beat him here. He rang the door bell. We ignored it. I'd told him to leave the luggage on the steps if we didn't answer. After a moment he pulled out and drove away. The bags could wait.

* * *

Somewhat later I went down and got my stuff. I stowed it in the bedroom, then went out to fire up the grill. Dana prepped some garlic bread and threw together a Caesar salad. The weather was a little brisk but not enough to keep us off the deck. Amid the aroma of thick, marbled steaks approaching sizzling perfection we stood at the railing, barefooted in our bathrobes, listening to the surf crash in the darkness down below, exchanging pecks, nuzzles and squeezes between sips of welcome-home champagne. Her silky welcome-home sheets hadn't pitched us off the bed, and I felt confident we'd survive the return bout just fine—starting the minute we finished our dinner. Inspection revealed that she hadn't disarranged my bathroom too drastically. The shower was still plenty big enough for two.

THE END

Because reviews are critical in spreading the word about the Jake Fonko series, **please leave a brief review on Amazon** if you enjoyed *The Jake Fonko Series: Books 4, 5 & 6*.

EDITOR'S AFTERWORD

Much to my great relief, I did not have to preface *The Mother of All Fonkos* with a "trigger warning." I greatly resented the notion that these books contain anything to offend any reader's sensibilities—after all, they only repeat the truth, which we know shall make us free. Ms. Mellowdee Coxbaum, Assistant Associate Dean in the Office of Student Succor and Solace, had stipulated that I include one, and I hated doing it. But then her wife took an administrative position at the University of California, Lompoc, and Dean Coxbaum was promised a post in the Womyn's Studies Institute as well, and away she went. Our university has not yet filled her vacated slot, and no one else in that office has ever paid attention to me, so we are home free. For the time being.

Concurrently with the final editing of *The Mother of All Fonkos*, I came across a recently published work on the Iraq invasion of Kuwait, *The Lid is Lifted*. The author, Paul D. Kennedy, is an Irishman who at the time of the invasion worked as a financial consultant in Kuwait City. This book, the first of a trilogy, recounts his experiences during the first several weeks of the invasion, and subsequent books will recount his entire adventure. He was located in the heart of the city and he enjoyed wide and deep connections with the expatriate community there. Thus his book is ripe with detail and insight. Jake Fonko's experiences differed widely from Mr. Kennedy's, of course, but where I noted similarities or coincidences I was gratified to find that their respective accounts were rarely in disagreement. As both are true and factual accounts, this is only to be expected.

The campus here at California State University, Cucamonga, has been in a state of chaos lately, and these unfortunate distractions impeded the release of the present book, which should have come out months ago. It is regrettable that the pursuit of scholarship and the quest for learning should be derailed by trivial matters but such is the unfortunate state of academe in our troubled age.

The root of the disturbances lay in the traditional mascot of our athletic teams—"The Fighting Chumash." The Chumash are a Native American Tribe indigenous to Southern California, and if Stanford University could have "Indians" why should not we have Indians also, was the thinking at the time. It fostered some rousing school anthems and stadium cheers, for example, "Cucamonga, Cucamonga, Ziss Boom Bah! / Mash 'em! Mash 'em! Rah Rah Rah!"

However, colleagues in the sociology department took it upon themselves to conduct a study to measure community sensitivities regarding our mascot. They visited the Chumash Casino in Santa Ynez and conducted a series of scientific interviews. Of the dozen actual Chumash they found there, 25% declined to answer, and 42% had never heard of the "Fighting Chumash" and couldn't care less. Seventeen percent had heard of them but couldn't care less. One respondent said he was flattered that anyone would ascribe war-like qualities to the Chumash, whom anthropologists tell us mostly were a blissed-out and laid-back tribe that lived along the beach and may have developed a rudimentary version of the bodyboard. Another respondent told the interviewer she was offended, but inasmuch as she was a blackjack dealer and he badgered her while she was on duty, said offense may have had no relation to the mascot situation. Nevertheless, the student newspaper headlined the story, "STUDY

FINDS MASCOT OFFENDS NATIVE AMERICAN NATION."

The school administration immediately set about expunging all mentions of Chumash or any other Native Americans on campus or in any of its publications or statements. A committee was formed to find a replacement mascot. After months of extensive search the committee proposed "The Potato Bugs." This insect, indigenous to Southern California, is a nasty little creature, certainly as suitable for a mascot as, say, tarantulas. The thinking was that if Stanford University (which had years ago dropped "Indians") could have a tree and U Cal Irvine could have an anteater, why not a potato bug?

All well and good, but then some malcontent found out that potato bugs also were known as "Jerusalem crickets" and wrote a letter to the editor. Well! You can imagine the protests and counter-protests, and the demonstrations and counter-demonstrations, that provoked. Rival factions have been raging for weeks with no end in sight, rendering getting any work done on campus a near impossibility.

One of my students approached me a few days ago with an unsettling news clipping. It was headlined "Nation's Historians Warn the Past Is Expanding at Alarming Rate." It showed how, just in the last century, the amount of the past had increased by a full 100 years. I'd never thought of it before, but it is true. And it shows no signs of abating. The next century may well expand the past by a like amount. I alerted my colleagues to this development, but they shrugged it off. My search of the history literature turned up nothing on this topic and a Google search located only one source, something called *The Onion*. On the one hand, having more past will create jobs for historians (and I could use a change of scene!). On the other, might we already have enough of the past to deal with for the time being?

I will pursue the matter further, but I feel heartened that my lectures have inspired at least one student to take a serious interest in historical scholarship. I noticed that when he returned to his group they were all giggling, no doubt out of embarrassment that one of their friends so diligently applied himself to his studies in a campus atmosphere that generally seems devoted to partying and frivolity. I think I shall award him an A+ in "Postmodern History 252", just to encourage further serious efforts.

B. Hesse Pflingger, PhD
Professor of Contemporary History
California State University, Cucamonga

FROM THE PUBLISHER

It has come to our attention that considerable controversy has arisen concerning the origins, accuracy and veracity of the (thus far) six books recounting the life and career of Jake Fonko. While we could present a positive case in our own favor on these matters, doubters could dismiss such an effort as being self-serving. And rightly so. Judgments must always be based on fair, balanced and neutral analysis. Therefore, we are fortunate to have found a definitive exegesis on the matter, recently penned by an eminent scholar in the field. We have appended it to this book with the permission of the author. It will, we hope, settle all questions that have arisen regarding this excellent series of books.

Dorwin Huxtable
Senior Editor in Chief

THE FONKO CONUNDRUM DECONSTRUCTED

By: Aethelstan Proudhoum, AB, MA, MFA (ABD)
Literary Critic
The Phlogiston Review

The recent release of a series of "history books"—purported to be "true and factual accounts"—concerning the involvement of a putative espionage agent, "Jake Fonko", in certain major world events has ignited considerable controversy throughout scholarly circles. "Are these stories genuinely true and factual?" many ask. Do they reveal history faithfully and accurately as claimed? Or do they constitute an elaborate, diabolically clever hoax at the expense of the scholarly community? Are they, in a word, some kind of "send-up" or "spoof", a snare set to entrap the intellectually gullible?

I pose these questions not lightly, for *au fond* they challenge the very integrity and foundations of the historians' purview. Can the past truly be unraveled and revealed? And if so via what voices and vehicles? The Fonko books constitute an assault threatening the foundations of historical knowledge, and I will endeavor to address and answer that assault with all the depth and diligence at my command.

Numerous aspects of this "historical" compendium raise troubling doubts. To begin with, it is by no means clear that the author, "B. Hesse Pflingger, PhD", actually exists. My exhaustive search unearthed no one else, anywhere in the world, with the surname, "Pflingger". Mr. "Pflingger" claims to be a "professor of contemporary history." *There is no such thing*! The concept is an oxymoron, an absurdity! He purports to seek tenure after holding his faculty position for nearly 20 years, during which he published absolutely nothing but the Fonko books. Preposterous! It is invariably the rule that by his or her seventh year a tenure-track professor faces an up or out decision, and with a curriculum vitae boasting zero publications in *bona fide* scholarly journals the candidate would be most definitely cast OUT.

"B. Hesse Pflingger" possibly serves as a *nom de plume*, and if so it is by no means either unique or original. One is reminded of one's sophomore year at Oberlin College, when classmates dubbed a particularly obscure and pedantic lecturer "B. S. Flinger", a joke name that, I am sure, has occurred to sophomores in many different places, times and contexts (c.f., B. F. Skinner). The more one considers the matter, the more one's conviction solidifies that it must be a *nom de plume*... but if so, why that particular one?

"Professor Pflingger" claims employment at "California State University, Cucamonga". Rancho Cucamonga is a prosperous Southern California community, blessed with the presence of several institutions of higher learning including: Chaffey College, University of La Verne, Cambridge College, University of Redlands, Everest College, and University of Phoenix. However, there is not, nor has there ever been, any campus of the California State University system located anywhere in that vicinity. So why was "Cucamonga" chosen as his affiliation? Other than being a running joke on the venerable Jack Benny Radio Program ("All aboard for for Anaheim, Azusa and Cuc... amonga!") and in Looney

Tunes cartoons, the town of Cucamonga has hitherto received scant notice or attention from the world at large.

On the other hand, "Professor Pflingger's" recountings of campus events, issues and policies in his "Editor's Afterwords" ring authentic and plausible. For example, only someone thoroughly immersed in contemporary campus life could so graphically describe his altercation with an Assistant Associate Dean in the Office of Student Succor and Solace. Or compose as comprehensive a "trigger warning" as the one preceding *Fonko Bolo*. Apparently he is intimately familiar with the current academic milieu, but then why would he claim a fictitious affiliation at a non-existent university?

The protagonist, "Jake Fonko", is introduced at the outset as a man of retirement age straightforwardly proffering a memoir, a chronicle of his adventures and exploits since 1975. An exhaustive search yielded no other people of the surname, "Fonko". He claims that an Ellis Island clerk bestowed that name on his great-grandfather, an immigrant arriving from Serbia, but even so, by this late date (more than a century after that event) other "Fonkos" must surely exist somewhere in the world, as he does allude to extant relatives. My inquiry as to his status at UCLA (from which he claims to have been expelled during his sophomore year) yielded no information—for reasons of student privacy, their registrar informed me. I could find no record of homeownership in Malibu, California, where he claims to reside in a beachside bachelor pad. Queries to the Central Intelligence Agency, with which he alleges a longstanding history, were politely deflected.

Mr. Fonko's exploits recounted in these volumes seem reasonably in correspondence with reality. If he was indeed a decorated Ranger (Distinguished Service Cross) and college athlete (tailback, freshman football), then his actions throughout the stories seem acceptably believable. Yet one aspect raises a red flag, as it were. If, as he claims, his family lived in a mansion in Pacific Palisades, California, and he attended a well-regarded second-tier university such as UCLA, how likely is his claim that he participated in combat in Vietnam as a Ranger in Long Range Reconnaissance Patrols? It is widely known that such assignments are given exclusively to "rednecks", "hillbillies" and minorities, not scions of the upper middle class. Answers to requests for clarifying information from the United States Army have yet to emerge from that bureaucratic morass.

One point stands in favor of his veracity: Skillful and resourceful he may be, and admittedly lucky on occasion, but his successes do not rely on superhuman expertise, strength, prescience, split-second timing or coincidental happenstance. At the least, the actions he reports in these books do not undermine his credibility, and certain quotidian chores—he counts his money, he goes to the bathroom—serve to bolster it. Nor do his accounts rely, as "thriller" fiction so tiresomely does, on preternaturally evil, relentless and implacable villains (more often than not, psychopathic serial killers). Mr. Fonko's adversaries and antagonists consistently are drawn from the domain of reality. Indeed, they invariably are well-known public figures.

Compounding the mystery, these books employ a first-person narrative style and therefore are entirely self-referential. "Mr. Fonko" speaks for himself, with no alternative perspectives available. "Professor Pflingger" proclaims himself the editor of this lengthy memoir and assures the reader of meticulous vetting, cross-checking and fact verification. Yet a diligent search for citations or other evidence of any scholarly effort on the part of "Professor Pflingger" yielded only a smattering of mentions of proof of "Mr. Fonko's" accuracy based on lack of evidence to the contrary.

Most disturbingly, "scholarly" though these "historical accounts" purport to be, it appears *they were not peer reviewed*.

In sum, we face the distinct possibility that we are confronted by "true and factual accounts" of the adventures of a man who does not exist, transcribed by an editor who does not exist. In other words, these books may be nothing more than pure fabrication. However, it also is possible that "the names have been changed to protect the innocent", a not uncommon literary disclaimer. I note the many instances where Mr. Fonko takes pains to label people he encounters with obviously false names "to spare them trouble or embarrassment." Perhaps this was done throughout every aspect of the work, for if the material reported therein is in fact the unvarnished truth, these tales suggest serious implications for national security. And perhaps for matters of "Mr. Fonko's" personal safety?

Thus, while a case, convincing to some, can be built that both the author, the subject and the substance of these books may be purely fictional creations, that assertion must for the time being be held in abeyance as "not proved."

Broaching the subject matter of the series conveys one into similarly shoal scholarly waters. On the one hand, Mr. Fonko claims to have played key roles in some of the major debacles of the later 20th Century: The collapse of Cambodia, the fall of Shah Pahlavi, John Delorean's failed venture, the Grenada invasion, the Amritsar Massacre, the deposing of Ferdinand Marcos and Operation Desert Storm, among others. That one man, acting as a "free lance whatever" (his description of his profession) but otherwise unlettered, unqualified and undistinguished, could find himself embroiled in such a wide spectrum of critical international events strains this reader's credulity, to say the least. On the other hand, where the history of these situations is publicly available, the books seem plausibly accurate. Mr. Fonko *could have been there*, but the reader must decide for him or her self whether or not to take as truth Mr. Fonko's reportage of behind the scenes occurrences. Maybe he saved Margaret Thatcher's life, but maybe not. Maybe he helped Corazon Aquino steal an election from Ferdinand Marcos, but maybe not. Maybe he saved the ruling family of Kuwait and outwitted Saddam Hussein, but maybe not. Maybe he arranged for the Shah's medical treatment in the United States, but maybe not. The purported outcomes of Mr. Fonko's adventures are public knowledge. The onus is on the reader whether to accept his word that he influenced world events as averred.

Mr. Fonko's relationship with the Central Intelligence Agency (CIA) is especially problematic. Initially, he claims, he was set up by a rogue agent who as part of an unauthorized scheme to "smoke out a mole" fabricated a fictitious "legend" for Mr. Fonko and dispatched him to Cambodia on the eve of the Khmer Rouge takeover. As a result of that assignment he received a Distinguished Intelligence Medal (or "jockstrap award"), he claims, and who can dispute it, given that disclosure of such awards is prevented by Top Secret classifications? One can justifiably wonder if the CIA is as devious, venal, corrupt and inept, as portrayed in *Jake Fonko MIA*. However, given that agency's ability to classify embarrassments and malfeasances on grounds of "national security", one cannot discount such a possibility. Other fictional treatments of the CIA, e.g., *Harlot's Ghost*, by Norman Mailer, *Shelley's Heart*, by Charles McCarry, Robert Ludlum's *Jason Bourne* series, the Coen Brothers' film, *Burn After Reading*, to name just a few, portray the CIA as devious, corrupt, venal and inept, and are there not invariably grains of truth interspersed through fictional tales?

Similarly, Mr. Fonko claims that a certain KGB agent, "Emil Grotesqcu", built a career in his agency for himself by both pursuing Fonko and perpetuating his legend, at times arriving opportunely to rescue him from seemingly hopeless situations (e.g., in Abu Ghraib prison). Agent Grotesqcu claims to have originated, as did Mr. Fonko's family, in Serbia, his family then fleeing from there to Kiev in Ukraine. The "cu" appendage to his name however, suggests neither Serbian nor Ukrainian, but *Romanian* origins. However, a search turned up no one else, from anywhere in the world, with the surname "Grotesqcu". Granted this name could be another pseudonym, or perhaps a "code name", but could that ruthless Russia espionage agency plausibly have allowed such a corruption in its own ranks to occur, let alone persist for nearly a quarter century? Comparably to the CIA, the KGB has ample capability to bury its embarrassments out of sight if need be, so once again proof may exist but may not be accessible. For what it is worth, one's exhaustive search of the Venona Files yielded no evidence one way or the other.

Most perplexing about these accounts are frequent excursions into literature and popular entertainment that Mr. Fonko enfolds into his narrative. Take, for example, his account in *Fonko Bolo* of his adventures in India and his rescue by (apparently) Mother Teresa. Portions of the tale are redolent of Voltaire's *Candide*—abject evil and depravity confronting naïve optimism. The adventures themselves, veering hither and yon and from pillar to post, as it were, appear reflective of Homer's *Odyssey* more than just coincidentally. And in their midst appears a guru who recites what might easily pass for one of Rudyard Kipling's *Just So Stories*. And, not least, from whence could the embedded "stories within stories" structure have arisen but Potocki's *The Manuscript Found in Saragossa?*

Or consider his forays in Northern Ireland's "Troubles", related in *Fonko's Errand Go Boom*. There are four plagiarisms from James Joyce's *Ulysses*, including the last lines of the book and a walking excursion through Dublin that corresponds suspiciously to Leopold Bloom's auspicious day. Mr. Fonko claimed never to have read *Ulysses*, though he "saw the movie" (Kirk Douglas portraying Ulysses in *The Odyssey*). One detects asides hinting at *Krapp's Last Tape* and *Waiting for Godot* by Irish author Samuel Beckett as well. "Professor Pflingger" explains these away as resulting from an over-zealous editorial assistant's attempts to enhance the text.

Or consider the numerous plagiarisms, allusions and references in *Fonko in the Sun* drawn from just about "everything under the sun" including: Hemingway's *To Have and Have Not* and *The Old Man and the Sea*; Graham Greene's *Our Man in Havana* and *The Comedians*; Ian Fleming's *Dr. No;* and Harry Belafonte's *Banana Boat Song*. Once again "Professor Pflingger" asks the reader to accept a glib explanation, that some ill-informed editorial assistants mistook ancillary materials he included with his notes for original material and incorporated it in the narrative.

Similarly, in *The Mother of All Fonkos*, the narrative includes an incident strongly suggestive of the *Alex Delaware* novels by Jonathan Kellerman; several tales taken from *1001 Nights*; and a poet Mr. Fonko meets in Abu Ghraib prison whose life story seems more than just vaguely similar to the musical, *Kismet*, and who spouts doggerel purloined from *The Wizard of Oz*, Hillaire Belloc, Ogden Nash, Gilbert and Sullivan, and the oldest limerick in the book.

And not only does Mr. Fonko inhabit literature and entertainment. It seems he also participates in urban legends (e.g., the abandoned stewardess) and hoary old jokes (e.g., "John the carpenter"). These fictions within fictions plunge the reader down metaphorical rabbit holes sufficient to have baffled even little Alice Pleasance Liddell.

One is reminded, perusing these texts, of the annual "Easter Egg Hunt", for which treats (e.g., candies and decorated eggs) are hidden for gleeful tots to ferret out. Regarding the *Jake Fonko* series of books, one wonders if perhaps little nuggets and treasures (or *tchotchkes*, as our Jewish friends are wont to put it) were secreted to reward the sharp-eyed and attuned. One cannot evade the question: Did these events happen as reported—"true and factual accounts"? Or were these myriad "borrowings" inserted in the texts for some indiscernible, perhaps sinister purpose?

In summary, although deconstruction reveals substantial reasons to question the authenticity and veracity of yarns written by a dubious author about a dubious personage, yet doubts linger: a tenuous case can be made in their favor. It is not inconceivable that the tales are based on phenomenological reality, actual events some of whose features have been transfigured and disguised for reasons pertaining to national security or privacy concerns.

In the final analysis one must parse "Professor Pflingger's" textualizations, decode inherent subtextual cryptocontent, dissect tangential quasi-visualizations, assay the evidence at hand, balance the pros and cons, and at the end of the day make one's case. I rest mine, and I leave it to the reader to resolve these polysemies to his or her own satisfaction.

One hopes one's modest efforts have helped clarify these issues.

AP 8/2015

FONKO GO HOME (BOOK 7)

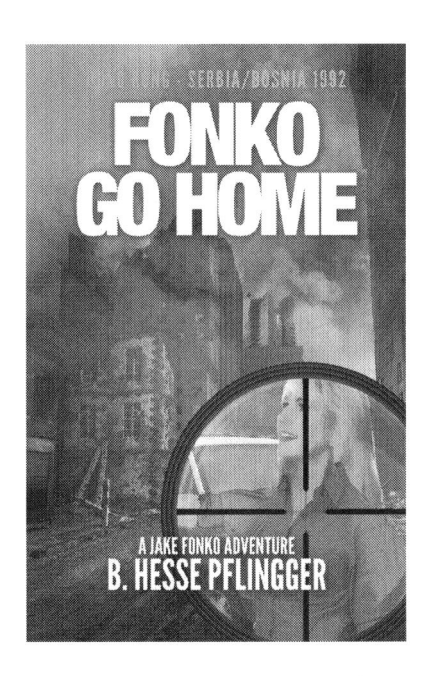

FONKO GO HOME (BOOK 7): Jake is caught in Sarajevo during the Serbian Civil War. But this time, he has to get a civilian friend safely out of the warzone, too.

Get Fonko Go Home on Amazon: bit.ly/jfgohome

Printed in Poland
by Amazon Fulfillment
Poland Sp. z o.o., Wrocław